TOGETHER

THE MACMILLAN COMPANY
NEW YORK · BOSTON · CHICAGO
ATLANTA · SAN FRANCISCO

MACMILLAN & CO., Limited
LONDON · BOMBAY · CALCUTTA
MELBOURNE

THE MACMILLAN CO. OF CANADA, Ltd.
TORONTO

TOGETHER

BY

ROBERT HERRICK

AUTHOR OF "THE REAL WORLD," "THE COMMON LOT," "THE MEMOIRS OF AN AMERICAN CITIZEN," ETC.

New York
THE MACMILLAN COMPANY
1908

Set up and electrotyped. Published July, 1908. Reprinted three times July, August, twice, September, twice, October, twice, 1908.

Norwood Press
J. S. Cushing Co. — Berwick & Smith Co.
Norwood, Mass., U.S.A.

TOGETHER

PART ONE

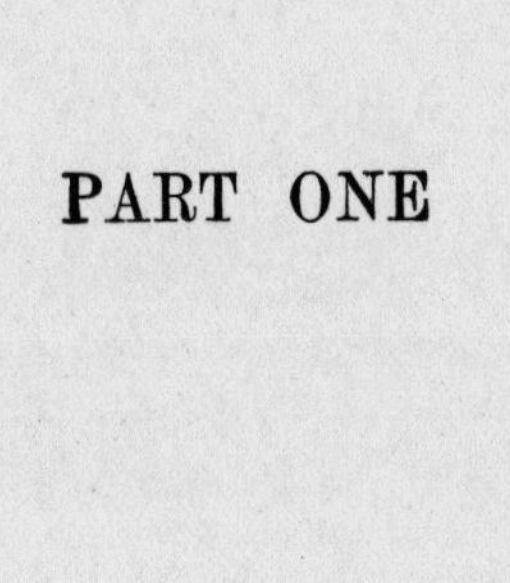

TOGETHER

CHAPTER I

She stood before the minister who was to marry them, very tall and straight. With lips slightly parted she looked at him steadfastly, not at the man beside her who was about to become her husband. Her father, with a last gentle pressure of her arm, had taken his place behind her. In the hush that had fallen throughout the little chapel, all the restless movement of the people who had gathered there this warm June morning was stilled, in the expectation of those ancient words that would unite the two before the altar. Through the open window behind the altar a spray of young woodbine had thrust its juicy green leaves and swayed slowly in the air, which was heavy with earthy odors of all the riotous new growth that was pushing forward in the fields outside. And beyond the vine could be seen a bit of the cloudless, rain-washed sky.

There before the minister, who was fumbling mechanically at his prayer-book, a great space seemed to divide the man and the woman from all the others, their friends and relatives, who had come to witness the ceremony of their union. In the woman's consciousness an unexpected stillness settled, as if for these few moments she were poised between the past of her whole life and the mysterious future. All the preoccupations of the engagement weeks, the strange colorings of mood and feeling, all the petty cares of the event itself, had suddenly vanished. She did not see even him, the man she was to marry, only the rugged face of the old minister, the bit of fluttering vine, the expanse of blue sky. She stood before the veil of her life, which was about to be drawn aside.

This hushed moment was broken by the resonant tones of the minister as he began the opening words of the sacrament that had been said over so many millions of human beings. Familiar as the phrases were, she did not realize them, could not summon back her attention from that depth within of awed expectancy. After a time she became aware of the subdued movements in the chapel, of people breaking into the remote circle of her mystery, — even here they must needs have their part, — and of the man beside her looking intently at her, with flushed face. It was this man, this one here at her side, whom she had chosen of all that might have come into her life; and suddenly he seemed a stranger, standing there, ready to become her husband! The woodbine waved, recalling to her flashing thoughts that day two years before when the chapel was dedicated, and they two, then mere friends, had planted this vine together. And now, after certain meetings, after some surface intercourse, they had willed to come here to be made one. . . .

"And who gives this woman in marriage?" the minister asked solemnly, following the primitive formula which symbolizes that the woman is to be made over from one family to another as a perpetual possession. She gave herself of course! The words were but an outgrown form. . . . There was the necessary pause while the Colonel came forward, and taking his daughter's hand from which the glove had been carefully turned back, laid it gently in the minister's large palm. The father's lips twitched, and she knew he was feeling the solemnity of his act, — that he was relinquishing a part of himself to another. Their marriage — her father's and mother's — had been happy, — oh, very peaceful! And yet — hers must be different, must strike deeper. For the first time she raised her shining eyes to the man at her side. . . .

"I, John, take thee Isabelle for my wedded wife, to have and to hold . . . in sickness and in health . . . until death us do part . . . and hereby I plight thee my troth."

Those old words, heard so many times, which heretofore

had echoed without meaning to her, — she had vaguely thought them beautiful, — now came freighted with sudden meaning, while from out the dreamlike space around sounded the firm tones of the man at her side repeating slowly, with grave pauses, word by word, the marriage oath. "I, John, take thee Isabelle," that voice was saying, and she knew that the man who spoke these words in his calm, grave manner was the one she had chosen, to whom she had willed to give herself for all time, — presently she would say it also, — for always, always, "until death us do part." He was promising it with tranquil assurance, — fidelity, the eternal bond, throughout the unknown years, out of the known present. "And hereby I plight thee my troth." Without a tremor the man's assured voice registered the oath— before God and man.

"I, Isabelle," and the priest took up with her this primal oath of fidelity, body and soul. All at once the full personal import of the words pierced her, and her low voice swelled unconsciously with her affirmation. She was to be for always as she was now. They two had not been one before: the words did not make them so now. It was their desire. But the old divided selves, the old impulses, they were to die, here, forever.

She heard herself repeating the words after the minister. Her strong young voice in the stillness of the chapel sounded strangely not her own voice, but the voice of some unknown woman within her, who was taking the oath for her in this barbaric ceremony whereby man and woman are bound together. "And hereby I plight thee my troth," — the voice sank to a whisper as of prayer. Her eyes came back to the man's face, searching for his eyes.

There were little beads of perspiration on his broad brow, and the shaven lips were closely pressed together, moulding the face into lines of will, — the look of mastery. What was he, this man, now her husband for always, his hand about hers in sign of perpetual possession and protection? What beneath all was he who had taken with her, thus publicly, the mighty oath of fidelity, "until death us do part"? Each had said it; each believed it; each desired it wholly. Perversely, here in the moment of her deepest feeling, intruded the consciousness of broken contracts, the waste of shattered purposes. Ah, but *theirs* was different! This absolute oath of fidelity one to the other, each with his own will and his own desire,—this irredeemable contract of union between man and woman, — it was not always a binding sacrament. Often twisted and broken, men and women promising in the belief of the best within them what was beyond their power to perform. There were those in that very chapel who had said these words and broken them, furtively or legally. . . . With them, of course, it would be different, would be the best; for she conceived their love to be of another kind, — the enduring kind. Nevertheless, just here, while the priest of society pronounced the final words of union, something spoke within the woman's soul that it was a strange oath to be taking, a strange manner of making two living beings one!

"And I pronounce you man and wife," the words ran. Then the minister hastened on into his little homily upon the marriage state. But the woman's thought rested at those fateful words, — "man and wife," — the knot of the contract. There should fall a new light in her heart that would make her know they were really one, having now been joined as the book said "in holy wedlock." From this sacramental union of persons there should issue to both a new spirit. . . .

Her husband was standing firm and erect, listening with all the concentration of his mind to what the minister was saying —not tumultuously distracted—as though he comprehended the exact gravity of this contract into which he was entering, as he might that of any other he could make, sure of his power to fulfil all, confident before Fate. She trembled strangely. Did she know him, this other self? In the swift apprehension of life's depths which came through her heightened mood she perceived that ultimate division lying between all human beings, that impregnable fortress of the individual soul. . . . It was all over. He looked tenderly at her. Her lips trembled with a serious smile, — yes, they would understand now!

The people behind them moved more audibly. The thing was done; the priest's words of exhortation were largely superfluous. All else that concerned married life these two would have to find out for themselves. The thing was done, as ordained by the church, according to the rules of society. Now it was for Man and Wife to make of it what they would or — could.

The minister closed his book in dismissal. The groom offered his arm to the bride. Facing the chapelful she came out of that dim world of wonder whither she had strayed. Her veil thrown back, head proudly erect, eyes mistily ranging above the onlookers, she descended the altar steps, gazing down the straight aisle over the black figures, to the sunny village green, beyond into the vista of life! . . . Triumphant organ notes beat through the chapel, as they passed between the rows of smiling faces, — familiar faces only vaguely perceived, yet each with its own expression, its own reaction from this ceremony. She swept on deliberately, with the grace of her long stride, her head raised, a little smile on her open lips, her hand just touching his, — going forward with him into life.

Only two faces stood out from the others at this moment, — the dark, mischievous face of Nancy Lawton, smiling sceptically. Her dark, little eyes seemed to say, 'Oh, you don't know yet!' And the other was the large, placid face of a blond woman, older than the bride, standing beside a stolid man at the end of a pew. The serene, soft eyes of this woman were dim with tears, and a tender smile still lingered on her lips. She at least, Alice Johnston, the bride's cousin, could smile through the tears — a smile that told of the sweetness in life. . . . .

At the door the frock-coated young ushers formed into double line through which the couple passed. The village green outside was flooded with sunshine, checkered by drooping elm branches. Bells began to ring from the library across the green and from the schoolhouse farther down. It was over — the fine old barbaric ceremony, the passing of the irredeemable contract between man and woman, the public proclamation of eternal union. Henceforth they were man and wife before the law, before their kind — one and one, and yet not two.

Thus together they passed out of the church.

CHAPTER II

THE company gathered within the chapel for the wedding now moved and talked with evident relief, each one expressing his feeling of the solemn service.

"Very well done, very lovely!" the Senator was murmuring to the bride's mother, just as he might give an opinion of a good dinner or some neat business transaction or of a smartly dressed woman. It was a function of life successfully performed — and he nodded gayly to a pretty woman three rows away. He was handsome and gray-haired, long a widower, and evidently considered weddings to be an attractive, ornamental feature of social life. Mrs. Price, the bride's mother, intent upon escaping with the Colonel by the side door and rejoining the bridal party at the house before the guests arrived on foot, scarcely heeded the amiable Senator's remarks. This affair of her daughter's marriage was, like most events, a matter of engrossing details. The Colonel, in his usual gregarious manner, had strayed among the guests, forgetful of his duties, listening with bent head to congratulatory remarks. She had to send her younger son, Vickers, after him where he lingered with Farrington Beals, the President of the great Atlantic and Pacific Railroad, in which his new son-in-law held a position. When the Colonel finally dragged himself away from the pleasant things that his old friend Beals had to say about young Lane, he looked at his impatient wife with his tender smile, as if he would like to pat her cheek and say, "Well, we've started them right, haven't we?"

The guests flowed conversationally towards the door and the sunny green, while the organ played deafeningly. But play as exultantly as it might, it could not drown the babble of human voices. Every one wanted to utter those excitable commonplaces that seem somehow to cover at such times deep meanings.

"What a perfect wedding!"

"How pretty it all was!"

"Not a hitch."

"She looked the part."

"Good fellow — nice girl — ought to be happy . . . Well, old man, when is your turn coming? . . . Could hear every word they said . . . looked as though they meant it, too! . . ."

In an eddy of the centre aisle a tall, blond young woman with handsome, square shoulders and dark eyes stood looking about her calmly, as if she were estimating the gathering, setting each one down at the proper social valuation, deciding, perhaps, in sum that they were a very "mixed lot," old friends and new, poor and rich. A thin girl, also blond, with deep blue eyes, and a fine bony contour of the face, was swept by the stream near the solitary observer and held out a hand: —

"Cornelia!"

"Margaret!"

"Isn't it ideal!" Margaret Lawton exclaimed, her nervous face still stirred by all that she had felt during the service, — "the day, the country, and this dear little chapel!"

"Very sweet," the large woman replied in a purring voice, properly modulated for the sentiment expressed. "Isabelle made an impressive bride." And these two school friends moved on towards the door. Cornelia Pallanton, still surveying the scene, nodded and said to her companion, "There's your cousin Nannie Lawton. Her husband isn't here, I suppose? There are a good many St. Louis people."

The guests were now scattered in little groups over the green, dawdling in talk and breathing happily the June-scented air. The stolid man and his placid wife who had sat near the rear had already started for the Colonel's house, following the foot-path across the fields. They walked silently side by side, as if long used to wordless companionship.

The amiable Senator and his friend Beals examined critically the little Gothic chapel, which had been a gift to his native town by the Colonel, as well as the stone library at the other end of the green. "Nice idea of Price," the Senator was saying, "handsome buildings — pleasant little village," and he moved in the direction of Miss Pallanton, who was alone.

Down below in the valley, on the railroad siding, lay the special train that had brought most of the guests from New York that morning. The engine emitted little puffs of white smoke in the still noon, ready to carry its load back to the city after the breakfast. About the library steps were the carriages of those who had driven over from neighboring towns; the whole village had a disturbed and festal air.

The procession was straggling across the village street through the stile and into the meadow, tramping down the thick young grass, up the slope to the comfortable old white house that opened its broad verandas like hospitable arms. The President of the Atlantic and Pacific, deserted by the Senator, had offered his arm to a stern old lady with knotty hands partly concealed in lace gloves. Her lined face had grown serious in age and contention with life. She clung stiffly to the arm of the railroad president, — proud, silent, and shy. She was *his* mother. From her one might conclude that the groom's people were less comfortably circumstanced than the bride's — that this was not a marriage of ambition on the woman's part. It was the first time Mrs. Lane had been "back east" since she had left her country home as a young bride. It was a proud moment, walking with her son's chief; but the old lady did not betray any elation, as she listened to the kindly words that Beals found to say about her son.

"A first-rate railroad man, Mrs. Lane, — he will move up rapidly. We can't get enough of that sort."

The mother, never relaxing her tight lips, drank it all in, treasured it as a reward for the hard years spent in keeping that boarding-house in Omaha, after the death of her husband, who had been a country doctor.

"He's a good son," she admitted as the eulogy flagged. "And he knows how to get on with all kinds of folks. . . ."

At their heels were Vickers Price and the thin Southern girl, Margaret Lawton. Vickers, just back from Munich for this event, had managed to give the conventional dress that he was obliged to wear a touch of strangeness, with an enormous flowing tie of delicate pink, a velvet waistcoat, and broad-brimmed hat. The clothes and the full beard, the rippling chestnut hair and pointed mustache, showed a desire for eccentricity on the part of the young man that distinguished him from all the other well-dressed young Americans. He carried a thin cane and balanced a cigarette between his lips.

"Yes," he was saying, "I had to come over to see Isabelle married, but I shall go back after a look around — not the place for me!" He laughed and waved his cane towards the company with an ironic sense of his inappropriateness to an American domestic scene.

"You are a composer, — music, isn't it?" the girl asked, a flash in her blue eyes at the thought of youth, Munich, music.

"I have written a few things; am getting ready, you know," Vickers Price admitted modestly.

Just there they were joined by a handsome, fashionably dressed man, his face red with rapid walking. He touched his long, well-brushed black mustache with his handkerchief as he explained: —

"Missed the train — missed the show — but got here in time for the fun, on the express."

He took his place beside the girl, whose color deepened and eyes turned away, — perhaps annoyed, or pleased?

"That's what you come for, isn't it?" she said, forcing a little joke. Noticing that the two men did not speak, she added hastily, "Don't you know Mr. Price, Mr. Vickers Price? Mr. Hollenby."

The newcomer raised his silk hat, sweeping Vickers, who was fanning himself with his broad-brimmed felt, in a light, critical stare. Then Mr. Hollenby at once appropriated the young woman's attention, as though he would indicate that it was for her sake he had taken this long, hot journey.

There were other little groups at different stages on the hill, — one gathered about a small, dark-haired woman, whose face burned duskily in the June sun. She was Aline Goring, — the Eros of that schoolgirl band at St. Mary's who had come to see their comrade married. And there was Elsie Beals, — quite elegant, the only daughter of the President of the A. and P. The Woodyards, Percy and Lancey, classmates of Vickers at the university, both slim young men, wearing their clothes carelessly, — clearly not of the Hollenby manner, —had attached themselves here. Behind them was Nan Lawton, too boisterous even for the open air. At the head of the procession, now nearly topping the hill beneath the house, was that silent married couple, the heavy, sober man and the serene, large-eyed woman, who did not mingle with the others. He had pointed out to her the amiable Senator and President Beals, both well-known figures in the railroad world where he worked, far down, obscurely, as a rate clerk. His wife looked at these two great ones, who indirectly controlled the petty destiny of the Johnstons, and squeezed her husband's hand more tightly, expressing thus many mixed feelings, — content with him, pride and confidence in him, in spite of his humble position in the race.

"It's just like the Pilgrim's Progress," she said with a little smile, looking backward at the stream.

"But who is Christian?" the literal husband asked. Her eyes answered that she knew, but would not tell.

Just as each one had reflected his own emotion at the marriage, so each one, looking up at the hospitable goal ahead,

— that irregular, broad white house poured over the little Connecticut hilltop, — had his word about the Colonel's home.

"No wonder they call it the Farm," sneered Nan Lawton to the Senator.

"It's like the dear old Colonel, the new and the old," the Senator sententiously interpreted.

Beals, overhearing this, added, "It's poor policy to do things that way. Better to pull the old thing down and go at it afresh, — you save time and money, and have it right in the end."

"It's been in the family a hundred years or more," some one remarked. "The Colonel used to mow this field himself, before he took to making hardware."

"Isabelle will pull it about their ears when she gets the chance," Mrs. Lawton said. "The present-day young haven't much sentiment for uncomfortable souvenirs."

Her cousin Margaret was remarking to Vickers, "What a good, homey sort of place, — like our old Virginia houses, — all but that great barn!"

It was, indeed, as the Senator had said, very like the Colonel, who could spare neither the old nor the new. It was also like him to give Grafton a new stone library and church, and piece on rooms here and there to his own house. In spite of these additions demanded by comfort there was something in the conglomeration to remind the Colonel, who had returned to Grafton after tasting strife and success in the Middle West, of the plain home of his youth.

"The dear old place!" Alice Johnston murmured to her husband. "It was never more attractive than to-day, as if it knew that it was marrying off an only daughter." To her, too, the Farm had memories, and no new villa spread out spaciously in Italian, Tudor, or Classic style could ever equal this white, four-chimneyed New England mansion.

On the west slope of the hill near the veranda a large tent had been erected, and into this black-coated waiters were running excitedly to and fro around a wing of the house which evidently held the servant quarters. Just beyond the tent a band was playing a loud march. There was to be dancing on the lawn after the breakfast, and in the evening on the village green for everybody, and later fireworks. The Colonel had insisted on the dancing and the fireworks, in spite of Vickers's jeers about pagan rites and the Fourth of July.

The bride and groom had already taken their places in the broad hall, which bisected the old house. The guests were to enter from the south veranda, pass through the hall, and after greeting the couple gain the refreshment tent through the library windows. The Colonel had worked it all out with that wonderful attention to detail that had built up his great hardware business. Upstairs in the front bedrooms the wedding presents had been arranged, and nicely ticketed with cards for the amusement of aged relatives, — a wonderful assortment of silver and gold and glass, — an exhibition of the wide relationships of the contracting pair, at least of the wife. And through these rooms soft-footed detectives patrolled, examining the guests. . . .

Isabelle Price had not wished her wedding to be of this kind, ordered so to speak like the refreshments from Sherry and the presents from Tiffany, with a special train on the siding. When she and John had decided to be married at the old farm, she had thought of a country feast, — her St. Mary's girls of course and one or two more, but quite to themselves! They were to walk with these few friends to the little chapel, where the dull old village parson would say the necessary words. The marriage over, and a simple breakfast in the old house, — the scene of their love, — they were to ride off among the hills to her camp on Dog Mountain, alone. And thus quietly, without flourish, they would enter the new life. But as happens to all such pretty idylls, reality had forced her hand. Colonel Price's daughter could not marry like an eloping schoolgirl, so her mother had declared. Even John had taken it as a matter of course, all this elaborate celebration, the guests, the special train, the overflowing house. And she had yielded her ideal of having something special in her wedding, acquiescing in the "usual thing."

But now that the first guests began to top the hill and enter the hall with warm, laughing greetings, all as gay as the June sunlight, the women in their fresh summer gowns, she felt the joy of the moment. "Isn't it jolly, so many of 'em!" she exclaimed to her husband, squeezing his arm gayly. He took it, like most things, as a matter of course. The hall soon filled with high tones and noisy laughter, as the guests crowded in from the lawn about the couple, to offer their congratulations, to make their little jokes and premeditated speeches. Standing at the foot of the broad stairs, her veil thrown back, her fair face flushed with color and her lips parted in a smile, one arm about a thick bunch of roses, the bride made a bright spot of light in the dark hall. All those whirling thoughts, the depths to which her spirit had descended during the service, had fled; she was excited by this throng of smiling, joking people, by the sense of her rôle. She had the feeling of its being *her* day, and she was eager to drink every drop in the sparkling cup. A great kindness for everybody, a sort of beaming sympathy for the world, bubbled up in her heart, making the repeated hand squeeze which she gave — sometimes a double pressure — a personal expression of her emotion. Her flashing hazel eyes, darting into each face in turn as it came before her, seemed to say: 'Of course, I am the happiest woman in the world, and you must be happy, too. It is such a good world!' While her voice was repeating again and again, with the same tremulous intensity, "Thank you — it is awfully nice of you — I am so glad you are here!"

To the amiable Senator's much worn compliment, — "It's the prettiest wedding I have seen since your mother's, and the prettiest bride, too," — she blushed a pleased reply, though she had confessed to John only the night before that the sprightly Senator was "horrid, — he has such a way of squeezing your hand, as if he would like to do more," — to which the young man had replied in his perplexity, due to the Senator's exalted position in the A. and P. Board, "I suppose it's only the old boy's way of being cordial."

Even when Nannie Lawton came loudly with Hollenby — she had captured him from her cousin — and threw her arms about the bride, Isabelle did not draw back. She forgot that she disliked the gay little woman, with her muddy eyes, whose "affairs" — one after the other — were condoned "for her husband's sake." Perhaps Nannie felt what it might be to be as happy and proud as she was, — she was large, generous, comprehending at this moment. And she passed the explosive little woman over to her husband, who received her with the calm courtesy that never made an enemy.

But when "her girls" came up the line, she felt happiest. Cornelia was first, large, handsome, stately, her broad black hat nodding above the feminine stream, her dark eyes observing all, while she slowly smiled to the witticisms Vickers murmured in her ear. Every one glanced at Miss Pallanton; she was a figure, as Isabelle realized when she finally stood before her, — a very handsome figure, and would get her due attention from her world. They had not cared very much for "Conny" at St. Mary's, though she was a handsome girl then and had what was called "a good mind." There was something coarse in the detail of this large figure, the plentiful reddish hair, the strong, straight nose, — all of which the girls of St. Mary's had interpreted their own way, and also the fact that she had come from Duluth, — probably of "ordinary" people. Surely not a girl's girl, nor a woman's woman! But one to be reckoned with when it came to men. Isabelle was conscious of her old reserve as she listened to Conny's piping, falsetto voice, — such a funny voice to come from that large person through that magnificent white throat.

"It makes me so happy, dear Isabelle," the voice piped; "it is all so ideal, so exactly what it ought to be for you, don't you know?" And as Percy Woodyard bore her off — he had hovered near all the time — she smiled again, leaving Isabelle to wonder what Conny thought would be "just right" for her.

"You must hurry, Conny," she called on over Vickers's head, "and make up your mind; you are almost our last!"

"You know I never hurry," the smiling lips piped languidly, and the large hat sailed into the library, piloted on either side by Woodyard and Vickers. Isabelle had a twinge of sisterly jealousy at seeing her younger brother so persistently in the wake of the large, blond girl. Dear Vick, her own chum, her girl's first ideal of a man, fascinatingly developed by his two years in Munich, must not go bobbing between Nan Lawton and Conny!

And here was Margaret Lawton — so different from her cousin's wife — with the delicate, high brow, the firm, aristocratic line from temple to chin. She was the rarest and best of the St. Mary's set, and though Isabelle had known her at school only a year, she had felt curiosity and admiration for the Virginian. Her low, almost drawling voice, which reflected a controlled spirit, always soothed her. The deep-set blue eyes had caught Isabelle's glance at Vickers, and with an amused smile the Southern girl said, "He's in the tide!"

Isabelle said, "I am so, so glad you could get here, Margaret."

"I wanted to — very much. I made mother put off our sailing."

"How is the Bishop?" she asked, as Margaret was pushed on.

"Oh, happy, riding about the mountains and converting the poor heathen, who prefer whiskey to religion. Mother's taking him to England this summer to show him off to the foreign clergy."

"And Washington?"

Margaret's thin, long lips curved ironically for answer. Hollenby, who seemed to have recollected a purpose, was waiting for her at the library door. . . . "Ah, my Eros!" Isabelle exclaimed with delight, holding forth two hands to a small, dark young woman, with waving brown hair and large eyes that were fixed on distant objects.

"Eros with a husband and two children," Aline Goring murmured, in her soft contralto. "You remember Eugene? At the Springs that summer?" The husband, a tall, smooth-shaven, young man with glasses and the delicate air of the steam-heated American scholar bowed stiffly.

"Of course! Didn't I aid and abet you two?"

"That's two years and a half ago," Aline remarked, as if the simple words covered a multitude of facts about life. "We are on our way to St. Louis to settle."

"Splendid!" Isabelle exclaimed. "We shall have you again. Torso, where we are exiled for the present, is only a night's ride from St. Louis."

Aline smiled that slow, warm smile, which seemed to come from the remote inner heart of her dreamy life. Isabelle looked at her eagerly, searching for the radiant, woodsy creature she had known, that Eros, with her dreamy, passionate, romantic temperament, a girl whom girls adored and kissed and petted, divining in her the feminine spirit of themselves. Surely, she should be happy, Aline, the beautiful girl made for love, poetic, tender. The lovely eyes were there, but veiled; the velvety skin had roughened; and the small body was almost heavy. The wood nymph had been submerged in matrimony.

Goring was saying in a twinkling manner: —

"I've been reckoning up, Mrs. Lane. You are the seventh most intimate girl friend Aline has married off the last two years. How many more of you are there?"

Aline, putting her arms about the bride's neck, drew her face to her lips and whispered: —

"Dearie, my darling! I hope you will be so happy, — that it will be all you can wish!" After these two had disappeared into the library, where there was much commotion about the punch-bowl, the bride wondered — were *they* happy? She had seen the engagement at Southern Springs, — the two most ecstatic, unearthly lovers she had ever known. . . . But now? . . .

Thus the stream of her little world flowed on, repeating its high-pitched note of gratulation, of jocular welcome to the married state, as if to say, 'Well, now you are one of us — you've been brought in — this is life.' That was what these smiling people were thinking, as they welcomed the neophytes to the large vale of human experience. 'We have seen you through this business, started you joyously on the common path. And now what will you make of it?' For the occasion they ignored, good naturedly, the stones along the road, the mistakes, the miserable failures that lined the path, assuming the bride's proper illusion of triumph and confidence. . . . Among the very last came the Johnstons, who had lingered outside while the more boisterous ones pressed about the couple. Isabelle noticed that the large brown eyes of the placid woman, who always seemed to her much older than herself, were moist, and her face was serious when she said, "May it be all that your heart desires — the Real Thing!"

A persistent aunt interrupted them here, and it was hours afterward when Isabelle's thought came back to these words and dwelt on them. 'The real thing!' Of course, that was what it was to be, her marriage, — the woman's symbol of the Perfect, not merely Success (though with John they could not fail of worldly success), nor humdrum content — but, as Alice said, the real thing, — a state of passionate and complete union. Something in those misty brown eyes, something in the warm, deep voice of the older woman, in the prayer-like form of the wish, sank deep into her consciousness.

She turned to her husband, who was chatting with Fosdick, a large, heavy man with a Dr. Johnson head on massive shoulders. One fat hand leaned heavily on a fat club, for Fosdick was slightly lame and rolled in his gait.

"Isabelle," he remarked with a windy sigh, "I salute my victor!"

Old Dick, Vickers's playmate in the boy-and-girl days, her playmate, too, — he had wanted to marry her for years, ever since Vick's freshman year when he had made them a visit at the Farm. He had grown very heavy since then,— time which he had spent roving about in odd corners of the earth. As he stood there, his head bent mockingly before the two, Isabelle felt herself Queen once more, the— American woman who, having surveyed all, and dominated all within the compass of her little world, has chosen the One. But not Dickie, humorous and charming as he was.

"How goes it, Dickie?"

"As always," he puffed; "I come from walking or rather limping up and down this weary earth and observing — men and women — how they go about to make themselves miserable."

"Stuff!"

"My dear friends," he continued, placing both hands on the big cane, "you are about to undergo a new and wonderful experience. You haven't the slightest conception of what it is. You think it is love; but it is the holy state of matrimony, — a very different proposition —"

They interrupted him with laughing abuse, but he persisted, — a serious undertone to his banter. "Yes, I have always observed the scepticism of youth, no matter what may be the age of the contracting parties and their previous experience, in this matter. But Love and Marriage are two distinct and entirely independent states of being, — one is the creation of God, the other of Society. I have observed that few make them coalesce."

As relatives again interposed, Fosdick rolled off, ostentatiously thumping his stick on the floor, and made straight for the punch-bowl, where he seemed to meet congenial company.

CHAPTER III

MEANWHILE inside the great tent the commotion was at its height, most of the guests — those who had escaped the fascination of the punch-bowl — having found their way thither. Perspiring waiters rushed back and forth with salad and champagne bottles, which were seized by the men and borne off to the women waiting suitably to be fed by the men whom they had attached. Near the entrance the Colonel, with his old friends Beals and Senator Thomas, was surveying the breakfast scene, a contented smile on his kind face, as he murmured assentingly, "So — so." He and the Senator had served in the same regiment during the War, Price retiring as Colonel and the Senator as Captain; while the bridegroom's father, Tyringham Lane, had been the regimental surgeon.

"What a good fellow Tyringham was, and how he would have liked to be here!" the Senator was saying sentimentally, as he held out a glass to be refilled. "Poor fellow! — he never got much out of his life; didn't know how to make the most of things,— went out there to that Iowa prairie after the War. You say he left his widow badly off?"

The Colonel nodded, and added with pride, "But John has made that right now."

The Senator, who had settled in Indianapolis and practised railroad law until his clients had elevated him to the Senate, considered complacently the various dispensations of Providence towards men. He said generously: —

"Well, Tyringham's son has good blood, and it will tell. He will make his way. We'll see to that, eh, Beals?" and the Senator sauntered over to a livelier group dominated by Cornelia Pallanton's waving black plumes.

"Oh, marriage!" Conny chaffed, "it's the easiest thing a woman can do, isn't it? Why should one be in a hurry when it's so hard to go back?"

"Matrimony," Fosdick remarked, "is an experiment where nobody's experience counts but your own." He had been torn from the punch-bowl and thus returned to his previous train of thought.

"Is that why some repeat it so often?" Elsie Beals inquired. She had broken her engagement the previous winter and had spent the summer hunting with Indian guides among the Canadian Rockies. She regarded herself as unusual, and turned sympathetically to Fosdick, who also had a reputation for being odd.

"So let us eat and be merry," that young man said, seizing a pâté and glass of champagne, "though I never could see why good people should make such an unholy rumpus when two poor souls decide to attempt the great experiment of converting illusion into reality."

"Some succeed," an earnest young man suggested.

Conny, who had turned from the constant Woodyard to the voluble fat man, who might be a Somebody, remarked:—

"I suppose you don't see the puddles when you are in their condition. It's always the belief that we are going to escape 'em that drives us all into your arms."

"What I object to," Fosdick persisted, feeding himself prodigiously, "is not the fact, but this savage glee over it. It's as though a lot of caged animals set up a howl of delight every time the cage door was opened and a new pair was introduced into the pen. They ought to perform the wedding ceremony in sackcloth and ashes, after duly fasting, accompanied by a few faithful friends garbed in black with torches."

Conny gave him a cold, surface smile, setting down his talk as "young" and beamed at the approaching Senator.

"Oh, what an idea!" giggled a little woman. "If you can't dance at your own wedding, you may never have another chance."

Conny, though intent upon the Senator, kept an eye upon Woodyard, introducing him to the distinguished man, thinking, no doubt, that the Chairman of the A. and P. Board might be useful to the young lawyer. For whatever she might be to women, this large blond creature with white neck, voluptuous lips, and slow gaze from childlike eyes had the power of drawing males to her, a power despised and also envied by women. Those simple eyes seemed always to seek information about obvious matters. But behind the eyes Conny was thinking, 'It's rather queer, this crowd. And these Prices with all their money might do so much better. That Fosdick is a silly fellow. The Senator is worn of course, but still important!' And yet Conny, with all her sureness, did not know all her own mental processes. For she, too, was really looking for a mate, weighing, estimating men to that end, and some day she would come to a conclusion,—would take a man, Woodyard or another, giving him her very handsome person, and her intelligence, in exchange for certain definite powers of brain and will.

The bride and groom entered the tent at last. Isabelle, in a renewed glow of triumph, stepped over to the table and with her husband's assistance plunged a knife into the huge cake, while her health was being drunk with cheers. As she firmly cut out a tiny piece, she exposed a thin but beautifully moulded arm.

"Handsome girl," the Senator murmured in Conny's ear. "Must be some sore hearts here to-day. I don't see how such a beauty could escape until she was twenty-six. But girls want their fling these days, same as the men!"

"Toast! Toast the bride!" came voices from all sides, while the waiters hurried here and there slopping the wine into empty glasses.

As the bride left the tent to get ready for departure, she caught sight of Margaret Lawton in a corner of the veranda with Hollenby, who was bending towards her, his eyes fastened on her face. Margaret was looking far away, across the fields to where Dog Mountain rose in the summer haze. Was Margaret deciding *her* fate at this moment, — attracted, repulsed, waiting for the deciding thrill, while her eyes searched for the ideal of happiness on the distant mountain? She turned to look at the man, drawing back as his hand reached forward. So little, so much — woman's fate was in the making this June day, all about the old house, — attracting, repulsing, weighing, — unconsciously moulding destiny that might easily be momentous in the outcome of the years. . . .

When the bride came down, a few couples had already begun to dance, but they followed the other guests to the north side where the carriage stood ready. Isabelle looked very smart in her new gown, a round travelling hat just framing her brilliant eyes and dark hair. Mrs. Price followed her daughter closely, her brows puckered in nervous fear lest something should be forgotten. She was especially anxious about a certain small bag, and had the maid take out all the hand luggage to make sure it had not been mislaid.

Some of the younger ones led by Vickers pelted the couple with rice, while this delay occurred. It was a silly custom that they felt bound to follow. There was no longer any meaning in the symbol of fertility. Multiply and be fruitful, the Bible might urge, following an ancient economic ideal of happiness. But the end of marriage no longer being this gross purpose, the sterile woman has at last come into honor! . . .

The bride was busy kissing a group of young women who had clustered about her, — Elsie Beals, Aline, Alice Johnston, Conny. Avoiding Nannie Lawton's wide open arms, she jumped laughingly into the carriage, then turned for a last kiss from the Colonel.

"Here, out with you Joe," Vickers exclaimed to the coachman. "I'll drive them down to the station. Quick now, — they mustn't lose the express!"

He bundled the old man from the seat, gathered up the

reins with a flourish, and whipped the fresh horses. The bride's last look, as the carriage shot through the bunch of oleanders at the gate, gathered in the group of waving, gesticulating men and women, and above them on the steps the Colonel, with his sweet, half-humorous smile, her mother at his side, already greatly relieved, and behind all the serious face of Alice Johnston, the one who knew the mysteries both tender and harsh, and who could still call it all good! . . .

Vickers whisked them to the station in a trice, soothing his excitement by driving diabolically, cutting corners and speeding down hill. At the platform President Beals's own car was standing ready for them, the two porters at the steps. The engine of the special was to take them to the junction where the "Bellefleur" would be attached to the night express, — a special favor for the President of the A. and P. The Senator had insisted on their having his camp in the Adirondacks for a month. Isabelle would have preferred her own little log hut in the firs of Dog Mountain, which she and Vickers had built. There they could be really quite alone, forced to care for themselves. But the Colonel could not understand her bit of sentiment, and John thought they ought not to offend the amiable Senator, who had shown himself distinctly friendly. So they were to enter upon their new life enjoying these luxuries of powerful friends.

The porters made haste to put the bags in the car, and the engine snorted.

"Good-by, Mr. Gerrish," Isabelle called to the station agent, who was watching them at a respectful distance. Suddenly he seemed to be an old friend, a part of all that she was leaving behind.

"Good-by, Miss Price — Mrs. Lane," he called back. "Good luck to you!"

"Dear old Vick," Isabelle murmured caressingly, "I hate most to leave you behind."

"Better stay, then, — it isn't too late," he joked. "We

could elope with the ponies, — you always said you would run off with me!"

She hugged him more tightly, burying her head in his neck, shaking him gently. "Dear old Vick! Don't be a fool! And be good to Dad, won't you?"

"I'll try not to abuse him."

"You know what I mean — about staying over for the summer. Oh dear, dear!" There was a queer sob in her voice, as if now for the first time she knew what it was. The old life was all over. Vick had been so much of that! And she had seen little or nothing of him since his return from Europe, so absorbed had she been in the bustle of her marriage. Up there on Dog Mountain which swam in the haze of the June afternoon they had walked on snowshoes one cold January night, over the new snow by moonlight, talking marvellously of all that life was to be. She believed then that she should never marry, but remain always Vick's comrade, — to guide him, to share his triumphs. Now she was abandoning that child's plan. She shook with nervous sobs.

"The engineer says we must start, dear," Lane suggested. "We have only just time to make the connection."

Vickers untwisted his sister's arms from his neck and placed them gently in her husband's hands.

"Good-by, girl," he called.

Sinking into a chair near the open door, Isabelle gazed back at the hills of Grafton until the car plunged into a cut. She gave a long sigh. "We're off!" her husband said joyously. He was standing beside her, one hand resting on her shoulder.

"Yes, dear!" She took his strong, muscled hand in hers. But when he tried to draw her to him, she shrank back involuntarily, startled, and looked at him with wide-open eyes as if she would read Destiny in him, — the Man, her husband.

For this was marriage, not the pantomime they had lived through all that day. That was demanded by custom;

but now, alone with this man, his eyes alight with love and desire, his lips caressing her hair, his hands drawing her to him, — this was marriage!

Her eyes closed as if to shut out his face, — "Don't, don't!" she murmured vaguely. Suddenly she started to her feet, her eyes wide open, and she held him away from her, looking into him, looking deep into his soul.

CHAPTER IV

It was a hot, close night. After the Bellefleur had been coupled to the Western express at the junction, Lane had the porters make up a bed for Isabelle on the floor of the little parlor next the observation platform, and here at the rear of the long train, with the door open, she lay sleepless through the night hours, listening to the rattle of the trucks, the thud of heavy wheels on the rails, disturbed only when the car was shifted to the Adirondack train by the blue glare of arc lights and phantom figures rushing to and fro in the pallid night.

The excitement of the day had utterly exhausted her; but her mind was extraordinarily alive with impressions, — faces and pictures from this great day of her existence, her marriage. And out of all these crowding images emerged persistently certain ones, — Aline, with the bloom almost gone, the worn air of something carelessly used. That was due to the children, to cares, — the Gorings were poor and the two years abroad must have been a strain. All the girls at St. Mary's had thought that marriage ideal, made all of love. For there was something of the poet in Eugene Goring, the slim scholar, walking with raised head and speaking with melodious voice. He was a girl's ideal. . . . And then came Nan Lawton, with her jesting tone, and sly, half-shut eyes. Isabelle remembered how brilliant Nan's marriage was, how proud she herself had been to have a part in it. Nan's face was blotted by Alice Johnston's with her phlegmatic husband. She was happy, serene, but old and acquainted with care.

Why should she think of them, of any other marriage? Hers was to be different, — oh, yes, quite exceptional and perfect, with an intimacy, a mutual helpfulness. . . . The girls at St. Mary's had all had their emotional experiences, which they confessed to one another; and she had had hers, of course, like her affair with Fosdick; but so innocent, so merely kittenish that they had almost disappeared from memory. These girls at St. Mary's read poetry, and had dreams of heroes, in the form of football players. They all thought about marriage, coming as they did from well-to-do parents, whose daughters might be expected to marry. Marriage, men, position in the world, — all that was their proper inheritance.

After St. Mary's there had been two winters in St. Louis, — her first real dinners and parties, her first real men. Then a brief season in Washington as Senator Thomas's guest, where the horizon, especially the man part of it, had considerably widened. She had made a fair success in Washington, thanks to her fresh beauty and spirit, and also, she was frank to confess, thanks to the Senator's interest and the reputation of her father's wealth. Then had come a six months with her mother and Vickers in Europe, from which she returned abruptly to get engaged, to begin life seriously.

These experimental years had seemed to her full of radiant avenues, any one of which she was free to enter, and for a while she had gone joyously on, discovering new avenues, pleasing herself with trying them all imaginatively. At the head of all these avenues had stood a man, of course. She could recall them all: the one in St. Louis who had followed her to Washington, up the Nile, would not be turned away. Once he had touched her, taken her hand, and she had felt cold, — she knew that his was not her way. In Washington there had been a brilliant congressman whom the Senator approved of, — an older man. She had given him some weeks of puzzled deliberation, then rejected him, as she considered sagely, because he spoke only to her mind. Perhaps the most dangerous had been the Austrian whom she had met in Rome. She almost yielded there; but once when they were alone together she had caught sight of depths in him, behind his black eyes and smiling lips, that made her afraid, — deep differences of race. The Prices were American in an old-fashioned, clean, plain sense. So when he persisted, she made her mother engage passage for home and fled with the feeling that she must put an ocean between herself and this man, fled to the arms of the man she was to marry, who somehow in the midst of his busy life managed to meet her in New York.

But why him? Out of all these avenues, her possibilities of various fate, why had she chosen him, the least promising outwardly? Was it done in a mood of reaction against the other men who had sought her? He was most unlike them all, with a background of hard struggle, with limitations instead of privileges such as they had. The Colonel's daughter could understand John Lane's persistent force, — patient, quiet, sure. She remembered his shy, inexperienced face when her father first brought him to the house for dinner. She had thought little of him then, — the Colonel was always bringing home some rough diamond, — but he had silently absorbed her as he did everything in his path, and selected her, so to speak, as he selected whatever he wanted. And after that whenever she came back to her father's home from her little expeditions into the world, he was always there, and she came to know that he wanted her, — was waiting until his moment should come. It came.

Never since then had she had a regret for those possibilities that had been hers, — for those other men standing at the other avenues and inviting her. From the moment that his arms had held her, she knew that he was the best, — so much stronger, finer, simpler than any other. She was proud that she had been able to divine this quality and could prefer real things to sham. During the engagement months she had learned, bit by bit, the story of his struggle, what had been denied to him of comfort and advantage, what he had done for himself and for his mother. She yearned to give him what he had never had, — pleasure, joy, the soft suavities of life, what she had had always.

Now she was his! Her wandering thoughts came back to that central fact.

Half frightened, she drew the blanket about her shoulders and listened. He had been so considerate of her, — had left her here to rest after making sure of her comfort and gone forward to the stuffy stateroom to sleep, divining that she was not yet ready to accept him; that if he took her now, he should violate something precious in her, — that she was not fully won. She realized this delicate instinct and was grateful to him. Of course she was his, — only his; all the other avenues had been closed forever by her love for him, her marriage to him. Ah, that should be wonderful for them both, all the years that were to come! Nevertheless, here on the threshold, her wayward soul had paused the merest moment to consider those other avenues, what they might have offered of experience, of knowledge, had she taken any other one of them. Were she here with another than him, destiny, her inmost self, the whole world of being would be changed, would be other than it was to be! What was that mysterious power that settled fate on its grooves? What were those other lives within her soul never to be lived, the lives she might have lived? Bewildered, weary, she stretched out her arms dreamily to life, and with parted lips sank into slumber. . . .

The sun was streaming through the open door; the train had come to a halt. Isabelle awoke with a start, afraid. Her husband was bending over her and she stared up directly into his amused eyes, looked steadily at him, remembering now all that she had thought the night before. This was her avenue — this was *he* . . . yet she closed her eyes as he bent still nearer to kiss her neck, her temples, her lips. Like a frightened child she drew the clothes close about her, and turned from his eager embraces. Beyond his face she saw a line of straight, stiff firs beside the track, and the blue foot-hills through which the train was winding its way upwards to the mountains. She stretched herself sleepily, murmuring: —

"Dear, I'm so tired! Is it late?"

"Ten o'clock. We're due in half an hour. I had to wake you."

"In half an hour!" She fled to the dressing-room, putting him off with a fleeting kiss.

One of the Senator's guides met them at the station with a buckboard. All the way driving upwards through the woods to the camp they were very gay. It was like one of those excursions she used to take with Vickers when he was in his best, most expansive mood, alternately chaffing and petting her. Lane was in high spirits, throwing off completely that sober self which made him so weighty in his world, revealing an unexpected boyishness. He joked with the guide, talked fishing and shooting. With the deep breaths of mountain air he expanded, his eyes flashing a new fire of joy at sight of the woods and streams. Once when they stopped to water the horses he seized the drinking-cup and dashed up the slope to a spring hidden among the trees. He brought back a brimming cupful of cold water, which she emptied. Then with a boyish, chivalrous smile he put his lips to the spot where she had drunk and drained the last drop. "That's enough for me!" he said, and they laughed self-consciously. His homage seemed to say that thus through life he would be content with what she left him to drink, — absurd fancy, but at this moment altogether delightful. . . . Later she rested, pillowing her head on his shoulder, covered by his coat, while the trap jolted on through the woods between high hills. Now and then he touched her face with the tips of his strong fingers, brushing away the wandering threads of hair. Very peaceful, happy, feeling that it was all as she would have wished it, she shut her eyes, content to rest on this comrade, so strong and so gentle. Life would be like this, always.

The Senator's camp was a camp only in name, of course; in fact it was an elaborate and expensive rustic establishment on a steep bluff above a little mountain lake. The Japanese cook had prepared a rich dinner, and the champagne was properly iced. The couple tiptoed about the place, looking at each other in some dismay, and John readily fell in with her suggestion that they should try sleeping in the open, with a rough shelter of boughs, — should make their first nest for themselves. The guide took them to a spot some distance up the lake and helped them cut the fir boughs, all but those for the bed, which they insisted upon gathering for themselves. After bringing up the blankets and the bags he paddled back to the camp, leaving them to themselves in the solitude of the woods, under the black, star-strewn sky.

Alone with him thus beside their little fire her heart was full of dream and content, of peace and love. They two seemed to have come up out of the world to some higher level of life. After the joyous day this solitude of the deep forest was perfect. When the fire had died down to the embers, he circled her with his arms and kissed her. Although her body yielded to his strong embrace her lips were cold, hard, and her eyes answered his passion with a strange, aloof look, as if her soul waited in fear. . . . She knew what marriage was to be, although she had never listened to the allusions whispered among married women and more experienced girls. Something in the sex side of the relations between men and women had always made her shrink. She was not so much pure in body and soul, as without sex, unborn. She knew the fact of nature, the eternal law of life repeating itself through desire and passion; but she realized it remotely, only in her mind, as some necessary physiological mechanism of living, like perspiration, fatigue, hunger. But it had not spoken in her body, in her soul; she did not feel that it ever could speak to her as it was speaking in the man's lighted eyes, in his lips. So now as always she was cold, tranquil beneath her lover's kisses.

And later on their bed of boughs, with her husband's arms about her, his heart throbbing against her breast, his warm breath covering her neck, she lay still, very still, — aloof, fearful of this mystery to be revealed, a little weary, wishing that she were back once more in the car or in her own room at the Farm, for this night, to return on the morrow to her comrade for another joyous, free day.

"My love! . . . Come to me! . . . I love you, love you!" . . .

The passionate tone beat against her ears, yet roused no thrilling response. The trembling voice, the intensity of the worn old words coming from him, — it was all like another man suddenly appearing in the guise of one she thought she knew so well! The taut muscles of his powerful arm pressing against her troubled her. She would have fled, — why could one be like this! Still she caressed his face and hair, kissing him gently. Oh, yes, she loved him, — she was his! He was her husband. Nevertheless she could not meet him wholly in this inmost intimacy, and her heart was troubled. If he could be content to be her companion, her lover! But this other thing was the male, the something which made all men differ from all women in the crisis of emotion — so she supposed — and must be endured. She lay passive in his arms, less yielding than merely acquiescent, drawn in upon herself to something smaller than she was before. . . .

When he slept at her side, his head pillowed close to hers on the fragrant fir, she still lay awake, her eyes staring up at the golden stars, still fearful, uncomprehending. At last she was his, as he would have her, — wholly his, so she said, seeking comfort, — and thus kissing his brow, with a long, wondering sigh she fell asleep by his side.

In the morning they dipped into the cold black lake, and as they paddled back to the camp for breakfast while the first rays of the warm sun shone through the firs in gold bars, she felt like herself once more, — a companion ready for a frolic. The next morning Lane insisted on cooking their breakfast, for he was a competent woodsman. She admired the deft way in which he built his little fire and toasted the bacon. In the undress of the woods he showed at his best, — self-reliant, capable. There followed a month of lovely days which they spent together from sunrise to starlight, walking, fishing, canoeing, swimming,—days of fine companionship when they learned the human quality in each other. He was strong, buoyant, perfectly sure of himself. No emergency could arise where he would be found wanting in the man's part. The man in him she admired,—it was what first had attracted her,—was proud of it, just as he was proud of her lithe figure, her beauty, her gayety, and her little air of worldliness. She began to assume that this was all of marriage, at least the essential part of it, and that the other, the passionate desire, was something desired by the man and to be avoided by the woman.

They liked their guide, one of those American gypsies, half poacher, half farmer. He kept a wife and family in a shack at the foot of the lake, and Isabelle, with a woman's need for the natural order of life, sought out and made friends with the wild little brood. The woman had been a mill-hand, discovered by the woodsman on a chance visit to the town where she worked, and made his wife, his woman. Not yet thirty, she had had eight children, and another was coming. Freckled, with a few wisps of thin blond hair, her front teeth imperfect, she was an untidy, bedraggled object, used and prematurely aged. Nevertheless the guide seemed attached to her, and when on a Sunday the family went down to the settlement, following the trail through the camp, Isabelle could see him help the woman at the wire fence, carrying on one arm the youngest child, trailing his gun in the other hand.

"He must care for her!" Isabelle remarked.

"Why, of course. Why not?" her husband asked.

"But think—" It was all she could say, not knowing how to put into words the mournful feeling this woman with her brood of young gave her. What joy, what life for herself could such a creature have? Isabelle, her imagination full of comfortable houses with little dinner parties, pretty furniture, books, theatres, charity committees,—

all that she conceived made up a properly married young woman's life, — could not understand the existence of the guide's wife. She was merely the man's woman, a creature to give him children, to cook the food, to keep the fire going. He had the woods, the wild things he hunted; he had, too, his time of drink and rioting; but she was merely his drudge and the instrument of his animal passion. Well, civilization had put a few milestones between herself and Molly Sewall! In the years to come her mind would revert often to this family as she saw it filing down the path to the settlement, the half-clothed children peeping shyly at her, the woman trailing an old shawl from her bent shoulders, the man striding on ahead with his gun and his youngest baby, careless so long as there was a fire, a bit of food, and the forest to roam in. . . .

So passed these days of their honeymoon, each one perfect, except for the occasional disquieting presence of passion, of unappeasable desire in the man. This male fire was as mysterious, as inexplicable to her as that first night, — something to be endured forgivingly, but feared, almost hated for its fierce invasion of her. If her husband could only take her as companion, — the deep, deep friend, the first and best for the long journey of life! Perhaps some day that would content him; perhaps this flower of passion came only at first, to be subdued by the work of life. She never dreamed that some day she herself might change, might be waked by passion. And yet she knew that she loved her husband, yearned to give him all that he desired. Taking his face between her hands, she would kiss it gently, tenderly, as a mother might kiss a hot, impulsive child trying to still a restless spirit within.

This mystery of passion! It swept over the man, transfiguring him as the summer storm swept across the little lake, blackening the sky with shadows through which the lightning played fearsomely. She saw this face hot with desire of her, as the face of a stranger, — another one than the strong, self-contained man she had married, — a face with strange animal and spiritual depths in it, all mixed and vivified. It was the brute, she said to herself, and feared. Brute and God lie close together; but she could not see the God, — felt only the fury of the brute.

Like the storm it passed off, leaving him as she loved him, her tender and worshipping husband. It never entered her thought that she might love any man more than she loved him, that perhaps some day she would long for a passion to meet her own heart. She saw now no lack in her cold limbs, her hard lips, her passionless eyes. She was still Diana, — long, shapely, muscular. In her heart she loved this Diana self, so aloof from desire!

The last night of their stay in the mountains she revolved all these things in her mind as they lay side by side on their fir couch, he asleep in a deep, dreamless fatigue, she alert and tense after the long day in the spirituous air, the night wind sighing to her from the upper branches of the firs. To-morrow they would start for the West, to begin the prose of life. Suddenly a thought flashed over her that stopped the beat of her pulse, — she might already have conceived! She did not wish to escape having children, at least one or two; she knew that it was to be expected, that it was necessary and good. He would want his child and she also, and her father and mother would be made happy by children. But her heart said, — not yet, already. Something in which her part had been so slight! She felt the injustice of Nature that let conception come to a woman indifferently, merely of desire in man and acquiescence in woman. How could that be! How could woman conceive so blindly? The child should be got with joy, should flower from a sublime moment of perfect union when the man and the woman were lifted out of themselves to some divine pinnacle of experience, of soul and body union and self-effacement. Then conception would be but the carrying over of their deep yearning, each for the other, the hunger of souls and bodies to create.

Now she saw that it could be otherwise, as perhaps with

her this very moment: that Nature took the seed, however it might fall, and nourished it wherever it fell, and made of it, regardless of human will, the New Life, — heedless of the emotion of the two that were concerned in the process. For the first time she saw that pitiless, indifferent face of Nature, intent only on the Result, the thing created, scorning the spiritual travail of the creator, ignoring any great revelation of the man and the woman that would seem to count for so much in this process of life-making. Thus a drunken beast might beget his child in the body of a loathing woman, blind souls sowing life blindly for a blind future.

The idea clutched her like fear: she would defy this fate that would use her like any other piece of matrix, merely to bear the seed and nourish it for a certain period of its way, one small step in the long process. Her heart demanded more than a passive part in the order of Nature. Her soul needed its share from the first moment of conception in making that which she was to give to the race. Some day a doctor would explain to her that she was but the soil on which the fertile germ grew like a vegetable, without her will, her consent, her creating soul! But she would reject that coarse interpretation, — the very blasphemy of love.

And here, at this point, as she lay in the dark beneath the sighing firs, it dawned in her dimly that something was wanting in her marriage, in the union with the man she had chosen. She had taken him of her own free choice; she was willingly his; she would bear his children if they came. Her body and her soul were committed to him by choice, and by that ceremony of marriage before the people in the chapel, — to take her part with him in the endless process of Fate, the continuance of life.

Nevertheless, lying there in full contemplation of this new life that might already be putting its clutch upon her life, to suck from her its own being, she rebelled at it all. Her heart cried for her part, her very own, for that mysterious exaltation that should make her really one with the father in the act of creation, in the fulfilment of Love. And somehow she knew assuredly that this could not be, not with this man by her side, not with her husband. . . .

She turned to him, pillowed there at her side, one hand resting fondly on her arm. Her eyes stared at him through the darkness, trying to read the familiar features. Did he, too, know this? Did he feel that it was impossible ever to be really one with her? Did he suspect the terrible defeat she was suffering now? A tear dropped from her eye and fell on the upturned face of the sleeper. He moved, murmured, "dearest," and settled back into his deep sleep, taking his hand from her arm. With a little cry she fell on him and kissed him, asking his forgiveness for the mistake between them. She put her head close to his, her lips to his lips; for she was his and yet not his, — a strange division separating them, a cleavage between their bodies and their souls.

"Why did we not know?" something whispered within. But she answered herself more calmly, — "It will all come right in the end — it must come right — for his sake!"

CHAPTER V

When young John Lane first came to St. Louis to work as a clerk in the traffic department of the Atlantic and Pacific, he had called on Colonel Price at his office, a dingy little room in the corner of the second story of the old brick building which had housed the wholesale hardware business of Parrott and Price for a generation. The old merchant had received the young man with the pleasant kindliness that kept his three hundred employees always devoted to him.

"I knew your father, sir!" he said, half-closing his eyes and leaning back in his padded old office chair. "Let me see — it was in sixty-two in camp before Vicksburg. I went to consult him about a boil on my leg. It was a bad boil, — it hurt me. . . . Your father was a fine man — What are you doing in St. Louis?" he concluded abruptly, looking out of his shrewd blue eyes at the fresh-colored young man whose strong hands gripped squarely the arms of his chair.

And from that day Lane knew that the Colonel never lost sight of him. When his chance came, as in time it did come through one of the mutations of the great corporation, he suspected that the old hardware merchant, who was a close friend of the chief men in the road, had spoken the needed word to lift the clerk out of the rut. At any rate the Colonel had not forgotten the son of Tyringham Lane, and the young man had often been to the generous, ugly Victorian house, — built when the hardware business made its first success.

Nevertheless, when three years later John Lane made another afternoon visit to that dingy office in the Parrott and Price establishment, his hands trembed nervously as he sat waiting while the Colonel scrawled his signature to several papers.

"Well, John!" the old man remarked finally, shoving the papers towards the waiting stenographer. "How's railroadin' these days?"

"All right," Lane answered buoyantly. "They have transferred me to the Indiana division, headquarters at Torso — superintendent of the Torso and Toledo."

"Indeed! But you'll be back here some day, eh?"

"I hope so!"

"That's good!" The Colonel smiled sympathetically, as he always did when he contemplated energetic youth, climbing the long ladder with a firm grip on each rung.

"I came to see you about another matter," Lane began hesitantly.

"Anything I can do for you?"

"Yes, sir; I want to marry your daughter, — and I'd like you to know it."

The old merchant's face became suddenly grave, the twinkle disappearing from his blue eyes. He listened thoughtfully while the young man explained himself. He was still a poor man, of course; his future was to be made. But he did not intend to remain poor. His salary was not much to offer a girl like the Colonel's daughter; but it would go far in Torso — and it was the first step. Finally he was silent, well aware that there was small possibility that he should ever be a rich man, as Colonel Price was, and that it was presumptuous of him to seek to marry his daughter, and therefore open to mean interpretation. But he felt that the Colonel was not one to impute low motives. He knew the very real democracy of the successful merchant, who never had forgotten his own story.

"What does Belle say?" the Colonel asked.

"I should not have come here if I didn't think —" the young man laughed.

"Of course!"

Then the Colonel pulled down the top of his desk, signifying that the day's business was done.

"We have never desired what is called a good match for our girl," he remarked slowly in reply to a further plea from Lane. "All we want is the best;" he laid grave emphasis on this watchword. "And the best is that Isabelle should be happy in her marriage. If she loves the man she marries, she must be that. . . . And I don't suppose you would be here if you weren't sure you could make her love you enough to be happy!"

The old man's smile returned for a fleeting moment, and then he mused.

"I am afraid it will be hard for her to settle down in a place like Torso — after all she's had," Lane conceded. "But I don't expect that Torso is the end of my rope. I shall give her a better chance than that, I hope."

The Colonel nodded sympathetically.

"I shouldn't consider it any hardship for my daughter to live in Torso or in any other place — if she has a good husband and loves him. That is all, my boy!"

Lane, who realized the grades of a plutocratic democracy better than three years before, and knew the position of the Prices in the city, comprehended the splendid simplicity, the single-mindedness of the man, who could thus completely ignore considerations of wealth and social position in the marriage of his only daughter.

"I shall do my best, sir, to make her happy all her life!" the young man stammered.

"I know you will, my boy, and I think you will succeed, if she loves you as you say she does."

Then the Colonel took his hat from the nail behind the door, and the two men continued their conversation in the street. They did not turn up town to the club and residence quarter, but descended towards the river, passing on their way the massive skeleton of the ten-story building that was to house, when completed, the Parrott and Price business. It rose in the smoky sunset, stretching out spidery tendons of steel to the heavens, and from its interior came a mighty clangor. The Colonel paused to look at the new building, — the monument of his success as a merchant.

"Pretty good? Corbin's doing it,—he's the best in the country, they tell me."

Soon they kept on past the new building into an old quarter of the city, the Colonel apparently having some purpose that guided his devious course through these unattractive streets.

"There!" he exclaimed at last, pointing across a dirty street to a shabby little brick house. "That's the place where Isabelle's mother and I started in St. Louis. We had a couple of rooms over there the first winter. The store was just a block further west. It's torn down now. I passed some of the best days of my life in those rooms on the second story. . . . It isn't the outside that counts, my boy!" The Colonel tucked his hand beneath the young man's arm, as they turned back to the newer quarters of the city.

Mrs. Price, it should be said, did not accept Lane's suit as easily as the Colonel. Her imagination had been expanded by that winter in Washington, and though she was glad that Isabelle had not accepted any of "those foreigners," yet Harmony Price had very definite ideas of the position that the Colonel's daughter might aspire to in America. . . . But her objections could not stand before the Colonel's flat consent and Isabelle's decision.

"They'll be a great deal better off than we were," her husband reminded her.

"That's no reason why Belle should have to start where we did, or anywhere near it!" his wife retorted. What one generation had been able to gain in the social fight, it seemed to her only natural that the next should at least hold.

The Colonel gave the couple their new home in Torso, selecting, with a fine eye for real estate values, a large "colonial" wooden house with ample grounds out beyond the smoke of the little city, near the new country club. Mrs. Price spent an exciting three months running back and forth between New York, St. Louis, and Torso furnishing the new home. Isabelle's liberal allowance was to continue indefinitely, and beyond this the Colonel promised nothing, now or later; nor would Lane have accepted more from his hand. It was to the Torso house that the Lanes went immediately after their month in the Adirondacks.

Torso, Indiana, is one of those towns in the Mississippi Valley which makes more impression the farther from New York one travels. New York has never heard of it, except as it appears occasionally on a hotel register among other queer places that Americans confess to as home. At Pittsburg it is a round black spot on the map, in the main ganglia of the great A. and P. and the junction point of two other railroads. At Cincinnati it is a commercial centre of considerable importance, almost a rival. While Torso to Torso is the coming pivot of the universe.

It is an old settlement — some families with French names still own the large distilleries — on the clay banks of a sluggish creek in the southern part of the state, and there are many Kentuckians in its population. Nourished by railroads, a division headquarters of the great A. and P., near the soft-coal beds, with a tin-plate factory, a carpet factory, a carriage factory, and a dozen other mills and factories, Torso is a black smudge in a flat green landscape from which many lines of electric railway radiate forth along the country roads. And along the same roads across the reaches of prairie, over the swelling hills, stalk towering poles, bearing many fine wires glistening in the sunlight and singing the importance of Torso to the world at large.

The Lanes arrived at night, and to Isabelle the prairie heavens seemed dark and far away, the long broad streets with their bushy maple trees empty, and the air filled with hoarse plaints, the rumbling speech of the railroad. She was homesick and fearful, as they mounted the steps to the new house and pushed open the shining oak door that stuck and smelled of varnish. The next morning Lane whisked off on a trolley to the A. and P. offices, while Isabelle walked around the house, which faced the main northern artery of Torso. From the western veranda she could see the roof of the new country club through a ragged group of trees. On the other side were dotted the ample houses of Torso aristocracy, similar to hers, as she knew, finished in hard wood, electric-lighted, telephoned, with many baths, large "picture" windows of plate glass, with potted ferns in them, and much the same furniture, — wholesome, comfortable "homes." Isabelle, turning back to her house to cope with the three Swedes that her mother had sent on from St. Louis, had a queer sense of anti-climax. She swept the landscape with a critical eye, feeling she knew it all, even to what the people were saying at this moment in those large American-Georgian mansions; what Torso was doing at this moment in its main street. . . . No, it could not be for the Lanes for long, — that was the conviction in her heart. Their destiny would be larger, fuller than any to be found in Torso. Just what she meant by a "large, full life," she had never stopped to set down; but she was sure it was not to be found here in Torso.

Here began, however, the routine of her married life. Each morning she watched her husband walk down the broad avenue to the electric car, — alert, strong, waving his newspaper to her as he turned the corner. Each afternoon she waited for him at the same place, or drove down to the office with the Kentucky horses that she had bought, to take him for a drive before dinner. He greeted her each time with the same satisfied smile, apparently not wilted by the long hours in a hot office. There was a smudged, work-a-day appearance to his face and linen, the mark of Torso, the same mark that the mill-hands across the street from the A. and P. offices brought home to their wives. . . . Thus the long summer days dragged. For distraction there was a mutiny in the crew of Swedish servants, but Isabelle, with her mother's instinct for domestic management, quickly produced order, in spite of the completely servantless state of Torso. She would telegraph to St. Louis for what she wanted and somehow always got it. The house ran, — that was her business. It was pretty and attractive, — that was also her business. But this woman's work she tossed off quickly. Then what? She pottered in the garden a little, but when the hot blasts of prairie heat in mid-August had shrivelled all the vines and flowers and cooked the beds into slabs of clay, she retired from the garden and sent to St. Louis for the daily flowers. She read a good deal, almost always novels, in the vague belief that she was "keeping up" with modern literature, and she played at translating some German lyrics.

Then people began to call, — the wives of the Torso great, her neighbors in those ample mansions scattered all about the prairie. These she reported to John with a mocking sense of their oddity.

"Mrs. Fraser came to-day. What is she? Tin-plate or coal?"

"He's the most important banker here," her husband explained seriously.

"Oh, — well, she asked me to join the 'travel-class.' They are going through the Holy Land. What do you suppose a 'travel-class' is?" . . .

Again it was the wife of the chief coal operator, Freke, "who wanted me to know that she always got her clothes from New York." She added gently, "I think she wished to find out if we are fit for Torso society. I did my best to give her the impression we were beneath it." . . .

These people, all the "society" of Torso, they met also at the country club, where they went Sundays for a game of golf, which Lane was learning. The wife of the A. and P. superintendent could not be ignored by Torso, and so in spite of Isabelle's efforts there was forming around her a social life. But the objective point of the day remained John, — his going and coming.

"Busy day?" she would ask when he bent to kiss her.

"They're all busy days!"

"Tell me what you did."

"Oh," he would answer vaguely, "just saw people and dictated letters and telegrams, — yes, it was a busy day." And he left her to dress for dinner.

She knew that he was weary after all the problems that he had thrust his busy mind into since the morning. She had no great curiosity to know what these problems were. She had been accustomed to the sanctity of business reserve in her father's house: men disappeared in the morning to their work and emerged to wash and dress and be as amusing as they might for the few remaining hours of the day. There were rumors of what went on in that mysterious world of business, but the right kind of men did not disclose the secrets of the office to women.

It never occurred to Lane to go over with her the minute detail of his full day: how he had considered an application from a large shipper for switching privileges, had discussed the action of the Torso and Northern in cutting the coal rates, had lunched with Freke, the president of a coal company that did business with the A. and P.; and had received, just as he left the office, the report of a serious freight wreck at one end of his division. As he had said, a busy day! And this business of life, like an endless steel chain, had caught hold of him at once and was carrying him fast in its revolution. It was his life; he liked it. With cool head and steady nerves he set himself at each problem, working it out according to known rules, calling on his trained experience. He did not look into the future, content with the preoccupation of the present, confident that the future, whatever and wherever it might be, would be crowded with affairs, activity, which he would meet competently. . . .

"Well, what have *you* been doing?" he asked as he sat down, fresh from his bath, and relaxed comfortably in anticipation of a pleasant dinner. Isabelle made a great point of dinner, having it served formally by two maids, with five courses and at least one wine, "to get used to living properly," as she explained vaguely.

"Mrs. Adams called." She was the wife of the manager of the baking-powder works and president of the country club, a young married woman from a Western city with pretensions to social experience. "John," Isabelle added after mentioning this name, "do you think we shall have to stay here long?"

Her husband paused in eating his soup to look at her. "Why — why?"

"It's so second-classy," she continued; "at least the women are, mostly. There's only one I've met so far that seemed like other people one has known."

"Who is she?" Lane inquired, ignoring the large question.

"Mrs. Falkner."

"Rob Falkner's wife? He's engineer at the Pleasant Valley mines."

"She came from Denver."

"They say he's a clever engineer."

"She is girlish and charming. She told me all about every one in Torso. She's been here two years, and she seems to know everybody."

"And she thinks Torso is second-class?" Lane inquired.

"She would like to get away, I think. But they are poor, I suppose. Her clothes look as if she knew what to wear, — pretty. She says there are some interesting people here when you find them out. . . . Who is Mr. Darnell? A lawyer."

"Tom Darnell? He's one of the local counsel for the road, — a Kentuckian, politician, talkative sort of fellow, very popular with all sorts. What did Mrs. Falkner have to say about Tom Darnell?"

"She told me all about his marriage, — how he ran away with his wife from a boarding-school in Kentucky — and was chased by her father and brothers, and they fired at him. A regular Southern scrimmage! But they got across the river and were married."

"Sounds like Darnell," Lane remarked contemptuously.

"It sounds exciting!" his wife said.

The story, as related by the vivacious Mrs. Falkner, had stirred Isabelle's curiosity; she could not dismiss this Kentucky politician as curtly as her husband had disposed of him. . . .

They were both wilted by the heat, and after dinner they strolled out into the garden to get more air, walking leisurely arm in arm, while Lane smoked his first cigar. Having finished the gossip for the day, they had little to say to each other, — Isabelle wondered that it should be so little! Two months of daily companionship after the intimate weeks of their engagement had exhausted the topics for mere talk which they had in common. To-night, as Lane wished to learn the latest news from the wreck, they went into the town, crossing on their way to the office the court-house square. This was the centre of old Torso, where the distillery aristocracy still lived in high, broad-eaved houses of the same pattern as the Colonel's city mansion. In one of these, which needed painting and was generally neglected, the long front windows on the first story were open, revealing a group of people sitting around a supper-table.

"There's Mrs. Falkner," Isabelle remarked; "the one at the end of the table, in white. This must be where they live."

Lane looked at the house with a mental estimate of the rent. "Large house," he observed.

Isabelle watched the people laughing and talking about the table, which was still covered with coffee cups and glasses. A sudden desire to be there, to hear what they were saying, seized her. A dark-haired man was leaning forward and emphasizing his remarks by tapping a wine glass with a long finger. That might be Tom Darnell, she thought. . . . The other houses about the square were dark and gloomy, most of them closed for the summer.

"There's a good deal of money in Torso," Lane commented, glancing at a brick house with wooden pillars. "It's a growing place, — more business coming all the time."

He looked at the town with the observant eye of the railroad officer, who sees in the prosperity of any community but one word writ large, — TRAFFIC.

And that word was blown through the soft night by the puffing locomotives in the valley below, by the pall of smoke that hung night and day over this quarter of the city, the dull glow of the coke-ovens on the distant hills. To the man this was enough — this and his home; business and the woman he had won, — they were his two poles!

CHAPTER VI

"YOU see," continued Bessie Falkner, drawing up her pretty feet into the piazza cot, "it was just love at first sight. I was up there at the hotel in the mountains, trying to make up my mind whether I could marry another man, who was awfully rich — owned a mine and a ranch; but he was so dull the horses would go to sleep when we were out driving. . . . And then just as I concluded it was the only thing for me to do, to take him and make the best of him, — then Rob rode up to the hotel in his old tattered suit — he was building a dam or something up in the mountains — and I knew I couldn't marry Mr. Mine-and-Ranch. That was all there was to it, my dear. The rest of the story? Why, of course he made the hotel his headquarters while he was at work on the dam; I stayed on, too, and it came along — naturally, you know."

Mrs. Falkner dipped into a box of candy and swung the cot gently to and fro. The men were still talking inside the house and the two wives had come outside for long confidences. Isabelle, amused by this sketch of the Colorado courtship, patted the blond woman's little hand. Mrs. Falkner had large blue eyes, with waving tendrils of hair, which gave her face the look of childish unsophistication, — especially at this moment when her voluptuous lips were closing over a specially desired piece of candy.

"Of course it would come along — with you!"

"I didn't do a thing — just waited," Bessie protested, fishing about the almost empty box for another delectable bit. "He did it all. He was in such a hurry he wanted to marry me then and there at the hotel and go live up in the mountains in a cabin above the dam where he was at work. He's romantic. Men are all like that then, don't you think? But of course it couldn't be that way; so we got married properly in the fall in Denver, and then came straight here. And," with a long sigh, "we've been here ever since. Stuck!"

"I should think you would have preferred the cabin above the dam," Isabelle suggested, recalling her own romantic notion of Dog Mountain. Mrs. Falkner made a little grimace.

"That might do for two or three months. But snowed in all the winter, even with the man you like best in all the world? He'd kill you or escape through the drifts. . . . You see we hadn't a thing, not a cent, except his salary and that ended with the dam. It was only eighty a month any way. This is better, a hundred and fifty," she explained with childish frankness. "But Rob has to work harder and likes the mountains, is always talking of going back. But I say there are better things than hiding yourself at the land's end. There's St. Louis, or maybe New York!"

Isabelle wondered how the Falkners were able to support such a hospitable house — they had two small children and Bessie had confided that another was coming in the spring — on the engineer's salary.

"And the other one," Mrs. Falkner added in revery, "is more than a millionnaire now."

Her face was full of speculation over what might have been as the wife of all that money.

"But we are happy, Rob and I, — except for the bills! Don't you hate bills?"

Isabelle's only answer was a hearty laugh. She found this pretty, frank little "Westerner" very attractive.

"It was bills that made my mother unhappy — broke her heart. Sometimes we had money, — most generally not. Such horrid fusses when there wasn't any. But what is one to do? You've got to go on living somehow. Rob says we can't afford this house, — Rob is always afraid we won't get through. But we do somehow. I tell him that the good time is coming, — we must just anticipate it, draw a little on the future."

At this point the men came through the window to the piazza. Bessie shook her box of candy coquettishly at Lane, who took the chair beside her. Evidently he thought her amusing, as most men did. Falkner leaned against the white pillar and stared up at the heavens. Isabelle, accustomed to men of more conventional social qualities, had found the young engineer glum and odd. He had a stern, rather handsome face, a deep furrow dividing his forehead and meeting the part of his thick brown hair, which curled slightly at the ends. "If he didn't look so cross, he would be quite handsome," thought Isabelle, wondering how long it might be before her host would speak to her. She could see him as he rode up to the hotel piazza that day, when Bessie Falkner had made up her mind on the moment that she could not marry "the other man." Finally Falkner broke his glum silence.

"Do you eat candy, Mrs. Lane? Pounds of it, I mean, — so that it is your staple article of diet."

"Tut, tut," remarked his wife from her cot. "Don't complain."

His next remark was equally abrupt.

"There's only one good thing in this Torso hole," he observed with more animation than he had shown all the evening, "and that's the coke-ovens at night — have you noticed them? They are like the fiery pits, smouldering, ready for the damned!"

It was not what she expected from a civil engineer, in Torso, Indiana, and she was at a loss for a reply.

"You'd rather have stayed in Colorado?" she asked frankly.

He turned his face to her and said earnestly, "Did you ever sleep out on a mountain with the stars close above you? — 'the vast tellurian galleons' voyaging through space?"

Isabelle suspected that he was quoting poetry, which also seemed odd in Torso.

"Yes, — my brother and I used to camp out at our home

in Connecticut. But I don't suppose you would call our Berkshire Hills mountains."

"No," he replied dryly, "I shouldn't."

And their conversation ended. Isabelle wished that the Darnells had not been obliged to go home immediately after supper. The young lawyer knew how to talk to women, and had made himself very agreeable, telling stories of his youth spent among the mountains with a primitive people. She had observed that he drank a good deal of whiskey, and there was something in his black eyes that made her uncomfortable. But he was a man that women liked to think about: he touched their imaginations. She did not talk about him to John on their way home, however, but discussed the Falkners.

"Don't you think she is perfectly charming?" (Charming was the word she had found for Bessie Falkner.) "So natural and amusing! She's very Western — she can't have seen much of life — but she isn't a bit ordinary."

"Yes, I like her," Lane replied unenthusiastically, "and he seems original. I shouldn't wonder if he were clever in his profession; he told me a lot about Freke's mines."

What he had learned about the Pleasant Valley mines was the chief thing in the evening to Lane. He did not understand why Isabelle seemed so much more eager to know these people — these Darnells and Falkners — than the Frasers and the Adamses. She had made fun of the solemn dinner that the Frasers had given to introduce them into Torso "society."

"I wonder how they can live on that salary," Isabelle remarked. "One hundred and fifty a month!"

"He must make something outside."

After the Lanes had gone, Bessie Falkner prepared yawningly for bed, leaving her husband to shut up the house. Her weekly excitement of entertaining people over, she always felt let down, like a poet after the stir of creation. It was useless to go over the affair with Rob, as he was merely bored. But she spent hours thinking what the women said and how they looked and deciding whom she could have the next time. On her way to bed she went into the nursery where her two little girls were asleep in their cots beside the nurse, and finding a window open woke the nurse to reprove her for her carelessness. In the hall she met her husband bringing up the silver.

"Emma is so thoughtless," she complained. "I shall have to let her go if I can find another servant in this town."

Her husband listened negligently. The Falkners were perpetually changing their two servants, or were getting on without them.

"Mrs. Lane's maids all wear caps," Mrs. Falkner had observed frequently to her husband.

Bessie had strict ideas of how a house should be run, ideas derived from the best houses that she was familiar with. Since the advent of the Lanes she had extended these ideas and strove all the harder to achieve magnificent results. Though the livery of service was practically unknown in Torso, she had resolved to induce her cook (and maid of all work) to serve the meals with cap and apron, and also endeavored to have the nursemaid open the door and help serve when company was expected.

"What's the use!" her husband protested. "They'll only get up and go."

He could not understand the amount of earnest attention and real feeling that his wife put into these things, — her pride to have her small domain somewhat resemble the more affluent ones that she admired. Though her family had been decidedly plain, they had given her "advantages" in education and dress, and her own prettiness, her vivacity and charm, had won her way into whatever society Kansas City and Denver could offer. She had also visited here and there in different parts of the country, — once in New York, and again at a cottage on the New England coast where there were eight servants, a yacht, and horses. These experiences of luxury, of an easy and large social life, she had absorbed through every pore. With that marvellous adaptability of her race she had quickly formed her ideals of "how people ought to live." It was frequently difficult to carry out these ideals on a circumscribed income, with a husband who cared nothing for appearances, and that was a source of constant discontent to Bessie.

"Coming to bed?" she asked her husband, as she looked in vain for the drinking water that the maid was supposed to bring to her bedside at night.

"No," Falkner answered shortly. "I've got to make out those estimates somehow before morning. If you will have people all the time — "

Bessie turned in at her door shrugging her shoulders. Rob was in one of his "cross" moods, — overworked, poor boy! She slowly began to undress before the mirror, thinking of Isabelle Lane's stylish figure and her perfect clothes. "She must have lots of money," she reflected, "and so nice and simple! He's attractive, too. Rob is foolish not to like them. He showed his worst side to-night. If he wants to get on, — why, they are the sort of people he ought to know." Her husband's freakish temper gave her much trouble, his unexpectedly bearish moods when she was doing her very best for him, "bringing him out" as she put it, making the right kind of friends, — influential ones, so that he might have some chance in the scramble for the good things of life. Surely that was a wife's part. Bessie was satisfied that she had done much for her husband in this way, developed him socially; for when he rode up to the mountain hotel, he was solitary, moody, shy. To-night he hadn't kissed her, — in fact hadn't done so for several days. He was tired by the prolonged heat, she supposed, and worried about the bills. He was always worried about expenses.

As the clothes slipped from her still shapely figure, she stood before the glass, thinking in a haze of those first lover-days that had departed so soon. Now instead of petting her, Rob spent his hours at home upstairs in his attic workroom, doing extra work or reading. Could it be that he was growing tired of her, so soon, in four years? She glanced over her shoulder at her pretty arms, her plump white neck reflected in the glass, and smiled unconsciously with assurance. Oh, he would come back to the lover-mood — she was still desirable! And as the smile curved her lip she thought, "I married him for love!" She was very proud of that. . . .

The house was now deliciously cool and quiet. Bessie sank into her bed with a sigh, putting out one hand for a magazine and turning on the electric light beside the bed. It had been a tiresome day, with the supper to bring off. There had been six courses, and everything had been very nice. The black cook she had engaged to prepare the meal was a treasure, could serve a better dinner than Mrs. Fraser's or Mrs. Adams's. She herself had made the salad and prepared the iced grape-fruit. Every limb ached — she was always so tired. She loved this last quiet hour of the day that she had by herself, now that the nurse took both the children. With her delicate health the nurse had been a necessity. She usually looked blooming and rosy, but was always tired, always had been as long as she could remember. The doctor had told Falkner after the second child came that his wife would always be a delicate woman, must be carefully protected, or she would collapse and have the fearful modern disease of nerves. So Falkner had insisted on having the best nurse obtainable to relieve her from the wearing nights, — though it meant that somehow eighteen hundred dollars must grow of itself!

As midnight sounded from the court-house clock, Bessie laid down the magazine and stretched her tired limbs, luxuriating in the comfort of her soft bed. The story she had been reading was sentimental, — the love of a cow-boy for the fair daughter of a railroad president. She longed for the caresses of her cow-boy lover, and wondered dreamily if Lane were a devoted husband. He seemed so; but all men were probably alike: their first desires gratified, they thought of other things. So she put out the light and closed her eyes, in faint discontent with life, which was proving less romantic than she had anticipated.

She had her own room. At first it had held two beds, her husband sharing the room with her. But as the house was large he had taken a room on the third story. Nowadays, as Bessie knew, the better sort of American household does not use the primitive double bed. For hygiene and comfort enlightened people have taken to separate beds, then separate quarters. A book might be written on the doing away of the conjugal bed in American life! There should be interesting observations on the effect of this change, social, and hygienic, and moral, — oh, most interesting! . . . A contented smile at last stole over the young wife's face. Was she dreaming of her babies, of those first days of love, when her husband never wished her out of his sight, or simply of the well-ordered, perfectly served, pretty supper that she had given for the Lanes whom she was most anxious to know well? The supper had quite met her aspirations except in the matter of caps and aprons, had satisfied her cherished ideal of how "nice people" lived in this world.

That ideal is constantly expanding these days. In America no one is classed by birth or profession. All is to make, and the women with their marvellous powers of absorption do the shaping. In a thousand ways they learn "how to live as other people do," — in magazines and on bill boards, in the theatre, the churches, the trains, the illustrated novel. Suggestions how to live!

Meantime upstairs in the mansard room of the old house Falkner was figuring over stresses and strains of an unemotional sort. When past midnight he shoved the papers into the drawer, a familiar thought coursed through his brain: somehow he must sell himself at a dearer price. Living was not cheap even in Torso, and the cost of living was ever going higher, so the papers said and the wives. There were four of them now, a fifth to come in a few months. There should be a third servant, he knew, if they were to live "like other people." With a gesture that said, "Oh, Hell!" he jumped from his chair and took down a volume of verse from the pine shelf above the mantel and lighted a cigarette. For a few minutes he might lose himself and forget the fret of life, in the glowing pictures of things not seen.

The book dropped from his hand. He had carried it in his mountain kit, had read it to Bessie when they were engaged. She had listened, flattered, looking at him and smoothing his hair. But after marriage she confessed flatly that she was not "literary." So they had read together a book of travels, then a novel, then a magazine, and latterly nothing. Taking another cigarette, the man read on, and before his tired eyes rose the purple peaks of the Rockies, the shining crests of snow, the azure sky. And also a cabin in a green meadow beside a still mountain lake, and a woman fair and tall and straight, with blue eyes and a caressing hand, — a child on one arm. But Bessie was sleeping downstairs. Putting out his light, the man went to bed.

The man on horseback riding up the trail to look into the girl's eyes that summer afternoon!

CHAPTER VII

The two young wives quickly became very intimate. They spent many mornings together "reading," that is, they sat on the cool west veranda of the Lanes's house, or less often on the balcony at the Falkners's, with a novel turned down where their attention had relaxed, chatting and sewing. Isabelle found Bessie Falkner "cunning," "amusing," "odd," and always "charming." She had "an air about her," a picturesque style of gossip that she used when instructing Isabelle in the intricacies of Torso society. Isabelle also enjoyed the homage that Bessie paid her.

Bessie frankly admired Isabelle's house, her clothes, her stylish self, and enjoyed her larger experience of life, — the Washington winter, Europe, even the St. Louis horizon, — all larger than anything she had ever known. Isabelle was very nearly the ideal of what she herself would have liked to be. So when they had exhausted Torso and their households, they filled the morning hours with long tales about people they had known, — "Did you ever hear of the Dysarts in St. Louis? Sallie Dysart was a great belle, — she had no end of affairs, and then she married Paul Potter. The Potters were very well-known people in Philadelphia, etc." Thus they gratified their curiosity about *lives*, all the interesting complications into which men and women might get. Often Bessie stayed for luncheon, a dainty affair served on a little table which the maid brought out and set between them. Sometimes Bessie had with her the baby girl, but oftener not, for she became exacting and interfered with the luncheon.

Bessie had endless tidbits of observation about Torsonians. "Mrs. Freke was a cashier in a Cleveland restaurant when he married her. Don't you see the bang in her hair still? . . . Mrs. Griscom came from Kentucky, — very old family. Tom Griscom, their only son, went to Harvard, — he was very wild. He's disappeared since. . . . Yes, Mrs. Adams is common, but the men seem to like her. I don't trust her green eyes. Mr. Darnell, they say, is always there. Oh, Mr. Adams isn't the one to care!"

Often they came back to Darnell, — that impetuous, black-haired young lawyer with his deep-set, fiery eyes, who had run away with his wife.

"She looks scared most of the time, don't you think? They say he drinks. Too bad, isn't it? Such a brilliant man, and with the best chances. He ran for Congress two years ago on the Democratic ticket, and just failed. He is going to try again this next fall, but his railroad connection is against him. . . . Oh, Sue Darnell, — she is nobody; she can't hold him — that's plain."

"What does she think of Mrs. Adams?"

Bessie shrugged her shoulders significantly.

"Sue has to have her out at their farm. Well, they say she was pretty gay herself, — engaged to three men at once, — one of them turned up in Torso last year. Tom was very polite to him, elaborately polite; but he left town very soon, and she seemed dazed. . . . I guess she has reason to be afraid of her husband. He looks sometimes — well, I shouldn't like to have Rob look at me that way, not for half a second!"

The two women clothed the brilliant Kentuckian with all the romance of unbridled passion. "He sends to Alabama every week for the jasmine Mrs. Adams wears — fancy!"

"Really! Oh, men! men!"

"It's probably *her* fault — she can't hold him."

That was the simple philosophy which they evolved about marriage, — men were uncertain creatures, only partly tamed, and it was the woman's business to "hold" them. So much the worse for the women if they happened to be tied to men they could not "hold." Isabelle, remembering on one occasion the flashing eyes of the Kentuckian, his passionate denunciation of mere commercialism in public life, felt that there might be some defence for poor Tom Darnell, — even in his flirtation with the "common" Mrs. Adams.

Then the two friends went deeper and talked husbands, both admiring, both hilariously amused at the masculine absurdities of their mates.

"I hate to see poor Rob so harassed with bills," Bessie confided. "It is hard for him, with his tastes, poor boy. But I don't know what I can do about it. When he complains, I tell him we eat everything we have, and I am sure I never get a dress!"

Isabelle, recollecting the delicious suppers she had had at the Falkners', thought that less might be eaten. In her mother's house there had always been comfort, but strict economy, even after the hardware business paid enormous profits. This thrift was in her blood. Bessie had said to Rob that Isabelle was "close." But Isabelle only laughed at Bessie when she was in these moods of dejection, usually at the first of the month. Bessie was so amusing about her troubles that she could not take her seriously.

"Never mind, Bessie!" she laughed. "He probably likes to work hard for you, — every man does for the woman he loves."

And then they would have luncheon, specially devised for Bessie's epicurean taste. For Bessie Falkner did devout homage to a properly cooked dish. Isabelle, watching the contented look with which the little woman swallowed a bit of jellied meat, felt that any man worth his salt would like to gratify her innocent tastes. Probably Falkner couldn't endure a less charming woman for his wife. So she condoned, as one does with a clever child, all the little manifestations of waywardness and selfishness that she was too intelligent not to see in her new friend. Isabelle liked to spoil Bessie Falkner. Everybody liked to indulge her, just as one likes to feed a pretty child with cake and candy, especially when the discomforts of the resulting indigestion fall on some one else.

"Oh, it will all come out right in the end!" Bessie usually exclaimed, after she had well lunched. She did not see things very vividly far ahead, — nothing beyond the pleasant luncheon, the attractive house, her adorable Isabelle. "I always tell Rob when he is blue that his chance will come some day; he'll make a lucky strike, do some work that attracts public attention, and then we'll all be as happy as can be."

She had the gambler's instinct; her whole life had been a gamble, now winning, now losing, even to that moment when her lover had ridden up to the hotel and solved her doubts about the rich suitor. In Colorado she had known men whose fortunes came over night, "millions and millions," as she told Isabelle, rolling the words in her little mouth toothsomely. Why not to her? She felt that any day fortune might smile.

"My husband says that Mr. Falkner is doing excellent work, — Mr. Freke said so," Isabelle told Bessie.

"And Rob talks as if he were going to lose his job next week! Sometimes I wish he would lose it — and we could go away to a large city."

Bessie thus echoed the feeling in Isabelle's own heart, — "I don't want to spend my life on an Indiana prairie!" To both of the women Torso was less a home, a corner of the earth into which to put down roots, than a way-station in the drama and mystery of life. Confident in their husbands' ability to achieve Success, they dreamed of other scenes, of a larger future, with that restlessness of a new civilization, which has latterly seized even women — the supposedly stable sex.

As the year wore on there were broader social levels into which Isabelle in company with Bessie dipped from time to time. The Woman's Club had a lecture course in art and sociology. They attended one of the lectures in the Normal

School building, and laughed furtively in their muffs at "Madam President" of the Club, — a portly, silk-dressed dame, — and at the ill-fitting black coat of the university professor who lectured. They came away before the reception.

"Dowds!" Bessie summed up succinctly.

"Rather crude," Isabelle agreed tolerantly.

During the winter Isabelle did some desultory visiting among the Hungarians employed at the coke-ovens, for Bessie's church society. Originally of Presbyterian faith, she had changed at St. Mary's to the Episcopal church, and latterly all church affiliations had grown faint. The Colonel maintained a pew in the first Presbyterian Church, but usually went to hear the excellent lectures of a Unitarian preacher. Isabelle's religious views were vague, broad, liberal, and unvital. Bessie's were simpler, but scarcely more effective. Lane took a lively interest in the railroad Y.M.C.A., which he believed to be helpful for young men. He himself had been a member in St. Louis and had used the gymnasium. Isabelle got up an entertainment for the Hungarian children, which was ended by a disastrous thunderstorm. She had an uneasy feeling that she "ought to do something for somebody." Alice Johnston, she knew, had lived at a settlement for a couple of years. But there were no settlements in Torso, and the acutely poor were looked after by the various churches. Just what there was to be done for others was not clear. When she expressed her desire "not to live selfishly" to her husband, he replied easily: —

"There are societies for those things, I suppose. It ought to be natural, what we do for others."

Just what was meant by "natural" was not clear to Isabelle, but the word accorded with the general belief of her class that the best way to help in the world was to help one's self, to become useful to others by becoming important in the community, — a comfortable philosophy. But there was one definite thing that they might accomplish, and that was to help the Falkners into easier circumstances.

"Don't you suppose we could do something for them? Now that the baby has come they are dreadfully poor,— can't think of going away for the summer, and poor Bessie needs it and the children. I meant to ask the Colonel when he was here last Christmas. Isn't there something Rob could do in the road?"

Lane shook his head.

"That is not my department. There might be a place in St. Louis when they begin work on the new terminals. I'll speak to Brundage the next time he's here."

"St. Louis — Bessie would like that. She's such a dear, and would enjoy pretty things so much! It seems as if she almost had a right to them."

"Why did she marry a poor man, then?" Lane demanded with masculine logic.

"Because she loved him, silly! She isn't mercenary."

"Well, then, — " but Lane did not finish his sentence, kissing his wife instead. "She's rather extravagant, isn't she?" he asked after a time.

"Oh, she'll learn to manage."

"I will do what I can for him, of course."

And Isabelle considered the Falkners' fate settled; John, like her father, always brought about what he wanted.

They spent the Christmas holidays that year with her parents. Lane was called to New York on railroad business, and Isabelle had a breathless ten days with old friends, dining and lunching, listening to threads of gossip that had been broken by her exile to Torso. She discovered an unexpected avidity for diversion, and felt almost ashamed to enjoy people so keenly, to miss her husband so little. She put it all down to the cramping effect of Torso. So when the Colonel asked her how she liked her new home, she burst forth, feeling that her opportunity had come: —

"It doesn't agree with me, I think. I've grown frightfully thin,—John says I mustn't spend another summer there. . . . I hope we can get away soon. John must have a wider field, don't you think?"

"He seems to find Torso pretty wide."

"He's done splendid work, I know. But I don't want him side-tracked all his life in a little Indiana town. Don't you think you could speak to the Senator or Mr. Beals?"

The Colonel smiled.

"Yes, I could speak to them, if John wants me to."

"He hasn't said anything about it," she hastened to add.

"So you are tired of Torso?" he asked, smiling still more.

"It seems so good to be here, to hear some music, and go to the theatre; to be near old friends," she explained apologetically. "Don't you and mother want us to be near you?"

"Of course, my dear! We want you to be happy."

"Why, we are happy there, — only it seems so out of the world, so second-class. And John is not second-class."

"No, John is not second-class," the Colonel admitted with another smile. "And for that reason I don't believe he will want me to interfere."

Nevertheless she kept at her idea, talking it over with her mother. All her friends were settled in the great cities, and it was only natural that she should aspire to something better than Torso — for the present, St. Louis. So the Colonel spoke to Lane, and Lane spoke to his wife when they were back once more in the Torso house. He was grave, almost hurt.

"I'm sorry, Belle, you are so tired of life here. I can take another position or ask to be transferred; but you must understand, dear, that whatever is done, it must be by myself. I don't want favors, not even from the Colonel!"

She felt ashamed and small, yet protested: "I don't see why you should object. Every one does the same, — uses all the pull he has."

"There are changes coming, — I prefer to wait. The man who uses least pull usually hangs on longest."

As he walked to the office that morning, the thought of Isabelle's restlessness occupied his mind. "It's dull for her here, of course. It isn't the kind of life she's been used to, or had the right to expect as the Colonel's daughter." He felt the obligation to live up to his wife, having won her from a superior position. Like a chivalrous American gentleman he was not aggrieved because even during the first two years of marriage, he — their life together — was not enough to satisfy his wife. He did not reflect that his mother had accepted unquestioningly the Iowa town to which his father had brought her after the War; nor that Isabelle's mother had accepted cheerfully the two rooms in the little brick house near the hardware store. Those were other days.

He saw the picture of Isabelle standing beside the dining-room window with the sun on her hair, — a developed type of human being, that demanded much of life for satisfaction and adjustment. He plunged into his affairs with an added grip, an unconscious feeling that he must by his exertions provide those satisfactions and adjustments which his wife's nature demanded for its perfect development.

CHAPTER VIII

It was to be Isabelle's first real dinner-party, a large affair for Torso. It had already absorbed her energies for a fortnight. The occasion was the arrival of a party of Atlantic and Pacific officials and directors, who were to inspect the Torso and Northern, with a view to its purchase and absorption. The Torso and Northern was only a little scab line of railroad, penetrating the soft-coal country for a couple of hundred miles, bankrupt and demoralized. When Lane saw President Beals at Christmas, he pointed out to him what might be made of this scrap-heap road, if it were rehabilitated and extended into new coal fields. Beals had shown no interest in the Torso and Northern at that time, and Lane forgot the matter until he noticed that there was a market for Torso and Northern equipment bonds, which before had been unsalable at twenty. Seeing them rise point by point for a month, he had bought all he could pay for; he knew the weather signs in the railroad world. When the inspection party was announced, his sagacity was proved.

Isabelle was excited by the prospect of her dinner for the distinguished visitors. Who should she have of Torso's best to meet them? The Frasers and the Griscoms, of course. John insisted on inviting the Frekes, and Isabelle wanted the Darnells and the Adamses, though her husband demurred at recognizing the bond. But Tom Darnell was so interesting, his wife urged, and she was presentable. And the Falkners? There was no special reason for having them, but Isabelle thought it might be a good thing for Rob to meet some influential people, and Bessie would surely amuse the men. Isabelle's executive energy was thoroughly aroused. The flowers and the wines were ordered from St. Louis, the terrapin from Philadelphia, the fish and the candies from New York. Should they have champagne? Lane thought not, because "it's not quite our style." But Isabelle overbore his objection: —

"The Adamses always have it, and the Senator will expect it and all the New York crowd."

Her husband acquiesced, feeling that in these things his wife knew the world better than he, — though he would have preferred to offer his superior officers a simpler meal.

The inspection party returned from their trip over the Torso and Northern in the best of spirits. Lane felt sure that the purchase had been decided upon by this inner coterie of the A. and P., of which the mouthpiece, Senator Thomas, had emitted prophetic phrases, — "valuable possibilities undeveloped," "would tap new fields, — good feeder," etc., etc. Lane thought pleasantly of the twenty equipment bonds in his safe, which would be redeemed by the Atlantic and Pacific at par and accrued interest, and he resolved to secure another block, if they were to be had, before the sale was officially confirmed by the directors. Altogether it had been an agreeable jaunt. He had met several influential directors and had been generally consulted as the man who knew the exact local conditions. And he was aware that he had made a favorable impression as a practical railroad man. . . .

When his guests came down to the drawing-room, he was proud of what his wife had done. The house was ablaze with candles — Bessie had persuaded Isabelle to dispense with the electric light — and bunches of heavy, thick-stemmed roses filled the vases. A large silver tray of decanters and cocktails was placed in the hall beside the blazing fire. The Senator had already possessed himself of a cocktail, and was making his little speeches to Isabelle, who in a Paris gown that gave due emphasis to her pretty shoulders and thin figure, was listening to him gayly.

"Did you think we lived in a log-cabin, Senator?" she protested to his compliments. "We eat with knives and forks, silver ones too, and sometimes we even have champagne in Torso!" . . .

Lane, coming up with the first Vice-president, Vernon Short, and a Mr. Stanton, one of the New York directors ("a great swell," and "not just money," "has brains, you know," as the Senator whispered), was proud of his competent wife. She was vivaciously awake, and seemed to have forgotten her girlish repugnance to the amorous Senator. As she stood by the drawing-room door receiving her guests, he felt how much superior to all the Torso "leaders" she was, — yes, she deserved a larger frame! And to-night he felt confident that he should be able before long to place her in it. . . . The Senator, having discharged his cargo of compliments, was saying: —

"Saw your friend Miss Pallanton that was — Mrs. Woodyard — at the Stantons's the other night, looking like a blond Cleopatra. She's married a bright fellow, and she'll be the making of him. He'll have to hop around to please her, — I expect that's what husbands are for, isn't it, Lane?"

And here Isabelle passed him over to Bessie, who had come without Falkner, he having made some silly excuse at the last moment, — "just cross," as Bessie confided to Isabelle. She was looking very fresh in a gown that she and Isabelle's seamstress had contrived, and she smiled up into the Senator's face with her blandest child-manner. The Senator, who liked all women, even those who asked his views on public questions, was especially fond of what he called the "unsophisticated" variety, with whom his title carried weight.

When they reached the dining room, Lane's elation rose to a higher pitch. The table, strewn with sweet jasmine and glossy leaves, was adorned with all the handsome gold and silver service and glass that Isabelle had received at her marriage. It was too barbarically laden to be really beautiful; but it was in the best prevailing taste of the time, and to Lane, who never regarded such matters attentively, "was as good as the best." Looking down the long table after they were seated, he smiled with satisfaction and expanded, a subtle suavity born of being host to distinguished folk unlocking his ordinarily reticent tongue, causing him even to joke with Mrs. Adams, whom he did not like.

The food was excellent, and the maids, some borrowed, some specially imported from St. Louis, made no mistakes, at least gross ones. The feast moved as smoothly as need be. Isabelle, glancing over the table as the game came on, had her moment of elation, too. This was a real dinner-party, as elaborate and sumptuous as any that her friends in St. Louis might give. The Farrington Beals, she remembered, had men servants, — most New York families kept them, but that could hardly be expected in Torso. The dinner was excellent, as the hungry visitors testified, and they seemed to find the women agreeable and the whole affair unexpectedly cosmopolitan, which was pleasing after spending a long week in a car, examining terminals and coal properties. Indeed, it was very much the same dinner that was being served at about that hour in thousands of well-to-do houses throughout the country all the way from New York to San Francisco, — the same dishes, the same wines, the same service, almost the same talk. Nothing in American life is so completely standardized as what is known as a "dinner" in good, that is well-to-do, society. Isabelle Lane, with all her executive ability, her real cleverness, aspired to do "the proper thing," just as it was done in the houses of the moderately rich everywhere.

The model of hospitality is set by the hotel manager and his chef, and all that the clever hostess aspires to do is to offer the nearest copy of this to her guests. Neither the Lanes nor any of their guests, however, felt this lack of distinction, this sameness, in the entertainment provided for them. They had the comfortable feeling of being in a cheerful house, well warmed and well lighted, of eating all this superfluous food, which they were accustomed to eat, of saying the things they always said on such occasions. . . .

Isabelle had distributed her Torsonians skilfully: Bessie was adorable and kept three men hanging on her stories. Mrs. Adams, on the other side of Stanton, was furtively eying Darnell, who was talking rather loudly, trying to capture the Senator's attention from Bessie. Across the table Mrs. Darnell, still the striking dark-haired schoolgirl, was watching her husband, with a pitiful something in her frightened eyes that made Isabelle shrink. . . . It was Darnell who finally brought the conversation to a full stop.

"No, Senator," he said in his emphatic voice, "it is not scum like the assassin of the President that this country should fear!"

"We're paying now for our liberal policy in giving homes to the anarchistic refuse of Europe," the Senator insisted. "Congress must pass legislation that will protect us from another Czolgocz."

Darnell threw up his head, his lips curving disdainfully. He had emptied his champagne glass frequently, and there was a reckless light in his dark eyes. Isabelle trembled for his next remark:—

"You are wrong, sir, if you will allow me to say so. The legislation that we need is not against poor, feeble-minded rats like that murderer. We have prisons and asylums enough for them. What the country needs is legislation against its honored thieves, the real anarchists among us. We don't get 'em from Europe, Senator; we breed 'em right here, — in Wall street."

If some one had discharged assafœtida over the table, there could not have been a more unpleasant sensation.

"You don't mean quite that, Darnell," Lane began; but the Kentuckian brushed him to one side.

"Just that; and some day you will see what Americans will do with their anarchists. I tell you this land is full of discontent, — men hating dishonesty, privilege, corruption, injustice! men ready to fight their oppressors for freedom!"

The men about the table were all good Republicans, devout believers in the gospel of prosperity, all sharers in it. They smiled contemptuously at Darnell's passion.

"Our martyred President was a great and good man," the Senator observed irrelevantly in his public tone.

"He was the greatest breeder of corruption that has ever held that office," retorted the Kentuckian. "With his connivance, a Mark Hanna has forged the worst industrial tyranny the world has ever seen, — the corrupt grip of corporations on the lives of the people."

"Pretty strong for a corporation lawyer!" Lane remarked, and the men laughed cynically.

"I am no longer a corporation hireling," Darnell said in a loud voice.

Isabelle noticed that Mrs. Adams's eyes glowed, as she gazed at the man.

"I sent in my resignation last week."

"Getting ready for the public platform?" some one suggested. "You won't find much enthusiasm for those sentiments; wages are too high!"

There was a moment of unpleasant silence. The Kentuckian raised his head as if to retort, then collected himself, and remarked meekly:—

"Pardon me, Mrs. Lane, this is not the occasion for such a discussion. I was carried away by my feelings. Sometimes the real thought will burst out."

The apology scarcely bettered matters, and Isabelle's response was flat.

"I am sure it is always interesting to hear both sides."

"But I can't see that to a good citizen there can be two sides to the lamentable massacre of our President," the Senator said severely. "I had the privilege of knowing our late President intimately, and I may say that I never knew a better man, — he was another Lincoln!"

"I don't see where Mr. Darnell can find this general discontent," the Vice-president of the A. and P. put in suavely. "The country has never been so prosperous as during the

McKinley-Hanna régime, — wages at the high level, exports increasing, crops abundant. What any honest and industrious man has to complain of, I can't see. Why, we are looking for men all the time, and we can't get them, at any price!"

"'Ye shall not live by bread alone,'" Darnell muttered. It was a curious remark for a dinner-party, Isabelle thought. Mrs. Adams's lips curled as if she understood it. But now that the fiery lawyer had taken to quoting the Bible no one paid any further attention to him, and the party sank back into little duologues appropriate to the occasion. Later Bessie confessed to Isabelle that she had been positively frightened lest the Kentuckian would do "something awful," — he had been drinking, she thought. But Darnell remained silent for the brief time before the ladies left the room, merely once raising his eyes apologetically to Isabelle with his wine-glass at his lips, murmuring so that she alone could hear him, — "I drink to the gods of Prosperity!" She smiled back her forgiveness. He had behaved very badly, almost wrecked her successful dinner; but somehow she could not dislike him. She did not understand what he was saying or why he should say it when people were having a good time; but she felt it was part of his interesting and uncertain nature. . . .

Presently the coffee and cigars came and the women went across the hall, while the men talked desultorily until the sound of Bessie's voice singing a French song to Isabelle's accompaniment attracted them. After the next song the visitors went, their car being due to leave on the Eastern express. They said many pleasant things to Isabelle, and the Senator, holding her hand in his broad, soft palm, whispered: —

"We can't let so much charm stay buried in Torso!"

So when the last home guest had departed and Lane sat down before the fire for another cigar, Isabelle drew her chair close to his, her heart beating with pleasant emotions.

"Well?" she said expectantly.

"Splendid—everything! They liked it, I am sure. I felt proud of you, Belle!"

"It was all good but the fish,—yes, I thought our party was very nice!" Then she told him what the Senator had said, and this time Lane did not repel the idea of their moving to wider fields. He had made a good impression on "the New York crowd," and he thought again complacently of the Torso and Northern equipment bonds.

"Something may turn up before long, perhaps."

New York! It made her heart leap. She felt that she was now doing the wife's part admirably, furthering John's interests by being a competent hostess, and she liked to further his interests by giving pleasant dinners, in an attractive gown, and receiving the admiration of clever men. It had not been the way that her mother had helped on the Colonel; but it was another way, the modern way, and a very agreeable way.

"Darnell is an awful fool," Lane commented. "If he can't hold on to himself any better than he did to-night, he won't get far."

"Did you know that he had resigned?"

"No,—it's just as well he has. I don't think the A. and P. would have much use for him. He's headed the wrong way;" and he added with hardly a pause, "I think we had better cut the Darnells out, Isabelle. They are not our sort."

Isabelle, thinking that this was the man's prejudice, made no reply.

"It was too bad Rob Falkner wouldn't come. It would have been a good thing for him to meet influential people."

Already she spoke with an air of commanding the right sort that her husband had referred to.

"He doesn't make a good impression on people," Lane remarked. "Perhaps he will make good with his work."

As a man who had made his own way he felt the great importance of being able to "get on" with people, to interest them, and keep them aware of one's presence. But he was broad enough to recognize other roads to success.

"So you were quite satisfied, John?" his wife asked as she kissed him good-night.

"Perfectly — it was the right thing — every way — all but Darnell's rot; and that didn't do much harm."

So the two went to their rest perfectly satisfied with themselves and their world. Lane's last conscious thought was a jumble of equipment bonds, and the idea of his wife at the head of a long dinner table in some very grand house — in New York.

CHAPTER IX

THE Darnells had a farm a few miles out of Torso, and this spring they had given up their house on the square and moved to the farm permanently. Bessie said it was for Mrs. Darnell's health; men said that the lawyer was in a tight place with the banks; and gossip suggested that Darnell preferred being in Torso without his wife whenever he was there. The farm was on a small hill above a sluggish river, and was surrounded by a growth of old sycamores and maples. There was a long stretch of fertile fields in front of the house, dotted by the huge barns and steel windmills of surrounding farms.

One Sunday in early May the Lanes were riding in the direction of the Darnell place, and Isabelle persuaded her husband to call there. "I promised to ride out here and show him the horses," she explained. The house was a shabby frame affair, large for a farmhouse, with porticoes and pillars in Southern style. They found the Darnells with the Falkners in the living-room. Tom Darnell was reading an Elizabethan play aloud, rolling out the verse in resounding declamation, punctuated by fervid appreciation, — "God! but that's fine!" "Hear this thing sing." "Just listen to this ripper."

> "O God! O God! that it were possible
> To undo things done; to call back yesterday!
> That Time could turn up his swift sandy glass,
> To untell the days, and to redeem the hours!" . . .

When the Lanes had found chairs before the fire, he kept on reading, but with less enthusiasm, as if he felt an alien atmosphere. Falkner listened to the lines with closed eyes, his grim jaw relaxed, the deep frown smoothed. Bessie stroked a white cat, — it was plain that her thoughts were far away. Mrs. Darnell, who looked slovenly but pretty, stared vacantly out of the window. The sun lay in broad streaks on the dusty floor; there was an air of drowsy peace, broken only by the warm tones of the lawyer as his voice rose and fell over the spirited verse. Isabelle enjoyed it all; here was something out of her usual routine. Darnell's face, which reflected the emotion of the lines, was attractive to her. He might not be the "right sort"; but he was unusual. . . . Finally Darnell flung the book into the corner and jumped up.

"Here I am boring you good people with stuff dead and gone these hundreds of years. Falkner always starts me off. Let's have a drink and take a look at the horses."

The living-room was a mess of furniture and books, wine-glasses, bottles, wraps, whips, and riding-boots. Lane looked it over critically, while Darnell found some tumblers and poured out wine. Then they all went to the stable and dawdled about, talking horse. The fields were green with the soft grass, already nearly a foot high. Over the house an old grape-vine was budding in purple balls. There was a languor and sweetness to the air that instigated laziness. Although Lane wished to be off, Isabelle lingered on, and Darnell exclaimed hospitably: "You stay to dinner, of course! It is just plain dinner, Mrs. Lane," — and he swept away all denial. Turning to his wife, who had said nothing, he remarked, "It's very good of them to come in on us like this, isn't it, Irene?"

Mrs. Darnell started and mumbled: —

"Yes, I am sure!"

His manners to his wife were always perfect, deferential, — why should she shrink before him? Isabelle wondered. . . . Dinner, plentiful and appetizing, was finally provided by the one negro woman. Darnell tried to talk to Lane, but to Isabelle's surprise her husband was at a disadvantage: — the two men could not find common ground. Then Darnell and Falkner quoted poetry, and Isabelle listened. It was all very different from anything she knew. While the others waited for their coffee, Darnell showed her the old orchard, —"to smell the first blossoms." It was languorously still there under the trees, with the misty fields beyond. Darnell said dreamily: —

"This is where I'd like to be always, — no, not six miles from Torso, but in some far-off country, a thousand miles from men!"

"You, a farmer!" laughed Isabelle. "And what about Congress, and the real anarchists?"

"Oh, you cannot understand! You do not belong to the fields as I do." He pointed ironically to her handsome riding skirt. "You are of the cities, of people. You will flit from this Indiana landscape one day, from provincial Torso, and spread your gay wings among the houses of men. While I —" He made a gesture of despair, — half comic, half serious, — and his dark face became gloomy.

Isabelle was amused at what she called his "heroics," but she felt interested to know what he was; and it flattered her that he should see her "spreading gay wings among the houses of men." These days she liked to think of herself that way.

"You will be in Washington, while we are still in Torso!" she answered.

"Maybe," he mused. "Well, we play the game — play the game — until it is played out!"

'He is not happy with his wife,' Isabelle concluded sagely; 'she doesn't understand him, and that's why she has that half-scared look.'

"I believe you really want to play the game as much as anybody," she ventured with a little thrill of surprise to find herself talking so personally with a man other than her husband.

"You think so?" he demanded, and his face grew wistful. "There is nothing in the game compared with the peace that one might have —"

Lane was calling to her, but she lingered to say: —

"How?"

"Far away — with love and the fields!"

They walked back to where John was holding the horses. She was oddly fluttered. For the first time since she had become engaged a man had somehow given her that special sensation, which women know, of confidence between them. She wished that John had not been so anxious to be off, and she did not repeat to him Darnell's talk, as she usually did every small item. All that she said was, after a time of reflection, "He is not a happy man."

"Who?"

"Mr. Darnell."

"From what I hear he is in a bad way. It is his own fault. He has plenty of ability, — a splendid chance."

She felt that this was an entirely inadequate judgment. What interested the man was the net result; what interested the woman was the human being in whom that result was being worked out. They talked a little longer about the fermenting tragedy of the household that they had just left, as the world talks, from a distance. But Isabelle made the silent reservation, — 'she doesn't understand him — with another woman, it would be different.' . . .

Their road home lay through a district devastated by the mammoth sheds of some collieries. A smudged sign bore the legend: —

PLEASANT VALLEY COAL COMPANY

Lane pulled up his horse and looked carefully about the place. Then he suggested turning west to examine another coal property.

"I suppose that Freke man is awfully rich," Isabelle remarked, associating the name of the coal company with its president; "but he's so common, — I can't see how you can stand him, John!"

Lane turned in his saddle and looked at the elegant figure that his wife made on horseback.

"He isn't half as interesting as Tom Darnell or Rob," she added.

"I stand him," he explained, smiling, "for the reason men stand each other most often,—we make money together."

"Why, how do you mean? He isn't in the railroad."

"I mean in coal mines," he replied vaguely, and Isabelle realized that she was trespassing on that territory of man's business which she had been brought up to keep away from. Nevertheless, as they rode homeward in the westering golden light, she thought of several things:—John was in other business than the railroad, and that puffy-faced German-American was in some way connected with it; business covered many mysteries; a man did business with people he would not ordinarily associate with. It even crossed her mind that what with sleep and business a very large part of her husband's life lay quite beyond her touch. Perhaps that was what the Kentuckian meant by his ideal,—to live life with some loved one far away in companionship altogether intimate.

But before long she was thinking of the set of her riding-skirt, and that led to the subject of summer gowns which she meant to get when she went East with her mother, and that led on to the question of the summer itself. It had been decided that Isabelle should not spend another summer in the Torso heat, but whether she should go to the Connecticut place or accept Margaret Lawton's invitation to the mountains, she was uncertain. Thus pleasantly her thoughts drifted on into her future.

CHAPTER X

If Isabelle had been curious about her husband's interest in the Pleasant Valley Coal Company, she might have developed a highly interesting chapter of commercial history, in which Mr. Freke and John Lane were enacting typical parts.

The Atlantic and Pacific railroad corporation is, as may easily be inferred, a vast organism, with a history, a life of its own, lying like a thick ganglia of nerves and blood-vessels a third of the way across our broad continent, sucking its nourishment from thousands of miles of rich and populous territory. To write its history humanly, not statistically, would be to reveal an important chapter in the national drama for the past forty years,—a drama buried in dusty archives, in auditors' reports, vouchers, mortgage deeds, general orders, etc. Some day there will come the great master of irony, the man of insight, who will make this mass of routine paper glow with meaning visible to all!

Meanwhile this Atlantic and Pacific, which to-day is a mighty system, was once only a handful of atoms. There was the period of Birth; there was the period of Conquest; and finally there has come the period of Domination. Now, with its hold on the industry, the life of eight states, complete, like the great Serpent it can grumble, "I lie here possessing!"

Farrington Beals came to be President of the Atlantic and Pacific at the close of the period of Conquest. The condottieri leaders, those splendid railroad brigands of the seventies and eighties, had retired with "the fruits of their industry." To Farrington Beals and his associate was left the care of the orchard. It was their task to solidify a conglomerate mass of interest-bearing burden, to operate the property with the greatest efficiency possible, in order that it might support the burdens laid upon it and yet other burdens to come as the land waxed rich, — all burdens being ultimately passed to the broad back of the Public, where burdens seem naturally to belong. To this end, Beals men, as they were called, gradually replaced throughout the length and breadth of the system the old operatives, whose methods belonged to the coarse days of brigandage! These Beals men were youngsters, — capable, active, full of "jump," with the word "traffic, traffic" singing always in their ears. Beals was a splendid "operator," and he rapidly brought the Atlantic and Pacific into the first rank of the world's railroads. That shrewd and conservative statesman, Senator Alonzo Thomas (who had skilfully marshalled the legal and political forces during the period of Conquest) was now chairman of the Board, and he and the President successfully readjusted the heterogeneous mass of bonds and stocks, notes and prior liens, taking advantage of a period of optimistic feeling in the market to float a tremendous general mortgage. When this "Readjustment" had been successfully put through, the burden was some forty or fifty millions larger than before,—where those millions went is one of the mysteries to reward that future Carlyle! — but the public load was adjusted more trimly. So it was spoken of as a "masterly stroke of finance," and the ex-statesman gained much credit in the highest circles.

The Senator and the President are excellent men, as any financier will tell you. They are charitable and genial, social beings, members of clubs, hard working and intelligent, public spirited, too,—oh, the very best that the Republic breeds! To see Farrington Beals, gray-haired, thoughtful, almost the student, clothed in a sober dark suit, with a simple flower in the buttonhole, and delicate glasses on the bridge of his shapely nose, — to see him modestly enter the general offices of the Atlantic and Pacific, any one would recognize an Industrial Flywheel of society. To accompany him over the system in his car, with a party of distinguished foreign stockholders, was in the nature of a religious ceremony, so much the interests of this giant property in his care seemed allied with the best interests of our great land!

Thus Beals men ran the road, — men like John Hamilton Lane, railroad men to the core, loyal men, devoted to the great A. and P. And traffic increased monthly, tonnage mounted, wheels turned faster, long freight trains wound their snaky coils through the Alleghanies, over the flat prairies, into Eastern ports, or Western terminals — Traffic, Traffic! And money poured into the treasury, more than enough to provide for all those securities that the Senator was so skilled in manufacturing. All worked in this blessed land of freedom to the glory of Farrington Beals and the profit of the great A. and P.

What has Isabelle to do with all this? Actually she was witness to one event, — rather, just the surface of it, the odd-looking, concrete outside! An afternoon early in her married life at Torso, she had gone down to the railroad office to take her husband for a drive in the pleasant autumn weather. As he was long in coming to meet her, she entered the brick building; the elevator boy, recognizing her with a pleasant nod, whisked her up to the floor where Lane had his private office. Entering the outer room, which happened to be empty at this hour, she heard voices through the half-open door that led to the inner office. It was first her husband's voice, so low that she could not hear what he was saying. Presently it was interrupted by a passionate treble. Through the door she could just see John's side face where he was seated at his desk, — the look she liked best, showing the firm cheek and jaw line, and resolute mouth. Over his desk a thin, roughly dressed man with a ragged reddish beard was leaning on both arms, and his shoulders trembled with the passion of his utterance.

"Mr. Lane," he was saying in that passionate treble, "I must have them cars — or I shall lose my contract!"

"As I have told you a dozen times, Mr. Simonds, I have done my best for you. I recognize your trouble, and it is most unfortunate,—but there seems to be a shortage of coalers just now."

"The Pleasant Valley company get all they want!" the man blurted out.

Lane merely drummed on his desk.

"If I can't get cars to ship my coal, I shall be broke, bankrupt," the thin man cried.

"I am very sorry —"

"Sorry be damned! Give me some cars!"

"You will have to see Mr. Brundage at St. Louis," Lane answered coldly. "He has final say on such matters for the Western division. I merely follow orders."

He rose and closed his desk. The thin man with an eloquent gesture turned and rushed out of the office, past Isabelle, who caught a glimpse of a white face working, of teeth chewing a scrubby mustache, of blood-shot eyes. John locked his desk, took down his hat and coat, and came into the outer office. He kissed his wife, and they went to drive behind the Kentucky horses, talking of pleasant matters. After a time, Isabelle asked irrelevantly:—

"John, why couldn't you give that man the cars he wanted?"

"Because I had no orders to do so."

"But aren't there cars to be had when the other company gets them?"

"There don't happen to be any cars for Simonds. The road is friendly to Mr. Freke."

And he closed his explanation by kissing his wife on her pretty neck, as though he would imply that more things than kisses go by favor in this world. Isabelle had exhausted her interest in the troubled man's desire for coal cars, and yet in that little phrase, "The road is friendly to Mr. Freke," she had touched close upon a great secret of the Beals régime. Unbeknownst to her, she had just witnessed one of those little modern tragedies as intense in their way as any Cæsarian welter of blood; she had seen a plain little man, one of the negligible millions, being "squeezed," in other words the operation in an ordinary case of the divine law of survival. Freke was to survive; Simonds was not. In what respects Simonds was inferior to Freke, the Divine Mind alone could say. When that convulsive face shot past Isabelle in Lane's office, it was merely the tragic moment when the conscious atom was realizing fully that he was not to be the one to survive! The moment when Suspense is converted into Despair. . . .

Nor could Isabelle trace the well-linked chain of cause and effect that led from Simonds about-to-be-a-bankrupt *viâ* Freke and the Pleasant Valley Coal Company through the glory of the A. and P. (incidentally creating in the Senator his fine patriotism and faith in the future of his country) to her husband's check-book and her own brilliant little dinner, "where they could afford to offer champagne." But in the maze of earthly affairs all these unlike matters were related, and the relationship is worth our notice, if not Isabelle's. If it had been expounded to her, if she had seen certain certificates of Pleasant Valley stock lying snugly side by side with Torso Northern bonds and other "good things" in her husband's safe, — and also in the strong boxes of Messrs. Beals, Thomas, Stanton, *et al.*, she would have said, as she had been brought up to say, "that is my husband's affair." . . .

The Atlantic and Pacific, under the shrewd guidance of the amiable Senator, was a law-abiding citizen, outwardly. When the anti-rebate laws were passed, the road reformed; it was glad to reform, it made money by reforming. But within the law there was ample room for "efficient" men to acquire more money than their salaries, and they naturally grasped their opportunities, as did the general officers. Freke, whom Isabelle disliked, with her trivial woman's prejudice about face and manners, embodied a Device, — in other words he was an instrument whereby some persons could make a profit, a very large profit, at the expense of other persons. The A. and P. 'was friendly to Freke.' The Pleasant Valley Coal Company never wanted cars, and it also enjoyed certain other valuable privileges, covered by the vague term "switching," that enabled it to deliver its coal into the gaping hulls at tidewater at seventy to eighty cents per ton cheaper than any of its competitors in the Torso district. No wonder that the Pleasant Valley company, with all this "friendliness" of the A. and P., prospered, and that Mr. Freke, under one name or another, swallowed presently, at a bargain, the little mine that the man Simonds had struggled to operate, as well as thousands of acres of bituminous coal lands along the Pleasant River, and along the Torso Northern road. (Perhaps the inwardness of that Inspection Party can now be seen, also.) The signs of the Pleasant Valley Coal Company and its aliases squatted here and there all through the Torso coal region. As the Senator would say, it was a very successful business, "thanks to the initiative of Mr. Freke." And that poor Simonds, who had amply demonstrated his inability to survive, his utter lack of adaptation to his environment, by not being able to be friendly with the great A. and P., went — where all the inefficient, non-adaptable human refuse goes — to the bottom. *Bien entendu!*

Freke was the Pleasant Valley Coal Company, — that is, he was its necessary physiognomy, — but really the coal company was an incorporated private farm of the officers and friends of the A. and P., — an immensely profitable farm. Lane in his callow youth did not know this fact; but he learned it after he had been in Torso a few weeks. He was quick to learn, a typical Beals man, thoroughly "efficient," one who could keep his eyes where they belonged, his tongue in his mouth, and his ears open. As he told Isabelle that Sunday afternoon, "he had had many business dealings with Freke," alias the Pleasant Valley Company, etc., and they had been uniformly profitable.

For the fatherly Senator and the shrewd Beals believed that the "right sort" should make a "good thing"; they believed in thrift. In a word, to cut short this lengthy explanation, the great Atlantic and Pacific, one of the two or three most efficiently operated railroads in the United

States, was honeycombed with that common thing "graft," or private "initiative"! From the President's office all the way down to subordinates in the traffic department, there were "good things" to be enjoyed. In that growing bunch of securities that Lane was accumulating in his safe, there were, as has been said, a number of certificates of stock in coal companies — and not small ones.

And this is why Lane maintained social as well as financial relations with the coarse Mr. Freke. And this is why, also, Lane felt that they could afford "the best," when they undertook to give a dinner to the distinguished gentlemen from New York. Of course he did not explain all this to Isabelle that pleasant Sunday afternoon. Would Isabelle have comprehended it, if he had? Her mind would have wandered off to another dinner, to that cottage at Bedmouth, which she thought of taking for the summer, or to the handsome figure that John made on horseback. At least nine out of ten American husbands would have treated the matter as Lane did, — given some sufficient general answer to their wives' amateurish curiosity about business and paid their figures due compliments, and thought complacently of the comfortable homes to which they were progressing and the cheerful dinners therein, — all, wife, home, dinner, the result of their fortunate adaptation to the environments they found themselves in. . . .

Perhaps may be seen by this time the remote connection between that tragic gesture of Frank Simonds on the Saturday afternoon, calling on heaven and the Divine Mind that pitilessly strains its little creatures through the holes of a mighty colander — between that tragic gesture, I say, and Isabelle's delightful dinner of ten courses, — champagne and terrapin!

But this tiresome chapter on the affairs of the Atlantic and Pacific railroad, — will it never be done! So sordid, so commonplace, so newspapery, so — just what everything in life is — when we might have expected for the dollar and a quarter expended on this pound of wood pulp and ink,—something less dull than a magazine article; something about a motor-car and a girl with a mischievous face whom a Russian baron seeks to carry away by force and is barely thwarted by the brave American college youth dashing in pursuit with a new eighty h. p., etc., etc. Or at least if one must have a railroad in a novel (when every one knows just what a railroad is), give us a private car and the lovely daughter of the President together with a cow-punching hero, as in Bessie's beloved story. But an entire chapter on graft and a common dinner-party with the champagne drunk so long ago — what a bore!

And yet in the infinite hues of this our human life, the methods by which our substantial hero, John Hamilton Lane, amassed his fortune, are worthy of contemplation. There is more, O yawning reader, in the tragic gesture of ragged-bearded Frank Simonds than in some tons of your favorite brand of "real American women"; more in the sublime complacency of Senator Alonzo Thomas, when he praised "that great and good man," and raised to his memory his glass of Pommery brut, triple sec, than in all the adventures of soldiers of fortune or yellow cars or mysterious yachts or hectic Russian baronesses; more — at least for the purpose of this history — in John's answer to Isabelle's random inquiry that Sunday afternoon than in all the "heart-interest" you have absorbed in a twelvemonth. For in the atmosphere of the Acts here recorded, you and I, my reader, live and have our being, such as it is — and also poor Frank Simonds (who will never appear again to trouble us). And to the seeing eye, mystery and beauty lie in the hidden meaning of things seen but not known. . . .

Patience! We move to something more intimate and domestic, if not more thrilling.

CHAPTER XI

The child was coming!

When Isabelle realized it, she had a shock, as if something quite outside her had suddenly interposed in her affairs. That cottage at Bedmouth for the summer would have to be given up and other plans as well. At first she had refused to heed the warning,—allowed John to go away to New York on business without confiding in him,—at last accepted it regretfully. Since the terrifying fear those first days in the Adirondack forest lest she might have conceived without her passionate consent, the thought of children had gradually slipped out of her mind. They had settled into a comfortable way of living, with their plans and their expectations. "That side of life," as she called it, was still distasteful to her,—she did not see why it had to be. Fortunately it did not play a large part in their life, and the other, the companionable thing, the being admired and petted, quite satisfied her. Children, of course, sometime; but "not just yet."

"It will be the wrong time,—September,—spoil everything!" she complained to Bessie.

"Oh, it's always the wrong time, no matter when it happens. But you'll get used to it. Rob had to keep me from going crazy at first. But in the end you like it."

"It settles Bedmouth this year!"

"It is a bore," Bessie agreed sympathetically, feeling sorry for herself, as she was to have spent six weeks with Isabelle. "It takes a year out of a woman's life, of course, no matter how she is situated. And I'm so fearfully ugly all the time. But you won't be,—your figure is better."

Bessie, like most childlike persons, took short views

of immediate matters. She repeated her idea of child-bearing: —

"I hated it each time, — especially the last time. It did seem so unnecessary — for us. . . . And it spoils your love, being so afraid. But when it comes, why you like it, of course!"

John arrived from his hurried trip to New York, smiling with news. He did not notice his wife's dejected appearance when he kissed her, in his eagerness to tell something.

"There is going to be a shake-up in the road," he announced. "That's why they sent for me."

"Is there?" she asked listlessly.

"Well, I am slated for fourth Vice-president. They were pleased to say handsome things about what I have done at Torso. Guess they heard of that offer from the D. and O."

"What is fourth Vice-president?" Isabelle inquired.

"In charge of traffic west — headquarters at St. Louis!"

He expected that his wife would be elated at this fulfilment of her desires; but instead Isabelle's eyes unaccountably filled with tears. When he understood, he was still more mystified at her dejection. Very tenderly holding her in his arms, he whispered his delight into her ears. His face was radiant; it was far greater news than his promotion to the fourth vice-presidency of the A. and P.

"And you knew all this time!" he exclaimed reproachfully.

"I wasn't sure!"

He seemed to take the event as natural and joyful, which irritated her still more. As Bessie had said, "Whatever ties a woman to the home, makes her a piece of domestic furniture, the men seem to approve of!"

"What a fright I look already!" Isabelle complained, gazing at the dark circles under her eyes in the glass. She thought of Aline, whose complexion like a Jacqueminot rose had been roughened and marred. Something still virginal in her soul rebelled against it all.

"Oh, not so bad," Lane protested. "You are just a little pinched. You'll be fitter than ever when it's over!"

The man doesn't care, she thought mutinously. It seems to him the proper thing,— what woman is made for. Isabelle was conscious that she was made for much more, for her own joy and her own activity, and she hated to part with even a little of it!

He could not understand her attitude. As a man he had retained the primitive joy in the coming of the child, any child, — but *his* child and the first one above all! Compared with that nothing was of the least importance. Seeing her pouting into the glass, he said reproachfully: —

"But you like children, Belle!"

And taking her again into his arms and kissing her, he added, "We'll give the little beggar a royal welcome, girl!"

His grave face took on a special look of content with the world and his share in it, while Isabelle continued to stare at herself in the glass and think of the change a child would make in her life. Thus the woman of the new generation, with her eagerness for a "large, full life," feels towards that process of nature for which the institution of marriage was primarily designed.

So for a time longer Isabelle tried to ignore the coming fact, to put it out of her mind, and grasp as much of her own life as she could before the life within her should deprive her of freedom. As Lane's new duties would not begin until the summer, it was arranged that Isabelle should spend the hot weeks at the Grafton farm with her mother, and then return to St. Louis for her confinement in her old home. Later they would settle themselves in the city at their leisure. . . . It was all so provoking, Isabelle persisted in thinking. They might have had at least a year of freedom in which to settle themselves in the new home. And she had had visions of a few months in Europe with Vickers, who was now in Rome. John might have come over after her. To give up all this for what any woman could do at any time!

As the months passed she could not evade the issue. By the time she was settled in her old room at the Farm she had grown anæmic, nervous. The coming of the child had sapped rather than created strength as it properly should have done. White and wasted she lay for long hours on the lounge near the window where she could see the gentle green hills. Here her cousin Alice Johnston found her, when she arrived with her children to make Mrs. Price a visit. The large, placid woman knelt by Isabelle's side and gathered her in her arms.

"I'm so glad, dear! When is it to be?"

"Oh, sometime in the fall," Isabelle replied vaguely, bored that her condition already revealed itself. "Did you want the first one?" she asked after a time.

"Well, not at the very first. You see it was just so much more of a risk. And our marriage was a risk without that. . . . I hated the idea of becoming a burden for Steve. But with you it will be so different, from the start. And then it always makes its own place, you see. When it comes, you will think you always wanted it!"

She smiled in her large human way, as if she had tested the trials of life and found that all held some sweet. Isabelle looked down at her thin arms. The Johnstons had four, and they were so poor! As if divining her thought, Alice said: —

"Every time I wondered how we were going to survive, but somehow we did. And now it will all be well, with Steve's new position — "

"What is that?"

"Hasn't John told you? It has just been settled; Steve is going into the A. and P., — John's assistant in St. Louis."

"I'm so glad for you," Isabelle responded listlessly. She recalled now something that her husband had said about Johnston being a good man, who hadn't had his chance, and that he hoped to do something for him.

"Tremendous rise in salary,— four thousand," Alice continued buoyantly. "We shan't know what to do with all that money! We can give the children the best education."

Isabelle reflected that John's salary had been five thousand at Torso, and as fourth Vice-president would be ten thousand. And she still had her twenty-five hundred dollars of allowance from her father. Alice's elation over Steve's rise gave her a sudden appreciation of her husband's growing power, — his ability to offer a struggling man his chance. Perhaps he could do something for the Falkners also. The thought took her out of herself for a little while. Men were free to work out their destiny in life, to go hither and thither, to alter fate. But a woman had to bear children. John was growing all this time, and she was separated from him. She tried to believe that this was the reason for her discontent, this separation from her husband; but she knew that when she had been perfectly free, she had not shared largely in his activity. . . .

"You must tell me all about the St. Mary's girls," Alice said. "Have you seen Aline?"

"Yes, — she has grown very faddy, I should think, — arts and crafts and all that. Isn't it queer? I asked her to visit us, but she has another one coming,— the third!"

Isabelle made a little grimace.

"And Margaret?"

"She has suddenly gone abroad with her husband — to Munich. He's given up his business. Didn't her marriage surprise you?"

"Yes, I thought she was going to marry that Englishman who was at your wedding."

"Mr. Hollenby? Yes, every one did. Something happened. Suddenly she became engaged to this Pole, — a New York man. Very well connected, and has money, I hear. Conny wrote me about him." . . .

So they gossiped on. When Alice rose to leave her, Isabelle held her large cool hand in hers. The older woman, whose experience had been so unlike hers, so difficult, soothed her, gave her a suggestion of other kinds of living than her own little life.

"I'm glad you are here," she said. "Come in often, won't you?"

And her cousin, leaning over to kiss her as she might a fretful child who had much to learn, murmured, "Of course, dear. It will be all right!"

CHAPTER XII

The Steve Johnstons had had a hard time, as Isabelle would have phrased it.

He had been a faithful, somewhat dull and plodding student at the technical school, where he took the civil engineering degree, and had gone forth to lay track in Montana. He laid it well; but this job finished, there seemed no permanent place for him. He was heavy and rather tongue-tied, and made no impression on his superiors except that of commonplace efficiency. He drifted into Canada, then back to the States, and finally found a place in Detroit.

Here, while working for thirty dollars a week, he met Alice Johnston, — she also was earning her living, being unwilling to accept from the Colonel more than the means for her education, — and from the first he wished to marry her, attracted by her gentle, calm beauty, her sincerity, and buoyant, healthy enjoyment of life. She was teaching in a girls' school, and was very happy. Other women had always left the heavy man on the road, so to speak, marking him as stupid. But Alice Johnston was keener or kinder than most young women: she perceived beneath the large body a will, an intelligence, a character, merely inhibited in their envelope of large bones and solid flesh, with an entire absence of nervous system. He was silent before the world, but not foolish, and with her he was not long silent. She loved him, and she consented to marry him on forty dollars a week, hopefully planning to add something from her teaching to the budget, until Steve's slow power might gain recognition.

"So we married," she said to Isabelle, recounting her little life history in the drowsy summer afternoon. "And we were so happy on what we had! It was real love. We took a little flat a long way out of the city, and when I came home afternoons from the school, I got the dinner and Steve cooked the breakfasts, — he's a splendid cook, learned on the plains. It all went merrily the first months, though Aunt Harmony thought I was such a fool to marry, you remember?" She laughed, and Isabelle smiled at the memory of the caustic comments which Mrs. Price had made when Alice Vance, a poor niece, had dared to marry a poor man, — "They'll be coming to your father for help before the year is out," she had said. But they hadn't gone to the Colonel yet.

"Then little Steve came, and I had to leave the school and stay at home. That was hard, but I had saved enough to pay for the doctor and the nurse. Then that piece of track elevation was finished and Steve was out of work for a couple of months. He tried so hard, poor boy! But he was never meant to be an engineer. I knew that, of course, all along. . . . Well, the baby came, and if it hadn't been for my savings, — why, I should have gone to the hospital!

"Just then Steve met a man he had known at the Tech, and was given that place on a railroad as clerk in the traffic department. He was doubtful about taking it, but I wasn't. I was sure it would open up, and even twenty-five dollars a week is something. So he left for Cleveland a week after the baby was born, and somehow I packed up and followed with the baby when I could.

"That wasn't the end of hard times by any means. You see Ned came the next year, — we're such healthy, normal specimens!" She laughed heartily at this admission of her powers of maternity. "And it wasn't eighteen months before Alice was coming. . . . Oh, I know that we belong to the thriftless pauper class that's always having children, — more than it can properly care for. We ought to be discouraged! But somehow we have fed and clothed 'em all, and we couldn't spare one of the kiddies. There's James, too, you know. He came last winter, just after Steve had the grippe and pneumonia; that was a pull. But it doesn't seem right to — to keep them from coming — and when you love each other — "

Her eyes shone with a certain joy as she frankly stated the woman's problem, while Isabelle looked away, embarrassed. Mrs. Johnston continued in her simple manner:—

"If Nature doesn't want us to have them, why does she give us the power? . . . I know that is wretched political economy and that Nature really has nothing to do with the modern civilized family. But as I see other women, the families about me, those that are always worrying over having children, trying to keep out of it, — why, they don't seem to be any better off. And it is — well, undignified, — not nice, you know. . . . We can't spare 'em, nor any more that may come! . . . As I said, I believed all along that Steve had it in him, that his mind and character must tell, and though it was discouraging to have men put over him, younger men too, at last the railroad found out what he could do."

Her face beamed with pride.

"You see Steve has a remarkable power of storing things up in that big head of his. Remembers a lot of pesky little detail when he's once fixed his mind on it, — the prices of things, figures, and distances, and rates and differentials. Mr. Mason — that was the traffic manager of our road — happened to take Steve to Buffalo with him about some rate-making business. Steve, it turned out, knew the situation better than all the traffic managers. He coached Mr. Mason, and so our road got something it wanted. It was about the lumber rate, in competition with Canadian roads. Mr. Mason made Steve his assistant — did you ever think what an awful lot the rate on lumber might mean to *you* and yours? It's a funny world. Because Steve happened to be there and knew that with a rate of so much a thousand feet our road could make money, — why, we had a house to live in for the first time!

"Of course," she bubbled, "it isn't just that. It's Steve's

head, — an ability to find his way through those great sheets of figures the railroads are always compiling. He stores the facts up in that big round head and pulls 'em out when they are wanted. Why, he can tell you just what it would cost to ship a car of tea from Seattle to New York!"

Isabelle had a vision of Steve Johnston's large, heavy head with its thick, black hair, and she began to feel a respect for the stolid man.

"John said he had great ability," she remarked. "I'm so glad it all came out right in the end."

"I had my first servant when the promotion came, and that spring we took a little house, — it was crowded in the flat, and noisy."

"You will find it so much easier now, and you will like St. Louis."

"Oh, yes! But it hasn't been really bad, — the struggle, the being poor. You see we were both well and strong, and we loved so much, and we always had the problem of how to live, — that draws you together if you have the real thing in you. It isn't sordid trying to see what a quarter can be made to do. It's exciting."

As she recalled the fight, a tender smile illuminated her face and curved her lips upward. To her poverty had not been limiting, grinding, but an exhilarating fight that taxed her resources of mind and body.

"Of course there are a lot of things you can't have. But most people have more than they know how to handle, no matter where they are!"

Isabelle was puzzled by this remark, and explained Alice Johnston's content by her age, her lack of experience, at least such experience as she had had. For life to her presented a tantalizing feast of opportunities, and it was her intention to grasp as many of these as one possibly could. Any other view of living seemed not only foolish but small-minded. Without any snobbishness she considered that her sphere and her husband's could not be compared with the Johnstons'. The Lanes, she felt, were somehow called to large issues.

Nevertheless, Isabelle could understand that Alice's marriage was quite a different thing from what hers was, — something to glorify all the petty, sordid details, to vivify the grimy struggle of keeping one's head above the social waters.

"Now," Alice concluded, "we can save! And start the children fairly. But I wonder if we shall ever be any happier than we have been, — any closer, Steve and I?"

Alice, by her very presence, her calm acceptance of life as it shaped itself, soothed Isabelle's restlessness, suggested trust and confidence.

"You are a dear," she whispered to her cousin. "I am so glad you are to be near me in St. Louis!"

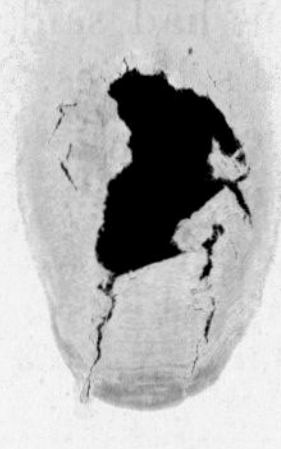

CHAPTER XIII

ISABELLE saw the fat headlines in the Pittsburg paper that the porter brought her, — "Congressman Darnell and his wife killed!" The bodies had been found at the bottom of an abandoned quarry. It was supposed that during a thunder-storm the night before, as he was driving from Torso to his farm in company with his wife, the horses had become uncontrollable and had dashed into the pit before Darnell could pull them up. He had just taken his seat in Congress. Isabelle remembered that he called the day before she left Torso, and when she had congratulated him on his election, had said jokingly: "Now I shall get after your husband's horses, Mrs. Lane. We shan't be on speaking terms when next we meet." He seemed gay and vital. So it had ended thus for the tempestuous Kentuckian. . . .

John was waiting for her at the station in Torso, where she was to break the journey. His face was eager and solicitous. He made many anxious inquiries about her health and the journey. But she put it all to one side.

"Tell me about the Darnells. Isn't it dreadful!"

"Yes," he said slowly, "it is very bad." Lane's voice was grave, as if he knew more than the published report.

"How could it have happened, — he was such a good driver? He must have been drunk."

"Tom Darnell could have driven all right, even if he had been drunk. I am afraid it's worse than that."

"Tell me!"

"There are all sorts of rumors. He came up from Washington unexpectedly, and his wife met him at the station with their team. They went to the hotel first, and then suddenly started for the farm in the midst of the storm. It was a terrible storm. . . . One story is that he had trouble with a bank; it is even said he had forged paper. I don't know! . . . Another story was about the Adams woman, — you know she followed him to Washington. . . . Too bad! He was a brilliant fellow, but he tied himself all up, tied himself all up," he observed sententiously, thus explaining the catastrophe of an unbalanced character.

"You mean it was — suicide?" Isabelle questioned.

"Looks that way!"

"How awful! and his wife killed, too!"

"He was always desperate — uncontrolled sort of fellow. You remember how he went off the handle the night of our dinner."

"So he ended it — that way," she murmured.

And she saw the man driving along the road in the black storm, his young wife by his side, with desperate purpose. She remembered his words in the orchard, his wistful desire for another kind of life. "The Adams woman, too," as John expressed it, and "he couldn't hold his horses." This nature had flown in pieces, liked a cracked wheel, in the swift revolution of life. To her husband it was only one of the messes recorded in the newspapers. But her mind was full of wonder and fear. As little as she had known the man, she had felt an interest in him altogether disproportionate to what he said or did. He was a man of possibilities, of streaks, of moods, one that could have been powerful, lived a rich life. And at thirty-three he had come to the end, where his passions and his ideals in perpetual warfare had held him bound. He had cut the knot! And she had chosen to go with him, the poor, timid wife! . . . Surely there were strange elements in people, Isabelle felt, not commonly seen in her little well-ordered existence, traits of character covered up before the world, fissures running back through the years into old impulses. Life might be terrible — when it got beyond your hand. She could not dismiss poor Tom Darnell as summarily as John did, — "a bad lot, I'm afraid!"

"You mustn't think anything more about it," her husband said anxiously, as she sat staring before her, trying to comprehend the tragedy. "I have arranged to take you on to-morrow. The Colonel writes that your brother Ezra is seedy, — touch of malaria, he thinks. The Colonel is looking forward a lot to your coming."

He talked on about the little domestic things, but she held that picture in the background of her mind and something within her said over and over, 'Why should it be like that for any one!'

And all the next day, on their way to St. Louis, she could not dismiss the thought from her mind: 'Why, I saw him only a few weeks ago. How well he read that poetry, as if he enjoyed it! And what he said that night at dinner he really meant, — oh, he believed it! And he was sorry for his wife, — yes, I am sure he was sorry for her. But he loved the other woman, — she understood him. And so he ended it. It's quite dreadful!'

The Colonel met them at the station with his new motor. His face was a bit grave as he said in answer to their inquiry: —

"No, it is not malaria, I am afraid. The doctors think it is typhoid. There has been a great deal of it in the city this summer, and the boy wouldn't take a vacation, was afraid I would stay here if he did. So I went up to Pelee, instead."

It was typhoid, and young Price died within the week. In the hush that followed the death of her brother Isabelle lay waiting for the coming of her child. . . . Her older brother Ezra! He was like a sturdy young tree in the forest, scarce noticed in the familiar landscape until his loss. Quiet, hard-working "Junior," as the family called him, — what would the Colonel do without him? The old man — now he was obviously old even to Isabelle — would come to her room and sit for long hours silent, as if he, too, was waiting for the coming of the new life into his house.

These two deaths so unlike, the tragic end of Darnell and

her brother's sudden removal, sank deep into her, sounding to her in the midst of her own childish preoccupation with her own life, the intricacy, the mystery of all existence. Life was larger than a private garden hedged with personal ambitions. She was the instrument of forces outside her being. And in her weakness she shrank into herself.

They told her that she had given birth to a daughter — another being like herself!

PART TWO

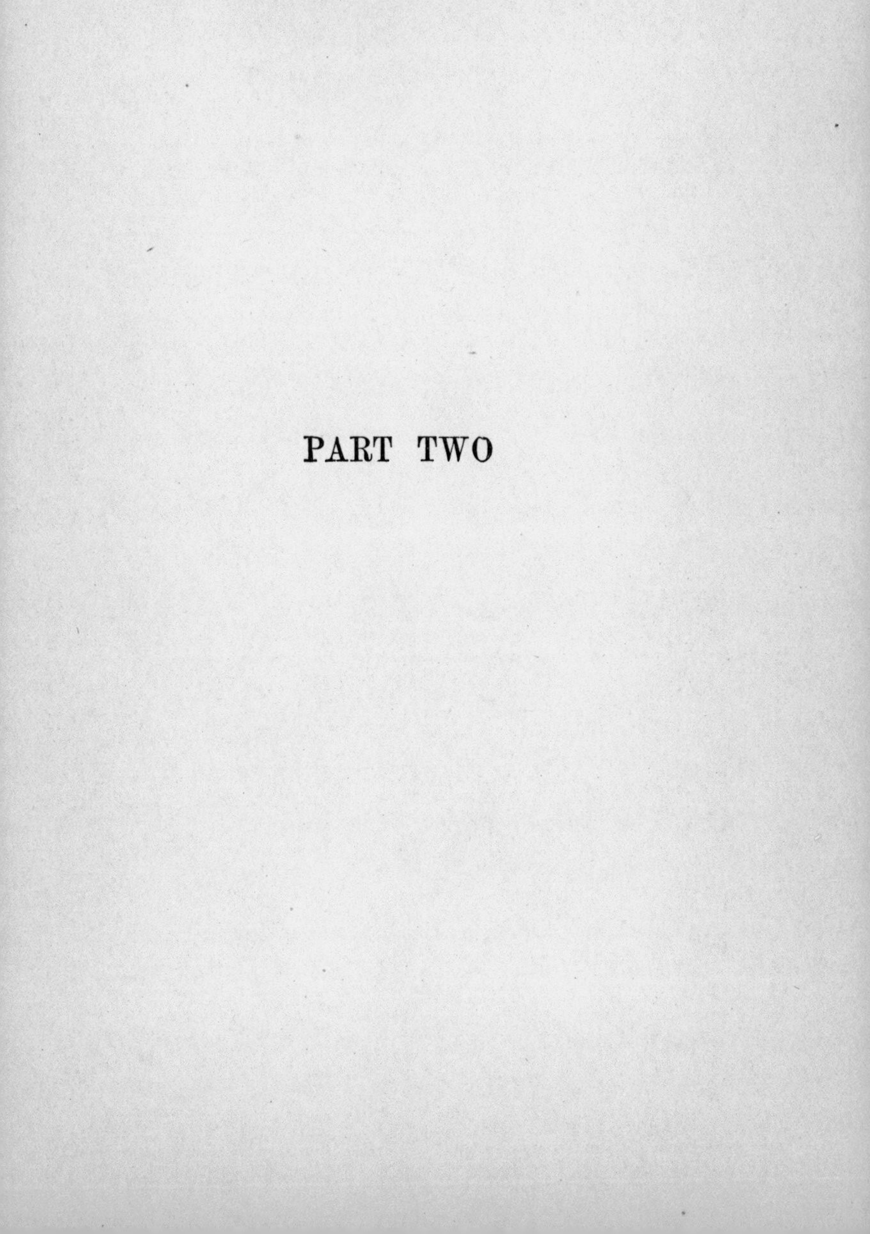

CHAPTER XIV

Colonel Price was a great merchant, one of those men who have been the energy, the spirit of the country since the War, now fast disappearing, giving way to another type in this era of "finance" as distinguished from "business." When the final review was ended, and he was free to journey back to the little Connecticut village where three years before he had left with his parents his young wife and their one child, he was a man just over thirty, very poor, and weak from a digestive complaint that troubled him all his life. But the spirit of the man was unbroken. Taking his little family with him, he moved to St. Louis, and falling in there with a couple of young men with like metal to himself, who happened also to possess some capital, he started the wholesale hardware business of Parrott, Price, and Co., which rapidly became the leading house in that branch of trade throughout the new West. The capital belonged to the other men, but the leadership from the start to Colonel Price. It was his genius as a trader, a diviner of needs, as an organizer, that within twenty years created the immense volume of business that rolled through the doors of their old warehouse. During the early years the Colonel was the chief salesman and spent his days "on the road" up and down the Mississippi Valley, sleeping in rough country taverns, dining on soda biscuit and milk, driving many miles over clayey, rutty roads, — dealing with men, making business.

Meanwhile the wife — her maiden name was Harmony Vickers — was doing her part in that little brick house which the Colonel had taken Lane to see. There she worked and saved, treating her husband's money like a sacred fund to be treasured. When the colonel came home from his weekly trips, he helped in the housework, and nursed the boy through the croup at night, saving his wife where he could. It was long after success had begun to look their way before Mrs. Price would consent to move into the wooden cottage on a quiet cross street that the Colonel wanted to buy, or employ more than one servant. But the younger children as they came on, first Vickers, then Isabelle, insensibly changed the family habits, — also the growing wealth and luxury of their friends, and the fast increasing income of the Colonel, no longer to be disguised. Yet when they built that lofty brick house in the older quarter of the city, she would have but two servants and used sparingly the livery carriage that her husband insisted on providing for her. The habit of fearsome spending never could wholly be eradicated. When the Colonel had become one of the leading merchants of the city, she consented grudgingly to the addition of one servant, also a coachman and a single pair of horses, although she preferred the street-cars on the next block as safer and less troublesome; and she began gradually to entertain her neighbors, to satisfy the Colonel's hospitable instincts, in the style in which they entertained her.

Mrs. Price had an enormous pride in the Colonel and in his reputation in St. Louis, a pride that no duke's wife could exceed. It was the Colonel who had started the movement for a Commercial Association and was its first president. As his wife she had entertained under her roof a President of the United States, not to mention a Russian prince and an English peer. It was the Colonel, as she told her children, who had carried through the agitation for a Water Commission; who urged the Park system; who saved the Second National Bank from failure in the panic days of ninety-three. She knew that he might have been governor, senator, possibly vice-president, if it had not been for his modesty and his disinclination to dip into the muddy pool of politics. As she drove into the city on her errands she was proudly conscious that she was the wife of the best-known private citizen, and as such recognized by every important resident and every quick-witted clerk in the stores where she dealt. To be plain Mrs. Ezra Price was ample reward for all the hardship and deprivation of those beginning years!

She was proud, too, of the fact that the money which she spent was honest money. For the hardware merchant belonged to the class that made its fortunes honestly, in the eye of the Law and of Society, also. Although latterly his investments had carried him into real estate, railroads, and banks, nevertheless it was as the seller of hardware that he wished to be known. He was prouder of the Lion brand of tools than of all his stock holdings. And though for many years a director in the Atlantic and Pacific and other great corporations, he had always resolutely refused to be drawn into the New York whirlpool; he was an American merchant and preferred to remain such all his life rather than add a number of millions to his estate "by playing faro in Wall Street."

The American merchant of this sort is fast disappearing, alas! As a class it has never held that position in the East that it had in the West. In the older states the manufacturer and the speculator have had precedence. Fortunes built on slaves and rum and cotton have brought more honor than those made in groceries and dry goods. Odd snobbery of trade! But in that broad, middle ground of the country, its great dorsal column, the merchant found his field, after the War, to develop and civilize. The character of those pioneers in trade, men from Vermont, New Hampshire, and Maine, was such as to make them leaders. They were brave and unselfish, faithful, and trusting of the future. With the plainest personal habits and tastes, taking no tarnish from the luxury that rose about them, seeing things larger than dollars on their horizon, they made the best aristocracy that this country has seen. Their coat of arms bore the legend: Integrity and Enterprise.

For their fortunes were built not speculatively, but on the ancient principles of trade, of barter between men, which is to divine needs and satisfy them, and hence they are the only fortunes in our rich land that do not represent, to some degree, human blood, the sacrifice of the many for the few. They were not fattened on a protective tariff, nor dug in wild speculation out of the earth, nor gambled into being over night on the price of foodstuffs, nor stolen from government lands, nor made of water in Wall Street. These merchants earned them, as the pedler earns the profit of his pack, as the farmer reaps the harvest of his seed. They earned them by labor and sagacity, and having them, they stood with heads erect, looking over their world and knowing that such as it is they helped to build it.

The day of the great merchant has already gone. Already the names of these honorable firms are mere symbols, cloaking corporate management, trading on the old personalities. No one saw the inevitable drift clearer than Colonel Price. In common with his class he cherished the desire of handing on the structure that he had built to the next generation, with the same sign-manual over the door, — to his son and his grandson. So he had resisted the temptation to incorporate the business and "take his profits." There was a son to sit in his seat. The sons of the other partners would not be fit: Starbird's only son, after a dissipated youth, was nursing himself somewhere on the Riviera; his daughter had married an Easterner, and beyond the quarterly check which the daughter and son received from the business, this family no longer had a share in it. As for Parrott there was a younger son serving somewhere in the immense establishment, but he had already proved his amiable incapacity for responsibility. The second generation, as the Colonel was forced to admit, was a disappointment. Somehow these merchants had failed to transmit the iron in their blood to their children. The sons and sons-in-law either lacked ability and grit, or were frankly degenerate, — withered limbs!

With the Colonel it had promised to be different; that first boy he had left behind when he went to the War had grown up under his eye, was saturated with the business idea. Young Ezra had preferred to leave the military academy where he had been at school and enter the store at eighteen. At thirty-six he had been made treasurer of the firm, only a few months before his death. . . . The Colonel's thin figure bent perceptibly after that autumn of ninety-seven. He erected a pseudo-Greek temple in Fairview Cemetery, with the name Price cut in deep Roman letters above the door, to hold the ashes of his son,— then devoted all his energies to measures for sanitary reform in the city. He was a fighter, even of death. . . .

Vickers had cabled at once when the news reached him that he was sailing for home. He and Isabelle had inherited their mother's nervous constitution and had come later in the family fortunes. They had known only ease and luxury, tempered as it was by their father's democratic simplicity and their mother's plain tastes. Insensibly they had acquired the outlook of the richer generation, the sense of freedom to do with themselves what they pleased. Both had been sent East to school, — to what the Colonel had been told were the best schools, — and Vickers had gone to a great university.

There for a time the boy had tried to compete in athletics, as the one inevitable path of ambition for an American boy at college; but realizing soon that he was too slightly built for this field, he had drifted into desultory reading and sketching for the college comic paper. Then a social talent and a gift for writing music gave him the composition of the score for the annual musical play. This was a hit, and from that time he began to think seriously of studying music. It was agreed in the family that after his graduation he should go abroad "to see what he could do." Ezra had already taken his place in the hardware business, and the younger son could be spared for the ornamental side of life, all the more as he was delicate in health and had not shown the slightest evidence of "practical ability." So the summer that he took his degree, a creditable degree with honors in music, the Prices sailed for Europe to undertake one of those elaborate tasting tours of foreign lands that well-to-do American families still essay. In the autumn it concluded by the Colonel's establishing the family in Munich and returning to his affairs. Vickers had been in Europe most of the time since, living leisurely, studying, writing "little things" that Isabelle played over for the Colonel on the piano.

Now he had come home at the family call, — an odd figure it must be confessed in St. Louis, with his little pointed beard, and thin mustache, his fondness for flowing neckwear and velveteen waistcoats, his little canes and varnished boots. And he stayed on; for the family seemed to need him, in a general way, though it was not clear to him what good he could do to them and there were tempting reasons for returning to Rome. In spite of the sadness of the family situation the young man could not repress his humorous sense of the futility of all hopes built upon himself.

"Just think of me selling nails," — he always referred to the hardware business as "selling nails," — he said to his mother when she spoke to him of the Colonel's hope that he would try to take his brother's place. "All I know about business is just enough to draw a check if the bank will keep the account straight. Poor Colonel! That germ ought to have got me instead of Junior!"

"You owe it to your father, Vick. You can't be more useless than Bob Parrott, and your father would like to see you in the office — for a time any way."

Vickers refrained from saying that there was an unmentioned difference between him and Bob Parrott. Young Parrott had never shown the desire to do anything, except play polo; while he might, — at least he had the passion for other things. The family, he thought, took his music very lightly, as a kind of elegant toy that should be put aside at the first call of real duty. Perhaps he had given them reason by his slow preparation, his waiting on the fulness of time and his own development to produce results for the world to see. Isabelle alone voiced a protest against this absorption of the young man into the family business.

"Why, he has his own life! It is too much of a sacrifice," she remonstrated.

"Nothing that can give your father comfort is too much of a sacrifice," Mrs. Price replied sharply.

"It can't last long," Isabelle said to Vickers. "The Colonel will see,—he is generous."

"He will see that I am no good fast enough!"

"He will understand what you are giving up, and he is too large hearted to want other people to do what they are not fitted to do."

"I don't suppose that the family fortunes need my strong right arm exactly?" the young man inquired.

"Of course not! It's the sentiment, don't you see?"

"Yes, of course, the sentiment for nails!" the young man accepted whimsically. "Poor Junior did the sentiment as well as the business so admirably, and I shall be such a hollow bluff at both, I fear."

Nevertheless, the next morning Vickers was at breakfast on time, and when the Colonel's motor came around at eight-thirty, he followed his father into the hall, put on an unobtrusive black hat, selected a sober pair of gloves, and leaving his little cane behind him took the seat beside his father. Their neighbor in the block was getting into his brougham at the same moment.

"Alexander Harmon," the Colonel explained, "president of the Commercial Trust Company."

They passed more of the Colonel's acquaintances on their way down the avenue, emerging from their comfortable houses for the day's work. It was the order of an industrial society, the young man realized, in a depressed frame of mind. He also realized, sympathetically, that he was occupying his brother's seat in the motor, and he was sorry for the old man at his side. The Colonel looked at him as if he were debating whether he should ask his son to stop at a barber shop and sacrifice his pointed beard,—but he refrained.

Vickers had never seen the towering steel and terra-cotta building in which the hardware business was now housed. It stood in a cloud of mist and smoke close by the river in the warehouse district. As the car drew up before its pillared entrance, the Colonel pointed with pride to the brass plaque beside the door on which was engraved the architect's name.

"Corbin did it,—you know him? They say he's the best man in America. It was his idea to sign it, the same as they do in Paris. Pretty good building, eh?"

The young man threw back his head and cast a critical glance over the twelve-story monster and again at the dwarfed classic entrance through which was pouring just now a stream of young men.

"Yes, Corbin is a good man," he assented vaguely, looking through the smoke drifts down the long crowded thoroughfare, on into a mass of telegraph wires, masts, and smokestacks, and lines of bulky freight cars. Some huge drays were backed against the Price building receiving bundles of iron rods that fell clanging into their place. Wagons rattled past over the uneven pavement, and below along the river locomotives whistled. Above all was the bass overtone of the city, swelling louder each minute with the day's work. A picture of a fair palace in the cavernous depths of a Sienna street came over the young man with a vivid sense of pain. Under his breath he muttered to himself, "Fierce!" Then he glanced with compunction at the gentle old face by his side. How had he kept so perfectly sweet, so fine in the midst of all this welter? The Colonel was like an old Venetian lord, shrewd with the wisdom of men, gentle with more than a woman's mercy; but the current that flowed by his palace was not that of the Grand Canal, the winds not those of the Levant!

But mayhap there was a harmony in this shrill battlefield, if it could be found. . . .

Within those long double doors there was a vast open area of floor space, dotted with iron beams, and divided economically into little plots by screens, in each one of which was a desk with the name of its occupant on an enamel sign.

"The city sales department," the Colonel explained as they crossed to the bank of shooting elevators. The Colonel was obliged to stop and speak and shake hands with many men, mostly in shirt sleeves, with hats on their heads, smoking cigars or pipes. They all smiled when they caught sight of the old man's face, and when he stopped to shake hands with some one, the man's face shone with pride. It was plain enough that the "old man" was popular with his employees. The mere handshake that he gave had something instinctively human and kind in it. He had a little habit of kneading gently the hand he held, of clinging to it a trifle longer than was needed. Every one of the six or seven hundred men in the building knew that the head of the business was at heart a plain man like themselves, who had never forgotten the day he sold his first bill of goods, and respected all his men each in his place as a man. They knew his "record" as a merchant and were proud of it. They thought him a "big man." Were he to drop out, they were convinced the business would run down, as if the main belt had slipped from the great fly-wheel of the machine shop. All the other "upstairs" men, as the firm members and managers of departments were called, were nonentities beside "our Colonel," the "whole thing," "it," as he was affectionately described.

So the progress to the elevators was slow, for the Colonel stopped to introduce his son to every man whose desk they passed or whose eye he caught.

"My boy, Vickers, Mr. Slason — Mr. Slason is our credit man, Vick — you'll know him better soon. . . . Mr. Jameson, just a moment, please; I want you to meet this young man!"

"If he's got any of your blood in him, Colonel, he's all right," a beefy, red-faced man jerked out, chewing at an unlighted cigar and looking Vickers hard in the face.

Even the porters had to be introduced. It was a democratic advance! But finally they reached the "upstairs" quarters, where in one corner was the Colonel's private den, partitioned off from the other offices by ground glass, — a bare space with a little old black walnut desk, a private safe, and a set of desk telephones. Here Vickers stood looking down at the turmoil of traffic in the street below, while his father glanced over a mass of telegrams and memoranda piled on his desk.

The roar of business that had begun to rumble through the streets at daybreak and was now approaching its meridian stunned the young man's nerves. Deadened by the sound of it all, he could not dissociate from the volume that particular note, which would be his note, and live oblivious to the rest. . . . So this was business! And what a feeble reed he was with which to prop it! Visions of that other life came thronging to his mind, — the human note of other cities he had learned to love, the placid hours of contemplation, visions of things beautiful in a world of joy! Humorously he thought of the hundreds of thousands of dollars this busy hive earned each year. A minute fraction of its profits would satisfy him, make him richer than all of it. And he suspected that the thrifty Colonel had much more wealth stored away in that old-fashioned iron safe. What was the use of throwing himself into this great machine? It would merely grind the soul out of him and spit him forth.

To keep it going, — that was the reason for sacrificing his youth, his desire. But why keep the thing going? Pride, sentiment? He did not know the Colonel's feeling of fatherhood towards all the men who worked for him, his conviction that in this enterprise which he had created, all these human beings were able to live happier lives because of him, his leadership. There was poetry in the old man, and imagination. But the young man, with his eyes filled with those other — more brilliant — glories, saw only the grime, heard only the dull roar of the wheels that turned out a meaningless flood of gold, like an engine contrived to supply desires and reap its percentage of profits.

"Father!" he cried involuntarily.

Hot words of protest were in his throat. Let some other young man be found to run the machine; or let them make a corporation of it and sell it in the market. Or close the doors, its work having been done. But give him his life, and a few dollars!

"Eh, Vick? Hungry? We'll go over to the club for luncheon in just a minute." And the old Colonel smiled affectionately at his son over his glasses.

"Not now — not just yet," Vickers said to himself, with a quick rush of comprehension.

But the "now" never seemed to come, the right moment for delivering the blow, through all those months that followed, while the young man was settling into his corner of the great establishment. When the mother or Isabelle confessed their doubts to the Colonel, the old man would say: —

"It will do him no harm, a little of it. He'll know how to look after your money, mother, when I am gone." And he added, "It's making a man of him, you'll see!"

There was another matter, little suspected by the Colonel, that was rapidly to make a man of his engaging young son.

CHAPTER XV

When Vickers Price raised his eyes from his desk and, losing for the moment the clattering note of business that surged all around him, looked through dusky panes into the cloud of mist and smoke, visions rose before him that were strange to the smoky horizon of the river city. . . .

From the little balcony of his room on the Pincio, all Rome lay spread before him, — Rome smiling under the blue heaven of an April morning! The cypresses in the garden pointed to a cloudless sky. Beyond the city roofs, where the domes of churches rose like little islands, was the green band of the Janiculum, and farther southwards the river cut the city and was lost behind the Aventine. And still beyond the Campagna reached to the hills about Albano.

Beneath he could see the Piazza del Popolo, with a line of tiny cabs standing lazily in the sunlight, and just below the balcony was a garden where a fountain poured softly, night and day. Brilliant balls of colored fruit hung from the orange trees, glossy against the yellow walls of the palazzo across the garden. From the steep street on the other side of the wall rose the thin voice of a girl, singing a song of the mountains, with a sad note of ancient woe, and farther away in the city sounded the hoarse call of a pedler. . . . This was not the Rome of the antiquary, not the tawdry Rome of the tourist. It was the Rome of sunshine and color and music, the Rome of joy, of youth! And the young man, leaning there over the iron railing, his eyes wandering up and down the city at his feet, drank deep of the blessed draught,— the beauty and the joy of it, the spirit of youth and romance in his heart. . . .

From some one of the rooms behind a neighboring balcony

floated a woman's voice, swelling into a full contralto note, then sinking low and sweet into brooding contemplation. After a time Vickers went to his work, trying to forget the golden city outside the open window, but when the voice he had heard burst forth joyously outside, he looked up and saw the singer standing on her balcony, shading her eyes with a hand, gazing out over the city, her voice breaking forth again and again in scattered notes, as though compelled by the light and the joy of it all. She was dressed in a loose black morning gown that rippled in the breeze over her figure. She clasped her hands above her bronze-colored hair, the action revealing the pure white tint of neck and arms, the well-knit body of small bones. She stood there singing to herself softly, the note of spring and Rome in her voice. Still singing she turned into her room, and Vickers could hear her, as she moved back and forth, singing to herself. And as he hung brooding over Rome, listening to the gurgle of the fountain in the garden, he often listened to this contralto voice echoing the spirit within him. . . . Sometimes a little girl came out on the balcony to play.

"Are you English?" she asked the young man one day.

"No, American, like you, eh?" Vickers replied.

They talked, and presently the little girl running back into the room spoke to some one: "There is a nice man out there, mother. He says he's American, too." Vickers could not hear what the woman said in reply. . . .

The child made them friends. Mrs. Conry, Vickers learned, was his neighbor's name, and she was taking lessons in singing, preparing herself, he gathered, for professional work, — a widow, he supposed, until he heard the little girl say one day, "when we go home to father, — we are going home, mother, aren't we? Soon?" And when the mother answered something unintelligible, the little girl with a child's subtle tact was silent. . . .

This woman standing there on the balcony above the city, — all gold and white and black, save for the gray eyes, the curving lines of her supple body, — this was what he saw of Europe, — all outside those vivid Roman weeks that he shared with her fading into a vague background. Together they tasted the city, — its sunny climbing streets, its white squares, and dark churches, the fields beyond the Colosseum, the green Campagna, the vivid mornings, the windless moonlight nights! All without this marvellous circle, this charmed being of Rome, had the formlessness of a distant planet. Here life began and closed, and neither wished to know what the other had been in the world behind.

That she was from some Southern state, — "a little tiny place near the Gulf, far from every civilized thing," Mrs. Conry told him; and it was plain enough that she was meagrely educated, — there had been few advantages in that "tiny place." But her sensuous temperament was now absorbing all that it touched. Rome meant little to her beyond the day's charm, the music it made in her heart; while the man vibrated to every association, every memory of the laden city. . . .

Thus the days and weeks slipped by until the gathering heat warned them of the passing of time. One June day that promised to be fresh and cool they walked through the woods above the lake of Albano. Stacia Conry hummed the words of a song that Vickers had written and set to music, one of a cycle they had planned for her to sing — the Songs of the Cities. This was the song of Rome, and in it Vickers had embedded the sad strain that the girl sang coming up the street, — the cry of the past.

"That is too high for me," she said, breaking off. "And it is melancholy. I hate sad things. It reminds me of that desolate place at the end of the earth where I came from."

"All the purest music has a strain of sadness," Vickers protested.

"No, no; it has longing, passion! . . . I escaped!" She looked down on the cuplike lake, shimmering in the sun below. "I knew in my heart that *this* lived, this world of sunshine and beauty and joy. I thirsted for it. Now I drink it!"

She turned on him her gray eyes, which were cool in spite of her emotion. She had begun again the song in a lower key, when at a turn in the path they came upon a little wooden shrine, one of those wayside altars still left in a land where religion has been life. Before the weather-stained blue-and-red madonna knelt a strangely mediæval figure, — a man wasted and bare-headed, with long hair falling matted over his eyes. An old sheepskin coat came to his bare knees. Dirty, forlorn, leaning wearily on his pilgrim's staff, the man was praying before the shrine, his lips moving silently.

"What a figure!" Vickers exclaimed in a low voice, taking from his pocket a little camera. As he tiptoed ahead of Mrs. Conry to get his picture before the pilgrim should rise, he saw the intense yearning on the man's face. Beckoning to his companion, Vickers put the camera into his pocket and passed on, Mrs. Conry following, shrinking to the opposite side of the way, a look of aversion on her mobile face.

"Why didn't you take him?" she asked as they turned the corner of the road.

"He was praying, — and he meant it," Vickers answered vaguely.

The woman's lips curved in disgust at the thought of the dirty pilgrim on his knees by the roadside.

"Only the weak pray! I hate that sort of thing, — prayer and penitence."

"Perhaps it is the only real thing in life," Vickers replied from some unknown depth within him.

"No, no! How can you say that? You who know what life can be. Never! That is what they tried to teach me at school. But I did not believe it. I escaped. I wanted to sing. I wanted my own life." She became grave, and added under her breath: "And I shall get it. That is best, best, best!" She broke into a run down the sun-flecked road, and they emerged breathless in an olive orchard beside the lake. Her body panted as she threw herself down on the grass. "Now!" she smiled, her skin all rose; "can you say that?" And her voice chanted, "To live, — my friend, — to LIVE! And you and I are made to live, — isn't it so?"

The artist in Vickers, the young man of romance, his heart tender with sentiment, responded to the creed. But woven with the threads of this artist temperament were other impulses that stirred. The pilgrim in the act of penitence and ecstatic devotion was beautiful, too, and real, — ah, very real, as he was to know. . . .

They supped that afternoon in a little wine shop looking towards the great dome swimming above Rome. And as the sun shot level and golden over the Campagna, lighting the old, gray tombs, they drove back to the city along the ancient Latin road. The wonderful plain, the most human landscape in the world, began to take twilight shadows. Rome hung, in a mist of sun, like a mirage in the far distance, and between them and the city flowed the massive arches of an aqueduct, and all about were the crumbling tombs, half hidden by the sod. The carriage rolled monotonously onwards. The woman's eyes nearly closed; she looked dreamily out through the white lids, fringed with heavy auburn lashes. She still hummed from time to time the old refrain of Vickers's song. Thus they returned, hearing the voice of the old world in its peculiar hour.

"I am glad that I have had it — that I have lived — a little. This, this! — I can sing to-night! You must come and sit on my balcony and look at the stars while I sing to you — the music of the day."

As the Porta San Paolo drew near, Vickers remarked: —

"I shall write you a song of Venice, — that is the music for you."

"Venice, and Paris, and Vienna, and Rome, — all! I love them all!"

She reached her arms to the great cities of the earth, seeing herself in triumph, singing to multitudes the joy of life. . . . "Come to-night, — I will sing for you!" . . .

On the porter's table at the hotel lay a thick letter for Mrs. Conry. It bore the printed business address, — THE

Conry Construction Company. Mrs. Conry took it negligently in her white hand. "You will come later?" she said, smiling back at the young man.

Sitting crowded in front of Arragno's and sipping a liqueur, Fosdick remarked to Vickers: "So you have run across the Conry? Of course I know her. I saw her in Munich the first time. The little girl still with her? Then it was Vienna. . . . She's got as far as Rome! Been over here two or three years studying music. Pretty good voice, and a better figure. Oh, Stacia is much of a siren."

Vickers moved uneasily and in reply to a question Fosdick continued:—

"Widow — grass widow — properly linked — who knows? Our pretty country-women have such a habit of trotting around by themselves for their own delectation that you never can tell how to place them. She may be divorced — she may be the other thing! You can't tell. But she is a very handsome woman." . . .

Mrs. Conry herself told Vickers the facts, as they sat at a little restaurant on the Aventine where they loved to go to watch the night steal across the Palatine.

". . . He offered me my education — my chance. I took it. I went to the conservatory at Cincinnati. Then he wanted to marry me, and promised to send me abroad to study more." . . . Her tone was dry, impartially recounting the fact. Then her eyes dropped, and Vickers's cigarette glowed between them as they leaned across the little iron table. . . . "I was a child then — did not know anything. I married him. The first years business was poor, and he could not let me have the money. When times got better, he let me come — kept his promise. I have been here nearly three years, back two or three times. And now," her voice dropped, "I must go back for good — soon."

Nothing more. But it seemed to Vickers as if a ghost had risen from the river mist and come to sit between them.

That the woman was paying a price for her chance, a heavy price, he could see. They walked back to the city between the deserted vineyards. As they crossed the river, Mrs. Conry stopped, and remarked sombrely, "A bargain is a bargain the world over, is it not?"

Vickers felt the warm breathing woman close to him, felt her brooding eyes. "One pays," he murmured, "I suppose!"

She threw up her hand in protest, and they walked on into the lighted city.

Occasionally Fosdick joined their excursions, and after one of them he said to Vickers:—

"My friend, she is wonderful; more so every time I see her. But beneath that soft, rounded body, with its smooth white skin, is something hard. Oh, I know the eyes and the hair and the throat and the voice! I, too, am a man. Paint her, if you like, or set her to music. She is for *bel canto* and moonlight and the voice of Rome. But there is a world outside this all, my friend, to which you and I belong, and *you* rather more than I. . . . Stacia Conry doesn't belong at all."

"Which means?" demanded Vickers steadily of the burly Fosdick.

"Take care that you don't get stuck in the sea of Sargasso. I think something bitter might rise out of all that loveliness."

Nevertheless, instead of going to the Maloya with Fosdick, Vickers stayed on in Rome, and September found him there and Mrs. Conry, too, having returned to the city from the mountain resort, where she had left the little girl with her governess. They roamed the deserted city, and again began to work on the songs which Mrs. Conry hoped to give in concerts on her return to America. Very foolish of the young man, and the woman, thus to prolong the moment of charm, to linger in the Sargasso Sea! But at least with the man, the feeling that kept him in Rome those summer months was pure and fine, the sweetest and the best that man may know, where he gives of his depths with no thought of reward, willing to accept the coming pain. . . . Little Delia, who had seen quite as much of Vickers as her mother, said to him the day she left with her governess: —

"We're going home soon — before Thanksgiving. I'm so glad! And you'll be there, too?"

"I suppose not, Delia," the young man replied. But as it happened he was the first to go back. . . .

That late September day they had returned from a ramble in the hills. It was nearly midnight when the cab rattled up the deserted streets to their hotel. As Vickers bade his companion good-night, with some word about a long-projected excursion to Volterra, she said: —

"Come in and I will sing for a while. I don't feel like sleep. . . . Yes, come! Perhaps it will be the last of all our good times."

In the large dark apartment the night wind was drawing over the roofs of the hill through the open windows, fluttering stray sheets of music along the stone floor. Mrs. Conry lighted a candle on the piano, and throwing aside her hat and veil, dropping her gloves on the floor, struck some heavy chords. She sang the song they had been working over, the song of Venice, with a swaying melody as of floating water-grasses. Then she plunged into a throbbing aria, — singing freely, none too accurately, but with a passion and self-forgetfulness which promised greater things than the concert performer. From this on to other snatches of opera, to songs, wandering as the mood took her, coming finally to the street song that Vickers had woven into his composition for Rome, with its high, sad note. There her voice stopped, died in a cry half stifled in the throat, and leaving the piano she came to the window. A puff of wind blew out the candle. With the curtains swaying in the night wind, they stood side by side looking down into the dark city, dotted irregularly with points of light, and up above the Janiculum to the shining stars.

"Rome, Rome," she murmured, and the words sighed past the young man's ears, — "and life — LIFE!"

It was life that was calling them, close together, looking forth into the night, their hearts beating, the longing to grasp it, to go out alone into the night for it. Freedom, and love, and life, — they beckoned! Vickers saw her eyes turn to him in the dark. . . .

"And now I go," he said softly. He found his way to the door in the dark salon, and as he turned he saw her white figure against the swaying curtain, and felt her eyes following him.

In his room he found the little blue despatch, sent up from his banker, which announced his brother's death, and the next morning he left by the early express for the north to catch the Cherbourg boat. As he passed Mrs. Conry's salon he slipped under the door the despatch with a note, which ended, "I know that we shall see each other again, somewhere, somehow!" and from the piazza he sent back an armful of great white *fleur-de-lys*. Later that morning, while Vickers was staring at the vintage in the Umbrian Valley and thinking of the woman all white and bronze with the gray eyes, Mrs. Conry was reading his note. A bitter smile curved her lips, as she gathered up the white flowers and laid them on the piano.

CHAPTER XVI

ONE winter day while Vickers Price was "selling nails," as he still expressed his business career, there came in his mail a queer little scrawl, postmarked Pittsburg. It was from Delia Conry, and it ran:—

"We've been home a month. We live in a hotel. I don't like it. The bird you gave me died. Mother says she'll get me a new one. I wish I could see you. Love from Delia."

But not a word from Mrs. Conry! Fosdick, drifting through Rome on his way to Turkestan, wrote: —

". . . What has become of the Conry? She has disappeared from the cities of Europe with her melodious songs and beautiful hair. Are you touring the States with her? Or has she rediscovered Mr. Conry — for a period of seclusion? . . . To think of you serving hardware to the barbarians across the counter enlivens my dull moments. From the Sargasso Sea to St. Louis, — there is a leap for you, my dear." . . .

While he "served hardware to the barbarians" and in other respects conformed to the life of a privileged young American gentleman, Vickers Price dreamed of those Roman days, the happiest of his life. If that night they two had taken life in their hands? . . . Could the old Colonel have read his son's heart, — if from the pinnacle of his years filled with ripe deeds he could have comprehended youth, — he might have been less sure that the hardware business was to be "the making of Vick"!

What had come to her? Had she accepted her lot, once back in the groove of fate, or had she rebelled, striking out for her own vivid desire of joy and song, of fame? Vickers would have liked to hear that she had rebelled, was making her own life, — had taken the other road than the one he had accepted for himself. His tender, idealizing heart could not hold a woman to the sterner courses of conduct.

For, as Fosdick had told him in Rome, the young man was a Sentimentalist with no exact vision of life. His heart was perpetually distorting whatever his mind told him was fact. This woman, with her beauty, her love of music, had touched him at the lyric moment of life, when reality was but the unstable foundation for dream. Life as might be, glowing, colored, and splendid, — life as it was within him, not as this hideous maelstrom all about him reported. And why not the I, the I! cried the spirit of youth, the egotistic spirit of the age. For all reply there was the bent, gray head of the Colonel at his desk in the office beside him. "One sentiment against another," Fosdick might say. . . .

Finally Stacia Conry wrote, a little note: she was to be in St. Louis on the fourteenth for a short time and hoped that he would call on her at the hotel. A perfectly proper, colorless little note, written in an unformed hand, with a word or two misspelled, — the kind of note that gave no indication of the writer, but seemed like the voice of a stranger. However, as Vickers reflected, literary skill, the power to write personal little notes did not go necessarily with a talent for music — or for life. Nannie Lawton wrote intimate notes, and other women, single and married, whom Vickers had come to know these past months. But their cleverest phrases could not stir his pulses as did this crude production.

The woman who was waiting for him in the little hotel parlor, however, gave him a curious shock, — she was so different in her rich street costume from the woman in black and white, whose picture had grown into his memory. She seemed older, he thought, thus accounting for that strange idealizing power of the mind to select from a face what that face has specially given it and create an altogether new being, with its own lineaments graven in place of actual bone and tissue. It takes time to correct this ideal misreport of the soul, to accept the fact! Except for the one glance from the gray eyes which she gave him as they shook hands, Stacia Conry did not stir the past. But she was voluble of the present.

"You did not expect this! You see my husband had some work to attend to near here, and I thought I would come with him. . . . No, we left Delia in Pittsburg with his mother, — she wanted to see you, but she would be in the way."

They came soon to her singing, and her face clouded.

"I haven't been able to get an opening. I wanted to sing the Cycle with an orchestra. But I haven't succeeded, — our Pittsburg orchestra won't look at any talent purely domestic. It is all pull over here. I haven't any influence. . . . You must start with some backing, — sing in private houses for great people! We don't know that kind, you see."

"And concerts?" Vickers inquired.

"The same way, — to get good engagements you must have something to show. . . . I've sung once or twice, — in little places, church affairs and that kind of thing."

Vickers laughed as Mrs. Conry's expressive lips curled.

"They tell you to take everything to begin with. But singing for church sociables in Frankfort and Alleghany, — that doesn't do much! I want to go to New York, — I know people there, but — "

Vickers understood that Mr. Conry objected.

"It must come sometime," she said vehemently; "only waiting is killing. It takes the life out of you, the power, don't you think?"

"Could you sing here?" Vickers asked, — "now, I mean? I might be able to arrange it."

"Oh, if you could!" Mrs. Conry's face glowed, and her fingers played nervously with her long chain. "If I could give the Cycle with your accompaniment, here in St. Louis where you are so well known — "

Vickers smiled at the picture of his début in St. Louis drawing-rooms.

"I will ask my sister to help," he said. "I should like her to call."

Mrs. Conry became suddenly animated, as if after a period of depressing darkness she saw a large ray of sunshine. She had thought of possibilities when she had persuaded her husband to take her to St. Louis, but had not expected them to develop at once.

"You see," she continued quickly, "if I can get a hearing here, it means that other people may want me,— I'll become known, a little."

"My mother couldn't have it," Vickers explained, "nor my sister, because of our mourning. But Mrs. Lawton,— that would be better any way." He thought of Nannie Lawton's love of *réclame*, and he knew that though she would never have considered inviting the unheralded Mrs. Conry to sing in her drawing-room, she would gladly have *him* appear there with any one, playing his own music.

"Yes, we'll put it through! The Songs of the Cities." He repeated the words with sentimental visions of the hours of their composition.

"And then I have some more, — Spanish songs. They take, you know! And folk-songs." Mrs. Conry talked on eagerly of her ambitions until Vickers left, having arranged for Isabelle to call the next day. As he took his way to the Lawtons' to use his influence with the volatile Nan in behalf of Mrs. Conry, his memory of their talk was sad. 'America, that's it,' he explained. 'She wants to do something for herself, to get her independence.' And he resolved to leave no stone unturned, no influence unused, to gratify her ambition.

So Isabelle called on Mrs. Conry in company with Nannie Lawton. Vickers little knew what an ordeal the woman he loved was passing through in this simple affair. A woman may present no difficulties to the most fastidiously bred man, and yet be found wanting in a thousand particulars by the women of his social class. As the two emerged from the hotel, Isabelle looked dubiously at Mrs. Lawton.

"Queer, isn't she?" that frank lady remarked. "Oh, she's one of those stray people you run across in Europe. Perhaps she can sing all right, though I don't care. The men will be crazy after her, — she's the kind, — red hair and soft skin and all that. . . . Better look out for that young brother of yours, Isabelle. She is just the one to nab our innocent Vickie."

Isabelle's report of her call had some reserves.

"Of course she is very striking, Vick. But, you see, — she — she isn't exactly our kind!"

"That is Nan," the young man retorted impatiently. "I never heard you say that sort of thing before. What on earth is 'our kind'? She is beautiful and has talent, a lot of it, — all she wants is her chance. And why shouldn't she have it?"

Isabelle smiled at his heat, and replied caressingly: —

"She shall have all that Nan and I can do for her here. But don't be foolish about her. I suspect you could be with a woman — because of your dear old heart. . . . If she can't sing a note, she'll make a hit with her looks, Nan says!"

So the musicale was arranged. There were mostly women in Mrs. Lawton's smart little music room when Mrs. Conry rose to sing a series of introductory songs. She was very striking, as Isabelle and Mrs. Lawton had foreseen that she would be, — rather bizarrely dressed in a white and gold costume that she had designed herself, with a girdle of old stones strung loosely about her waist. She was nervous and sang uncertainly at first so that Vickers had to favor her in his accompaniment. He could see the trembling of her white arm beside him. The Cycle of the Cities came near the end of the programme, and when Vickers took his seat to play the accompaniments, he was aware that a number of men had arrived and were standing in the hall, peering through the doors at the performance. He knew well enough what the men were thinking of him, sitting there playing his own songs, — that it was a queer, monkey performance for the son of Colonel Price! The fine arts are duly recognized in American cities; but the commercial class, as always has been its wont, places them in a category between millinery and theology.

She had chosen *Paris* to open with, and gave the song with assurance, eliciting especially from the men in the hall the first real applause. Then followed *Vienna, Munich.* She was singing well, gaining confidence. When it came to *Venice,* — Vickers remembered as he followed her swimming voice the twilight over the Campagna, the approaching mass of Rome, — even the women woke to something like enthusiasm. As she uttered the first note of *Rome,* she glanced down at Vickers, with a little smile, which said: —

"Do you remember? This is *ours,* — I am singing this for you!"

Her face was flushed and happy. She sang the difficult music as she had sung that last night in Rome, and Vickers, listening to the full voice so close to him, heard again the high sad note of the street singer, in the golden spring day, uttering this ancient melody of tears, — only this time it was woven with laughter and joy. When she finished, he sought her eyes; but Mrs. Conry was sweeping the gathering with a restless glance, thinking of her encore. . . .

Afterwards the women said agreeable things about Vickers's music, especially the *Paris* and the *Venice.* About Mrs. Conry they said that her voice was good, "somewhat uncultivated," "too loud for drawing-room music," — safe criticisms. The men said little about the music, but they clustered around the singer. Mrs. Lawton looked significantly at Isabelle and winked. One old gentleman, something of a beau as well as a successful lawyer, congratulated Vickers on his "tuneful" music. "It must be a pleasant avocation to write songs," he said. . . .

They dined at the Lawtons', and afterwards Vickers took

Mrs. Conry to the hotel. She was gay with the success she had had, the impression she had made on the men.

"Something'll come of this, I am sure. Do you think they liked me?"

"You sang well," Vickers replied evasively, "better than well, the *Rome*."

In the lobby of the hotel she turned as though to dismiss him, but Vickers, who was talking of a change to be made in one of the songs, accompanied her to the parlor above, where they had practised the music in preparation for the concert. Mrs. Conry glanced quickly into the room as they entered, as if expecting to find some one there. Vickers was saying:—

"I think we shall have to add another one to the Cycle, — *New York* or something to stand for — well, what it is over here, — just living!"

The door of the inner room opened and a man appeared, coatless, with a much-flowered waistcoat.

"So you're back," the man remarked in a heavy voice.

"My husband," Mrs. Conry explained, "Mr. Vickers Price!"

Mr. Conry shuffled heavily into the room. He was a large man with a big grizzled head and very red face, finely chased with purple veins. He gave Vickers a stubby hand.

"Pleased to meet you, Mr. Price. Heard about you from Delia. Sit down." Conry himself stood, swaying slightly on his stout legs. After a time he chose a seat with great deliberation and continued to stare at the young man. "Have a cigar?" He took one from his waistcoat pocket and held it towards the young man. "It's a good one,— none of your barroom smokes,— oh, I see you are one of those cigarette fiends, same as Stacia!"

There was a conversational hiatus, and Vickers was thinking of going.

"Well, how was the show?" Conry demanded of his wife. "Did you sing good,— make a hit with the swells? She thinks she wants to sing," he explained with a wink to

Vickers, "but I tell her she's after sassiety, — that's what the women want; ain't it so?"

"Mrs. Conry sang very well indeed," Vickers remarked in default of better, and rose to leave.

"Don't go, — what's your hurry? Have something to drink? I got some in there you don't see every day in the week, young man. A racing friend of mine from Kentuck sends it to me. What's yours, Stacy?" . . .

When the young man departed, Stacia Conry stared at the door through which he had disappeared, with a dead expression that had something disagreeable in it. Conry, who had had his drink, came back to the parlor and began to talk.

"I went to a show myself to-night, seeing you were amusing yourself. . . . There was a girl there who danced and sang, — you'd oughter seen her. . . . Well, what are you sittin' staring at? Ain't you coming to bed?"

His wife rose from her seat, exclaiming harshly, "Let me alone!" And Conry, with a half-sober scrutiny of the woman, who had flung herself face down on the lounge, mumbled: —

"Singing don't seem to agree with you. Well, I kept my word; gave you the money to educate yourself." . . .

"And I have paid you!" the wife flashed. "God, I have paid!"

The man stumbled off to bed.

Vickers, on leaving the hotel, walked home in the chill night, a sickening sensation in his heart. If he had been a shrewd young man, he might have foreseen the somewhat boozy Mr. Conry, the vulgar setting of the woman he loved. If there had been the least thing base in him, he might have welcomed it, for his own uses. But being a sentimentalist and simple in nature, the few moments of intercourse with Mr. Conry had come like a revelation to him. This was what she had sold herself to for her education. This was what she was tied to! And this what she sought to escape from by her music, to place herself and her child beyond the touch of that man!

Vickers in his disgust overlooked the fact that little Delia seemed to love her father, and that though Conry might not be to his taste, he might also be a perfectly worthy citizen, given occasionally to liquor. But love and youth and the idealizing temperament make few allowances. To give her that freedom which her beauty and her nature craved, he would do what he could, and he searched his memory for names and persons of influence in the professional world of music. He had the fragments of a score for an opera that he had scarce looked at since he had begun "to sell nails"; but to-night he took it from the drawer and ran it over, — "Love Among the Ruins," — and as he went to sleep he saw Stacia Conry singing as she had sung that last night in Rome, singing the music of his opera, success and fame at her feet. . . .

The something that Mrs. Conry hoped for did come from that introduction at the Lawtons'. The wife of one of those men she had charmed called on her and invited her to sing "those pleasant little songs Mr. Price wrote for you" (with Mr. Price's appearance, of course!). And several women, who were anxious to be counted as of the Lawton set, hastened to engage Mrs. Conry to sing at their houses, with the same condition. Vickers understood the meaning of this condition and disliked the position, but consented in his desire to give Mrs. Conry every chance in his power. Others understood the situation, and disliked it, — among them Isabelle. Nannie Lawton threw at her across a dinner-table the remark: "When is Vick going to offer his 'Love Among the Ruins'? Mrs. Conry is the 'ruins,' I suppose!"

And the musicales, in spite of all that Vickers could do, were only moderately successful. In any community, the people who hunt the latest novelty are limited in number, and that spring there arrived a Swedish portrait painter and an Antarctic traveller to push the beautiful singer from the centre of attention. So after the first weeks the engagements became farther spaced and less desirable, less influential. Mrs. Conry still stayed at the hotel, though her husband had been called to another city on a contract he had undertaken. She realized that her début had not been brilliant, but she clung to the opportunity, in the hope that something would come of it. And naturally enough Vickers saw a good deal of her; not merely the days they appeared together, but almost every day he found an excuse for dropping in at the hotel, to play over some music, to take her to ride in his new motor, which he ran himself, or to dine with her. Mrs. Conry was lonely. After Isabelle went to California for her health, she saw almost no one. The women she met at her engagements found her "not our kind," and Nan Lawton's witticism about "the ruins" and Vickers did not help matters. Vickers saw the situation and resented it. This loneliness and disappointment were bad for her. She worked at her music in a desultory fashion, dawdled over novels, and smoked too many cigarettes for the good of her voice. She seemed listless and discouraged. Vickers redoubled his efforts to have her sing before a celebrated manager, who was coming presently to the city with an opera company.

'She sees no way, no escape,' he said to himself. 'One ray of hope, and she would wake to what she was in Europe!'

In his blind, sentimental devotion, he blamed the accidents of life for her disappointment, not the woman herself. When he came, she awoke, and it was an unconscious joy to him, this power he had to rouse her from her apathy, to make her become for the time the woman he always saw just beneath the surface, eager to emerge if life would but grant her the chance.

His own situation had changed with the growing year. The Colonel, closely watching "the boy," was coming gradually to comprehend the sacrifice that he had accepted, all the more as Vickers never murmured but kept steadily at his work. Before Isabelle left for California, she spoke plainly to her father: —

"What's the use, Colonel! No matter how he tries, Vick can never be like you,— and why should he be any way?"

"It won't have done any harm," the old man replied dubiously. "We'll see!"

First he made his son independent of salary or allowance by giving him a small fortune in stocks and bonds. Then one day, while Mrs. Conry was still in the city, he suggested that Vickers might expect a considerable vacation in the summer. "You can go to Europe and write something," he remarked, in his simple faith that art could be laid down or resumed at will. Vickers smiled, but did not grasp the opportunity eagerly. When he told Mrs. Conry that afternoon of the proposed "vacation," she exclaimed enviously:—

"I knew you would go back!"

"I am not sure that I shall go."

She said perfunctorily: "Of course you must go— will you go back to Rome? I shall be so glad to think you are doing what you want to do."

He turned the matter off with a laugh:—

"The dear old boy thinks two months out of a year is long enough to give to composing an opera. It's like fishing,— a few weeks now and then if you can afford it!"

"But you wouldn't have to stay here at all, if you made up your mind not to," she remarked with a touch of hardness. "They'll give you what you want."

"I am not sure that I want it," he replied slowly, "at the price."

She looked at him uncomprehendingly, then perceiving another meaning in his words, lowered her eyes. She was thinking swiftly, 'If we could both go!' But he was reflecting rather bitterly on that new wealth which his father had given him, the dollars piling up to his credit, not one of which he might use as he most dearly desired to use them— for her! With all this power within his easy reach he could not stretch forth his hand to save a human soul. For thus he conceived the woman's need.

It came to Mrs. Conry's last engagement, — the last possible excuse for her lingering in the city. It was a suburban affair, and the place was difficult to reach. Vickers had invited the Falkners to go with them, to prevent gossip, and Bessie willingly accepted as a spree, though she had confided to Isabelle that "Mrs. Conry was dreadful ordinary," "not half good enough for our adorable Vickers to *afficher* himself with." Nevertheless, she was very sweet to the beautiful Mrs. Conry, as was Bessie's wont to be with pretty nearly all the world. It was late on their return, and the Falkners left them at the station. With the sense that to-night they must part, they walked slowly towards the hotel, then stopped at a little German restaurant for supper. They looked at each other across the marble-top table without speaking. The evening had been a depressing conclusion to the concert season they had had together. And that morning Vickers had found it impossible to arrange a meeting for Mrs. Conry with the director of a famous orchestra, who happened to be in the city.

"You must go to-morrow?" Vickers asked at last. "I may get a reply from Moller any day."

Mrs. Conry looked at him out of her gray eyes, as if she were thinking many things that a woman might think but could not say, before she replied slowly: —

"My husband's coming back to-morrow — to get me." As Vickers said nothing, she continued, slowly shaking the yellow wine in her glass until it circled, — "And it's no use — I'm not good enough for Moller — and you know it. I must have more training, more experience."

Vickers did know it, but had not let himself believe it.

"My little struggle does not matter, — I'm only a woman — and must do as most women do. . . . Perhaps, who knows! the combination may change some day, and —" she glanced fearlessly at him — "we shall all do as we want in another world!"

Then she looked at her watch. It was very late, and the tired waiters stood leaning listlessly against their tables.

"I am tired," she said at last. "Will you call a cab, please?"

They drove silently down the empty boulevard. A mist came through the cab window, touching her hair with fine points. Her hand lay close to his.

"How happy we were in Rome! Rome!" she looked out into the dark night, and there were tears in her eyes. "You have been very good to me, dear friend. Sometime I shall sing to you again, to you alone. Now good-by." . . .

His hand held hers, while his heart beat and words rose clamorously to his lips, — the words of rebellion, of protest and love, the words of youth. But he said nothing, — it was better that they should part without a spoken word, — better for her and better for him. His feeling for her, compact of tenderness, pity, and belief, had never been tested by any clear light. She was not his; and beyond that fact he had never looked.

So the carriage rolled on while the two sat silent with beating hearts, and as it approached the hotel he quickly bent his head and kissed the hand that was in his.

"Come to-morrow," she whispered, "in the morning, — once more."

"No," he said simply; "I can't. You know why."

As Vickers stepped out of the cab he recognized Conry. The contractor had been looking up and down the street, and had started to walk away, but turned at the sound of the carriage wheels and came over towards them. Something in his appearance, the slouch hat pulled forward over his face, the quick jerky step, suggested that he had been drinking. Vickers with a sensation of disgust foresaw a scene there on the pavement, and he could feel the shrinking of the woman by his side.

"Good evening, Mr. Conry," Vickers said coolly, turning to give Mrs. Conry his hand. A glance into Conry's eyes had convinced him that the man was in a drunken temper, and his one thought was to save her from a public brawl. Already a couple of people sauntering past had paused to look at them. Conry grasped the young man by the arm and flung him to one side, and thrusting his other hand into the cab jerked his wife out of it.

"Come here!" he roared. "I'll show you — you — "

Mrs. Conry, trembling and white, tried to free her arm and cross the pavement. The driver, arranging himself on the seat, looked down at Vickers, winked, and waited. Conry still dragged his wife by the arm, and as she tried to free herself he raised his other hand and slapped her across the face as he would cuff a struggling dog, then struck her again. She groaned and half sank to the pavement. The curious bystanders said nothing, made no move to interfere. Here was a domestic difference, about a woman apparently; and the husband was exerting his ancient, impregnable rights of domination over the woman, who was his. . . .

All these months Vickers had never even in imagination crossed the barrier of Fact. Now without a moment's wavering he raised his hand and struck Conry full in the face, and as the man staggered from the unexpected blow he struck him again, knocking him to the ground. Then swiftly disentangling the woman's hand from her husband's grasp, he motioned to the cab driver to pull up at the curb and carried her into the cab. When Vickers closed the door, the driver without further orders whipped up his horse and drove into a side street, leaving the group on the pavement staring at them and at Conry, who was staggering to his feet. . . .

Within the cab Mrs. Conry moaned inarticulately. Vickers held her in his arms, and slowly bending his head to hers he kissed her upon the lips. Her lips were cold, but after a time to the touch of his lips hers responded with a trembling, yielding kiss.

Thus they drove on, without words, away from the city.

CHAPTER XVII

It had all happened in a brief moment of time, — the blow, the rescue, the kiss. But it had changed the face of the world for Vickers. What hitherto had been clouded in dream, a mingling of sentiment, pity, tender yearning, became at once reality. With that blow, that kiss, his soul had opened to a new conception of life. . . .

They drove to the Lanes' house. Isabelle had returned that day from California, and her husband was away on business. Vickers, who had a latch-key, let himself into the house and tapped at his sister's door. When she saw him, she cried out, frightened by his white face: —

"Vick! What has happened?"

"Mrs. Conry is downstairs, Isabelle. I want her to stay here with you to-night!"

"Vick! What is it?" Isabelle demanded with staring eyes.

"I will tell you to-morrow."

"No — now!" She clutched her wrap about her shiveringly and drew him within the room.

"It's — I am going away, Isabelle, at once — with Mrs. Conry. There has been trouble — her husband struck her on the street, when she was with me. I took her from him."

"Vick!" Her voice trembled as she cried, "No, — it wasn't that!"

"No," he said gravely. "There was no cause, none at all. He was drunk. But I don't know that it would have made any difference. The man is a low brute, and her life is killing her. I love her — well, that is all!"

"Vick!" she cried; "I knew you would do some — " she hesitated before his glittering eyes — "something very risky," she faltered at last.

He waved this aside impatiently.

"What will you do now?" she asked hesitantly.

"I don't know, — we shall go away," he replied vaguely; "but she is waiting, needs me. Will you help her, — help *us?*" he demanded, turning to the door, "or shall we have to go to-night?"

"Wait," she said, putting her hands on his arms; "you can't do that! Just think what it will mean to father and mother, to everybody. . . . Let me dress and take her back!" she suggested half heartedly.

"Isabelle!" he cried. "She shall never go back to that brute."

"You love her so much?"

"Enough for anything," he answered gravely, turning to the door.

In the face of his set look, his short words, all the protesting considerations on the tip of her tongue seemed futile. To a man in a mood like his they would but drive him to further folly. And admiration rose unexpectedly in her heart for the man who could hold his fate in his hands like this and unshakenly cast it on the ground. The very madness of it all awed her. She threw her arms about him, murmuring: —

"Oh, Vick — for you — it seems so horrid, so — "

"It *is* mean," he admitted through his compressed lips. "For that very reason, don't you see, I will take her beyond where it can touch her, at once, this very night, — if you will not help us!"

And all that she could do was to kiss him, the tears falling from her eyes.

"I will, Vick, dear. . . . It makes no difference to me what happens, — if you are only happy!"

As he drove to his father's house in the damp April night, he tried to think of the steps he must take on the morrow. He had acted irresistibly, out of the depths of his nature, unconcerned that he was about to tear in pieces the fabric of his life. It was not until he had let himself into the silent house and noiselessly passed his mother's door that he realized in sudden pain what it must mean to others.

He lay awake thinking, thinking. First of all she must telegraph for Delia to meet them somewhere, — she must have the child with her at once; and they must leave the city before Conry could find her and make trouble. . . . And he must tell the Colonel. . . .

The next morning when Vickers entered his sister's library, Stacia Conry rose from the lounge where she had been lying reading a newspaper, and waited hesitantly while he came forward. She was very pretty this morning, with a faint touch of rose beneath her pale skin, her long lashes falling over fresh, shy eyes. In spite of it all she had slept, while the sleepless hours he had spent showed in his worn, white face. He put out his arms, and she clung to him.

"We must decide what to do," he said.

"You will not leave me?" she whispered, her head lying passive against his breast. Suddenly raising her head, she clasped her arms about his neck, drawing him passionately to her, crying, "I love you — love you, — you will never leave me?"

And the man looking down into her eyes answered from his heart in all truth: —

"Never, never so long as I live!" The words muttered in his broken voice had all the solemnity of a marriage oath; and he kissed her, sealing the promise, while she lay passive in his arms.

Holding her thus to him, her head against his beating heart, he felt the helplessness, the dependence of the woman, and it filled him with a subdued, sad joy. His part was to protect her, to defend her always, and his grip tightened about her yielding form. Their lips met again, and this time the sensuous appeal of the woman entered his senses, clouding for the time his delicate vision, submerging that nobler feeling which hitherto alone she had roused. She was a woman, — his to desire, to have!

"What shall we do?" she asked, sitting down, still holding his hand.

"First we must get Delia. We had better telegraph your mother at once to meet us somewhere."

"Oh!"

"You must have Delia, of course. He will probably make trouble, try to get hold of the child, and so we must leave here as soon as possible, to-day if we can."

"Where shall we go?" she asked, bewildered.

"Somewhere — out of the country," he replied slowly, looking at her significantly. "Of course it would be better to wait and have the divorce; but he might fight that, and make a mess, — try to keep the child, you understand."

She was silent, and he thought she objected to his summary plan. But it was on her lips to say, 'Why not leave Delia with him until it can all be arranged?' Something in the young man's stern face restrained her; she was afraid of outraging instincts, delicacies that were strange to her.

"Should you mind," he asked pleadingly, "going without the divorce? Of course to me it is the same thing. You are mine now, as I look at it, — any marriage would mean little to either of us after — the past! Somehow to hang about here, with the danger of trouble to you, waiting for a divorce, with the row and all, — I can't see you going through it. I think the — other way — is better."

She did not fully understand his feeling about it, which was that with the soiled experience of her marriage another ceremony with him would be a mere legal farce. To the pure idealism of his nature it seemed cleaner, nobler for them to take this step without any attempt to regularize it in the eyes of Society. To him she was justified in doing what she had done, in leaving her husband for him, and that would have to be enough for them both. He despised half measures, compromises. He was ready to cast all into his defiance of law. Meanwhile she pondered the matter with lowered eyes and presently she asked: —

"How long would it take to get a divorce?"

"If he fought it, a year perhaps, or longer."

"And I should have to stay here in the city?"

"Or go somewhere else to get a residence."

"And we —" she hesitated to complete the thought.

He drew her to him and kissed her.

"I think we shall be enough for each other," he said.

"I will do whatever you wish," she murmured, thus softly putting on his shoulders the burden of the step.

He was the man, the strong protector that had come to her in her distress, to whom she fled as naturally as a hunted animal flies to a hole, as a crippled bird to the deep underbrush. Her beauty, her sex, herself, had somehow attracted to her this male arm, and the right to take it never occurred to her. He loved her, of course, and she would make him love her more, and all would be well. If he had been penniless, unable to give her the full protection that she needed, then they would have been obliged to consider this step more carefully, and doubts might have forced themselves upon her. But as it was she clung to him, trusting to the power of her sex to hold him constant, to shield her. . . .

"Now I must go down to the office to see my father," Vickers said finally. "I'll be back early in the afternoon, and then — we will make our plans."

"Will you tell him, your father?" Mrs. Conry asked tensely.

"He will have to know, of course." As he spoke a wave of pain shot over the young man's face. He stepped to the door and then turned: —

"You will telegraph about Delia, — she might meet us in New York — in two days."

"Very well," Mrs. Conry murmured submissively.

The Colonel was sitting in his little corner office before the old-fashioned dingy desk, where he had transacted so many affairs of one sort or another for nearly thirty years. He was not even reading his mail this morning, but musing, as he often was when the clerks thought that he was more busily employed. Isabelle and her child had returned from California, the day before. She had not recovered from bearing the child, and the St. Louis doctors who had been consulted had not helped her. It might be well to see some one in New York. . . . But the Colonel was thinking most of all this morning of his son. The tenacious old merchant was wondering whether he had done right in accepting the young man's sacrifice. In his disgust for the do-nothing, parasitic offspring about him, perhaps he had taken a delicate instrument and blunted it by setting it at coarse work. Well, it was not too late to change that.

'The boy didn't start right,' the Colonel mused sadly. 'He didn't start selling hardware on the road. He's done his best, and he's no such duffer as Parrott's boy anyhow. But he would make only a front office kind of business man. The business must get on by itself pretty soon. Perhaps that idea for a selling company would not be a bad thing. And that would be the end of Parrott and Price.'

Nevertheless, the old man's heart having come slowly to this generous decision was not light, — if the other boy had lived, if Belle had married some one who could have gone into the business. The bricks and mortar of the building were part of his own being, and he longed to live out these last few years in the shadow of his great enterprise. . . .

"Father, can I see you about something important?"

The Colonel, startled from his revery, looked up at his son with his sweet smile.

"Why, yes, my boy, — I wasn't doing much, and I had something to say to you. Sit down. You got away from home early this morning."

He glanced inquiringly at his son's white, set face and tense lips. Playing with his eye-glasses, he began to talk lightly of other matters, as was his wont when he felt the coming of a storm.

Vickers listened patiently, staring straight across his father to the wall, and when the Colonel came to a full pause, he said abruptly: —

"Father, you said you were ready for me to take a vacation. I must go at once, to-day if possible. And, father, I can't come back."

The old man moved slightly in his chair. It was his intention to offer the young man his freedom, but it hurt him to have it taken for granted in this light manner. He waited.

"Something has happened," Vickers continued in a low voice, "something which will alter my whole life."

The Colonel still waited.

"I love a woman, and I must take her away from here at once."

"Who is she?" the old man asked gently.

"Mrs. Conry —"

"But she's a married woman, isn't she, Vick?"

"She has a dirty brute of a husband — she's left him forever!"

The Colonel's blue eyes opened in speechless surprise, as his son went on to tell rapidly what had happened the previous night. Before he had finished the old man interrupted by a low exclamation: —

"But she is a married woman, Vickers!"

"Her marriage was a mistake, and she's paid for it, poor woman, — paid with soul and body! She will not pay any longer."

"But what are you going to do, my boy?"

"I love her, father. I mean to take her away, at once, take her and her child."

"Run away with a married woman?" The Colonel's pale face flushed slightly, less in anger than in shame, and his eyes fell from his son's face.

"I wish with all my heart it wasn't so, of course; that she wasn't married, or that she had left him long ago. But that can't be helped. And I don't see how a divorce could make any difference, and it would take a long time, and cause a dirty mess. He's the kind who would fight it for spite, or blackmail. Perhaps later it will come. Now she must not suffer any more. I love her all the deeper for what she has been through. I want to make her life happy, make it up to her somehow, if I can."

The Colonel rose and with an old man's slow step went over to the office door and locked it.

"Vickers," he said as he turned around from the door, still averting his shamed face, "you must be crazy, out of your mind, my son!"

"No, father," the young man replied calmly; "I was never surer of anything in my life! I knew it would hurt you and mother, — you can't understand. But you must trust me in this. It has to be."

"Why does it have to be?"

"Because I love her!" he burst out. "Because I want to save her from that man, from the degradation she's lived in. With me she will have some joy, at last,— her life, her soul, — oh, father, you can't say these things to any one! You can't give good reasons."

The old merchant's face became stern as he replied: —

"You wish to do all this for her, and yet you do not mean to marry her."

"I can't marry her! I would to-day if I could. Some day perhaps we can, — for the sake of the child it would be better. But that makes no difference to me. It is the same as marriage for us —"

"'Doesn't make any difference' — 'the same as marriage' — what are you talking about?"

The young man tried to find words which would fully express his feeling. He had come a long way these last hours in his ideas of life; he saw things naked and clear cut, without dubious shades. But he had to realize now that what *his* soul accepted as incontrovertible logic was meaningless to others.

"I mean," he said at last slowly, "that this woman is the woman I love. I care more for her happiness, for her well-being than for anything else in life. And so no matter how we arrange to live, she is all that a woman can be to a man, married or not as it may happen."

"To take another man's wife and live with her!" the Colonel summed up bitterly. "No, Vick, you don't mean that. You can't do a dirty thing like that. Think it over!"

So they argued a little while longer, and finally the old man pleaded with his son for time, offering to see Mrs. Conry, to help her get a separation from her husband, to send her abroad with her child, — to all of which Vickers replied steadily: —

"But I love her, father — you forget that! And she needs me now!"

"Love her!" the old man cried. "Don't call that love!"

Vickers shut his lips and rose, very white.

"I must go now. Let's not say any more. We've never had any bitter words between us, father. You don't understand this — do you think I would hurt you and mother, if it didn't have to be? I gave up my own life, when it was only myself at stake; but I cannot give her up — and everything it will mean to her."

The Colonel turned away his face and refused to see his son's outstretched hand. He could not think without a blush that his son should be able to contemplate this thing. Vickers, as he turned the handle of the door, recollected something and came back.

"Oh, you must cancel that stock agreement. I shouldn't want to own it now that I have quit. The other things, the money, I shall keep. You would like me to have it, father, and it will be quite enough."

The old man made a gesture as if to wave aside the money matter.

"Good-by, father!" he said slowly, tenderly.

"You'll see your mother?"

"Yes — I'm going there now."

Thus father and son parted.

Nothing, it seemed to Vickers, after this painful half hour, could be as miserable as what he had been through, and as a matter of fact his interview with his mother was comparatively easy.

To Mrs. Price her son's determination was merely an unexpected outburst of wild folly, such as happened in other families, — coming rather late in Vick's life, but by no means irremediable. Vickers had fallen into the hands of a designing woman, who intended to capture a rich man's son. Her first thought was that the Colonel would have to buy Mrs. Conry off, as Mr. Stewart had done in a similar accident that befell Ted Stewart, and when Vickers finally made it plain to her that his was not that kind of case, she fell to berating him for the scandal he would create by "trapesing off to Europe with a singer." Oddly enough that delicate modesty, like a woman's, which had made it almost impossible for the Colonel to mention the affair, did not seem to trouble her. To live with another man's wife was in the Colonel's eyes a sin little short of incest, and more shocking than many kinds of murder. But his wife, with a deeper comprehension of the powers of her sex, of the appeal of woman to man, saw in it merely a weakness that threatened to become a family disgrace. When she found after an hour's talk that her arguments made no impression, while Vickers sat, harassed and silent, his head resting on his hands, she burst into tears.

"It's just like those things you read of in the papers," she sobbed, "those queer Pittsburg people, who are always doing some nasty thing, and no decent folks will associate with them."

"It's not the thing you do, mother; it's the way you do it, the purpose, the feeling," the young man protested. "And there won't be a scandal, if that's what's troubling you. You can tell your friends that I have gone abroad suddenly for my health."

"Who would believe that? Do you think her husband's going to keep quiet?" Mrs. Price sniffled, with considerable worldly wisdom.

"Well, let them believe what they like. They'll forget me in a week."

"Where are you going?"

"To Europe, somewhere, — I haven't thought about the place. I'll let you know."

"And how about her child?"

"We shall take her with us."

"She wants her along, does she?"

"Of course!"

Vickers rose impatiently.

"Good-by, mother."

She let him kiss her.

"I shall come to see you sometimes, if you want me to."

"Oh, you'll be coming back fast enough," she retorted quickly.

And then she straightened the sofa pillows where he had been sitting and picked up a book she had been reading. As Vickers went to his room to get a bag, Isabelle opened the door of her mother's room, where she had been waiting for him. She put her arms about his neck, as she had that night of her marriage on the station platform at Grafton, and pressed him tightly to her.

"Vick! Vick!" she cried. "That it had to be like this, your love! Like this!"

"It had to be, Belle," he answered with a smile. "It comes to us in different ways, old girl."

"But you! You!" She led him by the hand to the sofa, where she threw herself, a white exhausted look coming into her face. He stroked her hair with the ends of his fingers. Suddenly she half turned, grasping his hand with both of hers.

"Can you be happy — really happy?"

"I think so; but even that makes no difference, perhaps. I should do it all the same, if I knew it meant no happiness for me."

She looked at him searchingly, trying to read his heart in his eyes. After the year of her marriage, knowing now the mystery of human relations, she wondered whether he might not be right. That precious something, pain or joy, which was wanting in her union he might find in this forbidden by-path, in this woman who seemed to her so immeasurably beneath her brother. She kissed him, and he went away.

When the hall door clicked, she rose from the lounge and dragged herself to the window to watch him, holding her breath, her heart beating rapidly, almost glad that he was strong enough to take his fate in his hands, to test life, to break the rules, to defy reason! "Vick, dear Vick," she murmured.

In the room below Mrs. Price, also, was looking out of the bay window, watching her son disappear down the avenue. She had not been reading, and she had heard him come down into the hall, but let him go without another word. He walked slowly, erect as the Colonel used to walk. Tears dropped from her eyes, — tears of mortification. For in her heart she knew that he would come back some day, this woman who had lured him having fallen from him like a dead leaf. She sat on at the window until the Colonel's figure appeared in the distance coming up the avenue. His head was bent; he looked neither to the right nor to the left; and he walked very slowly, like an old man, dragging his feet after him. He was crushed. It would not have been thus if he had lost his fortune, the work of all his years. Such a fate he would have looked in the eye, with raised head. . . .

That night Vickers and Stacia Conry left for New York, and a few days later Mrs. Price read their names in a list of outgoing passengers for Genoa. She did not show the list to the Colonel, and their son's name was never mentioned in the house.

When the people who knew the Prices intimately began to whisper, then chatter, they said many hard things of Vickers, chiefly that he was a Fool, a judgment that could not be gainsaid. Nevertheless the heart of a Fool may be pure.

CHAPTER XVIII

ISABELLE did not regain her strength after the birth of her child. She lay nerveless and white, so that her husband, her mother, the Colonel, all became alarmed. The celebrated accoucheur who had attended her alarmed them still more.

"Something's wrong, — she couldn't stand the strain. Oh, it's another case of American woman, — too finely organized for the plain animal duties. A lot of my women patients are the same way. They take child-bearing hard, — damned hard. . . . What's the matter with them? I don't know!" he concluded irritably. "She must just go slow until she gets back her strength."

She went "slow," but Nature refused to assert itself, to proclaim the will to live. For months the days crept by with hardly a sign of change in her condition, and then began the period of doctors. The family physician, who had a reputation for diagnosis, pronounced her case "anæmia and nervous debility." "She must be built up, — baths, massage, distraction." Of course she was not to nurse her child, and the little girl was handed over to a trained nurse. Then this doctor called in another, a specialist in nerves, who listened to all that the others said, tapped her here and there, and wished the opinion of an obstetrical surgeon. After his examination there was a discussion of the advisability of "surgical interference," and the conclusion "to wait."

"It may be a long time — years — before Mrs. Lane fully recovers her tone," the nerve specialist told the husband. "We must have patience. It would be a good thing to take her to Europe for a change."

This was the invariable suggestion that he made to his wealthy patients when he saw no immediate results from his treatment. It could do no harm, Europe, and most of his patients liked the prescription. They returned, to be sure, in many cases in about the same condition as when they left, or merely rested temporarily, — but of course that was the fault of the patient.

When Lane objected that it would be almost impossible for him to leave his duties for a trip abroad and that he did not like to have his wife go without him, the specialist advised California: —

"A mild climate where she can be out-of-doors and relaxed."

Isabelle went to California with her mother, the trained nurse, and the child. But instead of the "mild climate," Pasadena happened to be raw and rainy. She disliked the hotel, and the hosts of idle, overdressed, and vulgar women. So her mother brought her back, as we have seen, and then there was talk of the Virginia Springs, "an excellent spring climate."

A new doctor was called in, who had his own peculiar régime of sprays and baths, of subcutaneous medicine, and then a third nerve specialist, who said, "We must find the right key," and looked as if he might have it in his office.

"The right key?"

"Her combination, the secret of her vitality. We must find it for her, — distraction, a system of physical exercises, perhaps. But we must occupy the mind. Those Christian Scientists have an idea, you know, — not that I recommend their tomfoolery; but we must accomplish their results by scientific means." And he went away highly satisfied with his liberality of view. . . .

On one vital point the doctors were hopelessly divided. Some thought Isabelle should have another child, "as soon as may be," — it was a chance that Nature might take to right matters. The others strongly dissented: a child in the patient's present debilitated condition would be criminal. As these doctors seemed to have the best of the argument, it was decided that for the present the wife should remain sterile, and the physicians undertook to watch over the life process, to guard against its asserting its rights.

The last illusions of romance seemed to go at this period. The simple old tale that a man and a woman loving each other marry and have the children that live within them and come from their mutual love has been rewritten for the higher classes of American women, with the aid of science. Health, economic pressure, the hectic struggle to survive in an ambitious world have altered the simple axioms of nature. Isabelle accepted easily the judgment of the doctors, — she had known so many women in a like case. Yet when she referred to this matter in talking to Alice Johnston, she caught an odd look on her cousin's face.

"I wonder if they know, the doctors — they seem always to be finding excuses for women not to have children. . . . We've been all through that, Steve and I; and decided we wouldn't have anything to do with it, no matter what happened. It — tarnishes you somehow, and after all does it help? There's Lulu Baxter, living in daily fear of having a child because they think they are too poor. He gets twenty-five hundred from the road — he's under Steve, you know — and they live in a nice apartment with two servants and entertain. They are afraid of falling in the social scale, if they should live differently. But she's as nervous as a witch, never wholly well, and they'll just go on, as he rises and gets more money, adding to their expenses. They will never have money enough for children, or only for one, maybe, — no, I don't believe it pays!"

"But she's so pretty, and they live nicely," Isabelle protested, and added, "There are other things to live for besides having a lot of children —"

"What?" the older woman asked gravely.

"Your husband"; and thinking of John's present homeless condition, she continued hastily, "and life itself, — to be some one, — you owe something to yourself."

"Yes," Alice assented, smiling, — "if we only knew what it was!"

"Besides if we were all like you, Alice dear, we should be paupers. Even we can't afford —"

"We should be paupers together, then! No, you can't convince me — it's against Nature."

"All modern life is against Nature," the young woman retorted glibly; "just at present I regard Nature as a mighty poor thing."

She stretched her thin arms behind her head and turned on the lounge.

"That's why the people who made this country are dying out so rapidly, giving way before Swedes and Slavs and others, — because those people are willing to have children."

"Meantime we have the success!" Isabelle cried languidly. "*Après nous* the Slavs, — we are the flower! An aristocracy is always nourished on sterility!"

"Dr. Fuller!" Alice commented. . . . "So the Colonel is going with you to the Springs?"

"Yes, poor old Colonel! — he must get away — he's awfully broken up," and she added sombrely. "That's one trouble with having children, — you expect them to think and act like you. You can't be willing to let them be themselves."

"But, Isabelle!"

"Oh, I know what you are going to say about Vick. I have heard it over and over. John has said it. Mother has said it. Father looks it. You needn't bother to say it, Alice!" She glanced at her cousin mutinously. "John thought I was partly to blame; that I ought to have been able to control Vick. He speaks as if the poor boy were insane or drunk or something — because he did what he did!"

"And you?"

Isabelle sat upright, leaning her head thoughtfully on her hands, and staring with bright eyes at Alice.

"Do you want to know what I really believe? . . . I have done a lot of thinking these months, all by myself. Well, I admire Vick tremendously; he had the courage —"

"Does that take courage?"

"Yes! For a man like Vickers. . . . Oh, I suppose she is horrid and not worth it — I only hope he will never find it out! But to love any one enough to be willing, to be glad to give up your life for him, for her — why, it is tremendous, Alice! . . . Here is Tots," she broke off as the nurse wheeled the baby through the hall, — "Miss Marian Lane. . . . Nurse, cover up her face with the veil so her ladyship won't get frostbitten," and Isabelle sank back again with a sigh on the lounge and resumed the thread of her thought. "And I am not so sure that what John objects to isn't largely the mess, — the papers, the scandal, the fact they went off without waiting for a divorce and all that. Of course that wasn't pleasant for respectable folk like the Lanes and the Prices. But why should Vickers have given up what seemed to him right, what was his life and hers, just for our prejudices about not having our names in the papers?"

"That wasn't all!"

"Well, I shall always believe in Vick, no matter what comes of it. . . . Marriage — the regular thing — doesn't seem to be such a great success with many people, I know. Perhaps life would be better if more people had Vick's courage!"

Isabelle forced her point with an invalid's desire to relieve a wayward feeling and also a childish wish to shock this good cousin, who saw life simply and was so sure of herself. Alice Johnston rose with a smile.

"I hope you will be a great deal stronger when you come back, dear."

"I shall be — or I shall have an operation. I don't intend to remain in the noble army of N.P.'s."

"How is John?"

"Flourishing and busy — oh, tremendously busy! He might just as well live in New York or Washington for all I see of him."

"Steve says he is very clever and successful, — you must be so proud!"

Isabelle smiled. "Of course! But sometimes I think

I should like a substitute husband, one for everyday use, you know!"

"There are plenty of that kind!" laughed Alice. "But I don't believe they would satisfy you wholly."

"Perhaps not. . . . How is Steve? Does he like his new work?"

"Yes," Alice replied without enthusiasm. "He's working very hard, too."

"Oh, men love it, — it makes them feel important."

"Did you ever think, Belle, that men have difficulties to meet, — problems that we never dream of?"

"Worse than the child-bearing question?" queried Isabelle, kicking out the folds of her tea-gown with a slippered foot.

"Well, different; harder, perhaps. . . . Steve doesn't talk them over as he used to with me."

"Too tired. John never talks to me about business. We discuss what the last doctor thinks, and how the baby is, and whether we'll take the Jackson house or build or live at the Monopole and go abroad, and Nan Lawton's latest, — really vital things, you see! Business is such a bore."

The older woman seemed to have something on her mind and sat down again at the end of the lounge.

"By the way," Isabelle continued idly, "did you know that the Falkners were coming to St. Louis to live? John found Rob a place in the terminal work. It isn't permanent, but Bessie was crazy to come, and it may be an opening. She is a nice thing, — mad about people."

"But, Isabelle," her cousin persisted, "don't you want to know the things that make your husband's life, — that go down to the roots?"

"If you mean business, no, I don't. Besides they are confidential matters, I suppose. He couldn't make me understand. . . ."

"They have to face the fight, the men; make the decisions that count — for character."

"Of course, — John attends to that side and I to mine. We should be treading on each other's toes if I tried to decide his matters for him!"

"But when they are questions of right and wrong —"

"Don't worry. Steve and John are all right. Besides they are only officers. You don't believe all that stuff in the magazines about Senator Thomas and the railroads? John says that is a form of modern blackmail."

"I don't know what to believe," the older woman replied. "I know it's terrible, — it's like war!"

"Of course it's war, and men must do the fighting."

"And fight fair."

"Of course, — as fair as the others. What are you driving at?"

"I wonder if the A. and P. always fights fair?"

"It isn't a charitable organization, my dear. . . . But Steve and John are just officers. They don't have to decide. They take their orders from headquarters and carry them out."

"No matter what they are?"

"Naturally, — that's what officers are for, isn't it? If they don't want to carry them out, they must resign."

"But they can't always resign."

"Why not?"

"Because of you and me and the children!"

"Oh, don't worry about it! They don't worry. That's what I like a man for. If he's good for anything, he isn't perpetually pawing himself over."

This did not seem wholly to satisfy Alice, but she leaned over Isabelle and kissed her: —

"Only get well, my dear, and paw some of your notions over, — it won't do you any harm!"

That evening when the Lanes were alone, after they had discussed the topics that Isabelle had enumerated, with the addition of the arrangements for the trip to the Springs, Isabelle asked casually: —

"John, is it easy to be honest in business?"

"That depends," he replied guardedly, "on the business and the man. Why?"

"You don't believe what those magazine articles say about the Senator and the others?"

"I don't read them."

"Why?"

"Because the men who write them don't understand the facts, and what they know they distort — for money."

"Um," she observed thoughtfully. "But are there facts — like those? *You* know the facts."

"I don't know all of them."

"Are those you know straight or crooked?" she asked, feeling considerable interest in the question, now that it was started.

"I don't know what you would mean by crooked, — what is it you want to know?"

"Are you honest?" she asked with mild curiosity. "I mean in the way of railroad business. Of course I know you are other ways."

Lane smiled at her childlike seriousness.

"I always try to do what seems to me right under the circumstances."

"But the circumstances are sometimes — queer?"

"The circumstances are usually complex."

"The circumstances are complex," she mused aloud. "I'll tell Alice that."

"What has Alice to do with it?"

"She seems bothered about the circumstances — that's all, — the circumstances and Steve."

"I guess Steve can manage the circumstances by himself," he replied coldly, turning over the evening paper. "She probably reads the magazines and believes all she hears."

"All intelligent women read the magazines — and believe what they hear or else what their husbands tell them," she rejoined flippantly. Presently, as Lane continued to look over the stock page of the paper, she observed: —

"Don't you suppose that in Vickers's case the circumstances may have been — complex?"

Lane looked at her steadily.

"I can't see what that has to do with the question."

"Oh?" she queried mischievously. He considered the working of her mind as merely whimsical, but she had a sense of logical triumph over the man. Apparently he would make allowances of "circumstances" in business, his life, that he would not admit in private affairs. As he kissed her and was turning out the light, before joining the Colonel for another cigar, she asked: —

"Supposing that you refused to be involved in circumstances that were — complex? What would happen?"

"What a girl!" he laughed cheerfully. "For one thing I think we should not be going to the Springs to-morrow in a private car, or buying the Jackson house — or any other. Now put it all out of your head and have a good rest."

He kissed her again, and she murmured wearily: —

"I'm so useless, — they should kill things like me! How can you love me?"

She was confident that he did love her, that like so many husbands he had accepted her invalidism cheerfully, with an unconscious chivalry for the wife who instead of flowering forth in marriage had for the time being withered. His confidence, in her sinking moods like this, that it would all come right, buoyed her up. And John was a wise man as well as a good husband; the Colonel trusted him, admired him. Alice Johnston's doubts slipped easily from her mind. Nevertheless, there were now two subjects of serious interest that husband and wife would always avoid, — Vickers, and business honesty!

She lay there feeling weak and forlorn before the journey, preoccupied with herself. These days she was beset with a tantalizing sense that life was slipping past her just beyond her reach, flowing like a mighty river to issues that she was not permitted to share. And while she was forced to lie useless on the bank, her youth, her own life, was somehow running out, too. Just what it was that she was missing she could not say, — something alluring, something more than her husband's activity, than her child, something that made her stretch out longing hands in the dark. . . . She would not submit to invalidism.

CHAPTER XIX

The Virginia mountains made a narrow horizon of brilliant blue. On their lower slopes the misty outlines of early spring had begun with the budding trees. Here and there the feathery forest was spotted by dashes of pink coolness where the wild peach and plum had blossomed, and the faint blue of the rhododendron bushes mounted to the sky-line. The morning was brilliant after a rain and the fresh mountain air blew invigoratingly, as Isabelle left the car on her husband's arm. With the quick change of mood of the nervous invalid she already felt stronger, more hopeful. There was color in her thin face, and her eyes had again the vivacious sparkle that had been so largely her charm.

"We must find some good horses," she said to her father as they approached the hotel cottage which had been engaged; "I want to get up in those hills. Margaret promised to come for a week. . . . Oh, I am going to be all right now!"

The hotel was one of those huge structures dropped down in the mountains or by the sea to provide for the taste for fresh air, the need for recuperation, of a wealthy society that crams its pleasures and its business into small periods, — days and hours. It rambled over an acre or two and provided as nearly as possible the same luxuries and occupations that its frequenters had at home. At this season it was crowded with rich people, who had sought the balm of early spring in the Virginia mountains after their weeks of frantic activity in the cities, instead of taking the steamers to Europe. They were sitting, beautifully wrapped in furs, on the long verandas, or smartly costumed were setting out for the links or for horseback excursions. The

Colonel and Lane quickly discovered acquaintances in the broker's office where prominent "operators" were sitting, smoking cigars and looking at the country through large plate-glass windows, while the ticker chattered within hearing. There was music in the hall, and fresh arrivals with spotless luggage poured in from the trains. This mountain inn was a little piece of New York moved out into the country.

But it was peaceful on the piazza of the cottage, which was somewhat removed from the great caravansary, where Isabelle lay and watched the blue recesses of the receding hills. Here her husband found her when it was time to say good-by.

"You'll be very well off," he remarked, laying his hand affectionately on his wife's arm. "The Stantons are here — you remember him at Torso? — and the Blakes from St. Louis, and no doubt a lot more people your father knows, — so you won't be lonely. I have arranged about the horses and selected a quiet table for you."

"That is very good of you, — I don't want to see people," she replied, her eyes still on the hills. "When will you be back?"

"In a week or ten days I can run up again and stay for a couple of days, over Sunday."

"You'll telegraph about Marian?"

"Of course."

And bending over to kiss her forehead, he hurried away. It seemed to her that he was always leaving, always going somewhere. When he was away, he wrote or telegraphed her each day as a matter of course, and sent her flowers every other day, and brought her some piece of jewellery when he went to New York. Yes, he was very fond of her, she felt, and his was a loyal nature, — she never need fear that in these many absences from his wife he might become entangled with women, as other men did. He was not that kind. . . .

The Colonel crossed the lawn in the direction of the golf

links with a party of young old men. It was fortunate that the Colonel had become interested, almost boyishly, in golf; for since that morning when his son had left him he had lost all zest for business. A year ago he would never have thought it possible to come away like this for a month in the busy season. To Isabelle it was sad and also curious the way he took this matter of Vickers. He seemed to feel that he had but one child now, had put his boy quite out of his mind. He was gradually arranging his affairs — already there was talk of incorporating the hardware business and taking in new blood. And he had aged still more. But he was so tremendously vital, — the Colonel! No one could say he was heart-broken. He took more interest than ever in public affairs, like the General Hospital, and the Park Board. But he was different, as Isabelle felt, — abstracted, more silent, apparently revising his philosophy of life at an advanced age, and that is always painful. If she had only given him a man child, something male and vital like himself! He was fond of John, but no one could take the place of his own blood. That, too, was a curious limitation in the eyes of the younger generation.

"Isabelle!"

She was wakened from her brooding by a soft Southern voice, and perceived Margaret Pole coming up the steps. With the grasp of Margaret's small hands, the kiss, all the years since St. Mary's seemed to fall away. The two women drew off and looked at each other, Margaret smiling enigmatically, understanding that Isabelle was trying to read the record of the years, the experience of marriage on her. Coloring slightly, she turned away and drew up a chair.

"Is your husband with you?" Isabelle asked. "I do so want to meet him."

"No; I left him at my father's with the children. He's very good with the children," she added with a mocking smile, "and he doesn't like little trips. He doesn't understand how I can get up at five in the morning and travel all day across country to see an old friend. . . . Men don't understand things, do you think?"

"So you are going abroad to live?"

"Yes," Margaret answered without enthusiasm. "We are going to study music, — the voice. My husband doesn't like business!"

Isabelle had heard that Mr. Pole, agreeable as he was, had not been successful in business. But the Poles and the Lawtons were all comfortably off, and it was natural that he should follow his tastes.

"He has a very good voice," Margaret added.

"How exciting — to change your whole life like that!" Isabelle exclaimed, fired by the prospect of escape from routine, from the known.

"Think so?" Margaret remarked in a dull voice. "Well, perhaps. Tell me how you are — everything."

And they began to talk, and yet carefully avoided what was uppermost in the minds of both, — 'How has it been with you? How has marriage been? Has it given you all that you looked for? Are you happy?' For in spite of all the education, the freedom so much talked about for women, that remains the central theme of their existence, — the emotional and material satisfaction of their natures through marriage. Margaret Pole was accounted intellectual among women, with bookish tastes, thoughtful, and she knew many women who had been educated in colleges. "They are all like us," she once said to Isabelle; "just like us. They want to marry a man who will give them everything, and they aren't any wiser in their choice, either. The only difference is that a smaller number of them have the chance to marry, and when they can't be married, they have something besides cats and maiden aunts to fall back upon. But interests in common with their husbands, intellectual interests, — rubbish! A man who amounts to anything is always a specialist, and he doesn't care for feminine amateurishness. An acquaintance with Dante and the housing of the poor doesn't broaden the breakfast table, not a little bit."

When Margaret Pole talked in this strain, men thought her intelligent and women cynical. Isabelle felt that this cynicism had grown upon her. It appeared in little things, as when she said: "I can stay only a week. I must see to breaking up the house and a lot of business. We shall never sail if I don't go back and get at it. Men are supposed to be practical and attend to the details, but they don't if they can get out of them." When Isabelle complimented her on her pretty figure, Margaret said with a mocking grimace: "Yes, the figure is there yet. The face goes first usually." Isabelle had to admit that Margaret's delicate, girlish face had grown strangely old and grave. The smile about the thin lips was there, but it was a mocking or a wistful smile. The blue eyes were deeper underneath the high brow. Life was writing its record on this fine face, — a record not easily read, however. They fell to talking over the St. Mary's girls.

"Aline, — have you seen much of her?" Margaret asked.

"Not as much as I hoped to, — I have been so useless," Isabelle replied. "She's grown queer!"

"Queer?"

"She is rather dowdy, and they live in such a funny way, — always in a mess. Of course they haven't much money, but they needn't be so — squalid, — the children and the mussy house and all."

"Aline doesn't care for things," Margaret observed.

"But one must care enough to be clean! And she has gone in for fads, — she has taken to spinning and weaving and designing jewellery and I don't know what."

"That is her escape," Margaret explained.

"Escape? It must be horrid for her husband and awful for the children."

"What would you have her do? Scrub and wash and mend and keep a tidy house? That would take all the poetry out of Aline, destroy her personality. Isn't it better for her husband and for the children that she should keep herself alive and give them something better than a good housewife?"

"Keep herself alive by making weird cloths and impossible bracelets?"

Margaret laughed at Isabelle's philistine horror of the Goring household, and amused herself with suggesting more of the philosophy of the Intellectuals, the creed of Woman's Independence. She pointed out that Aline did not interfere with Goring's pursuit of his profession though it might not interest her or benefit her. Why should Goring interfere with Aline's endeavors to develop herself, to be something more than a mother and a nurse?

"She has kept something of her own soul, — that is it!"

"Her own soul!" mocked Isabelle. "If you were to take a meal with them, you would wish there was less soul, and more clean table napkins."

"My dear little *bourgeoise*," Margaret commented with amusement, "you must get a larger point of view. The housewife ideal is doomed. Women won't submit to it, — intelligent ones. And Goring probably likes Aline better as she is than he would any competent wife of the old sort."

"I don't believe any sane man likes to see his children dirty, and never know where to find a clean towel, — don't tell me!"

"Then men must change their characters," Margaret replied vaguely; "we women have been changing our characters for centuries to conform to men's desires. It's time that the men adjusted themselves to us."

"I wonder what John would say if I told him he must change his character," mused Isabelle.

"There is Cornelia Woodyard," Margaret continued; "she combines the two ideals — but she is very clever."

"We never thought so at St. Mary's."

"That's because we judged her by woman's standards, sentimental ones, — old-fashioned ones. But she is New."

"How new?" asked Isabelle, who felt that she had been dwelling in a dark place the past three years.

"Why, she made up her mind just what she wanted out of life, — a certain kind of husband, a certain kind of married life, a certain set of associates, — and she's got just what she planned. She isn't an opportunist like most of us, who take the husbands we marry because they are there, we don't know why, and take the children they give us because they come, and live and do what turns up in the circumstances chosen for us by the Male. No, Conny is very clever!"

"But how?"

"Eugene Woodyard is not a rich man, — Conny was not after money, — but he is a clever lawyer, well connected, — in with a lot of interesting people, and has possibilities. Conny saw those and has developed them, — that has been her success. You see she combines the old and the new. She makes the mould of their life, but she works through him. As a result she has just what she wants, and her husband adores her, — he is the outward and visible symbol of Conny's inward and material strength!"

Isabelle laughed, and Margaret continued in her pleasant drawl, painting the Woodyard firmament.

"She understood her man better than he did himself. She knew that he would never be a great money-getter, hadn't the mental or the physical qualifications for it. So she turns him deftly into a reformer, a kind of gentlemanly politician. She'll make him Congressman or better, — much better! Meantime she has given him a delightful home, one of the nicest I know, — on a street down town near a little park, where the herd does not know enough to live. And there Conny receives the best picked set of people I ever see. It is all quite wonderful!"

"And we thought her coarse," mused Isabelle.

"Perhaps she is, — I don't think she is fine. But a strong hand is rarely fine. I don't think she would hesitate to use any means to arrive, — and that is Power, my dear little girl!"

Margaret Pole rose, the enigmatic smile on her lips.

"I must leave you now to your nap and the peace of the hills," she said lightly. "We'll meet at luncheon. By the way, I ran across a cousin of mine coming in on the train, — a Virginian cousin, which means that he is close enough to ask favors when he wants them. He wishes to meet you, — he is a great favorite of the Woodyards, of Conny, I should say, — Tom Cairy. . . . He was at college with your brother, I think. I will bring him over in the afternoon if you say so. He's amusing, Thomas; but I don't vouch for him. Good-by, girl."

Isabelle watched Margaret Pole cross the light green of the lawn, walking leisurely, her head raised towards the mountains. 'She is not happy,' thought Isabelle. 'There is something wrong in her marriage. I wonder if it is always so!' Margaret had given her so much to think about, with her sharp suggestions of strange, new views, that she felt extraordinarily refreshed. And Margaret, her eyes on the blue hills, was thinking, 'She is still the girl, — she doesn't know herself yet, does not know life!' Her lips smiled wistfully, as though to add: 'But she is eager. She will have to learn, as we all do.' Thus the two young women, carefully avoiding any reference to the thought nearest their hearts, discovered in a brief half hour what each wanted to know. . . .

After the noisy luncheon, with its interminable variety of food, in the crowded, hot dining room, Isabelle and Margaret with Cairy sought refuge in one of the foot-paths that led up into the hills. Cairy dragged his left leg with a perceptible limp. He was slight, blond hair with auburn tinge, smooth shaven, with appealing eyes that, like Margaret's, were recessed beneath delicate brows. He had pleased Isabelle by talking to her about Vickers, whom he had known slightly at the university, talking warmly and naturally, as if nothing had happened to Vickers. Now he devoted himself to her quite personally, while Margaret walked on ahead. Cairy had a way of seeing but one woman at a time, no matter what the circumstances might be, because his emotional horizon was always limited. That was one reason why he was liked so much by women. He had a good deal to say about the Woodyards, especially Conny.

"She is so sure in her judgments," he said. "I always show her everything I write!" (He had already explained that he was a literary "jobber," as he called it, at the Springs to see a well-known Wall Street man for an article on "the other side" that he was preparing for *The People's Magazine,* and also hinted that his ambitions rose above his magazine efforts.)

"But I did not know that Conny was literary," Isabelle remarked in surprise.

The young Southerner smiled at her simplicity.

"I don't know that she is what *you* mean by literary; perhaps that is the reason she is such a good judge. She knows what people want to read, at least what the editors think they want and will pay for. If Con — Mrs. Woodyard likes a thing, I know I shall get a check for it. If she throws it down, I might as well save postage stamps."

"A valuable friend," Margaret called back lightly, "for a struggling man of letters!"

"Rather," Cairy agreed. "You see," turning to Isabelle again, "that sort of judgment is worth reams of literary criticism."

"It's practical."

"Yes, that is just what she is, — the genius of the practical; it's an instinct with her. That is why she can give really elaborate dinners in her little house, and you have the feeling that there are at least a dozen servants where they ought to be, and all that."

From the Woodyards they digressed to New York and insensibly to Cairy's life there. Before they had turned back for tea Isabelle knew that the lame young Southerner had written a play which he hoped to induce some actress to take, and that meantime he was supporting himself in the various ways that modern genius has found as a substitute for Grub Street. He had also told her that New York was the only place one could live in, if one was interested in the arts, and that in his opinion the drama was the coming art of America, — "real American drama with blood in it"; and had said something about the necessity of a knowledge of life, "a broad understanding of the national forces," if a man were to write anything worth while.

"You mean dinner-parties?" Margaret asked at this point. . . .

When he left the women, he had arranged to ride with Isabelle.

"It's the only sport I can indulge in," he said, referring to his physical infirmity, "and I don't get much of it in New York."

As he limped away across the lawn, Margaret asked mischievously: —

"Well, what do you think of Cousin Thomas? He lets you know a good deal about himself all at once."

"He is so interesting — and appealing, don't you think so, with those eyes? Isn't it a pity he is lame?"

"I don't know about that. He's used that lameness of his very effectively. It's procured him no end of sympathy, and sympathy is what Thomas likes, — from women. He will tell you all about it some time, — how his negro nurse was frightened by a snake and dropped him on a stone step when he was a baby."

"We don't have men like him in St. Louis," Isabelle reflected aloud; "men who write or do things that are really interesting, — it is all business or gossip. I should like to see Conny, — it must be exciting to live in New York, and *be* somebody!"

"Come and try it; you will, I suppose?"

In spite of Margaret's gibes at her distant cousin, Isabelle enjoyed Cairy. He was the kind of man she had rarely seen and never known: by birth a gentleman, by education and ambition a writer, with a distinct social sense and the charm of an artist. In spite of his poverty he had found the means to run about the world — the habited part of it — a good deal, and had always managed to meet the right people, — the ones "whose names mean something." He was of the parasite species, but of the higher types. To Isabelle his rapid talk, about plays, people, pictures, the opera, books, was a revelation of some of that flowing stream of life which she felt she was missing. And he gave her the pleasant illusion of "being worth while." The way he would look at her as he rolled a cigarette on the veranda steps, awaiting her least word, flattered her woman's sympathy. When he left for Washington, going, as he said, "where the *People's* call me," she missed him distinctly.

"I hope I shall meet him again!"

"You will," Margaret replied. "Thomas is the kind one meets pretty often if you are his sort. And I take it you are!"

Isabelle believed that Margaret Pole was jealous of her young cousin or piqued because of a sentimental encounter in their youth. Cairy had hinted at something of this kind. Margaret patted Isabelle's pretty head.

"My little girl," she mocked, "how wonderful the world is, and all the creatures in it!"

From this month's visit at the Springs the Colonel got some good golf, Mrs. Price a vivid sense of the way people threw their money about these days ("They say that Wall Street broker gave the head waiter a hundred dollar bill when he left!"). And Isabelle had absorbed a miscellaneous assortment of ideas, the dominant one being that intelligent Americans who really wished to have interesting lives went East to live, particularly to New York. And incidentally there was inserted in the nether layers of her consciousness the belief that the world was changing its ideas about women and marriage, "and all that." She desired eagerly to be in the current of these new ideas.

CHAPTER XX

"WHAT makes a happy marriage?" Rob Falkner queried in his brutal and ironical mood, which made his wife shiver for the proprieties of pleasant society. It was at one of Bessie's famous Torso suppers, when the Lanes and Darnells were present.

"A good cook and a good provider," Lane suggested pleasantly, to keep the topic off conversational reefs.

"A husband who thinks everything you do just right!" sighed Bessie.

"Plenty of money and a few children — for appearances," some one threw in.

Isabelle remarked sagely, "A husband who knows what is best for you in the big things, and a wife who does what is best in the small ones."

"Unity of Purpose — Unity of Souls," Tom Darnell announced in his oratorical voice, with an earnestness that made the party self-conscious. His wife said nothing, and Falkner summed up cynically: —

"You've won, Lane! The American husband must be a good provider, but it doesn't follow that the wife must be a good cook. Say a good entertainer, and there you have a complete formula of matrimony: PROVIDER (Hustler, Money-getter, Liberal) and ENTERTAINER (A woman pretty, charming, social)."

"Here's to the Falkner household, — the perfect example!"

Thus the talk drifted off with a laugh into a discussion of masculine deficiencies and feminine endurances. Isabelle, looking back with the experience of after years, remembered this "puppy-dog" conversation. How young they all were and how they played with ideas! Bessie, also, remembered the occasion, with an injured feeling. On the way home that night Lane had remarked to his wife:—

"Falkner is a queer chap, — he was too personal to-night."

"I suppose it is hard on him; Bessie is rather wilful and extravagant. He looked badly to-night. And he told me he had to take an early train to examine some new work."

Lane shrugged his shoulders, as does the man of imperturbable will, perfect digestion, and constant equilibrium, for the troubles of a weaker vessel.

"If he doesn't like what his wife does, he should have character enough to control her. Besides he should have known all that before he married!"

Isabelle smiled at this piece of masculine complacency,— as if a man could know any essential fact about a woman from the way she did her hair to the way she spent money before he had lived with her!

"I do hope he will get a better place," Isabelle remarked good-naturedly. "It would do them both so much good."

As we have seen, Falkner's chance came at last through Lane, who recommended him to the A. and P. engineer in charge of the great terminal works that the road had undertaken in St. Louis. The salary of the new position was four thousand dollars a year, — a very considerable advance over the Torso position, and the work gave Falkner an opportunity such as he had never had before. The railroad system had other large projects in contemplation also.

"Bessie has written me such a letter, — the child!" Isabelle told her husband. "You would think they had inherited a million. And yet she seems sad to leave Torso, after all the ragging she gave the place. She has a good word to say even for Mrs. Fraser!"

Bessie Falkner was one of those who put down many small roots wherever chance places them. She had settled into Torso more solidly than she knew until she came to pull up her roots and put them down in a large, strange city. "We won't know any one there," she said dolefully to her Torso friends. "The Lanes, of course; but they are such grand folk now — and Isabelle has all her old friends about her." Nevertheless, it scarcely entered her mind to remain "in this prairie village all our days." Bessie had to the full the American ambition to move on and up as far as possible. . . .

Fortune, having turned its attention to the Falkners, seemed determined to smile on them this year. An uncle of Bessie's died on his lonely ranch in Wyoming, and when the infrequent local authorities got around to settling his affairs, they found that he had left his little estate to Elizabeth Bissell, who was now Mrs. Robert Falkner of Torso. The lonely old rancher, it seemed, had remembered the pretty, vivacious blond girl of eighteen, who had taken the trouble to show him the sights of Denver the one time he had visited his sister ten years before. Bessie, amused at his eccentric appearance, had tried to give "Uncle Billy" a good time. "Uncle Billy," she would say, "you must do this, — you will remember it all your life. Uncle Billy, won't you lunch with me down town to-day? You must go to the theatre, while you are here. Uncle, I am going to make you a necktie!" So she had chirped from morning until night, flattering, coaxing, and also making sport of the old man. "Bess has a good heart," her mother said to Uncle Bill, and it must be added Bessie also had a woman's instinct to please a possible benefactor. Uncle Billy when he returned to the lonely ranch wrote a letter to his pretty niece, which Bessie neglected to answer. Nevertheless, when Uncle Billy made ready to die, he bestowed all that he had to give upon the girl who had smiled on him once.

Thus Bessie's purring good nature bore fruit. Before the property could be sold, the most imaginative ideas about her inheritance filled Bessie's dreams. Day and night she planned what they would do with this fortune, — everything from a year in Europe to new dresses for the children! When it came finally in the form of a draft for thirteen thousand and some odd dollars, her visions were dampened for a time, — so many of her castles could not be acquired for thirteen thousand and some odd dollars.

Falkner was for investing the legacy in Freke's mines, which, he had good reason to believe, were better than gold mines. But when Bessie learned that the annual dividends would only be about twelve hundred dollars, she demurred. That was too slow. Secretly she thought that "if Rob were only clever about money," he might in a few years make a real fortune out of this capital. There were men she had known in Denver, as she told her husband, "who hadn't half of that and who had bought mines that had brought them hundreds of thousands of dollars." To which remark, Rob had replied curtly that he was not in that sort of business and that there were many more suckers than millionnaires in Denver — and elsewhere.

So, finally, after paying some Torso debts, it came down to buying a house in St. Louis; for the flat that they had first rented was crowded and Bessie found great difficulty in keeping a servant longer than a week. Rob thought that it would be more prudent to rent a house for six to nine hundred than to buy outright or build, until they saw how his work for the A. and P. developed. But Bessie wanted a home, — a house of her own. So they began the wearisome search for a house. Bessie already had her views about the desirable section to live in, — outside the smoke in one of "those private estate parks," — where the Lanes were thinking of settling. (A few months had been sufficient for Bessie to orientate herself socially in her new surroundings.) "That's where all the nice young people are going," she announced. In vain Rob pointed out that there were no houses to be bought for less than eighteen thousand in this fashionable neighborhood. "You never dare!" she retorted reproachfully. "You have to take risks if you want anything in this world! How many houses in St. Louis that aren't mortgaged do you suppose there are?"

"But there is only about eleven thousand of Uncle Billy's

money left, and those houses in Buena Vista Park cost from eighteen to twenty-four thousand dollars."

"And they have only one bath-room," sighed Bessie.

The summer went by in "looking," and the more houses they looked at the less satisfied was Bessie. She had in the foreground of her mind an image of the Lanes' Torso house, only "more artistic"; but Falkner convinced her that such a house in St. Louis would cost thirty thousand dollars at the present cost of building materials.

"It is so difficult," she explained to Mrs. Price, "to find anything small and your own, don't you know?" She arched her brows prettily over her dilemma. Mrs. Price, who, in spite of the fascination that Bessie exerted, had prim ideas "of what young persons in moderate circumstances" should do, suggested that the Johnstons were buying a very good house in the new suburb of Bryn Mawr on the installment plan.

"As if we could bury ourselves in that swamp, — we might as well stay in Torso!" Bessie said to her husband disgustedly.

Falkner reflected that the train service to Bryn Mawr made it easier of access to his work than the newer residential quarter inside the city which Bessie was considering. But that was the kind of remark he had learned not to make. . . .

In the end it came to their building. For Bessie found nothing "small and pretty, and just her own," with three bath-rooms, two maids' rooms, etc., in any "possible" neighborhood. She had met at a dinner-party an attractive young architect, who had recently come from the East to settle in St. Louis. Mr. Bowles prepared some water-color sketches which were so pretty that she decided to engage him. With misgivings Rob gave his consent. A narrow strip of frontage was found next a large house in the desired section. They had to pay three thousand dollars for the strip of land. Mr. Bowles thought the house could be built for eight or ten thousand dollars, depending on the price of materials, which seemed to be going up with astonishing rapidity.

Then Bessie plunged into plans. It was a gusty March day when the Falkners went out with the architect to consider the lot, and spent an afternoon trying to decide how to secure the most sun. Falkner, weary of the whole matter, listened to the glib young architect. Another windy day in April they returned to the lot to look at the excavation. The contracts were not yet signed. Lumber had gone soaring, and there was a strike in the brick business, the kind of brick they had chosen being unobtainable, while hardware seemed unaccountably precious. Already it was impossible to build the house for less than twelve thousand, even after sacrificing Bessie's private bath. Falkner had consented to the mortgage, — "only four thousand," Bessie said; "we'll save our rent and pay it off in a year or two!" Bessie's periods of economy were always just dawning!

Falkner, looking at the contractor's tool shed, had a sense of depressing fatality. From the moment that the first spadeful of ground had been dug, it seemed to him that the foundation of his domestic peace had begun to crumble. But this depression was only an attack of the grippe, he said to himself, and he tried to take an interest in the architect's description of how they should terrace the front of the lot. . . .

Of course, as the novelists tell us, the man of Strong Will, of Mature Character, of Determined Purpose, would not have allowed his wife to entangle him in this house business (or in matrimony, perhaps, in the first instance)! But if society were composed of men of S. W., M. C., and D. P., there would be no real novels, — merely epics of Slaughter and Success, of Passionate Love and Heroic Accomplishment. . . . At this period Falkner still loved his wife, — wanted to give her every gratification within his power, and some just beyond, — though that love had been strained by five hard years, when her efforts as an economic partner had not been intelligent. (Bessie would have scorned such an unromantic term as "economic partner.") They still had their times of amiable understanding, of pleasant comradeship, even of passionate endearment. But by the time the young architect's creation at number 26 Buena Vista Pleasance had become their residence, that love was in a moribund condition. . . . Yet after all, as Bessie sometimes reminded him, it was *her* money that was building the house, at least the larger part of it; and further it was all her life that was to be spent in it, presumably. The woman's home was her world.

Thus, in the division that had come between them, the man began to consider his wife's rights, what he owed to her as a woman that he had taken under his protection, — a very dangerous state of mind in matrimony. If he had discovered that her conception of the desirable end of life was not his, he must respect her individuality, and so far as possible provide for her that which she seemed to need. The faithful husband, or dray-horse interpretation of marriage, this.

CHAPTER XXI

If it takes Strong Will, Mature Character, and Determined Purpose to live effectively, it takes all of that and more — humor and patience — to build a house in America, unless one can afford to order his habitation as he does a suit of clothes and spend the season in Europe until the contractor and the architect have fought it out between them. But Bessie was a young woman of visions. She had improved all her opportunities to acquire taste, — the young architect said she had "very intelligent ideas." And he, Bertram Bowles, fresh from Paris, with haunting memories of chateaux and villas, and a knowledge of what the leading young architects of the East were turning out, had visions too, in carrying out this first real commission that he had received in St. Louis. "Something *chic*, with his stamp on it," he said. . . .

The hours with the contractors to persuade them that they could do something they had never seen done before! The debates over wood finish, and lumber going up while you talked! The intricacies of heating, plumbing, electric lighting, and house telephones — when all men are discovered to be liars! Falkner thought it would be easier to lay out the entire terminal system of the A. and P. than to build one "small house, pretty and just your own, you know." Occasionally even Bessie and the polite Bertram Bowles fell out, when Falkner was called in to arbitrate. Before the question of interior decoration came up the house had already cost fourteen thousand dollars, which would necessitate a mortgage of six thousand dollars at once. Here Falkner put his foot down, — no more; they would live in it with bare walls. Bessie pleaded and sulked, — "only another thousand." And "not to be perfectly ridiculous," Falkner was forced to concede another thousand. "Not much when you consider," as the architect said to Bessie. . . . Time dragged on, and the house was not ready. The apartment hotel into which they had moved was expensive and bad for the children. In June Falkner insisted on moving into the unfinished house, with carpenters, painters, decorators still hanging on through the sultry summer months.

"I met your poor little friend Mrs. Falkner at Sneeson's this morning," Nan Lawton said to Isabelle. "She was looking over hangings and curtains for her house. . . . She is nothing but a bag of bones, she's so worn. That husband of hers must be a brute to let her wear herself all out. She was telling me some long yarn about their troubles with the gas men, — very amusing and bright. She is a charming little thing."

"Yes," Isabelle replied; "I am afraid the house has been too much for them both."

She had been Bessie's confidant in all her troubles, and sympathized — who could not sympathize with Bessie? — though she thought her rather foolish to undertake so much.

"We'll simply have to have rugs, I tell Rob," Bessie said to her. "He is in such bad humor these days, and says we must go on the bare floors or use the old Torso carpets. Fancy!"

And Isabelle said, as she was expected to say, "Of course you will have to have rugs. They are having a sale at Moritz's, — some beauties and cheap."

Yet she had a sneaking sympathy for Falkner. Isabelle did not suspect that she herself was the chief undoing of the Falkner household, nor did any one else suspect it. It was Bessie's ideal of Isabelle that rode her hard from the beginning of her acquaintance with the Lanes. And it was Isabelle who very naturally introduced them to most of the people they had come to know in their new world. Isabelle herself had much of her mother's thrift and her father's sagacity in practical matters. She would never have done what Bessie was doing in Bessie's circumstances. But in her own circumstances she did unconsciously a great deal more, —

and she disliked to fill her mind with money matters, considering it vulgar and underbred to dwell long on them. The rich and the very wise can indulge in these aristocratic refinements! Isabelle, to be sure, felt flattered by Bessie's admiring discipleship,—who does not like to lead a friend? She never dreamed of her evil influence. The power of suggestion, subtle, far-reaching, ever working on plastic human souls! Society evolves out of these petty reactions. . . .

The rugs came.

"We simply have to have rugs,—the house calls for it," asserted Bessie, using one of Mr. Bertram Bowles's favorite expressions.

"My purse doesn't," growled Falkner.

Nevertheless Bessie selected some pretty cheap rugs at Moritz's, which could be had on credit. In the great rug room of the department store she met Alice Johnston, who was looking at a drugget. The two women exchanged experiences as the perspiring clerks rolled and rerolled rugs.

"Yes, we shall like Bryn Mawr," Mrs. Johnston said, "now that the foliage covers up the tin cans and real estate signs. The schools are really very good, and there is plenty of room for the boys to make rough house in. We are to have a garden another year. . . . Oh, yes, it is rural middle class,—that's why I can get drugget for the halls."

Bessie thought of her pretty house and shuddered.

"We are planning to call and see the house — Isabelle says it's wonderful — but it will have to be on a Sunday — the distance —"

"Can't you come next Sunday for luncheon? I will ask Isabelle and her husband," Bessie interrupted hospitably, proud to show off her new toy.

And on Sunday they all had a very good time and the new "toy" was much admired, although the paint was still sticky, — the painter had been optimistic when he took the contract and had tried to save himself later, — the colors wrong, and the furniture, which had done well enough in Torso, looked decidedly shabby.

"It's the prettiest house I know," Isabelle said warmly, and Bessie felt repaid.

She was very tired, and to-day looked worn. The new toy was dragging her out. As the long St. Louis summer drew to an end, she was always tired. Some obscure woman's trouble, something in the delicate organism that had never been quite right, was becoming acutely wrong. She lived in fear of having another child,— the last baby had died. By the new year she was in care of Isabelle's specialist, who advised an operation. When that was over, it was nearly spring, and though she was still delicate, she wished to give some dinners "to return their obligations." Falkner objected for many reasons, and she thought him very hard.

"It is always sickness and babies for me," she pouted; "and when I want a little fun, you think we can't afford it or something."

Her hospitable heart was so bent on this project, it seemed so natural that she should desire to show off her toy, after her struggle for it, so innocent "to have our friends about us," that he yielded in part. A good deal might be told about that dinner, from an economic, a social, a domestic point of view. But we must lose it and hasten on. Imagine merely, what a charming woman like Bessie Falkner, whose scheme of the universe was founded on the giving of "pleasant little dinners," would do, — a woman who was making her life, building her wigwam, filling it with those she wished to have as friends, and you will see it all. It was, of course, a great success. Mrs. Anstruthers Leason said of the hostess (reported by Nan Lawton through Isabelle), "Little Mrs. Falkner has the real social gift, — a very rare thing among our women!" And when an invitation came from Mrs. Anstruthers Leason to dinner and her box at the French opera, Bessie was sure that she had found her sphere.

Falkner seemed to Bessie these days to be growing harder, — he was "exacting," "unsympathetic," "tyrannical." "He won't go places, and he won't have people, — isn't nice to them, even in his own house," Bessie said sadly to Isabelle. "I suppose that marriage usually comes to that: the wife stands for bills and trouble, and the husband scolds. Most people squabble, don't they?"

"Of course he loves you, dear," Isabelle consoled her. "American husbands always take their wives for granted, as Nannie says. A foreigner pays attentions to his wife after marriage that our husbands don't think are necessary once they have us. Our husbands take us too much as a matter of course, — and pay the bills!"

Bessie felt and said that Rob took life too hard, worried too much. After all, when a man married a woman and had children, he must expect a certain amount of trouble and anxiety. She wasn't sure but that wives were needed to keep men spurred to their highest pitch of working efficiency. She had an obscure idea that the male was by nature lazy and self-indulgent, and required the steel prod of necessity to do his best work. As she looked about her among the struggling households, it seemed such was the rule, — that if it weren't for the fact of wife and children and bills, the men would deteriorate. . . . Naturally there were differences, — "squabbles," as she called them; but she would have been horrified if any one had suggested that these petty squabbles, the state of mind they produced or indicated, were infinitely more degrading, more deteriorating to them both, than adultery. It never entered her mind that either she or her husband could be unfaithful, that Falkner could ever care for any other woman than her. "Why, we married for love!"

Love! That divine unreason of the gods, which lures man as a universal solvent of his sorrow, the great solution to the great enigma! Where was it? Bessie asked when Rob passed her door in the morning on his way to his solitary breakfast without a word of greeting or a kiss, and finally left the house without remembering to go upstairs again. And Falkner asked himself much the same thing, when

Bessie persisted in doing certain things "because everybody does," or when he realized that after two years in his new position, with a five hundred dollars' increase in his salary the second year, he was nearly a thousand dollars in debt, and losing steadily each quarter. Something must be done — and by him! — for in marriage, he perceived with a certain bitterness, Man was the Forager, the Provider. And in America if he didn't bring in enough from the day's hunt to satisfy the charming squaw that he had made his consort, why, — he must trudge forth again and get it! A poor hunter does not deserve the embellishment of a Bessie and two pretty children.

So he went forth to bring in more game, and he read no poetry these days.

CHAPTER XXII

THE calm male observer might marvel at Bessie's elation over the prospect of sitting in Mrs. Anstruthers Leason's box at the performance of "Faust" given by the French Opera Company on tour. But no candid woman will. It could be explained partly by the natural desire to associate with entertaining, well-dressed folk, who were generally considered to be "the best," "the leaders" of local society. Sitting there in the stuffy box, which was a poor place for seeing or hearing, Bessie felt the satisfaction of being in the right company. She had discovered in one of the serried rows of the first balcony Kitty Sanders, whom she had known as a girl in Kansas City, where Bessie had once lived in the peregrinations of the Bissell family. Kitty had married a prosperous dentist and enjoyed with him an income nearly twice that of Rob Falkner. Kitty, scanning the boxes closely, also spied Bessie, and exclaimed to her husband: —

"Why, there's Bessie Bissell in that box! You know she married a young fellow, an engineer or something." And she added either aloud or to herself, "They seem to be *in it*,— that's the Leason box." While the alluring strains of the overture floated across the house, she mused at the strange mutations of fortune, which had landed Bessie Bissell there and herself here beside the dentist, — with some envy, in spite of three beloved children at home and a motor-car. . . .

To the dispassionate male observer this state of mind might be more comprehensible if Bessie had appeared in Mrs. Corporation's box on a gala night at the Metropolitan, or in the Duchess of Thatshire's box at Covent Garden. But the strange fact of democracy is that instead of discouraging social desires it has multiplied them ten thousand fold. Every city in the land has its own Mrs. Anstruthers Leason or Mrs. Corporation, to form the local constellation, towards which the active-minded women of a certain type will always strive or gravitate, as you choose to put it. This being so, the American husband, one might suppose, would sigh for an absolute monarchy, where there is but one fixed social firmament, admission to which is determined by a despot's edict. Then the great middle class could rest content, knowing that forever, no matter what their gifts might be, their wives could not aspire to social heights. With us the field is clear, the race open to money and brains, and the result? Each one can answer for himself.

Isabelle, returning to her home that fall, with a slight surplus of vitality, was eager for life. "I have been dead so long," she said to her husband. "I want to see people!" Born inside the local constellation, as she had been, that was not difficult. Yet she realized soon enough that the Prices, prominent as they were, had never belonged to the heart of the constellation. It remained for her to penetrate there, under the guidance of the same Nannie Lawton whom as a girl she had rather despised. For every constellation has its inner circle, the members of which touch telepathically all other inner circles. The fact that Nannie Lawton called her by her first name would help her socially more than the Colonel's record as a citizen or her husband's position in the railroad or their ample means. Before her second winter of married life had elapsed, she had begun to exhaust this form of excitement, to find herself always tired. After all, although the smudge of St. Louis on the level alluvial plains of America was a number of times larger than the smudge of Torso, the human formula, at least in its ornamental form, remained much the same. She was patroness where she should be patroness, she was invited where she would have felt neglected not to be invited, she entertained very much as the others she knew entertained, and she and her husband had more engagements than they could keep. She saw this existence stretching down the years with monotonous iteration, and began to ask herself what else there was to satisfy the thirst for experience which had never been assuaged.

Bessie, with a keener social sense, kept her eye on the game, — she had to, and her little triumphs satisfied her. Nan Lawton varied the monotony of "the ordinary round" by emotional dissipations that Isabelle felt herself to be above. Other women of their set got variety by running about the country to New York or Washington, to a hotel in Florida or in the mountains of Carolina, or as a perpetual resource to Paris and Aix and Trouville and London. . . .

Isabelle was too intelligent, too much the daughter of her father, to believe that a part of the world did not exist outside the social constellation, and an interesting part, too. Some of those outside she touched as time went on. She was one of the board of governors for the Society of Country Homes for Girls, and here and on the Orphanage board she met energetic and well-bred young married women, who apparently genuinely preferred their charities, their reading clubs, the little country places where they spent the summers, to the glory of Mrs. Anstruthers Leason's opera box or dinner dance. As she shot about the city on her errands, social and philanthropic, Isabelle sometimes mused on the lives of the "others," — all those thousands that filled the streets and great buildings of the city. Of course the poor, — that was simple enough; the struggle for life settled how one would live with ruthless severity. If it was a daily question how you could keep yourself housed and fed, why it did not matter what you did with your life. In the ranks above the poor, the little people who lived in steam-heated apartments and in small suburban boxes had their small fixed round of church and friends, still closely circumscribed and to Isabelle, in her present mood, — simply dreadful. When she expressed this to Fosdick, whom she was taking one morning to a gallery to see the work of a local artist that fashionable people were patronizing, he had scoffed at her: —

"*Madame la princesse,*" he said, waving his hand towards the throng of morning shoppers, "don't you suppose that the same capacity for human sensation exists in every unit of that crowd bent towards Sneeson's as in you?"

"No," protested Isabelle, promptly; "they haven't the same experience."

"As thrilling a drama can be unrolled in a twenty-five dollar flat as in a palace."

"Stuff! There isn't one of those women who wouldn't be keen to try the palace!"

"As you ought to be to try the flat, in a normally constituted society."

"What do you mean by a normally constituted society?"

"One where the goal of ease is not merely entertainment."

"You are preaching now, aren't you?" demanded Isabelle. "Society has always been pretty much the same, hasn't it? First necessities, then comforts, then luxuries, and then — "

"Well, what?"

"Oh, experience, art, culture, I suppose."

"Isabelle," the big man smilingly commented, "you are the same woman you were six years ago."

"I am not!" she protested, really irritated. "I have done a lot of thinking, and I have seen a good deal of life. Besides I am a good wife, and a mother, which I wasn't six years ago, and a member of the Country Homes Society and the Orphanage, and a lot more." They laughed at her defence, and Isabelle added as a concession: "I know that there are plenty of women not in society who lead interesting lives, are intelligent and all that. But I am a good wife, and a good mother, and I am intelligent, and what is more, I see amusing people and more of them than the others, — the just plain women. What would you have me do?"

"Live," Fosdick replied enigmatically.

"We all live."

"Very few do."

"You mean emotional — heart experiences, like Nan's

affairs? . . . Sometimes I wonder if that wouldn't be — interesting. But it would give John such a shock! . . . Well, here are the pictures. There's Mrs. Leason's portrait, — flatters her, don't you think?"

Fosdick, leaning his fat hands on his heavy stick, slowly made the round of the canvasses, concluding with the portrait of Mrs. Leason.

"Got some talent in him," he pronounced; "a penny worth. If he can only keep away from this sort of thing," pointing with his stick to the portrait, "he might paint in twenty years."

"But why shouldn't he do portraits? They all have to, to live."

"It isn't the portrait, — it's the sort of thing it brings with it. You met him, I suppose?"

"Yes; dined with him at Mrs. Leason's last week."

"I thought so. That's the beginning of his end."

"You silly! Art has always been parasitic, — why shouldn't the young man go to pleasant people's houses and have a good time and be agreeable and get them to buy his pictures?"

"Isabelle, you have fallen into the bad habit of echoing phrases. 'Art has always been parasitic.' That's the second commonplace of the drawing-room you have got off this morning."

"Come over here and tell me something. . . . I can't quarrel with you, Dickie!" Isabelle said, leading the way to a secluded bench.

"If I were not modest, I should say you were flirting with me."

"I never flirt with any man; I am known as the Saint, the Puritan, — I might try it, but I couldn't — with you. . . . Tell me about Vick. Have you seen him?"

"Yes," Fosdick replied gravely. "I ran across him in Venice."

"How was he?"

"He looked well, has grown rather stout. . . . The first

time I saw him was on the Grand Canal; met him in a smart gondola, with men all togged out, no end of a get-up!"

"You saw them *both?*"

"Of course, — I looked him up at once. They have an old place on the Giudecca, you know. I spent a week with them. He's still working on the opera, — it doesn't get on very fast, I gather. He played me some of the music, — it's great, parts of it. And he has written other things."

"I know all that," Isabelle interrupted impatiently. "But is he happy?"

"A man like Vickers doesn't tell you that, you know."

"But you can tell — how did they seem?"

"Well," Fosdick replied slowly, "when I saw them in the gondola the first time, I thought — it was too bad!"

"I was afraid so," Isabelle cried. "Why don't they marry and come to New York or go to London or some place and make a life? — people can't live like that."

"I think he wants to marry her," Fosdick replied.

"But she won't?"

"Precisely, — not now."

"Why — what?"

Fosdick avoided the answer, and observed, "Vick seems awfully fond of the little girl, Delia."

"Poor, poor Vick!" Isabelle sighed. "He ought to leave that creature."

"He won't; Vick was the kind that the world sells cheap, — it's best kind. He lives the dream and believes his shadows; it was always so. It will be so until the end. Life will stab him at every corner."

"Dear, dear Vick!" Isabelle said softly; "some days I feel as if I would have done as he did."

"But fortunately there is John to puncture your dream with solid fact."

"John even might not be able to do it! . . . I am going over to see Vick this summer."

"Wouldn't that make complications — family ones?"

Isabelle threw up her head wilfully.

"Dickie, I think there is something in me deeper than my love for John or for the child, — and that is the feeling I have about Vick!"

Fosdick looked at her penetratingly.

"You ought not to have married, Isabelle."

"Why? Every one marries — and John and I are very happy. . . . Come; there are some people I don't want to meet."

As they descended the steps into the murky light of the noisy city, Isabelle remarked: —

"Don't forget to-night, promptly at seven, — we are going to the theatre afterwards. I shall show you some of our smart people and let you see if they aren't more interesting than the mob."

She nodded gayly and drove off. As she went to a luncheon engagement, she thought of Vickers, of Fosdick's remarks about living, and a great wave of dissatisfaction swept over her. "It's this ugly city," she said to herself, letting down the window. "Or it's nerves again, — I must do something!" That phrase was often on her lips these days. In her restlessness nothing seemed just right, — she was ever trying to find something beyond the horizon. As Fosdick would have said, "The race vitality being exhausted in its primitive force, nothing has come to take its place." But at luncheon she was gay and talkative, the excitement of human contact stimulating her. And afterwards she packed the afternoon with trivial engagements until it was time to dress for her guests.

The dinner and the theatre might have passed off uneventfully, if it had not been for Fosdick. That unwieldy social vessel broke early in the dinner. Isabelle had placed him next Mrs. Leason because the lady liked celebrities, and Fosdick, having lately been put gently but firmly beyond the confines of the Tzar's realm for undue intimacy with the rebellious majority of the Tzar's subjects, might be counted such. For the time being he had come to a momentary equilibrium in the city of his birth. Fosdick and Mrs.

Leason seemed to find common ground, while the other men, the usual speechless contingent of tired business men, allowed themselves to be talked at by the women. Presently Fosdick's voice boomed forth: —

"Let me tell you a story which will illustrate my point, Mrs. Leason. Some years ago I was riding through the Kentucky mountains, and after a wretched luncheon in one of the log-and-mud huts I was sitting on the bench in front of the cabin trying to make peace with my digestion. The ground in that spot sloped down towards me, and on the side of this little hill there lay a large hog, a razor-back sow. There were eight little pigs clustered in voracious attitudes about her, and she could supply but six at a time, — I mean that she was provided by nature with but six teats."

Mrs. Leason visibly moved away from her neighbor, and for the rest of his story Fosdick had a silent dinner table.

"The mother was asleep," Fosdick continued, turning his great head closer to Mrs. Leason, "probably attending to her digestion as I was to mine, and she left her offspring to fight it out among themselves for the possession of her teats. There was a lively scrap, a lot of hollerin' and squealin' from that bunch of porkers, grunts from the ins and yaps from the outs, you know. Every now and then one of the outs would make a flying start, get a wedge in and take a nip, forcing some one of his brothers out of the heap so that he would roll down the hill into the path. Up he'd get and start over, and maybe he would dislodge some other porker. And the old sow kept grunting and sleeping peacefully in the sun while her children got their dinner in the usual free-fight fashion.

"Now," Fosdick raised his heavy, square-pointed finger and shook it at the horrified Mrs. Leason and also across the table, noticing what seemed to him serious interest in his allegory, "I observed that there was a difference among those little porkers, — some were fat and some were peaked, and the peaked fellers got little show at the mother. Now what I ask myself is, — were they weak because they couldn't manage to get a square feed, or were they hustled out more than the others because they were naturally weak? I leave that to my friends the sociologists to determine —"

"Isabelle," Lane interposed from his end of the table, "if Mr. Fosdick has finished his pig story, perhaps —"

Isabelle, divided between a desire to laugh and a very vivid sense of Mrs. Leason's feelings, rose, but Fosdick had not finished and she sat down again.

"But what I meant to say was this, madam, — there's only one difference between that old sow and her brood and society as it is run at present, and that is there are a thousand mouths to every teat, and a few big, fat fellows are getting all the food."

He looked up triumphantly from his exposition. There was a titter at Mrs. Lawton's end of the table. This lady had been listening to an indecent story told in French-English when Fosdick had upset things. Now she remarked in an audible tone: —

"Disgusting, I say!"

"Eh! What's the matter? Don't you believe what I told you?" Fosdick demanded.

"Oh, yes, Dickie, — anything you say, — only don't repeat it!" Isabelle exclaimed, rising from the table.

"Does he come from a farm?" one woman murmured indignantly. "Such *gros mots!*" She too had been listening to the story of adultery at Mrs. Lawton's end of the table. Isabelle, who had taken in the whole situation from her husband's shocked face, Nan Lawton's sly giggle over the salacious tidbit, and Mrs. Leason's offended countenance, felt that she must shriek to relieve her feelings.

The party finally reached the theatre and saw a "sex" play, which caused a furious discussion among the women. "No woman would have done that." "The man was not worth the sacrifice," etc. And Fosdick gloomily remarked in Isabelle's ears: "Rot like this is all you see on the modern stage. And it's because women want it, — they must forever be fooling with sex. Why don't they —"

"Hush, Dickie! you have exploded enough to-night. Don't say that to Mrs. Leason!"

Her world appeared to her that night a harlequin tangle, and, above all, meaningless — yes, dispiritedly without sense. John, somehow, seemed displeased with her, as if she were responsible for Dickie's breaks. She laughed again as she thought of the sow story, and the way the women took it. "What a silly world, — talk and flutter and gadding, all about nothing!"

CHAPTER XXIII

ISABELLE did not see much of the Falkners as time went on. Little lines of social divergence began to separate them more and more widely. "After all, one sees chiefly the people who do the same things one does," Isabelle explained to herself. Bessie thought Isabelle "uncertain," perhaps snobbish, and felt hurt; though she remarked to Rob merely, "The Lanes are very successful, of course."

Affairs in the Buena Vista Pleasance house had progressed meantime. There were, naturally, so many meals to be got and eaten, so many little illnesses of the children, and other roughnesses of the road of life. There was also Bessie's developing social talent, and above all there was the infinitely complex action and reaction of the man and the wife upon each other. Seen as an all-seeing eye might observe, with all the emotional shading, the perspective of each act, the most commonplace household created by man and woman would be a wonderful cosmography. But the novelist, even he who has the courage to write a dull book, can touch but here and there, on the little promontories of daily life, where it seems to him the spiritual lava boils up near the surface and betrays most poignantly the nature of the fire beneath. . . .

It was a little over three years since the Falkners had moved into the Buena Vista Pleasance house. Husband and wife sat in the front room after their silent dinner alone, with the September breeze playing through the windows, which after a hot day had been thrown open. There was the débris of a children's party in the room and the hall, — dolls and toys, half-nibbled cakes and saucers of ice-cream. Bessie, who was very neat about herself, was quite

Southern in her disregard for order. She was also an adorable hostess for children, because she gave them loose rein.

"What is it you wish to say?" she asked her husband in a cold, defensive tone that had grown almost habitual.

Though pale she was looking very pretty in a new dress that she had worn at a woman's luncheon, where she had spent the first part of the afternoon. She had been much admired at the luncheon, had taken the lead in the talk about a new novel which was making a ten days' sensation. Her mind was still occupied partly with what she had said about the book. These discussions with Rob on household matters, at increasingly frequent periods, always froze her. "He makes me show my worst side," she said to herself. At the children's tea, moreover, an attack of indigestion had developed. Bessie was fond of rich food, and in her nervous condition, which was almost chronic, it did not agree with her, and made her irritable.

"I have been going over our affairs," Falkner began in measured tones. That was the usual formula! Bessie thought he understood women very badly. She wondered if he ever did anything else those evenings he spent at home except "go over their affairs." She wished he would devote himself to some more profitable occupation.

"Well?"

Falkner looked tired and listless. The summer was always his hardest time, and this summer the road had been pushing its terminal work with actual ferocity. He wore glasses now, and was perceptibly bald. He was also slouchy about dress; Bessie could rarely induce him to put on evening clothes when they dined alone.

"Well?" she asked again. It was not polite of him to sit staring there as if his mind were a thousand miles away. A husband should show some good manners to a woman, even if she was his wife!

Their chairs were not far apart, but the tones of their voices indicated an immeasurable gulf that had been deepening for years. Falkner cleared his voice.

"As I have told you so often, Bessie, we are running behind all the time. It has got to a point where it must stop."

"What do you suggest?"

"You say that three servants are necessary?"

"You can see for yourself that they are busy all the time. There's work for four persons in this house, and there ought to be a governess beside. I don't at all like the influence of that school on Mildred —"

"Ought!" he exclaimed.

"If people live in a certain kind of house, in a certain neighborhood, they must live up to it, — that is all. If you wish to live as the Johnstons live, why that is another matter altogether."

Her logic was imperturbable. There was an unexpressed axiom: "If you want a dowd for your wife who can't dress or talk and whom nobody cares to know, — why you should have married some one else." Bessie awaited his reply in unassailable attractiveness.

"Very well," Falkner said slowly. "That being so, I have made up my mind what to do."

Mildred entered the room at this moment, looking for a book. She was eight, and one swift glance at her parents' faces was enough to show her quick intelligence that they were "discussing."

"What is it, Mildred?" Bessie asked in the cooing voice she always had for children.

"I want my *Jungle Book*," the little girl replied, taking a book from the table.

"Run along, girlie," Bessie said; and Mildred, having decided that it was not an opportune moment to make affectionate good-nights, went upstairs.

"Well, what is it?" Bessie demanded in the other tone.

"I have a purchaser for the house, at fair terms."

"Please remember that it is *my* house."

"Wait! Whatever remains after paying off the mortgage and our debts, not more than six thousand dollars, I suppose, will be placed to your credit in the trust company."

"Why should I pay all our debts?"

Her husband looked at her, and she continued hastily:—

"What do you mean to do then? We can't live on the street."

"We can hire a smaller house somewhere else, or live in a flat."

Bessie waved her hand in despair; they had been over this so many times and she had proved so conclusively the impossibility of their squeezing into a flat. Men never stay convinced!

"Or board."

"Never!" she said firmly.

"You will have to choose."

This was the leading topic of their discussion, and enough has been said to reveal the lines along which it developed. There was much of a discursive nature, naturally, introduced by Bessie, who sought thereby to fog the issue and effect a compromise. She had found that was a good way to deal with a husband. But to-night Falkner kept steadily at his object.

"No, no, no!" he iterated in weary cadence. "It's no use to keep on expecting; five thousand is all they will pay me, and it is all I am really worth to them. And after this terminal work is finished, they may have nothing to offer me. . . . We must make a clean sweep to start afresh, right, on the proper basis." After a moment, he added by way of appeal, "And I think that will be the best for us, also."

"You expect me to do all the work?"

"Expect!" Falkner leaned his head wearily against the chair-back. Words seemed useless at this point. Bessie continued rather pitilessly:—

"Don't you want a home? Don't you want your children brought up decently with friends about them?"

"God knows I want a home!" the husband murmured.

"I think I have made a very good one,—other people think so."

"That's the trouble — too good for me!"

"I should think it would be an incentive for a man —"

"God!" Falkner thundered; "that you should say that!"

It had been in her heart a long time, but she had never dared to express it before, — the feeling that other men, no abler than Rob, contrived to give their wives, no more seductive than she, so much more than she had had.

"Other men find the means —"

She was thinking of John Lane, of Purrington, — a lively young broker of their acquaintance, — of Dr. Larned, — all men whose earning power had leaped ahead of Falkner's. Bessie resented the economic dependence of married women on their husbands. She believed in the foreign *dot* system. "My daughters shall never marry as I did," she would say frankly to her friends. "There can be no perfectly happy marriage unless the woman is independent of her husband in money matters to a certain extent." . . . For she felt that she had a right to her ideals, so long as they were not bad, vicious; a right to her own life as distinct from her husband's life, or the family life. "The old idea of the woman's complete subordination has gone," she would say. "It is better for the men, too, that women are no longer mere possessions without wills of their own." It was such ideas as this that earned for Bessie among her acquaintances the reputation of being "intelligent" and "modern."

And Falkner, a vision of the mountains and the lonely cabin before his eyes, remarked with ironic calm: —

"And why should I earn more than I do, assuming that I could sell myself at a higher figure?"

For the man, too, had his dumb idea, — the feeling that something precious inside him was being murdered by this pressing struggle to earn more, always more. As man he did not accept the simple theory that men were better off the harder they were pushed, that the male brute needed the spur of necessity to function, that all the man was good for was to be the competent forager. No! Within him there was a protest to the whole spirit of his times, — to the fierce competitive struggle. Something inside him proclaimed that he was not a mere maker of dollars, that life was more than food and lodging, even for those he loved most.

"What do I get out of it?" he added bitterly. "Perhaps I have done too much."

"Oh, if that is the way you feel, — if you don't love me!" Bessie exclaimed with wounded pride. "Probably you are tired of me. When a man is sick of his wife, he finds his family a burden, naturally."

And there they paused at the brink of domestic vulgarity.

Falkner saw the girl on the veranda of the mountain hotel, with her golden hair, her fresh complexion, her allurement. Bessie, most men would think, was even more desirable this minute than then as an unformed girl. The arched eyebrows, so clearly marked, the full lips, the dimpled neck, all spake: —

"Come kiss me, and stop talking like that!"

For a moment the old lure seized the man, the call of the woman who had once been sweet to him. Then his blood turned cold within him. That was the last shame of marriage, — that a wife should throw this lure into the reasoning, a husband to console himself — that way! Falkner rose to his feet.

"I shall make arrangements to sell the house."

"Very well; then I shall take the children and go to my mother in Denver."

"As you please."

Without looking again at his wife, he left the room.

Bessie had played blindly her last card, the wife's last card, and lost! There was bitterness and rebellion in her heart. She had loved her husband, — hadn't she shown it by marrying him instead of the mine owner? She had been a good woman, not because she hadn't had her chances of other men's admiration, as she sometimes let her husband know. Dickie Lawton had made love to her outrageously, and the last time the old Senator had been in St. Louis, —

well, he would never come again to her house. Not a shadow of disloyalty had ever crossed her heart.

Bessie thought that a good wife must be chaste, of course; other matters of wifely duty were less distinct.

No! her husband did not care for her any more, — that was the real cause of their troubles. It was hard to wake up to such a fact after nine years of marriage with a man whom you loved!

There was a tragedy between, but not the one that Bessie suspected, nor the mere tragedy of extravagance. Each realized dimly that the other hindered rather than promoted that something within which each held tenaciously as most precious. Instead of giving mutually, they stole mutually, and the end of that sort of life must be concubinage or the divorce court — or a spiritual readjustment beyond the horizon of either Falkner or his wife.

"Did you know that the Falkners were going to give up their house?" Lane asked his wife.

"No, indeed. I saw Bessie at the symphony the other day, and she spoke of going out to Denver to visit her mother; but she didn't say anything about the house. Are you sure?"

"Yes; Falkner told Bainbridge he was selling it. And he wanted Bainbridge to see if there was an opening for him on the road in the East. I am afraid things haven't gone well with them."

"After all the trouble they had building, and such a pretty house! What a shame!"

Lane was in his outing clothes, about to go to the country club for an afternoon of golf with the Colonel. He looked very strong and handsome in his Scotch tweeds. Lately he had begun to take more exercise than he had found time for the first years of his marriage, had developed a taste for sport, and often found a day or two to fish or hunt when friends turned up from the East. Isabelle encouraged this taste, though she saw all the less of her husband; she had a feeling that it was good for him to relax, made him more of the gentleman, less of the hard-working clerk. The motor was at the door, but he dawdled.

"It is a pity about the Falkners, — I am afraid they are not getting on well together. He's a peculiar fellow. Bainbridge tells me his work is only pretty good, — doesn't put his back into it the way a man must who means to get up in his profession these days. There is a lot doing in his line, too. It will be a shame if trouble comes to Bessie."

"The old difficulty, I suppose," Isabelle remarked; "not enough money — same story everywhere!"

It was the same story everywhere, even in these piping times of prosperity, with fortunes doubling, salaries going up, and the country pouring out its wealth. So few of her friends, even the wealthy ones, seemed to have enough money for their necessities or desires. If they had four servants, they needed six; if they had one motor, they must have two; and the new idea of country houses had simply doubled or trebled domestic budgets. It wasn't merely in the homes of ambitious middle-class folk that the cry went up, — "We must have more!" Isabelle herself had begun to feel that the Colonel might very well have given her a package of stocks and bonds at her wedding. Even with her skilful management, and John's excellent salary, there was so much they could not do that seemed highly desirable to do. "Everything costs so these days!" And to live meant to spend, — to live!

CHAPTER XXIV

Isabelle did not go to Vickers as she firmly intended to that summer. Lane offered a stubborn if silent opposition to the idea of her joining her brother, — "so long as that woman is with him." He could not understand Isabelle's passionate longing for her brother, nor the fact that his loyalty to his mistake endeared Vickers all the more to her. She divined the ashes in her brother's heart, the waste in which he dwelt, and the fact that he "had made a complete mess of life" did not subtract from her love. After all, did the others, their respectable acquaintance, often make much of living?

It was not John's opposition, however, that prevented the journey, but the alarming weakness of the Colonel. In spite of his activity and his exercise the old man had been growing perceptibly weaker, and his digestive trouble had developed until the doctors hinted at cancer. To leave the Colonel now and go to the son he had put out of his life would be mere brutality. Vickers might come back, but Mrs. Price felt that this would cause the Colonel more pain than pleasure.

During the spring Isabelle made many expeditions about the city in company with her father, who gave as an excuse for penetrating all sorts of new neighborhoods that he wished to look at his real estate, which was widely scattered. But this was merely an excuse, as Isabelle easily perceived; what he really cared about was to see the city itself, the building, the evidences of growth, of thriving.

"When your mother and I came to live in the city," he would say, laying a large white hand on his daughter's knee, "it was all swamp out this way, — we used to bring Ezra with us in the early spring and pick pussy-willows. Now look at it!" And what Isabelle saw, when she looked in the direction that the old man waved his hand, was a row of ugly brick apartment houses or little suburban cottages, or brick stores and tenements. There was nothing in the scene, for her, to inspire enthusiasm, and yet the Colonel would smile and gaze fondly out of those kindly blue eyes at the acres of human hive. It was not pride in his shrewd foresight in investing his money, so much as a generous sympathy for the growth of the city, the forthputting of a strong organism.

"I bought this tract in eighty-two," he said, pointing to a stretch of factories and grain elevators. "Had to borrow part of the money to do it. Parrott thought I was a fool, but I knew the time would come when it would be sold by the foot, — folks are born and must work and live," he mused. He made the man drive the car slowly through the rutty street while he looked keenly at the hands pouring from the mills, the elevators, the railroad yards. "Too many of those Polaks," he commented, "but they are better than niggers. It is a great country!"

In the old man's pride there was more than selfish satisfaction, more than flamboyant patriotism over his "big" country; there was an almost pathetic belief in the goodness of life, merely as life. These breeding millions, in this teeming country, were working out their destiny, — on the whole a better destiny than the world had yet seen. And the old man, who had lived his life and fought vitally, felt deep in the inner recesses of his being that all was good; the more chance for the human organism to be born and work out its day, the better. In the eyes of the woman of the newer generation this was a singular pantheism, — incomprehensible. Unless one were born under favorable conditions, what good was there in the struggle? Mere life was not interesting.

They went, too, to see the site of the coming Exposition. The great trees were being cut down and uprooted to give space for the vast buildings. The Colonel lamented the loss of the trees. "Your mother and I used to come out here Sundays in summer," he said regretfully. "It was a great way from town then — there was only a steam road — and those oaks were grateful, after the heat. I used to lie on the ground and your mother would read to me. She had a very sweet voice, Isabelle!"

But he believed in the Exposition, even if the old trees must be sacrificed for it. He had contributed largely to the fund, and had been made a director, though the days of his leadership were over. "It is good for people to see how strong they are," he said. "These fairs are our Olympic games!"

At first he did not wish to leave the city, which was part of his bone and flesh; but as the summer drew on and he was unable to endure the motor his thoughts turned back to his Connecticut hills, to the old farm and the woods and the fields. Something deeper than all was calling to him to return to the land that was first in his blood. So they carried him — now a bony simulacrum of his vigorous self — to the old house at Grafton. For a few weeks he lay wrapped in rugs on the veranda, his eyes on Dog Mountain. At first he liked to talk with the farm-hands, who slouched past the veranda. But more and more his spirit withdrew even from this peaceful scene of his activity, and at last he died, as one who has no more concern about life. . . .

To Isabelle, who had been with him constantly these last fading months, there was much that remained for a long time inexplicable in her father's attitude towards life. He seemed to regret nothing, not even the death of his elder son, nor his estrangement from Vickers, and he had little of the old man's pessimism. There were certain modern manifestations that she knew he disliked; but he seemed to have a fine tolerance even for them, as being of no special concern to him. He had lived his life, such as it was, without swerving, without doubts or hesitations, which beset the younger generation, and now that it was over he had neither regret nor desire to grasp more.

When the Colonel's will was opened, it caused surprise not only in his family, but in the city where he had lived. It was long talked about. In the first place his estate was much larger than even those nearest him had supposed; it mounted upwards from eight millions. The will apparently had been most carefully considered, largely rewritten after the departure of Vickers. His son was not mentioned in the document. Nor were there the large bequests, at least outright, to charities that had been expected of so public spirited a man. The will was a document in the trust field. To sum it all up, it seemed as if the old man had little faith in the immediate generation, even in his daughter and her successful husband. For he left Isabelle only the farm at Grafton and a few hundred thousand dollars. To be sure, after his wife's death the bulk of the estate would be held in trust for her child, or children, should her marriage prove more fruitful in the future. Failing heirs, he willed that the bulk of the estate should go to certain specified charities, — an Old Man's Home, The Home for Crippled Children, etc. And it was arranged that the business should be continued under the direction of the trustees. The name of Parrott and Price should still stand for another generation!

"A singular will!" Lane, who was one of the trustees, said to his wife.

Isabelle was more hurt than she cared to have known. She had always supposed that some day she would be a rich woman in her own right. But it was the silent comment, the mark of disapproval, that she read in the lines of the will which hurt. The Colonel had never criticised, never chided her; but she had felt at times that he did not like the kind of life she had elected to lead latterly.

"He thought we were extravagant, probably," she replied to her husband.

"I can't see why, — we never went to him for help!"

She knew that was not exactly the reason, — extravagance. The old man did not like the modern spirit — at least the spirit of so many of her friends — of spending for themselves. The Colonel did not trust the present generation; he preferred that his money should wait until possibly the passing of the years had brought wisdom.

"A selfish will!" the public said.

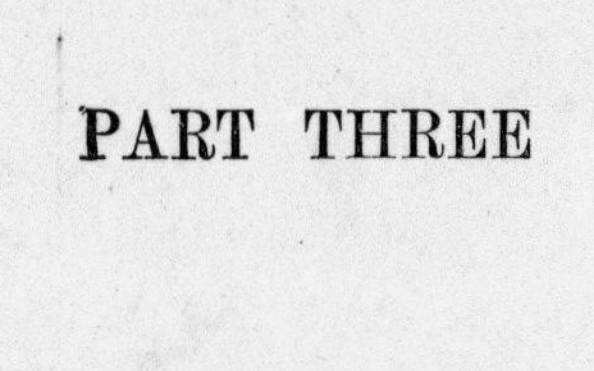

PART THREE

CHAPTER XXV

Fosdick had called Cornelia Woodyard the "Vampire," — why, none of her admirers could say. She did not look the part this afternoon, standing before the fire in her library, negligently holding a cup of tea in one hand, while she nibbled gourmandizingly at a frosted cake. She had come in from an expedition with Cairy, and had not removed her hat and gloves, merely letting her furs slip off to the floor. While she had her tea, Cairy was looking through the diamond panes of a bank of windows at a strip of small park, which was dripping in the fog of a dubious December day. Conny, having finished her tea, examined lazily some notes, pushed them back into their envelopes with a disgusted curl of her long lips, and glancing over her shoulder at Cairy drawled in an exhausted voice: —

"Poke the fire, please, Tommy!"

Cairy did as he was told, then lighted a cigarette and stood expectantly. Conny seemed lost in a maze of dreary thoughts, and the man looked about the room for amusement. It was a pleasant little room, with sufficient color of flowers and personal disorderliness of letters and books and papers to soften the severity of the Empire furniture. Evidently the architect who had done over this small down-town house had been supplemented by the strong hand of its mistress. Outside and inside he had done his best to create something French out of the old-fashioned New York block house, but Cornelia Woodyard had Americanized his creation enough to make it intimate, livable.

"Can't you say something, Tommy?" Conny murmured in her childish treble.

"I have said a good deal first and last, haven't I?"

"Don't be cross, Tommy! I am down on my job to-day."

"Suppose you quit it! Shall we go to the Bahamas? Or Paris? Or Rio?"

"Do you think that you could manage the excursion, Tommy?" Although she smiled good-naturedly, the remark seemed to cut. The young man slumped into a chair and leaned his head on his hands.

"Besides, where would Percy come in?"

Cairy asked half humorously, "And where, may I ask, do I come in?"

"Oh, Tommy, don't look like that!" Conny complained. "You *do* come in, you know!"

Cairy brought his chair and placed himself near the fire; then leaned forward, looking intently into the woman's eyes.

"I think sometimes the women must be right about you, you know."

"What do they say?"

. . . "That you are a calculating machine, — one of those things they have in banks to do arithmetic stunts!"

"No, you don't, . . . silly! Tell me what Gossom said about the place."

"He didn't say much about that; he talked about G. Lafayette Gossom and *The People's Magazine* chiefly. . . . The mess of pottage is three hundred a month. I am to be understudy to the great fount of ideas. When he has an inspiration he will push a bell, and I am to run and catch it as it flows red hot from his lips and put it into shape, — if I can."

Cairy nursed his injured leg with a disgusted air.

"Don't sniff, Tommy, — there are lots of men who would like to be in your shoes."

"I know. . . . Oh, I am not ungrateful for my daily bread. I kiss the hand that found it, — the hand of power!"

"Silly! Don't be literary with me. Perhaps I put the idea into old Noddy Gossom's head when he was here the other night. You'll have to humor him, listen to his pomposity. But he has made a success of that *People's Magazine*. It is an influence, and it pays!"

"Four hundred thousand a year, chiefly automobile and corset ads, I should say."

"Nearly half a million a year!" Conny cried with the air of 'See what I have done for you!'

"Yes!" the Southerner remarked with scornful emphasis. . . . "I shall harness myself once more to the car of triumphant prosperity, and stretch forth my hungry hands to catch the grains that dribble in the rear. Compromise! Compromise! All is Compromise!"

"Now you are literary again," Conny pronounced severely. "Your play wasn't a success, — there was no compromise about that! The managers don't want your new play. Gossom does want your little articles. You have to live, and you take the best you can get, — pretty good, too."

"Madam Materialist!"

Conny made a little face, and continued in the same lecturing tone.

"Had you rather go back to that cross-roads in the Virginia mountains — something Court-house — or go to London and write slop home to the papers, as Ted Stevens does?"

"You know why I don't go back to the something Court-house and live on corn-bread and bacon!" Cairy sat down once more very near the blond woman and leaned forward slowly. Conny's mouth relaxed, and her eyes softened.

"You are dear," she said with a little laugh; "but you are silly about things." As the young man leaned still farther forward, his hand touching her arm, Conny's large brown eyes opened speculatively on him. . . .

The other night he had kissed her for the first time, that is, really kissed her in unequivocal fashion, and she had been debating since whether she should mention the matter to Percy. The right moment for such a confidence had not yet come. She must tell him some day. She prided herself that her relation with her husband had always been honest and frank, and this seemed the kind of thing he ought to know about, if she were going to keep that relation what it had been. She had had tender intimacies — "emotional friendships," her phrase was — before this affair with Cairy. They had always been perfectly open: she had lunched and dined them, so to speak, in public as well as at the domestic table. Percy had rather liked her special friends, had been nice to them always.

But looking into the Southerner's eyes, she felt that there was something different in this case; it had troubled her from the time he kissed her, it troubled her now — what she could read in his eyes. He would not be content with that "emotional friendship" she had given the others. Perhaps, and this was the strangest thrill in her consciousness, she might not be content to have him satisfied so easily. . . . Little Wrexton Grant had sent her flowers and written notes — and kissed her strong fingers, once. Bertie Sollowell had dedicated one of his books to her (the author's copy was somewhere in Percy's study), and hinted that his life missed the guiding hand that she could have afforded him. He had since found a guiding hand that seemed satisfactory. Dear old Royal Salters had squired her, bought her silver in Europe, and Jevons had painted her portrait the year he opened his studio in New York, and kissed a very beautiful white shoulder, — purely by way of compliment to the shoulder. All these marks of gallantry had been duly reported to Percy, and laughed at together by husband and wife in that morning hour when Conny had her coffee in bed. Nevertheless, they had touched her vanity, as evidences that she was still attractive as a woman. No woman — few women at any rate — of thirty-one resents the fact that some man other than her husband can feel tenderly towards her. And "these friends" — the special ones — had all been respecters of the law; not one would have thought of coveting his neighbor's wife, any more than of looting his safe.

But with Tom Cairy it was different. Not merely because he was Southern and hence presumably ardent in temperament, nor because of his reputation for being "successful" with women; not wholly because he appealed to her on account of his physical disability, — that unfortunate slip by the negro nurse. But because there was in this man the strain of feminine understanding, of vibrating sentiment — the lyric chord of temperament — which made him lover first and last! That is why he had stirred most women he had known well, — women in whom the emotional life had been dormant, or unappeased, or petrified.

"You are such a dear!" Conny murmured, looking at him with her full soft eyes, realizing in her own way that in this fragile body there was the soul of the lover, — born to love, to burn in some fashion before some altar, always.

The special aroma that Cairy brought to his love-making was this sense that for the time it was all there was in life, that it shut out past and future. The special woman enveloped by his sentiment did not hear the steps of other women echoing through outer rooms. She was, for the moment, first and last. He was able to create this emotional delusion genuinely; for into each new love he poured himself, like a fiery liquor, that swept the heart clean.

"Dearest," he had murmured that night to Conny, "you are wonderful, — woman and man, — the soul of a woman, the mind of a man! To love you is to love life."

And Conny, in whose ears the style of lover's sighs was immaterial, was stirred with an unaccountable feeling. When Cairy put his hand on hers, and his lips quivered beneath his mustache, her face inevitably softened and her eyes widened like a child's eyes. For Conny, even Conny, with her robust intelligence and strong will to grasp that out of life which seemed good to her, wanted to love — in a way she had never loved before. Like many women she had passed thirty with a husband of her choice, two children, and an establishment entirely of her making before she became aware that she had missed something on the way, — a something that other women had. She had seen Severine Wilson go white when a certain man entered the room — then light brilliantly with joy when his eyes sought her. . . . That must be worth having, too! . . .

Her relations with her husband were perfect, — she had said so for years and every one said the same thing about the Woodyards. They were very intimate friends, close comrades. She knew that Percy respected and admired her more than any woman in the world, and paid her the last flattery of conceding to her will, respecting her intelligence. But there was something that he had not done, could not do, and that was a something that Cairy seemed able to do, — give her a sensation partly physical, wholly emotional, like the effect of stimulant, touching every nerve. Conny, with her sure grasp of herself, however, had no mind to submit blindly to this intoxication; she would examine it, like other matters, — was testing it now in her capacious intelligence, as the man bent his eyes upon her, so close to her lips.

Had she only been the "other sort," the conventional ordinary sort, she would have either gulped her sensation blindly, — "let herself go," — or trembled with horror and run away as from some evil thing. Being as she was, modern, intellectual, proudly questioning all maxims, she kept this new phenomenon in her hand, saying, "What does it mean for *me?*" The note of the Intellectuals!

CHAPTER XXVI

There was the soft sound of a footstep on the padded stairs, and Percy Woodyard glanced into the room.

"Hello, Tom!" he said briskly, and crossed to Conny, whose smooth brow he touched softly with the tips of his fingers. "How goes it, Tom?"

"You are home early," Conny complained in her treble drawl.

"Must go to Albany to-night," Percy explained, a weary note in his voice. "Not dining out to-night, Tom?"

It was a little joke they had, that when Cairy was not with them he was "dining out." . . .

When Cairy had left, Conny rose from her lounging position as if to resume the burden of life.

"It's the Commission?" she inquired.

"Yes! I sent you the governor's letter."

For a time they discussed the political situation in the new Commission, to which Woodyard had recently been appointed, his first conspicuous public position. Then his wife observed wearily: "I was at Potts's this morning and saw Isabelle Lane there. She was in mourning."

"Her father died, — you know we saw it in the papers."

"She must be awfully rich."

"He left considerable property, — I don't know to whom."

"Well, they are in New York. Her husband has been made something or other in the railroad, so they are going to live here."

"He is a very able man, I am told."

After a time Conny drawled: "I suppose we must have 'em here to dinner, — they are at a hotel up town. Whom shall we have?"

Evidently after due consideration Conny had concluded

that the Lanes must come under her cognizance. She ran over half a dozen names from her best dinner list, and added, "And Tom."

"Why Tom this time?" Percy demanded.

"He's met Isabelle — and we always have Tommy! You aren't jealous, are you, Percy?" She glanced at him in amusement.

"I must dress," Percy observed negligently, setting down his cup of tea.

"Come here and tell me you are not jealous," Conny commanded. As her husband smiled and brushed her fair hair with his lips, she muttered, "You silly!" just as she had to Cairy's unreasonableness. Why! She was Percy's destiny and he knew it. . . . She had a contempt for people who ruffled themselves over petty emotions. This sex matter had been exaggerated by Poets and Prudes, and their hysterical utterances should not inhibit her impulses.

Nevertheless she did not consider it a suitable opportunity to tell Percy about the kiss.

Percy Woodyard and Cornelia Pallanton had married on a new, radical basis. They had first met in the house of an intellectual woman, the wife of a university professor, where clever young persons were drawn in and taught to read Schopenhauer and Nietzsche, Ibsen and George Moore, and to engage gracefully in perilous topics. They had been rather conscious that they were radicals, — "did their own thinking," as they phrased it, these young persons. They were not willing to accept the current morality, not even that part of it engraved in law; but so far as regarded all of morality that lay outside the domain of sex their actions were not in conflict with society, though they were Idealists, and in most cases Sentimentalists. But in the matter of sex relation, which is the knot of the tangle for youth, they believed in the "development of the individual." It must be determined by him, or her, whether this development could be obtained best through regular or irregular relations.

The end of all this individual development? "The fullest activity, the largest experience, the most complete presentation of personality," etc. Or as Fosdick railed, "Suck all and spit out what you don't like!"

So when these two young souls had felt sufficiently moved, one to the other, to contemplate marriage, they had had an "understanding": they would go through with the customary formula and oaths of marriage, to please their relatives and a foolish world; but neither was to be "bound" by any such piece of silly archaism as the marriage contract. Both recognized that both had diversified natures, which might require in either case more varied experience than the other could give. In their enlightened affection for each other, neither would stand in the light of the other's best good. . . . There are many such young people, in whom intellectual pride has erased deeper human instincts. But as middle life draws on, they conform — or seek refuge in the divorce court.

Neither Percy nor Cornelia had any intention of practising adultery as a habit: they merely wished to be honest with themselves, and felt superior to the herd in recognizing the errant or variant possibilities in themselves. Conny took pleasure in throwing temptation in Percy's way, in encouraging him to know other women, — secretly gratified that he proved hopelessly domestic. And on her side we have seen the innocent lengths to which she had hitherto gone.

For it proved as life began in earnest for these two that much of their clear philosophy crumbled. Instead of the vision of feminine Idealism that the young lawyer had worshipped, Conny developed a neat, practical nature, immensely capable of "making things go." As her husband was the most obvious channel through which things could move, her husband became her chief care. She had no theory of exploiting him, — she had no theories at all. She saw him as so much capacity to be utilized. Just as she never was entrapped into a useless acquaintance, never had a "wrong person" at her house, never wasted her energies on the mere ebullition of good feeling, so she never allowed Percy to waste his energies on fruitless works. Everything must count. Their life was a pattern of simple and pronounced design, from the situation of their house to the footing on which it was established and the people who were encouraged to attach themselves there.

Woodyard had been interested in social good works, and as a young man had served the Legal Aid Society. A merely worldly woman would have discouraged this mild weakness for philanthropy. But Conny knew her material; out of such as Percy, corporation lawyers — those gross feeders at the public trough — were not made. Woodyard was a man of fine fibre, rather unaggressive. He must either be steered into a shady pool of legal sinecure, or take the more dangerous course through the rapids of public life. It was the moment of Reform. Conny realized the capabilities of Reform, and Percy's especial fitness for it; Reform, if not remunerative, was fashionable and prominent.

So Conny had steered their little bark, hoisting sail to every favorable wind, no matter how slight the puff, until Woodyard now was a minor figure in the political world. When his name occurred in the newspapers, a good many people knew who he was, and his remarks at dinners and his occasional speeches were quoted from, if there was not more valuable matter. He had been spoken of for Congress. (Conny, of course, would never permit him to engulf himself in that hopeless sea.) Just what Conny designed as the ultimate end, she herself did not know; like all great generals, she was an opportunist and took what seemed to her worth taking from the fortunes of the day. The last good thing which had floated up on her shore was this Commissionership. She had fished that up with the aid of the amiable Senator, who had spoken a word here and a word there in behalf of young Woodyard.

Conny was very well pleased with herself as a wife, and she knew that her husband was pleased with her. Moreover, she had not the slightest intention of permitting anything to interfere with her wifely duties as she saw them. . . .

Percy had gone upstairs to that roof story where in New York children are housed, to see his boy and girl. He was very fond of his children. When he came down, his thoughtful face was worried.

"The kids seem always to have colds," he remarked.

"I know it," Conny admitted. "I must take them to Dr. Snow to-morrow." (They had their own doctor, and also their own throat specialist.)

"I wonder if it is good for them here, so far down in the city, — they have only that scrap of park to play in."

Conny, who had been over this question a good many times, answered irrefutably, —

"There seem to be a good many children growing up all right in the same conditions."

She knew that Percy would like some excuse to escape into the country. Conny had no liking for suburban life, and with her husband's career at the critical point the real country was out of the question.

"I suppose Jack will have to go to boarding school another year," Percy said with a sigh.

He was not a strong man himself, though of solid build and barely thirty. He had that bloodless whiteness of skin so often found among young American men, which contrasted with his dark mustache, and after a long day's work like this his step dragged. He wore glasses over his blue eyes, and when he removed them the dark circles could be seen. Conny knew the limits of his strength and looked carefully to his physical exercise.

"You didn't get your squash this afternoon?"

When Percy was worried about anything, she immediately searched for a physical cause.

"No! I had to finish up things at the office so that I could get away to-night."

Then husband and wife went to their dinner, and Woodyard gave Conny a short-hand account of his doings, the people he had seen, what they had said, the events at the office. Conny required this account each day, either in the morning or in the evening. And Woodyard yielded quite unconsciously to his wife's strong will, to her singularly definite idea of "what is best." He admired her deeply, was grateful to her for that complete mastery of the detail of life which she had shown, aware that if it were not for the dominating personality of this woman he had somehow had the good fortune to marry, life would have been a smaller matter for him.

"Con," he said when they had gone back to the library for their coffee, "I am afraid this Commission is going to be ticklish business."

"Why?" she demanded alertly.

"There are some dreadful grafters on it,— I suspect that the chairman is a wolf. I suspect further that it has been arranged to whitewash certain rank deals."

"But why should the governor have appointed you?"

"Possibly to hold the whitewash brush."

"You think that the Senator knows that?"

"You can't tell where the Senator's tracks lead."

"Well, don't worry! Keep your eyes open. You can always resign, you know."

Woodyard went off to his train after kissing his wife affectionately. Conny called out as he was getting into his coat:—

"Will you be back Sunday? Shall I have the Lanes then?"

"Yes, — and you will go to the Hillyers to-morrow?"

"I think so, — Tom will take me."

After the door closed Conny went to her desk and wrote the note to Isabelle. Then after meditating a few moments, more notes of invitation. She had decided on her combination, — Gossom, the Silvers, the Hillyers (to get them off her mind), Senator Thomas, and Cairy. She did not take Percy's objection to Tom seriously.

She had decided to present a variety of people to the Lanes. Isabelle and she had never been intimate, and Conny had a woman's desire to show an accomplished superiority to the rich friend, who had been inclined to snub her in boarding school. Conny was eminently skilful in "combinations." Every one that composed her circle or even entered it might some day be of use in creating what is called "publicity." That, as Cornelia Woodyard felt, was the note of the day. "You must be talked about by the right people, if you want to be heard, if you want your show!" she had said to Cairy. Thanks to Lane's rapid rise in the railroad corporation, Isabelle had come legitimately within the zone of interest.

After she had settled this matter to her satisfaction, she turned to some house accounts and made various calculations. It was a wonder to every one who knew them how the Woodyards "could do so much on what they had." As a matter of fact, with the rising scale of living, it required all Conny's practical adroitness to make the household come out nearly even. Thanks to a great-aunt who admired Percy, they had been able to buy this house and alter it over, and with good business judgment it had been done so that the property was now worth nearly a third more than when they took it. But a second man-servant had been added, and Conny felt that she must have a motor; she pushed away the papers and glanced up, thinking, planning.

The Senator and she had talked investments the last time they had met. She had a little money of her own. If the old fox would only take it and roll it up into a big snowball! Isabelle, now, with all that wealth! Conny pursed her lips in disgust to think that so much of the ammunition of war had fallen into such incompetent hands. "Yes," she said to herself, "the Senator must show me how to do it." Perhaps it flitted vaguely through her mind that Percy might object to using stock market tips from the Senator. But Percy must accept her judgment on this matter. They could not go on any longer with only twenty thousand a year.

Turning out the lights, she went to her bedroom. It was very plain and bare, with none of the little toilette elegances or chamber comforts that women usually love. Conny never spent except where it showed saliently. Her evening gowns were sometimes almost splendid, but her dressing gowns were dowdy, and poor little Bessie Falkner spent twice as much on lingerie.

Having discharged the duties of her day, her mind returned to Cairy, to his work for Gossom, to his appealing self, and her lips relaxed in a gentle smile. Hers was a simple nature, the cue once caught. She had come of rather plain people, who knew the worth of a dollar, and had spent their lives saving or investing money. The energy of the proletariat had been handed to her undiminished. The blood was evident in the large bones, the solid figure, and tenacious fingers, as well as in the shrewdness with which she had created this household. It was her instinct to push out into the troubled waters of the material world. She never weakened herself by questioning values. She knew — what she wanted.

Nevertheless, as she reached up her hand to turn out the night light, she was smiling with dreamy eyes, and her thoughts were no longer practical!

CHAPTER XXVII

When Isabelle emerged from the great hotel and turned down the avenue to walk to the office of Dr. Potts, as he required her to do every day, she had a momentary thrill of exultation. Descending the gentle incline, she could see a good part of the city extending into a distant blue horizon before her. The vast buildings rose like islands in the morning mist. It reminded her, this general panorama, of the awe-compelling spaces of the Arizona cañon into which she had once descended. Here were the same irregular, beetling cliffs, the same isolated crags, with sharply outlined lower and minor levels of building. The delicate blue, the many grays of storm and mist gave it color, also. But in place of the cañon's eternal quiet, — the solitude of the remote gods, — this city boiled and hummed. That, too, — the realization of multitudinous humanity, — made Isabelle's pulses leap.

In spite of her poor health, she had the satisfaction of at last being here, in the big hive, where she had wished to be so long. She was a part of it, a painfully insignificant mite as yet, but still a part of it. Hitherto New York had been a sort of varied hotel, an entertainment. Now it was to be her scene, and she had begun already to take possession. It had all come about very naturally, shortly after her father's death. While she was dreading the return to St. Louis, which must be emptier than ever without the Colonel, and she and her mother were discussing the possibility of Europe, John's new position had come. A Western road had made him an offer; for he had a splendid record as a "traffic getter." The Atlantic and Pacific could not lose him; they gave him the third vice-presidency with headquarters in New York and general charge of traffic. Thus the Lanes' horizon shifted, and it was decided that the first year in the city they should spend in a hotel with Mrs. Price. Isabelle's health was again miserable; there had been the delayed operation; and now she was in the care of the famous Potts, trying to recover from the operation, from the old fatigue and the recent strains, "to be made fit."

The move to New York had not meant much to Lane. He had spent a great deal of his time there these last years, as well as in Washington, Pittsburg, — in this city and that, — as business called him. His was what is usually regarded as a cosmopolitan view of life, — it might better be called a hotel-view. Home still meant to him the city where his wife and child were temporarily housed, but he was equally familiar with half a dozen cities. Isabelle, too, had the same rootless feeling. She had spent but a short time in any one place since she had left her father's house to go to St. Mary's. That is the privilege or the curse of the prosperous American. Life thus becomes a shifting panorama of surfaces. Even in the same city there are a dozen spots where the family ark has rested, which for the sake of a better term may be called "homes." That sense of rooted attachment which comes from long habituation to one set of physical images is practically a lost emotion to Americans. . . .

There were days when New York roared too loudly for Isabelle's nerves, when the jammed streets, the buzzing shops, the overflowing hotels and theatres, made her long for quiet. Then she thought of the Farm as the most stable memory of a fixed condition, and she had an unformed plan of "doing over" the old place, which was now her own, and making it the centre of the family's centrifugal energy. Meantime there was the great Potts, who promised her health, and the flashing charm of the city.

Occasionally she felt lonely in this packed procession, this hotel existence, with its multitude of strange faces, and longed for something familiar, even Torso! At such times when she saw the face of an old acquaintance, perhaps in a cab at a standstill in the press of the avenue, her heart warmed. Even a fleeting glimpse of something known was a relief. Clearly she must settle herself into this whirlpool, put out her tentacles, and grasp an anchorage. But where? What?

One morning as she and her mother were making slow progress down the avenue, she caught sight of Margaret Pole on the sidewalk, waiting to cross the stream, a little boy's hand in hers. Isabelle waved to her frantically, and then leaped from the cab, dodged between the pushing motors, and grasped Margaret.

"You here!" she gasped.

"We came back some months ago," Margaret explained.

She was thin, Isabelle thought, and her face seemed much older than the years warranted. Margaret, raising her voice above the roar, explained that they were living out of town, "in the country, in Westchester," and promised to come to lunch the next time she was in the city. Then with a nod and a smile she slipped into the stream again as if anxious to be lost, and Isabelle rejoined her mother.

"She looks as if she were saving her clothes," Mrs. Price announced with her precise view of what she observed. Isabelle, while she waited for the doctor, mused on the momentary vision of her old friend at the street corner. Margaret turned up in the noise and mist of the city, as everybody might turn up; but Margaret old, worn, and almost shabby! Then the nurse came for her and she went into the doctor's room, with a depressing sensation compounded of a bad night, the city roar, the vision of Margaret.

"Well, my lady, what's the story to-day?"

Dr. Potts looked up from his desk, and scrutinized the new patient out of his shaggy eyebrows. Isabelle began at once the neurasthenic's involved and particularized tale of woe, breaking at the end with almost a sob: —

"I am so useless! I am never going to be well, — what is the matter with me?"

"So it's a bad world this morning, eh?" the doctor quizzed in an indulgent voice. "We'll try to make it better, — shake up the combination." He broke off suddenly and remarked in an ordinary, conversational voice: "Your friend Mrs. Woodyard was in here this morning, — a clever woman! My, but she is clever!"

"What is the matter with her?"

"Same thing,—Americanitis; but she'll pull out if she will give herself half a chance."

Then he returned to Isabelle, wrote her a prescription, talked to her for ten minutes, and when she left the office she felt better, was sure it would "all come out right."

The great Dr. Potts! He served as God to several hundred neurasthenic women. Born in a back street of a small town, he had emerged into the fashionable light after prodigious labor and exercise of will. Physically he stood six feet, with a heavy head covered with thick black hair, and deep-set black eyes. He had been well educated professionally, but his training, his medical attainments, had little to do with his success. He had the power to look through the small souls of his women patients, and he found generally Fear, and sometimes Hypocrisy, — a desire to evade, to get pleasure and escape the bill. These he bullied. Others he found struggling, feeble of purpose, desiring light, willingly confessing their weakness, and begging for strength. These he despised; he gave them drugs and flattered them. There were some, like Conny, who were perfectly poised, with a plain philosophy of selfishness. These he understood, being of fellow clay, and plotted with them how to entrap what they desired.

Power! That was Potts's keynote, — power, effectiveness, accomplishment, at any and all cost. He was the spirit of the city, nay of the country itself! "Results — get results at all costs," that was the one lesson of life which he had learned from the back street, where luckier men had shouldered him. . . . "I must supply backbone," he would say to his patients. "I am your temporary dynamo!"

To Isabelle this mass of energy, Dr. Alexander Potts, seemed like the incarnate will to live of the great city. After her visit at his office she came out into the sharp air, the shrill discords of the busy streets, attuned — with purpose, — "I am going to be well now! I am going to do this. Life will arrange itself, and at last I shall be able to live as others live." This borrowed purpose might last the day out, and she would plunge into a dozen matters; or it might wear off in an hour or two. Then back she went the next day to be keyed up once more.

"Do something! Deliver the goods, no matter what goods or how you get them into the premises!" Potts thundered, beating the desk in the energy of his lecture. "Live! That's what we must all do. Never mind *how* you live, — don't waste good tissue worrying over that. *Live!*"

Dr. Potts was an education to Isabelle. His moods of brutality and of sympathy came like the shifting shadows of a gusty day. His perfectly material philosophy frightened her and allured her. He was Mephistopheles, — one hand on the medicine chest of life, the other pointing satirically towards the towered city.

"See, my child," he purred; "I will tinker this little toy of your body for you; then run along down there and play with your brothers and sisters."

In the mood of reaction that the neurasthenic must meet, the trough of the wave, Isabelle doubted. Potts had not yet found the key to her mechanism; the old listless cloud befogged her still. After a sleepless night she would sit by her window, high up in the mountain of stone, and look out over the city, its voice dull at this hour of dawn, — a dozing monster. Something like terror filled her at these times, fear of herself, of the slumbering monster, so soon to wake and roar. "Act, do!" thundered Potts; "don't think! Live and get what you want." . . . Was that all? The peaceful pastures at Grafton, the still September afternoon when the Colonel died, the old man himself, — there was something in them beyond mere energy, quite outside the Potts philosophy.

Once she ventured to suggest this doubt to Cornelia

Woodyard, who, being temporarily in need of a bracer, had resorted to "old Pot." She had planned to go to the opera that night and wanted to "be herself."

"I wonder if he's right about it all," said Isabelle; "if we are just machines, with a need to be oiled now and then, — to take this drug or that? Is it all as simple as he makes out? All just autointoxication, chemistry, and delusion?"

"You're ill, — that's why you doubt," Conny replied with tranquil positiveness. "When you've got the poison out of your system, you'll see, or rather you won't see crooked, — won't have ideas."

"It's all a formula?"

Conny nodded, shutting her large mouth firmly.

"And he has the key. You are merely an organ, and he pulls out this stop or that; gives you one thing to take and then another. You tell him this dotty idea you've got in your head and he'll pull the right stop to shake it out."

"I wonder! Some days I feel that I must go away by myself, get out of all the noise, and live up among the mountains far off —"

She stopped. For Conny was not one to whom to confide a longing for the stars and the winds in the pines and the scent of the earth. Such vaporing would be merely another symptom!

"What would you go mooning off by yourself for? You'd be crazy, for a fact. Better come down to Palm Beach with me next month."

The great Potts had the unfortunate habit of gossiping about his patients with one another. He had said to Conny: "Your friend Isabelle interests me. I should say that she had a case of festering conscience." He crossed his legs and gazed wisely up at the ceiling. "A rudimentary organ left over from her hard-working ancestors. She is inhibited, tied, thinks she can't do this and that. What she needs" — Potts had found the answer to his riddle and brought his eyes from the ceiling — "is a lover! Can't you find her one?"

"Women usually prefer to select *that* for themselves."

"Oh, no, — one is as good as another. What she needs is a counter-irritant. That husband of hers, what is he like?"

"Just husband, very successful, good-natured, gives her what she wants, — I should say they pull well together."

"That's it! He's one of the smooth, get-everything-the-dear-woman-wants kind, eh? And then busies himself about his old railroad? Well, it is the worst sort for her. She needs a man who will beat her."

"Is that what the lover would do?"

"Bless you, no! He would make her stop thinking she had an ache." When Conny went, the doctor came to the door with her and as he held her hand cried breezily: "Remember what I said about your friend. Look up some nice young man, who will hang around and make her think she's got a soul." He pressed Conny's hand and smiled.

CHAPTER XXVIII

When the Lanes went to Sunday luncheon at the Woodyards', the impression on Isabelle was exactly what Conny wished it to be. The little house had a distinct "atmosphere," Conny herself had an "atmosphere," and the people, who seemed much at home there and very gay, were what is termed "interesting." That is, each person had his ticket of "distinction," as Isabelle quickly found out. One was a lawyer whose name often appeared in the newspapers as counsel for powerful interests; another was a woman novelist, whose last book was then running serially in a magazine and causing discussion; a third — a small man with a boyish open face — Isabelle discovered with a thrill of delight was the Ned Silver whose clever little articles on the current drama she had read in a fashionable weekly paper.

Isabelle found her hostess leaning against the mantelpiece with the air of having just come in and discovered her guests.

"How are you, dearie?" she drawled in greeting. "This is Mr. Thomas Randall Cairy, Margaret's cousin, — do you remember? He says he has met you before, but Thomas usually believes he has met ladies whom he wants to know!" Then Conny turned away, and thereafter paid little attention to the Lanes, as though she wished them to understand that the luncheon was not given for them.

"In this case," Cairy remarked, "Mrs. Woodyard's gibe happens to miss. I haven't forgotten the Virginian hills, and I hope you haven't."

It was Cairy who explained the people to Isabelle: —

"There is Gossom, the little moth-eaten, fat man at the door. He is the mouthpiece of the *People's*, but he doesn't dislike to feast with the classes. He is probably telling

Woodyard at this moment what the President said to him last week about Princhard's articles on the distillery trust!"

Among the Colonel's friends the magazine reporter Princhard had been considered an ignorant and malicious liar. Isabelle looked eagerly as Cairy pointed him out, — a short, bespectacled man with a thin beard, who was talking to Silver.

"There is the only representative of the fashionable world present, Mrs. George Bertram, just coming in the door. We do not go in for the purely fashionable — yet," he remarked mockingly. "Mrs. Bertram is interested in music, — she has a history, too." . . .

By the time the company were ready to lunch, Isabelle's pulse had risen with excitement. She had known, hitherto, but two methods of assimilating friends and acquaintances, — pure friendship, a good-natured acceptance of those likable or endurable people fate threw in one's way; and fashion, — the desire to know people who were generally supposed to be the people best worth knowing. But here she perceived quickly there was a third principle of selection, — "interest." And as she glanced about the appointments of Conny's smart little house, her admiration for her old schoolmate rose. Conny evidently had a definite purpose in life, and had the power and intelligence to pursue it. To the purposeless person, such as Isabelle had been, the evidences of this power were almost mysterious.

At first the talk at the table went quite over Isabelle's head. It consisted of light gibe and allusion to persons and things she had never heard of, — a new actress whom the serious Percy was supposed to be in love with, Princhard's adventure with a political notability, a new very "American" play. Isabelle glanced apprehensively at her husband, who was at Conny's end of the table. Lane was listening appreciatively, now and then exchanging a remark with the lawyer across the table. John Lane had that solid acquaintance with life which made him at home in almost all circumstances. If he felt as she did, hopelessly countrified, he would never betray it. Presently the conversation got to politics, the President, the situation at Albany. Conny, with her negligent manner and her childish treble voice, gave the talk a poke here and there and steered it skilfully, never allowing it to get into serious pools or become mere noise. In one of the shifts Cairy asked Isabelle, "Have you seen Margaret since her return?"

"Yes; tell me why they came back!"

Cairy raised his eyebrows. "Too much husband, I should say, — shouldn't you?"

"I don't know him. Margaret seemed older, not strong, — what is the matter with us all!"

"You'll understand what is the matter with Margaret when you see Larry! And then she has three children, — an indecent excess, with her health and that husband." . . .

The company broke up after the prolonged luncheon almost at once, to Isabelle's regret; for she wished to see more of these people. As they strolled upstairs to the library Cairy followed her and said: —

"Are you going to Mrs. Bertram's with us? She has some music and people Sundays — I'll tell Mrs. Woodyard," and before she could reply he had slipped over to Conny. That lady glanced at Isabelle, smiled on Cairy, and nodded. What she said to Cairy was: "So you've got a new interest. Take care, Tommy, — you'll complicate your life!" But apparently she did not regard Isabelle seriously; for presently she was saying to her, "Mrs. Bertram wants me to bring you around with us this afternoon, — you'll like it."

Lane begged off and walked back to the hotel in company with the lawyer. After a time which was filled with the flutter of amiable little speeches, appointments, and good-bys, Isabelle found herself in company with the Silvers and Gossom, Cornelia and Cairy on her way to Mrs. Bertram's, which was "just around the corner," — that is, half a dozen blocks farther up town on Madison Avenue. Mrs. Silver was a pretty, girlish woman with a troubled face, who seemed to be making great efforts to be gay.

She and Cornelia called each other by first names, and when Isabelle asked about her later, Conny replied with a preoccupied drawl: —

"Yes, Annie Silver is a nice little thing, — an awful drag on him, you know. They haven't a dollar, and she is going to have a baby; she is in fits about it."

As a matter of fact Silver managed to earn by his swiftly flowing pen over four thousand dollars a year, without any more application than the average clerk.

"But in New York, you know!" as Conny explained. "They have lived in a little apartment, very comfortably, and know nice people. Their friends are good to them. But if they take to having children!" It meant, according to Conny's expressive gesture, suburban life, or something "way up town," "no friends." Small wonder that Annie Silver's face was drawn, and that she was making nervous efforts to keep up to the last. Isabelle felt that it must be a tragedy, and as Conny said, "Such a clever man, too!"

Mrs. Bertram's deep rooms were well filled, and Cairy, who still served as her monitor, told Isabelle that most of the women were merely fashionable. The men — and there was a good sprinkling of them — counted; they all had tickets of one sort or another, and he told them off with a keen phrase for each. When the music began, Isabelle found herself in a recess of the farther room with several people whom she did not know. Cairy had disappeared, and Isabelle settled back to enjoy the music and study the company. In the kaleidoscope of the day, however, another change was to come, — one that at the time made no special impression on her, but one that she was to remember years afterward.

A young man had been singing some songs. When he rose from the piano, the people near Isabelle began to chatter: —

"Isn't he good looking! . . . That was his own music, —

the Granite City . . . Can't you see the tall buildings, hear the wind sweeping from the sea and rushing through the streets!" etc. Presently there was a piece of music for a quartette. At its conclusion a voice said to Isabelle from behind her chair: —

"Pardon me, but do you know what that was?"

She looked over her shoulder expecting to see an acquaintance. The man who had spoken was leaning forwards, resting one elbow on her chair, his hand carelessly plucking his gray hair. He had deep piercing black eyes, and an odd bony face. In spite of his gray hair and lined face she saw that he was not old.

"Something Russian, I heard some one say," Isabelle replied.

"I don't like to sit through music and not know anything about it," the stranger continued with a delicate, deliberate enunciation. "I don't believe that I should be any wiser if I heard the name of the piece; but it flatters your vanity, I suppose, to know it. There is Carova standing beside Mrs. Bertram; he's going to sing."

"Who is Carova?" Isabelle demanded eagerly.

"The new tenor at the Manhattan, — you haven't heard him?"

"No," Isabelle faltered and felt ashamed as she added, "You see I am almost a stranger in New York."

"Mrs. Bertram knows a lot of these musical chaps."

Then the tenor sang, and after the applause had given way to another rustle of talk, the gray-haired man continued as if there had been no interruption: —

"So you don't live in New York? — lucky woman!"

Isabelle moved her chair to look at this person, who wanted to talk. She thought him unusual in appearance, and liked his friendliness. His face was lined and thin, and the long, thin hand on his knee was muscular. Isabelle decided that he must be Somebody.

"I am here for my health, but I expect to live in New York," she explained.

"In New York for your health?" he asked in a puzzled tone. "You see, I am a doctor."

"Yes — I came to consult Dr. Potts. I gave out, — am always giving out," Isabelle continued with that confiding frankness that always pleased men. "I'm like so many women these days, — no good, nerves! If you are a doctor, please tell me why we should all go to pieces in this foolish fashion?"

"If I could do that satisfactorily and also tell you how not to go to pieces, I should be a very famous man," he replied pleasantly.

"Perhaps you are!"

"Perhaps. But I haven't discovered *that* secret, yet."

"Dr. Potts says it's all the chemistry inside us — auto-intoxication, poison!"

"Yes, that is the latest theory."

"It seems reasonable; but why didn't our grandmothers get poisoned?"

"Perhaps they did, — but they didn't know what to call it."

"You think that is so, — that we are poor little chemical retorts? It sounds — horrid."

"It sounds sensible, but it isn't the whole of it."

"Tell me what you think!"

"I don't like to interfere with Dr. Potts," he suggested.

"I shouldn't talk to you professionally, I know; but it is in my mind most of the time. What is the matter? What is wrong?"

"I, too, have thought about it a great deal." He smiled and his black eyes had a kindly gleam.

"Do you believe as Dr. Potts does that it is all what you eat, just matter? If your mind is so much troubled, if you have these queer ideas, it can't be altogether the chemistry?"

"It might be the soul."

"Don't laugh — "

"But I really think it might be the soul."

The music burst upon them, and when there was another interval, Isabelle persisted with the topic which filled her mind.

"Will you tell me what you mean by the soul?"

"Can *you* answer the question? . . . Well, since we are both in doubt, let us drop the term for a while and get back to the body."

"Only we must not end with it, as Potts does!"

"No, we must not end with the body."

"First, what causes it, — hysterics, nerves, no-goodness, — the whole thing?"

"Improper food, bad education, steam heat, variable climate, inbreeding, lack of children, — shall I stop?"

"No! I can't find a reasonable cause yet."

"I haven't really begun. . . . The brain is a delicate instrument. It can do a good deal of work in its own way, if you don't abuse it —"

"Overwork it?" suggested Isabelle.

"I never knew an American woman who overworked her brain," he retorted impatiently. "I mean *abuse* it. It's grossly abused."

"Wrong ideas?"

"No ideas at all, in the proper sense, — it's stuffed with all sorts of things, — sensations, emotions. . . . Where are you living?"

"At the Metropole."

"And where were you last month?"

"In St. Louis."

"And the month before?"

"I went to Washington with my husband and —"

"Precisely — that's enough!" he waved his thin hand.

"But it rests me to travel," Isabelle protested.

"It seems to rest you. Did you ever think what all those whisking changes in your environment mean to the brain cells? And it isn't just travelling, with new scenes, new people; it is everything in your life, — every act from the time you get up to the time you go to bed. You are cramming those brain cells all the time, giving them new records to make, — even when you lie down with an illustrated paper. Why, the merest backwoodsman in Iowa is living faster in a sense than Cicero or Webster. . . . The gray matter cannot stand the strain. It isn't the quality of what it has to do; it is the mere amount! Understand?"

"I see! I never thought before what it means to be tired. I have worked the machine foolishly. But one must travel fast — be geared up, as you say — or fall behind and become dull and uninteresting. What is living if we can't keep the pace others do?"

"Must we? Is that *living?*" he asked ironically. "I have a diary kept by an old great-aunt of mine. She was a country clergyman's wife, away back in a little village. She brought up four sons, helped her husband fit them for college as well as pupils he took in, and baked and washed and sewed. And learned German for amusement when she was fifty! I think she lived somewhat, but she probably never lived at the pressure you have the past month."

"One can't repeat — can't go back to old conditions. Each generation has its own lesson, its own way."

"But is our way *living?* Are we living now this very minute, listening to music we don't apparently care for, that means nothing to us, with our mind crammed full of distracting purposes and reflections? When I read my aunt Merelda's journal of the silent winter days on the snowy farm, I think *she* lived, as much as one should live. Living doesn't consist in the number of muscular or nervous reactions that you undergo."

"What is your formula?"

"We haven't yet mentioned the most formidable reason for the American plague," he continued, ignoring her question. "It has to do with that troublesome term we evaded, — the Soul."

"The Soul?" . . .

The music had come to an end, and the people were moving about them. Cornelia came up and drawled: —

"Tom and I are going on, — will you go with us?"

When Isabelle reached her hostess, she had but one idea in her mind, and exclaimed impulsively to that somewhat bored lady: —

"Who is that man just going out? With gray hair? The tall, thin man?"

"Dr. Renault? He's a surgeon, operates on children, — has done something or other lately." . . .

She smiled at Isabelle's impulsiveness, and turned to another.

'A surgeon,' Isabelle thought. 'What has he to do with the soul?'

In a few moments she had a chance to repeat her question aloud to Dr. Renault when they left the house together.

"Did you ever hear," he replied directly, "that a house divided against itself will fall?"

"Of course."

"I should say that this national disease, which we have been discussing, is one of the results of trying to live with divided souls, — souls torn, distraught!"

"And we need —?"

"A religion."

The doctor raised his hat and sauntered down the avenue.

"A religion!" Isabelle murmured, — a queer word, here at the close of Mrs. Bertram's pleasantly pagan Sunday afternoon, with ladies of undoubted social position getting into their motors, and men lighting cigarettes and cigars to solace them on the way to their clubs. Religion! and the need of it suggested by a surgeon, a man of science. . . .

When the three reached the Woodyards' house, Conny paused with, "When shall I see you again?" which Isabelle understood as a polite dismissal. Cairy to her surprise proposed to walk to the hotel with her. Isabelle felt that this arrangement was not in the plan, but Conny merely waved her hand with a smile, — "By-by, children."

They sauntered up the avenue, at the pace required by Cairy's disability. The city, although filled with people loitering in holiday ease, had a strange air of subdued life, of Sunday peace, not disturbed even by the dashing motors. Isabelle, bubbling with the day's impressions, was eager to talk, and Cairy, as she had found him before at the Virginia Springs, was a sympathetic man to be with. He told her the little semi-scandalous story of her recent hostess. . . . "And now they have settled down to bring up the children like any good couple, and it threatens to end on the 'live happy ever after' note. Sam Bertram is really domestic, — you can see he admires her tremendously. He sits and listens to the music and nods his sleepy old head."

"And the — other one?" Isabelle asked, laughing in spite of the fact that she felt a little shocked.

"Who knows? . . . The lady disappears at rare intervals, and there are rumors. But she is a good sort, and you see Sam admires her, needs her."

"But it is rather awful when you stop to think of it!"

"Why more awful than if Sam had stuck a knife into the other's ribs or punctured him with a bullet? . . . I think it is rather more intelligent."

Cairy did not know Renault. "Mrs. Bertram gets everybody," he said. Isabelle felt no inclination to discuss with Cairy her talk about neurasthenia and religion. So their chatter drifted from the people they had seen to Cairy himself, his last play, "which was a rank fizzle," and the plan of the new one. One got on fast and far with Cairy, if one were a woman and felt his charm. By the time they had reached the hotel, he was counselling Isabelle most wisely how she should settle herself in New York. "But why don't you live in the country? in that old village Mrs. Woodyard told me about? The city is nothing but a club, a way-station these days, a sort of Fair, you know, where you come two or three times a year to see your dressmaker and hear the gossip."

"But there's my husband!" Isabelle suggested. "You see his business is here."

"I forgot the husband, — make him change his business. Besides, men like country life."

Isabelle found her husband comfortably settled near a hot radiator, reading a novel. Lane occasionally read novels on a Sunday when there was absolutely nothing else to do. He read them slowly, with a curious interest in the world they depicted, the same kind of interest that he would take in a strange civilization, like that of the Esquimaux, where phenomena would have only an amusing significance. He dropped his glasses when his wife appeared and helped himself to a fresh cigar from the box beside him.

"Have a good time?"

It was the formula that he used for almost every occupation pursued by women. Isabelle, throbbing with her new impressions and ideas, found the question depressing. John was not the person to pour out one's mind to when that mind was in a tumult. He would listen kindly, assent at the wrong place, and yawn at the end. Undoubtedly his life was exciting, but it had no fine shades. He was growing stout, Isabelle perceived, and a little heavy. New York life was not good for him.

"I thought Conny's house and the people so — interesting," — she used the universal term for a new sensation, — "didn't you?"

"Yes, — very pleasant," he assented as he would have if it had been the Falkners or the Lawtons or the Frasers.

In the same undiscriminating manner he agreed with her other remarks about the Woodyards. People were people to him, and life was life, — more or less the same thing everywhere; while Isabelle felt the fine shades.

"I think it would be delightful to know people worth while," she observed almost childishly, "people who *do* something."

"You mean writers and artists and that kind? I guess it isn't very difficult," Lane replied indulgently.

Isabelle sighed. Such a remark betrayed his remoteness

from her idea; she would have it all to do for herself, when she started her life in New York.

"I think I shall make over the place at Grafton," she said after a time. Her husband looked at her with some surprise. She was standing at the window, gazing down into the cavernous city in the twilight. He could not possibly follow the erratic course of ideas through her brain, the tissue of impression and suggestion, that resulted in such a conclusion.

"Why? what do you want to do with it? I thought you didn't care for the country."

"One must have a background," she replied vaguely, and continued to stare at the city. This was the sum of her new experience, with all its elements. The man calmly smoking there did not realize that his life, their life, was to be affected profoundly by such trivial matters as a Sunday luncheon, a remark by Tom Cairy, the savage aspect of the great city seen through April mist, and the low vitality of a nervous organism. But everything plays its part with an impressionable character in which the equilibrium is not found and fixed. As the woman stared down into the twilight, she seemed to see afar off what she had longed for, held out her hands towards, — life.

Pictures, music, the play of interesting personalities, books, plays, — ideas, — that was the note of the higher civilization that Conny had caught. If Conny had absorbed all this so quickly, why could not she? Cornelia Woodyard — that somewhat ordinary schoolmate of her youth — was becoming for Isabelle a powerful source of suggestion, just as Isabelle had been for Bessie Falkner in the Torso days.

CHAPTER XXIX

When Mrs. Woodyard returned to her house at nine o'clock in the evening and found it dark, no lights in the drawing-room or the library, no fire lighted in either room, she pushed the button disgustedly and flung her cloak into a chair.

"Why is the house like a tomb?" she demanded sharply of the servant, who appeared tardily.

"Mrs. Woodyard was not expected until later."

"That should make no difference," she observed curtly, and the flustered servant hastened to pull curtains, light lamps, and build up the fire.

Conny disliked entering a gloomy house. Moreover, she disliked explaining things to servants. Her attitude was that of the grand marshal of life, who once having expressed an idea or wish expects that it will be properly fulfilled. This attitude worked perfectly with Percy and the children, and usually with servants. No one "got more results" in her establishment with less worry and thought than Mrs. Woodyard. The resolutely expectant attitude is a large part of efficiency.

After the servant had gathered up her wrap and gloves, Conny looked over the room, gave another curve to the dark curtains, and ordered whiskey and cigarettes. It was plain that she was expecting some one. She had gone to the Hillyers' to dinner as she had promised Percy, and just as the party was about to leave for the opera had pleaded a headache and returned home. It was true that she was not well; the winter had taxed her strength, and she lived quite up to the margin of her vitality. That was her plan, also. Moreover, the day had contained rather more than its share of problems. . . .

When Cairy's light step pressed the stair, she turned quickly from the fire.

"Ah, Tommy, — so you got my message?" She greeted him with a slow smile. "Where were you dining?"

"With the Lanes. Mrs. Lane and I saw *The Doll's House* this afternoon." As Conny did not look pleased, he added, "It is amusing to show Ibsen to a child."

"Isabelle Lane is no child."

"She takes Shaw and Ibsen with that childlike earnestness which has given those two great fakirs a posthumous vogue," Cairy remarked with a yawn. "If it were not for America, — for the Mississippi Valley of America, one might say, — Ibsen would have had a quiet grave, and Shaw might remain the Celtic buffoon. But the women of the Mississippi Valley have made a gospel out of them. . . . It is as interesting to hear them discuss the new dogmas on marriage as it is to see a child eat candy."

"You seem to find it so — with Isabelle."

"She is very intelligent — she will get over the Shaw-measles quickly."

"You think so?" Conny queried. "Well, with all that money she might do something, if she had it in her. . . . But she is middle class, in ideas, — always was."

That afternoon Isabelle had confided her schoolgirl opinion of Mrs. Woodyard to Cairy. The young man balancing the two judgments smiled.

"She is good to behold," he observed, helping himself to whiskey.

"Not your kind, Tommy!" Conny warned with a laugh. "The Prices are very *good* people. You'll find that Isabelle will keep you at the proper distance."

Cairy yawned as if the topic did not touch him. "I thought you were going to *Manon* with the Hillyers."

"I was, — but I came home instead!" Conny replied softly, and their eyes met.

"That was kind of you," he murmured, and they were silent a long time.

It had come over her suddenly in the afternoon that she must see Cairy, must drink again the peculiar and potent draught which he alone of men seemed to be able to offer her. So she had written the note and made the excuse. She would not have given up the Hillyers altogether. They were important to Percy just now, and she expected to see the Senator there and accomplish something with him. It was clearly her duty, her plan of life as she saw it, for her to go to the Hillyers'. But having put in an appearance, flattered the old lawyer, and had her little talk with Senator Thomas before dinner, she felt that she had earned her right to a few hours of sentimental indulgence. . . .

Conny, sitting there before the fire, looking her most seductive best, had the clear conscience of a child. Her life, she thought, was arduous, and she met its demands admirably, she also thought. The subtleties of feeling and perception never troubled her. She felt entitled to her sentimental repose with Cairy as she felt entitled to her well-ordered house. She did not see that her "affair" interfered with her duties, or with Percy, or with the children. If it should, — then it would be time to consider. . . .

"Tommy," she murmured plaintively, "I am so tired! You are the only person who rests me."

She meant it quite literally, that he always rested and soothed her, and that she was grateful to him for it. But the Southerner's pulses leaped at the purring words. To him they meant more, oh, much more! He gave her strength; his love was the one vital thing she had missed in life. The sentimentalist must believe that; must believe that he is giving, and that some generous issue justifies his passion. Cairy leaning forward caressingly said:—

"You make me feel your love to-night! . . . Wonderful one! . . . It is all ours to-night, in this still room."

She did not always make him feel that she loved him, far from it. And it hurt his sentimental soul, and injured his vanity. He would be capable of a great folly with sufficient delusion, but he was not capable of loving intensely a woman who did not love him. To-night they seemed in harmony, and as their lips met at last, the man had the desired illusion — she was his!

They are not coarsely physiological, — these Cairys, the born lovers. They look abhorrently on mere flesh. With them it must always be the spirit that leads to the flesh, and that is their peculiar danger. Society can always take care of the simply licentious males; women know them and for the most part hate them. But the poet lovers — the men of "temperament" — are fatal to its prosaic peace. These must "love" before they can desire, must gratify that emotional longing first, pour themselves out, and have the ecstasy before the union. That is their fatal nature. The state of love is their opiate, and each time they dream, it is the only dream. Each woman who can give them the dream is the only woman, — she calls to them with a single voice. And they divine afar off those women whose voices will call. . . .

What would come after? . . . The woman looked up at the man with a peculiar light in her eyes, a gentleness which never appeared except for him, and held him from her, dreaming intangible things. . . . She, too, could dream with him, — that was the wonder of it all to her! This was the force that had taken her out of her ordinary self. She slipped into nothing — never drifted — looked blind fate between the eyes. But now she dreamed! . . . And as the man spoke to her, covered her with his warm terms of endearment, she listened — and forgot her little world.

Even the most selfish woman has something of the large mother, the giving quality, when a man's arms hold her. She reads the man's need and would supply it. She would comfort the inner sore, supply the lack. And for this moment, Conny was not selfish: she was thinking of her lover's needs, and how she could meet them.

Thus the hour sped.

"You love — you love!" the man said again and again, — to convince himself.

Conny smiled disdainfully, as at the childish iteration of a child, but said nothing. Finally with a long sigh, coming back from her dream, she rose and stood thoughtfully before the fire, looking down at Cairy reflectively. He had the bewildered feeling of not understanding what was in her mind.

"I will dine with you to-morrow," she remarked at last.

Cairy laughed ironically. It was the perfect anti-climax,— after all this unfathomable silence, after resting in his arms, —"I will dine with you to-morrow!"

But Conny never wasted words,—the commonest had a meaning. While he was searching for the meaning under this commonplace, there was the noise of some one entering the hall below. Conny frowned. Another interruption in her ordered household! Some servant was coming in at the front door. Or a burglar?

If it were a burglar, it was a very well assured one that closed the door carefully, took time to lay down hat and coat, and then with well-bred quiet ascended the stairs.

"It must be Percy," Conny observed, with a puzzled frown. "Something must have happened to bring him back to-night."

Woodyard, seeing a light in the library, looked in, the traveller's weary smile on his face.

"Hello, Percy!" Conny drawled. "What brings you back at this time?"

Woodyard came into the room draggingly, nodded to Cairy, and drew a chair up to the fire. His manner showed no surprise at the situation.

"Some things came up at Albany," he replied vaguely. "I shall have to go back to-morrow."

"What is it?" his wife demanded quickly.

"Will you give me a cigarette, Tom?" he asked equably, indicating that he preferred not to mention his business, whatever it might be. Cairy handed him his cigarette case.

"These are so much better than the brand Con supplies me with," he observed lightly.

He examined the cigarette closely, then lit it, and remarked: —

"The train was beastly hot. You seem very comfortable here."

Cairy threw away his cigarette and said good-by.

"Tom," Conny called from the door, as he descended, "don't forget the dinner." She turned to Percy, — "Tom is taking me to dinner to-morrow."

There was silence between husband and wife until the door below clicked, and then Conny murmured interrogatively, "Well?"

"I came back," Percy remarked calmly, "because I made up my mind that there is something rotten on in that Commission."

Conny, after her talk with the Senator, knew rather more about the Commission than her husband; but she merely asked, "What do you mean?"

"I mean that I want to find just who is interested in this up-state water-power grant before I go any farther. That is why I came down, — to see one or two men, especially Princhard."

While Cornelia was thinking of certain remarks that the Senator had made, Percy added, "I am not the Senator's hired man."

"Of course not!"

Her husband's next remark was startling, — "I have almost made up my mind to get out, Con, — to take Jackson's offer of a partnership and stick to the law."

Here, Conny recognized, was a crisis, and like most crises it came unexpectedly. Conny rose to meet it. Husband and wife discussed the situation, personal and political, of Percy's fortunes for a long time, and it was not settled when it was time for bed.

"Con," her husband said, still sitting before the fire as she turned out the lights and selected a book for night reading, "aren't you going pretty far with Tom?"

Conny paused and looked at him questioningly.

"Yes," she admitted in an even voice. "I have gone pretty far. . . . I wanted to tell you about it. But this political business has worried you so much lately that I didn't like to add anything."

As Percy made no reply, she said tentatively: —

"I may go farther, Percy. . . . Tom loves me — very much!"

"It means that — you care for him — the same way?"

"He's given me something," Conny replied evasively, "something I never felt — just that way — before."

"Yes, Tom is of an emotional nature," Woodyard remarked dryly.

"You don't like Tom. Men wouldn't, I can understand. He isn't like most men. . . . But women like him!"

Then for a while they waited, until he spoke, a little wearily, dispassionately.

"You know, Con, I always want you to have everything that is best for you — that you feel you need to complete your life. We have been the best sort of partners, trying not to limit each other in any way. . . . I know I have never been enough for you, given you all that you ought to have, in some ways. I am not emotional, as Tom is! And you have done everything for me. I shall never forget that. So if another can do something for you, make your life happier, fuller, — you must do it, take it. I should be a beastly pig to interfere!"

He spoke evenly, and at the end he smiled rather wanly.

"I know you mean it, Percy, — every word. But I shouldn't want you to be unhappy," replied Conny, in a subdued voice.

"You need not think of me — if you feel sure that this is best for you."

"You know that I could not do anything that might hurt our life, — *that* is the most important!"

Her husband nodded.

"The trouble is that I want both!" she analyzed gravely; "both in different ways."

A slight smile crept under her husband's mustache, but he made no comment.

"I shall always be honest with you, Percy, and if at any time it becomes —"

"You needn't explain," Percy interrupted hurriedly. "I don't ask! I don't want to know what is peculiarly your own affair, as this. . . . As I said, you must live your life as you choose, not hampered by me. We have always believed that was the best way, and meant it, too, haven't we?"

"But you have never wanted your own life," Conny remarked reflectively.

"No, not that way!" The look on Percy's face made Conny frown. She was afraid that he was keeping something back.

"I suppose it is different with a man."

"No, not always," and the smile reappeared under the mustache, a painful smile. "But you see in my case I never wanted — more."

"Oh!" murmured Conny, more troubled than ever.

"You won't do it lightly, whatever you do, I know! . . . And I'll manage — I shall be away a good deal this winter."

There was another long silence, and when Conny sighed and prepared to leave the room, Percy spoke: —

"There's one thing, Conny. . . . This mustn't affect the children."

"Oh, Percy!" she protested. "Of course not."

"You must be careful that it won't — in any way, you understand. That would be very — wrong."

"Of course," Conny admitted in the same slightly injured tone, as if he were undervaluing her character. "Whatever I do," she added, "I shall not sacrifice you or the children, naturally."

"We needn't talk more about it, then, need we?"

Conny slowly crossed the room to her husband, and putting one hand on his shoulder she leaned down and pushed up the hair from his forehead, murmuring: —

"You know I love you, Percy!"

"I know it, dear," he answered, caressing her face with his fingers. "If I don't happen to be enough for you, it is my fault — not yours."

"It isn't that!" she protested. But she could not explain what else it was that drew her to Cairy so strongly. "It mustn't make any difference between us. It won't, will it?"

Percy hesitated a moment, still caressing the lovely face. "I don't think so, Con. . . . But you can't tell that now — do you think?"

"It mustn't!" she said decisively, as if the matter was wholly in her own hands. And leaning still closer towards him, she whispered: "You are wonderful to me. A man who can take things as you do is really — big!" She meant him to understand that she admired him more than ever, that in respect to character she recognized that he was larger and finer than the other man.

Percy kissed the cheek so close to his lips. Conny shrank back perceptibly. Some elemental instinct of the female pushed its way through her broad-minded modern philosophy and made her shudder at the double embrace. She controlled herself at once and again bowed her beautiful head to his. But Percy did not offer to kiss her.

"There are other things in life than passion," she remarked slowly.

Percy looking directly into her eyes observed dryly: "Oh, many more. . . . But passion plays the deuce with the rest sometimes!"

And he held open the door for his wife to leave the room.

CHAPTER XXX

"THAT snipe!" Conny called Margaret's husband, Mr. Lawrence Pole. Larry, as he was known in his flourishing days when he loafed in brokers' offices, and idiotically dribbled away his own fortune and most of his wife's, rarely earned a better word than this epithet. "She ought to leave him — divorce him — get rid of such rubbish somehow," Conny continued with unwonted heat, as the tired motor chugged up the steep Westchester hillside on its way to Dudley Farms where the Poles lived.

"Perhaps Margaret has prejudices," Isabelle suggested. "You know she used to be religious, and there's her father, the Bishop."

"It would take a good many bishops to keep me tied to Larry!"

Conny was enjoying the early spring air, the virginal complexion of the April landscape. She surveyed the scene from Isabelle's motor with complacent superiority. How much better she had arranged her life than either Margaret or Isabelle! After the talk with Percy the previous evening, she felt a new sense of power and competency, with a touch of gratitude for that husband who had so frankly and unselfishly "accepted her point of view" and allowed her "to have her own life" without a distressing sense of wrecking anything. Conny's conscience was simple, almost rudimentary; but it had to be satisfied, such as it was. To-day it was completely satisfied, and she took an ample pleasure in realizing how well she had managed a difficult situation,— and also in the prospect of dinner with her lover in the evening.

That morning before the motor had come for her, she had gone over with Percy the complicated situation that had developed at Albany. It was her way in a crisis to let him talk it all out first, and then later, preferably when he came to her room in the morning after his breakfast with the children, to suggest those points which she wished to determine his action. Thus her husband absorbed her views when they would make most impression and in time came to believe that they were all evolved from his inner being. . . . To-day when he appeared shortly before her coffee, she had glanced at him apprehensively out of her sleepy eyes. But he betrayed no sign of travail of spirit. Though naturally weary after his brief rest, he had the same calm, friendly manner that was habitual with him. So they got at once to the political situation.

She was content with the way in which she had led him, for the time at least, to resolve his doubts and suspicions. They had no reason to suspect the Senator, — he had always encouraged Woodyard's independent position in politics and pushed him. There was not yet sufficient evidence of fraud in the hearings before the Commission to warrant aggressive action. It would be a pity to fire too soon, or to resign and lose an opportunity later. It would mean not only political oblivion, but also put him in a ridiculous light in the press, and suggest cowardice, etc. So he had gone away to attend to some matters at his office, and take an afternoon train back to Albany, with the conviction that "he must do nothing hurriedly, before the situation had cleared up." Those were his own phrases; Conny always preferred to have Percy use his own words to express his resolves.

There was only one small matter on her mind: she must see the Senator and find out — well, as much as she could discreetly, and be prepared for the next crisis. . . .

"I don't see why Margaret buries herself like this," Conny remarked, coming back to the present foreground, with a disgusted glance at the little settlement of Dudley Farms, a sorry combination of the suburb and the village, which they were approaching. "She might at least have a flat in the city somewhere, like others."

"Margaret wants the children to be in the country. Probably she gets less of Larry out here, — that may compensate!"

"As for the children," Conny pronounced with lazy dogmatism, "I don't believe in fussing. Children must camp where it's best for the parents. They can get fresh air in the Park."

The motor turned in at a neglected driveway, forbidding with black tree-trunks, and whirled up to the piazza of a brick house, an ugly survival of the early country mansion. Mrs. Pole, who was bending over a baby carriage within a sun parlor, came forward, a smile of welcome on her pale face. She seemed very small and fragile as she stood above them on the steps, and her thin, delicate face had the marked lines of a woman of forty. She said in her slow, Southern voice, which had a pleasant human quality: —

"I hope you weren't mired. The roads are something awful about here. I am so glad to see you both."

When she spoke her face lost some of the years.

"It is a long way out, — one can't exactly run in on you, Margaret! If it hadn't been for Isabelle's magnificent car, you might have died without seeing me!" Conny poured forth.

"It *is* a journey; but you see people don't run in on us often."

"You've got a landscape," Conny continued, turning to look across the bare treetops towards the Sound. It would have been a pleasant prospect except for the eruption of small houses on every side. "But how can you stand it the whole year round? Are there any civilized people — in those houses?" She indicated vaguely the patch of wooden villas below.

"Very few, I suppose, according to your standard, Cornelia. But we don't know them. I pulled up the drawbridge when we first came."

Mrs. Pole's thin lips twitched with mirth, and Conny, who was never content with mere inference, asked bluntly: —

"Then what do you do with yourselves — evenings?" Her tone reflected the emptiness of the landscape, and she added with a treble laugh, "I've always wondered what suburban life is like!"

"Oh, you eat and read and sleep. Then there are the children daytimes. I help teach 'em. We live the model life, — flowers and shrubs in the summer, I suppose. . . . The Bishop was with me for a time."

The large bare drawing-room, which was sunnily lighted from the southwest, was singularly without the usual furniture of what Conny called "civilized life." There were no rugs, few chairs, but one table, such as might be made by the village carpenter and stained black, which was littered with books and magazines. There was also a large writing cabinet of mahogany, — a magnificent piece of Southern colonial design, — and before the fire a modern couch. Conny inventoried all this in a glance. She could not "make it out." 'They can't be as poor as that,' she reflected, and turned to the books on the table.

"Weiniger's *Sex and Character*," she announced, "Brieux's *Maternité*, Lavedan, Stendhal, Strobel on Child Life, — well, you do read! And this?" She held up a yellow volume of French plays. "What do you do with this when the Bishop comes?"

"The Bishop is used to me now. Besides, he doesn't see very well, poor dear, and has forgotten his French. Have you read that book of Weiniger's? It is a good dose for woman's conceit these days."

There was a touch of playful cynicism in the tone, which went with the fleeting smile. Mrs. Pole understood Cornelia Woodyard perfectly, and was amused by her. But Conny's coarse and determined handling of life did not fascinate her fastidious nature as it had fascinated Isabelle's.

Conny continued to poke among the books, emitting comments as she happened upon unexpected things. It was the heterogeneous reading of an untrained woman, who was seeking blindly in many directions for guidance, for light, trying to appease an awakened intellect, and to answer certain gnawing questions of her soul. . . .

Isabelle and Margaret talked of their visit at the Virginia Springs. In the mature face, Isabelle was seeking the blond-haired girl, with deep-set blue eyes, and sensitive mouth, that she had admired at St. Mary's. Now it was not even pretty, although it spoke of race, for the bony features, the high brow, the thin nose, had emerged, as if chiselled from the flesh by pain.

'She has suffered,' Isabelle thought, 'suffered — and lived.'

Conny had recounted to Isabelle on their way out some of the rumors about the Poles. Larry Pole was a weakling, had gone wrong in money matters, — nothing that had flared up in scandal, merely family transactions. Margaret had taken the family abroad — she had inherited something from her mother — and suddenly they had come back to New York, and Larry had found a petty job in the city. Evidently, from the bare house, their hiding themselves out here, most of the wife's money had gone, too.

Pity! because Margaret was proud. She had her Virginian mother's pride with a note of difference. The mother had been proud in the conventional way, of her family, her position, — things. Margaret had the pride of accomplishment, — of deeds. She was the kind who would have gone ragged with a poet or lived content in a sod hut with a Man. And she had married this Larry Pole, who according to Conny looked seedy and was often rather "boozy." How could she have made such a mistake, — Margaret of all women? That Englishman Hollenby, who really was somebody, had been much interested in her. Why hadn't she married him? Nobody would know the reason. . . .

The luncheon was very good. The black cook, "a relic of my mother's establishment," as Margaret explained, gave them a few savory family dishes, and there was a light French wine. Margaret ate little and talked little, seeming to enjoy the vivacity of the other women.

"Tell about your visit to the Gorings," Conny drawled. "Percy's cousin, Eugene Goring, who married Aline, you know. Boots in the bath-tub, and the babies running around naked, and Aline lost in the metaphysics of the arts, making chairs."

And Isabelle recounted what she had seen of Aline's establishment in St. Louis, with its total disregard of what Conny called the "decencies" of life. They all laughed at her picture of their "wood-nymph," as they had named Aline.

"And Eugene talking anarchy, and washing the dishes, — it sounds like a Weber and Field's farce," gurgled Conny. "He wrote Percy about lecturing in New York, — wanted to come East. But Percy couldn't do anything for him. It isn't a combination to make a drawing-room impression."

"But," Margaret protested, "Aline is a person, and that is more than you can say of most of us married women. She has kept her personality."

"If I were 'Gene," Conny replied contemptuously, "I'd tone her 'personality' down."

"He's probably big enough to respect it."

There followed a discussion of the woman's part in marriage, Margaret defending independence, "the woman's right to live for herself," and Conny taking the practical view.

"She can't be anything any way, just by herself. She had better make the most of the material she's got to work with — or get another helping," she added, thinking of Larry.

"And Aline isn't happy," Isabelle remarked; "she has a look on her face as if she were a thousand miles away, and had forgotten her marriage as much as she could. Her chairs and tables are just ways of forgetting."

"But they have something to think about, — those two. They don't vegetate."

"I should say they had, — but no anarchy in my domestic circle, thank you!" Conny observed.

"I shouldn't object to anarchy," sighed Margaret, with her whimsical smile.

"Margaret is bored," Isabelle pronounced, "simply awfully bored. She's so bored that I expect some day she will poison herself and the children, merely to find out what comes next."

"No wonder — buried in the snowdrifts out here," Conny agreed. "Isn't there anything you want to do, even something wicked?"

"Yes," Mrs. Pole answered half seriously. "There is *one* thing I'd like to do before I die."

"Tell us!"

"I'd like to find Somebody — man or woman — who cared for the things I care for — sky and clouds and mountains, — and go away with him anywhere for — a little while, just a little while," she drawled dreamily, resting her elbows on the table.

"Elope! Fie, fie!" Conny laughed.

"My mother's father had a plantation in one of the Windward Islands," Margaret continued. "It must be nice down there — warm and sunny. I'd like to lie out on the beach and forget children and servants and husbands, and stop wondering what life is. Yes, I'd like a vacation — in the Windward Islands, with somebody who understood."

"To wit, a man!" added Conny.

"Yes, a man! But only for the trip."

They laughed a good deal about Margaret's vacation, called her the "Windward Islands," and asked her to make reservations for them in her Paradise when they had found desirable partners.

"Only, I should have to bring John, and he wouldn't know what to do with himself on a beach," Isabelle remarked. "I don't know any one else to take."

"You mustn't go Windwarding until you have to," Margaret explained. . . .

At the dessert, the children came in, — two boys and a girl. The elder boy was eight, with his mother's fair hair, blue eyes, and fine features, and the same suggestion of race in the narrow high brow, the upward poise of the head.

His younger brother was nondescript, with dark hair and full lips. Margaret observed her children with a curiously detached air, Isabelle thought. Was she looking for signs of Larry in that second son? Alas, she might see Larry always, with the cold apprehension of a woman too wise to deceive herself! The little girl, fresh from her nap, was round and undefined, and the mother took her into her arms, cuddling her close to her breast, as if nothing, not even the seed of Larry, could separate her from this one; as if she felt in her heart all the ills and sorrows, the woman's pains to be, — the eternal feminine defeat, — in this tiny ball of freshness. And the ironical smile subtly softened to a glow of affection. Here, at least, was an illusion!

Isabelle, watching these two, understood — all the lines, the smile, the light cynicism — the Windward Islands! She put her arms impulsively about the mother and the child, hugging them closely. Margaret looked up into her shining eyes and pressed her hand. . . .

"There are some cigarettes in the other room," Margaret suggested; "we'll build up the fire and continue the argument in favor of the Windward Islands."

"It is a long way to New York over that road," Conny observed. "I have an engagement."

Now that she had satisfied her curiosity about "how the Poles lived," she began to think of her dinner with Cairy, and was fearful lest she might be delayed.

"Spend the night," suggested Margaret; but Isabelle, who understood Conny, telephoned at once for the motor.

"You aren't going back to the West, Isabelle?" Margaret asked, while they waited for the motor. "Won't you miss it?"

"Miss the West? Did you ever know a woman that had escaped from the Mississippi Valley who would go back there?" Conny drawled. "Why, Belle is like a girl just out of school, looking at the shop windows!"

Cornelia Woodyard, who had lived a number of years in a corner of that same vast valley, looked from metropolitan heights on the monotony of the "middle West." She had the New Yorker's amusing incapacity to comprehend existence outside the neighborhood of Fifth Avenue and Central Park.

"One lives out there," Margaret protested with sudden fire, "in those great spaces. Men grow there. They *do* things. When my boys are educated I shall take them away from New York, to the Virginia mountains, perhaps, and have them grow up there, doing things, real things, working with their hands, becoming men! Perhaps not there," she mused, recollecting that the acres of timber and coal in the mountains, her sons' inheritance from her vigorous ancestors, had been lost to them in a vulgar stock dealer's gamble by their father,—"perhaps out to Oregon, where I have an uncle. His father rode his horse all the way from Louisiana across the continent, after the War! He had nothing but his horse—and before he died he built a city in his new country. That is where men do things!"

Margaret had flashed into life again. As Tom Cairy would have said, "*Vraiment, ma petite cousine a une grande âme — étouffée*" (For Cairy always made his acute observations in the French tongue).

"There's something of the Amazon in you, Margaret," Conny remarked, "in spite of your desire to seclude yourself in the Windward Islands with a suitable mate."

The motor finally came puffing up the drive, and the women stood on the veranda, prolonging their farewells. A round, red, important sun peeped from under the gray cloud bank that had lowered all the afternoon, flooding the thin branches of the budding trees, falling warm and gold across the dead fields.

"See!" Margaret cried, raising her thin arms to the sun. "The Promise!"

"I hope it will hold until we reach Jerome Avenue," Conny replied practically, preparing to enter the car.

"The promise of another life!"

Margaret was standing in the sun, her nostrils dilated, absorbing the light, the source of joy and life.

"Windward Islands, eh?" Conny coughed, settling herself comfortably in her corner.

"The real land," Margaret murmured to herself.

The chauffeur had reached for the lever when there appeared on the drive two men bearing something between them, a human something, carefully.

"What's that!" exclaimed Conny in a frightened voice. "What is it?" she repeated to the chauffeur, — demanding of a man something in his province to know.

"Looks though they had a child—hurt," the chauffeur replied.

Margaret, shading her eyes with a thin hand, looked down the avenue. She made no movement to go towards the men, — merely waited motionless for the thing to come. And the men came slowly forward, past the car, up the steps.

It was the older boy. The man who held the head and shoulders of the child said, "An accident — not serious, I believe."

Margaret opened the door and pointed to the lounge before the fire. The man who had spoken laid the boy down very gently with his head on a cushion, and smoothed back the rumpled hair.

"I will go for the doctor," the other man said, and presently there was the sound of the motor leaping down the hill.

Margaret had dropped on her knees beside the unconscious boy, and placed one hand on his brow. "Bring some water," she said to Isabelle, and began to unbutton the torn sweater.

Conny, with one look at the white face and closed eyes, went softly out into the hall and sat down.

"Will you telephone to Dr. W. S. Rogers in New York, and ask him to send some one if he can't come himself?" Margaret asked the stranger, who was helping her with the boy's clothes.

"Can I telephone any one else — his father?" the man suggested, as he turned to the door.

"No — it would be no use — it's too late to reach him."

Then she turned again to the boy, who was still unconscious. . . .

When the man had finished telephoning, he came back through the hall, where Conny was sitting.

"How did it happen?" she asked.

"He fell over the culvert, — the high one just as you leave the station, you know. He was riding his bicycle, — I saw the little chap pushing it up the hill as I got out of the train. Then a big touring car passed me, and met another one coming down at full speed. I suppose the boy was frightened and tried to get too far out on the culvert and fell over. The motors didn't notice him; but when I reached the spot, I saw his bicycle hanging on the edge and looked over for him, — could just see his head in the bushes and leaves. Poor little fellow! It was a nasty fall. But the leaves and the rubbish must have broken it somewhat."

"Rob! Rob Falkner!" Isabelle exclaimed, as the man turned and met her at the door. "I didn't recognize you — with your beard! How is Bessie?"

"Very well, I believe. She is in Denver, you know."

When he had gone back to the boy, Isabelle said to Conny:—

"We used to know the Falkners very well. There is a story! . . . Strange he should be *here*. But I heard he was in the East somewhere."

Conny did not seem interested in Rob Falkner and his turning up at this juncture. She sat with a solemn face, wondering how she could get back to the city. Finally she resolved to telephone Cairy.

Falkner went over to the unconscious boy, and taking his hand, counted the pulse. "It's all right so far," he said to the mother, who did not hear him. After a time she looked up, and her low voice dragged hoarsely, — "You mustn't wait. The doctor will be here soon, and we can do everything now."

"I will wait until the doctor comes," Falkner replied gently, and stepped to the window to watch for the motor.

After the local doctor had come and said, "A slight concussion, — nothing serious, I expect," and the boy had revived somewhat, Conny departed alone in the motor, Isabelle having decided to stay with Margaret over the night. Falkner helped the doctor carry the patient upstairs, and then started to leave. Isabelle waited for him at the door.

"Mrs. Pole wishes me to thank you for all your kindness."

"I shall look in to-morrow morning," he replied hurriedly. "I would stay now until the boy's father came; but I don't suppose there is anything I can do. I am living at the hotel below, and you can telephone if you want me."

"You are living here?"

"Yes; I am working on the new dam, a few miles from this place."

"I am so glad to see you again," Isabelle said, the only words she could think of.

"Thank you."

Then with a curt nod he was off. He had not shown in any way that he was glad to see her, Isabelle reflected. Falkner was always moody, but she had thought he liked her, — and after all their friendship! Something had kept her from asking more about Bessie.

CHAPTER XXXI

LARRY did not return for dinner, which Isabelle ate by herself in sombre silence. When she went upstairs to take the mother's place with the boy, Margaret did not seem to notice her husband's absence, though she inquired repeatedly whether the New York doctor had telephoned. Later in the evening when Isabelle suggested that some effort should be made to find the boy's father, Margaret exclaimed impatiently: —

"I can't tell where he is! . . . It is easier for me that he isn't here." And in answer to Isabelle's expression, she added: "Don't look so shocked, B! Larry gets on my nerves frightfully when there is anything extra to bear or do. Of course I shall telephone his office in the morning, and he will come out at once. That doctor said there would be no change before morning. Do you suppose he knows anything, that doctor? He had the look of polite ignorance!"

The New York doctor arrived towards midnight with a nurse, and stayed the night to await developments. Margaret still sat by the boy's bed, and Isabelle left her huddled in a large chair, her eyes staring at the shadow on the faintly lighted bed. She had listened to what Dr. Rogers had to say without a word. She was almost stone, Isabelle felt, looking at her with some awe. What could have made her like this!

She was still in this stony mood the next morning when Larry reached the house. Dressed in a loose black gown that clung to her slight figure and brought out the perfect whiteness of her skin, she stood and listened indifferently to the vague explanation of his absence that her husband poured out profusely. Then with a remark that the doctor would see him before he went, she left the room. Isabelle, who was present, watched the two keenly, trying to divine the secret. To be sure, Larry was not attractive, she decided, — too effusive, too anxious to make the right impression, as if he were acting a part before Isabelle, and full of wordy concern for every one. A little below the medium height, he stood very erect, consciously making the most of his inches. His sandy hair was thin, and he wore glasses, behind which one eye kept winking nervously. Neatly, almost fashionably dressed, he bore no evident marks of dissipation. After Conny's description, Isabelle had expected to see his shortcomings written all over him. Though he was over-mannered and talkative, there was nothing to mark him as of the outcast class. "One doesn't despise one's husband because he's foolish or unfortunate about money matters," Isabelle said to herself. And the sympathy that she had felt for Margaret began to evaporate.

"You say that he fell off that embankment?" Larry remarked to her. "I was afraid he was too young to ride about here by himself with all the motors there are in this neighborhood. But Margaret was anxious to have him fearless. . . . People who motor are so careless — it has become a curse in the country. . . . Mrs. Woodyard came out with you? I am so sorry this frightful accident spoiled your day." . . .

He ran on from remark to remark, with no prompting from Isabelle, and had got to their life in Germany when the doctor entered the room. Larry shook hands punctiliously with him, inquiring in a special tone: "I hope you have good news of the little fellow, Doctor? I thought I would not go up until I had seen you first." . . .

The doctor cut short the father's prolixity in a burly voice: —

"It's concussion, passing off, I think. But nobody can say what will happen then, — whether there is anything wrong with the cord. It may clear up in a few days. It may not. No use speculating. . . . I shall be back to-morrow or send some one. Good day."

Larry followed him into the hall, talking, questioning,

exclaiming. Isabelle noticed that the doctor gave Pole a quick, impatient glance, shaking him off with a curt reply, and jumped into the waiting carriage. In some ways men read men more rapidly than women can. They look for fewer details, with an eye to the essential stuff of character.

What had the doctor said to Margaret? Had he let her know his evident fears? When she came into the room for a moment, there was an expression of fixed will in her white face, as if she had gone down into herself and found there the courage to meet whatever was coming. . . . 'The older boy, too,' thought Isabelle, — 'the one so like her, with no outward trace of the father!'

While Margaret was giving directions for telephoning, making in brief phrases her arrangements for the day, Falkner came in. He was in his working clothes, and with his thick beard and scrubby mustache looked quite rough beside the trim Larry.

"How is the boy?" he demanded directly, going up to the mother.

"Better, I think, — comfortable at least," she answered gently. There was a warm gleam in her eyes as she spoke to this stranger, as if she had felt his fibre and liked it.

"I will come in this afternoon. I should like to see him when I can."

"Yes, this afternoon," Margaret replied. "I should be glad to have you come."

Isabelle had told Pole that Falkner was the man who had found the boy and brought him home. Larry, with the subtle air of superiority that clothes seem to give a small man, thanked Falkner in suitable language. Isabelle had the suspicion that he was debating with himself whether he should give this workingman a couple of dollars for his trouble, and with an hysterical desire to laugh interposed: —

"Mr. Pole, this is Mr. Falkner, an old friend of ours!"

"Oh," Larry remarked, "I didn't understand!" and he looked at Falkner again, still from a distance.

"Rob," Isabelle continued, turning to Falkner, "you

didn't tell me yesterday how Bessie is. I haven't heard from her for a long while, — and Mildred?"

"They are well, I believe. Bessie doesn't write often."

Pole followed him into the hall, making remarks. Isabelle heard Falkner reply gruffly: "Yes, it was a nasty fall. But a kid can fall a good way without hurting himself seriously."

When Pole came back and began to talk to her, Isabelle's sympathy for his wife revived. The house had settled into the dreary imitation of its customary routine that the house of suspense takes on. To live in this, with the mild irritation of Larry's conversational fluency, was quite intolerable. It was not what he said, but the fact that he was forever saying it. "A bag of words," Isabelle called him. "Poor Margaret!" And she concluded that there was nothing more useful for her to do than to take upon herself the burden of Larry until he should dispose of himself in some harmless way.

CHAPTER XXXII

No, women such as Margaret Pole do not "despise their husbands because they are unfortunate in money matters," — not altogether because they prove themselves generally incompetent in the man's struggle for life! This process of the petrification of a woman's heart, slow or rapid as it may be, is always interesting, — if the woman is endowed in the first place with the power to feel. How Margaret Lawton may have come to marry Lawrence Pole, we can defer for the present, as a matter of post-mortem psychology, unprofitable, melancholy, and inexact, however interesting. How does any woman come to marry any man? Poets, psychologists, and philosophers have failed to account for the accidents of this emotional nexus.

What is determinable and more to our purpose is the subsequent process of dissolution, or petrifaction. All that need be said is that Margaret married her husband when she was twenty-four, with confidence, belief in him, and a spiritual aspiration concerning marriage not possible to many who marry. However foolishly she may have deluded herself, — betrayed a fatal incapacity to divine, — she believed when she went to the altar with Lawrence Pole that she was marrying a Man,— one whom she could respect as well as love, and to whom she should remain loyally bound in mind and heart and soul.

She was ardent, this delicate Southern girl. Under a manner that had seemed to comrades at St. Mary's cold because of its reticence, there burned the fire of a crusading race, — of those Southerners who had pushed from the fat lowlands about the sea into the mountains and across them to the wilderness; of that uncle, who after the defeat of his cause had ridden his cavalry horse across the entire country in search of a new opening, to build at forty-three a new life for himself and his wife — after defeat! There was courage, aspiration, the power of deeds in that blood, — note the high forehead, the moulded chin, the deep eyes of this woman. And there was also in her religious faith, received from her father the Bishop, piety, and accepted beliefs in honor, loyalty, love to one's family and friends, and charity to the world. All this was untested, handed down to her wrapped in the prayer-book by the Bishop. And she had seen a bit of what we call the world, there in Washington among her mother's friends, — had been gay, perhaps reckless, played like a girl with love and life, those hours of sunshine. She knew vaguely that some men were liars, and some were carnal; but she came to her marriage virgin in soul as well as body, without a spot from living, without a vicious nerve in her body, ready to learn.

And folly with money, mere incompetence, did not turn that heart to stone, — not that alone. The small segment of the world that knew the Poles might think so, hearing how Larry had gone into Wall Street and fatuously left there his own small fortune, and later, going back after his lesson, had lost what he could of his wife's property. To be sure, after that first "ill luck," Margaret's eyes had opened to the fact that her husband was not "practical," was easily led by vanity. In the Lawton family it had been the Man's part to deal effectively with practical life, and women did not concern themselves with their judgments. But as Margaret had never expected to be rich, — had no ambition for place in the social race, — she would have gone back to her blue-capped mountains and lived there contented, "with something to look at." She had urged this course upon her husband after the first disaster; but he was too vain to "get out," to "quit the game," to leave New York. So with the understanding that henceforth he would stick to prosaic methods of money making, he had started again in his brokerage business. This was at the time when Margaret was occupied with her babies. As the indubitable clay of her idol revealed itself, she had thought that child-bearing, child-having would be a tolerable compensation for her idyl. Margaret Pole was one who "didn't mind having babies," and did not consider the fatal nine months a serious deprivation of life. She liked it all, she told Isabelle, and was completely happy only when the children were coming and while they were helpless babies. One real interest suffices for all.

Then one day, after the second boy was born, Larry came in, shaking in hand and heart, and the miserable news was soon out, — "caught in the panic," "unexpected turn of the market." But how could he be caught, his wife demanded, with contracting blue eyes? Had his firm failed? And after a little, — lie and subterfuge within lie and subterfuge being unwrapped, — it appeared, — the fact. He had "gone into cotton" — with whose money? His mother's estate, — those excellent four per cent gold bonds that the thrifty judge had put aside for his widow!

With the look that Margaret gave her husband, he might have seen that the process of petrifaction had set in, had gone far, indeed.

Margaret loved her mother-in-law, — the sweet old woman of gentle fancies who lived in an old house in an old town on the Massachusetts coast, the town where she and the judge had grown up. An unworldly, gentle woman, who had somehow told her daughter-in-law without words that she knew what was missing in her woman's heart. No, the judge's widow should not pay for her son's folly! So Margaret sold the New York house, which was hers, and also some of those mountain lands that had a growing value now, realizing bitterly that by this early sale she was sacrificing her boys' heritage — the gift of her forefathers — for a miserable tithe of its real value, — just because their father was too weak to hold what others had given him; and hadn't kept faith with her like a frank comrade. . . . What was left she took into her own possession.

So the Poles went abroad, after this. In doubt and distress, in sickness and divorce, what else does an American do? Margaret had one lingering hope for her husband. He had a good voice. At college it was considered remarkable, — a clear, high tenor. He had done little with his gift except make social capital out of it. And he had some aptitude for acting. He had been a four years' star in the college operas. If the judge had not belonged to the settled classes, Larry might have adorned a "Broadway show." Instead, through his father's influence, he had attempted finance — and remained an amateur, a "gentleman." But now, Margaret said to herself, over there, away from trivial society, — the bungled business career ended, — Larry might turn to his gift seriously. He was only thirty-two, — not too old, with hard work and steady persistence, which she would supply, to achieve something. For she would have been content to have him in the Broadway show; it mattered not to her now what he should do. And then she beguiled herself with the hope that some of that intellectual life, the interests in books, music, art — in ideas — could come to them in common, — a little of what she had dreamed the husband-and-wife life might be like. Thus with clear insight into her husband's nature, with few illusions, but with tolerance and hope, Margaret betook herself to Munich and settled her family in a little villa on the outskirts, conformable to their income, — *her* income, which was all they had. But it mattered not what she had to live on; her mother had shown her how to make a little answer. . . .

At first Larry liked this Munich life. It saved his vanity, and offered an easy solution for his catastrophe in cotton. He was the artist, not fitted for business, as his wife saw. He liked to go to concerts and opera, and take lessons, — but he had to learn German and he was lazy about that. Margaret studied German with him, until the little girl came. Then Larry was left to amuse himself, and did it. First he found some idle American students, and ran about with them, and through them he fell in with a woman of the Stacia Conry type, of which there is always a supply in every agreeable European centre. When Margaret emerged from her retirement and began to look about, she found this Englishwoman very prominent on the horizon. Larry sang with her and drove with her and did the other things that he could not do with his wife. He was the kind of man who finds the nine months of his wife's disability socially irksome, and amuses himself more or less innocently.

Margaret understood. Whether Larry's fondness for Mrs. Demarest was innocent or not, she did not care; she was surprised with herself to find that she had no jealousy whatever. Mrs. Demarest did not exist for her. This Mrs. Conry had a husband who came to Munich after her and bore her back to London. When Larry proposed that they should spend the next season in London, his wife said calmly: —

"You may if you like. I am going to return to America."

"And my work?"

Margaret waved a hand ironically: —

"You will be better alone. . . . My father is getting old and feeble; I must see him." . . .

When the family sailed, Larry was in the party. Mrs. Demarest had written him the proper thing to write after such an intimacy, and Larry felt that he must "get a job." . . .

In those months of the coming of the little girl and the summer afterwards, the new Margaret had been born. It was a quiet woman, outwardly calm, inwardly thinking its way slowly to conclusions, — thoughts that would have surprised the good Bishop. For when her heart had begun to grow cold in the process of petrifaction, there had awakened a new faculty, — her mind. She began to digest the world. Those little rules of life, the ones handed down with the prayer-book, having failed, she asked questions, — 'What is life? What is a woman's life? What is *my* life? What is duty? A woman's duty? *My* duty, married to Larry?' . . .

And one by one with relentless clarity she stripped bare all those platitudinous precepts that she had inherited, had accepted, as one accepts the physical facts of the world. When the untrained mind of a woman, driven in on itself by some spiritual bruise, begins to reach out for light, the end may be social Anarchy. Margaret read and understood French and German, and she had ample time to read. She saw modern plays that presented facts, naked and raw, and women's lives from the inside, without regard to the moral convention. She perceived that she had a soul, an inner life of her own, apart from her husband, her children, her father, from all the world. That soul had its own rights, — must be respected. What it might compel her to do in the years to come, was not yet clear. She waited, — growing. If it had not been for her father, she would have been content to stay on in Europe as she was, reading, thinking, loving her children.

On the way back to America, Larry, becoming conscious in the monotony of the voyage of his own insufficiency and failure, hinted that he was ready to accept the mountain home, which Margaret still retained, her mother's old house. "We might try living in the country," he suggested. But Margaret, focussing in one rapid image the picture of her husband always before her in the intimacy of a lonely country life, Larry disintegrating in small ways, shook her head firmly, giving as an excuse, "The children must have schools." She would set him at some petty job in the city, anything to keep him from rotting completely. For he was the father of her children!

The good old Bishop met them at the pier in New York. In spite of his hardened convictions about life, the little rule of thumb by which he lived, he knew something of men and women; and he suspected that process of petrifaction in his daughter's heart. So he took occasion to say in their first intimate talk: —

"I am glad that you and Lawrence have decided to come home to live. It is not well for people to remain long away from their own country, to evade the responsibilities of our social brotherhood. The Church preaches the highest communism, . . . and you must help your husband to find some definite service in life, and do it."

Margaret's lips curved dangerously, and the Bishop, as if answering this sign, continued: —

"Lawrence does not show great power, I know, my dear. But he is a good man, — a faithful husband and a kind father. That is much, Margaret. It rests with you to make him more!"

'Does it?' Margaret was asking herself behind her blank countenance. 'One cannot make bricks without straw. . . . What is that sort of goodness worth in a man? I had rather my husband were what you call a bad man — and a Man.' But she said nothing.

"Thus our Lord has ordered it in this life," continued the Bishop, feeling that he was making headway; "that one who is weak is bound to one who is stronger, — perchance for the good of both."

Margaret smiled.

"And a good woman has always the comfort of her children, — when she has been blessed with them, — who will grow to fill the desolate places in her heart," concluded the good Bishop, feeling that he had irrefutably presented to his daughter the right ideas. But the daughter was thinking, with the new faculty that was awakening in her: —

'Do children fill the desolate spots in a woman's heart completely? I love mine, even if they are spotted with *his* weaknesses. I am a good mother, — I know that I am, — yet I could love, — oh, I could love grandly some one else, and love them more because of it! At thirty a woman is not done with loving, even though she has three children.'

But she did not dispute her father's words, merely saying in a weary voice, "I suppose Larry and I will make a life of it, as most people do, somehow!"

Nevertheless, as she spoke these words of endurance, there was welling up within her the spirit of rebellion against her lot, — the ordinary lot of acceptance. She had a consciousness of power in herself to live, to be something other than the prosaic animal that endures.

The Poles took the house at Dudley Farms and began the routine of American suburban life, forty miles from New York. After several months of futile effort, spaced by periods of laziness that Margaret put an end to, a gentleman's job was secured for Larry, through the kindness of one of his father's friends. At first Larry was inclined to think that the work would belittle him, spoil his chances of "better things." But Margaret, seeing that as assistant secretary to the Malachite Company he could do no harm, could neither gamble nor loaf, replied to these doubts in a tone of cold irony: —

"You can resign when you find something better suited to your talents."

Thus at thirty-five Larry was *rangé* and a commuter. He dressed well, kept up one of his clubs, talked the condition of the country, and was a kind father to his boys. . . . 'What more should a woman expect?' Margaret asked herself, thinking of her father's words and enumerating her blessings. Three healthy children, a home and enough to eat and wear, a husband who (in spite of Conny's gossip) neither drank to excess nor was unfaithful nor beat her, — who had none of the obvious vices of the male! Good God! Margaret sighed with a bitter sense of irony.

"I must be a wicked woman," her mother would have said under similar circumstances, — and there lies the change in woman's attitude.

Looking across the table at Larry in his neat evening clothes, — he was growing a trifle stout these days, — listening to his observations on the railroad service, or his suggestion that she should pay more attention to dress, Margaret felt that some day she must shriek maniacally. But instead her heart grew still and cold, and her blue eyes icy.

"What is there in woman that makes trifles so important?" she asked Isabelle in a rare effusion of truth-speaking. "Why do some voices — correct and well-bred ones — exasperate you, and others, no better, fill you with content, comfort? Why do little acts — the way a man holds a book or strokes his mustache — annoy you? Why are you dead and bored when you walk with one person, and are gay when you walk by yourself?"

To all of which Isabelle sagely replied: "You think too much, Margaret dear. As John says when I ask him profound questions, 'Get up against something real!'"

For Isabelle could be admirably wise where another was concerned.

"Yes," Margaret admitted, "I suppose I am at fault. It is my job to make life worth living for all of us, — the Bishop, mother-in-law, children, Larry, — all but myself. That's a woman's privilege."

So she did her "job." But within her the lassitude of dead things was ever growing, sapping her physical buoyancy, sapping her will. She called to her soul, and the weary spirit seemed to have withdrawn.

"A case of low vitality," in the medical jargon of the day. And hers was a vital stock, too.

'In time,' she said, 'I shall be dead, and then I shall be a good woman, — wholly good! The Bishop will be content.' And she smiled in denial of her own words. For even then, at the lowest ebb, her soul spoke: there was wonder and joy and beauty somewhere in this gray procession of phenomena, and it must come to her sometime. And when it came, her heart said, she would grasp it!

CHAPTER XXXIII

These days Larry Pole began to think well of himself once more. He had made his mistakes, — what man hasn't? — but he had wiped out the score, and he was fulfilling the office of under-secretary to the great Malachite Company admirably. He was conscious that the men in the office felt that his personality, his bearing, and associations gave distinction to the place. And he still secretly looked for some turn in the game which would put him where he desired to be. In New York the game is always on, the tables always set: from the newsboy to the magnate the gambler's hope is open to every man.

Only one thing disturbed his self-complacency, — Margaret treated him indifferently, coldly. He even suspected that though by some accident she had borne him three children he had never won her love, that she had never been really his. Since their return from Europe and establishing themselves in the country, she had withdrawn more and more from him — where? Into herself. She had her own room and dressing-room, beyond the children's quarters, in the rear of the rambling house, and her life seemed to go on in those rooms more and more. It was almost, Larry observed discontentedly, as if there were not a husband in the situation. Well, he reflected philosophically, women were like that, — American women; they thought they owned themselves even after they had married. If a wife took that attitude, she must not complain if the husband went his way, too. Larry in these injured moods felt vague possibilities of wickedness within him, — justified errancies. . . .

One day he was to see deep into that privacy, to learn all — all he was capable of understanding — about his wife. Margaret had been to the city, — a rare event, — had lunched with Isabelle, and gone to see a new actress in a clever little German play. She and Isabelle had talked it over, — very animatedly. Then she had brought back with her some new books and foreign reviews. After dinner she was lying on the great lounge before the fire, curled up in a soft dress of pale lilac, seriously absorbing an article on a Russian playwright. Hers was a little face, — pale, thin, with sunken eyes. The brow was too high, and latterly Margaret paid no attention to arranging her hair becomingly. It was not a face that could be called pretty; it would not be attractive to most men, her husband thought as he watched her. But it had drawn some men strongly, fired them; and Larry still longed for its smiles, — desired her.

He had felt talkative that evening, had chattered all through dinner, and she had listened tolerantly, as she might to her younger boy when he had a great deal to say about nothing. But now she had taken refuge in this review, and Larry had dropped from sight. When he had finished his cigarette, he sat down on the edge of the lounge, taking her idle hand in his. She let him caress it, still reading on. After a time, as he continued to press the hand, his wife said without raising her eyes: —

"What do you want?"

"'What do you want?'" Larry mimicked! "Lord! you American women are as hard as stone."

"Are the others different?" Margaret asked, raising her eyes.

"They say they are — how should I know?"

"I thought you might know from experience," she observed equably.

"I have never loved any woman but you, Margaret!" he said tenderly. "You know that!"

Margaret made no response. The statement seemed to demand something of her which she could not give. He took her hand again, caressed it, and finally kissed her. She looked at him steadily, coldly.

"Please — sit over there!" As her husband continued to

caress her, she sat upright. "I want to say something to you, Larry."

"What is it?"

"There can't be any more of *that* — you understand? — between us."

"What do you mean?"

"I mean — *that*, what you call love, passion, is over between us."

"Why? . . . what have I done?"

Margaret waved her hand impatiently: —

"It makes no difference, — I don't want it — I can't — that is all."

"You refuse to be my wife?"

"Yes, — that way."

"You take back your marriage vow?" (Larry was a high churchman, which fact had condoned much in the Bishop's eyes.)

"I take back — myself!"

Margaret's eyes shone, but her voice was calm.

"If you loved any other man — but you are as cold as ice!"

"Am I?"

"Yes! . . . I have been faithful to you always," he observed by way of defence and accusation.

Margaret rose from the couch, and looked down at her husband, almost compassionately. But when she spoke, her low voice shook with scorn: —

"That is your affair, — I have never wanted to know. . . . You seem to pride yourself on that. Good God! if you were more of a man, — if you were man enough to *want* anything, even sin, — I might love you!"

It was like a bolt of white fire from the clear heavens. Her husband gasped, scarcely comprehending the words.

"I don't believe you know what you are saying. Something has upset you. . . . Would you like me to love another woman? That's a pretty idea for a wife to advance!"

"I want you to — oh, what's the use of talking about it, Larry? You know what I mean — what I think, what I have felt — for a long time, even before little Elsa came. How can you want love with a woman who feels towards you as I do?"

"It is natural enough for a man who cares for his wife —"

"Too natural," Margaret laughed bitterly. "No, Larry; that's all over! You can do as you like, — I shan't ask questions. And we shall get on very well, like this."

"This comes of the rotten books you read!" he fumed.

"I do my own thinking."

"Suppose I don't want the freedom you hand out so readily?" he asked with an appealing note. "Suppose I still love you, my wife? have always loved you! You married me. . . . I've been unfortunate —"

"It isn't that, you know! It isn't the money — the fact that you would have beggared your mother — not quite that. It's everything — *you!* Why go into it? I don't blame you, Larry. But I know you now, and I don't love you — that is all."

"You knew me when you married me. Why did you marry me?"

"Why — why did I marry you?"

Margaret's voice had the habit of growing lower and stiller as passion touched her heart. "Yes — you may well ask that! Why does a woman see those things she wants to see in a man, and is blind to what she might see! . . . Oh, why does any woman marry, my husband?"

And in the silence that followed they were both thinking of those days in Washington, eight years before, when they had met. He was acting as secretary to some great man then, and was flashing in the pleasant light of youth, popularity, social approbation. He had "won out" against the Englishman, Hollenby, — why, he had never exactly known. Margaret was thinking of that why, as a woman does think at times for long years afterwards, trying to solve the psychological puzzle of her foolish youth! Hollenby was certainly the abler man, as well as the more brilliant prospect. And there were others who had loved her, and whom even as a girl she had wit enough to value. . . . A girl's choice, when her heart speaks, as the novelists say, is a curious process, compounded of an infinite number of subtle elements, — suggestions, traits of character, and above all temporary atmospheric conditions of mind. It is a marvel if it ever can be resolved into its elements! . . . The Englishman — she was almost his — had lost her because once he had betrayed to the girl the brute. One frightened glimpse of the animal in his nature had been enough. And in the rebound from this chance perception of man as brute, she had listened to Lawrence Pole, because he seemed to her all that the other was not, — high-souled, poetic, restrained, tender, — all the ideals. With him life would be a communion of lovely and lovable things. He would secure some place in the diplomatic service abroad, and they would live on the heights, with art, ideas, beauty. . . .

"Wasn't I a fool — not to know!" she remarked aloud. She was thinking, with the tolerance of mature womanhood: 'I could have tamed the brute in the other one. At least he was a man!' "Well, we dream our dreams, sentimental little girls that we are! And after a time we open our eyes like kittens on life. I have opened mine, Larry, — very wide open. There isn't a sentimental chord in my being that you can twang any longer. . . . But we can be good-tempered and sensible about it. Run along now and have your cigar, or go over to the country club and find some one to play billiards, — only let me finish what you are pleased to call my rotten reading, — it is so amusing!"

She had descended from the crest of her passion, and could play with the situation. But her husband, realizing in some small way the significance of these words they had exchanged, still probed the ground: —

"If you feel like that, why do you still live with me? Why do you consent to bear my name?"

The pomposity of the last words roused a wicked gleam in his wife's eyes. She looked up from her article again.

"Perhaps I shan't always 'consent to bear your name,' Larry. I'm still thinking, and I haven't thought it all out yet. When I do, I may give up your name, — go away. Meanwhile I think we get on very well: I make a comfortable home for you; you have your children, — and they are well brought up. I have kept you trying to toe the mark, too. Take it all in all, I haven't been a bad wife, — if we are to present references?"

"No," Larry admitted generously; "I have always said you were too good for me, — too fine."

"And so, still being a good wife, I have decided to take myself back." She drew her small body together, clasping her arms about the review. "My body and my soul, — what is personally most mine. But I will serve you — make you comfortable. And after a time you won't mind, and you will see that it was best."

"It goes deeper than that," her husband protested, groping for the idea that he caught imperfectly; "it means practically that we are living under the same roof but aren't married!"

"With perfect respectability, Larry, which is more than is always the case when a man and a woman live under the same roof, either married or unmarried! . . . I am afraid that is it in plain words. But I will do my best to make it tolerable for you."

"Perhaps some day you'll find a man, — what then?"

Margaret looked at him for a long minute before replying. "And if I should find a Man, God alone knows what would happen!"

Then in reply to the frightened look on her husband's face, she added lightly: —

"Don't worry, Larry! No immediate scandal. I haven't any one in view, and living as I do it isn't likely that I shall be tempted by some knightly or idiotic man, who wants to run away with a middle-aged woman and three children. I am anchored safely — at any rate as long as dad lives and your mother, and the children need my good name.

Oh!" she broke off suddenly; "don't let us talk any more about it!" . . .

Leaning her head on her hands, she looked into the fire, and murmured to herself as if she had forgotten Larry's presence: —

"God! why are we so blind, so blind, — and our feet caught in the net of life before we know what is in our souls!"

For she realized that when she said she was middle-aged and anchored, it was but the surface truth. At thirty, with three children, she was more the woman, more capable of love, passion, understanding, devotion — more capable of giving herself wholly and greatly to a mate — than any girl could be. The well of life still poured its flood into her! Her husband could never know that agony of longing, those arms stretched out to — what? When would this torture of defeated capacity be ended — when had God set the term for her to suffer!

In the black silence that had fallen between them, Pole betook himself to the club, as his wife had suggested, for the consolation of billiards and talk among sensible folk, "who didn't take life so damned hard." In the intervals of these distractions his mind would revert to what had passed between him and his wife that evening. Margaret's last remarks comforted him somewhat. Nothing of a scandalous or public demonstration of her feeling about her marriage was imminent. Nevertheless, his pride was hurt. In spite of the fact that he had suspected for a long time that his wife was cold, — was not "won," — he had hitherto travelled along in complacent egotism. "They were a fairly happy couple" or "they geed as well as most," as he would have expressed it. He had not suspected that Margaret might feel the need of more than that. To-night he had heard and understood the truth, — and it was a blow. Deep down in his masculine heart he felt that he had been unjustly put in the wrong, somehow. No woman had the right — no wife — to say without cause that having thought better of the marriage bargain she had "taken herself back." There was something preposterous in the idea. It was due to the modern fad of a woman's reading all sorts of stuff, when her mind was inflammable. He recognized that his wife was the more important, the stronger person of the two, — that was the trouble with American women (Larry always made national generalizations when he wished to express a personal truth) — they knew when they were strong, — felt their oats. They needed to be "tamed."

But Larry was aware that he was not fitted for the task of woman-tamer, and moreover it should have been begun long before this.

So having won his game of billiards Larry had a drink, which made him even more philosophical. "Margaret is all right," he said to himself. "She was strung up to-night, — something made her go loose. But she'll come around, — she'll never do the other thing!" Yet in spite of a second whiskey and soda before starting for home, he was not absolutely convinced of this last statement.

What makes a man like Larry Pole content to remain the master of the fort merely in name, when the woman has escaped him in spirit? Why will such men as he live on for years, aye and get children, with women, who do not even pretend to love them?

Meanwhile the wife sat there before the fire, her reading forgotten, thinking, thinking. She had said more than she herself knew to be in her heart. For one lives on monotonously, from day to day, unresolved, and then on occasion there flame forth unsuspected ideas, resolves. For the soul has not been idle. . . . It was true that their marriage was at an end. And it was not because of her husband's failures, his follies, — not the money mistakes. It was himself, — the petty nature he revealed in every act. For women like Margaret Pole can endure vice and folly and disappointment, but not a petty, trivial, chattering biped that masquerades as Man.

CHAPTER XXXIV

In the weeks that followed the accident Margaret Pole saw much of Falkner. The engineer would come up the hill to the old house late in the afternoon after his work, or ride up on his bicycle in the morning on his way to the dam he was building. Ned — "the Little Man" as Falkner called him — came to expect this daily visit as one of his invalid rights. Several times Falkner stayed to dinner; but he bored Larry, who called him "a Western bounder," and grumbled, "He hasn't anything to say for himself." It was true that Falkner developed chronic dumbness in Larry's conversational presence. But Margaret seemed to like the "bounder." She discovered that he carried in his pocket a volume of verse. An engineer who went to his job these days with a poetry book in his coat pocket was not ordinary, as she remarked to her husband. . . .

Falkner's was one of those commonplace figures to be seen by the thousands in an American city. He dressed neither well nor ill, as if long ago the question of appearances had ceased to interest him, and he bought what was necessary for decency in the nearest shop. His manners, though brusque, indicated that he had always been within that vague line which marks off the modern "gentleman." His face, largely covered by beard and mustache, was pale and thoughtful, and his eyes were tired, usually dull. He was merely one of the undistinguished units in the industrial army. Obviously he had not "arrived," had not pushed into the circle of power. Some lack of energy, or natal unfitness for the present environment? Or was he inhibited by a twist of fate, needing an incentive, a spur?

At any rate the day when Margaret met him, the day when he had brought her boy home in his arms, the book of life seemed closed and fastened for him forever. The fellow-units in the industrial scheme in which he had become fixed, might say of him, — "Yes, a good fellow, steady, intelligent, but lacks push, — he'll never get there." Such are the trite summaries of man among men. Of all the inner territory of the man's soul, which had resolved him in its history to what he was, had left him this negative unit of life, his fellows were ignorant, as man must be of man. They saw the Result, and in the rough arithmetic of life results are all that count with most people.

But the woman — Margaret, — possessing her own hidden territory of soul existence, had divined more, even in that first tragic moment, when he had borne her maimed child into the house and laid his burden tenderly on the lounge. As he came and went, telephoning, doing the little that could be done, she saw more than the commonplace figure, clothed in ready-made garments; more than the dull, bearded face, the strong, thin hands, the rumpled hair. Something out of that vast beyond which this stranger had in common with her had spoken through the husk, even then. . . .

And it had not ended there, as it would have ended, had Falkner been the mere "bounder" Larry saw. It was Falkner to whom the mother first told the doctors' decision about the boy. Certain days impress their atmosphere indelibly; they have being to them like persons, and through years the odor, the light, the sense of their few hours may be recalled as vividly as when they were lived. This May day the birds were twittering beside the veranda where Margaret was reading to the Little Man, when Falkner came up the drive. The long windows of the house were opened to admit the soft air, for it was already summer. Margaret was dressed in a black gown that relieved the pallor of her neck and face like the dark background of an old portrait. As the boy called, "There's big Bob!" she looked up from her book and smiled. Yet in spite of the placid scene, the welcoming smile, Falkner knew that something had happened, — something of moment. The three talked and the birds chattered; the haze of the gentle brooding day deepened. Far away above the feathery treetops, which did their best to hide the little houses, there was the blue line of sea, gleaming in the sun. It seemed to Falkner after the long day's work the very spot of Peace, and yet in the woman's controlled manner there was the something not peace. When Falkner rose to go, Margaret accompanied him to the steps.

"It's like the South to-day, all this sun and windless air. You have never been in the South? Some days I ache for it."

In the full light she seemed a slight, worn figure with a blanched face.

"Bring me my puppy, please, Bob!" the child called from his couch. "He's in the garden."

Falkner searched among the flower-beds beneath the veranda and finally captured the fat puppy and carried him up to the boy, who hugged him as a girl would a doll, crooning to him. Margaret was still staring into space.

"What has happened?" Falkner asked.

She looked at him out of her deep eyes, as if he might read there what had happened. They descended the steps and walked away from the house.

"He hears so quickly," she explained; "I don't want him to know yet."

So they kept on down the drive.

"Dr. Rogers was here this morning. . . . He brought two other doctors with him. . . . There is no longer any doubt — it is paralysis of the lower limbs. He will never walk, they think."

They kept on down the drive, Falkner looking before him. He knew that the woman was not crying, would never betray her pain that watery way; but he could not bear to see the misery of those eyes.

"My father the Bishop has written me . . . spiritual consolation for Ned's illness. Should I feel thankful for the chastening to my rebellious spirit administered to me through my poor boy? Should I thank God for the lash of the whip on my stubborn back?"

Falkner smiled.

"My father the Bishop is a good man, a kind man in his way, yet he never considered my mother, — he lived his own life with his own God. . . . It would surprise him if he knew what I thought about God, — *his* God, at least." . . .

Falkner looked at her at last, and they stopped. Afterwards he knew that he already loved Margaret Pole. He, too, had divined that the woman, stricken through her child, was essentially alone in the world, and in her hungry eyes lay the story of the same dreary road over which he had passed. And these two, defeated ones in the riotous world of circumstance, silently, instinctively held out hands across the void and looked at each other with closed lips.

Among the trees the golden haze deepened, and the birds sang. Down below in the village sounded the deep throbs of an engine: the evening train had come from the city. It was the only disturbing note in the peace, the silence. The old house had caught the full western sun, and its dull red bricks glowed. On the veranda the small boy was still caressing the puppy.

"Mother!" a thin voice sounded. Margaret started.

"Good-by," Falkner said. "I shall come to-morrow."

At the gate he met Pole, lightly swinging a neat green bag, his gloves in his hand. Larry stopped to talk, but Falkner, with a short, "Pleasant afternoon," kept on. Somehow the sight of Pole made the thing he had just learned all the worse.

Thus it happened that in the space of a few weeks Margaret knew Falkner more intimately than Isabelle had ever known him or ever could know him. Two beings meeting in this illusive, glimmering world of ours may come to a ready knowledge of each other, as two travellers on a dark road, who have made the greater part of the stormy journey alone. It would be difficult to record the growth of that inner intimacy, — so much happening in wordless moments or so much being bodied forth in little words that would be as meaningless as newspaper print. But these weeks of the child's invalidism, there was growing within them another life that no one shared or would have understood. When Larry observed, "That bounder is always here," Margaret did not seem to hear. Already the food that the "bounder" had given her parched self was too precious to lose. She had begun to live again the stifled memories, the life laid away, — to talk of her girlhood, of her Virginia hills, her people.

And Falkner had told her something of those earlier years in the Rockies, when he had lived in the world of open spaces and felt the thrill of life, but never a word of what had passed since he had left the cañons and the peaks. Sometimes these days there was a gleam in his dark eyes, a smile on the bearded lips that indicated the reopening of the closed book once more. His fellow-units in the industrial world might not see it; but Margaret felt it. Here was a human being pressed into the service of the machine and held there, at pay, powerless to extract himself, sacrificed. And she saw what there was beneath the mistake; she felt the pioneer blood, like her own, close to the earth in its broad spaces, living under the sky in a new land. She saw the man that should be, that once was, that must be again! And in this world of their other selves, which had been denied them, these two touched hands. They needed little explanation.

Rarely Margaret spoke of her present life, and then with irony, as if an inner and unsentimental honesty compelled utterance: "You see," she remarked once when her husband called her, "we dress for dinner because when we started in New York we belonged to the dining-out class. If we didn't keep up the habit, we should lose our self-respect. . . . My neck is thin and I don't look well in evening dress. But that makes no matter. . . . We have prayers on Sunday morning; religion is part of the substantial life." . . .

Conny had said once, hearing Margaret rail like this: "She ought to make a better bluff, or get out, — not guy old Larry like that ; it isn't decent, embarrasses one so. You can't guy him, too." . . .

But Falkner understood how the acid of her daily life eating into her had touched, at these times, a sensitive nerve and compelled such self-revelations.

It was Falkner who first spoke to the Poles about Dr. Renault. In some way he had heard of the surgeon and learned of the wonderful things he had done.

"Anyhow it is worth while seeing him. It is best to try everything."

"Yes," Margaret assented quickly; "I shall not give up — never!"

Through a doctor whom he knew Falkner arranged the visit to the surgeon, who was difficult of access. And he went in the evening after the visit to learn the result.

"He thinks there is a chance!" and Margaret added more slowly: "It is a great risk. I supposed it must be so."

"You will take it?"

"I think," she said slowly, "that Ned would want me to. You see he is like me. It may accomplish nothing, Dr. Renault said. It may be partially successful. . . . Or it may be — fatal. He was very kind, — spent all the afternoon here. I liked him immensely; he was so direct."

"When will it be?"

"Next week."

The operation took place, and was not fatal. "Now we shall have to wait," the surgeon said to the mother, — "and hope! It will be months before we shall know finally what is the result."

"I shall wait and hope!" Margaret replied to him. Renault, who had a chord in common with this Southern woman, stroked her hand gently as he left. "Better take the little chap away somewhere and get a change yourself," he said.

It was a still, hot night of late June, the last time that Falkner climbed the hill to the old place. The summer, long delayed, had burst these last days with scorching fury. Margaret was to leave on the morrow for Bedmouth, where she would spend the summer with old Mrs. Pole. She was lying on the veranda couch. She smiled as Falkner drew a chair to her side, the frank smile from the deep blue eyes, that she gave only to her children and to him, and there was a joyous note in her voice: —

"At last there is a sign. I have a little more hope now!"

She told him of the first faint indications of life in the still limbs of the child.

"It will be months before we can tell really. But to-night I have strong hope!"

"What we need most in life is hope," he mused. "It keeps the thing going."

"As long as a man can work, he has hope," she replied stoutly.

"I suppose so, — at least he must think so."

Margaret knew that the work the engineer was engaged on was nearly finished. It might last at the most another six weeks, and he did not know where he should go then; but it was altogether unlikely that the fall would find him at Dudley Farms.

"I was in the city to-day," he said after a time, "and in the company's office I ran across my old chief. He's going to Panama in the fall." . . .

Margaret waited with strange expectancy for what Falkner might say next. She rarely asked questions, sought directly to know. She had the power of patience, and an unconscious belief that life shaped itself largely without the help of speech. Here and there in the drama of events the spoken word might be called for — but rarely.

"They have interesting problems down there," Falkner continued; "it is really big work, you know. A man might do something worth while. But it is a hole!"

She still waited, and what she expected came: —

"He asked me to go with him, — promised me charge of one of the dams, my own work, — it is the biggest thing that ever came my way."

And then the word fell from her almost without her will: —

"You must go! *Must* go!"

"Yes," he mused on; "I thought so. There was a time when it would have made me crazy, such a chance. . . . It's odd after all these years, when I thought I was dead —"

"Don't say dead!"

"Well, rutted deep in the mire, then, — that this should happen."

She had said "go," with all the truth of her nature. It was the thing for him to do. But she did not have the strength to say another word. In the moment she had seen with blinding clearness all that this man meant in her little firmament. 'This was a Man!' She knew him. She loved him! yes, she loved him, thank God! And now he must go out of her life as suddenly as he had come into it, — must leave her alone, stranded as before in the dark.

"It isn't so easy to decide," Falkner continued. "There isn't much money in it, — not for the under men, you know."

"What difference does that make!" she flashed.

"Not to me," he explained, and there was a pause. "But I have my wife and child to think of. I need all the money I can earn."

It was the first time any reference had been made to his family. After a time Margaret said: —

"But they pay fair salaries, and any woman would rather be pinched and have her husband in the front ranks —" And then she hesitated, something in Falkner's eyes troubling her.

"I shall not decide just yet. . . . The offer has stirred my blood, — I feel that I have some youth left!"

They said little more. Margaret walked with him down the avenue. In her summer dress she looked wasted, infinitely fragile.

"This is not good-by," he said at last. "I shall go down the coast in a boat for a week, as I used to do when I was a boy, and my sister has a cottage at Lancaster. That is not far from Bedmouth?"

"No, it isn't far," she answered softly.

They paused and then walked back, as if all was not said yet.

"There is another reason," Falkner exclaimed abruptly, "why I did not wish to go — and you must know it."

She raised her head and looked at him, murmuring, —

"Yes! I know it! . . . But *nothing* should keep you here."

"No, not keep me. . . . But there is something infinitely precious to lose by going. . . . You have made me live again, Margaret. I was dead, dead, — a dead soul."

"We were both dead . . . and now we live!"

"It were better not said, perhaps —"

"No!" she interrupted passionately. "It *ought* to be said! Why not?"

"There can be nothing for us," he muttered dully.

"No!" and her hands touched his. "Don't say that! We are both in the world, — don't you see?"

His face drew near to hers, they kissed, and she clung to him for the moment, then whispered: "Now go! You must live, live, — live greatly, — for us both!"

Margaret fled to her room, knelt down beside the boy's bed, with clasped hands, her eyes shining down on the sleeping child, a smile on her face.

CHAPTER XXXV

Cornelia Woodyard's expression was not pleasant when she was deliberating or in perplexity. Her broad brow wrinkled, and her mouth drew down at the corners, adding a number of years to her face. She did not allow this condition of perplexity to appear in public, reserving her "heavy thinking," as Tom Cairy called these moments, for the early morning hours of privacy. This languid spring day while Conny turned over her mail that lay strewn in disorder on her bed, she apparently had one of her worst fits of dubitation. She poked about in the mass of letters, bills, and newspapers until she found the sheet she was looking for, — it was in her husband's handwriting, — reread it, the scowl deepening, pushed it back thoughtfully into its envelope, and rang for the maid that looked after her personally as well as performed other offices in the well-organized household. When Conny emerged at the end of the hour in street costume, the frown had disappeared, but her fair face wore a preoccupied air.

"Hello, Tom!" she said wanly to Cairy, who was dawdling over the paper in the library. "How is it out?"

"Warm, — a perfect day!" Cairy replied, smiling at her and jumping to his feet.

"Is the cab there?"

"Yes, — shall we start?"

"I can't go to-day, Tom, — something has turned up."

"Something has turned up?" he queried. He was an expert in Conny's moods, but he had seen little of this mood lately.

"Business," Conny explained shortly. "Leave the cab, please. I may want it. . . . No," she added as Cairy came towards her with a question on his lips. "I can't bother to explain, — but it's important. We must give up our day."

She turned to her desk, and then remarked as if she felt Cairy's disappointment: "You can come in after dinner if you like, Tom! We can have the evening, perhaps."

He looked at her questioningly, as if he would insist on an explanation. But Conny was not one of whom even a lover would demand explanations when she was in this mood.

"We can't always play, Tommy!" she sighed.

But after he had left the room she called him back.

"You didn't kiss me," she said sweetly. "You may if you like, just once. . . . There!" she raised her head and smiled at Cairy, with that satisfaction which emotional moments brought to her. "You had better get to work, too. You can't have been of much use to Gossom lately." And she settled herself at her desk with the telephone book. As she called the hotel where Senator Thomas usually stayed when he was in the city, the scowl returned to her brow. Her mind had already begun to grapple with the problems suggested by Percy's letter of the morning. But by the time she had succeeded in getting the Senator, her voice was gentle and sweet. . . .

. . . "Yes, at luncheon, — that will be very nice!" And she hung up the receiver with an air of swift accomplishment.

It is not necessary to go into what had passed between Cornelia Woodyard and Cairy in the weeks that had elapsed since that day when Conny had been so anxious to get back to New York from the Poles'. It would gratify merely a vulgar curiosity. Suffice it to say that never before had Conny been so pleased with life or her own competent handling of her affairs in it. Up to this morning she felt that she had admirably fulfilled all claims upon her as well as satisfied herself. Things had seemed "to come her way" during this period. The troublesome matter before the

Commission that had roused her husband's conscience and fighting blood had gone over for the time. The Commission had reserved its decision, and the newspapers had gone off on a number of other scents of wrong-doing that seemed more odorously promising. Percy's conscience had returned to its normal unsuspecting state, and he had been absorbed to an unwonted degree in private business of one sort or another.

Meantime the Senator and Cornelia had had a number of little talks. The Senator had advised her about the reinvestment of her money, and all her small fortune was now placed in certain stocks and bonds of a paper company that "had great prospects in the near future," as the Senator conservatively phrased it. Percy, naturally, had known about this, and though he was slightly troubled by the growing intimacy with the Senator, he was also flattered and trusted his wife's judgment. "A shrewd business head," the Senator said of Conny, and the Senator ought to know. "It is as easy to do business with her as with a man." Which did not mean that Cornelia Woodyard had sold her husband to the Senator, — nothing as crude as that, but merely that she "knew the values" of this life.

The Senator and Conny often talked of Percy, the promise he had shown, his ability and popularity among all kinds of men. "If he steers right now," the Senator had said to his wife, "there is a great future ahead of Woodyard, and" — with a pleasant glance at Conny — "I have no doubt he will avoid false steps." The Senator thought that Congress would be a mistake. So did Conny. "It takes luck or genius to survive the lower house," the Senator said. They had talked of something in diplomacy, and now that the stocks and bonds of the paper-mill were to be so profitable, they could afford to consider diplomacy. Moreover, the amiable Senator, who knew how to "keep in" with an aggressively moral administration at Washington without altogether giving up the pleasing habit of "good things," promised to have Woodyard in mind "for the proper place."

So Conny had dreamed her little dream, which among many other things included the splendor of a career in some European capital, where Conny had no doubt that she could properly shine, and she felt proud that she could do so much for Percy. The world, this one at any rate, was for the able, — those who knew what to take from the table and how to take it. She was of those who had the instinct and the power. Then Percy's letter: —

. . . "Princhard came up to see me yesterday. From the facts he gave me I have no doubt at all what is the inner meaning of the Water Power bill. I shall get after Dillon [the chairman of the Commission] and find out what he means by delaying matters as he has. . . . It looks also as though the Senator had some connection with this steal. . . . I am sorrier than I can say that we have been so intimate with him, and that you followed his advice about your money. I may be down Sunday, and we will talk it over. Perhaps it is not too late to withdraw from that investment. It will make no difference, however, in my action here." . . .

Simply according to Conny's crisp version, "Percy has flown the track again!"

After a pleasant little luncheon with the Senator, Conny sent a telegram to her husband that she would meet him at the station on the arrival of a certain train from Albany that evening, adding the one word, "urgent," which was a code word between them. Then she telephoned the office of *The People's*, but Cairy was not there, and he had not returned when later in the afternoon she telephoned again.

"Well," she mused, a troubled expression on her face, "perhaps it is just as well, — Tom might not be easy to manage. He's more exacting than Percy about some things." So while the cab was waiting to take her to the station, she sat down at her desk and wrote a note, — a brief little note: —

"DEAR TOM: I am just starting for the station to meet Percy. Something very important has come up, which for the present must change things for us all. . . . You know that we agreed the one thing we could not do would be to let our feelings interfere with our duties — to any one. . . . I don't know when I can see you. But I will let you know soon. Good-by. C."

"Give this to Mr. Cairy when he calls and tell him not to wait," she said to the maid who opened the door for her. Conny did not believe in "writing foolish things to men," and her letter of farewell had the brevity of telegraphic despatch. Nevertheless she sank into the corner of the cab wearily and closed her eyes on the brilliant street, which usually amused her as it would divert a child. "He'll know sometime!" she said to herself. "He'll understand or have to get along without understanding!" and her lips drew together. It was a different world to-night from that of the day before; but unhappy as she was she had a subtle satisfaction in her willingness and her ability to meet it whatever side it turned towards her.

The train was a halfhour late, and as she paced the court slowly, she realized that Cairy had come to the house, — he was always prompt these days, — had received the note, and was walking away, reading it, — thinking what of her? Her lips tightened a trifle, as she glanced at the clock. "He will go to Isabelle's," she said to herself. "He likes Isabelle." She knew Cairy well enough to feel that the Southerner could not long endure a lonely world. And Conny had a tolerant nature; she did not despise him for going where he could find amusement and comfort; nor did she think his love less worth having. But she bit her lip as she repeated, "He will go to Isabelle." If Percy wanted to know the extent of his wife's devotion to their married life, their common interests, he should have seen her at this moment. As the train drew in, she had already thought, "But he will come back — when it is possible."

She met her husband with a frank smile.

"You'll have to take me somewhere to dinner," she drawled. "There isn't any at home, — besides I want to talk at once. Glad to see me?"

When they were finally by themselves in a small private room of a restaurant where Conny loved to go with her husband, — "because it seems so naughty," — she said in answer to his look of inquiry: "Percy, I want you to take me away — to Europe, just for a few weeks!"

Woodyard's face reflected surprise and concern.

"But, Con!" he stammered.

"Please, Percy!" She put her hand softly on his arm. "No matter what is in the way, — only for a few weeks!" and her eyes filled with tears, quite genuine tears, which dropped slowly to her pale face. "Percy," she murmured, "don't you love me any longer?" . . .

CHAPTER XXXVI

It was perfectly true, as Conny surmised, that Cairy went to Isabelle. But not that evening — the blow was too hard and too little expected — nor on the whole more frequently than he had been in the habit of going during the winter. Isabelle interested him, — "her problem," as he called it; that is, given her husband and her circumstances, how she would settle herself into New York, — how far she might go there. It flattered him also to serve as intellectual and æsthetic mentor to an attractive, untrained woman, who frankly liked him and bowed to his opinion. It was Cairy, through Isabelle, much more than Lane, who decided on the house in that up-town cross street, on the "right" side of the Park, which the Lanes finally bought. It was in an excellent neighborhood, "just around the corner" from a number of houses where well-known people lived. In the same block the Gossoms had established themselves, on the profits of *The People's*, and only two doors away, on the same side of the street, a successful novelist had housed himself behind what looked like a Venetian façade. Close by were the Rogerses, — he was a fashionable physician; the Hillary Peytons; the Dentons, — all people, according to Cairy, "one might know."

When Isabelle came to look more closely into this matter of settling herself in the city, she regretted the Colonel's illiberal will. They might easily have had a house nearer "the Avenue," instead of belonging to the polite poor-rich class two blocks east. Nevertheless, she tried to comfort herself by the thought that even with the Colonel's millions at their disposal they would have been "little people" in the New York scale of means. And the other thing, the "interesting," "right" society was much better worth while. "You make your own life, — it isn't made for you," Cairy said.

Isabelle was very busy these days. Thanks to the Potts régime, she was feeling almost well generally, and when she "went down," Dr. Potts was always there with the right drug to pull her up to the level. So she plunged into the question of altering the house, furnishing it, and getting it ready for the autumn. Her mother and John could not understand her perplexity about furnishing. What with the contents of two houses on hand, it seemed incomprehensible that the new home should demand a clean sweep. But Isabelle realized the solid atrocity of the Torso establishment and of the St. Louis one as well. She was determined that this time she should be right. With Cairy for guide and adviser she took to visiting the old furniture shops, selecting piece by piece what was to go into the new house. She was planning, also, to make that deferred trip to Europe to see her brother, and she should complete her selection over there, although Cairy warned her that everything she was likely to buy in Europe these days would be "fake." Once launched on the sea of household art, she found herself in a torturing maze. What was "right" seemed to alter with marvellous rapidity; the subject, she soon realized, demanded a culture, an experience that she had never suspected. Then there was the matter of the Farm at Grafton, which must be altered. The architect, who was making over the New York house, had visited Grafton and had ideas as to what could be done with the rambling old house without removing it bodily. "Tear down the barn — throw out a beautiful room here — terrace it — a formal garden there," etc. In the blue prints the old place was marvellously transformed.

"Aren't you doing too much, all at once?" Lane remonstrated in the mild way of husbands who have experienced nervous prostration with their wives.

"Oh, no; it interests me so! Dr. Potts thinks I should

keep occupied reasonably, with things that really interest me. . . . Besides I am only directing it all, you know."

And glad to see her once more satisfied, eager, he went his way to his work, which demanded quite all his large energy. After all, women had to do just about so much, and find their limit themselves.

Isabelle had learned to "look after herself," as she phrased it, by which she meant exercise, baths, massage, days off when she ran down to Lakewood, electricity, — all the physical devices for keeping a nervous people in condition. It is a science, and it takes time, — but it is a duty, as Isabelle reflected. Then there was the little girl. She was four now, and though the child was almost never on her hands, thanks to the excellent Miss Butts, Molly, as they called her, had her place in her mother's busy thoughts: what was the best regimen, whether she ought to have a French or a German governess next year, how she should dress, and in the distance the right school to be selected. Isabelle meant to do her best for the little girl, and looked back on her own bringing up — even the St. Mary's part of it — as distressingly haphazard, and limiting. Her daughter should be fitted "to make the most of life," which was what Isabelle felt that she herself was now beginning to do.

So Isabelle was occupied, as she believed profitably, spending her new energy wisely, and though she was getting worn, it was only a month to the date she had set for sailing. Vickers had promised to meet her at Genoa and take her into the Dolomites and then to San Moritz, where she could rest. As her life filled up, she saw less of her husband than ever, for he, too, was busy, "with that railroad thing," as she called the great Atlantic and Pacific. She made him buy a horse and ride in the Park afternoons when he could get the time, because he was growing too heavy. He had developed laziness socially, liked to go to some restaurant for dinner with chance friends that were drifting continually through New York, and afterwards to the theatre, — "to see something lively," as he put it, preferably Weber and

Fields', or Broadway opera. Isabelle felt that this was not the right thing, and boring, too; but it would all be changed when they were "settled." Meantime she went out more or less by herself, as the wives of busy men have to do.

"It is so much better not to bring a yawning husband home at midnight," she laughed to Cairy on one of these occasions when she had given him a seat down town in her cab. "By the way, you haven't spoken of Conny lately, — don't you see her any more?"

Isabelle still had her girlish habit of asking indiscreet, impertinent questions. She carried them off with a lively good nature, but they irritated Cairy occasionally.

"I have been busy with my play," he replied shortly.

As a matter of fact he had been attacked by one of those fits of intense occupation which came upon him in the intervals of his devotions. At such times he worked to better effect, with a kind of abandoned fury, than when his thoughts and feelings were engaged, as if to make up to his muse for his periods of neglect. The experience, he philosophized, which had stored itself, was now finding vent, — the spiritual travail as well as the knowledge of life. A man, an artist, had but one real passion, he told Isabelle, — and that was his work. Everything else was mere fertilizer or waste. Since the night that Conny had turned him from the door, he had completed his new play, which had been hanging fire all winter, and he was convinced it was his best. "Yes, a man's work, no matter what it may be, is God's solace for living." In response to which Isabelle mischievously remarked: —

"So you and Conny really have had a tiff? I must get her to tell me about it."

"Do you think she would tell you the truth?"

"No."

Isabelle, in spite of Cairy's protestations about his work, was gratified with her discovery, as she called it. She had decided that Conny was "a bad influence" on the Southerner; that Cairy was simple and ingenuous, — "really a nice boy," so she told her husband. Just what evil Conny had done to Cairy Isabelle could not say, ending always with the phrase, "but I don't trust her," or "she is so selfish." She had made these comments to Margaret Pole, and Margaret had answered with one of her enigmatic smiles and the remark:—

"Conny's no more selfish than most of us women,—only her methods are more direct—and successful."

"That is cynical," Isabelle retorted. "Most of us women are not selfish; I am not!"

And in her childlike way she asked her husband that very night:—

"John, do you think I am selfish?"

John answered this large question with a laugh and a pleasant compliment.

"I suppose Margaret means that I don't go in for charities, like that Mrs. Knop of the Relief and Aid, or for her old Consumers' League. Well, I had enough of that sort of thing in St. Louis. And I don't believe it does any good; it is better to give money to those who know how to spend it. . . . Have you any poor relatives we could be good to, John? . . . Any cousins that ought to be sent to college, any old aunts pining for a trip to California?"

"Lots of 'em, I suppose," her husband responded amiably. "They turn up every now and then, and I do what I can for them. I believe I am sending two young women to college to fit themselves for teaching."

Lane was generous, though he had the successful man's suspicion of all those who wanted help. He had no more formulated ideas about doing for others than his wife had. But when anything appealed to him, he gave and had a comfortable sense that he was helping things along.

Isabelle, in spite of the disquiet caused by Margaret's statement, felt convinced that she was doing her duty in life broadly, "in that station where Providence had called her." She was sure that she was a good wife, a good daughter, a good mother. And now she meant to be more than these humdrum things, — she meant to be Somebody, she meant to live! . . .

When she found time to call at the Woodyards', she saw that the house was closed, and the caretaker, who was routed out with difficulty, informed her that the master and mistress had sailed for Europe the week before.

'Very sudden,' mused Isabelle. 'I don't see how Percy could get away.'

Half the houses on the neighboring square were closed already, however, and she thought as she drove up town that it was time for her to be going. The city was becoming hot and dusty, and she was rather tired of it, too. Mrs. Price was to open the Farm for the summer and have Miss Butts and the little girl with her. John promised "to run over and get her" in September, if he could find time. Her little world was all arranged for, she reflected complacently. John would stay at the hotel and go up to Grafton over Sundays, and he had joined a club. Yes, the Lanes were shaking into place in New York.

Cairy sent her some roses when she sailed and was in the mob at the pier to bid her good-by.

"Perhaps I shall be over myself later on," he said, "to see if I can place the play."

"Oh, do!" Isabelle exclaimed. "And we'll buy things. I am going to ruin John."

Lane smiled placidly, as one not easily ruined. When the visitors were driven down the gangway, Isabelle called to Cairy: —

"Come on and go back in the tug with John!"

So Cairy limped back. Isabelle was nervous and tired, and now that she was actually on the steamer felt sad at seeing accustomed people and things about to slip away. She wanted to hold on to them as long as possible. Presently the hulking steamer was pulled out into the stream and headed for the sea. It was a hot June morning and through the haze the great buildings towered loftily. The long city raised a jagged sky-line of human immensity, and the harbor swarmed with craft, — car ferries, and sailing vessels dropping down stream carefully to take the sea breeze, steamers lined with black figures, screeching tugs, and occasionally a gleaming yacht. The three stood together on the deck looking at the scene.

"It always gives me the same old thrill," Cairy said. "Coming or going, it makes no difference, — it is the biggest fact in the modern world."

"I love it!" murmured Isabelle, her eyes fastened on the serried walls about the end of the island. "I shall never forget when I saw it as a child, the first time. It was mystery, like a story-book then, and it has been the same ever since."

Lane said nothing, but watched the city with smiling lips. To him the squat car ferries, the lighters, the dirty tramp steamers, the railroad yards across the river, as well as the lofty buildings of the long city — all the teeming life here at the mouth of the country — meant Traffic, the intercourse of men. And he, too, loved the great roaring city. He looked at it with a vista that reached from the Iowa town where he had first "railroaded it," up through the intervening steps at St. Louis and Torso, to his niche in the largest of these buildings, — all the busy years which he had spent dealing with men.

Isabelle touched his arm.

"I wish you were coming, too, John," she said as the breeze struck in from the open sea. "Do you remember how we talked of going over when we were in Torso?"

What a stretch of time there was between those first years of marriage and to-day! She would never have considered in the Torso days that she could sail off like this alone with a maid and leave her husband behind.

"Oh, it will be only a few weeks, — you'll enjoy yourself," he replied. He had been very good about her going over to join Vickers, made no objections to it this time. They were both growing more tolerant, as they grew older and saw more of life.

"What is in the paper?" she asked idly, as her husband rolled it up.

"There's a dirty roast on your friend, Percy Woodyard,— nothing else!"

"See, that must be the tug!" exclaimed Isabelle, pushing up her veil to kiss her husband. "Good-by — I wish you were going, too — I shall miss you so — be sure you exercise and keep thin!" . . .

She watched the two men climb down into the bobbing tug and take places beside the pilot room, — her tall, square-shouldered husband, and the slighter man, leaning on a cane, both looking up at her with smiles. John waved his paper at her, — the one that had the "roast" about Percy Woodyard. She had meant to read that, — she might see the Woodyards in Paris. Then the tug moved off, both men still waving to her. She hurried to the rear deck to get a last look, sentimental forlornness at leaving her husband coming over her afresh. As she gazed back at the retreating tug there was also in her heart a warm feeling for Cairy. "Poor Tom!" she murmured without knowing why.

On this great ship, among the thousand or more first-class passengers, there were a goodly number of women like her, leaving home and husband for a foreign trip. After all, as she had often said, it was a good idea for husbands and wives to have vacations from each other. There was no real reason why two people should stick together in an endless daily intimacy because they were married. . . .

Thus the great city — the city of her ambitions — sank mistily on the horizon.

PART FOUR

CHAPTER XXXVII

MRS. POLE's house stood on the outskirts of the old town of Bedmouth, facing the narrow road that ran eastward to the Point. In the days of Mrs. Pole's father the ships passing to and from Bedmouth on the river could be seen from the front windows. Now the wires of a trolley road disfigured the old street and cheap wooden houses cut off the view of the river. In the rear there was a small garden, sloping down to an inlet of the sea, from which could be seen Bedmouth-way the slender spires of two churches that rose among the drooping branches of the elms, and seaward the squat outline of a great summer hotel, bedecked with many flags. In the black mould of the old garden grew tall syringa bushes, lilacs, pampas grass, and a few tiger lilies, and over the crumbling brick walls hung dusty leaves of grapevines. When the gate at the bottom of the garden was open, there was a view of the inlet, bordered with marsh grass, and farther away a segment of the open sea, with the lighthouse on Goose Rock.

Here the Judge's wife had come to live when her husband died, forsaking Washington, which had grown "too busy for an old woman." . . .

At the end of the garden, which was shaded by the high wall, Margaret sat, an uncut book on her knees, her eyes resting on the green marsh to be seen through the open door. Near by Ned in his little invalid chair was picking the mortar from the brick wall with a nail he had been able to reach. The two were often alone like this for hours, silent.

"Mother," the child said at last, as Margaret took up the book.

"What is it, Ned?"

"Must I sit like this always,—forever and ever?"

"I hope not, dear. You must remember Dr. Renault said it would take patience."

"But I have been patient."

"Yes, I know, dear!"

"If I didn't get any better, should I have to sit like this always?" At last the question which she feared had come, the child's first doubt. It had been uncertain, the recovery of the lost power; at times it seemed as if there were no progress. The mother answered in her slow, deep voice:—

"Yes, dear; you would have to be patient always. But we are going to hope!"

"Mother," the child persisted, "why does it have to be so?"

And the mother answered steadily:—

"I don't know, my boy. Nobody knows why."

Ned resumed his scratching at the wall, pondering this mystery of an inexplicable world. Presently there was a sound of oars beyond the wall, and the child exclaimed:—

"There's Big Bob! He said he'd take me for a row."

Falkner carried off the Little Man for his promised boat ride, leaving Margaret to cut the leaves of her book and to think. It was the week before, the end of August, that Falkner had put into Bedmouth in his small sloop. He was staying with his sister at Lancaster, only a short walk on the other side of the Point. After a few days more at the most he would have to turn back southwards, and then? . . . She threw down her book and paced slowly back and forth along the garden walk. As the sun sank low, her mother-in-law appeared, a frail little lady, who looked gently into Margaret's face.

"I am afraid you feel the heat, Margaret. It has been a very hot day."

"Is it hot?" Margaret asked vaguely, shading her eyes with her hand to look out over the marsh.

There was the sound of oars and a child's laugh, loud and careless, just beyond the wall. "Look out!" Ned cried.

"There, you've wet your feet!" The two women smiled. That boyish laugh was rare these days.

When the grandmother wheeled Ned into the house for his supper, Margaret and Falkner strolled out of the garden beside the marsh to a rocky knoll that jutted into the sea. They seated themselves under a scrawny pine whose roots were bathed by the incoming tide, and watched the twilight stillness steal across the marshes and the sea. There was no air and yet the ships out by Goose Island passed across the horizon, sails full set, as though moved by an unseen hand.

They knew each other so well! And yet in silent times like these their intimacy seemed always to go deeper, to reveal without the aid of speech new levels of understanding.

"I had a letter this morning from Marvin," Falkner remarked at last.

Margaret scooped up a handful of pebbles and let them fall through her thin fingers, waiting for the expected words.

"It is settled. We sail from New York the tenth."

"The tenth?"

"Yes, . . . so I must go back soon and get ready."

The decision about Panama had been in the balance when Falkner left New York, she knew. Another opportunity of work in the States had come meanwhile; the decision had not been easy to make. When Falkner had written his wife, Bessie had replied: "You must do what seems best to you, as you have always done in the past. . . . Of course I cannot take the children to Panama." And when Falkner had written of the other work nearer home, Bessie said: "I don't care to make another move and settle in a new place. . . . We seem to get on better like this. Go to Panama if you want to, and we will see when you get back." So he had debated the matter with himself all the way up the coast. . . .

"When must you leave?"

"To-morrow," he answered slowly, and again they were silent.

It was as she wished, as she had urged. The new work would reopen the man's ambition, and that *must* be. Where a man's work was concerned, nothing—nothing surely of any woman—should intervene. That was her feeling. No woman's pining or longing to fetter the man: clear the decks for action!

"To-morrow!" she murmured. She was smiling bravely, a smile that belied the tenseness within. Falkner picked the long spines from a pine branch, and arranged them methodically one by one in a row. They were not all alike, differing in minute characteristics of size and length and color. Nature at her wholesale task of turning out these millions of needles varied the product infinitely. And so with human beings!

They two were at peace together, their inner hunger appeased, with a sustaining content in life neither had ever known before. When they were together in this intimate silence, their spirits were freed from all bondage, free to rise, to leap upwards out of the encircling abysm of things. And this state of perfect meeting — spiritual equilibrium — must end. . . .

"To-morrow?" she repeated, raising her eyes and gazing far out to the sunlit sea. And her heart was saying, "To-morrow, and to-morrow, and the days thereafter, — and all empty of this!"

"It is best so," he said. "It could not go on like this!"

"No! We are human, after all!" and smiling wanly she rose to return to the house. When they reached his boat, Falkner took her hand, — a hand with finely tapering fingers, broad in the palm and oval, — a woman's hand, firm to hold, gentle to caress. The fingers tightened about his slowly. He looked into the blue eyes; they were dry and shining. And in those shining eyes he read the same unspoken words of revolt that rose within his heart, — 'Why thus too late! too late! Why has life declared itself in all its meaning — too late? Why were we caught by the mistakes of half knowledge, and then received the revelation?' The futile questions of human hearts.

"You will come to-night — after dinner?" Margaret asked. "Bring the boat. We will go to Lawlor's Cove. I want to get away — from everything!"

As she mounted the garden steps to the house, she heard the whirr of a motor in the street. It stopped in front of the house, and as Margaret waited she heard Mrs. Hillyer's thin voice: "I am so sorry! Please tell Mrs. Pole that I came over from Lancaster to get her for dinner." Presently the motor whirled away in the direction of the great hotel, a cloud of dust following in its wake. Margaret stood for a moment watching the car disappear into the distance, thankful that she had escaped Mrs. Hillyer and her new motor just now. . . . The sun, sinking into the Bedmouth elms across the green marshes, fell full and golden upon her face. It was still and hot and brooding, this sunset hour, like the silent reaches of her heart. But slowly a smile broke from her lips, and she raised her arms to the light. It had touched her, the Sun God! It had burned her with its heat, its life. She knew! And she was glad. Nothing could take its fire wholly from her.

"To-night!" she murmured to herself.

CHAPTER XXXVIII

SHE had written him in that fierce honesty which spoke in every penstroke on the paper:—

. . . "Yes, I love you! I am proud when I say it over to myself, when I see it written here. I want you to know just how it is with me and my husband. . . . So our marriage was a mistake, one of the millions women make out of the girlish guess. Ignorance, blind ignorance of self and life! And my husband knows how it is between us. He knows that when the man comes to me whom I can love, I shall love him. . . . The man has come. . . . When it is time, I shall go to him and tell him honestly what has happened. I hate the little, lying women, — those who are afraid. I am not afraid! But these last hours I will have my heart's joy to myself, — we will draw a circle about ourselves." . . .

"As I kiss you, I love you with that spirit you have given me," she said to Falkner. "That is right, and this is right. You have given me life, and thus I give it back to you." . . .

When they were alone beside the sea this last evening, Margaret said: "Dearest, you must know as I know, that nothing which we have had together is sin. I would not yield even to you where I felt the right. To my father the Bishop, this would be Sin. To that dear old lady over there in Bedmouth, who suffered all her life from a bullying husband and from a selfish son, — and who is now too broken to think for herself, — it would be Sin, anything not suffering would be Sin! But I know!" She raised her head proudly from his arms. "I know within me that this is the rightest thing in all my life. When it came, I was sure that I should take it, and that it would save me from worse than death. . . . It came . . . and we were strong enough to take it, thank God!"

On the other side of the shingle rampart, which rose sheer behind them, the slow swells of the sea fell at distant intervals with solemn resonance, the only sound that broke the stillness of the night. This surge rising and falling on the land from out the great body of the sea was like a deep voice in the woman's soul, echoing her instinct of a reason beyond reasons that compelled.

But the man, holding her close to him, his lips upon her lips, did not heed her hot words of justification. His was the hunger which took what satisfied it without debate.

"It makes little difference, the right and the wrong, after to-night," he replied grimly, "in all the days to come. . . . We have lived and we have loved, that is enough."

"No, no, — we are not weak, blind fools!" she spoke on swiftly. "I will not have it so! I will not have you leave me to-night with the thought that some day you will feel that of me. You must understand — you must always remember through all the years of life — that I — the woman you love — am sinless, am pure. . . . I can go with your kisses upon my lips to my children, to little Ned, and hold them tight, and know that I am pure in the sight of God! . . .

"I give them my life, my all, — I am giving them this, too. A woman's heart is not filled with the love of children. A woman's life is not closed at thirty-two! . . . I have a soul — a life to be satisfied, — ah, dearest, a soul of my own to be filled, in order to give. Most men don't know that a woman has a life of her own — apart from her children, from her husband, from all. It's hers, hers, her very own!" she cried with a sob of joy and anguish.

In these words escaped the essence of that creed which had taken the place of the Bishop's teaching, — the creed that is breathed insensibly in the atmosphere of the age, — 'I, the woman, have a soul that is mine which has its rights, and what it bids me take, that I will take and hold!'

The man listened to the solemn rhythm of the sea pounding upon the rocky coast, and it spoke to him of fatality, of the surge of life striking blindly, carrying in its mighty grip the little human atoms. It had borne him up to the stars, and in a few hours it would roll him back, down into the gulf, from which no effort of his will could take him. With this hunger, which was his human birthright, he must labor on, unappeased. It was given him merely to know what would recreate living for him, what would make of the days joy instead of pain, and it was not to be his, except for this moment of time.

"I think," he said, "there is enough to suffer and endure. We will not quibble about the law. In the face of the gulf, why argue?" and he took her once more in his arms, where she rested content. . . .

Lawlor's Point was a little neck of shingle, curving inwards from the open sea, making a small harbor. On the landward side the still, salty marsh was fringed by evergreens that rose dark in the night. Once it had been a farm, its few acres swept by the full Atlantic winds, its shore pounded by the rock drift of the coast. Within the shingle the waves had washed a sandy beach. . . . Margaret knew the place years before, and they had found it to-night in the dark. The abandoned farm-house, windowless, loomed above them, desolate, forlorn, emitting an odor of the past from its damp rooms. About the old walnut tree where they had been sitting there grew in the long grass fleur-de-lys and myrtle.

"Let us go nearer to the water!" Margaret exclaimed. "I want to hear its voice close to my ears. This place is musty with dead lives. Dead lives!" She laughed softly. "I was like them once, only I walked and spoke, instead of lying still in a grave. And then you found me, dearest, and touched me. I shall never be dead like that again."

And when they had picked their way over the rough shingle to the water, she said in another passionate outburst, as if nature dammed for a long time were pouring itself forth in torrent: —

"Pain! Don't say the word. Do you think that we can count the pain — ever? Now that we have lived? What is Pain against Being!"

"A man's thought, that!" he reflected, surprised by the piercing insight, the triumphant answer of the spirit to the backward dragging surge of circumstance. "A woman suffers — always more than a man."

Margaret, flinging up her head to the dark heaven, the deep guttural note of the sea in her ears, chanted low, "Some pain is tonic. . . . Though to-night we are together, one and undivided — for the last time, the last time," she whispered, "yet I cannot feel the pain."

The man rebelled: —

"The last time? . . . But we are not ready, Margaret, — not yet!"

"We should never be ready!"

"We have had so little."

"Yes! So little — oh, so little of all the splendid chance of living."

The same thought lay between them. They had come but to the edge of experience, and beyond lay the vision of recreated life. Like souls that touched the confines of a new existence and turned back, so must they turn back to earth. So little! A few hours of meeting, a few spoken words, a few caresses, a few moments like this of mute understanding, out of all conscious time, and then nothing, — the blank!

There was something cowardly, thus to turn back at the edge of experience, incomplete and wistfully desirous. Yet the man would not ask her to venture on. What the woman would gladly give, he would not take as sacrifice. She understood.

"Would it be easier?" she asked slowly, "if for a time we had all?"

"Yes!"

"If for a little while we left the world behind us and went away — to know — all?"

"We should be happier then, always. . . . But I cannot ask it."

"It would be better so," she whispered dreamily. "I will go!"

Her hands clasped about him and her lips trembled.

"We will take our life!" She smiled as the vision of joy — food for a lifetime — filled her heart. "For a few hours I will be yours, all yours."

Thus, there beside the grumbling sea, these two — full man and woman, having weighed the issues of this life, the complex threads of soul and body, obligation and right, willed that they would take to themselves out of all eternity a few days, a few nights, a few mornings and a few evenings, — entire hours to be theirs, from which must be born courage for the future.

Old Mrs. Pole looked up at the sound of Margaret's step. The younger woman's face was pale, but still radiant with a complete joy. She patted the old lady's cheek and glanced down at the magazine in her lap. Between these two there was a depth of unspoken sympathy.

"Found a good story, mother dear?" Margaret asked.

The old woman's lips trembled. Many times that evening she had resolved to speak to Margaret of something her heart ached over. For she had seen far these last days with those old eyes that had seen so much. She could divine the dead waste in her daughter-in-law's heart, having lived with father and son, and out of the wisdom of suffering years endured she wished to speak to-night. But the deeper wisdom of age restrained her.

"Yes, my dear, — a very good story."

Each ache must find its own healing.

CHAPTER XXXIX

THE long train pulled slowly into the station of the little seaport town. It was late, as always at this turning-point of the season, when the summer population was changing its roost from sea to mountain or from the north to the south shore. Falkner, glancing anxiously along the line of cars for a certain figure, said again to himself, 'If she shouldn't come — at the last moment!' and ashamed of his doubt, replied, 'She will, if humanly possible.' . . . At last his eye caught sight of Margaret as she stepped from the last car. She had seen him at the instant, and she smiled rapidly above the crowd, one of her fleeting smiles, like a ray of April sun. Another smile, he took her bag from the porter's hand, and their meeting was over. It was not until they were seated at a table in a sheltered corner of the station restaurant that he spoke: —

"The *Swallow* is waiting at the wharf. But we had best get something hot to eat here. We shall have a long sail."

He took charge, at once, and while he ordered the luncheon, she looked at the travellers swarming to their food. Once during the long ride she had thought, "If we were seen by some one!" and her face had burned at the miserable fear. Now looking at the passing faces, she had a fierce wish that she might be seen by all the world! To speak out, to act unashamed, — but not yet, — no; the time was not ripe. As her look returned to Falkner, who was dressed in yachting flannels with a white sweater she smiled again: —

"I am so hungry!"

"I am afraid it will be bad. However —"

"It doesn't matter. Nothing matters — to-day!"

Neither of them, she reflected, cared for the detail of life, for luxury, mere comfort. They had shed superfluity, unlike those around them, who lived for it.

"Is it all right?" he asked as the waitress slung the dishes on the table.

"Everything!" and she added: "I can telephone Ned? I promised to speak to him every day."

"Of course!"

"Now let us forget. . . . What a lot of people there are in the world running about!"

"We'll say good-by to them all very soon," he replied.

Their spirits rose as they ate. It was festive and joyous, even this dirty country station. The September sun was shining brightly through the window, and a faint breeze came straying in, smelling of the salt water. She had given no thought to what they would do, to where they would go. She did not ask. It was good to trust all to him, just to step forth from the old maze into this dreamed existence, which somehow had been made true, where there was no need to take thought. She pushed away her ice untouched and began slowly to draw on her gloves.

"All the way here from Bedmouth I had a queer feeling that I was making a journey that I had made before, though I was never here in my life. And now it seems as if we had sat by this window some other day,—it is all so expected!" she mused. And she thought how that morning when she got up, she had gone to her little girl, the baby Lilla, and kissed her. With her arms about the child she had felt again that her act was right and that some day when the little one was a woman she would know and understand.

Her lips trembled, and then a slow smile suffused her face, bringing color, and leaning forward she murmured:—

"I am so happy! . . . As never before, so happy!"

Their eyes met, and for the moment they were lost in wonder, unconscious of the noisy room. . . .

With a familiarity of old knowledge, Falkner descended the winding streets to the water front. In this lower part of the town the dingy old houses had an air of ancient grandeur, and tall elms drooped dust-laden branches over the street.

"Dear old place!" he exclaimed, memories reviving of his boyhood cruises. "It was in ninety-one when I was here last. I never expected to put in here again."

The streets were empty, a noon stillness brooding in them. Margaret slipped her hand into his, the joy, the freedom, the sense of the open road sweeping over her afresh. The world was already fading behind them. . . . They came out upon the wharves, and threaded their way among the sagging gray buildings that smelt of salt fish, until the harbor water lapped at the piles beneath their feet.

"There's the *Swallow!*" Falkner cried, pointing into the stream.

They were soon aboard, and Margaret curled herself in the cockpit on a rug, while Falkner ran up the sails. Little waves were dancing across the harbor. Taking the tiller, he crouched beside her and whispered: —

"Now we are off — to the islands of the blest!"

It was all so in her dream, even to the white sail slowly filling before the breeze. They glided past hulking schooners lying idle with grimy sails all set, and from their decks above black-faced men looked down curiously at the white figure in the cockpit of the little sloop. Behind the schooners the wharves and the red brick warehouses, the elms and the white houses on the hill, the tall spires — all drew backwards into the westering sun. A low gray lighthouse came into sight; the *Swallow* dipped and rose; and the breeze freshened as they entered the lower bay. A great ship was slowly rounding the point, bound outward, too, laboring into the deep — for what? For some noisy port beneath the horizon. But for her the port of starlight and a man's arm, — the world was wonderful, this day! Falkner raised his hand and pointed far away to the eastward where a shadow lay like a finger on the sea.

"Our harbor is over there!"

Away to the east, to the broad open ocean, it was fitting they should speed, — they who had shaken themselves loose from the land. . . .

She held the tiller when he rummaged below for a chart, and while she was there alone, a pot-bellied pleasure steamer, swarming with people, rolled past, shaking the *Swallow* with its wake. The people on the decks spied the sail-boat, raised glasses, looked down, and had their say. 'A bit of the chattering world that is left,' thought Margaret, 'like all the rest.' And something joyful within cried: 'Not to-day! To-day I defy you. To-day I have escaped — I am a rebel. You can do nothing with me. Oh, to-day I am happy, happy, happy, — can you say that?' Falkner came up from the cabin with his chart, and shading his eyes, swept the sea for the landmarks of their course. And the *Swallow* sped on out of the noisy to-day through a path of gold and blue to the radiant to-morrow.

"See!" Falkner pointed back to the old seaport grown dim in the distance behind them. The sun was falling behind the steeples, and only the black smoke from engine and chimney marked the edge of the shore. Far away to the north opened a long reach of blue water and at the head of the bay green fields descending gently to the sea. The *Swallow* was a lonely dot in the open waters, dipping, rising, the sun on its white sail, — fleeing always. Falkner sat beside her, circling her shoulders with his arm, talking of the sea and the boat as if they had sailed for many days like this together and were familiar with all. His arm as it touched her said, 'I love you!' And his eyes resting on her face said, 'But we are happy, together, you and I, — so strangely happy!'

What was left there behind — the city and the vessels, the land itself — was all the mirage of life, had never been lived by them. And this — the swaying, sweeping boat, a dot upon the ocean and they together, heart by heart, going outward to the sea and night — was all that was real. Could it be possible that they two would ever land again on that far shore of circumstance, hemmed in by petty and sorrowful thoughts?

Yet across the dream came the thought of the Little Man, waiting behind there, and the woman knew that on the morrow after the morrow she should wake. For life is stronger than a single soul! . . .

To the west and north there were islands, long stretches of sea opening between their green shores, far up into the coast land. The wind freshened and died, until at last in the twilight with scarcely a ripple the *Swallow* floated into a sheltered cove on the outermost of all the islands. A forest of stiff little spruces covered the sea point, and behind this was a smooth green field, and above on the crest of the island a small white farm-house.

"A man named Viney used to live there," Falkner said, breaking a long silence. "Either he or some one else will take us in." Margaret helped him anchor, furl the sails, and then they went ashore, pulling the tender far up on the shingle beech beside the lobster-pots. They crossed the field — it was nearly dark and the *Swallow* was a speck on the dark water beneath — and knocked at the white farm-house.

"It is like what you knew must be so when you were a child," whispered Margaret.

"But suppose they turn us away?"

"Why, we'll go back to the *Swallow* or sleep under the firs! But they won't. There is a charm in all our doings this day, dearest."

The Vineys welcomed them, and gave them supper. Then Mr. Viney, divining that with these two wanderers a love matter was concerned, remarked suggestively: —

"Maybe you'd like to go over to my son's place to sleep. My son's folks built a camp over there on the Pint. It's a sightly spot, and they've gone back to the city. Here, Joe, you show 'em the path!"

So in the starlight they threaded the spruce forest down by the sea, and found the "camp," a wooden box, with a broad veranda hanging over the eastern cliff.

"Yes!" exclaimed Margaret, taking now her woman's place of command; "this is the very spot. We'll sleep here on the veranda. You can bring out the bedding. If we had ordered it all, we could not have discovered the perfect thing, like this!"

The gray pathway of the ocean lay at their feet, and from the headlands up and down the coast, from distant islands, the lights began to call and answer each other. A cloud of smoke far eastward hung over a seagoing steamer. And throughout the little island, over the floor of the ocean, in the wood about them, there was perfect stillness, a cessation of all movement.

"Peace! Such large and splendid peace!" Margaret murmured, as they stood gazing at the beauty of the coming night. Peace without and answering peace within. Surely they had come to the heart of solitude, removed from the tumultuous earth.

"Come!" he whispered at her ear, and she slowly turned her face to him.

"Now, I know!" she said triumphantly. "This has been sent to answer me, — all the glory and the wonder and the peace of life, my dearest! I know it all. We have lived all our years with this vision in our hearts, and it has been given to us to have it at last."

And as they lay down beside each other she murmured: —

"Peace that is above joy, — see the stars!"

And there beneath the tranquil stars in the calm night came the ecstasy of union, transcending Fate and Sorrow. . . .

Thus at the extreme verge of human experience these two realized that inner state of harmony, that equilibrium of spirit, towards which conscious beings strive blindly, and which sanctioning what man forbids gives reason to life. The spirit within them declared that it was best so to gain the heights, whether in the final sum of life it should lie as Sin or Glory. For this night, for these immediate hours, as man and woman they would rise to wider kingdoms of themselves than ever otherwise might be reached.

Thus far to them had come revelation.

In the morning Margaret would play housewife. Sending Falkner to the Vineys' for the things needed, she cooked the meal while he swam out to the *Swallow* and made ready for the day's sail. Whimsically she insisted on doing all without his help, and when he was ready, she served him before she would eat herself, — "Just as Mrs. Viney would her man."

Did she wish to show him that she was equal to the common surface of living, — a comrade to do her part? Or, rather, was the act symbolical, — woman serving joyfully where she yields real mastery? The woman, so often capricious and disdainful, was submissive, as if she would say: "This man is my mate. I am forever his. It is my best joy to be through him myself."

And after the meal she insisted on completing the task by washing the dishes, putting all to rights in the camp; then mended a rent in his coat which he had got from a stumble in the dark the night before. He laughed, but her eyes shone.

"Let me *do* as long as I can! . . . There — wouldn't you and I shed things! That's the way to live, — to shed things." As they passed the Vineys' house on their way to the boat, Margaret observed: —

"That would do very well for us, don't you think? You could go lobstering, and I would have a garden. Can you milk a cow?" She was picturing the mould for their lives.

And all that day as they sailed among the islands, up thoroughfares, across the reaches of the sea, they played a little game of selecting the right cottage from the little white farm-houses dotted along the shores, and said, "We'd take this or that, and we'd do thus and so with it — and live this way!" Then they would laugh, and grow pensive, as if the land with its smoke wreaths had suddenly drifted past their eyes, reminding them of the future. 'You are bound with invisible cords,' a voice said. 'You have escaped in fancy, but to-morrow you will find the world wagging its old way.' But the woman knew that no matter what came, the morrow and all the morrows could never be again as her days once had been. For the subtle virtue of a great fulfilment is its power to alter the inner aspect of all things thereafter. Nothing could ever be the same to either of them. The stuff of their inner lives had been changed. . . .

They sailed the day long in the full sun, which beat down with a memory of summer that already had departed. At noon they landed on a rocky islet, a mere clump of firs water bound, and after eating their luncheon they lay under the fragrant trees and talked long hours.

"If this hadn't been," Falkner said with deep gratitude, "we should not have known each other."

She smiled back triumphantly. That was the truth she had divined the night he was to have left her.

"No," she assented, "we should have been almost strangers and been dissatisfied always."

"And now nothing can come between us, not time nor circumstance, nor pain. Nothing! It is sealed for all time — our union."

"Our life together, which has been and will be forever."

None of the surface ways of life, no exchange of words, no companionship, could have created anything to resemble this inner union which had come about. The woman giving herself with full knowledge, the man possessing with full insight,—this experience had made a spirit common to both, in which both might live apart from each other, so long as they could see with the spirit, — an existence new, deep, inner.

So they talked of the life to be with perfect willingness, as two might who were to part soon for a long journey, which both would share intimately and real loneliness never seize them.

"And beyond this luminous moment," suggested the man,

— his the speculative imagination, — "there must lie other levels of intimacy, of comradeship. If we could go on into the years like this, why, the world would ever be new, — we should go deeper into the mysteries every day, discovering ourselves, creating ourselves!"

The warm sunlight, the islands mirrored in the waveless sea, the aromatic breath of the spruce and fir, the salty scent of the tidal shore — this physical world in which they lay — and that other more remote physical world of men and cities — all, all was but the pictured drama of man's inner life. As he lived, each day dying and recreated, with an atmosphere of the soul as subtly shifting as the atmosphere of the earth, so this wonderful panorama of his faded, dissolved, was made anew. For out of the panorama of sense man builds his tabernacle, and calls it life, but within the veil there lies hidden beneath a power, that can unlock other worlds, — strange, beautiful worlds, like the mazes of the firmament through which the earth pursues its way. And the tide ebbing past this islet to the sea, flowing fast outward into the deep, carried them in its silent depths out into the new, the mysterious places of the spirit.

The sun sank, covering the islands and the sea with a rare amethystine glow deepening to a band of purple, like some old dyed cloth, then fading to pale green at the rim of the earth. There ensued a hush, a pause in life, that filled the air. 'We are fading, we are withdrawing,' whispered the elements. 'Our hour is past, the riotous hour, the springtime flood, the passionate will. And in our place the night will come and bring you peace.' The sadness of change, the sense of something passing, of moments slipping away to eternity! . . .

"Tell me," she said as they drifted back with the tide, "what is it?"

"Only," he answered, "the thought of waste, — that it should have come late, too late!"

Proudly denying the flaw in the perfect image, she protested: —

"Not late, — the exact hour. Don't you see that it could never have been until now? Neither of us was ready to understand until we had lived all the mistakes, suffered all. That is the law of the soul, — its great moments can neither be hastened nor delayed. All is appointed."

Her gentle voice touched his heart like a soothing hand, — 'Accept — rejoice — be strong — it must be so! And it is good!'

"Dearest, we should have passed each other in the dark, without knowing, earlier. You could not have seen me, the thing you love in me, nor I you, until we were stricken with the hunger. . . . It takes time to know this babbling life, to know what is real and what is counterfeit. Before or after, who knows how it might have been? This was the time for us to meet!"

In these paths her eyes were bright to see the way, her feet accustomed. So it was true. By what they had suffered, apart, by what they had tested and rejected, they had fitted themselves to come together, for this point of time, this flame of fulfilment. Mystery of waste to be accepted. No wistfulness for loss! Brave smiles for that which had been given. And resolved hearts for that to come. . . .

Slowly, with the mood of the day in her lingering feet, Margaret crossed the field towards the Vineys' cottage, while Falkner stayed to make the *Swallow* ready for its homeward journey in the morning. Joe Viney rowed out to the boat with him. Nodding towards the slight figure on the path above, the fisherman observed simply: —

"She ain't strong, your wife?"

With that illumined face! He had thought her this day pure force. Later as he followed her slow steps to the camp, he said over the old man's words, "She ain't strong." She lived behind her eyes in the land of will and spirit. And the man's arms ached to take her frail body to him, and keep her safe in some island of rest.

CHAPTER XL

After supper Margaret sat and talked with Mrs. Viney. The fisherman's wife was a woman of fifty, with a dragging voice, a faint curiosity in her manner. Her iron-gray hair smoothed flat was tied in a little knot behind. Her husband, a good ten years older, had the vitality of a young man compared with his wife. He was grizzled and squat, with thick red face and powerful shoulders. His eyes twinkled sharply under their fleshy lids; but he exhibited no outward curiosity over the two strangers who had dropped down on his island.

"That woman!" Margaret exclaimed disgustedly to Falkner as they went back to the camp.

"Our excellent hostess? What is the matter with her?"

"She's a whiner!" Margaret replied hotly. "The woman is always the whiner, — it makes me despise my sex. What do you suppose she wants? She has a sister in Lawrence, Mass., and Lawrence, Mass., is her Paris! She wants her husband to give up this, all the life he's known since he was a boy, and go to live in Lawrence, Mass., so that she can walk on brick sidewalks and look into shop windows. There's an ideal for you, my dear!"

Falkner laughed at her outburst. After all an ambition for Lawrence, Mass., was not criminal.

"Oh, women! . . . She wanted me to know that she had seen life, — knew a lady who had rings like mine, — the social instinct in women, — phew! And he smoked his pipe like an honest man and said not a word. He'll never die in Lawrence, Mass."

"But it must be lonely for the poor thing here winters; their children have all gone to the city."

"There are ten families at the other end of the island, if she must have some one to clack with."

"Perhaps she doesn't find the island society congenial," Falkner suggested slyly. He had heard Margaret inveigh against certain less restricted societies.

"But the old man said, 'Winters are best of all — when it's fierce outside, and there's nothing but yourself to amuse yourself with!' That's the man. And he said: 'I like the blows, too. I've been on the sea all my life, and I don't know nothing about it to speak on.' He has a sense of what it means, — all this greatness about him."

"But her element, you forget, is Lawrence, Mass."

"The man has the imagination, if he is a man! If he is a man! Woman just tails on, — as I cling to you, dearest!"

"And sometimes I think you would want to take the lead, — to have your own little way."

"Yes, I like my way, too! But the women who think they can strike out alone — live their own lives, as they say — are foolish. The wise women work through men, — accomplish themselves in those they love. Isn't that bigger than doing all the work yourself?"

"Women create the necessity for man's work."

"You know I don't mean that! . . . What is bliss is to make the way clear for the one you loved. . . . I could do that! I'd set my little brain working to smooth away the immediate difficulties, those that hinder, the little things that stick in the way. I'd clean the armor for my lord and bring him nourishing food."

"And point out the particular castle you would like him to capture for your dwelling?"

"Never! If the man were worth serving, he would mark his own game." . . .

They had walked to the eastern point of the island, where nothing was to be seen but the wide sea. The wind had utterly fallen, leaving the surface of the water mottled with currents from beneath. Far away on the horizon some ships seemed to be sailing — they had wind out there — and their sails still shone in the twilight. About the cliff at their feet the tide ran in black circles. It was still, and the earth was warm and fragrant from the hot day. Margaret rested her head upon his arm and closed her eyes.

"It has been too much for you," he said, concerned.

"No," she murmured, "I am not tired. This is content, at the day's end. It is marvellous," — she opened her eyes again upon him with a smile of wonder. "I haven't had a moment of fatigue, and I have done so much since yesterday, — more than I have done for years. I wonder what it is gives us women strength or weakness."

"Joy gives strength!"

"Peace gives strength. Sometimes I think that all the weakness in life — women's weakness — is merely wrong adjustment. It is never work that kills — it isn't just living, no matter how hard it is. But it is trying to live when you are dead. . . . Dearest, if we stayed here, I should be always strong! I know it. All the weariness and the pain and the languor would go; I should be what I was meant to be, what every human being is meant to be, — strong to bear."

"It is a bitter thought."

"I suppose that is why men and women struggle so blindly to set themselves right, why they run away and commit all sorts of follies. They feel within them the capacity for health, for happiness, if they can only get right somehow. And when they find the way —"

She made a little gesture with her hand that swept the troubles from the road.

"If they can be sure, it is almost a duty — to put themselves right, isn't it?"

Here they had come to the temptation which in all their intimate moments they had avoided. . . . 'Others have remade the pattern of their lives, — why not we?' The woman answered the thought in the man's mind.

"I should never take it, even knowing that it is my one chance for health and all that I desire, not while my father lives, not while my mother-in-law lives; it would add another sorrow to their graves. Nor while my husband has a right to his children. We are all bound in criss-cross in life. Nor would you, dearest, have me; you would hate me, — it would turn our glory to gall!"

It was not her habit to put her hands before her eyes. She was clear with herself, and without the sentimental fog. For the Bishop's creed she cared nothing. For her mother-in-law's prejudices she cared as little. The punishment of Society she would have met with gleeful contempt. People could not take from her what she valued, for she had stripped so much that there was little left in her heart to be deprived of. As for her husband, he did not exist for her; towards him she was spiritually blind. Her children were so much a part of her that she never thought of them as away from her. Where she went, they would be, as a matter of course.

They had never laid all this on the table before them, so to speak, but both had realized it from the beginning. They had walked beside the social precipice serene, but aware of the depths — and the heights.

"I hate to be limited by the opinions, the prejudices, of other people, of any one," the man protested. "There seems a cowardice in silently acquiescing in social laws that I don't respect, because the majority so wills it."

"Not because it is the will of the majority — not that; but because others near you will be made wretched. That is the only morality I have!"

The law of pity in the place of the law of God! A fragile leash for passion and egotism. They both shuddered.

The dusk gathered all about them. Her head still rested on his breast, and her hand stole to his face. She whispered, "So we pay the forfeit — for our blindness!"

"And if I stay —"

"Don't say it! Don't say that! Do you think that I could be here this moment in your arms if *that* were possible?"

Her voice trembled with scorn, disgust of the adulterous world.

"Hiding and corner lies for us? No, no, my lover, — not for *you!* Not even for *me.* That is the one price too great to pay for happiness. It would kill it all. Kill it! Surely. I should become in your eyes — like one of — *them.* It would be — oh, you understand!" She buried her head in his coat.

Again she had saved them, kept the balance of their ideal. She would have love, not hidden lust. What she had done this once could never be done again without defilement. She had come to him as to a man condemned to die, to leave the earth forever, and the one most precious thing he wanted and the one most precious thing that she had to give, — that she had given freely — to the man condemned to death.

"We have come all the hard way up the heights to infinite joy, to Peace! Shall we throw ourselves down into the gulf?" . . .

In the night Falkner woke with a start, putting out his hand to fend off a catastrophe. She was not there by his side! For one moment fear filled his mind, and then as he sprang up he saw her in the faint moonlight, leaning against the post of the veranda, looking out into the night. At his movement she turned.

"The night was too beautiful to sleep through, dearest! I have so much to think about."

She came back to his side and knelt above him, drawing her cloak around her. "See! we are all alone here under the stars." The fog had stolen in from the sea, risen as high as the trees, and lay close over land and ocean. The heavens were cloudless, and the little moon was low. "Those tranquil stars up there! They give us our benediction for the time to come. . . . We have had our supreme joy — our desire of desires — and now Peace shall enter our hearts and remain there. That is what the night says.

. . . It can never be as it was before for you or me. We shall carry away something from our feast to feed on all our lives. We shall have enough to give others. Love makes you rich — so rich! We must give it away, all our lives. We shall, dearest, never fear."

For the soul has its own sensualities, — its self-delight in pain, in humiliation, — its mood of generosity, too. The penetrating warmth of a great passion irradiates life about it.

"My children, my children," she murmured, "I love them more — I can do for them more. And for dear Mother Pole — and even for him. I shall be gentler — I shall understand. . . . Love was set before me. I have taken it, and it has made me strong. I will be glad and love the world, all of it, for your sake, because you have blessed me. . . . Ours is not the fire that turns inward and feeds upon itself!"

"Oh, Margaret, Margaret! —"

"Listen," she murmured, clasping his neck, "you are the Man! You must spread the flame where I cannot. I kiss you. I have eaten of life with you. Together we have understood. Forget me, cease to love me; but always you must be stronger, greater, nobler because you have held me in your arms and loved me. If you cannot carry us upwards, it has been base, — the mere hunger of animals, — my lover! You have made of my weakness strength, and I have given you peace! Pour it out for me in deeds that I may know I have loved a Man, that my hero lives!"

Like a cry of the spirit it rang out into the night between the mist-hidden earth and the silent stars. In the stillness there had come a revelation of life, — the eternal battle of man between the spirit and the flesh, between the seen and the unseen, the struggle infinite and always. Where life is, that must be. And the vision of man's little, misshapen existence, — the incomplete and infinitesimal unit he is, — and also the significance of him, — this material atom, the symbol, the weapon of the spirit, shone forth before them. This the woman had felt in giving herself to him, that the spirit within was freed by the touch of flesh. . . .

Already in the calm night desire and passion seemed to fade from them. Here had ended their passion, and now must begin the accomplishment. When the revelation comes, and the spirit thus speaks through the flesh, it is peace with human beings. . . .

They lay there awake but silent into the gray hours of dawn, and when the mist had spread upwards to the sky, shutting out the stars, they slept.

CHAPTER XLI

At breakfast Joe Viney said: —

"I was lobsterin' this morning."

"It must have been the thud of your oars that we heard when we woke."

"Mos' likely, — I was down there at the end of the island, hauling in the pots. It's goin' to be a greasy day. But there's wind comin'."

They could hear the long call of a steamer's whistle and the wail of the fog-horn beyond the next island. The little white house was swathed in the sea mist.

"Better take the steamer at the Neck, if you're going to the city," Mrs. Viney suggested. "It'll be cold and damp sailing this morning."

"Never!" Margaret protested.

Mrs. Viney looked at Margaret pityingly. That a woman from the city should care to come to this forlorn, lonesome spot, "when the summer folks had gone," and sleep out of doors on fir boughs, and go off in a messy sail-boat in a fog, when there was a clean, fast steamer that would take her in an hour to the city — it was a mystery. As she packed some pieces of soggy bread, a little meat, and still soggier cake into a box for their luncheon she shook her head, protesting: —

"You'll spoil that hat o' yourn. It wasn't meant for sailin'."

"No, it wasn't; that's true!" She took off the flower-bedecked hat with its filmy veiling. "Would you like it? I shall find a cap in the boat."

'Clearly,' thought Mrs. Viney, 'the woman is crazy;' but she accepted the hat. Afterwards she said to her husband: —

"I can't make them two out. She ain't young, and she ain't exactly old, and she ain't pretty, — well, she's got the best of the bargain, a little wisp like her." For, womanlike, she admired Falkner in his sweater and flannels, strong and male, with a dark coat of tan on his face.

Viney accompanied them to the boat, waddling across the field, his hands in the armholes of his vest. He said little, but as he shoved them off in their tender, he observed: —

"It's the sort of day you could get lost in mighty easy."

"Oh," Falkner called back cheerily, "I guess I know my way."

"Well, I guess you *do!*"

As Viney had said, the wind came through the fog, driving the boat in unseen fashion, while the sail hung almost limp. There was a little eddy of oily water at the stern; they were slipping, sliding through the fog-bank, back to the earth.

"Back to life," Falkner hummed, "back; back, to the land, to the world!"

The fog clung in Margaret's hair, and dimmed her eyes. She bared her arms to feel the cool touch of it on her skin. Clean things, like the sun yesterday, the resinous firs, the salty fog, — clean elemental things, — how she loved them!

"And suppose," Falkner suggested, "I should lose my way in this nest of reefs and islands and we got shipwrecked or carried out to sea?"

"I should hear Ned calling through the fog." A simple answer, but withal enough. Their hour, which they had set themselves, was past. And lying here in the impalpable mist, slipping towards the hidden port, she was filled with ineffable content. . . .

"You are still radiant!" Falkner said wonderingly.

"It can't fade — never wholly! I cherish it." She drew her arms close about her. "Sacred things never utterly die!"

They had found it, they had lived it, they knew — what the unspiritual and carnal millions that clutter God's earth may never know — ecstasy, the secret behind the stars, beyond the verge of the sea, in the great lunar spaces of spirit.

On they glided through the thoroughfares, around island points, across reaches of the sea, sweeping onward now with an audible gurgle in their wake, the sails bellying forward; veering this way, falling off there, as the impassive man touched the tiller, obeying an instinct, seeing into the dark beyond. Now a bit of cliff loomed in the fog, again a shingled roof or a cluster of firs, and the whistling buoy at the harbor's mouth began to bellow sadly, — reminders all of the shell of that world towards which they sailed. And at last the harbor, with its echoing bells and fog-whistles, the protesting shrieks of its man-machines; suddenly the colossal hull of a schooner at anchor. Then the ghostly outlines of the huddled shipping, the city roofs, the steeples, the shriek of engines in the freight yards — they touched the earth! It had ended. The noise of living reverberated in their ears.

Margaret rose with a sigh, and looked back through the closing curtain of fog to an island headland misty and vague.

"My heaven — oh, my heaven! our haven, my master!"

Like two newly wakened beings, stunned by the light and sound around them, they stumbled over the wharf. A large sailing vessel was loading there for its voyage, — a Portuguese ship bound for Demerara, so the black sailor said whom Falkner questioned. With a last look at its tall masts they took their way into the city and so to the station.

Here was the same crowd coming from the trains, — the little human motes pushing hither and thither, hurrying from train to train, dashing, dawdling, loitering. Were they the same motes as two days before? Were they always the same, — marionettes wound to perform the clamorous motions of life? Or were they men and women like themselves, with their own great secrets in their hearts? Above all, the secret that transforms! Had these others, too, gone into the great high places?

They walked to the bridge while they waited for the Bedmouth train. Far down the harbor rose the tall masts of the Portuguese ship.

"Bound for Demerara," murmured Falkner, with a smile; "we might be sailing for the Windward Islands?"

"No," Margaret smiled back; "we love too much for that, — you and I."

CHAPTER XLII

WITHIN the old parlor of the Bedmouth house Mrs. Pole was waiting for a step. It came at last.

"The children?" Margaret demanded, kissing the old lady.

"Perfectly well."

"I must go up to them," and she started for the door.

"Wait!" Mrs. Pole said, looking up sadly into the younger woman's pale face, which still held the glow.

"Yes, mother?" The voice rang with a note of vitality, of life, as if to chant, 'I have come back to you from a long way off!' Mrs. Pole said slowly: —

"Lawrence is upstairs. He came on from New York yesterday."

"Oh!"

At the head of the stairs she met her husband, who had heard her voice below.

"You have been away!" he said sharply, an unwonted touch of authority in his voice.

It was in her heart to say: 'Yes, in heaven! Can't you see it in my face?' She replied gently: —

"Yes, I have been — away!"

"Where?"

She looked at him out of her deep eyes, and said slowly: —

"Do you wish me to tell you?"

And after a moment, as if her husband was not there and she were looking through him at something beyond, she went on into the children's room. Pole, steadying himself by the hand-rail, descended the stairs.

He no longer existed, even as a convention, for his wife.

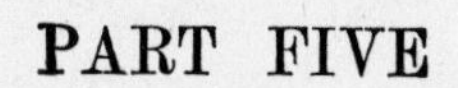

PART FIVE

CHAPTER XLIII

Isabelle had not succeeded in bringing Vickers home with her that first time she had gone abroad. They had had a very pleasant month in the Dolomites, and he had taken her to Paris to join the Woodyards, with whom she returned. Whenever she had spoken to Vickers of coming home he had smiled and made a little joke. Once he said, "Not yet, — I cannot go yet, Belle," and she understood that it was "that beast of a woman," as she called Mrs. Conry, who kept him. She wanted to say to him, "Well, Vick, if you won't leave her, why don't you marry her then!" But gentle as her brother was to her, she did not like to touch on that topic.

She had meant to go over the next spring, but the new house was under way then. A year later a letter from Fosdick, who was returning from Russia by the way of Venice, made her start for Europe at once.

. . . "Madam," Fosdick wrote, "having sucked our Vickers dry, has left him at last, I am happy to say. Gone off with a fresh orange. Vick doesn't realize his luck, — he's plain dazed. Before the other orange becomes dry, it is our simple duty — yours and mine — to remove the stranded hero out of reach. I think you can do it now. . . . I forgot to say that the Conry left with him a pledge of her return in the shape of a lump of a girl, her daughter by Conry. Vick seems idiotically tied to this little Conry. . . . Oh, it is a shame, a shame!"

Isabelle cabled Fosdick to bring Vickers with him to Paris and started with her mother. "No sermons, you know, mother," she warned Mrs. Price. "It's something you and I don't understand."

When Vickers came to their hotel in Paris, it seemed to

Isabelle that the last two years had worked more damage than the previous six. There was a dazed and submissive air about her brother that brought the tears to her eyes. In the languid, colorless face before her, she could scarcely find a trace of the pale, tense boy, who had roused her in the middle of the night the day before he left St. Louis. . . .

"Why don't you come to this hotel?" Mrs. Price had demanded.

Vickers had made an excuse, and when his mother had left the room, he said to Isabelle, "You will have to explain to mother that I am not alone."

Isabelle gasped, and Vickers hastened to say, "You see Delia is with me."

"Dick wrote me that she left her child!"

"Yes. . . . I am really very fond of the poor little thing."

"The beast!" Isabelle muttered.

Vickers shuddered, and Isabelle resolved that no matter what happened she would not allow herself to refer again to either mother or child. Later she walked back with him to his rooms and saw the girl. Delia Conry was a heavily built and homely girl of thirteen, with light gray eyes. All but the eyes were like her father, the builder. There was no hint of the mother's soft, seductive physique.

"Delia," Vickers said gently, "come and speak to my sister, Mrs. Lane."

As the child awkwardly held out a hand, Isabelle felt the tears come into her eyes. Here was her old Vickers, — the gentle, idealistic soul she had loved, the only being it seemed to her then that she had ever really loved.

"Delia and I have been tramping the Louvre," Vickers remarked. "That's the way we are learning history."

Isabelle glanced about the forlorn little sitting-room of the third-class hotel.

"Why did you come here?"

"It does well enough, and it's near the Louvre and places. . . . It is very reasonable."

Then Isabelle remembered what Fosdick had said about

Vickers's gift of half his fortune to Mrs. Conry. "You see the idiot hadn't sense enough to run off with a man who had money. Some damn fool artist! That's why you must pack Vick away as soon as you can get him to go."

With this in her mind she exclaimed impulsively: —

"You are coming back with us, Vick!"

"To live in America?" he queried with bitter humor. "So you came out as a rescue party!"

"You must get back into life," Isabelle urged vaguely.

"What life? You don't mean the hardware business?"

"Don't be silly! . . . You can't go on living over here alone by yourself with that child."

"Why not?"

"Oh, because — you must *do* something, Vick! I want you to be famous."

"That doesn't seem quite possible, now," he replied gently.

"You'll come and live with me — oh, I need you, Vick!"

She threw her arms about him and hugged him tightly to her as she had as a girl. The intensity of her feeling moved him strangely, and her words also. What was it she meant by "needing him"?

"You must — that's the thing!"

Holding her head away she searched his face critically, and her heart was wrung again by the sense of waste in it all. "Poor brother," she murmured, tightening her clasp.

"I'm not going over as a helpless dependent!" he protested, and suddenly without warning he shot out his question, — "And what have *you* made out of it? How have the years been?"

"Oh, we jog on, John and I, — just the usual thing, you know, — no heights and no depths!"

An expression of futility came momentarily into her eyes. It wasn't what she had pictured to herself, her marriage and life. Somehow she had never quite caught hold of life. But that was a common fate. Why, after all, should she commiserate her brother, take the 'poor Vick' tone that everybody did about him? Had she attained to a much more satisfactory level than he, or had the others who 'poor Vickered' him? There was something in both their natures, perhaps, at jar with life, incapable of effectiveness.

Vickers finally consented to return to America with his mother and sister "for a visit." Delia, he said, ought to see her father, who was a broken man, living in some small place in the West. (Isabelle suspected that Vickers had sent him also money.) Conry had written him lately, asking for news of his daughter.

"Does Vick intend to tote that lump of a girl around with him for the next twenty years?" Mrs. Price demanded of Isabelle, when she heard that Delia was to be of their party.

"I suppose so, unless she totes herself off!"

"The woman dumped her child on him! Well, well, the Colonel had something of the fool in him where women were concerned, — only I looked after that!"

"Mother," Isabelle retorted mischievously, "I am afraid you'll never be able to keep down the fool in us; Vick is pretty nearly all fool, the dear!"

Her brother's return being settled, Isabelle plunged into her shopping, buying many things for both the houses, as well as her dresses. There were friends flitting back and forth, snatches of sight-seeing, and theatres. By the time they took the steamer Isabelle confessed she was a "wreck." Yet she talked of taking an apartment in Paris the next spring and sending her child to a convent, as Mrs. Rogers had done. "It would be nice to have my own corner over here to run to," she explained. "Only Potts wants me to bury myself at Schwalbach."

Cairy joined them at Plymouth. He had been in London making arrangements for the production of a play there, and had hopes of enlarging his sphere.

"Coming home?" he asked Vickers. "That's good!"

"Thank you," Vickers replied dryly.

Cairy had already the atmosphere of success about him. He still limped in a distinguished manner, and his clothes marked him even in the company of well-dressed American men. He had grown stouter, — was worried by the fear of flesh, as he confided to Vickers, — and generally took himself with serious consideration. It was a far call from the days when he had been Gossom's ready pen. He now spoke of his "work" importantly, and was kind to Vickers, who "had made such a mess of things," "with all that money, too." With his large egotism, his uniform success where women were concerned, Vickers's career seemed peculiarly stupid. "No woman," he said to Isabelle, "should be able to break a man." And he thought thankfully of the square blow between the eyes that Conny had dealt him.

In the large gay party of returning Americans that surrounded Isabelle and Cairy on the ship Vickers was like a queer little ghost. He occupied himself with his small charge, reading and walking with her most of the days. Isabelle was conscious of the odd figure Vickers made, in his ill-fitting Italian clothes, with an old Tyrolean cloak of faded green hanging about him, his pale face half hidden by a scrubby beard, his unseeing eyes, wandering over the great steamer, a little girl's hand in his, or reading in a corner of the deserted dining hall.

Vickers was not so dull of eye, however, that he did not observe Isabelle and Cairy, sitting side by side on the deck, talking and reading. They tried to "bring him in," but they had a little language of jokes and references personal to themselves. If Vickers wondered what his sister, as he knew her, found so engrossing in the Southerner, he was answered by a remark Isabelle made: —

"Tom is so charming! . . . There are few men in America who understand how to talk to a woman, you know."

When Vickers had left his native land, the art of talking to a woman as distinguished from a man had not been developed. . . .

Lane met the party at Quarantine. That was his domestic office, — "meeting" and "seeing off." As he stood on the deck of the bobbing tug waving to his wife, he was a symbol of the American husband, Cairy jokingly pointed out. "There's John holding out the welcoming arms to roving wife." And there were hundreds of them, roving wives, on the deck, very smartly dressed for their return to domesticity, with laden trunks coming up out of the holds, and long customs bills to pay, the expectant husbands waiting at the pier with the necessary money. And there were others with their husbands beside them on the decks, having carried them through Europe, bill-payers and arrangers extraordinary for their majesties, the American wives. Cairy was writing a farce about it with the title, "Coming Home."

Vickers, who scarcely remembered his brother-in-law, looked curiously at the self-possessed, rather heavy man on the tug. He was an effective person, "one who had done something," the kind his countrymen much admired. "Had a pleasant voyage, I suppose, and all well?" Then he had turned to Vickers, and with slight hesitation, as if not sure of his ground, observed, "You will find considerable changes, I suppose."

"I suppose so," Vickers assented, feeling that conversation between them would be limited. In the confusion at the pier while the numerous trunks were being disgorged, Vickers stood apart with Delia Conry and had an opportunity to observe the quiet, efficient manner in which John Lane arranged everything. He had greeted Isabelle and his mother impartially, with a family kiss for both. Vickers caught his brother-in-law's eye on him several times as they were waiting, and once Lane made as if to speak and was silent. Vickers was sensitively aware that this man of affairs could not pretend to understand him, — could at the best merely conceal under general tolerance and family good feeling his real contempt for one who had so completely "made a mess of things." He had foreseen the brother-in-law, and that had been one reason why he had hesitated to return, even for a visit. Lane soon made another effort, saying: "You will find it rather warm in the city. We have had a good deal of hot weather this summer."

"Yes," Vickers replied; "I remember New York in September. But I am used to long summers."

As the stranger's eyes roved over the noisy pier, Lane looked at the little girl, who was rendered dumb by the confusion and clung to Vickers's hand, and then he eyed his brother-in-law again, as if he were recollecting the old Colonel and thinking of the irony in the fact that his only surviving son should be this queer, half-foreign chap.

A large motor waited outside the pier to take the party to the hotel.

"Aren't you coming, Tom?" Isabelle asked, as Cairy made for a cab with his luggage.

"I will meet you at the station to-morrow," Cairy called back. "Business!"

"Well, — how is everything?" she asked her husband. "Glad to see me back?"

"Of course."

They darted swiftly up town to an immense hotel, where Lane had engaged rooms for the party. Having seen them into the elevator, he returned by the motor to his office.

CHAPTER XLIV

THE old Farm at Grafton had been marvellously transformed. Vickers Price, standing on the terrace the evening of his arrival, looked wistfully for landmarks, for something to recall the place he had loved as a boy, which had gathered charm in his imaginative memory these years of his exile. The Georgian façade of the new house faced the broad meadow through which the wedding party had wandered back to the Farm the day of Isabelle's marriage. Below the brick terrace, elaborate gardens, suggesting remotely Italy, had been laid out on the slope of the New England hill. The thin poplars, struggling to maintain themselves in the bitter blasts of an American winter, gave an unreal air to the place as much as anything. The village of Grafton, which had once been visible as a homely white-dotted road beyond the meadow, had been "planted out." There was a formal garden now where the old barn stood, from which the Colonel's pointers had once yapped their greetings on the arrival of strangers. The new brick stables and the garage were in the woods across the road, connected with the house by telephone.

On their arrival by the late train they had had supper quite informally. It had been served by two men, however, and there was a housekeeper to relieve the mistress of the care of the increased establishment. What had bewildered Vickers on his return to America after an absence of ten years, from the moment he had taken ship until the Lanes' new French motor had whisked him up to the Farm — Isabelle still clung to the old name — was the lavish luxury, the increased pace of living, on this side of the ocean. The years he had spent in Italy had been the richest period of our industrial renaissance. In the rising tide of wealth the signs of the old order — the simplicity of the Colonel's day — had been swept away.

As Vickers stood rather apart from the others, who were strolling about the terrace, and looked at Dog Mountain, the only perfectly familiar feature in the scene, Isabelle tucked her arm under his and led him towards the gardens: —

"Vick, I want you to see what I have done. Don't you think it's much better? I am not altogether satisfied." She glanced back at the long façade: "I think I should have done better with Herring rather than Osgood. But when we started to alter the old place, I didn't mean to do so much to it."

Isabelle knew more now than when Osgood had been engaged, two years before, and Herring's reputation had meanwhile quite overshadowed the older architect's.

"I told Isabelle at the start," said Cairy, who joined them, "she had better pull the old place down, and have a fresh deal. You had to come to it practically in the end?" He turned to Isabelle teasingly.

"Yes," she admitted half regretfully; "that's the way I always do a thing, — walk backwards into it, as John says. But if we had built from the ground up, it wouldn't have been this place, I suppose. . . . And I don't see why we did it, — Grafton is so far from anything."

"It's neither Tuxedo nor Lenox," Cairy suggested.

"Just plain Connecticut. Well, you see the Colonel left the place to me, — that was the reason."

And also the fact that he had left her only a small portion of his fortune besides. It was an ironical rebuke for his act that much of the small fortune he had given her had gone to transform his beloved Farm into something he would never have recognized. Vickers thought sadly, "If the old Colonel's ghost should haunt this terrace, he couldn't find his way about!"

"But it's snug and amusing, — the Farm? Isn't it?" Cairy demanded of Vickers in a consoling manner.

"I shouldn't call it snug," Vickers replied, unconsciously edging away from the Southerner, "nor wholly amusing!"

"You don't like my efforts!" Isabelle exclaimed wearily. She herself, as she had said, was not satisfied; but money as well as strength and her husband's dislike of "more building" had held her hand.

"We all change," Vickers replied humorously. "I can't blame the old place for looking different. I have changed somewhat myself, and you, Cairy," — he glanced at the figure by his sister's side, which had sleek marks of prosperity as well as the Farm, — "too. All changed but you, Isabelle!"

"But I have changed a lot!" she protested. "I have grown better looking, Vickie, and my mind has developed, hasn't it, Tom? One's family never sees any change but the wrinkles!" . . .

Vickers, turning back to the terrace where Fosdick and Gossom were smoking, had a depressed feeling that of all the changes his was the greatest.

"I must look in on my little girl," he explained to Isabelle, as he left her and Cairy.

Isabelle watched him mount the steps. His small figure had grown heavy from his inactive life abroad. The thick hair had almost gone from the top of his head, and the neat pointed beard had become bushy. In his negligent clothes he looked quite slouchy, she had felt that evening, as if he had long ceased to have any interest in his person. "It's all that beast of a woman," she said resentfully to Cairy, remembering the slender, quite elegant brother of the old days. "And to think of his saddling himself with her brat and lugging her around with him! I couldn't make him drop her in New York with her governess. But it's impossible!"

"The lady left him her husband's child, as a souvenir, didn't she?"

"I can't think of it!" Isabelle exclaimed, shrugging her shoulders. "To go off with that other man — after all he had given up for her! The beast!"

"Perhaps that was the best she could do for him under the circumstances," Cairy remarked philosophically. "But the child must be a bore." He laughed at the comical situation.

"Just like Vick!"

It was also like Vickers to give Mrs. Conry a large share of his small fortune when she had seen fit to leave him, as Fosdick had told her. . . .

After visiting his small charge, who was lonely this first night in the strange house, Vickers had gone to his room and sat down by the window. Below him on the terrace Fosdick and Gossom were discussing Socialism, the Russian revolution, and the War of Classes. New topics, or rather new forms of old themes, they seemed to Vickers. Fosdick, from his rolling around the earth, had become an expert on the social revolution; he could tell the approximate dates when it "would be pulled off" in all the great countries. He had bought a farm somewhere in Vermont, and had sat down to wait for the social revolution; meantime he was raising apples, and at intervals descended upon the houses of his friends to inveigh against predatory wealth or visited the city for the sake of more robust amusement. Gossom, whose former radicalism was slowly modifying into an "intelligent conservatism," was mildly opposing Fosdick's views. "We have gone too far in this campaign of vilification of wealth, — Americans are sound at the core, — what they want is conservative individualism, a sense of the law," etc. Vickers smiled to himself, and looking out over the old meadow forgot all about the talkers.

From the meadow came the sweet scent of the September crop of hay. There was the river at the end of the vista, disappearing into a piece of woodland. The place was sown with memories, and Vickers's eyes were moist as he leaned there, looking forth into the night. It was but a shallow New England brook, this river, meandering through cranberry bogs, with alders and bilberry bushes on either side. He remembered the cranberry picking at this season, and later when the meadow had been flooded, the skating over the bushes that were frozen in the ice, and the snaky forms of the cranberry plants visible at the bottom. All these years he had thought of this little meadow as he had conceived it when a child, — a mighty river flowing on mysteriously through the dark valley, — on, around the woods that made out like a bold headland, then on and on to the remote sea. It was dim and wild, this meadow of his childhood, and the brook was like that river on which was borne to Camelot the silent bark with the fair Elaine. His older brother had taken him down that same brook in a canoe, — a quite wonderful journey. They had started early, just as the August moon was setting; and as they passed the headland of woods — pines and maples fearful in their dark recesses — an early thrush had broken the silence of the glimmering dawn with its sweet call. And another had answered from the depth of the wood, and then another, while the little canoe had slipped noiselessly past into strange lands, — a country altogether new and mysterious. . . . To-night that old boyhood thrill came over him, as when kneeling in the canoe with suspended paddle, in the half light of dawn, he had heard the thrushes calling from the woods. Then it had seemed that life was like this adventurous journey through the gray meadows, past the silent woods, on into the river below, and the great sea, far, far away! A wonderful journey of enlarging mystery from experience to experience into some great ocean of understanding. . . .

Vickers sat down at the piano by the window, and forgetting all that had taken the place of his dream, — the searing flame of his manhood, — struck the gentle chords of that boyhood journey, something of the river and the meadow and the woods and the gray dawn, which had often sounded in his ears far away in Venice.

Isabelle and Cairy, coming up the terrace steps, heard the notes and stopped to listen.

"Charming!" Cairy murmured. "His own?"

"How I wish he would try to do something, and get

his work played by our orchestras! He could if he would only interest himself enough. But the ambition seems gone out of him. He merely smiles when I talk about it."

"He'll come back to it," Cairy grinned. "It's in the air here to put your talent in the front window."

Vickers played on softly, dreaming of the boy's river of life, at home once more in the old Farm.

Early the next morning as Vickers stole softly through the corridor, on his way for a stroll, a door opened and Isabelle looked out.

"You'll find coffee downstairs, Vick. I remembered your dawn-wandering habit and asked Mrs. Stevens to have it ready for you. I'll join you in a few moments."

Before he had finished his coffee, Isabelle appeared and sleepily poured out a cup for herself. The servant was making ready a tray at the sideboard.

"Tom is one of your sleepless kind, too," she explained. "He does his writing before the house is awake, so as not to be disturbed, or he says he does. I believe he just turns over and takes another nap!"

"Cairy seems at home here," Vickers observed, sipping his coffee.

"Of course, Tommy is one of the family," Isabelle replied lightly. "He is much more domesticated than John, though, since his great success last winter, he hasn't been up very much."

"Has he made a great success?" Vickers inquired. "What at?"

"Haven't you heard of his play! It ran all the winter, and this new one they say will also make a great hit."

Vickers, who remembered Cairy in college as one always endeavoring after things out of his reach, looked mildly surprised.

"I hadn't heard that he was a dramatist," he said.

"I wish *you* would do something!" Isabelle remarked,

feeling that Cairy's success might point for Vickers his own defeat, and stir him into healthy action.

"What? Write a play?"

"No — you old dear!" She caressed his hand. "I think it would be good for you — to feel you were doing something in the world, instead of running about with that absurd child." She wanted to say much more about Delia Conry, but bided a more fitting time.

"I haven't run much so far," was all that Vickers replied. "You shouldn't have bothered to come down," he added when the coffee was finished. "I just wanted to poke around the old place as I used to."

"I know, — and I wanted to be with you, of course, this first time. Don't you remember how we got our own breakfasts when we went shooting in the autumn?"

Her brother nodded.

"Those were good times, Vick! . . . They were the best for both of us," she added less buoyantly. She pushed away her cup, put her arm about his shoulders, and kissed him.

"You shouldn't say that, Belle!"

"Vickie, it's so nice to hug you and have you all to myself before the others are up. I've missed some one to go batting with me, to hug and bully and chatter with. Now you've come I shall be a girl all over again."

And Isabelle was her old self for the first time since Vickers had joined her in Paris a month before, — no longer preoccupied, striving after some satisfaction that never perfectly arrived. Here the past was upon them both, — in spite of Osgood's transformations, — a past when they had been close, in the precious intimacy of brother and sister. Outside in the new, very new Dutch garden, Isabelle resumed her anxieties of the day.

"The gardener ought not to have put those bulbs there, — he knows nothing really! I shall have to find another man. . . . I hope the chauffeur John engaged will get along with the houseman. The last one fought. . . . Oh, did

I tell you that Potts is coming out Saturday, — the great Dr. Potts? He wants to look me over, — get me ready for the winter campaign. . . . There's Tom, writing at the desk by his window. Hello, Tommy!" Isabelle waved a hand gayly at the balcony above them. Vickers smiled at the disconnected remarks, so like Isabelle. Her conversation was a loose bundle of impressions, reflections, wishes, and feelings, especially her feelings about other people. And Isabelle had a taste for lame cats, as her mother said, — at least those cats that obviously felt their lameness.

"You don't like Tom," she rambled on. "Why not? Poor Tommy! he's so sweet and clever. Why don't you like Tom, Vickers? You must like him — because he'll be here a lot, and I am awfully fond of him."

"Why 'poor Tom'?" Vickers asked laconically.

"He's had such a hard time, a struggle to get on, — his people were poor, very nice though, — the best Virginia, you know. . . . He's ambitious, and he isn't strong. If this play shouldn't go — he's counting on it so much!"

Vickers smilingly drew her hand beneath his arm and led her out through the garden into the meadow. "The same old Belle after all," he murmured. "I don't see that Brother Cairy is badly off, — he has a good deal of petting, I fancy. I have heard all about that Virginia childhood and the rest of it. . . . Do you remember, Belle, when we used to go over to the Ed Prices' and were scared when we saw a tramp in the bushes on the hill? And how we ran through the willows as if the devil was after us? — Who have the Ed Prices' farm now?"

"Don't you know that father gave it to Alice Johnston? Wasn't it nice of him! Her husband is in the road, in St. Louis, doing very well, John says. Alice is over there now, — she brings the children on for the summer. . . . I don't see much of her — she is so enveloped in children!"

"What's become of the brother, — the one I licked and threw into Beaty's pond?"

"The world seems to have licked him, too," Isabelle replied, laughing at the old memory. "The last time Alice spoke of him she said he was on some newspaper in Spokane, — had been in the Klondike, I believe. . . . There's Mr. Gossom and Tom! We must go back for breakfast."

"Thanks! I have had mine. I think I'll walk over to the Price place and see Alice. Don't look for me before noon."

"But there are people coming for luncheon," Isabelle protested.

Vickers waved his hand to her and called back, "I think you'll get on very well without me!"

Isabelle was already answering Cairy's shout from the terrace. As Vickers took his way through the meadow, he thought how sweet she was, the real Isabelle, when one got to her as he had this morning. But she had never once mentioned John; her husband seemed to be very little in her mind.

CHAPTER XLV

VICKERS strode off through the meadow that morning in the hope of finding familiar things, and indulging in old memories. The country roads had been widened and improved, and many of the farm-houses had given way to more or less pretentious "places." Motors whirled past him. The hill that he remembered as a veritable mountain was a mere rise in the straightened road over which a fast car plunged at full speed, covering him with dust and leaving behind a sickening odor. He struck off into a wood-lot; here and in the pastures and meadows he found himself again. It was nearly noon before he came up the lane that led to the Ed Price farm.

This was off the beat of the motors, away from the new "estates," at the end of a grassy road bordered by gray birches. The ample old house he remembered very well with its square central chimney and stretch of outbuildings that joined the yellow barn. At his knock a broad-shouldered, smiling woman came to the door, and after a moment's hesitation exclaimed: —

"Why, Vick, — can it be you?"

"Yes, Cousin Alice."

She led him to the orchard in the rear, where with the aid of two little boys she was preparing vegetables for dinner. Tying on a large apron, she said: —

"You see we all have to take a hand. Won't you have a bib and dip in, too? . . . Children, this is your uncle — cousin. Which is it, Vickers?"

It was pleasant in the long grass under the apple tree, looking across the orchard of gnarled and stubby trees to the lane. Mrs. Johnston worked and talked, while the little boys with furtive glances pecked at the peas like two birds.

"I heard you were coming — I did not know just when. It is good to see you back, Vick!"

There was a comfortable largeness in the atmosphere of this woman, which suited the homely background of the square farm-house and the peaceful orchard. And there was a pleasant warmth in her tone.

"How do you find it?" she asked; "or perhaps you haven't had time yet to know."

"It hardly seems like being home," Vickers admitted, "everything is so changed — everything but this!" he added gratefully, thinking of Alice as well as the farm.

"Yes, — the country has changed, so many rich people have bought places. And your old home —" She hesitated to complete her sentence.

"I can't find my way around there." Vickers laughed. "What would the Colonel say!"

Alice looked as if she preferred not to think what the Colonel might say of his daughter's alterations.

"I suppose Isabelle had to have more room, — she has so many people with her. And you will find that life has changed over here in ten years."

"Nothing but change!"

"Except among the poor! . . . No, Tot, you can't eat the pods. There, boys, take sister and run out to the barn to help Charlie wash the buggy. . . . How does Isabelle seem to you?"

"I scarcely know — I haven't made up my mind. How does she seem to *you?*"

"She does too much, — she's not strong enough," Alice replied evasively.

"No, she doesn't seem strong; but she can't keep still!"

"She gets so little comfort out of anything, — that is the worst of it. Sometimes I wish John weren't so strong, — that he would have an illness, so that Isabelle would have something definite to do."

"She would have a trained nurse!" Vickers suggested with a laugh.

"She is such a dear, — I wish she were happier!"

"Perhaps that isn't in the blood."

"But I never saw a happier creature than she was the day she was married! And John is a fine fellow, and she has everything a woman could want."

"A woman wants a good many things these days." . . .

They chatted on about Isabelle and her love of people, and then about St. Louis and the old days at Grafton. For the first time since he had landed, it seemed to Vickers, he was permitted to ignore his failure, — he was at home. When he rose to go, Alice protested: —

"But you aren't going back, — it is just our dinner-time, and we haven't said half what we have to say!"

So he dined with the brood of children in the large front room, and afterwards Alice walked down the lane with him.

"I hope you are going to stay here?" she asked warmly.

"Oh, I don't know! America doesn't seem to need me," he replied, endeavoring to joke; "not that I know any place which does. I am waiting to be called."

In spite of the joking manner there was sadness in the voice. Alice was silent for a time and then replied earnestly: —

"Perhaps you are called *here* — for the present."

"You mean over there?" he asked quickly, nodding in the direction of Grafton.

"Yes!"

"Why do you think so?"

"You know Isabelle really cares for you as she doesn't for any one else in the world!"

"Yes, — we have always been close."

"But she cares for what you *think* —"

Vickers made a gesture, as if it were impossible that any one could do that.

"Yes," Alice continued gently; "a woman never gets wholly away from the influence of one she has admired as Isabelle admired you."

"But one's experience," he mused, "no matter how costly it has been, never seems to be of any use to any one else."

"Can you tell — until the end? . . . What we don't see in life is so much more than what we see!"

Vickers looked at her gratefully. He would like to feel that he was needed somewhere in this hurried world. Presently there was a childish uproar behind them, and Alice turned back.

"My brood is getting tempestuous; I must say good-by!"

She held Vickers's hand in her warm, firm grasp.

"I hope we shall see you often. . . . I think that you are called *here!*"

Vickers returned to the Farm, thinking of Alice Johnston. She had given him of her peace, of her confidence, her large way of taking the issues of life. 'And I used to say that she was a commonplace dumpy country girl!' he mused. He pondered what she had spoken, — the suggestion, vague but comforting, of purpose, of a place for him in the world to fill. Just what was she thinking of? "We'll see," he murmured, as he mounted the steps of the terrace. As Alice had said, the unseen in life was so much more than the seen.

In the formal garden the pretty little English governess was conducting the social game for the two girls. Marian Lane, having shown Delia her pony and her rabbits without eliciting much enthusiasm, now sat and stared at her with politely suppressed scorn for the dull red frock that Vickers had designed for his charge.

"Have you been to dancing school?" she demanded.

"What is that?" Delia asked.

She was dully uncomfortable in the company of this very dainty little creature, who was always dressed in delicate, light fabrics, and seemed to have many possessions. And Miss Betterton had a well-bred manner of putting the stranger outside the little social game. So when Delia spied Vickers, she cried, "There's father!" and ran towards him.

"Uncle Vickers is not Mabel's father," Marian asserted to Miss Betterton.

"Hush, dearie!" the well-bred Miss Betterton replied; "we mustn't talk about that."

When Isabelle and Cairy came up to the house from their afternoon ride, they found Vickers playing croquet with Miss Betterton and the two little girls, who in his society were approaching something like informality in their manner of addressing each other.

"He looks quite domestic," Cairy jeered.

"Hello, Vick! Come over and see the horses," Isabelle called.

At the stable Marian's new pony that Cairy had selected was exhibited. Lane drove up with a friend he had brought from the city for the week end, and the party played with the pony and laughed at his tricks, which Cairy showed off.

"He looks like a cross between an Angora cat and a Newfoundland dog," Cairy remarked, leaning down to feel of his legs. As he stooped the ivory handle of a small revolver pushed out of the hip pocket of his riding breeches.

"What's that, Uncle Tom?" Marian asked, pointing to the pistol.

Cairy drew out the pistol and held it up, with a slight flourish, — "A family weapon!"

Holding the pony with one hand and pointing the revolver at a blossom on a magnolia tree a few paces away, he fired and the white petals came fluttering down. A second report and another blossom fell. The pony jumped and snorted, but it did not disturb Cairy's aim. A third blossom fell, and then he quickly shot the descending bud which had been cut by the previous shot.

"Steady hand!" Lane commented.

"It's an old habit of mine to carry it and practise when I have a chance," Cairy remarked, breaking the revolver. After extracting the shells, he handed the pistol to Isabelle.

"Made in Paris," she read from the chased plate.

"Yes; it's a pretty toy, don't you think?"

"It's a curious shell," Lane remarked, picking up one of the empty shells from the ground.

"Yes, I have to have them specially made," replied Cairy. The toy was handed around and much admired.

"But, Uncle Tom," Marian asked, "why do you carry a pistol?"

"In the South gentlemen always carry pistols."

"Is it very dangerous in the South?" the little girl inquired. Then the older people laughed, and Cairy looked rather foolish.

CHAPTER XLVI

Isabelle's house appeared to Vickers more like a comfortable country club or a small country inn than the home of a private family. There were people coming and going all the time. Isabelle seemed at a loss without a peopled background. "And they are all interesting," she said to her brother, with a touch of pride. "It's the only place Dickie will stay in for any time, — he says I have the best collection of fakes he knows. But he likes to chatter with them." So far as Vickers could discover there was no special principle of selection in the conglomerate, except the vague test of being "interesting." Besides Gossom and Cairy and the Silvers and others of their kind there were Lane's business friends, officers of the railroad, and men that Lane brought out to golf with or ride with. "We don't go in for society," Isabelle explained, affecting a stronger indifference than she really felt for "merely smart people." She wished her brother to know that she had profited by her two years of New York life to gather about her intellectual people, and there was much clever talk at the Farm, to which Vickers paid an amused and bewildered attention.

From the quiet corner where Vickers looked on at the household these autumn days, he watched especially his brother-in-law. Lane could be at the Farm only for occasional days, and while there spent his time out of doors. He took small part in all the talk, but it amused him as might the vivacity of children. He left this personal side of life to Isabelle, content to be a passive spectator of the little game she was playing; while, as Vickers judged from what Gossom and other men said, Lane himself had a more absorbing, more exacting game in the city, which he was playing with eminent success. "He's getting close to the king row," Isabelle remarked to Vickers. "He was offered the presidency of some road or other out West. But we couldn't go out there again to live!"

Of all the men and women who came and went at the Farm, Cairy was on the most familiar footing. "He likes to work here," Isabelle explained with pride, "and he amuses John more than most of them. Besides he's very useful about the place!" Surely Cairy was pleasantly installed, as Conny would have said. He was delightful with the governess, who admired his light conversation, and he selected the pony for Molly, and taught her how to fall off gracefully. At domestic moments, which were rare, he effaced himself. He had a curious position in the household that puzzled Vickers. He was accepted, — the wheels ran around him. Isabelle treated him with a jesting, frank intimacy, very much as she treated her brother. And Lane, Vickers decided, had distinctly more use for the limping Southerner than he had for most of the people at the house, including his brother-in-law. Cairy was so completely out of Lane's world of men that there were no standards of comparison for him.

"Tommy distracts John," Isabelle explained to Vickers. "If he only could play golf, I suspect John would steal him from me."

As the weeks passed, however, Cairy was drawn to the city for longer intervals. The new play had not been a "Broadway success," in fact had been taken off after a short run, and Cairy's money affairs were again becoming precarious, much to Isabelle's frank concern. "It's the wretched condition of the theatre in our country," she complained; "to think that a few miserable newspaper writers can ruin the chances of a dramatist's being heard! The managers become panicky, if it doesn't go at once in New York. . . . There is a chance that they will put it on again somewhere West. But Tom hasn't much hope."

"It was a poor play," Fosdick asserted flatly. "And if you hadn't heard it line by line from Tommy, you'd know it."

"No," Isabelle protested; "it's lots cleverer than most things."

"I do not know how it may be with the theatre," Gossom put in at this point, "but more literature is produced in America to-day than at any other time in the world's history!"

"Oh!"

"I don't mean mere rhetoric, college writing," Gossom went on dogmatically; "but literature, things with blood to them in the language people use. Why, in the story contest for the *People's* there were at least fourteen masterpieces submitted, and not one of them had any reference to Europe, or showed the least trace of what college professors call style!" He turned triumphantly to Vickers, to whom he had previously expressed his conviction that America was the future home of all the arts. This was an item in his patriotic creed.

"Fourteen masterpieces,—really!" drawled Fosdick; "and how much a masterpiece, please? I must send you mine."

They had heard a good deal this week about the famous story contest for the *People's*. Gossom, ignoring the gibe, continued:—

"We publish every month real literature, the kind that comes from the heart, the stuff of real human lives. I am tired of this silly whine about the lack of opportunities for genius in our country."

"It's hard on Tommy, all the same," Isabelle concluded irrelevantly.

When Isabelle moved to New York for the winter, Vickers took Delia Conry West, and on his return after a few days in the city went up to the Farm, where Miss Betterton and Marian were still staying. He felt relieved to get back once more in the country that was now beginning its quiet preparation for winter. New York had overwhelmed him. And he could not but see that in the city he was something of a problem to his beautiful sister. She would not hear of his going to a hotel, and yet he was in the way. Vickers was not one to make an impression. And one must make an impression of some sort in Isabelle's world. "He's quaint, your brother," one of her friends said. "But he's locked up and the key is lost. Most people won't take the time to hunt for keys or even open doors."

If he had been more the artist, had some *réclame* from his music or his father's money, he would have fitted in. But a subdued little man with a sandy beard, sunken eyes, and careless clothes, — no, he was queer, but not "interesting"! And Isabelle, in spite of her strong sisterly loyalty, was relieved when she saw him off at the station.

"It's nice to think of you, Vickie, snugged away in the country, going around in your velveteens with a pipe in your mouth. Keep an eye on Molly and don't flirt with Miss Betterton. I shall run up often, and you must come down for the opera when you want to hear some music."

So Vickers betook himself to his seclusion. And when he did run down for the opera, he found himself jostled in a worse jam of Isabelle's occupations than before. Although she had just recovered from her yearly attack of grippe, and felt perpetually tired and exhausted, she kept up with her engagement list, besides going once a week to her boys' club, where Cairy helped her. Seeing her tired, restless face, Vickers asked her why she did it all.

"I should die if I sat back!" she answered irritably. "But I'll go up to the Farm with you for a day or two. . . . There's the masseuse — you'll find some cigarettes in the drawer — don't forget we dine early." . . .

When they reached the Farm the next afternoon, little Marian met them in the hall, dressed like a white doll. "How do you do, Mamma?" she said very prettily. "I am so glad to see you." And she held up her face to be kissed. The little girl had thought all day of her mother's coming, but she had not dared to ask the governess to meet her at the station; for "Mamma has not arranged it so." Isabelle looked at her daughter critically, and said in French to the English governess, "Too pale, my darling, — does she take her ride each day?"

Everything about the child's life was perfectly arranged, all thought out, from her baths and her frocks and her meals to the books she read and the friends she should have. But to Vickers, who stood near, it seemed a strange meeting between mother and child.

That evening as Isabelle lay with a new novel before the blazing fire, too listless to read, Vickers remarked: —

"A month of this would make you over, sis!"

"A month! I couldn't stand it a week, even with you, Bud!"

"You can't stand the other."

"Come! The rest cure idea is exploded. The thing to do nowadays is to vary your pursuits, employ different sets of nerve centres!" Isabelle quoted the famous Potts with a mocking smile. "You should see how I vary my activities, — I use a different group of cells every half hour. You don't know how well I look after the family, too. I don't neglect my job. Aren't you comfortable here? Mary cooks very well, I think."

"Oh, Mary is all right. . . . You may shift the batteries, Belle, but you are burning up the wires, all the same."

"Let 'em burn, then, — I've got to live! . . . You see, Vickie, I am not the little girl you remember. I've grown up! When I was *down* after Marian came, I did such a lot of thinking. . . . I was simple when I married, Vick. I thought John and I would spoon out the days, — at least read together and be great chums. But it didn't turn out that way; you can't live that sort of life these days, and it would be stupid. Each one has to develop his talent, you see, and then combine the gifts. John thinks and breathes the railroad. And when he's off duty, he wants to exercise or go to the theatre and see some fool show. That's natural, too, — he works hard. But I can't do *his* things, — so I do *my* things. He doesn't care. . . . To tell the truth, Vick, I suspect John wouldn't miss me before the month's bills were due, if I should elope to-night!"

"I am not so sure, Belle."

"Of course — don't I know? That must be the case with most marriages, and it's a good thing, perhaps."

Vickers suggested softly, "The Colonel's way was good, too."

"Women didn't expect much those days. They do now. Even the architects recognize the change in our habits."

"I don't believe the architects have made any changes for Alice."

"Oh, Alice!" Isabelle pished. "She is just a mother."

"And the millions of others, men and women?"

"They copy those on top as fast as they can; the simple life is either compulsory or an affectation. . . . I don't care for the unexpressive millions!"

(A Cairy phrase — Vickers recognized the mint.)

Isabelle rose, and drawing aside the curtains, looked out at the snowy gardens.

"See how stunning the poplars are against the white background! Do you remember, Vick, when we ran away from school and came up here together and spent two nights while they were telegraphing all over for us? What a different world! . . . Well, good night, Buddie, — I must sleep up."

Yes, thought Vickers, as he lighted another cigarette, what a different world! That summed up the months since he had taken the steamer at Cherbourg. And what different people! Had he stood still while Isabelle and her friends had expanded, thrown off limitations? For her and the many others like her the intoxicating feast of life seemed to have been spread lavishly. With full purses and never sated appetites they rushed to the tables, — all running, out of breath, scenting opportunities, avid to know, to feel, to experience! "We are passing through another renaissance," as Gossom had pompously phrased it. But with what a difference!

To-night as Vickers looked across the still white fields from his bedroom window, he was less concerned with the national aspect of the case than with what this renaissance meant to his sister. Even with the aid of the great Potts she could never keep the nerve-racking pace that she had set herself.

And yet in actual expenditure of force, either mental or physical, what Isabelle did or any of her acquaintance did was not enough to tire healthy, full-grown women. There was maladjustment somewhere. What ailed this race that was so rapidly becoming neurasthenic as it flowered?

One thing was plain, — that so far as emotional satisfaction went Isabelle's marriage was null, merely a convention like furniture. And John, as Vickers recognized in spite of his brother-in-law's indifference to him, was a good husband. Fortunately Isabelle, in spite of all her talk, was not the kind to fill an empty heart with another love. . . . A suspicion of that had crossed his mental vision, but had faded almost at once. . . . Isabelle was another sort!

CHAPTER XLVII

Isabelle had agreed to stay out the week with Vickers, and in spite of her restlessness, her desire to be doing something new, the old self in her — the frank, girlish, affectionate self — revived, as it always did when she was alone with her brother. He said: —

"I am coming to agree with Potts, Isabelle; you need to elope."

As she looked up, startled, he added, "With me! I'll take you to South America and bring you back a new woman."

"South America, — no thanks, brother."

"Then stay here." . . .

That evening Isabelle was called to the telephone, and when she came back her face was solemn.

"Percy Woodyard died last night, — pneumonia after grippe. Too bad! I haven't seen him this winter; he has been very delicate. . . . I must go in for the funeral."

"I thought you and Cornelia were intimate," Vickers remarked; "but I haven't heard you mention her name since I've been home."

"We were, at first; but I haven't seen much of her the last two years. . . . Too bad — poor Percy! Conny has killed him."

"What do you mean?"

"Oh, she's worked him to death, — made him do this and that. Tom says —" Isabelle hesitated.

"What does Tom say?"

"Oh, there was a lot of talk about something he did, — went off to Europe two years ago, and let some politicians make money — I don't know just what. But he's not been the same since, — he had to drop out of politics."

This and something more Isabelle had learned from Cairy, who had heard the gossip among men. Woodyard was too unimportant a man to occupy the public eye, even when it was a question of a "gigantic steal," for more than a few brief hours. By the time the Woodyards had returned from that journey to Europe, so hastily undertaken, the public had forgotten about the Northern Mill Company's franchise. But the men who follow things and remember, knew; and Percy Woodyard, when he sailed up the bay on his return in October, realized that politically he was buried, — that is, in the manner of politics he cared about. And he could never explain, not to his most intimate friend, how he had happened to desert his post, to betray the trust of men who trusted him. It was small satisfaction to believe that it would all have happened just as it had, even if he had been there to block the path of the determined majority.

When, towards the end of their stay abroad, a letter had come from the Senator in regard to "that post in the diplomatic service," Percy had flatly refused to consider it.

"But why, Percy?" his wife had asked gently, — she was very sweet with him since their departure from New York. "We can afford it, — you know my property is paying very well."

In the look that Percy gave her, Conny saw that her husband had plumbed her farther than she had ever dreamed him capable of doing, and she trembled.

"I am going back to New York to practise my profession," Percy said shortly. "And we shall live henceforth on *my* earnings, solely."

So he had gone back to his office and taken up his practice. He was a delicate man, and the past year had strained him. His practice was not large or especially profitable. The franchise scandal stood in his way, and though he succeeded in securing some of the corporation practice that he had once scorned, his earnings were never sufficient to support the establishment Conny had created. In fact that able mistress of domestic finance increased the establishment by buying a place at Lancaster for their country home. She was weaving a new web for her life and Percy's, the political one having failed, and no doubt she would have succeeded this time in making the strands hold, had it not been for Percy's delicate health. He faded out, the inner fire having been quenched. . . .

At the funeral Isabelle was surprised to see Cairy. Without knowing anything exactly about it, she had inferred that in some way Conny had treated Tom "badly," and she had not seen him the last times she had been at the Woodyards'. But that had not been lately. Somehow they had drifted apart these last two years, — their paths had diverged in the great social whirlpool ever more and more, though they still retained certain common friends, like the Silvers, who exchanged the current small gossip of each other's doings. Isabelle was thinking of this and many other things about Percy and Conny as she waited in the still drawing-room for the funeral service to begin. She had admired Conny extravagantly at first, and now though she tried to think of her in her widowhood sympathetically, she found it impossible to pity her; while of poor Percy, who it seemed "had been too much under his wife's thumb," she thought affectionately. . . . The hall and the two rooms on this floor where the people had gathered were exquisitely prepared. Isabelle could see Conny's masterly hand in it all. . . .

When the service was over, Isabelle waited to speak with Conny, who had asked her to stay. She saw Cairy go out behind the Senator, who looked properly grave and concerned, his black frock-coat setting off the thick white hair on the back of his head.

The two men walked down the street together, and the Senator, who had met Cairy at the Woodyards' a number of times and remembered him as an inmate of the house, fell to talking about the dead man.

"Poor chap!" he said meditatively; "he had fine talents."

"Yes," assented Cairy. "It was a shame!" His tone

left it doubtful just what was a shame, but the Senator, assuming that it was Percy's untimely death, continued: —

"And yet Woodyard seemed to lack something to give practical effectiveness to his abilities. He did not have the power to 'seize that tide which leads men on to victory,' — to size up the situation comprehensively, you know." (The Senator was fond of quoting inaccurately and then paraphrasing from his own accumulated wisdom.)

"I doubt very much," he went on expansively, "if he would have counted for as much as he did — as he promised at one time to count at any rate — if it had not been for his wife. Mrs. Woodyard is a very remarkable woman!"

"Yes, she is a strong personality, — she was the stronger of the two undoubtedly."

"She has one of the ablest business heads that I know of," the Senator said emphatically, nodding his own head. "She should have been a man."

"One would miss a good deal — if she were a man," suggested Cairy.

"Her beauty, — yes, very striking. But she has the brain of a man."

"She is the sort that must make destiny," agreed Cairy, feeling a literary satisfaction in the phrase and also pride that he could so generously play chorus to the Senator's praise. "I fancy she will marry again!"

He wondered at the moment whether the Senator might not venture now to break his long widowerhood. The great man, stopping on the step of his club, remarked in a curious voice: —

"I suppose so, — she is young and beautiful, and would naturally not consider her life ended. And yet — she is not exactly the sort of woman a man marries — unless he is very young!"

With a nod and a little smile the Senator went briskly up the steps of his club.

CHAPTER XLVIII

THE time, almost the very minute, when Isabelle realized the peculiar feeling she had come to have for Cairy, was strangely clear to her. It was shortly after Percy Woodyard's funeral. She had been to Lakewood with her mother, and having left her comfortably settled in her favorite hotel, had taken the train for New York. Tom was to go to the theatre with her that evening, and had suggested that they dine at a little down-town restaurant he used to frequent when he was Gossom's slave. He was to meet her at the ferry.

She had been thinking of Percy Woodyard, of Fosdick's epithet for Conny, — the Vampire. And there flashed across her the thought, 'She will try to get Tom back!' (Cairy had told her that he had gone to the funeral because Conny had written him a little note.) 'And she is so bad for him, so bad for any man!' Then looking out on the brown March landscape, she felt a pleasant glow of expectation, of something desirable in immediate prospect, which she did not at once attribute to anything more definite than the fact she was partly rested, after her two days at Lakewood. But when in the stream of outgoing passengers that filled the echoing terminal she caught sight of Tom's face, looking expectantly over the heads of the crowd, a vivid ray of joy darted through her.

'He's here!' she thought. 'He has come across the ferry to meet me!'

She smiled and waved the bunch of violets she was wearing — those he had sent down to Lakewood for her — above the intervening heads.

"I thought I would snatch a few more minutes," he explained, as they walked slowly through the long hall to the ferry.

The bleak March day had suddenly turned into something warm and gay for her; the dreary terminal was a spot to linger in.

"That was very nice of you," she replied gently, "and so are these!"

She held up his flowers, and in the look they exchanged they went far in that progress of emotional friendship, the steps of which Cairy knew so well. . . . The city was already lighted, tier on tier of twinkling dots in the great hives across the river, and as they sat out on the upper deck of the ferry for the sake of fresh air, Isabelle thought she had never seen the city so marvellous. There was an enchantment in the moving lights on the river, the millions of fixed lights in the long city. The scent of sea water reached them, strong and vital, with its ever witching associations of far-off lands. Isabelle turned and met Cairy's eyes looking intently at her.

"You seem so joyous to-night!" he said almost reproachfully.

She smiled at him softly.

"But I am! Very happy! — it is good to be here."

That was it, — the nearest description of her feeling, — it was all so good. She was so much alive! And as she settled back against the hard seat, she thought pleasantly of the hours to come, the dinner, the play, and then Tom would take her home and they would talk it over. . . . She had asked John to go with her. But he had declined on the ground that "he could not stand Ibsen," and "he didn't like that little Russian actress." Really, he was getting very lazy, Isabelle had thought. He would probably smoke too many cigars, yawn over a book, and go to bed at ten. That was what he usually did unless he went out to a public dinner, or brought home work from the office, or had late business meetings. Nothing for his wife, she had complained once. . . .

This wonderful feeling of light-hearted content continued as they walked through dingy streets to the old brick building that housed the restaurant, half café, half saloon, where the Irish wife of the Italian proprietor cooked extraordinary

Italian dishes, according to Cairy. He was pensive. He had been generally subdued this winter on account of the failure of his play. And, after all, the London opening had not come about. It was distinctly "his off year" — and he found it hard to work. "Nothing so takes the ideas out of you as failure," he had said, "and nothing makes you feel that you can do things like success."

Isabelle wanted to help him; she was afraid that he was being troubled again by lack of money. Art and letters were badly paid, and Tom, she was forced to admit, was not provident.

"But you are happy to-night," she had said coaxingly on the ferry. "We are going to be very gay, and forget things!" That was what Tom did for her, — made her forget things, and return to the mood of youth where all seemed shining and gay. She did that for him, too, — amused and distracted him, with her little impetuosities and girlish frankness. "You are such a good fellow — you put heart into a man," he had said.

She was happy that she could affect him, could really influence a man whose talent she admired, whom she believed in.

"I can't do anything to John except make him yawn!" she had replied.

So to-night she devoted her happy mood to brushing away care from Cairy's mind, and by the time they were seated at the little table with its coarse, wine-stained napkin, he was laughing at her, teasing her about growing stout, of which she pretended to be greatly afraid.

"Oh, dear!" she sighed. "I stand after meals and roll and roll, and Mrs. Peet pounds me until I am black and blue, but it's no use. I am gaining! Tommy, you'll have to find some younger woman to say your pretty things to. I am growing frightfully homely! . . . That's one comfort with John, — he'll never know it."

As the meal passed their mood became serious once more and tender, as it had been when they met. Cairy, lighting cigarette after cigarette, talked on, about himself. He was very despondent. He had made a hard fight for recognition; he thought he had won. And then had come discouragement after discouragement. It looked as if he should be obliged to accept an offer from a new magazine that was advertising its way into notice and do some articles for them. No, he would not go back to be Gossom's private mouthpiece at any price!

He did not whine, — Cairy never did that exactly; but he presented himself for sympathy. The odds had been against him from the start. And Isabelle was touched by this very need for sunshine in the emotional temperament of the man. Conny had appraised the possibilities of his talent intelligently, believed that if properly exploited he should "arrive." But Isabelle was moved by the possibilities of his failure, — a much more dangerous state of mind. . . .

It was long past the time for the theatre, but Cairy made no move. It was pleasantly quiet in the little room. The few diners had left long ago, and the debilitated old waiter had retreated to the bar. Cairy had said, "If it were not for you, for what you give me —" And she had thought, 'Yes, what I *might* give him, what he needs! And we are so happy together here.' . . .

Another hour passed. The waiter had returned and clattered dishes suggestively and departed again. Cairy had not finished saying all he wanted to say. . . . There were long pauses between his words, of which even the least carried feeling. Isabelle, her pretty mutinous face touched with tenderness, listened, one hand resting on the table. Cairy covered the hand with his, and at the touch of his warm fingers Isabelle flushed. Was it the mood of this day, or something deeper in her nature that thrilled at this touch as she had never thrilled before in her life? It held her there listening to his words, her breath coming tightly. She wanted to run away, and she did not move. . . . The love that he was telling her she seemed to have heard whispering in her heart long before. . . .

The way to Isabelle's heart was through pity, the desire to give, as with many women. Cairy felt it instinctively, and followed the path. Few men can blaze their way to glory, but all can offer the opportunity to a woman of splendid sacrifice in love!

"You know I care!" she had murmured. "But, oh, Tom —" That "but" and the sigh covered much, — John, the little girl, the world as it is. If she could only give John what she felt she could give this man, with his pleading eyes that said, 'With you I should be happy, I should conquer!'

"I know — I ask for nothing!"

(Nothing! Oh, damnable lover's lie! Do the Cairys ever content themselves with nothings?)

"I will do as you say — in all things. We will forget this talk, or I will not go back to the Farm; but I am glad we understand!"

"No, no," she said quickly. "You must come to the Farm! It must be just as it has been." She knew as she said the words that it could never be "as it had been." She liked to close her eyes now to the dark future; but after to-day, after this new sense of tenderness and love, the old complexion of life must be different.

Cairy still held her hand. As she looked up with misty eyes, very happy and very miserable, a little figure came into the empty room followed by the waiter, and glanced aimlessly about for a table.

"Vick!" Isabelle cried in astonishment. "Where did you come from?"

Vickers had a music score under his arm, and he tapped it as he stood above them at the end of their table.

"I've been trying over some things with Lester at his rooms, and came in for a bite. I thought you were going to the theatre, Belle?"

"We are!" Cairy exclaimed, looking at his watch. "We'll about get the last act!"

Vickers fingered his roll and did not look at Isabelle. Suddenly she cried: —

"Take me home, Vick! . . . Good-night, Tom!"

She hurried nervously from the place. Vickers hailed a cab, and as they rode up town neither spoke at first. Then Vickers put his hand on hers and held it very tightly. She knew that he had seen — her tear-stained eyes and Cairy's intent face, — that he had seen and understood.

"Vick," she moaned, "why is it all such a muddle? Life — what you mean to do, and what you can do! John doesn't care, doesn't understand. . . . I'm such a fool, Vick!" She leaned her head on his shoulder and sobbed. He caressed her hand gently, saying nothing.

He was sure now that he was called somewhere on this earth.

CHAPTER XLIX

When Lane went West early in May for his annual inspection trip, Isabelle moved to the Farm for the season. She was wan and listless. She had talked of going abroad with Vickers, but had suddenly given up the plan. A box of books arrived with her, and she announced to Vickers that she meant to read Italian with him; she must do something to kill the time. But the first evening when she opened a volume of French plays, she dropped it; books could not hold her attention any more. All the little details about her house annoyed her, — nothing went smoothly. The governess must be changed. Her French was horrible. Marian followed her mother about with great eyes, fearful of annoying her, yet fascinated. Isabelle exclaimed in sudden irritation: —

"Haven't you anything to do, Molly!" And to Vickers she complained: "Children nowadays seem perfectly helpless. Unless they are provided with amusement every minute, they dawdle about, waiting for you to do something for them. Miss Betterton should make Molly more independent."

And the next day in a fit of compunction she arranged to have a children's party, sending the motor for some ten-mile-away neighbors.

In her mood she found even Vickers unsatisfactory: "Now you have me here, cooped up, you don't say a word to me. You are as bad as John. That portentous silence is a husband's privilege, Vick. . . . You and I used to *jaser* all the time. Other men don't find me dull, anyway. They tell me things!"

She pouted like a child. Vickers recalled that when she had said something like this one day at breakfast with

John and Cairy present, Lane had lifted his head from his plate and remarked with a quiet man's irony: "The other men are specials, — they go on for an occasion. The husband's is a steady job."

Cairy had laughed immoderately. Isabelle had laughed with him, — "Yes, I suppose you are all alike; you would slump every morning at breakfast."

This spring Isabelle had grown tired, even of people. "Conny wants to come next month, and I suppose I must have her. I wanted Margaret, but she has got to take the little boy up to some place in the country and can't come. . . . There's a woman, now," she mused to Vickers, her mind departing on a train of association with Margaret Pole. "I wonder how she possibly stands life with that husband of hers. He's getting worse all the time. Drinks now! Margaret asked me if John could give him something in the railroad, and John sent him out to a place in the country where he would be out of harm. . . . There's marriage for you! Margaret is the most intelligent woman I know, and full of life if she had only half a chance to express herself. But everything is ruined by that mistake she made years ago. If I were she —" Isabelle waved a rebellious hand expressively. "I thought at one time that she was in love with Rob Falkner, — she saw a lot of him. But he has gone off to Panama. Margaret won't say a word about him; perhaps she is in love with him still, — who knows!"

One day she looked up from a book at Vickers, who was at the piano, and observed casually: —

"Tom is coming up to spend June when he gets back from the South." She waited for an expected remark, and then added, "If you dislike him as much as you used to, you had better take that time for Fosdick."

"Do you want me to go?"

"No, — only I thought it might be more comfortable for you —"

"Cairy doesn't make me uncomfortable."

"Oh — well, you needn't worry about me, brother dear!"

She blushed and came across the room to kiss him. "I am well harnessed; I shan't break the traces — yet." . . .

It was a summerish day, and at luncheon Isabelle seemed less moody than she had been since her arrival. "Let's take one of our old long rides, — just ride anywhere, as we used to," she suggested.

They talked of many things that afternoon, slipping back into the past and rising again to the present. Vickers, happy in her quieter, gentler mood, talked of himself, the impressions he had received these months in his own land.

"What strikes me most," he said, "at least with the people that I see about you, Belle, is the sharp line between work and play. I see you women all at play, and I see the men only when they are wearily watching you play or playing with you. One hears so much about business in America. But with you people it is as much suppressed as if your husbands and brothers went off to some other star every day to do their work and came back at night by air ship to see their families."

"Business is dull," Isabelle explained, — "most men's business. They want to forget it themselves when they leave the office."

"But it is so much a part of life," Vickers protested, thinking of the hours and days Lane spent absorbed in affairs that Isabelle hadn't the curiosity to inquire about.

"Too much over here."

"And not enough." . . .

On their way home in the cool of the evening, over a hilly road through the leafing woods, their horses walked close together, and Isabelle, putting an arm affectionately on her brother's shoulder, mused: —

"One feels so differently different days. Tell me, Vick, what makes the atmosphere, — the color of life in one's mind? Look over there, along the river. See all the gray mist and up above on the mountain the purple — and to-morrow it will be gone! Changing, always changing! It's just so inside you; the color is changing all the time. . . . There is the old village. It doesn't seem to me any longer the place you and I lived in as boy and girl, the place I was married from."

"It is we who have changed, not Grafton."

"Of course; it's what we have lived through, felt, — and we can't get back! We can't get back, — that's the sad thing."

"Perhaps it isn't best to get back altogether."

Isabelle gave him a curious glance, and then in a hard tone remarked, "Sometimes I think, Vick, that in spite of your experience you are the same soft, sentimental youth you were before it happened."

"Not quite."

"Did you ever regret it, Vick?"

"Yes," he said bravely, "many times; but I am not so sure now that one can really regret anything that is done out of one's full impulse."

"Well, — that was different," Isabelle remarked vaguely. "Did you ever consider, Vick, that marriage is an awful problem for a woman, — any woman who has individuality, who thinks? . . . A man takes it easily. If it doesn't fit, why he hangs it up in the closet, so to speak, and takes it out just as little as he has to. But a woman, — she must wear it pretty much all of the time — or give it up altogether. It's unfair to the woman. If she wants to be loved, and there are precious few women who don't want a man to love them, don't want that first of all, and her husband hasn't time to bother with love, — what does she get out of marriage? I know what you are going to say! John loves me, when he thinks about it, and I have my child, and I am happily placed, in very comfortable circumstances, and —"

"I wasn't going to say that," Vickers interrupted.

"But," continued Isabelle, with rising intensity, "you know that has nothing to do with happiness. . . . One might as well be married to a hitching-post as to John. Women simply don't count in his life. Sometimes I wish they did — that he would make me jealous! Give him the railroad and golf and a man to talk to, and he is perfectly happy. . . . Where do I come in?"

"Where do you put yourself in?"

"As housekeeper," she laughed, the mood breaking. "The Johnstons are coming next week, all eight — or is it nine? — of them. I must go over and see that the place is opened. . . . They live like tramps, with one servant, but they seem very happy. He is awfully good, but dull,— John is a social lion compared to Steve Johnston. John says he's very clever in his line. And as for Alice, she always was big, but she's become enormous. I don't suppose she ever thinks of anything so frivolous as a waist-line."

"I thought she had a beautiful face."

"Vick, I don't believe that you know whether a woman has a figure! You might write a *Symphonie Colossale* with Alice and her brood as the theme."

"She is Woman," suggested Vickers.

"Woman!" Isabelle scoffed. "Why is child-bearing considered the corner-stone of womanhood? Having young? Cows do that. Women are good for other things,— inspiration, love, perhaps!" She curved her pretty lips at her brother mockingly. . . .

There were two telegrams at the house. Isabelle, opening the first, read aloud, "Reach Grafton three thirty, Tuesday. John," and dropped it on the table. The other she did not read aloud, but telephoned an answer to the telegraph office. Later she remarked casually, "Tom finds he can get back earlier; he'll be here by the end of the week."

CHAPTER L

"THERE'S Steve," Isabelle said to Vickers, "coming across the meadow with his boys. He *is* an old dear, so nice and fatherly!"

The heavy man was plodding slowly along the path, the four boys frisking around him in the tall June grass like puppies.

"He has come to see John about some business. Let us take the boys and have a swim in the pool!"

Isabelle was gay and happy this morning, with one of those rapid changes in mood over night that had become habitual with her. When they returned from their romp in the pool, the boys having departed to the stable in search of further amusement, Lane and Johnston were still talking while they slowly paced the brick terrace.

"Still at it!" exclaimed Isabelle. "Goodness! what can it be to make John talk as fast as that! Why, he hasn't said half as many words to me since he's been back. Just look at 'em, Vick!"

Outside on the terrace Steve Johnston was saying, stuttering in his endeavor to get hastily all the words he needed to express his feelings: —

"It's no use, Jack! I tell you I am sick of the whole business. I know it's big pay, — more than I ever expected to earn in my life. But Alice and I have been poor before, and I guess we can be poor again if it comes to that."

"A man with your obligations has no right to give up such an opportunity."

"Alice is with me; we have talked the thing all through. . . . No, I may be a jackass, but I can't see it any different.

I don't like the business of loading the dice, — that is all. I have stood behind the counter, so to speak, and seen the dice loaded, fifteen years. But I wasn't responsible myself. Now in this new place you offer me I should be IT, — the man who loads. . . . I have been watching this thing for fifteen years. When I was a rate clerk on the Canada Southern, I could guess how it was, — the little fellows paid the rate as published and the big fellows didn't. Then when I went into the A. and P. I came a step nearer, could watch how it was done — didn't have to guess. Then I went with the Texas and Northern as assistant to the traffic manager, and I loaded the dice — under orders. Now —"

"Now," interrupted Lane, "you'll take your orders from *my* office."

"I know it, — that's part of the trouble, Jack!" the heavy man blurted out. "You want a safe man out there, you say. I know what that means! I don't want to talk good to you, Jack. But you see things differently from me." . . .

"All this newspaper gossip and scandal has got on your nerves," Lane said irritably.

"No, it hasn't. And it isn't any fear of being pulled up before the Commission. That doesn't mean anything to me. . . . No, I have seen it coming ever since I was a clerk at sixty a month. And somehow I felt if it ever got near enough me so that I should have to fix the game — for that's all it amounts to, Jack, and you know it — why, I should have to get out. At last it's got up to me, and so I am getting out!"

The stolid man puffed with the exertion of expressing himself so fully, inadequate as his confused sentences were to describe all that fermenting mass of observation, impression, revulsion, disgust that his experience in the rate-making side of his employment had stored up within him the last fifteen years. Out of it had come a result — a resolve. And it was this that Lane was combating heatedly. It was not merely that he liked Johnston personally and did not want him "to make a fool of himself," as he had expressed it, not altogether because he had made up his mind that the heavy man's qualities were exactly what he needed for this position he had offered him; rather, because the unexpected opposition, Johnston's scruples, irritated him personally. It was a part of the sentimental newspaper clamor, half ignorance, half envy, that he despised. When he had used the words, "womanish hysteria," descriptive of the agitation against the railroads, Steve had protested in the only humorous remark he was ever known to make: —

"Do I look hysterical, Jack?"

So the two men talked on. What they said would not have been wholly understood by Isabelle, and would not have interested her. And yet it contained more elements of pathos, of modern tragedy, than all the novels she read and the plays she went to see. The homely, heavy man — "He looks just like a bag of meal with a yellow pumpkin on top," Isabelle had said — replied to a thrust by Lane: —

"Yes, maybe I shall fail in the lumber business. It's pretty late to swap horses at forty-three. But Alice and I have talked it over, and we had rather run that risk than the other —"

"You mean?"

"That I should do what Satters of the L. P. has just testified he's been doing — under orders — to make traffic."

It was a shrewd blow. Satters was a clear case where the powerful L. P. road had been caught breaking the rate law by an ingenious device that aroused admiration in the railroad world. He had been fined a few thousand dollars, which was a cheap forfeit. This reference to Satters closed the discussion.

"I hope you will find the lumber business all you want it to suit your conscience, Steve. Come in and have some lunch!"

The heavy man refused, — he was in no mood for one of Isabelle's luncheons, and he had but one more day of vacation. Gathering up his brood, he retraced his way across the meadow, the four small boys following in his track.

"Well!" exclaimed Isabelle to her husband. "What was your business all about? Luncheon has been waiting half an hour. It was as good as a play watching you two out there. Steve looked really awake."

"He was awake all right," Lane replied.

"Tell us all about it — there, Vick, see if he doesn't put me off with 'Just business, my dear'!"

"It *was* just business. Steve has declined a good position I made for him, at nearly twice the salary he has ever earned."

"And all those boys to put through college!"

"What was it?" Vickers asked.

Something made Lane unusually communicative, — his irritation with Steve or his wife's taunt.

"Did you ever hear of the Interstate Commerce Commission?" he asked his brother-in-law, in a slightly ironical tone. And he began to state the situation, and stated it remarkably well from his point of view, explaining the spirit of interference that had been growing throughout the country with railroad management, corporation management in general, — its disastrous effect if persisted in, and also "emotionalism" in the press. He talked very ably, and held his wife's attention. Isabelle said: —

"But it was rather fine of Steve, if he felt that way!"

"He's kept his mouth shut fifteen years."

"He's slow, is Steve, but when he sees — he acts!"

Vickers said nothing, but a warm sense of comfort spread through his heart, as he thought, 'Splendid! — she did that for him, Alice.'

"I hope he won't come to grief in the lumber business," Lane concluded. "Steve is not fitted for general business. And he can't have much capital. Only their savings."

Then he yawned and went to the library for a cigar, dismissing Steve and his scruples and the railroad business altogether from his mind, in the manner of a well-trained man of affairs, who has learned that it is a useless waste of energy to speculate on what has been done and to wonder why men should feel and act as they do feel and act.

And Isabelle, with a "It will come hard on Alice!" — went off to cut some flowers for the vases, still light-hearted, humming a gay little French song that Tom had taught her.

If it were hard for Alice Johnston, the large woman did not betray it when Vickers saw her a few days later. With the help of her oldest boy she was unharnessing the horse from the Concord buggy.

"You see," she explained, as Vickers tried to put the head halter on the horse, "we are economizing on Joe, who used to do the chores when he did not forget them, which was every other day!"

When Vickers referred to Steve's new business, she said cheerfully: —

"I think there is a good chance of success. The men Steve is going in with have bought a large tract of land in the southern part of Missouri. They have experience in the lumber business, and Steve is to look after the city end, — he's well known in St. Louis."

"I do so hope it will go right," Vickers remarked, wishing that in some way he could help in this brave venture.

"Yes!" Alice smiled. "It had to be, this risk, — you know there come times when there is only one thing to do. If Steve hadn't taken the step, left the railroad, I think that neither of us would have been happy afterwards. But these are anxious days for us. We have put all the money in our stocking into it, — seven thousand dollars; all we have in the world but this old farm, which the Colonel gave me. I wanted to mortgage the farm, but Steve wouldn't let me. So all our eggs are in one basket. Not so many eggs, but we can't spare one!"

She laughed serenely, with a broad sense of humor over the family venture, yet with a full realization of its risk.

Vickers marvelled at her strong faith in Steve, in the future, in life. As he had said to Isabelle, this was Woman, one who had learned the deeper lessons of life from her children, from her birth-pangs.

She took him into the vegetable garden which she and the children had planted. "We are truck-farmers," she explained. "I have the potatoes, little Steve the corn, Ezra the peas, and so on to Tot, who looks after the carrots and beets because they are close to the ground and don't need much attention. The family is cultivating on shares."

They walked through the rows of green vegetables that were growing lustily in the June weather, and then turned back to the house. Alice stopped to fasten up a riotous branch of woodbine that had poked its way through a screen.

"If the worst comes to the worst, I shall turn farmer in earnest and raise vegetables for my wealthy neighbors. And there is the orchard! We have been poor so much of the time that we know what it means. . . . I have no doubt it will come out all right, — and we don't worry, Steve and I. We aren't ambitious enough to worry."

It was a pleasant place, the Price farm, tucked away in a fold of gentle hills, at the end of a grassy lane. The bees hummed in the apple trees, and the June breeze swayed through the house, where all the windows and doors were open. Vickers, looking at the calm, healthy woman sitting beside him on the porch, did not pity the Johnstons, nor fear for them. Alice, surely, was the kind that no great misfortune could live with long.

"I am really a farmer, — it's all the blood in my veins," Alice remarked. "And when I get back here summers, the soil seems to speak to me. I've known horses and cows and pigs and crops and seasons for centuries. It's only skin deep, the city coating, and is easily scraped off. . . . Your father, Vickers, was a wise man. He gave me the exact thing that was best for me when he died, — this old farm of my people. Just as he had given me the best thing in my life, — my education. If he had done more, I should be less able to get along now."

They had dinner, a noisy meal at which the children served in turns, Alice sitting like a queen bee at the head of the table, governing the brood. Vickers liked these midday meals with the chattering, chirping youngsters.

"And how has it been with the music?" Alice asked. "Have you been able to work? You spent most of the winter up here, didn't you?"

"I have done some things," Vickers said; "not much. I am not at home yet, and what seems familiar is this, the past. But I shall get broken in, no doubt. And," he added thoughtfully, "I have come to see that this is the place for me — for the present."

"I am glad," she said softly.

CHAPTER LI

As Vickers crossed the village on his way back from the Johnstons', Lane emerged from the telegraph office and joined him. On the rare occasions when they were thrown together alone like this, John Lane's taciturnity reached to positive dumbness. Vickers supposed that his brother-in-law disliked him, possibly despised him. It was, however, a case of absolute non-understanding. It must remain forever a problem to the man with a firm grasp on concrete fact how any one could do what Vickers had done, except through "woman-weakness," for which Lane had no tolerance. Moreover, the quiet little man, with his dull eyes, who moved about as if his faculties had been forgotten in the morning when he got up, who could sit for hours dawdling at the piano striking chords, or staring at the keys, seemed merely queer to the man of action. "I wish he would do something," Isabelle had said of Vickers, using his own words of her, and her husband had replied, "Do? . . . What could he do!"

"I've just been to see Alice," Vickers remarked timidly. "She takes Steve's change of business very calmly."

"She doesn't know," Lane answered curtly. "And I am afraid he doesn't either."

He let the topic drop, and they walked on in silence, turning off at the stile into an old by-path that led up to the new house through a small grove of beeches, which Isabelle had saved at her brother's plea from the destructive hand of the landscape artist. Vickers was thinking about Lane. He understood his brother-in-law as little as the latter comprehended him. He had often wondered these past months: 'Doesn't he *see* what is happening to Isabelle? Doesn't he care! It isn't surely helpless yet, —

they aren't so wholly incompatible, and Isabelle is frank, is honest!' But if Lane saw the state of affairs in his house, he never showed that he perceived it. His manner with his wife was placid, — although, as Isabelle often said, he was very little with her. But that state of separation in which the two lived seemed less due to incompatibility than to the accident of the way they lived. Lane was a very busy man with much on his mind; he had no time for emotional tribulations.

Since his return from the West — these five days which he had allowed himself as vacation — he had been irritable at times, easily disturbed, as he had been with Steve Johnston, but never short with his wife. Vickers supposed that some business affair was weighing on him, and as was his habit he locked it up tight within. . . .

And Lane would never have told what it was that gnawed at him, last of all to Vickers. It was pride that made him seem not to see, not to know the change that had come into his house. And something more, which might be found only in this kind of American gentleman, — a deep well of loyalty to his wife, a feeling of: 'What she wishes, no matter what it may be to me!' 'I shall trust her to the last, and if she fails me, I will still trust her to be true to herself.' A chivalry this, unsuspected by Vickers! Something of that old admiration for his wife which made him feel that he should provide her with the opportunities she craved, that somehow she had stooped in marrying him, still survived in spite of his successful career. And love? To define the sort of sentiment Lane at forty-two had for his wife, modified by his activities, by his lack of children, by her evident lack of passion for him, would not be an easy matter. But that he loved her more deeply than mere pride, than habit would account for, was sure. In that afterglow between men and women which comes when the storms of life have been lived through, Lane might be found a sufficient lover. . . .

As they entered the narrow path that led through the

beechwood, Lane stepped aside to allow Vickers to precede him. The afternoon sun falling on the glossy new leaves made a pleasant light. They had come to a point in the path where the western wing of the house was visible through the trees when suddenly Vickers stopped, hesitated, as if he would turn back, and said aloud hastily: "I always like this side of the house best, — don't you? It is quieter, less open than the south façade, more *intime* —" He talked on aimlessly, blocking the path, staring at the house, gesticulating. When he moved, he glanced at Lane's face. . . .

Just below in a hollow where a stone bench had been placed, Isabelle was sitting with Cairy, his arm about her, her eyes looking up at him, something gay and happy in the face like that little French song she was singing these days, as if a voice had stilled the restless craving in her, had touched to life that dead pulse, which had refused to beat for her husband. . . . This was what Vickers had seen, and it was on his lips to say, "When did Cairy come? Isabelle did not tell me." But instead he had faltered out nonsense, while the two, hearing his voice, betook themselves to the upper terrace. Had her husband seen them? Vickers wondered. Something in the man's perfect control, his manner of listening to Vickers's phrases, made him feel that he had seen — all. But Lane in his ordinary monosyllabic manner pointed to a nest of ground sparrows beside the path. "Guess we had better move this establishment to a safer place," he remarked, as he carefully put the nest into the thicket.

When they reached the hall, Isabelle, followed by Cairy, entered from the opposite door. "Hello, Tom; when did you get in?" Lane asked in his ordinary equable voice. "I sent your message, Isabelle." And he went to dress for dinner.

The dinner that night of the three men and the woman was tense and still at first. All the radiance had faded from Isabelle's face, leaving it white, and she moved as if she were numb. Vickers, watching her face, was sad at heart, miserable as he had been since he had seen her and Cairy together. Already it had gone so far! . . . Cairy was talkative, as always, telling stories of his trip to the South. At some light jeer over the California railroad situation, Lane suddenly spoke: —

"That is only one side, Tom. There is another."

Ordinarily he would have laughed at Cairy's flippant handling of the topics of the day. But to-night he was ready to challenge.

"The public doesn't want to hear the other side, it seems," Cairy retorted quickly.

Lane looked at him slowly as he might at a mosquito that he purposed to crush. "I think that some of the public wants to hear all sides," he replied quietly. "Let us see what the facts are." . . .

To-night he did not intend to be silenced by trivialities. Cairy had given him an opening on his own ground, — the vast field of fact. And he talked astonishingly well, with a grip not merely of the much-discussed railroad situation, but of business in general, economic conditions in America and abroad, — the trend of development. He talked in a large and leisurely way all through the courses, and when Cairy would interpose some objection, his judicious consideration eddied about it with a deferential sweep, then tossed it high on the shore of his buttressed conclusions. Vickers listened in astonishment to the argument, while Isabelle, her hands clasped tight before her, did not eat, but shifted her eyes from her husband's face to Cairy's and back again as the talk flowed.

. . . "And granted," Lane said by way of conclusion, having thoroughly riddled Cairy's contentions, "that in some cases there has been trickery and fraud, is that any reason why we should indict the corporate management of all great properties? Even if all the law-breaking of which our roads are accused could be proved to be true, nevertheless any philosophic investigator would conclude that the good they have done — the efficient service for civilization — far outbalances the wrong — "

"Useful thieves and parasites!" Cairy interposed.

"Yes, — if you like to put it in those words," Lane resumed quietly. "The law of payment for service in this world of ours is not a simple one. For large services and great sacrifices, the rewards must be large. For large risks and daring efforts, the pay must be alluring. Every excellence of a high degree costs, — every advance is made at the sacrifice of a lower order of good."

"Isn't that a pleasant defence for crime?" Isabelle asked.

Lane looked at his wife for a long moment of complete silence.

"Haven't you observed that people break laws, and seem to feel that they are justified in doing so by the force of higher laws?"

Isabelle's eyes fell. He had seen, Vickers knew, — not only this afternoon, but all along! . . . Presently they rose from the table, and as they passed out of the room Isabelle's scarf fell from her neck. Lane and Cairy stooped to pick it up. Cairy had his hands on it first, but in some way it was the husband who took possession of it and handed it to the wife. Her hand trembled as she took it from him, and she hurried to her room.

"If you are interested in this matter of the Pacific roads, Tom," Lane continued, handing Cairy the cigarette box, "I will have my secretary look up the data and send it out here. . . . You will be with us some time, I suppose?"

Cairy mumbled his thanks.

After this scene Vickers felt nothing but admiration for his brother-in-law. The man knew the risks. He cared, — yes, he cared! Vickers was very sure of that. At dinner it had been a sort of modern duel, as if, with perfect courtesy and openness, Lane had taken the opportunity to try conclusions with the rival his wife had chosen to give him, — to tease him with his rapier, to turn his mind to her gaze. . . . And yet, even he must know how useless victory was to him, victory of this nature. Isabelle did not love Cairy because of his intellectual grasp, though in the matters she cared for he seemed brilliant.

'It's to be a fight between them,' thought Vickers. 'He is giving the other one every chance. Oh, it is magnificent, this way of winning one's wife. But the danger in it!' And Vickers knew now that Lane scorned to hold a woman, even his wife, in any other way. His wife should not be bound to him by oath, nor by custom, nor even by their child. Nor would he plead for himself in this contest. Against the other man, he would play merely himself, — the decent years of their common life, their home, her own heart. And he was losing, — Vickers felt sure of that.

CHAPTER LII

DID he know that he had virtually lost when at the end of his brief vacation he went back to the city, leaving his rival alone in the field? During those tense days Vickers's admiration for the man grew. He was good tempered and considerate, even of Cairy. Lane had always been a pleasant host, and now instead of avoiding Cairy he seemed to seek his society, made an effort to talk to him about his work, and advised him shrewdly in a certain transaction with a theatrical manager.

"If she should go away with Cairy," Vickers said to himself, "he will look out for them always!"

Husband and wife, so Vickers judged, did not talk together during all this time. Perhaps they did not dare to meet the issue openly. At any rate when Isabelle proposed driving John to the station the last night, he said kindly, "It's raining, my dear, — I think you had better not." So he kissed her in the hall before the others, made some commonplace suggestion about the place, and with his bag in hand left, nodding to them all as he got into the carriage. Isabelle, who had appeared dazed these days, as if, her heart and mind occupied in desperate inner struggle, her body lived mechanically, left the two men to themselves and went to her room. And shortly afterwards Cairy, who had become subdued, thoughtful, pleaded work and went upstairs.

When Vickers rose early the next morning, the country was swathed in a thin white mist. The elevation on which the house stood just pierced the fog, and, here and there below, the head of a tall pine emerged. Vickers had slept badly with a suffocating sense of impending danger. When he stepped out of the drawing-room on the terrace, the coolness of the damp fog and the stillness of the June morning not yet broken by bird notes soothed his troubled mind. All this silent beauty, serenely ordered nature — and tumultuous man! Out of the earthy elements of which man was compounded, he had sucked passions which drove him hither and yon. . . . As he walked towards the west garden, the window above the terrace opened, and Isabelle, dressed in her morning clothes, looked down on her brother.

"I heard your step, Vick," she said in a whisper. Her face in the gray light was colorless, and her eyes were dull, veiled. "Wait for me, Bud!"

In a few moments she appeared, covered with a gray cloak, a soft saffron-colored veil drawn about her head. Slipping one hand under his arm, — her little fingers tightening on his flesh, — she led the way through the garden to the beech copse, which was filled with mist, then down to the stone bench, where she and Cairy had sat that other afternoon.

"How still it is!" she murmured, shivering slightly. She looked back to the copse, vague in the mist, and said: "Do you remember the tent we had here in the summers? We slept in it one night. . . . It was then I used to say that I was going to marry you, brother, and live with you for always because nobody else could be half so nice. . . . I wish I had! Oh, how I wish I had! We should have been happy, you and I. And it would have been better for both of us."

She smiled at him wanly. He understood the reference she made to his misadventure, but said nothing. Suddenly she leaned her head on his shoulder.

"Vick, dear, do you think that any one could care enough to forgive everything? Do you love me enough, so you would love me, no matter what I did? . . . That's real love, the only kind, that loves because it must and forgives because it loves! Could you, Vick? Could you?"

Vickers smoothed back her rumpled hair and drew the veil over it.

"You know that nothing would make any difference to me."

"Ah, you don't know! But perhaps you could —" Then raising her head she spoke with a harder voice. "But that's weak. One must expect to pay for what one does, — pay everything. Oh, my God!"

The fog had retreated slowly from their level. They stood on the edge looking into its depth. Suddenly Vickers exclaimed with energy: —

"You must end this, Isabelle! It will kill you."

"I wish it might!"

"End it!" and he added slowly, "Send him away — or let me take you away!"

"I — I — can't, — Vick!" she cried. "It has got beyond me. . . . It is not just for myself — just me. It's for *him*, too. He needs me. I could do so much for him! And here I can do nothing."

"And John?"

"Oh, John! He doesn't care, really — "

"Don't say that!"

"If he did — "

"Isabelle, he saw you and Tom, here, the afternoon Tom came!"

She flushed and drew herself away from her brother's arms.

"I know it — it was the first time that — that anything happened! . . . If he cared, why didn't he say something then, do something, strike me — "

"That is not right, Belle; you know he is not that kind of animal."

"If a man cares for a woman, he hasn't such godlike control! . . . No, John wants to preserve appearances, to have things around him smooth, — he's too cold to care!"

"That's ungenerous."

"Haven't I lived with him years enough to know what

is in his heart? He hates scandal. That's his nature, — he doesn't want unpleasant words, a fuss. There won't be any, either. . . . But I'm not the calculating kind, Vick. If I do it, I do it for the whole world to know and to see. I'm not Conny, — no sneaking compromises; I'll do it as you did it, — for the whole world to see and know."

"But you'll not do it!"

"You think I haven't the courage? You don't know me, Vick. I am not a girl any longer. I am thirty-two, and I know life *now*, my life at any rate. . . . It was all wrong between John and me from the beginning, — yes, from the beginning!"

"What makes you say that! You don't really believe it in your heart. You loved John when you married him. You were happy with him afterwards."

"I don't believe that any girl, no matter what experience she has had, can really love a man before she is married to him. I was sentimental, romantic, and I thought my liking for a man was love. I wanted to love, — all girls do. But I didn't know enough to love. It is all blind, blind! I might have had that feeling about other men, the feeling I had for John before. . . . Then comes marriage, and it's luck, all luck, whether love comes, whether it is right — the thing for you — the only one. Sometimes it is, — often enough for those who don't ask much, perhaps. But it was *wrong* for John and me. I knew it from the first days, — those when we tried to think we were happiest. I have never confessed this to a human being, — never to John. But it was so, Vick! I didn't know then what was the matter — why it was wrong. But a woman suspects then. . . . Those first days I was wretched, — I wanted to cry out to him: 'Can't you see it is wrong? You and I must part; our way is not the same!' But he seemed content. And there was father and mother and everything to hold us to the mistake. And of course I felt that it might come in time, that somehow it was my fault. I even thought that love as I wanted it was impossible, could never exist for a woman.

. . . So the child came, and I went through the motions. And the gap grew between us each year as I came to be a woman. I saw the gap, but I thought it was always so, almost always, between husbands and wives, and I went on going through the motions. . . . That was why I was ill, — yes, the real reason, because we were not fitted to be married. Because I tried to do something against nature, — tried to live married to a man who wasn't really my husband!"

Her voice sank exhausted. Never before even to herself had she said it all, — summed up that within her which must justify her revolt. Vickers felt the hot truth to her of her words; but granted the truth, was it enough?

Before he could speak she went on wearily, as if compelled: —

"But it might have gone on so until the end, until I died. Perhaps I could have got used to it, living like that, and fussed around like other women over amusements and charities and houses, — all the sawdust stuffing of life — and become a useless old woman, and not cared, not known."

She drew a deep breath.

"But you see — I know *now* — what the other is! I have known since" — her voice sank to a whisper — "that afternoon when I kissed him for the first time." She shuddered. "I am not a stick, Vick! I — am a woman! . . . No, don't say it!" She clasped his arm tightly. "You don't like Tom. You can't understand. He may not be what I feel he is — he may be less of a man for men than John. But I think it makes little difference to a woman so long as she loves — what the man is to others. To her he is *all* men!"

With this cry her voice softened, and now she spoke calmly. "And you see I can give him something! I can give HIM love and joy. And more — I could make it possible for him to do what he wants to do with his life. I would go with him to some beautiful spot, where he could be all that he has it in him to be, and I could watch and love. Oh, we should be enough, he and I!"

"Dear, that you can never tell! . . . It was not enough for us — for her. You can't tell when you are like this, ready to give all, whether it's what the other most needs or really wants."

In spite of Isabelle's doubting smile, Vickers hurried on, — willing now to show his scar.

"I have never told you how it was over there all these years. I could not speak of it. . . . I thought *we* should be enough, as you say. We had our love and our music. . . . But we weren't enough, almost from the start. She was unhappy. She really wanted those things we had given up, which she might have had if it had been otherwise — I mean if she had been my wife. I was too much of a fool to see that at once. I didn't want divorce and marriage — there were difficulties in the way, too. We had thrown over the world, defied it. I didn't care to sneak back into the fold. . . . Our love turned bad. All the sentiment and lofty feeling somehow went out of it. We became two animals, tied together first by our passion, and afterwards by — the situation. I can't tell you all. It was kiliing. . . . It did kill the best in me."

"It was *her* fault. The woman makes the kind of love always."

"No, she might have been different, another way! But I tell you the facts. She became dissatisfied, restless. She was unfaithful to me. I knew it, and I shielded her — because in part I had made her what she was. But it was awful. And at the end she went away with that other man. He will leave her. Then she'll take another. . . . Love turns sour, I tell you — love taken that way. Life becomes just cruddled milk. And it eats you like poison. Look at me, — the marrow of a man is all gone!"

"Dear Vick, it was all *her* fault. Any decent woman would have made you happy, — you would have worked, written great music, — lived a large life."

His story did not touch her except with pity for him. To her thinking each case was distinct, and her lips curved unconsciously into a smile, as if she were picturing how different it would be with *them*. . . .

The fog had broken, and was rising from the meadows below, revealing the trees and the sun. The birds had begun to sing in the beeches. It was fresh and cool and moist before the warmth of the coming day. Isabelle drew deep breaths and loosened her scarf.

Vickers sat silent, miserable. As he had said to Alice, the wreck of his life, where he had got knowledge so dearly, availed nothing when most he would have it count for another.

"No, Vick! Whatever happens it will be our own fate, nobody's else — and I want it!"

There was cool deliberation in her tone as if the resolve had been made already.

"Not John's fate, too?"

"He's not the kind to let a thing like this upset him long. While the railroad runs and the housekeeper stays — "

"And Molly's fate?"

"Of course I have thought about Marian. There are ways. It is often done. She would be with me until she went to school, which won't be long now."

"But just think what it would mean to her if her mother left her father."

"Oh, not so much, perhaps! I have been a good mother. . . . And why should I kill the twenty, thirty, maybe forty years left of my life for a child's sentiment for her mother? Very likely by the time she grows up, people will think differently about marriage."

She talked rapidly, as if eager to round all the corners.

"She may even decide to do the same thing some day."

"And you would want her to?"

"Yes! Rather than have the kind of marriage I have had."

"Isabelle!"

"You are an old sentimental dreamer, Vick. You don't understand modern life. And you don't know women —

they're lots more like men, too, than you think. They write such fool things about women. There are so many silly ideas about them that they don't dare to be themselves half the time, except a few like Margaret. She is honest with herself. Of course she loves Rob Falkner. He's in Panama now, but when he gets back I have no doubt Margaret will go and live with him. And she's got three children!"

"Isabelle, you aren't Margaret Pole or Cornelia Woodyard or any other woman but yourself. There are some things *you* can't do. I know you. There's the same twist in us both. You simply can't do this! You think you can, and you talk like this to me to make yourself think that you can. . . . But when it comes to the point, when you pack your bag, you know you will just unpack it again — and darn the stockings!"

"No, no!" Isabelle laughed in spite of herself; "I can't — I won't. . . . Why do I sniffle so like this? It's your fault, Vick; you always stir the pathetic note in me, you old fraud!"

She was crying now in long sobs, the tears falling to his hand.

"I know you because we are built the same foolish, idiotic way. There are many women who can play that game, who can live one way for ten or a dozen years, and then leave all that they have been — without ever looking back. But you are not one of them. I am afraid you and I are sentimentalists. It's a bad thing to be, Belle, but we can't help ourselves. We want the freedom of our feelings, but we want to keep a halo about them. You talked of cutting down these beeches. But you would never let one be touched, not one."

"I'll have 'em all cut down to-morrow," Isabelle murmured through her tears.

"Then you'll cry over them! No, Belle, it's no use going dead against your nature — the way you were made to run. You may like to soar, but you were meant to walk."

"You think there is nothing to me,—that I haven't a soul!"

"I know the soul."

Isabelle flung her arms about her brother and clung there, breathing hard. The long night had worn her out with its incessant alternation of doubt and resolve, endlessly weaving through her brain.

"Better to suffer on in this cloudy world than to make others suffer," he murmured.

"Don't talk! I am so tired — so tired." . . .

From the hillside below came a whistled note, then the bar of a song, like a bird call. Some workman on the place going to his work, Vickers thought. It was repeated, and suddenly Isabelle took her arms from his neck, — her eyes clear and a look of determination on her lips.

"No, Vick; you don't convince me. . . . You did the other thing when it came to you. Perhaps we *are* alike. Well, then, I shall do it! I shall dare to live!" . . .

And with that last defiance, — the curt expression of the floating beliefs which she had acquired, — she turned towards the house.

"Come, it is breakfast time."

She waited for him to rise and join her. For several silent moments they lingered to look at Dog Mountain across the river, as if they were looking at it for the last time, at something they had both so much loved.

"You are dear, brother," she murmured, taking his hand. "But don't lecture me. You see I am a woman now!"

And looking into her grave, tear-stained face, Vickers saw that he had lost. She had made her resolution; she would "dare to live," and that life would be with Cairy! His heart was sad. Though he had tried to free himself of his old dislike of Cairy and see him through Isabelle's eyes, it was useless. He read Tom Cairy's excitable, inflammable, lightly poised nature, with the artist glamour in him that attracted women. He would be all flame — for a time, — then dead until his flame was lighted before another shrine. And Isabelle, proud, exacting, who had always been served,

— no, it was hopeless! Inevitable tragedy, to be waited for like the expected motions of nature!

And beneath this misery for Isabelle was the bitterest of human feelings, — personal defeat, personal inadequacy. 'If I had been another!' "Don't lecture me!" she had said almost coldly. The spiritual power of guidance had gone from him, because of what he had done. Inwardly he felt that it had gone. That was part of the "marrow of the man" that had been burned out. The soul of him was impotent; he was a shell, something dead, that could not kindle another to life.

'I could have saved her,' he thought. 'Once I could have saved her. She has found me lacking *now,* when she needs me most!'

The whistle sounded nearer.

"Will you do one thing for me, Isabelle?"

"All — but one thing!"

"Let me know first."

"You will know."

Cairy was coming down the terrace, cigarette in hand. His auburn hair shone in the sunlight. After his sleep, his bath, his cup of early coffee, he was bright with physical content, and he felt the beauty of the misty morning in every sense. Seeing the brother and sister coming from the beeches together, he scrutinized them quickly; like the perfect egotist, he was swiftly measuring what this particular conjunction of personalities might mean to him. Then he limped towards them, his face in smiles, and bowing in mock veneration, he laid at Isabelle's feet a rose still dewy with mist.

Vickers turned on his heel, his face twitching. But Isabelle with parted lips and gleaming eyes looked at the man, her whole soul glad, as a woman looks who is blind to all but one thought, — 'I love him.'

"The breath of the morn," Cairy said, lifting the rose. "The morn of morns, — this is to be a great day, my lady! I read it in your eyes."

CHAPTER LIII

It was still sultry at four o'clock in the afternoon, and the two men walked slowly in the direction of the river. Cairy, who had been summoned by telegram to the city, would have preferred to be driven to the junction by Isabelle, but when Vickers had suggested that he knew a short cut by a shady path along the river, he had felt obliged to accept the implied invitation. He was debating why Price had suddenly evinced this desire to be with him, for he felt sure that Vickers disliked him. But Isabelle had shown plainly that she would like him to accept her brother's offer, — she was too tired to go out again, she said, and the only horse that could be used was a burden to drive. So he set forth on the two-mile walk this oppressive afternoon, not in the best mood, determined to let Vickers do the talking.

They plodded across the meadow in silence, Cairy thinking of the interview in the city, his spirits rising as they always soared at the slightest hint of an "opening." "I'll make her take the play," he said to himself; "she isn't much good as an actress, but I must get the thing on. I'll need the money." He hoped to finish his business with this minor star, who had expressed a desire to see him, and return to Grafton by the morning express. Isabelle would be disappointed if he should not be back for luncheon.

Vickers's head was bent to the path. He had seized this chance of being alone with Cairy, and now that they were beyond the danger of interruption his blood beat uncomfortably in his head and he could not speak — for fear of uttering the wrong word. . . . When they reached the river, the two men paused involuntarily in the shade and looked back up the slope to the Farm, lying in the warm haze on the brow of the hill. As they stood there, the shutter of an upper chamber was drawn in, and Cairy smiled to himself.

"The house looks well from here," he remarked. "It's a pleasant spot."

"It is a dear old place!" Vickers answered, forgetting for the moment the changes that Isabelle had wrought at the Farm. "It's grown into our lives, — Isabelle's and mine. We used to come here as boy and girl in vacations. . . . It was a day something like this when my sister was married. I remember seeing her as she came out of the house and crossed the meadow on my father's arm. We watched her from the green in front of the chapel. . . . She was very beautiful — and happy!"

"I can well imagine it," Cairy replied dryly, surprised at Vickers's sudden loquacity on family matters. "But I suppose we ought to be moving on, hadn't we, to get that express? You see I am a poor walker at the best."

Vickers struck off by the river path, leading the way. Suddenly he stopped, and with flushed face said: —

"Tom, I wish you wouldn't come back to-morrow!"

"And why the devil —"

"I know it isn't *my* house, it isn't *my* wife, it isn't *my* affair. But, Tom, my sister and I have been closer than most, — even husband and wife. I love her, — well, that's neither here nor there!"

"What are you driving at, may I ask?" Cairy demanded coldly.

"What I am going to say isn't usual—it isn't conventional. But I don't know any conventional manner of doing what I want to do. I think we have to drop all that sometimes, and speak out like plain human beings. That's the way I am going to speak to you, — as man to man. . . . I don't want to beat about the bush, Tom. I think it would be better if you did not come back to-morrow, — never came back to the Farm!"

He had not said it as he meant to phrase it. He was aware that he had lost ground by blurting it out like this.

Cairy waited until he had lighted a cigarette before he replied, with a laugh: —

"It is a little — brusque, your idea. May I ask why I am not to come back?"

"You know well enough! . . . I had hoped we could keep — other names out of this."

"We can't."

"My sister is very unhappy —"

"You think I make your sister unhappy?"

"Yes."

"I prefer to let her be the judge of that," Cairy retorted, walking ahead stiffly and exaggerating his limp.

"You know she cannot be a judge of what is best — just now."

"I think she can judge of herself better than any — outsider!"

Vickers flushed, controlled himself, and said almost humbly: —

"I know you care for her, Tom. We both do. So I thought we might discuss it amicably."

"This doesn't seem to me a discussable matter."

"But anything that concerns one I love as I do Isabelle *must* be discussable in some way."

"Your sister told me about her talk with you this morning. . . . You did your best then, it seems. If you couldn't succeed in changing *her* mind, — what do you expect from me?"

"That you will be generous! . . . There are some things that Isabelle can't see straight just now. She doesn't know herself, altogether."

"I should think that her husband —"

"Can't you feel his position? His lips are closed by his pride, by his love!"

"I should say, Vickers," Cairy remarked with a sneer, "that you had better follow Lane's sensible course. This is a matter for the two most concerned and for them alone to discuss. . . . With your experience you must understand that ours is the situation which a mature man and a mature woman must settle for themselves. Nothing that an outsider says can count."

And turning around to face Vickers, he added slowly, "Isabelle and I will do what seems best to us, just as under similar circumstances you did what you thought was best for you without consulting anybody, as I remember."

Vickers quivered as his eye met Cairy's glance, but he accepted the sneer quietly.

"The circumstances were not the same. And I may have learned that it is a serious matter to do what you wish to do, — to take another man's wife, no matter what the circumstances are."

"Oh, that's a mere phrase. There's usually not much taking! When a woman is unhappy in her marriage, when she can be happy with another man, when no one can be really hurt —"

"Somebody always is hurt."

"The only thing I am greatly interested in is Isabelle's happiness, her life. She has been stifled all these years of marriage, intellectually, emotionally stifled. She has begun to live lately — we have both begun to live. Do you think we shall give that up? Do you think any of your little preachments can alter the life currents of two strong people who love and find their fulfilment in each other? You know men and women very little if you think so! We are living to-day at the threshold of a new social epoch, — an honester one than the world has seen yet, thank God! Men and women are daring to throw off the bonds of convention, to think for themselves, and determine what is best for them, for their highest good, undisturbed by the bogies so long held up. I will take my life, I will live, I will not be suffocated by a false respect for my neighbor's opinion."

Cairy paused in the full career of his phrases. He was gesticulating with his hands, almost forgetful of Vickers, launched as it were on a dramatic monologue. He was accustomed thus to dramatize an emotional state, as those of his temperament are wont to do, living in a world of their own feelings imaginatively projected. While Vickers listened to Cairy's torrent of words, he had but one thought: 'It's no use. He can't be reached that way — any way!'

A stone wall stopped their progress. As Cairy slowly dragged himself over the wall, Vickers saw the outline of the pistol in the revolver pocket, and remembered the afternoon when Cairy had shown them the weapon and displayed his excellent marksmanship. And now, as then, the feeling of contempt that the peaceable Anglo-Saxon has for the man who always goes armed in a peaceable land came over him.

Cairy resumed his monologue on the other side of the wall. "It is the silliest piece of barbaric tradition for a civilized man to think that because a woman has once seen fit to give herself to him, she is his possession for all time. Because she has gone through some form, some ceremony, repeated a horrible oath that she doesn't understand, to say that she belongs to that man, is *his*, like his horse or his house, — phew! That's mere animalism. Human souls belong to themselves! Most of all the soul of a delicately sensitive woman like Isabelle! She gives, and she can take away. It's her duty to take herself back when she realizes that it no longer means anything to her, that her life is degraded by —"

"Rot!" Vickers exclaimed impatiently. He had scarcely heard what Cairy had been saying. His sickening sense of failure, of impotency, when he wished most for strength, had been succeeded by rage against the man, not because of his fluent argument, but because of himself; not against his theory of license, but against him. He saw Isabelle's life broken on the point of this glib egotism. "We needn't discuss your theories. The one fact is that my sister's life shall not be ruined by you!"

Cairy, dropping back at once to his tone of worldly convention, replied calmly: —

"That I think we shall have to let the lady decide for herself, — whether I shall ruin her life or not. And I beg to point out that this topic is of your own choosing. I regard it as an impertinence. Let us drop it. And if you will point out the direction, I think I will hurry on by myself and get my train."

"My God, no! We won't drop it — not yet. Not until you have heard a little more what I have in mind. . . . I think I know you, Cairy, better than my sister knows you. Would you make love to a *poor* woman, who had a lot of children, and take *her?* Would you take her and her children, like a man, and work for them? . . . In this case you will be given what you want —"

"I did not look for vulgarity from you! But with the *bourgeoisie*, I suppose, it all comes down to dollars and cents. I have not considered Mrs. Lane's circumstances."

"It's not mere dollars and cents! Though that is a test, — what a man will do for a woman, not what a woman will do for a man she loves and — pities."

As Cairy shot an ugly glance at him, Vickers saw that he was fast angering the man past all hope of influence. But he was careless now, having utterly failed to avert evil from the one he loved most in the world, and he poured out recklessly his bitter feeling: —

"The only success you have to offer a woman is success with other women! That little nurse in the hospital, you remember? The one who took care of you —"

"If you merely wish to insult me —" the Southerner stammered.

They were in the midst of a thicket of alders near the river, and the sinking sun, falling through the young green leaves, mottled the path with light and shade. The river, flushed with spring water, gurgled pleasantly over pebbly shallows. It was very still and drowsy; the birds had not begun their evening song.

The two men faced each other, their hands clenched in their coat pockets, and each read the hate in the other's face.

"Insult you!" Vickers muttered. "Cairy, you are scum to me — scum!"

Through the darkness of his rage a purpose was struggling — a blind purpose — that urged him on.

. . . "I don't know how many other women after the nurse have served to fatten your ego. But you will never feed on my sister's blood while I live!"

He stepped closer unconsciously, and as he advanced Cairy retreated, taking his clenched hand from his pocket.

"Why don't you strike?" Vickers cried.

Suddenly he knew that purpose; it had emerged with still clearness in his hot brain. His heart whispered, 'She will never do it over my body!' And the thought calmed him at once. He saw Cairy's trembling arm and angry face. 'He'll shoot,' he said to himself coldly. 'It's in his blood, and he's a coward. He'll shoot!' Standing very still, his hands in his pockets, he looked quietly at the enraged man. He was master now!

"Why don't you strike?" he repeated.

And as the Southerner still hesitated, he added slowly: —

"Do you want to hear more?"

The memory of old gossip came back to him. 'He is not the real Virginia Cairy,' some one had said once; 'he has the taint, — that mountain branch of the family, — the mother, you know, they say!' Very slowly Vickers spoke: —

"No decent man would want his sister living with a fellow whose mother —"

As the words fell he could see it coming, — the sudden snatch backwards of the arm, the little pistol not even raised elbow high. And in the drowsy June day, with the flash of the shot, the thought leapt upwards in his clear mind, 'At last I am not impotent — I have saved her!' . . .

And when he sank back into the meadow grass without a groan, seeing Cairy's face mistily through the smoke, and behind him the blur of the sky, he thought happily, 'She will never go to him, now — never!' — and then his eyes closed.

It was after sunset when some men fishing along the river heard a groan and hunting through the alders and swamp grass found Vickers, lying face down in the thicket. One of the men knew who he was, and as they lifted him from the pool of blood where he lay and felt the stiff fold of his coat, one said: —

"He must have been here some time. He's lost an awful lot of blood! The wound is low down."

They looked about for the weapon in the dusk, and not finding it, took the unconscious man into their boat and started up stream.

"Suicide?" one queried.

"Looks that way, — I'll go back after the pistol, later."

Isabelle had had tea with Marian and the governess out in the garden, and afterwards strolled about through the beds, plucking a flower here and there. To the agitation of the morning the calm of settled resolve had succeeded. She looked at the house and the gardens thoughtfully, as one looks who is about to depart on a long journey. In her heart was the stillness after the storm, not joy, — that would come later when the step was taken; when all was irrevocably settled. She thought quite methodically of how it would all be, — what must be done to cut the cords of the old life, to establish the new. John would see the necessity, — he would not make difficulties. He might even be glad to have it all over! Of course her mother would wail, but she would learn to accept. She would leave Molly at first, and John naturally must have his share in her always. That could be worked out later. As for the Farm, they might come back to it afterwards. John had better stay on here for the present, — it was good for Molly. They would probably live in the South, if they decided to live in America. She would prefer London, however. . . . She was surprised at the sure way in which she could think it all out. That must be because it was right and there was no wavering in her purpose. . . . Poor Vick! he would care most. But he would come to realize how much better it was thus, how much more right really than to go dragging through a loveless, empty life.

And when he saw her happy with Tom — but she wished he liked Tom better.

The failure of Vickers to return in time for tea had not troubled her. He had a desultory, irregular habit of life. He might have stopped at Alice's or even decided to go on to the city with Tom, or merely wandered off across the country by himself. . . .

In the last twilight three men came up the meadow path, carrying something among them, walking slowly. Isabelle caught sight of them as they reached the lower terrace and with her eyes fastened on them, trying to make out the burden they were carrying so carefully, stood waiting before the house.

"What is it?" she asked at last as the men drew nearer, seeing in the gloom only the figures staggering slightly as they mounted the steps.

"Your brother's been hurt, Mrs. Lane," a voice said.

"Hurt!" That nameless fear of supernatural interference, the quiver of the human nerve at the possible message from the infinite, stopped the beating of her heart.

"Yes'm — shot!" the voice said. "Where shall we take him?"

They carried Vickers upstairs and placed him in Isabelle's bed, as she directed. Bending over him, she tried to unbutton the stiff coat with her trembling fingers, and suddenly she felt something warm — his blood. It was red on her hand. She shuddered before an unknown horror, and with mysterious speed the knowledge came to her heart that Fate had overtaken her — here!

CHAPTER LIV

THE doctors had come, probed for the bullet, and gone. They had not found the bullet. The wound was crooked, they said, entering the fleshy part of the abdomen, ranging upwards in the direction of the heart, then to the back. The wounded man was still unconscious. There was a chance, so the New York surgeon told Isabelle, — only they had not been able to locate the bullet, and the heart was beating feebly. There had been a great loss of blood. If he had been found earlier, perhaps — they did not know. . . .

Outside on the drive the doctors exchanged glances, low words, and signs. Accident? But how, the ball ranging upwards like that? He would have to be on his knees. Well, then, suicide! Had the pistol been found? . . . There need be no scandal — the family was much loved in the village. Accident, of course. The fellow was always odd, the local practitioner explained to the city doctor, as he carried his distinguished colleague home in his car for breakfast. There was that scandal with a woman in Venice. They said it was all over, but you could never tell about those things. . . .

Upstairs the nurse made ready the room for illness, while Isabelle sat by the bed, watching her brother. Vickers was still unconscious, scarcely breathing. The nurse, having tried a number of ways to get her out of the room, now ignored her, and Isabelle sat in a kind of stupor, waiting for that Fate which had overtaken her to be worked out. When the gray dawn of the morning stole into the dark room, the nurse unbolted the shutters and threw open the window. In the uncertain light Dog Mountain loomed large and distant. Isabelle turned her head from Vickers's face and watched the wooded peak as it came nearer and nearer in the deepening light. . . . It was this hill that she and Vickers had climbed in the winter morning so long ago! How wonderful it had been then, life, for them both, with glorious possibilities of living! She had put forth her hands to grasp them, these possibilities, one after another, to grasp them for herself. Now they had come to an end — for both. There was no more to grasp. . . .

When she turned back to the silent form by her side, she saw that Vickers had opened his eyes. His face was very white and the eyes were buried deep beneath the eyebrows as of a man long sick, and he lay motionless. But the eyes had meaning in them; they were the eyes of the living. So brother and sister looked into each other, thus, and without words, without a murmur, it was all known between them. She understood! He had thrown his life into the abyss before her that she might be kept to that vision they had had as boy and girl. It was not to be for him. But for her!

"Vick!" she whispered, falling on her knees by his side. For reply there was that steady searching look, which spoke to unknown depths within her. "Vick!" she moaned. The white lips of the dying man trembled, and a faint flutter of breath crossed them — but no words. His fingers touched her hair. When she looked at him again through her tears, the eyes were closed, and the face bore an austere look of preoccupation, as of one withdrawn from the business of life. . . . Afterwards the nurse touched the kneeling woman, the doctor came, she was led away. She knew that Vickers was dead.

Late that afternoon there came a knock at the door of the room where Isabelle was, and her husband, hearing no sound, entered. She looked up wonderingly from the lounge where she lay. She did not know that John was in the house, that he had been sent for. She was unaware what time had elapsed since the evening before.

"Isabelle," he said and stopped. She looked at him

questioningly. The irritation that of late his very presence had caused her she was not conscious of now. All the irritations of life had been suddenly wiped out in the great fact. As she looked at her husband's grave face, she saw it with a new sense, — she saw what was behind it, as if she had had the power given her to read beneath matter. She saw his concern, his real sorrow, his consideration, the distress for her in the heart of this man, whom she had thrust out of her life. . . .

"Isabelle," he said very gently, hesitantly. "Tom has come — is downstairs — wants to see you. He asked me if you would see him for a moment."

This also did not surprise her. She was silent for a moment, and her husband said: —

"Do you want to see him?"

"Yes," she replied finally. "I will see him. . . . I will go down at once."

She rose and stepped towards the door.

"Isabelle!" Her husband's voice broke. Still standing with one hand on the knob of the door, he took from his pocket with the other a small pistol, and held it towards her on the palm of his hand. "Isabelle," he said, "this was in the river — near where they found him!"

She looked at it calmly. It was that little gold and ivory chased toy which she remembered Tom had used one afternoon to shoot the magnolia blossoms with. She remembered it well. It was broken open, and a cartridge half protruded from the breach.

"I thought you should know," Lane added.

"Yes," Isabelle whispered. "I know. I knew! . . . But I will go down and see him."

Her husband replaced the pistol in his pocket and opened the door for her.

Cairy was waiting before the fireplace in the library, nervously pacing to and fro across the rug. Would she see him? How much did she know? How much did they all know?

How much would she forgive? . . . These questions had racked him every hour since in a spasm of nervous terror he had flung the pistol over the bushes and heard it splash in the river, and with one terrified look at the wounded man, whom he had dragged into the thicket, had got himself in some unremembered fashion to the junction in time for the express. These and other considerations — what story should he tell? — had racked him all through the evening, which he had been obliged to spend with the actress, answering her silly objections to this and that in his play. Then during the night it became clear to him that he must return to the Farm in the morning as he had planned, as if nothing had happened. His story would be that Vickers had turned back before they reached the junction, and had borrowed his pistol to shoot at woodchucks. . . . Would Isabelle believe this? She *must* believe it! . . . It took courage to walk up to the familiar house, but he must see her. It was the only way. And he had been steadying himself for his part ever since he had left the city.

When Isabelle entered the room, she closed the door behind her and stood with her back against it for support. She wore the same white dress that she had had on when Cairy and Vickers had left her, not having changed it for tea. It had across the breast a small red stain, — the stain of her brother's blood. Cairy reached out his hands and started towards her, crying: —

"Isabelle! Isabelle! how awful! Isabelle, — I —"

She raised her arm as if to forbid him to advance, and he stood still, his words dying on his lips. Looking at him out of her weary eyes, Isabelle seemed to see through the man, with that same curious insight that had come when she had read the truth in her brother's eyes; the same insight that had enabled her to see the kindness and the pity beneath her husband's impassive gravity. So now she knew what he was going to say, the lie he would try to tell her. It was as if she knew every secret corner of the man's soul, had known it always really, and had merely veiled her eyes to him wilfully. Now the veil had been torn aside. Had Vickers given her this power to see into the heart of things, for always, so that the truths behind the veil she made should never be hid?

'Why does he try to lie to me?' she seemed to ask herself. 'It is so weak to lie in this world where all becomes known.' She merely gazed at him in wonder, seeing the deformed soul of the deformed body, eaten by egotism and passions. And this last — cowardice! And he was the man she had loved! That she had been ready to die for, to throw away all for, even the happiness of others! . . . It was all strangely dead. A body stood there before her in its nakedness.

"What do you want?" she demanded almost indifferently.

"I had to see you!" He had forgotten his story, his emotion, — everything beneath that piercing stare, which stripped him to the bone.

"Haven't you — a word —" he muttered.

Her eyes cried: 'I know. I know! I know ALL — even as those who are dead know.'

"Nothing!" she said.

"Isabelle!" he cried, and moved nearer. But the warning hand stopped him again, and the empty voice said, "Nothing!"

Then he saw that it was all ended between them, that this brother's blood, which stained her breast, lay forever between them, could not be crossed by any human will. And more, that the verity of life itself lay like a blinding light between them, revealing him and her and their love. It was dead, that love which they had thought was sacred and eternal, in the clear light of truth.

Without a word he walked to the open window and stepped into the garden, and his footstep on the gravel died away. Then Isabelle went back to the dead body in her room above.

On the terrace Lane was sitting beside his little girl, the father talking in low tones to the child, explaining what is death.

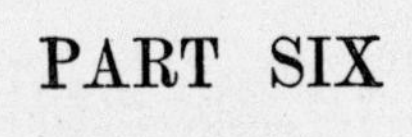

PART SIX

CHAPTER LV

It was a long, cold drive from the station at White River up into the hills. In the gloom of the December afternoon the aspect of the austere, pitiless northern winter was intensified. A thin crust of snow through which the young pines and firs forced their green tips covered the dead blackberry vines along the roadside. The ice of the brooks was broken in the centre like cracked sheets of glass, revealing the black water gurgling between the frozen banks. The road lay steadily uphill, and the two rough-coated farm horses pulled heavily at the stiff harness, slipping constantly in the track that was worn smooth and polished by the shoes of the wood-sleds. As the valley fell behind, the country opened out in broad sheets of snow-covered fields where frozen wisps of dead weeds fluttered above the crust. Then came the woods, dark with "black growth," and more distant hillsides, gray and black, where the leafless deciduous growth mingled with the evergreens. At infrequent intervals along the road appeared little farm-houses, — two rooms and an attic, with rickety outhouses and barns, all banked with earth to protect them from the winter. These were forlorn enough when they showed marks of life; but again and again they were deserted, with their special air of decay, the wind sucking through the paneless windows, the snow lying in unbroken drifts up to the rotting sills. Sometimes a lane led from the highroad to where one or perhaps two houses were hidden under the shelter of a hill, removed still farther from the artery of life. Already the lamps had begun to glimmer from these remote habitations, dotting the hillsides like widely scattered candles.

Lonely and desolate! These human beings lived in an isolation of snow and frozen earth. So thought Isabelle Lane, chilled beneath the old fur robe, cold to the heart. . . . Ahead the hills lifted with broader lines, higher, more lonely, and the gray clouds almost touched their tops. In a cleft of the range towards which the road was winding, there shone a saffron light, the last effort of the December sun to break through the heavy sky. And for a few moments there gleamed far away to the left a spot of bright light, marvellously clear and illuming, where the white breast of a clearing on the mountain had received these last few rays of sun. A warm golden pathway led through the forest to it from the sun. That distant spot of sunny snow was radiant, still, uplifting. Suddenly gloom again! The saffron glow faded from the Pass between the hills, and the north wind drew down into the valley, drifting the manes and the tails of the plodding horses. Soft wisps of snow circled and fell, — the heralding flakes of winter storm. . . .

It seemed to Isabelle that she had been journeying on like this for uncounted time, and would plod on like this always, — chilled, numbed to the heart, moving through a frozen, lonely world far from the voices of men, remote from the multitudinous feet bent on the joyous errands of life. . . . She had sunk into a lethargy of body and mind, in which the cheerless physical atmosphere reflected the condition of being within, — something empty or dead, with a dull ache instead of consciousness. . . .

The sleigh surmounted the long hill, swept at a trot around the edge of the mountain through dark woods, then out into an unexpected plateau of open fields. There was a cluster of lights in a small village, and they came to a sudden stop before a little brick house that was swathed in spruce boughs, like a blanket drawn close about the feet, to keep out the storm. The door opened and against the lighted room a small black figure stood out. Isabelle, stumbling numbly up the steps, fell into the arms of Margaret Pole.

"You must be nearly dead, poor dear! I have lighted a

fire in your room upstairs. . . . I am so glad you have come. I have hoped for it so long!"

When they were before the blazing wood fire, Margaret unfastened Isabelle's long cloak and they stood, both in black, pale in the firelight, and looked at each other, then embraced without a word.

"I wanted to come," Isabelle said at last when she was settled into the old arm-chair beside the fire, "when you first wrote. But I was too ill. I seemed to have lost not only strength but will to move. . . . It's good to be here."

"They are the nicest people, these Shorts! He's a wheelwright and blacksmith, and she used to teach school. It's all very plain, like one of our mountain places in Virginia; but it's heavenly peaceful — removed. You'll feel in a day or two that you have left everything behind you, down there below!"

"And the children?"

"They are splendidly. And Ned is really getting better — the doctor has worked a miracle for the poor little man. We think it won't be long now before he can walk and do what the others do. And he is happy. He used to have sullen fits, — resented his misfortune just like a grown person. He's different now!"

There was a buoyant note in Margaret's deep tones. Pale as she was in her black dress and slight, — "the mere spirit of a woman," as Falkner had called her, — there was a gentler curve to the lips, less chafing in the sunken eyes.

'I suppose it is a great relief,' thought Isabelle, — 'Larry's death, even with all its horror, — she can breathe once more, poor Margaret!'

"Tell me!" she said idly, as Margaret wheeled the lounge to the fire for Isabelle to rest on; "however did you happen to come up here to the land's end in Vermont — or is it Canada?"

"Grosvenor is just inside the line. . . . Why, it was the doctor — Dr. Renault, you know, the one who operated on Ned. I wanted to be near him. It was in July after

Larry's death that we came, and I haven't been away since. And I shall stay, always perhaps, at least as long as the doctor can do anything for the little man. And for me. . . . I like it. At first it seemed a bit lonesome and far away, this tiny village shut in among the hills, with nobody to talk to. But after a time you come to see a lot just here in this mite of a village. One's glasses become adjusted, as the doctor says, and you can see what you have never taken the time to see before. There's a stirring world up here on Grosvenor Flat! And the country is so lovely, — bigger and sterner than my old Virginia hills, but not unlike them."

"And why does your wonderful doctor live out of the world like this?"

"Dr. Renault used to be in New York, you know, — had his own private hospital there for his operations. He had to leave the city and his work because he was threatened with consumption. For a year he went the usual round of cures, — to the Adirondacks, out West; and he told me that one night while he was camping on the plains in Arizona, lying awake watching the stars, it came to him suddenly that the one thing for him to do was to stop this health-hunt, go back where he came from, and go to work — and forget he was ill until he died. The next morning he broke camp, rode out to the railroad, came straight here from Arizona, and has been here ever since."

"But why *here?*"

"Because he came from Grosvenor as a boy. It must be a French family — Renault — and it is only a few miles north to the line. . . . So he came here, and the climate or the life or something suits him wonderfully. He works like a horse!"

"Is he interesting, your doctor?" Isabelle asked idly.

"That's as you take him," Margaret replied with a little smile. "Not from Conny Woodyard's point of view, I should say. He has too many blind sides. But I have come to think him a really great man! And that, my dear, is more than what we used to call 'interesting.'"

"But how can he do his work up here?"

"That's the wonderful part of it all! He's *made* the world come to him, — what he needs of it. He says there is nothing marvellous in it; that all through the middle ages the sick and the needy flocked to remote spots, to deserts and mountain villages, wherever they thought help was to be found. Most great cures are not made even now in the cities."

"But hospitals?"

"He has his own, right here in Grosvenor Flat, and a perfect one. The great surgeons and doctors come up here and send patients here. He has all he can do, with two assistants."

"He must be a strong man."

"You will see! The place is Renault. It all bears the print of his hand. He says himself that given a man with a real idea, a persistent idea, and he will make the desert blossom like a garden or move mountains, — in some way he will make that idea part of the organism of life! . . . There! I am quoting the doctor again, the third time. It's a habit one gets into up here!"

At the tinkle of a bell below, Margaret exclaimed: —

"It's six and supper, and you have had no real rest. You see the hours are primitive here, — breakfast at seven, dinner noon, and supper six. You will get used to it in a few days."

The dining room was a corner of the old kitchen that had been partitioned off. It was warm and bright, with an open fire, and the supper that Mrs. Short put on the table excellent. Mr. Short came in presently and took his seat at the head of the table. He was a large man, with a bony face softened by a thick grizzled beard. He said grace in a low voice, and then served the food. Isabelle noticed that his large hands were finely formed. His manner was kindly, in a subtle way that of the host at his own table; but he said little or nothing at first. The children made the conversation, piping up like little birds about the table and keeping the older people laughing. Isabelle had always felt that children at the table were a bore, either forward and a nuisance, or like little lynxes uncomfortably absorbing conversation that was not suited to them. Perhaps that was because she knew few families where children were socially educated to take their place at the table, being relegated for the most part to the nurse or the governess.

Isabelle was much interested in Mr. Short. His wife, a thin, gray-haired woman, who wore spectacles and had a timid manner of speaking, was less of a person than the blacksmith. Sol Short, she found out later, had never been fifty miles from Grosvenor Flat in his life, but he had the poise, the self-contained air of a man who had acquired all needed worldly experience.

"Was it chilly coming up the Pass?" he asked Isabelle. "I thought 'twould be when it came on to blow some from the mountains. And Pete Jackson's horses *are* slow."

"They seemed frozen!"

The large man laughed.

"Well, you would take your time if you made that journey twice a day most every day in the year. You can't expect them to get exactly excited over it, can you?"

"Mr. Short," Margaret remarked, "I saw a light this evening in the house on Wing Hill. What can it be?"

"Some folks from down state have moved in, — renters, I take it."

"How do you know that?"

"From the look of the stuff Bailey's boy was hauling up there this morning. It's travelled often."

"Mr. Short," Margaret explained merrily, "is the Grosvenor *Times*. His shop is the centre of our universe. From it he sees all that happens in our world — or his cronies tell him what he can't see. He knows what is going on in the remotest corner of the township, — what Hiram Bailey got for his potatoes, where Bill King sold his apples, whether Mrs. Beans's second son has gone to the Academy at White

River. He knows the color and the power of every horse, the number of cows on every farm, the make of every wagon, — everything!"

"Not so bad as all that!" the blacksmith protested. It was evidently a family joke. "We don't gossip, do we, Jenny?"

"We don't gossip! But we keep our eyes open and tell what we see."

It was a pleasant, human sort of atmosphere. After the meal the two friends went back to Isabelle's couch and fire, Mrs. Short offering to put the youngest child to bed for Margaret.

"She likes to," Margaret explained. "Her daughter has gone away to college. . . . It is marvellous what that frail-looking woman can do; she does most of the cooking and housework, and never seems really busy. She prepared this daughter for college! She makes me ashamed of the little I accomplish, — and she reads, too, half a dozen magazines and all the stray books that come her way."

"But how can you stand it?" Isabelle asked bluntly; "I mean for months."

"Stand it? You mean the hours, the Strongs, Grosvenor? . . . Why, I feel positively afraid when I think that some day I may be shaken out of this nest! You will see. It is all so simple and easy, so human and natural, just like Mr. Short's day's work, — the same thing for thirty years, ever since he married the school teacher and took this house. You'll hear him building the fires to-morrow before daylight. He is at his shop at six-thirty, home at twelve, back again at one, milks the cow at five, and supper at six, bed at nine. Why, it's an Odyssey, that day, — as Mr. Short lives it!"

Margaret opened the window and drew in the shutters. Outside it was very still, and the snow was falling in fine flakes.

"The children will be so glad to-morrow," she remarked, "with all this snow. They are building a large bob-sled under Mr. Short's direction. . . . No!" she resumed her former thread of thought. "It doesn't count so much as we used to think — the variety of the thing you do, the change, — the novelty. It's the mind you do it with that makes it worth while."

Isabelle stared at the ceiling which was revealed fitfully by the dying fire. She still felt dead, numb, but this was a peaceful sort of grave, so remote, so silent. That endless torturing thought — the chain of weary reproach and useless speculation, which beset every waking moment — had ceased for the moment. It was like quiet after a perpetual whirring sound.

She liked to look at Margaret, to feel her near, but she mused over her. She was changed. Margaret had had this disease, too, this weariness of living, the torturing doubt, — if this or that, the one thing or the other, had happened, it might have been different, — the haggling of defeated will! No wonder she was glad to be out of the city up here at peace. . . .

"But one can't stay out of life for always," she remonstrated.

"Why not? What you call the world seems to get along very well without us, without any one in particular. And I don't feel the siren call, not yet!"

"But life can't be over at thirty-three, — one can't be really dead, I suppose."

"No, — just beginning!" Margaret responded with an elasticity that amazed Isabelle, who remembered the languid woman she had known so many years. "Just beginning," she murmured, "after the journey in the dark."

'Of course,' mused Isabelle, 'she means the relief from Larry, the anxiety over the boy, — all that she has had to bear. Yes, for her there is some beginning anew. She might possibly marry Rob Falkner now, if his wife got somebody else to look after her silly existence. Why shouldn't she? Margaret is still young, — she might even be pretty again.' And Isabelle wished to know what the situation was between Margaret and Falkner.

Nothing, it seemed, could make any difference to herself! She ached to tell some one of the despair in her heart, but even to Margaret she could not speak. Since that summer morning six months before when Vickers had died without a spoken word, she had never said his name. Her husband had mutely respected her muteness. Then she had been ill, — too ill to think or plan, too ill for everything but remembrance. Now it was all shut up, her tragedy, festering at the bottom of her heart like an undrained wound, poisoning her soul. . . . Suddenly in the midst of her brooding she woke with a start at something Margaret was saying, so unlike her reticent self.

. . . "You knew, of course, about Larry's death?"

"Yes, John told me."

"It was in the papers, too."

"Poor Margaret! — I was so sorry for you — it was terrible!"

"You mustn't think of it that way, — I mean for me. It was terrible that any human being should be where Larry got, — where he was hunted like a dog by his own acts, and in sheer despair made an end of himself. I often think of that — think what it must be not to have the courage to go on, not to feel the strength in yourself to live another hour!"

"It's always insanity. No sane person would do such a thing!"

"We call it insanity. But what difference does the name make?" Margaret said. "A human being falls into a state of mind where he is without one hope, one consideration, — all is misery. Then he takes what seems the only relief — death — as he would food or drink; that is sad."

"It was Larry's own doing, Margaret; he had his chance!"

"Of course, more than his chance — more than many chances. He was the kind of protoplasm that could not endure life, that carried in itself the seed of decay, — yet — yet — " She raised her pale face with the luminous eyes and said softly: "Sometimes I wonder if it had to be. When I look at little Ned and see how health is coming to that crippled body — the processes are righting themselves — sound and healthy, ready to be helped back to life — I wonder if it may not be so with other processes not wholly physical. I wonder! . . . Did you ever think, Isabelle, that we are waiting close to other worlds, — we can almost hear from them with our ears, — but we only hear confusedly so far. Some day we may hear more clearly!"

Margaret had reverted, Isabelle concluded, to the religion of her father, the Bishop! What she was vaguely talking about was the Bishop's heaven, in which the widow and orphan were counselled to take comfort.

"I wish I could feel it, — what the church teaches," Isabelle replied. "But I can't, — it isn't real. I go to church and say over the creed and ask myself what it means, and feel the same way when I come out — or worse!"

"I don't mean religion — the church," Margaret smiled back. "That has been dead for me a long time. It's something you come to feel within you about life. I can't explain — only there might have been a light even for poor Larry in that last dreadful darkness! . . . Some day I want to tell you all about myself, something I have never told any one, — but it will help to explain, perhaps. . . . Now you must go to bed, — I will send my black Sue up with your coffee in the morning." . . .

Isabelle, as she lay awake in the stillness, the absolute hush of the snowy night, thought of what Margaret had said about her husband. John had told her how Larry had gradually gone to the bad in a desultory, weak-kneed fashion, — had lost his clerkship in the A. and P. that Lane had got for him; then had taken to hanging about the down-town hotels, betting a little, drinking a little, and finally one morning the curt paragraph in the paper: "Found, in the North River, body of a respectably dressed man about forty years. Papers on him show that he was Lawrence Pole of Westchester," etc., etc.

And John's brief comment, — "Pity that he hadn't done it ten years ago." Yes, thought Isabelle, pity that he was ever born, the derelict, ever came into this difficult world to complicate further its issues. Margaret apparently had towards this worthless being who had marred her life a softened feeling. But it was absurd of her now to think that she might have loved him!

CHAPTER LVI

LONG before it was light the next morning Isabelle heard the heavy tread of the blacksmith as he was going his rounds to light the fires; then she snuggled deeper into bed. When Margaret's maid finally came with the coffee and pushed back the heavy shutters, Isabelle looked out into another world from the one she had come to half frozen the afternoon before. She had entered the village from the rear, and now she looked off south and west from the level shelf on which the houses sat, across a broad valley, to black woods and a sloping breast of hills, freshly powdered with snow, to the blue sky-line, all as clear in the snow-washed mountain air as in a desert. The sun striking down into the valley brought out the faint azure of the inner folds of the hills.

There was scarcely a footprint in the road to break the soft mass of new-fallen snow. Isabelle could see a black cat deliberately stealing its way from the barn across the road to the house. It lifted each paw with delicate precision and pushed it firmly into the snow, casting a deep shadow on the gleaming surface of white. The black cat, lean and muscular, stretching itself across the snow, was the touch of art needed to complete the silent scene. . . .

A wood-sled drawn by two heavy horses came around the corner of the house, softly churning the new snow before its runners. A man clad in a burly sheepskin coat and fur cap, his feet in enormous rubber shoes, stood on the sled, slowly thrashing his arms and breathing frostily.

"Hello, Sol!" the man cried to the blacksmith, who was shovelling a path from the barn to the house.

"Morning, Ed. Going up to Cross's lot?"

"Ye—as — "

"Hard sledding?"

The two men exchanged amicable nothings in the crisp, brilliant air through which their voices rang with a peculiar timbre. To Isabelle, looking and listening from her window, it was all so fresh, so simple, like a picture on a Japanese print! For the first time in months she had a distinct desire, — to get outside and look at the hills.

"You are commanded," announced Margaret, a little later, "to the doctor's for supper at six. That wasn't the way it was put exactly, but it amounts to the same thing. The doctor's least word is a command here. . . . Now I am off to help the housekeeper with the accounts, — it's all I am good for!" . . .

So Isabelle was left to set forth on her ramble of exploration by herself. She pushed through the snow to the last house on the village street, where the road dipped down a long hill, and the wide arc of northern mountains was revealed in a glittering rampart. Her eyes filled involuntarily with tears.

"I must be very weak," she said to herself, "to cry because it's beautiful!" And sitting down on a rock by the road, she cried more, with a feeling of self-pity and a little self-contempt. An old woman came to the door of the house she had just passed with a dish-pan of water and looked curiously at the stranger. At first the countrywoman opened her lips as if she intended to speak, but stood with her dish-pan and said nothing. Isabelle could see through her tears the bent figure and battered face of the old woman, — a being without one line of beauty or even animal grace. What a fight life must have been to reduce any woman's body to that! And the purpose, — to keep the breath of life in a worn old body, just to live?

"Pleasant morning!" Isabelle said with a smile through her tears.

"It ain't bad," the old woman admitted, emptying her dish-pan.

As Isabelle retraced her steps into the village the old

woman followed her with curious eyes, thinking no doubt that a woman like this stranger, well dressed, young, and apparently well fed, ought not to be sitting on a rock on a winter's day crying!

"And she's quite right!" Isabelle said to herself.

The jewelled morning was the same to them both, — the outer world was imperturbable in its circular variety. But the inner world, the vision, — ah, there was the extraordinary variation in human lives! From heaven to hell through all gradations, and whether it were heaven or hell did not depend on being like this crone at the end of the road or like herself in its sheltered nooks, — it was something else.

"I will have to see Margaret's wonderful doctor, if this keeps on," she said, still dropping tears.

The blacksmith stood beside the open door of his shop, gazing reflectively across the white fields to the upland. Beside him was a broken wood-sled that he was mending. Seeing Isabelle, he waved her a slow salute with the sled-runner he had ready in his hand.

"Morning!" he called out in his deep voice. "Seeing the country? The hills are extra fine this morning."

He proceeded slowly to brush the snow from the frame of the sled, still glancing now and then over the fields. Isabelle felt that she had caught his characteristic moment, *his* inner vision.

"You have a good view from your shop."

"The best in the town! I've always been grateful to my father for one thing, — well, for many things, — but specially because he had the good sense to set the old smithy right here where you can see something. When there isn't much going on, I come out of doors here and take a long look at the mountains. It rests your back so."

Isabelle sat down in the shop and watched Mr. Short repair the sled, interested in the slow, sure movements he made, the painstaking way in which he fitted iron and wood and riveted the pieces together. It must be a relief, she thought, to work with one's hands like that, — which men could do, forgetting the number of manual movements Mrs. Short also made during the same time. The blacksmith talked as he worked, in a gentle voice without a trace of self-consciousness, and Isabelle had again that sense of VISION, of something inward and sustaining in this man of remote and narrow range, — something that expressed itself in the slow speech, the peaceful, self-contained manner. As she went back up the street to the house the thick cloud of depression, of intangible misery, in which she had been living as it seemed to her for eternity, settled down once more, — the habitual gait of her mind, like the dragging gait of her feet. She at least was powerless to escape the bitter food of idle recollection.

The doctor's house was a plain, square, white building, a little way above the main road, from which there was a drive winding through the spruces. On the sides and behind the house stretched one-story wings, also white and severely plain. "Those are the wards, and the one behind is the operating room," Margaret explained.

The house inside was as plain as on the outside: there were no pictures, no rugs, no useless furniture. The large hall divided the first floor in two. On the right was the office and the dining room, on the left with a southerly exposure the large living room. There were great, blazing fires in all the rooms and in the hall at either side, — there was no other heat, — and the odor of burning fir boughs permeated the atmosphere.

"It's like a hospital almost," Isabelle commented as they waited in the living room. "And he has French blood! How can he stand it so — bare and cold?"

"The doctor's limitations are as interesting as his powers. He never has a newspaper in the house, nor a magazine, — burns them up if he finds them lying about. Yet he reads a great deal. He has a contempt for all the froth of immediate living, and still the whole place is the most modern, up-to-date contemporary machine of its kind!"

Outside was the blackness of the cold winter night; inside the grayness of stained walls lighted by the glow from the blazing fires. A few pieces of statuary, copies of the work of the idealistic Greek period, stood in the hall and the living room. All that meant merely comfort, homelikeness — all in a word that was characteristically American — was wanting. Nevertheless, as Isabelle waited in the room she was aware of a peculiar grave beauty in its very exclusions. This house had the atmosphere of a mind.

Some nurse came in and nodded to Margaret, then Mrs. Beck the matron appeared, and a couple of young doctors followed. They had been across the valley on snow-shoes in the afternoon and were talking of their adventures in the woods. There was much laughter and gayety — as if gathered here in the wilderness these people all knew one another very well. After some time Isabelle became aware of the entrance of another person, and turning around saw a thin, slight man with a thick head of gray hair. His smooth-shaven face was modelled with many lines, and under the dark eyebrows that had not yet turned gray there were piercing black eyes. Although the talk and the laughter did not die at once, there was the subtle movement among the persons in the room which indicated that the master of the house had appeared. Dr. Renault walked directly to Isabelle.

"Good evening, Mrs. Lane. Will you come in to supper?"

He offered her his arm, and without further word of ceremony they went into the dining room. At the table the doctor said little to her at first. He leaned back in his chair, his eyes half closed, listening to the talk of the others, as if weary after a long day. Isabelle was puzzled by a sense of something familiar in the man at her side; she must have met him before, she could not tell where. The dining room, like the living room, was square, panelled with white wood, and the walls stained. It was bare except for several copies of Tanagra figurines in a recess above the chimney and two large photographs of Greek athletes. The long table, made of heavy oak planks, had no cloth, and the dishes were of the coarsest earthenware, such as French peasants use.

The talk was lively enough, — about two new cases that had arrived that afternoon, the deer-hunting season that had just closed, bear tracks discovered on Bolton Hill near the lumber-camp, and a new piano that a friend had sent for the convalescent or "dotty" ward, as they called it. The young doctor who sat at Isabelle's right asked her if she could play or sing, and when she said no, he asked her if she could skee. Those were the only personal remarks of the meal. Margaret, who was very much at home, entered into the talk with unwonted liveliness. It was a workshop of busy men and women who had finished the day's labor with enough vitality left to react. The food, Isabelle noticed, was plentiful and more than good. At the end of the meal the young men lighted cigarettes, and one of the nurses also smoked, while a box of cigars was placed before Renault. Some one began to sing, and the table joined the chorus, gathering about the chimney, where there were a couple of settles.

It was a life, so Isabelle saw, with an order of its own, a direction of its own, a strong undercurrent. Its oddity and nonchalance were refreshing. Like one of the mountain brooks it ran its own course, strong and liquid beneath the snow, to its own end.

"You seem to have a very good time up here among yourselves!" Isabelle said to the doctor, expressing her wonder frankly.

"And why not?" he asked, a smile on his thin lips. He helped himself to a cigar, still looking at her whimsically, and biting off its end held a match ready to strike, as if awaiting her next remark.

"But don't you ever want to get away, to go back to the city? Don't you feel — isolated?"

"Why should we? Because there's no opera or dinner

parties? We have a dinner party every night." He lighted his cigar and grinned at Isabelle. "The city delusion is one of the chief idiocies of our day. City people encourage the idea that you can't get on without their society. Man was not meant to live herded along sidewalks. The cities breed the diseases for us doctors, — that is their one great occupation."

He threw the match into the fire, leaned back in his chair with his hands knit behind his head, and fastening his black eyes on Isabelle began to talk.

"I lived upwards of twenty years in cities with that same delusion, — not daring to get more than a trolley-car fare away from the muck and noise. Then I was kicked out, — had to go, thank God! On the Arizona plains I learned to know what an idiot I had been to throw away the better half of a life in a place where you have to breathe other peoples' bad air. Why, there isn't room to think in a city! I never used to think, or only at odd moments. I lived from one nervous reflex to another, and took most of my ideas from other folks. Now I do my own thinking. Just try it, young woman; it is a great relief!"

"But — but — " Isabelle stammered, laughing in spite of herself.

"You know," Renault bore on tranquilly, "there's a new form of mental disease you might call 'pavementitis' — the pavement itch. When the patient has it badly, so that he can't be happy when removed from his customary environment, he is incurable. A man isn't a sound man, nor a woman a healthy woman, who can't stand alone on his own two legs and be nourished intellectually and emotionally away from the herd. . . . That young fellow who has just gone out was a bad case of pavementitis when he came to me, — couldn't breathe comfortably outside the air of New York. Hard worker, too. He came up here to "rest." Rest! Almost nobody needs rest. What they want is hard work and tranquil minds. I put him on his job the day he came. You couldn't drive him away now! Last fall I sent him back to see if the cure was complete. Telegraphed me in a week that he was coming up, — life was too dull down there! . . . And that little black-haired woman who is talking to Mrs. Pole, — similar case, only it was complicated. She was neurotic, hysterical, insomniac, melancholy, — the usual neurasthenic ticket. Had a husband who didn't suit or a lover, I suspect, and it got fastened in the brain, — rode her. She's my chief nurse in the surgical ward now, — a tremendous worker; can go three nights without sleep if necessary and knows enough to sleep soundly when she gets the chance. . . . Has relapses of pavementitis now and then, when some of her fool friends write her; but I fix that! . . . So it goes; I have had incurable cases of course, as in everything else. The only thing to do with 'em then is to send them back to suck their poison until it kills."

The whimsical tone of irony and invective made Isabelle laugh, and also subtly changed her self-preoccupation. Evidently Dr. Renault was not a Potts to go to with a long story of woe.

"I thought it was surgery, your specialty," she remarked, "not nervous prostration."

"We do pretty much everything here — as it is needed. Come in to-morrow morning sometime and look the shop over."

He rose, threw away his cigar, and at this signal the group scattered. Renault, Margaret, and Isabelle went back to the bare living room, where the doctor stood silently in front of the fireplace for a few minutes, as though expecting his guests to leave. When they started, he threw open a long window and beckoned to Isabelle to follow him. Outside there was a broad platform running out over the crest of the hill on which the house was built. The land beyond fell away sharply, then rose in a wooded swell to the northern mountains. The night was dark with glittering starlight above, and the presence of the white masses of the hills could be felt rather than seen, — brooding under the stars.

There was the tinkle of a sleigh-bell on the road below,—the only sound in the still night.

"There!" Renault exclaimed. "Is there anything you would like to swap for this?"

He breathed deeply of the frosty air.

"It seems almost as if a voice were speaking in the silence!"

"Yes," Renault assented gravely. "There *is* a voice, and you can hear it up here—if you listen."

CHAPTER LVII

On their way home the two women discussed the doctor eagerly.

"I must have seen Dr. Renault somewhere," Isabelle said, "or rather what he might have been once. He's a person!"

"That is it, — he is a person, — not just a doctor or a clever surgeon."

"Has he other regular patients besides the children, the surgical cases?"

"He started with those alone. But latterly, they tell me, he has become more interested in the nervous ward, — what he calls the 'dotty' ward, — where there are chiefly convalescent children or incurable nervous diseases of children. It is wonderful what he does with them. The power he has over them is like the power of the old saints who worked miracles, — a religious power,— or the pure force of the will, if you prefer."

After her evening with Renault, Isabelle felt that Margaret's description might not be too fervid.

Towards morning Isabelle woke, and in the sudden clarity of the silent hour thoughts flowed through her with wonderful vividness. She saw Renault's face and manner, his sharp eyes, his air of dictation, arrogant and at the same time kindly, — yes, there was a power in the man! As Margaret had put it, — a religious power. The word set loose numberless thoughts, distasteful ones, dead ones. She saw the respectable Presbyterian caravansary in St. Louis where the family worshipped, — sermons, creeds, dogmas, — the little stone chapel at Grafton where she had been confirmed, and her attempt to believe herself moved by some spiritual force, expressed in the formulas that the old clergyman had taught her. Then the phrases rose in her mind. It might have done her good once, — people found it helpful, — women especially in their hours of trial. She disliked the idea of leaning for help on something which in her hours of vigor she rejected. A refuge, an explanation, — no, it was not possible! The story of the atonement, the rewards, the mystical attempt to explain the tragedy of life, its sorrow and pain, — no, it was childish! So the word "religious" had something in it repellent, sickly, and self-deceptive. . . . Suddenly the words stood out sharply in her mind, — "What we need is a new religion!" A new religion, — where had she heard that? . . . Another flash in her brooding consciousness and there came the face of the doctor, the face of the man who had talked to her one Sunday afternoon at the house where there had been music. She remembered that she wished the music would not interrupt their conversation. Yes, he was bidding her good-by, at the steps, his hat raised in his hand, and he had said with that same whimsical smile, "What we need is a new religion!" It was an odd thing to say in the New York street, after an entirely delightful Sunday afternoon of music. Now the face was older, more tense, yet with added calm. Had he found his religion? And with a wistful desire to know what it was, the religion that made Renault live as he did, Isabelle dropped once more to sleep.

When Isabelle presented herself at the doctor's house the next morning, as he had suggested, the little black-haired nurse met her and made Renault's excuses. The doctor was occupied, but would try to join her later. Meanwhile would she like to look over the operating room and the surgical ward? The young doctor who had been afflicted with pavementitis — a large, florid, blond young man — showed her through the operating room, explaining to her the many devices, the endless well-thought-out detail, from the plumbing to the special electric lighting.

"It's absolutely perfect, Mrs. Lane!" he summed up, and

when Isabelle smiled at his enthusiasm, he grew red of face and stuttered in his effort to make her comprehend all that his superlative meant. "I know what I am saying. I have been all over Europe and this country. Every surgeon who comes here says the same thing. You can't even *imagine* anything that might be better. There isn't much in the world where you can't imagine a something better, an improvement. There's almost always a better to be had if you could get it. But here, no! . . . Porowitz, the great Vienna orthopædic surgeon, was here last winter, and he told me there wasn't a hospital in the whole world where the chances for recovery, taking it all round, were as large as up here in Grosvenor Flat, Vermont. Think of it! And there is no hospital that keeps a record where the percentage of successful operations is as high as ours. . . . That's enough to say, I guess," he concluded solemnly, wiping his brow.

In the surgical ward the wasted, white faces of the sick children disturbed Isabelle. It all seemed neat, quiet, pleasant. But the physical dislike of suffering, cultivated by the refinement of a highly individualistic age, made her shudder. So much there was that was wrong in life to be made right, — partly right, never wholly right. . . . It seemed useless, almost sentimentalism, to attempt this patching of diseased humanity. . . .

In the convalescent ward, Margaret was sitting beside a cot reading to her boy.

"He'll be home in a few days now!" she said in answer to Isabelle's glance. "Some day he will be a great football player."

The child colored at the reference to his ailment.

"I can walk now," he said, "a little."

Dr. Renault was at the other end of the ward sitting beside a girl of twelve, with one arm about her thin back, talking to her. The child's face was stained with half-dried tears. Presently the doctor took the child up and carried her to the window, and continued to talk to her, pointing out of the window. After a time he joined Isabelle, saying: —

"I was kept from meeting you when you came by that little girl over there. She is, by the way, one of our most interesting cases. Came here for hip disease. She is an orphan, — nothing known about her parents, — probably alcoholic from the mental symptoms. She has hysteria and undeveloped suicidal mania."

"What can you do for her?"

"What we can with medicine and surgery, and where that fails — we try other means."

Isabelle was eager to know what were those "other means," but the doctor was not a man to be questioned. Presently as he sauntered through the room he volunteered: —

"I have been talking to her, — telling her how the hills are made. . . . You see we have to clean out their minds as well as their bodies, get rid so far as we can of the muddy deposit, both the images associated with their environment — that is done by bringing them up here — and also what might be called inherited thought processes. Give 'em a sort of spiritual purge, in other words," he said with a smile. "Then we can build up, feed their minds something fresh. Sarah Stern there is an obstinate case, — she has a deep deposit of ancestral gloom."

"But you can't overcome the temperament, the inherited nature!"

Renault waved his hand impatiently.

"You've been told that since you were born. We have all grown up in that belief, — it is the curse of the day! . . . It can't be done altogether — yet. Sarah may revert and cut her throat when she leaves here. . . . But the vital work for medicine to-day is to see just how much can be done to change temperament, — inherited nature, as you call it. In other words, to put new forces to work in diseased brains. Perhaps some day we can do it all, — who knows?"

"Plant new souls in place of the old!"

Renault nodded gravely.

"That's the true medicine — the root medicine, — to take an imperfect organism and develop it, mould it to the perfected idea. Life is plastic, — human beings are plastic, — that is one important thing to remember!"

"But you are a surgeon?"

Renault's lips quivered with one of his ironical smiles.

"I *was* a surgeon, just as I was a materialist. When I was young, I was caught by the lure of so-called science, and became a surgeon, because it was precise, definite, — and I am something of a dab at it now — ask the boys here! . . . But surgery is artisan work. Younger hands will always beat you. Pallegrew in there is as good as I am now. There is nothing creative in surgery; it is on the order of mending shoes. One needs to get beyond that. . . . And here is where we get beyond patching. . . . Don't think we are just cranks here. We do what we can with the accepted tools, — the knife and the pill. But we try to go farther — a little way."

They descended to the basement of the main house where the more active children were playing games.

"We have to teach some of them the primitive instincts,— the play instinct, for example, — and we have a work-room, where we try to teach them the absorbing excitement of work. . . . I am thinking of starting a school next. Don't you want to try a hand at a new sort of education?"

So, pausing now and then to joke with a child or speak to an assistant, Renault took Isabelle over his "shop" once more, explaining casually his purposes. As a whole, it developed before her eyes that here was a laboratory of the human being, a place where by different processes the diseased, the twisted, the maimed, the inhibited, the incomplete were analyzed and reconstructed. As they emerged on the broad platform where they had stood the night before, Isabelle asked: —

"Why is it you work only with children?"

"Because I started with the little beggars. . . . And they are more plastic, too. But some day the same sort of thing will be done with adults. For we are all plastic. . . .

Good-day!" and he walked away rapidly in the direction of his office.

Isabelle returned to the village in a strange excitement of impressions and thoughts. She felt as if she had been taken up out of the world that she had lived in and suddenly introduced to a planet which was motived by totally other ideas than those of the world she knew. Here was a life laboratory, a place for making over human character as well as tissue. And in bravado, as it were, the mere refuse of human material was chosen to be made anew, with happiness, effectiveness, health! She realized that a satisfactory understanding of it would come slowly; but walking here in the winter sunshine along the village street, she had that sensation of strangeness which the child has on coming from the lighted playhouse into the street. . . . The set vision that tormented her within — that, too, might it not be erased?

About the post-office people were gathered gossiping and laughing, waiting for the noon mail to be distributed. Country-women in fur coats drove up in dingy cutters to do their Saturday shopping. The wood-sleds went jogging past towards the valley. School children were recklessly sliding down the cross street into the main road. Sol Short was coming over from his shop to get his paper . . . Here the old world was moving along its wonted grooves in this backwater community. But over it all like the color swimming over the hills was SOMETHING more, — some aspect of life unseen! And faintly, very dimly, Isabelle began to realize that she had never really been alive, — these thirty years and more.

"We are all plastic," she murmured, and looked away to the hills.

CHAPTER LVIII

LIFE at Grosvenor moved on in a placid routine, day after day. What with her children and the engrossing work at the doctor's Margaret was busy every morning, and Isabelle rarely saw her before the noon meal. Then at the plentiful dinner over which the blacksmith presided with a gentle courtesy and sweetness there was gossip of the hospital and the village, while Short, who had the father instinct, entertained the children. He knew all the resources of the country, every animal wild or tame, every rod of wood and pasture and hill. The little Poles opened him like an atlas or encyclopædia.

"Mr. Wilson begins to haul from his lot to-morrow," he would announce for their benefit. "I guess he'll take you up to the clearing where the men are cutting if you look for him sharp. And when you get there, you want to find a very tall man with a small head. That's Sam Tisdell, — and you tell him I said he would show you the deer run and the yard the deer have made back there a piece behind the clearing."

Then he told them how, when he was a young man, he had hunted for deer on the mountains and been caught one time in a great snowstorm, almost losing his life.

"The children have so much to do and to think about here in Grosvenor that they are no trouble at all. They never have to be entertained," Margaret remarked. "Mr. Short is much better for them than a Swiss governess with three languages!"

There were long evenings after the six o'clock suppers, which the two friends spent together usually, reading or talking before Isabelle's fire. Wherever the talk started, it would often gravitate to Renault, his personality dominating like some mountain figure the community. Margaret had been absorbed into the life of the hospital with its exciting yet orderly movement. There were new arrivals, departures, difficult cases, improvements and failures to record. She related some of the slowly wrought miracles she had witnessed during the months that she had been there.

"It all sounds like magic," Isabelle had said doubtfully.

"No, that is just what it isn't," Margaret protested; "the doctor's processes are not tricks, — they are evident."

And the two discussed endlessly these "processes" whereby minds were used to cure matter, the cleansing of the soul, — thought substitution, suggestion, the relationship of body and mind. And through all the talk, through the busy routine of the place, in the men and women working in the hospital, there emerged always that something unseen, — Idea, Will, Spirit, the motiving force of the whole. Isabelle felt this nowhere more strongly than in the change in Margaret herself. It was not merely that she seemed alert and active, wholly absorbed in the things about her, but more in the marvellous content which filled her. And, as Isabelle reflected, Margaret was the most discontented woman she had known; even before she married, she was ever hunting for something.

"But you can't stay here always," Isabelle said to her one evening. "You will have to go back to the city to educate the children if for no other reason."

"Sometimes I think I shan't go back! Why should I? . . . You know I have almost no money to live on." (Isabelle suspected that Larry's last years had eaten into the little that had been left of Margaret's fortune). "The children will go to school here. It would be useless to educate them above their future, which must be very plain."

"But you have a lot of relatives who would gladly help you — and them."

"They might, but I don't think I want their help — even for the children. I am not so sure that what we call advantages, a good start in life, and all that, is worth while. I had the chance — you had it, too — and what did we make of it?"

"Our children need not repeat our mistakes," Isabelle replied with a sigh.

"If they were surrounded with the same ideas, they probably would!" . . .

"The doctor has thrown his charm over you!"

"He has saved my life!" Margaret murmured; "at least he has shown me how to save it," she corrected.

There it was again, the mysterious Peace that possessed her, that had touched Margaret's hard, defiant spirit and tamed it. But Isabelle, remembering the letters with the Panama postmark she had seen lying on the hall table, wondered, and she could not help saying: —

"You are young yet, Margaret, — oh, it might be — happiness, all that you have missed!"

"No!" Margaret replied, with a little smile. "I — think not!"

She closed her eyes as if she were contemplating that other happiness, and after a silence she opened them and touched Isabelle's hand.

"I want to tell you something, dear. . . . I loved Rob Falkner, very much, the most a woman can."

"I knew it! . . . I felt it. . . . That it only might be!"

"He came to me," Margaret continued, "when I was hard and bitter about life, when I was dead. . . . It was the kind of love that women dream of, ours, — the perfect thing you feel in your heart has always been there, — that takes all of you! . . . It was good for us both — he needed me, and I needed him."

"Margaret!"

"I was wonderfully happy, with a dreadful happiness that was two parts pain, pain for myself, and more pain for him, because he needed me, you understand, and it could not be — I could not live with him and give him the food he hungered for — love."

Isabelle kissed the wistful face. "I know," she said.

"I want to tell you more — but you may not understand! . . . He had to go away. It was best; it was his work, his life, and I should have been a poor weak fool to let our love stand in the way. So it was decided, and I urged him to go. He came to see me at Bedmouth before he left, — a few days, a few hours of love. And we saw how it would have to be, that we should have to go on loving and living in the spirit, for as long as our love lasted, apart. We faced that. But — but —"

Margaret hesitated and then with shining eyes went on in a low voice.

"It was not enough what we had had! I was not ready to let him go, to see him go — without all. He never asked — I gave him all. We went away to have our love by ourselves, — to live for each other just a few days. He took me away in his boat, and for a few days, a few nights, we had our love — we saw our souls."

She waited, breathing fast, then controlled herself.

"Those hours were more than ordinary life. They do not seem to me real even now, or perhaps they are the most real thing in all I have known. It was love before the parting — before Fate. . . . When it was all over, we went back to earth. I returned to Mother Pole's house in Bedmouth, and I went up to the children's room and took my baby in my arms and kissed her, my little girl. And I knew that it had been right, all pure and holy, and I was glad, oh, so glad that it had been, that we had had the courage!"

Isabelle pressed the hand she held close to her breast and watched the shining face.

"And I have never felt differently — never for one moment since. It was the greatest thing that ever came to me, and it seems to me that I should never really have lived if it had not been for those days — those nights and days — and the heaven that we saw!"

"Then how can you speak as if life were ended now —"

Margaret held her hand before her face and did not answer.

"It might be possible — for you both. . . . She never

really cared for Rob, — she left him and took her child when they sold their house — because she was disappointed. And she has refused to go to him ever since."

"I know all that," Margaret murmured; "that is not it wholly. I can't tell. I don't know yet. It is not clear. . . . But I know that I am proud and glad of what has been, — of our love in its fulness and glory. And I know it was not sin! Nothing can make it so to me."

She had risen and stood proudly before Isabelle.

"It has made living possible for him and for me, — it has made it something noble and great, to feel this in our souls. . . . I wanted to tell you; I thought you would understand, and I did not want you to be wrong about me, — not to know me all!"

She knelt and buried her head in Isabelle's lap, and when she raised her face there were tears falling from the eyes.

"I don't know why I should cry!" she exclaimed with a smile. "I don't often. . . . It was all so beautiful. But we women cry when we can't express ourselves any other way!"

"I shall always hope —"

Margaret shook her head.

"I don't know. . . . There are other things coming, — another revelation, perhaps! I don't think of what will be, dear."

But womanwise, Isabelle thought on after Margaret had left, of Falkner and Margaret, of their love. And why shouldn't it come to them, she asked herself? The other, Falkner's marriage, had been a mistake for both, a terrible mistake, and they had both paid for it. Bessie could have made it possible if she had wanted to, if she had had it in her. She had her chance. For him to go back to her now, with the gulf between them of all this past, was mere folly, — just conventional wrong-headedness. And it would probably be no better for Bessie if he were to make the sacrifice. . . . The revelation that Margaret had hinted of had not come to Isabelle. She lay awake thinking with aching heart of her own story, — its tragic ending. But *he* was not a man, — that, too, had been a mistake!

Isabelle, largely left to herself, for occupation drove about the snowy hills, sometimes taking with her for company one of the convalescents or a nurse, often alone, liking the solitude of the winter spaces. Sometimes she went to the blacksmith's shop and talked with the old man, learning the genealogy and the sociology of the neighborhood. The text for Sol Short's wisdom was ever at hand in the passers-by. Ending one of his transcripts, he made a phrase that lingered in Isabelle's mind long afterward. "So she was left a charge upon the property," he said of an old woman that had come out of one of the village houses. "Aunt Mehitabel went with the house. When it was sold, she had to be taken over by the new owner, and her keep provided. And there she is now, an old woman in ill health and ill temper. I don't know as there is a worse combination." . . .

"I wonder why I stay," Isabelle said to Margaret after nearly two months had slipped by. "I am quite rested, as well as I shall ever be, I believe. You don't need me. Nobody does exactly! Molly writes me very contented little letters. Mother is staying with her, and she is at the party age, and would be terribly bored to come here, as you suggested. John is in St. Louis; he seems to have a good deal to do out there this winter. So you see my little world gets on perfectly without me."

"Better stay here, then," Margaret urged, "until spring. It will do you good. You haven't exhausted the doctor yet!"

"I almost never see him, and when he does remember me he chaffs me as if I were a silly child. No, I think I will go next week."

But she did not wish to leave. The winter peace of the little village had been like an enveloping anodyne to her weary body and mind. Removed from all her past, from the sights and the people that suggested those obsessing thoughts which had filled her waking hours with dreariness, she had sunk into the simple routine of Grosvenor as the tired body sinks into a soft bed. The daily sight of the snowy fields, the frozen hillsides black with forests, and the dry spirituous air, lifted her. Now and then the effect of the anodyne wore off and the old gnawing pain, or a sodden sense of futility, overwhelmed her afresh. "It will never get straight!" she said, thinking in the terms of Potts's specifics. "I am somehow wrong, and I must go all my life with this torture — or worse — until I die!" And the whole panorama of her little life would unroll before her in the sleepless hours of the still night: her girl ambitions, her mistaken marriage, her striving for experience, for life, to satisfy — what? Then her mistaken love, and Vickers's sacrifice, and the blackness afterwards, — the mistake of it all! "They'll be better without me, — mother and Molly and John! Let me die!" she cried. Then illogically she would think of Renault and wonder what *he* could do for her. But she shrank from baring herself before his piercing gaze. "He would say I was a fool, and he would be right!"

So she went out into the cold country and walked miles over the frozen fields through the still woods, trying to forget, only to return still ridden by her thoughts, — bitter tears for Vickers, sometimes almost reproach for his act. "If he had let me plunge to my fate, it would have been better than this! I might never have known my mistake, — it would have been different, all of it different. Now there is nothing!" And at the end of one of these black moods she resolved to return to her world and "go through the motions as others do. What else? Perhaps it will be better when I am distracted. Potts will give me something to brace me." . . .

But Isabelle did not return to the city and get that prescription from the great Potts.

CHAPTER LIX

Just as Isabelle had completed her packing on Sunday afternoon, a message came to her from Dr. Renault through Margaret. "We need another woman, — two of our nurses have been called away and a third is sick. Will you give us some help?"

"I am going up myself for the night," Margaret added. "They are badly pushed, — six new cases the last three days."

So the night found Isabelle under the direction of Mrs. Felton, the little black-haired woman whose "case" the doctor had analyzed for her. It was a long night, and the next morning, all the experienced nurses being needed at an operation, Isabelle went on. The day was full and also the next two. The hospital force was inadequate, and though the doctor had telegraphed for help there would be no relief for a week. So Isabelle was caught up in the pressing activity of this organism and worked by it, impelled without her own will, driven hard as all around her were driven by the circumstances behind her. Dr. Renault abhorred noise, disorder, excitement, confusion of any kind. All had to run smoothly and quietly as if in perfect condition. He himself was evident, at all hours of day or night, chaffing, dropping his ironical comments, listening, directing, — the inner force of the organism. One night the little nurse dropped asleep, clearly worn out, and Isabelle sent her to bed. The ward was quiet; there was nothing to be done. Isabelle, pacing to and fro in the glass sun parlor to keep herself awake, suddenly became aware of the stillness within her. It was as if some noisy piece of machinery had ceased to revolve without her having noticed it. It was possible for her in this quiet moment to realize this: for the first time in five days she had not thought of herself. For five days she had not consciously thought! Doubtless she would have to pay for this debauch of work. She would collapse. But for five days she had not known whether she felt ill or well, was happy or distressed. Excitement — to be paid for! She shrank from the weary round of old thought that must come, the revolution of the wheels within. For five days she had not thought, she had not cared, she had not known herself! That must be the opiate of the poor, driven by labor to feed and clothe themselves; of the ambitious, driven by hope and desire. . . . She must work, too; work was a good thing. Why had Potts not included it in his panaceas? . . .

Later when she walked back into the still ward, she thought she heard a stifled breathing, but when she went the rounds of the cots, all was still. It was not until nearly morning that she noticed something wrong with a little boy, observing the huddled position of the limbs drawn up beneath the blanket. She felt of his face — it was cold. Frightened, she hurried to the bell to summon the night doctor. As she reached it Renault entered the ward and with a warning hand brought her back to the cot. He put his fingers swiftly here and there on the child's body.

"Where is Mrs. Felton?" he demanded severely.

"She was so worn out I persuaded her to get some rest. Have I neglected anything? — is anything wrong?"

"The child is dead," Renault replied, straightening himself and covering up the little form.

"Oh, I have — done something wrong!"

"It would have made no difference what you did," the doctor replied dryly. "Nothing would have made any difference. There was the millionth part of a chance, and it was not for him."

As they stood looking down at the dead face, it seemed to Isabelle that suddenly he had become a person, this dead child, with his lost millionth of a chance, — not merely one of the invalids sleeping in the room. For this brief moment when life had ceased to beat in his frail body, and before decay had begun, there was an individuality given him that he had never achieved in life.

"Poor little fellow!" Isabelle murmured softly. "He must have suffered so much." Then with that common consolation with which the living evade the thought of death, she added, "He has escaped more pain; it is better so, perhaps!"

"No — that is wrong!"

Renault, standing beside the bed, his arms folded across his breast, looked up from the dead child straight into the woman's eyes.

"That is false!" he cried with sudden passion. "Life is GOOD — all of it — for every one."

He held her eyes with his glance while his words reverberated through her being like the CREDO of a new faith.

When another nurse had come to relieve Isabelle, she left the ward with the doctor. As they went through the passageway that led to the house, Renault said in his usual abrupt tone: —

"You had better run home, Mrs. Lane, and get some sleep. To-morrow will be another hard day."

She wheeled suddenly and faced him.

"How dare you say that life is good for any other human being! What do *you* know of another's agony, — the misery that existence may mean, the daily woe?"

Her passionate burst of protest died in a sob.

"I say it because I believe it, because I *know* it!"

"No one can know that for another."

"For animals the account of good and evil may be struck, the pains set against the satisfactions that life offers. When we judge that the balance is on the wrong side, we are merciful, — put the creature out of its misery, as we say. But no human being is an animal in that sense. And no human being can cast his balance of good and evil in that mechanical way — nor any one else for him!"

"But one knows for himself! When you suffer, when all is blank within and you cry as Job cried, — 'would God it were morning, and in the morning would God it were night!' then life is *not* good. If you could be some one else for a few hours, then you might understand — what defeat and living death —"

Oh, if she could tell! The impulse to reveal surged in her heart, that deep human desire to call to another across the desert, so that some one besides the silent stars and the wretched Self may know! Renault waited, his compelling eyes on her face.

"When you have lost the most in your life — hope, love! When you have killed the best!" she murmured brokenly. "Oh, I can't say it! . . . I can never say it — tell the whole."

Tears fell, tears of pity for the dead child, for herself, for the fine-wrought agony of life.

"But I know!" Renault's voice, low and calm, came as it were from a shut corner of his heart. "I have felt and I have seen — yes, Defeat, Despair, Regret — all the black ghosts that walk."

Isabelle raised her eyes questioningly.

"And it is because of that, that I can raise my face to the stars and say, 'It is good, all good — all that life contains.' And the time will come when you will repeat my words and say to them, 'Amen.'"

"That I could!"

"We are not animals, — there is the Unseen behind the Seen; the Unknown behind the Observed. There is a Spirit that rises within us to slay the ghosts, to give them the lie. Call upon it, and it will answer. . . . For Peace is the rightful heritage of every soul that is born."

"Not Peace."

"Yes, — I say Peace! Health, perhaps; happiness, perhaps; efficiency, perhaps. But Peace always lies within the grasp of whomsoever will stretch out his hand to possess it." . . .

As they stopped at the house door and waited in the deep

silence of the dark morning, Renault put his hands on Isabelle's shoulders: —

"Call to it, and it will come from the depths! . . . Good-night."

There in the still dawning hour, when the vaulted heavens seemed brooding close to the hills and the forests, these two affirmations of a creed rang in Isabelle's soul like the reverberating chords of some mystic promise: —

"Life is good — all of it — for every one!" And, "Peace is the rightful heritage of every soul. It lies within the grasp of whomsoever will stretch out his hand to possess it."

It was still within her.

CHAPTER LX

When Isabelle woke, the morning sun fretted the green shutters. She was tired in every limb, — limp, content to lie in bed while Mrs. Strong lighted the fire, threw open the shutters, and brought breakfast and the mail. Through the east windows the sun streamed in solidly, flooding the counterpane, warming the faded roses of the wall paper. A bit of the north range of hills, the flat summit of Belton's Top with a glittering ice-cap, she could see above the gray gable of the barn. The sky was a soft, cloudless blue, and the eaves were busily dripping in a drowsy persistency.

She liked to lie there, watching the sun, listening to the drip, her letters unopened, her breakfast untouched. She was delightfully empty of thoughts. But one idea lay in her mind, — she should stay on, here, just here. Since she had packed her trunk the Sunday before, a great deal seemed to have happened, — a space had been placed between the outer world that she had restlessly turned back towards and herself. Some day she should go back to that other world — to Molly and John and all the rest. But not now — no! . . .

As she lay there, slowly the little things of the past weeks since she had travelled the cold road from White River — the impressions, the sights, the ideas — settled into her thought, pushing back the obstinate obsessions that had possessed her for months. The present began to be important, to drive out the past. Outside in the street some one whistled, the bells of the passing sleds jangled, a boy's treble halloa sounded far away, — unconscious voices of the living world, like the floating clouds, the noise of running water, the drip of the melting snow on the eaves, — so good it all was and real! . . .

Margaret had found that Peace the doctor had spoken of, Margaret whose delicate curving lips had always seemed to her the symbol of discontent, of the inadequacy of life. Margaret had found it, and why not she? . . . That explained the difference she felt these days in Margaret. There had always been something fine and sweet in the Southern woman, something sympathetic in her touch, in the tone of her voice even when she said cynical things. Now Margaret never said bitter things, even about the wretched Larry. She had always been a listener rather than a talker, but now there was a balm in her very presence, a touch upon the spirit, like a cool hand on the brow. Yes! She had found that rightful heritage of Peace and breathed it all around her, like warmth and light.

Margaret came in with the noon mail, which she had collected from the box in the post-office. As she tossed the papers and letters on the bed, Isabelle noticed another of the oblong letters in the familiar handwriting from Panama. . . .

"Or is it that?" she asked herself for a moment, and then was ashamed. The smile, the clear look out of the deep eyes, the caressing hand that stroked her face, all said no, — it was not that! And if it were, it must be good.

"So you are going to stay with us a while longer, Isabelle. . . . I shall unpack your trunk and hide it," Margaret said with smiling conviction.

"Yes, — I shall stay, for the present. . . . Now I must get into my clothes. I've been lazing away the whole morning here — not even reading my letters!"

"That's right," Margaret drawled. "Doing nothing is splendid for the temperament. That's why the darkies have such delightful natures. They can sit whole days in the sun and never think a thought." With her hand on the door she turned: "You must send for Molly, — it will be good for her to forget the dancing lessons and frocks. My children will take her down to Mill Hill and make a boy of her."

"Well, — but she will be a nuisance, I am afraid. She is such a young lady." . . .

At last Isabelle tore open a letter from her husband, one that Margaret had just brought. It was concise and dry, in the economical epistolary style into which they had dropped with each other. He was glad to hear that her rest in the country was doing her good. If it agreed with her and she was content, she had better stay on for the present. He should be detained in the West longer than he had expected. There were important suits coming on against the railroad in which he should be needed, hearings, etc. At the close there was an unusually passionate sentence or two about "the public unrest and suspicion," and the President and the newspapers. "They seem to like the smell of filth so much that they make a supply when they can't find any."

Broils of the world! The endless struggle between those who had and those who envied them what they had. There was another side, she supposed, and in the past Cairy had been at some pains to explain that other side to her. Her husband must of course be prejudiced, like her father; they saw it all too close. However, it was a man's affair to settle, unless a woman wished to play Conny's rôle and move her husband about the board. Broils! How infinitely far away it seemed, all the noise of the world! . . . She began to dress hurriedly to report at the hospital for the afternoon. As she glanced again at her husband's letter, she saw a postscript, with some scraps of St. Louis gossip: —

"I hear that Bessie is to get a divorce from Falkner. I wonder if it can be true. . . . I saw Steve in the street last week. From what I learn the lumber business isn't flourishing. . . . Pity he didn't swallow his scruples and stay with us where he would be safe!"

Poor Alice — if Steve should fail now, with all those children! And then she remembered what Alice Johnston had said to Vickers, "You see we have been poor so much of the time that we know what it is like." It would take a good deal to discourage Alice and Steve. But John must keep an eye on them, and try to help Steve. John, it occurred to her then for the first time, was that kind, — the substantial sort of man that never needed help himself, on which others might lean.

So Isabelle stayed in the mountain village through the winter months. Molly came with her governess, and both endeavored to suppress politely their wonder that any one could imprison herself in this dreary, cold place. The regular nurses came back to the hospital, but Isabelle, once having been drawn in, was not released.

"He's a hard master," Margaret said of the doctor. "If he once gets his hand on you, he never lets go — until he is ready to."

Apparently Renault was not ready to let go of Isabelle. Without explaining himself to her, he kept her supplied with work, and though she saw him often every day, they rarely talked, never seriously. He seemed to avoid after that first night any opportunity for personal revelation. The doctor was fond of jokes and had the manner of conducting his affairs as if they were a game in which he took a detached and whimsical interest. If there was sentiment in his nature, an emotional feeling towards the work he was doing, it was well concealed, first with drollery, and then with scientific application. So far as any one could observe the daily routine, there was nothing, at least in the surgical side of the hospital, that was not coldly scientific. As Renault had said, "We do what we can with every instrument known to man, every device, drug, or pathological theory." And his mind seemed mostly engrossed with this "artisan" side of his profession, in applying his skill and learning and directing the skill and learning of others. It was only in the convalescent ward that the other side showed itself, — that belief in the something spiritual, beyond the physical, to be called upon. One of the doctors, a young Norwegian named Norden, was his assistant in this work. And every one in the place felt that Norden was closest of all to the doctor. Norden in his experiments with nervous diseases used hypnotism, suggestion, psychotherapy, — all the modern forms of supernaturalism. His attitude was ever, as he said to Isabelle, "It might be — who knows?" — "There is truth, some little truth in all the ages, in all the theories and beliefs." Isabelle had a strong liking for this uncouth Northman with his bony figure and sunken eyes that seemed always burning with an unattained desire, an inexpressible belief. Norden said to her, the only way is "to recognize both soul and body in dealing with the organism. Medicine is a Religion, a Faith, a great Solution. It ought to be supported by the state, free to all. . . . The old medicine is either machine work or quackery, like the blood-letting of barbers." . . .

It was an exhilarating place to live in, Renault's hospital, — an atmosphere of intense activity, mental and physical, with a spirit of some large, unexpressed truth, a passionate faith, that raised the immediate finite and petty task to a step in the glorious ranks of eternity. The personality of Renault alone kept this atmosphere from becoming hectic and sentimental. He held this ship that he steered so steadily in the path of fact that there was no opportunity for emotional explosions. But he himself was the undefined incarnate Faith that made the voyage of the last importance to every one concerned. Small wonder that the doctors and nurses — the instruments of his will — "could not be driven away"! They had caught the note, each one of them, of that unseen power and lived always in the hope of greater revelations to come.

As the order of the days settled into a rhythmic routine with the passing of the weeks, Isabelle Lane desired more and more to come closer to this man who had touched her to the quick, to search more clearly for her personal Solution which evaded her grasp. There were many questions she wished to have answered! But Renault had few intimate moments. He avoided personalities, as if they were a useless drain upon energy. His message was delivered at casual moments. One day he came up behind Isabelle in the ward, and nodding towards Molly, who was reading a story to one of the little girl patients, said: —

"So you have put daughter to some use?"

"Yes!" Isabelle exclaimed irritably. "I found her going over her dresses for the tenth time and brought her along. . . . However does she get that air of condescension! Look at her over there playing the grand lady in her pretty frock for the benefit of these children. Little Snob! She didn't get *that* from me."

"Don't worry. Wait a day or two and you will see the small girl she is reading to hand her one between the eyes," Renault joked. "She's on to Miss Molly's patronage and airs, and she has Spanish blood in her. Look at her mouth now. Doesn't it say, 'I am something of a swell myself'?"

"They say children are a comfort!" Isabelle remarked disgustedly. "They are first a care and then a torment. In them you see all that you dislike in yourself popping up — and much more besides. Molly thinks of nothing but clothes and parties and etiquette. She has twice the social instinct I ever had. I can see myself ten years hence being led around by her through all the social stuff I have learned enough to avoid."

"You can't be sure."

"They change, but not the fundamentals. Molly is a little *mondaine*, — she showed it in the cradle."

"But you don't know what is inside her besides that tendency, any more than you know now what is inside yourself and will come out a year hence."

"If I don't know myself at my age, I must be an idiot!"

"No one knows the whole story until the end. Even really aged people develop surprising qualities of character. It's a Christmas box — the inside of us; you can always find another package if you put your hand in deep enough and feel around. Molly's top package seems to be finery. She may dip lower down."

'So I am dipping here in Grosvenor,' thought Isabelle,

'and I may find the unexpected!' . . . This was an empty quarter of an hour before dinner and Renault was talkative.

"Who knows?" he resumed whimsically. "You might have a good sense of humor somewhere, Mrs. Lane, pretty well buried."

Isabelle flushed with mortification.

"You are witty enough, young woman. But I mean real humor, not the rattle of dry peas in the pod that goes for humor at a dinner party. Do you know why I keep Sam about the place, — that fat lazy beggar who takes half an hour to fetch an armful of wood? Because he knows how to laugh. He is a splendid teacher of mirth. When I hear him laugh down in the cellar, I always open the door and try to get the whole of it. It shakes my stomach sympathetically. The old cuss knows it, too, which is a pity! . . . Well, young mademoiselle over there is play-acting to herself; she thinks she will be a grand lady like mamma. God knows what she will find more interesting before she reaches the bottom of the box. Don't worry! And did you ever think where they catch the tricks, these kids? If you went into it, you could trace every one down to some suggestion; it wouldn't take you long to account for that high and mighty air in your child that you don't fancy. If you don't want her to pick up undesirable packages, see that they aren't handed out to her."

"But she has had the best —"

"Yes, of course. Lord! the best! Americans are mad for the best. Which means the highest priced. I've no doubt, Mrs. Lane, you have given Molly all the disadvantages. . . . Did you ever sit down for five minutes and ask yourself seriously what is the best, humanly speaking, for that child? What things *are* best any way? . . . Do you want her to end where you are at your age?"

Isabelle shook her head sadly: —

"No, — not that!"

"Cultivate the garden, then. . . . Or, to change the figure, see what is handed out to her. . . . For every thought and feeling in your body, every act of your will, makes its trace upon her, — upon countless others, but upon her first because she is nearest."

Molly, having closed her book and said good-evening to the little patient, came up to her mother.

"It is time, I think, mamma, for me to go home to dress for dinner." She looked at the little watch pinned to her dress. Renault and Isabelle laughed heartily.

"What pebble that you tossed into the pool produced that ripple, do you think?" the doctor quizzed, twirling Molly about by her neck, much to her discomfort.

"He treats me like a child, too," Isabelle complained to Margaret; "gives me a little lesson now and then, and then says 'Run along now and be a good girl.'"

"It is a long lesson," Margaret admitted, "learning how to live, especially when you begin when we did. But after you have turned the pages for a while, somehow it counts."

CHAPTER LXI

The first of March was still deep winter in Grosvenor, but during the night the southwest wind had begun to blow, coming in at Isabelle's window with the cool freshness of anticipated spring. The day was calm and soft, with films of cloud floating over the hills, and the indefinable suggestion of change in the air, of the breaking of the frost. The southwest wind had brought with it from the low land the haze, as if it had come from far warm countries about the Gulf, where the flowers were already blooming and the birds preparing for the northward flight. It touched the earth through the thick mantle of ice and snow, and underneath in the rocky crust of frozen ground there was the movement of water. The brooks on the hills began to gurgle below the ice.

Up there in the north the snow had come early in the autumn, covering as with a warm blanket this rocky crust before the frost could strike deep. "An early spring," Sol Short announced at dinner, a dreamy look in his eyes, like the soft sky outside, the look of unconscious gladness that rises in man at the thought of the coming year, the great revival of life. . . . That afternoon Margaret and Isabelle drove over the snowy upland, where the deep drifts in the fields had shrivelled perceptibly, sucked by the warm sun above and the opening earth beneath. The runners of the sleigh cut into the trodden snow, and in the sheltered levels of the road the horse's feet plashed in slush. The birches and alders lifted their bare stems hardily from the retreating drifts. Soft violet lights hovered in the valleys.

"It is coming, Spring!" Margaret cried.

"Remember, Mr. Short said there would be many a freeze before it really came to stay!"

"Yes, but it is the first call; I feel it all through me."

The week before Ned had left the hospital, and for the first time in three years had sat at the table with his brother and sister. His face had lost wholly the gray look of disappointed childhood. Spring, arrested, was coming to him at last. . . .

As they climbed upward into the hills the stern aspect of winter returned, with the deep drifts of snow, the untracked road. When they topped the Pass and looked down over the village and beyond to the northern mountains, the wind caught the sharp edges of the drifts and swept a snowy foam in their faces. But the sun was sinking into a gulf of misty azure and gold, and the breath of awakening earth was rising to meet the sun.

Up here it was still winter, the Past; beneath was the sign of change, the coming of the New. And as Isabelle contemplated the broad sweep below, her heart was still, waiting for whatever should come out of the New.

The sun fell behind the Altar, as they called the flat top of Belton's Mountain, and all about the hills played the upward radiance from its descending beams. . . . Margaret touched the loafing horse with the whip, and he jogged down into the forest-covered road.

"Rob Falkner lands to-day in New York," Margaret remarked with a steady voice.

Isabelle started from her revery and asked: —

"Does he mean to go back to Panama?"

"I don't believe he knows yet. The life down there is, of course, terribly lonely and unfruitful. The work is interesting. I think he would like to go on with it until he had finished his part. But there are changes; the man he went out with has resigned."

Margaret wanted to talk about him, apparently, for she continued: —

"He has done some very good work, — has been in charge

of a difficult cut, — and he has been specially mentioned several times. Did you see the illustrated article in the last *People's?* There were sketches and photographs of his section. . . . But he hasn't been well lately, had a touch of fever, and needs a rest."

"My husband wrote that they were to be divorced — he had heard so."

"I don't believe it," Margaret replied evenly. "His wife hasn't been down there. . . . It isn't exactly the place for a woman, at least for one who can't stand monotony, loneliness, and hardship. She has been in Europe with her mother, this last year."

"You know I used to know her very well years ago. She was very pretty then. Everybody liked Bessie," Isabelle mused.

And later she remarked: —

"Singular that *her* marriage should be such a failure."

"Is it singular that any given marriage should be a failure?" Margaret asked with a touch of her old irony. "It is more singular to me that any marriage, made as they must be made to-day, should be anything but a dismal failure."

"But Bessie was the kind to be adored. She was pretty, and clever, and amusing, — a great talker and crazy about people. She had real social instinct, — the kind you read of in books, you know. She could make her circle anywhere. She couldn't be alone five minutes, — people clustered around her like bees. Her life might have been a romance, you would suppose, — pretty girl, poor, marries an ambitious, clever man, who arrives with her social help, goes into politics — oh, anything you will!"

"But the real thing," Margaret observed.

"What do you mean?"

"Love! . . . Love that understands and helps."

"Well, I saw the most dazzling future for her when she used to give garden parties in Torso, with only two unattached men who were possible in the place! And at least she might have had a small home in the suburbs and an adoring husband home at five-thirty, — but she wasn't that kind. . . . Poor Bess! I am sorry for her."

"I suppose the reason why a man and a woman hurt instead of help each other in marriage is never known to any one but themselves," Margaret observed dryly, urging on the horse. "And perhaps not even to themselves!"

There was a change in Margaret, an inner ferment that displayed itself in the haze in her clear eyes, — the look of one whose mind broods over the past, — a heightened color, a controlled restlessness of mood. 'No, it is not settled,' thought Isabelle. 'Poor Margaret!' She went about her many duties with the same silent sureness, the same poise as before. Whatever was happening to her was according to the discipline of her nature, controlled, suppressed. 'If she would only splutter,' Isabelle wished, 'instead of looking like a glowing sphinx!'

"Margaret!" she exclaimed in the evening, after a long silence between them. "You are so young — so pretty these days!"

"You think so? Thanks!" Margaret replied, stretching her thin arms above her head, which was crushed against one of Mrs. Short's hard pillows. "I suppose it is the Indian summer, the last warm glow before the end!" She opened her trembling lips in one of her ironical smiles. "There always comes a time of ripeness to a woman before she goes over the hill into old age."

"Nonsense! You are younger than you were twelve years ago!"

"Yes, I am younger in a sense than I ever was. I am well and strong, and I am in equilibrium, as I never was before. . . . And it's more than that. We become more vital if we survive the tangle of youth. We see more — we feel more! When I hear girls talk about love, I always want to say: 'What do you know, what *can* you know about it! Love isn't born in a woman before she is thirty, — she hasn't the power. She can have children, but she can't love a man.'"

Margaret pressed her hands tensely together and murmured to herself, "For love is born with the soul, — and is the last thing that comes into the heart!"

Isabelle with caressing impulsiveness put her arms about the slight figure.

"I love you, Margaret; it seems as if you were the only person I really loved now! It has been heaven to be with you all these weeks. You calm me, you breathe peace to me. . . . And I want to help you, now."

Margaret smiled sadly and drew Isabelle's dark head to her and kissed it.

"Nobody can help, dear. . . . It will come right! It must come right, I am sure."

With the feelings that are beyond expression they held each other thus. Finally Margaret said in a low voice: —

"Rob comes day after to-morrow; he will be at the Inn."

Isabelle rose from the couch with a sudden revulsion in her heart. After all, was this calm, this peace that she had admired in Margaret and longed to possess herself, this Something which she had achieved and which seemed to put her beyond and above ordinary women, nothing but the woman's satisfaction in love, whose lover is seeking her? She found herself almost despising Margaret unreasonably. Some man! That created the firmament of women's heaven, with its sun and its moon and its stars. Remembered caresses and expected joys, — the woman's bliss of yielding to her chosen master, — was that all!

Margaret, following Isabelle with her eyes, seemed to comprehend this sudden change in her heart. But she merely remarked: —

"He cannot stay long, — only a couple of days, I believe."

"Tell me," Isabelle demanded sharply, as if she had the right to know, must know, "what are you going to do?"

Margaret closed her eyes, and after a time of utter stillness she said in a voice beseechingly tender: —

"Dear, perhaps I do not know, yet."

Her eyes were wet with unaccustomed tears. Stretching a hand to Isabelle and smiling again, she murmured: —

"Whatever it will be, you must trust that it will be right for me and for him, — you must know that."

Isabelle pressed her hand gently: —

"Forgive me."

"And some day I will tell you."

CHAPTER LXII

Mrs. Short peered through the dining-room window on the snow field, — a dazzling white under the March sun now well above the hills, — and watched the two black figures tracking their way on snow-shoes towards the forest. Margaret's slight figure swept ahead with a skill and assurance that the taller one did not show. "I guess," mused the blacksmith's wife, "that life on the Isthmus of Panama don't fit a man much to distinguish himself on those things." Nevertheless, the man tramped laboriously behind the woman until the two were halted by a fence, now visible through the sunken drift. They faced each other, and were evidently discussing mirthfully how the obstacle was to be met. The man stooped to untie the shoes, his pockets bulging with the day's luncheon; but suddenly the woman backed away and began to climb the fence, a difficult feat. The man lumbered after her, catching one shoe in the top rail, finally freeing himself. Then the two black figures were lost over the dip of the hill. The smile still lingered on Mrs. Short's face, — the smile that two beings, man and woman, still young and vital, must always bring, as though saying, 'There's spring yet in the world, and years of life and hope to come!'

Behind the hill in the hollow Margaret was showing Falkner how to squat on his shoes and coast over the crust. At the bottom of the slide the brook was gurgling under a film of ice. The upward slope, untouched by the sun, was glare ice, and they toiled. Beyond was the forest with its black tree trunks amid the clotted clumps of snowy underbrush. Falkner pushed on with awkward strength to reach Margaret, who lingered at the opening of the wood. How wonderful she was, he thought, so well, so full of life and fire, — O God!

all woman! And his heart beat hard, now that what he had seen these two years behind the curtain of his eyes was so near, — after all the weary months of heat and toil and desire! Only she was more, so much more — as the achieved beauty of the day is more than memory or anticipation. . . .

She smiled a welcome when he reached her, and pointed away to the misty hills. "The beauty of it!" she whispered passionately. "I adore these hills, I worship them. I have seen them morning and night all these months. I know every color, every rock and curving line. It is like the face of a great austere God, this world up here, a God that may be seen."

"You have made me feel the hills in your letters."

"Now we see them together. . . . Isn't it wonderful to be here in it all, you and I, together?"

He held his arms to her.

"Not yet," she whispered, and sped on into the still darkness between the fir branches. He followed.

So on, on over the buried bushes, across the trickly, thawing streams, through a thick swamp, close with alder and birch, on up the slope into woods more largely spaced, where great oaks towered among the fir and the spruce, and tall white birches glimmered in the dusk — all still and as yet dead. And on far up the mountain slope until beneath the Altar they came to a little circle, hedged round with thick young firs, where the deep snow was tracked with footprints of birds and foxes. Margaret leaned against the root of a fallen birch and breathed deeply. She had come like the wind, swift and elusive, darting through the forest under the snowy branches, as if — so felt the man with his leashed desire of her — the mere physical joy of motion and air and sun and still woods were enough, and love had been lost in the glory of the day! . . .

"Here," she murmured with trembling lips, "at last!"

"At last!" he echoed, her eyes close to his. And as they waited a moment before their lips met, the woman's face softened and changed and pleaded with him wistfully, all the sorrow of waiting and hunger, of struggle and triumph in her eyes, and memory of joy and ecstasy that had been. . . . Her head fell to his shoulder, all will gone from her body, and she lay in his arms.

"Love!" she murmured; "my soul's desire, at last!" . . .

They had their luncheon there, in the sunny circle among the firs, and spoke of their two years' separation.

"And I am not going back!" Falkner cried joyously.

"You have decided already?"

"My chief has resigned, you know, — and there is a piece of work up North here he wants me for. . . . But that is not all the reason!"

Her face blanched. They had begun their journey again, and were following the ridge of the mountain in the light of the westering sun. They walked slowly side by side so that they might talk. Margaret looked up questioningly.

"You and I have always been honest — direct with each other," he said.

She nodded gravely.

"We have never slipped into things; we have looked ahead, looked it all in the face."

"Yes!" she assented proudly.

"Then we will look this in the face together. . . . I have come back for one thing — for you!"

As he drew her to him, she laid her hands on his breast and looked at him sadly.

"The other was not enough!"

"Never! — nothing could ever be enough but to have you always."

"Dearest, that I might forever give you all that you ever desired! All!" she cried out of the tenderest depth of a woman's heart, — the desire to give all, the best, to the man loved, the sacrificial triumph of woman, this offering of body and soul and life from the need to give, give, give!

"I have come for one thing," he said hoarsely; "for you!"

She drew herself back from his arms unconsciously and said: —

"You must understand. . . . Dearest, I love you as I never loved you before. Not even when you came to me and gave me life. . . . I long to give you all — for always. But, dearest, for us it — cannot be."

"I do not understand," Falkner protested. "You think I am not free, — but I have come to tell you —"

"No, — listen first! And you and I will be one in this as we always have been one since the beginning. . . . When we went away together those days, we climbed the heights — you gave me my soul — it was born in your arms. And I have lived since with that life. And it has grown, grown — I see so much farther now into the infinite that we reached out to then. And I see clearly what has been in the past — oh, so clearly!"

"But why should that divide us now?"

"Listen! . . . Now it is different. He, my husband, would be between us always, as he was not then. I took what I needed then — took it fiercely. I never thought of him. But now I see how all along from the beginning I withdrew my hand from him. Perhaps that was the reason he went so desperately to pieces at the end. I could not have made him a strong man. But, dearest, he died utterly alone, disgraced in his own heart — alone! That is awful to think of!"

"It was his nature," Falkner protested sternly.

"It was his nature to be weak and small and petty. . . . But don't you see that I deserted him — I took back my hand! And now I should let you take back yours. . . . Yes, — I have changed, dearest. I have come to understand that the weak must be the burden of the strong — always!"

Falkner's lean face grew hard with the lines of hunger, — repressed but not buried, — the lines of inner strife. In a dry voice he said: —

"I thought that we had settled all that once, Margaret."

"One cannot settle such things so. . . . It has come to

me — the light — slowly, so slowly. And it is not all clear yet. But I see a larger segment of the circle than we could see two years ago." . . .

Without more words they began to descend towards the village. The hills that compassed their view were rimmed with the green and saffron lights of the afterglow. Their summits were sharp edged as if drawn by a titanic hand against a sea of glowing color. But within the forests on the slope there was already the gloom of night. Slowly the words fell from his lips: —

"I will never believe it! Why should a man and a woman who can together make the world brave and noble and full of joy be parted — by anything? A sacrifice that gives nothing to any one else!"

That cry was the fruit of the man's two years' battle alone with his heart. To that point of hunger and desire he had come from the day when they parted, when they made their great refusal. . . .

Both remembered that evening, two years before, when they had sailed back to the land — to part. They remembered the Portuguese ship that was weighing anchor for a distant port. As they looked at it wistfully, he had said, "And why not? And she had replied with shining eyes, "Because we love too much for that." Then he had accepted, — they had found the heights and on them they would remain, apart in the world of effort, always together in their own world which they had created. Then he had understood and gone away to his struggle. Now he could live no longer in that shadowy union: he had come back to possess his desire.

With her it had been different, this separation. . . . How much more she loved now than then! Her love had entered into her these two years, deeper to the depths of her being, stronger as she was stronger in body, more vital. It had given her strength even for the great denial to him, — and this she realized miserably; their love had given her strength, had unfolded her soul to herself until she had come to large new spheres of feeling, and could see dimly others beyond. While with him it had burned away all else but one human, personal want. He thought to go back now to their island in the sea, — as if one could ever go back in this life, even to the fairest point of the past! . . .

She laid a caressing hand on his arm.

"Don't you see, dearest, that we could never come out again on the heights where we were?"

From the sombre mood of his defeat, he said bitterly:—

"So it was all wrong, — a mistake, a delusion!"

"Never!" she flashed. "Never! Not for one moment since we parted would I give up what has been between us. . . . You do not understand, dearest! . . . Life began for me there. If it had not been for that, this could not be now. But one journeys on from knowledge to knowledge."

"Then why not other heights — together?"

And she whispered back very low:—

"Because we should kill it! All of it . . . now that I see it would be base. We have risen above that glory, — yes, *both* of us! We have risen above it, divine as it was. It would be no longer divine, my dearest. I should be but a woman's body in your arms, my lover. . . . Now we shall rise always, always, together — each in the other!"

The lights of the village shone just below them. A sleigh went tinkling loudly along the road, with the voices of talking people in the dark night. Margaret stopped before they reached the road, and turning to him put her arms about his neck and drew him to her.

"Don't you know that I shall be yours always? Ah, dearest, dearest!"

In the passionate tenderness of her kiss he felt the fulness of victory and defeat. She was his, but never to be his. He kissed her burning eyes.

CHAPTER LXIII

SUPPER at the Shorts' was the pleasantest time of the day. The small, plain room, warm and light and homely, the old blacksmith's contented face as he sat at the head of his table and served the food, glancing now and then with a meaning look at his wife, mutely talking with her, and the two friends in light summer dresses chatting of the day, — it was all so remote from the bustle of life, so simply peaceful that to Isabelle supper at the Shorts' was the symbol of Grosvenor life as much as Renault's hospital. It was the hour when the blacksmith's ripest wisdom and best humor came to the surface; when, having pounded existence and lassitude out of iron and wood in the little shop down the street, he relaxed the muscles of his tired body and looked over to his wife and found the world good.

"Theirs is the figure of perfect marriage," Margaret had said; "interlocked activity, with emotional satisfaction. Mrs. Short's climax of the day is her hot supper laid before her lord. . . . Do you see how they talk without words across the table? They know what the other is thinking always. So the Shorts have found what so many millions miss, — a real marriage!"

To-night when Falkner came back with Margaret for supper, this note of perfect domesticity was at its best. Mr. Short had gone to the cellar for a bottle of cider wine in honor of the guest from Panama, and his wife rustled in black silk. She had made a marvellous cake that sat proudly on the sideboard, looking down on the feast. The blacksmith carved the hot meat, and in his gentle voice talked to the stranger.

"You must have found it hard work when the snow got soft on the hills. As I felt the sun coming down warm, I said to myself, 'Those shoes will seem as big as cart-wheels to him.' . . . You were up by Belton's? There's big timber in there still, back on the mountain, where they found it too hard to get out. You come across a great log now and then that looks like a fallen giant. . . . But I remember on my father's farm, twenty miles from here in the back country, when I was a boy" —

He held the carving-knife suspended above the steak, lost in the vista of years. These anecdotal attacks worried his wife, who feared for her hot food; but the others encouraged him.

— "there were trees lying on the ground in the pasture rotting, that must have been five feet through at the butt end. I used to sit atop of them and think how big they would have been standing up with their tops waving. . . . Yes, wood was cheap in those days." . . .

Isabelle, as she watched Margaret and Falkner, was puzzled. Margaret in her rose-colored tea-gown was like a glowing coal, but Falkner seemed glum and listless. "Tired, poor man!" Mrs. Short thought, and the blacksmith had full scope for his memories. But gradually Falkner became interested and asked questions. As a boy he had lived in the country, and in the atmosphere of the Shorts the warm memories of those days revived, and he talked of his own country up in the "big timber" of Michigan. Margaret, resting her head on her hands, watched his eager eyes. She knew, so well, what was in his mind below his memories. 'These good people have all this! these simple people, just the plain, elementary, ordinary things of life, — a peaceful shelter, warmth, comfort, happiness. And we, she and I, might have this and so much more, — a thousand interests and ecstasies, but we who are still young must live on in cheerless separation, missing all this — and for what?'

She read it in his eyes. She knew the man-nature, how it develops when middle life comes, — the desire for home, for the settled and ordered spot, the accustomed shelter. When the zest of the wandering days no longer thrills, the adventurous and experimenting impulse is spent, that is what man, even a passionate lover, craves to find in a woman, — peace and the ordered life. And she could give it to this man, who had never had it, — companionship and comradeship as well, and make an inner spot of peace where the man might withdraw from the fighting world. Oh, she knew how to fit his life like a spirit! . . .

When Falkner rose to leave, Margaret slipped on a long coat, saying: —

"I will show you the way to the Inn; you would never find it alone!"

As she took his arm outside, he asked dully: —

"Which way now?"

"This is our way first," and Margaret turned up the road away from the village, past the doctor's house. They walked in silence. When she pointed out Renault's hospital, Falkner looked at it indifferently. "Queer sort of place for a hospital. What kind of a man is he?"

"A queer sort of man," Margaret replied.

Beyond the hospital the road mounted the hillside, passing through dark woods. Beneath their feet the frozen snow crunched icily.

"Good people that blacksmith and his wife," Falkner remarked. "That was the kind of thing I dreamed it would be, — a place, a spot, of our own, no matter how plain and small, and some one to look across the table as that gray-haired woman looks at the old fellow, as if she knew him to the roots. . . . I hope it will be some time before they get the apartment hotel in Grosvenor! . . . A man has his work," he mused.

"Yes, the man has his work."

"And a woman her children."

"And the woman her children."

"So that is what life comes to in the middle distance, — the man has his work and the woman her children. . . . But one doesn't marry for that! There is something else."

Her clasp tightened on his arm, and he turned quickly

and taking the fingers in his hand separated them one by one between his. In the starlight he could see the fine line of her face from brow to pointed chin, and he could hear her breathing.

"This, this!" he muttered fiercely. "Your touch, so; your look, so — your voice in my ear — what makes it magic for me? Why not another? Any other — why *this?* To go to the heart of one! Yours — which will never be mine."

The sweep of dominating desire, the male sense of mastery and will to possess, surged up again in the man, tempting him to break the barriers she had erected between them, to take her beyond her scruples, and carry her with him, as the strong man of all time has carried away the woman whom he would have for mate.

She held her face upwards for his kiss, and as she trembled once more in the arms of the man she had consented to, there was answered in her the mystery he had propounded, — 'Because of the *I* within me that he loves and respects, because of that *I* which is mine and no other's, not even his, — therefore he loves me of all the world, — I am his soul!' . . .

It was all snowy upland near the crest of the hill. They leaned against a rock, close together, and listened to the stillness around them, his arm beneath her cloak drawing her closer, closer to him, away from herself. In the forgetfulness of joy she seemed mounting, floating, high up above all, the man's desire bearing her on wings away from the earth with its failure and sorrow, up to the freedom she had thirsted for, up to fulfilment. . . .

Now his eyes, once more victorious, looked close into hers, and something within her spoke, — low and sweet and far away. . . .

"I love you, dearest! I will be yours, as you will have me, — as we were those other days, and more. Much more! I will be your slave, your mistress, — to do with as you wish, to take and leave. . . . There can be no marriage, none. Will you have me? Will you take me like that? To be your thing? Will you . . . and throw me away when I am used and finished for you? . . . I will give you all! Now! . . . And when the time comes that must come, I will go out."

Then, at last, the man saw! She would give all, even her own soul, if he would take it. But first, there was something he must kill, — there in her body within his close embrace, with her breath on his face, — something she offered him as a last gift to kill. . . . The body was but a symbol, a piece of clothing, a rag. . . . So he understood, and after a long time his arms loosened about her.

"I see," he whispered, and as he kissed her lips, "Never that!"

The summit of the mountain loomed above them, — the Altar. Margaret as they turned towards the village stretched her arms upwards to the Altar, — there where she had lain as it were naked for the sacrifice before the man she loved. "Come!" he said gently.

They had kissed for the last time.

As they approached the Inn at the farther end of the village, Falkner was saying in reply to her question: —

"Yes, after I have seen something of Mildred, I shall go to Washington to join the chief. He will want me to live up in the country at the works. I shall like that. . . . The dam will take three years at least, I suppose. It must be like the work of the ancient Egyptians, for all time and colossal. I wish the work might last out my day!"

The woman's heart tightened. Already he had swung, as she willed, to the one steadfast star in his firmament, — work, accomplishment, — accepting the destiny she had willed, to struggle upwards apart from her to that high altar where they both had stood this night. . . .

When Margaret entered the house, Isabelle's light was still burning and her door was open. She paused as she passed to her room, her coat flung back revealing the soft rose color beneath, and in her white face her eyes shone softly.

"Rob leaves to-morrow morning by the early train," she remarked.

"So soon!"

"Yes, — for the West."

And then Isabelle knew, as Margaret had promised.

CHAPTER LXIV

Dr. Renault's private office was a large, square room with a north window that gave a broad view of the pointed Albany mountains. Along the walls were rows of unpainted wooden shelves on which were stacked books and pamphlets. One small piece of bronze on the shelf above the fireplace — a copy of the seated Mercury in the Naples museum — was the sole ornament in the room. A fire was dying on the hearth this gray March afternoon, and flashes of light from a breaking log revealed the faces of Renault and Isabelle, standing on opposite sides of his work table. They had stood like this a long time while the gray day came to an end outside and the trees lashed by the north wind bent and groaned. Isabelle was passing the office, after dinner, on some errand, and the doctor had called her. Accident had led to this long talk, the longest and the deepest she had had with Renault. One thing had touched another until she had bared to him her heart, had laid before his searching gaze the story of her restless, futile life. And the words that he had spoken had dropped like hot metal upon her wounds and burned until her hands trembled as they leaned upon his desk. . . .

"The discipline of life!" he had said. The phrase was hateful to her. It stirred within her all the antagonism of her generation to the creed of her people, to the Puritan ideal, cold, narrow, repressive. And yet Renault was far from being a Puritan. But he, too, believed in the "discipline of life." And again when she had confessed her ambitions for "a broad life," "for experience," he had said: "Egotism is the pestilence of our day, — the sort of base intellectual egotism that seeks to taste for the sake of tasting. Egotism is rampant. And worst of all it has corrupted the women, in whom should lie nature's great conservative element. So our body social is rotten with intellectual egotism. Yes, I mean just what you have prided yourself on, — Culture, Education, Individuality, Cleverness, — 'leading your own lives,' Refinement, Experience, Development, call it what you will, — it is the same, the inturning of the spirit to cherish self. Not one of all you women has a tenth of the experience my mother had, who, after bringing up her family of eight, at fifty-seven went to the town school to learn Latin, because before she had not had the time." . . . To some defence of her ideal by Isabelle, he retorted with fine scorn: —

"Oh, I know the pretty impression our American women make in the eyes of visiting foreigners, — so 'clever,' so 'fascinating,' so 'original,' so 'independent,' and such 'charm'! Those are the words, aren't they? While their dull husbands are 'money-getters.' They at least are doers, not talkers! . . .

"Do you know what you are, women like you, who have money and freedom to 'live your own lives'? You are sexless; you haven't nature's great apology for the animal, — desire. Such women sin, when they sin, with their minds. Great God! I had rather those broad-hipped Italian peasant women of Calabria, with solid red-brown flesh, bred bastards for the country than have these thin, anæmic, nervous, sexless creatures, with their 'souls' and their 'charm,' marry and become mothers! What have you done to the race? The race of blond giants from the forests of the north? Watch the avenue in New York!"

Again, — "So what have you made of marriage, 'leading your own lives'? You make marriage a sort of intelligent and intellectual prostitution — and you develop divorce. The best among you — those who will not marry unless the man can arouse their 'best selves' — will not bear children even then. And you think you have the right to choose again when your so-called souls have played you false the first time. . . . And man, what of him? You leave him to his two gross temptations, — Power and Lust. Man is given you to protect, and you drive him into the market-place, where he fights for your ease, and then relaxes in the refined sensualities you offer him as the reward for his toil. With the fall of man into the beast's trough must come the degradation of women. They cannot travel apart; they must pull together. What have *you* done for your husband?" He turned sharply on Isabelle. "Where is he now? where has he been all these years? What is he doing this hour? Have you nursed his spirit, sharpened his sword? . . . I am not speaking of the dumb ones far down in the mass, nor of the humdrum philistines that still make homes, have traces of the nest-instinct left; but of you, *you*, — the developed intelligences who flatter yourselves that you lead because you are free to do as you like. By your minds you are betrayed!"

Before the blast of his scorching words Isabelle saw her ambitions shrivel into petty nothings, — all the desires from her first married days to find a suitable expression of her individuality, her wish to escape Torso, her contempt for St. Louis, her admiration for Cornelia Woodyard, her seeking for "interesting" people and a cultivated and charming background for herself, and last of all her dissatisfaction in her marriage because it failed to evoke in her the passion she desired. It was a petty story, she felt, — ashamed before Renault's irony.

He knew her life, more than she had told him, much more. He knew *her*. He read below the surface and had known her from the first hour they had met. It was all true, — she had wanted many things that now she saw were futile. She had accepted her marriage as failure — almost with relief, as an excuse for her restlessness. Yes, she had made mistakes; what was worse, was a mistake herself! Crushed with this sense of futility, of failure, she cried: —

"But we are caught in the stream when we are young and eager. The world seems so big and rich if you but reach out your hand to take."

"And from its feast you took — what?"

She was silent, self-convicted; for she had taken chaff! . . . Nevertheless, it was not dead within her — the self. It cried out under Renault's pitiless scorn for satisfaction, for life. The rebellious surge of desire still suffocated her at times. There was beauty, the loveliness of the earth, the magic wonder of music and art, — all the clamor of emotion for an expression of self. And love? Ah, that was dead for her. But the life within, the self, still hungered for possession at times more fiercely than ever. Why should it be killed at her age? Why were they not good, these hungry desires, this fierce self that beat in her blood for recognition? The conquering, achieving SELF! That was the spirit of her race, to see and take that which was good in their eyes, to feed the SELF with all that the world contained of emotions, ideas, experience; to be big, and strong, and rich, — to have Power! That was what life had meant for her ancestors ever since the blond race emerged from their forests to conquer. All else was death to the self, was merely sentimental deception, a playing at resignation. . . .

As if he traced her fast thoughts, Renault said: —

"A house divided against itself — "

"But even if I have failed — "

"Failed because you did not look deep enough within!"

Renault's voice insensibly softened from his tone of harsh invective as he added: —

"And now you know what I meant when I said that a neurasthenic world needed a new religion!"

So he had remembered her, — knew her all the time!

"But you can't get it because you need it — "

"Yes, because you feel the need! . . . Not the old religion of abnegation, the impossible myths that come to us out of the pessimistic East, created for a relief, a soporific, a means of evasion, — I do not mean that as religion. But another faith, which abides in each one of us, if we look for it. We rise with it in the morning. It is a faith in life apart from our own personal fate. . . . Because we live on the surface, we despair, we get sick. Look below into the sustaining depths beyond desire, beyond self, to the depths, — and you will find it. It will uplift you. . . . When you wake in the morning, there will come to you some mysterious power that was not there before, some belief, some hope, some faith. Grasp it! . . . When the clouds lift, the physical clouds and the mental clouds, then appears the Vision and the knowledge. They are the truth from the depths within, — the voice of the spirit that lives always. And by that voice man himself lives or dies, as he wills, — by the voice of the spirit within."

So as the drear day of the dying winter drew to a close, as the ashes powdered on the hearth and the face of Renault became obscure in the twilight, the dim outlines of a great meaning rose before her, reconciling all. . . . The Vision that abides within apart from the teasing phantasmagoria of sense, the Vision that comes, now dim, now vivid, as the flash of white light in the storm, the Vision towards which mankind blindly reaches, the Vision by which he may learn to live and endure all!

And this Vision was all that really mattered, — to see it, to follow where it pointed the way!

. . . "The waste in life, the wrong steps, the futile years!" she murmured.

"Rather the cost, the infinite cost of human souls — and their infinite value once born," Renault corrected. "Do not distress yourself about what to do, the claims of this or that. The thing to do will always be clear, once you trust yourself, seek wholly the Vision. And as for beauty and satisfaction and significance, — it is infinite in every moment of every life — when the eyes are once open to see!"

There was the sound of footsteps outside, and Isabelle moved to the door.

"So," Renault concluded, putting his hands on her shoulders, "it is not the End but the Beginning. And always so, — a mysterious journey, this life, with countless beginnings.

. . . We go out into the night. But the light comes — when we forget to see ourselves."

The wind raged in the trees outside, sweeping across the earth, tearing the forest, cleansing and breaking its repose, preparing for the renewal to come. Like a mighty voice it shouted to man; like the whirlwind it shook his earth. . . . For the first time since Vickers lay dead in the dawn of the June morning Isabelle could bear to look at the past, — to accept it calmly as part of herself out of which she had lived, in recognition of that beginning within.

CHAPTER LXV

"They seem to be in such a pother, out in the world," Isabelle remarked to Margaret, as she turned over the leaves of her husband's letter. "The President is calling names, and a lot of good people are calling names back. And neither side seems to like being called names. John doesn't like it, and he calls names. And they sulk and won't play marbles. It all sounds like childish squabbling."

Margaret, who was unusually absent-minded this evening, sighed: —

"So many desires of men, always struggling at cross-purposes! I haven't read the papers for months! They don't seem real up here, somehow. What's happening?"

"I haven't opened my papers, either. Look there!" Isabelle pointed to a pile of wrapped newspapers in the corner. "But I must go through them and see what John is grumbling about. It isn't like John to grumble at anything." Then she read from her husband's letter: "The President in his besotted vanity and colossal ignorance has succeeded in creating trouble that twenty Presidents won't be able to settle. The evils which he may have corrected are nothing to those he has brought upon innocent people. . . . So far as our road is concerned, this prejudiced and partisan investigation, instigated by the newspapers and notoriety seekers, will do no great harm. . . . I suppose you have seen the garbled press account of my cross-examination, — don't let it disturb you." . . .

Isabelle looked up.

"I wonder what he means by that! 'My cross-examination'? It must be something rather out of the ordinary to stir John to such expression, — 'Besotted vanity and colossal ignorance.' Whew!"

After Margaret left, Isabelle began abstractedly to strip the wrappers from the newspapers, glancing at the thickest headlines:—

BANK FAILURE — SUICIDE OF BANK PRESIDENT — SENSATIONAL DIVORCE, etc.

Here it was at last:—

THE ATLANTIC AND PACIFIC ON THE GRILL!! INVESTIGATION OF THE GREAT RAILROAD'S COAL BUSINESS

Isabelle scanned the newspaper column indifferently. As Margaret had said, the squabbles of the great, conglomerate, writhing business world seemed remote indeed. They had never been actual to her, though she was the daughter of a merchant. In the Colonel's house, as in most American homes of the well-to-do, the newspaper was regarded as a necessary evil, largely composed of lies and garbled rumors. It was taken for granted that almost everything to be seen in print was vitiated by sensational falsehood, and so far as "business" — mystic word! — was concerned, all "news" was pure fabrication. This sceptical attitude had been intensified by John, who regarded any criticism of the actions of capital as dictated by envy, as "unpatriotic," aimed at the efforts of the most energetic and respectable element in the community; moreover, "socialistic," that is, subversive of the established order, etc. According to John the ablest men would always "get on top," no matter what laws were made. And getting on top meant that they would do what they wished with their own, *i.e.* capital. Thus without thinking about it Isabelle had always assumed that men in general were envious of their betters. Sometimes, to be sure, she had suspected that this simple theory might be incomplete, that her husband and his friends might be "narrow." Some people whose opinion she respected even approved of the President's policy in seeking to curb the activities of capital. But she had slight interest in the vexed question, and skipped all references to industrial turmoil in her reading.

So to-night her eyes slipped carelessly down the column, which was not intelligible without previous accounts, and she continued to rip the wrappers from newspapers, letting the stiff parcels of paper drop to the floor. She was thinking of what Renault had said, bits of his phrases constantly floating through her mind. If he had only been more precise! She wanted to know *what* to do, — here, now. He had said: "Wait! It will all be clear. It makes little difference what it is. You will find the path." With her eager temperament that was all baffling. Margaret had found her path, — had seen her Vision, and it had brought to her peace. Her restless, bitter nature had been wonderfully changed into something exquisitely calm and poised, so that her very presence, silent in the room, could be felt. . . .

Isabelle's eyes caught the headline in the paper she was opening: —

OFFICIALS OF THE ATLANTIC AND PACIFIC BEFORE THE FEDERAL GRAND JURY

JOHN S. LANE, THIRD VICE-PRESIDENT OF THE ROAD, INDICTED

Isabelle's mind suddenly woke to the present, and she began to read breathlessly: "As a result of the recent investigations by the Interstate Commerce Commission of the relation between the Atlantic and Pacific and certain coal properties, officials of that system have been examined by a special Grand Jury, and it is rumored," etc. Isabelle glanced at the date of the paper. It was a month old! Even now, perhaps, her husband was on trial or had already been tried for illegal acts in the conduct of his business, and she knew nothing about it! Another paper had the item: "This time the district attorney under direction from Washington will not be content to convict a few rate clerks or other underlings. The indictment found against one of the vice-presidents of this great corporation that has so successfully and impudently defied the law will create a profound impression upon the whole country. It is a warning to the corporation criminals that the President and his advisers are not to be frightened by calamity-howlers, and will steadfastly pursue their policy of going higher up in their effort to bring the real offenders before the courts. The coming trial before federal Judge Barstow will be followed with intense interest," etc., etc.

Isabelle rapidly uncovered the remaining newspapers, arranging them in the order of dates, and then glanced through every column in search of news about the trial, even to the editorial comments on the action of the Grand Jury. The earlier papers that had the account of the investigation by the Commission had been destroyed unread, but she inferred from what she saw that the affair rose from the complaint of independent mine-owners in Missouri and Indiana that they were discriminated against by the railroad. The federal authorities were trying to establish the fact of conspiracy on the part of the Atlantic and Pacific to control the coal business along its lines. There were hints of an "inside ring," whose operations tended to defraud both stockholders and public. . . .

As she read the wordy columns of report and suspicion, there suddenly shot into Isabelle's mind a memory of a Sunday afternoon in Torso when she and John had ridden by Mr. Freke's mines and John had said in reply to her question, "Mr. Freke and I do business together." Mr. Freke was the president of the Pleasant Valley Coal Company, — a name that occurred often in the newspaper report, the name which had been spread across the black sheds she had seen that Sunday afternoon. Now she remembered, also, that she had had to sign certain papers for transfer of stock when John had sold something to put the money — into coal. And last of all she remembered at the very beginning of her life in Torso the face of that man in her husband's office and how he had begged for cars, and his cry, "My God! I shall go bankrupt!" Out of it all — the newspaper paragraphs, the legal terms, the editorial innuendoes, the memories — there was shaped something like a coherent picture of what this dispute really meant, and her husband's concern in it.

It was now midnight. Isabelle's mind was stung to keen apprehension. She did not know whether John was guilty of what the government was seeking to prove him guilty. She could not judge whether the government was justified in bringing suit against the railroad and its officials. There was doubtless the other side, John's side. Perhaps it was a technical crime, a formal slip, as she had been told it was in other cases where the government had prosecuted railroads. That would come out clearly at the trial, of course. But the fact that stared her in the face was that her husband was to be *tried* — perhaps was on trial this very day — and she did not even know it! She reached for the papers again and searched for the date of the trial of the coal cases in the federal court. It was to open the nineteenth of March — it was now the twenty-second! And the last paper to reach her was the issue of the eighteenth. The trial had already begun.

Isabelle paced the narrow breadth of her chamber. Her husband was on trial, and he had not written her. His last letters, which she had destroyed, had betrayed signs of irritation, disturbance. . . . Renault's charge, "The curse of our day is egotism," rang in her ears. She had been so much concerned over her own peace of mind, her own soul, that she had had no room for any perception — even for the man with whom she had lived side by side for ten years! Love or not, satisfaction or not in marriage, it must mean something to live for ten years of life with another human being, eat bread with him, sleep under the same roof with him, bear a child to him. . . . And there in her silent room Isabelle began to see that there was something in marriage other than emotional satisfaction, other than conventional cohabitation. "Men are given to you women to protect — the best in them!" "You live off their strength, — what do you give them? Sensuality or spirit?" Her husband was a stranger; she had given him nothing but one child.

Isabelle opened her trunks and began to pack. There was a train south from White River at eight-thirty, which connected with the New York express. Molly could follow later with the governess. . . . She flung the things loosely into the trunks, her mind filled with but one idea. She must get to St. Louis as soon as possible. 'John — my husband — is being tried out there for dishonest conduct in his business, and we are so far apart that he doesn't even mention it in his letters!'

At last, the packing over, she crouched by the embers and tried to warm her numb hands. This burst of decided will which had made her swiftly prepare for the journey gave out for the moment. . . . What should she do out there, after all? She would merely be in the way and annoy John. And with a strength that startled her came the answer, 'After all, we are man and wife; he is my husband, and he is in trouble!'

It would not be possible to see Renault before she left. Well, he had spoken his message to her, having chosen his own time. And already his prophecy was coming about. The thing to do was plain. The Vision was there, and the voice had spoken out of the depths. She was extraordinarily calm, as if raised above doubt, the confusing calls of personal consideration. There might be disgrace to come for her husband. There was the undoubted miserable failure of her marriage, — the strong possibility of her husband's impassive coldness at her futile flight to his side, at this hour. But there was no Fear! . . . And serenely she dropped into sleep.

CHAPTER LXVI

MARGARET and the children drove down to White River with her the next morning. Just as Margaret had previously opposed her restless desire to leave Grosvenor, with gentle suggestions and quiet persuasion, so this time she accepted her going as inevitable.

"But you may come back; I wish it might be!" was all she said, not very hopefully.

Isabelle shook her head. She made no plans, but she felt that no matter what the outcome of the trial might be it was hardly probable that her path would lead back to this retreat. As she got into the sleigh she looked up the hillside to the hospital, its many windows glistening in the rising sun, its severe outlines sharp against the snowy field, and her eyes roved on to the dusky firs in the valley, up to the purple hilltop of the Altar, on to the distant peaks rising behind, with crests already bare. Her eyes were misty as she drove through the familiar village street, past the blacksmith's shop, where Sol Short waved a second good-by with a glowing bar of steel caught from the forge, on towards the Pass and the descent, — it was a haven of peace, this hillside village! Within that circle of snowy hills, in the silent beauty of the Northern winter, she had lived more, lived deeper, than anywhere else in the world. But she should not come back, — there would be no place for that. Grosvenor had given its benediction, — the hills and the woods, the snowy expanses and frozen brooks, the sunsets and starlit firmament, — the blacksmith's simple content and Renault's beacon lights, Margaret's peace, — all had done their work in her. As the lumbering sleigh dragged over the Pass, she gazed back to fix its image in her mind forever. The fresh March wind blew in her face, chill but full of distant promise, as if in its sweep from the north it had heard the tidings of spring, the stirrings deep below snow and frost. And the sky shimmered cloudless from horizon to horizon, a soft blue. . . .

The agitations before and the struggle to come were interspaced by this lofty place of Peace — wherein she had found herself!

The frost-covered train from the north drew up at the platform in a cloud of steam. The fireman, a lad of eighteen, with a curl waving from under his cap, was leaning far out of the cab, smoking a cigarette and looking up at the snowy mountains just visible from White River. He was careless, — alive, and content this fine morning, — his grimy arms bare on the sill of the cab window, the broad earth and its hills spread before him. As the engine shot past, he looked down at Isabelle, curiously, and then up to the mountains again, as if his life were complete enough. A careless figure of the human routine of the world, endlessly moving, changing, energizing, functioning in its destined orbit! And all lives were tied together in the fine mesh of circumstance, — one destiny running into another as the steel band of railroad ran on and on into distant places, just as the lad in the engine cab was somehow concerned with the whole human system that ended, perchance, in the courtroom at St. Louis. . . .

Isabelle took Margaret in her arms and holding her close, as if she would seize her very spirit, kissed her.

"Tell the doctor," she said, "that I am beginning to understand — a little."

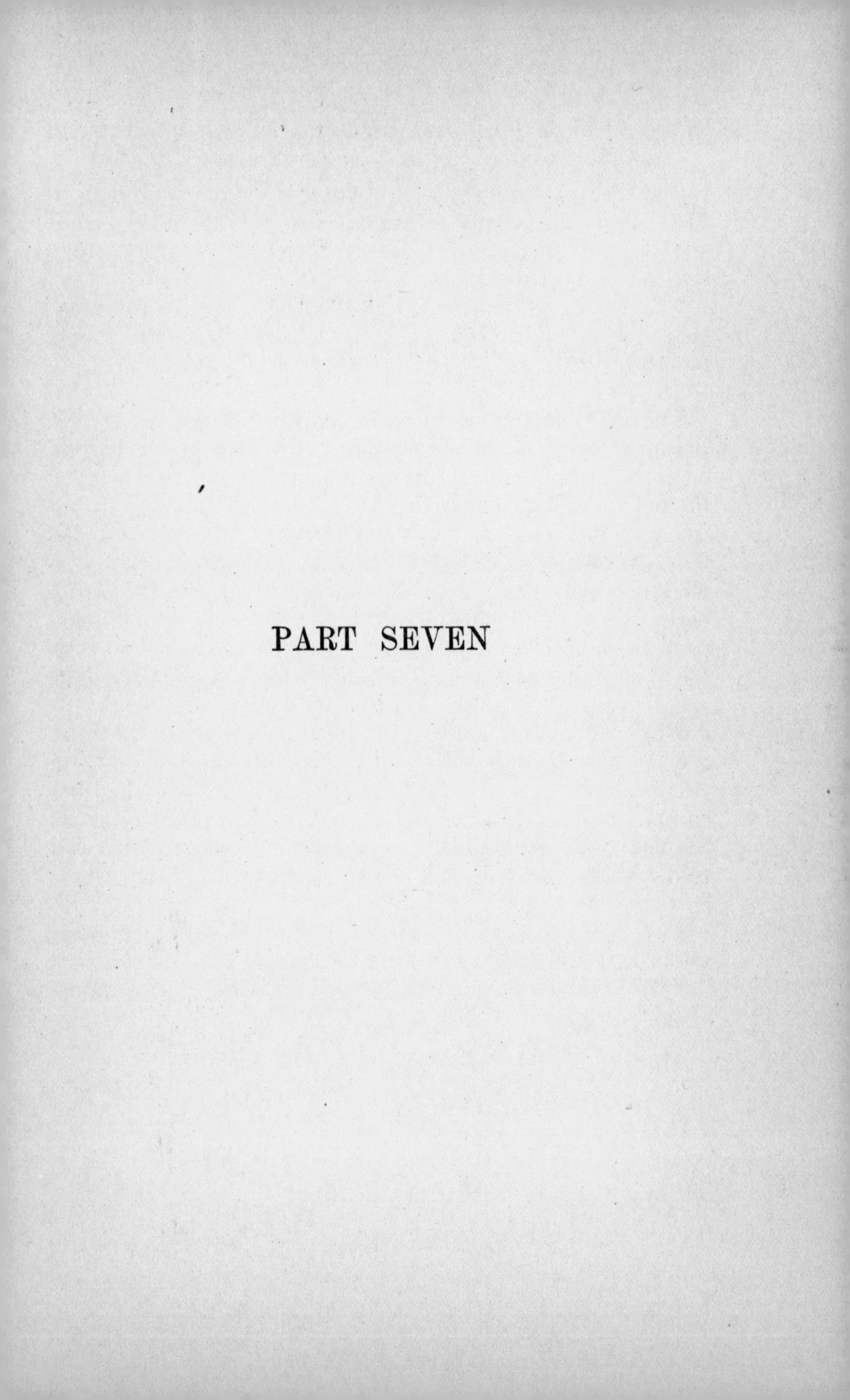

PART SEVEN

CHAPTER LXVII

What is marriage? At least in these United States where men once dreamed they would create a new society of ideal form based on that poetic illusion, "All men" — presumably women, too! — "are born free and equal!"

Yes, what has marriage been, — first among the pioneers pushing their way to new land through the forest, their women at their sides, or in the ox-cart behind them with the implements of conquest, — pushing out together into the wide wilderness, there to fight side by side, to tame Nature and win from her a small circle of economic order for their support? Together these two cut the trees, build the cabin, clear the land and sow it, thus making shelter and food. And then the Woman draws apart to bring *her* increment, the children, to fight with them, to follow in their steps. In that warfare against stubborn Nature and Chaos, against the Brute, against the Enemy in whatever form, the Man and the Woman are free and equal, — they stand together and win or lose together, live or die in the life-long battle. And the end? If they triumph in this primitive struggle for existence, they have won a few acres of cleared land for the harvest, a habitation, and food, and children who will take up from their hands the warfare for life, to win further concessions from Nature, a wider circle of order from chaos. This is the marriage type of the pioneer, — a primitive, body-wracking struggle of two against all, a perfect type, elemental but whole, — and this remains the large pattern of marriage to-day wherever sound. Two bodies, two souls are united for the life struggle to wring order out of chaos, — physical and spiritual.

Generations are born and die. The circles grow wider,

more diversified, overlap, intersect. But the type remains of that primitive wilderness struggle of the family. Then comes to this breeding society the Crisis. There came to us the great War, — the conflict of ideals. Now Man leaves behind in the home the Woman and her children, and goes forth alone to fight for the unseen, — the Idea that is in him, that is stronger than woman or child, greater than life itself. Giving over the selfish struggle with the Brute, he battles against articulate voices. And the Woman is left to keep warm the forsaken nest, to nurse the brood there, to wait and want, perchance to follow after her man to the battle-field and pick out her dead and bear it back to burial. She, too, has her part in the struggle; not merely the patient, economic part, but the cherishing and the shaping of man's impulse, — the stuff of his soul that sends him into the battle-field. Alone she cannot fight; her Man is her weapon. He makes to prevail those Ideals which she has given him with her embraces. This also is the perfect type of Marriage, — comradeship, togethership, — and yet larger than before because the two share sacrifice and sorrow and truth, — things of the spirit. Together they wage War for others.

And there follows a third condition of Marriage. The wilderness reduced, society organized, wars fought, there is the time of peace. Now Man, free to choose his task, goes down into the market-place to sell his force, and here he fights with new weapons a harder fight; while his Woman waits behind the firing line to care for him, — to equip him and to hoard his pelf. On the strength and wisdom of her commissariatship the fate of this battle in good part depends. Of such a nature was Colonel Price's marriage. "He made the money, I saved it," Harmony Price proudly repeated in the after-time. "We lived our lives together, your mother and I," her husband said to their daughter. It was *his* force that won the dollars, made the economic position, and *her* thrift and willingness to forego present ease that created future plenty. Living thus together for an economic end, saving the surplus of their energies, they were prosperous — and they were happy. The generation of money-earners after the War, when the country already largely reclaimed began to bear fruit abundantly, were happy, if in no greatly idealistic manner, yet peacefully, contentedly happy, and usefully preparing the way for the upward step of humanity to a little nearer realization of that poetic illusion, — the brotherhood of man.

In all these three stages of the marriage state, the union of Man and Woman is based on effort in common, together; not on sentiment, not on emotion, not on passion, not on individual gratification of sense or soul. The two are partners in living, and the fruit of their bodies is but another proof of partnership. . . .

And now emerges another economic condition, the inexorable successor of the previous one, and another kind of Marriage. Society is complexly organized, minutely interrelated; great power here and great weakness there, vast accumulations of surplus energies, hoarded goods, many possessions, — oh, a long gamut up and down the human scale! And the CHANCE, the great gamble, always dangles before Man's eyes; not the hope of a hard-won existence for woman and children, not a few acres of cleared wilderness, but a dream of the Aladdin lamp of human desires, — excitements, emotions, ecstasies, — all the world of the mind and the body. So Woman, no longer the Pioneer, no longer the defender of the house, no longer the economist, blossoms — as what? The Spender! She is the fine flower of the modern game, of the barbaric gamble. At last she is Queen and will rule. The Man has the money, and the Woman has — herself, her body and her charm. She traffics with man for what he will give, and she pays with her soul. . . . To her the man comes from the market-place soiled and worn, and lays at her feet his gain, and in return she gives him of her wit, of her handsome person, gowned and jewelled, of her beauty, of her body itself. She is Queen! She amuses her lord, she beguiles him, she whets his appetite and pushes him forth to the morrow's fight, to bring back to her more pelf, to make her greater yet. She sits idle in her cabin-palace, attended by servants, or goes forth on her errands to show herself before the world as her man's Queen. So long as she may but please this lord of hers, so long as she may hold him by her mind or her body, she will be Queen. She has found something softer than labor with her hands, easier than the pains of childbirth, — she has found the secret of rule, — mastery over her former master, the slave ruling the lord. Like the last wife of the barbarian king she is heaped with jewels and served with fine wines and foods and lives in the palace, — the favorite.

And Woman, now the mistress rather than the wife, has longings for Love. She listens to her heart, and it whispers strange fancies. "I cannot love this man whom I have married, though he feeds me and gives me of his best. My soul will have none of him, — I will not consent to live with him and bear children for him and thus be a slave. Lo, am I not a Queen, to give and take back, to swear and then swear again? I will divorce this man who can no longer thrill me, and I will take another dearer to my heart, — and thus I shall be nobler than I was. I shall be a person with a soul of my own. To have me man must win me not once, but daily. For marriage without the love of my soul is beastly." So she cheats herself with fine phrases and shirks. Small comradeship here! Marriage to this woman is a state of personal gratification, the best bargain she can make with man. . . .

To this state has come the honorable condition of marriage in a country where "men" — and surely women! — "are born free and equal." The flower of successful womanhood — those who have bargained shrewdly — are to be found overfed, overdressed, sensualized, in great hotels, on mammoth steamers and luxurious trains, rushing hither and thither on idle errands. They have lost their prime function: they will not or they cannot get children. They are free! As never women were before. And these wives are the custodians of men, not merely of their purses but of their souls. They whisper to them the Ideals of their hearts: "Come bring me money, and I will kiss you. Make me a name before the world, and I will noise it abroad. Build me a house more splendid than other houses, set me above my sisters, and I will reflect honor on you among men for the clothes I wear and the excellent shape of my figure."

And thus, unwittingly, Woman becomes again in the revolution of the ages what she was at first, the female creature, the possession, the thing for lust and for amusement, — the cherished slave. For the death of woman's soul follows when she pays with her body, — a simple, immutable law. . . . Woman in America, splendidly free and Queen! What have you done with the men who were given into your charge? Clever, beautiful, brilliant, — our most shining prize, — but what have you done for the souls of the men given into your keeping? . . . The answer roars up from the city streets, — the most material age and the most material men and the least lovely civilization on God's earth. No longer the fighting companion at man's side, but reaching out for yourselves, after your own desires, you have become the slave of the Brute as you were before. And a neurotic slave. For when Woman is no longer comrade of man in the struggle, she is either Nothing or a — but blot the word!

Perfect justice, a complete picture of society in a civilization of eighty millions, requires many shades. The darker shades are true only of the rotting refuse, the scum of the whole. Among the married millions most are, fortunately, still struggling through the earlier types from the pioneer to the economist. But as the water runs there lies the sea beyond. From the prairie village to the city tenement, the American woman sees in marriage the fulfilment of her heart's desire, — to be Queen, to rule and not work. Thus for emancipated Woman.

And the poor creature Man, who fights for his Queen? A trained energy, a vessel of careless passion, a blind doer, dreaming great truths and seeing little ends, — Man is still abroad ranging his forest, his hunting blood up, "playing the game." There are moments when his sleep is troubled with feverish dreams in which he hears murmurs, — "The body is more than raiment," and "The soul is more than the body"; "There are other hunting-grounds, another warfare." But roused from these idle fancies he sallies forth from his cabin-palace, or his hotel apartment, or his steam-heated and childless flat into the old fray, to kill his meat and bring it home. . . . We chatter of the curse of Castle Garden, unmindful that in the dumb animal hordes, who labor and breed children, lies the future. FOR THEIRS WILL BE THE LAND, when the blond hunter of the market and his pampered female are swept into the dust heap.

CHAPTER LXVIII

In the vast eighteen-story, thousand-room New York hotel where Isabelle Lane stayed for the night on her way west, there was the usual constant bustle of arriving and departing people. The heat, the crowd, the luxury of this cliff-city with its throngs of much-dressed men and women overwhelmed Isabelle with a sense of startling unreality. It was not simply that she had been removed from the noise of city life for a number of months, secluded in the quiet of open spaces, and that the latest novelty in New York hotels contrasted sharply with primitive Grosvenor. But she found herself examining the scene, from the moment she entered the crowded foyer with its stucco-marble columns and bronze railings, its heavy hangings and warm atmosphere, with eyes that seemed to observe what was there before her for the first time. She looked at the thick rugs, the uniformed servants, the line of pale, sleek young men in the office enclosure, the swarming "guests" (according to the euphemistic slang of American hotels!), — all these women in evening gowns, much jewelled, on their way to dinner, with their attendant males; and she asked herself if it were the same world that she had always known.

The little bronze doors in the bank of elevators opened and shut, taking in and disgorging men and women, to shoot upwards to the tiers of partitioned privacy above or to hurry forth on their errands. Waiting for the hotel maid to fetch her key, Isabelle felt like a soul resurrected from a grave, come back to experience what had once been its theatre of activity and joy. She felt the tense hum of life in the activity of the clerks behind the desk, the servants hurrying on their errands, the coming and going of the horde of people, among whom watchful house detectives moved about silently. She knew that across the narrow street was another even larger cliff-city, where the same picture of life was repeating itself, and around the corner there were four or five more, and farther away dozens almost exactly like this one, — all crowded, humming with people, with the same heavy atmosphere of human beings hived together in hot air, men and women dressed like these, feeding like these in great halls, spending lavishly for comfort, pleasure, and repose! . . .

This mammoth caravansary was a symbol of the broad, riotously rich country, — a spiritual and material symbol, representing its thoughts, its ideals, its art, its beauty, its joy. Into these metropolitan cliff-cities flowed the stream of dominant, successful lives of the nation, seeking to find satisfaction for their efforts, their rightful triumph. Once Isabelle had had the child's pleasure in the hotel pageant. Later it had been an accepted convenience. Now she sat there looking on as from a great distance, and she said over and over wonderingly: "Can this be life? No, this is not life, — it is not real!"

At the news-stand near by a group of men and women were loitering, the men buying theatre tickets, the women turning over the leaves of magazines, scanning lazily the titles of novels. The magazines were stacked in rows, each with a gaudy cover, — "artistic" or designed merely to capture the eye by a blaze of color. One of the women turned the leaves of several novels, idly, with a kind of fat ennui, as if loath to be tempted even by mental dissipation. Then noting a title that had somehow lodged itself with favorable associations in her brain, she said to the girl behind the counter, "You may send this up to my room."

So the work of imagination, the picture of life, the soul of the poet creator, was slipped from the pile to be sent upwards along with the other purchases of the day, — clothes and jewellery and candy, — what the woman had desired that day. This group moved on and another took its place. The books and the magazines disappeared like the theatre tickets and the cigars and cigarettes at the neighboring stand, — feeding the maw of the multitude, which sought to tickle different groups of brain cells. Gay little books, saucy little books, cheap little books, pleasant little books, — all making their bid to certain cells in the gray matter of these sated human beings! A literature composed chiefly by women for women, — tons of wood pulp, miles of linen covers, rivers of ink, — all to feed the prevailing taste, like the ribbons, the jewels, the candy, the theatre tickets! A great age, as Mr. Gossom, swelling with pride, would have said, and a great people, that has standardized its pleasures and has them marketed in convenient packages for all tastes! An age of women's ideals, a literature by women for women!...

Isabelle bought a copy of Mr. Gossom's patriotic magazine for the People, and turned its fresh pages with a curiosity to see what it was like, and who was writing now. The sentimental novel by the popular English novelist that she had looked at when it first appeared came to its conclusion in this number. And it not having met with the expected popular approval, for all its sentiment, Mr. Gossom had abandoned the idyllic in favor of a startling series of articles on "Our National Crimes," plentifully and personally illustrated. Mr. Gossom would have preferred to prolong the sentimental note, — "pleasant reading," as he called it; personally he did not approve of hanging up the nation's wash in the front yard, for he himself was an investor in corporations. But what could he do? It was his business to give the People what the People wanted. And just now they wanted to be shocked and outraged by revelations of business perfidy. Another six months, perhaps, when the public was tired of contemplating rascality, the editor would find something sweet, full of country charm and suburban peace, to feed them. . . . On the title-page there were the old names and some new ones, but the same grist, — a "homely" story of "real life" among the tenements, a "humorous" story of the new school, an article on a marvellous invention to set the public on the gape, etc. . . . Fosdick had an article of a serious nature, on Trades Unions and Socialism. 'So Dickie, having ceased to roll about the world,' thought Isabelle, 'has begun to write about it.' She turned down the page at his article and looked into the advertising section. That was where the *People's* excelled, — in its thick advertising section. Between the automobiles and the pianolas were inserted some pages of personal puff, photographs of the coming contributors, and an account of their deeds, — the menus prepared for the coming months. Isabelle looked at the faces of the contributors, among whom was Dick's face, very smooth and serious. As a whole the photographs might be those of any Modern Order of Redmen, consciously posed before the camera of Fame. But they gave that personal touch so necessary to please the democratic taste. Thus from Æschylus to Mr. Gossom's "literature." . . . It seemed no more real, no more a part of what life is in its essence, than the hotel and the sleek people thronging it.

When Isabelle entered the dining room, the head waiter placed her in a sheltered nook behind one of the stucco pillars, not far from the stringed instruments concealed in a little Gothic choir loft over the entrance. There were flowers on the tables and multitudinous electric candles in pink silk shades. The open-timbered ceiling had been decorated by an artist of some fame, who had sought in vain to give to this rich feeding place of the herd the grace of an Italian palace. Two long mural paintings adorned the end walls, and six highly colored tapestries were hung at equal spaces laterally. In spite of the large proportions of the room, it was insufferably hot and heavy with the odors of wilting flowers and perspiring humanity, somewhat perfumed, and of foods and wines. The early diners were leaving for the theatres and opera, the women trailing their rich gowns over the rugged floor as they stared about them. (They were mostly strangers from inland cities who had been attracted by the fame of this newest hotel.) Their places were quickly taken by others in couples and in parties, and the hum of talk was feebly punctuated by occasional bursts of teasing sound from the stringed instruments. Isabelle felt curiously alone, sitting here in the crowded dining room, — alone as she had not felt on the most solitary hillside of Grosvenor. She closed her eyes and saw the village in its cup among the mountains glittering white in the March sun. The thin, pure air of the forests filled her nostrils. She was homesick — for the first time in her life! With a little shake she roused herself and turned to Fosdick's article that she had brought with her to the table. It was all about the progress of the socialist parties abroad, their aims and accomplishments, showing first-hand observation and knowledge; also a vivaciously critical spirit, — in short what Gossom would call "a smart article." . . . There was another "serious" article on the problem of housing the poor, amply illustrated. In the newspapers that she had glanced through on her long journey, there had been likewise much about "movements," political and social, speeches and societies organized to promote this interest or that, and endless references to the eternal conflict of capital and labor, in the struggle for their respective shares of the human cake. It was the same with all the more serious magazines at the news-stand; they were filled with discussion of "movements" for the betterment of humanity, of talk about this means or that to make the world run a little more smoothly. It was proof, according to the editors, of the sound spirit of democracy, fighting for ideals, making progress along right lines. In other days Isabelle would have considered Fosdick's article brilliant, if not profound. She would have felt that here was something very important for serious people to know, and believed she was thinking. . . . To-night Fosdick's phrases seemed dead, like this hotel life, this hotel reading matter. Even the impassioned editorial she had seen on child-labor laws, and the article on factory inspection, and the bill to regulate the hours of labor on railroads — all the "uplift" movements — seemed dead, wooden, — part of the futile machinery with which earnest people deluded themselves that they were doing something. Would all of them, even if successful, right the wrong of life in any deep sense? . . .

Isabelle laid down the magazine and looked over the room again. Her eyes fell on a party of four at one of the tables in front of her, beneath the mural painting. While the food she had ordered was being slowly put before her, she watched them. There seemed something familiar about the black back of the man at the nearer side of the table, about the way he leaned forward, gesticulating from his wrists, and also about the large woman at his right with her head turned away. After a time this head came around and looked down the room. It was Conny! Conny splendidly blond and large, in half-mourning, with a fresh touch of color on her pale face, her beautiful shoulders quite bare. And that full mouth and competent chin, — no one but Conny! Isabelle hastily looked down at her plate. She had not recognized the others at the table. Conny was seated just beneath the pink and white painting representing spring, — a mixture of Botticelli brought to date and Puvis. And Conny carried on the allegory of Flora into full-blown summer. She was drinking her wine meditatively, and her firm chin — the Senator had said it was moulded for an empress — was slightly tilted, revealing the thick, muscular neck.

So long ago it was when Isabelle had been thrilled by her luncheon at the Woodyards'. She hurried her dinner now to escape the necessity of talking to Conny when her party passed out. But as she prepared to rise, she saw that they were coming towards her and sat down again, opening the magazine. From it she could see them, Conny in the lead sweeping forward in that consciously unconscious manner with which she took her world. The man behind her had some trouble in keeping up with her pace; he limped, and almost tripped on Conny's train. Isabelle saw him out of her lowered eyelids. It was Tom Cairy. They almost brushed her table as they passed, Conny and after her Tom. Conny was drawling in her treble note, "She made a great sensation in Herndon's piece over in London."

. . . And Isabelle was conscious that she was sitting alone at the hotel table, staring into vacancy, with a waiter impatiently eying the coin in her hand. . . .

She had looked at him for half an hour, not knowing him! And suddenly she saw how dead it all was: not merely her feeling for Cairy, but her whole past, the petty things done or felt by that petty other self, ending with the tragic fact of Vickers's sacrifice. She had passed through into another world. . . . This man who had sat there near her all the evening she had once believed that she loved more than life itself, — his mere voice had made her tremble, — this God she had created to worship! And she had not recognized him.

High up in her corner of the brick and stone cliff above the twinkling city, Isabelle knelt by the open window, looking out into the foggy night. Unconscious of the city sounds rising in one roar from the pavement, — the voice of the giant metropolis, — she knelt there thinking of that dead past, that dead self, and of Vickers, a solemn unearthly music like the march of life in her ears. She knelt there, wide-eyed, able to see it all calmly, something like prayer struggling upwards in her heart for expression.

CHAPTER LXIX

All night long in the corridors of the cliff-city the elevator doors had clicked, as they were opened and shut on the ceaseless trips to pack away the people in the eighteen stories. In the morning they became even livelier in their effort to take down the hungry guests for breakfast and the day's business. The corridors and the lobbies and the foyer were thronged with the same people, freshly dressed for the day, fat or lean, heavy eyed or alert, pale, nervous, with quick tones and jerky movements. And there was a line of new arrivals before a fresh row of pale clerks. The prominent people of the city, especially the women, had already left town for the Springs or Florida or Paris or the Mediterranean, anywhere but here! Their flitting, however, had made no impression on the hotels or the honey-hives along the avenue. What they abandoned — the city in March with its theatres, opera, restaurants, and shops — the provincials came hungrily to suck. For the cast-off, the spurned, is always Somebody's desired.

It was the same on the other side of the ferry in the railroad terminal, hurrying throngs pressing through the little wickets that bore the legend of the destination of each train, — "The Florida East Coast Limited," "New Orleans, Texas, and the South," "Washington and Virginia," etc. From this centre the strands of travel ran outwards to many beguiling points. And there were two perpetual motions, — the crowd flowing out to some joy beyond the horizon, and the crowd flowing back irresistibly to the sucking whirlpool. Always movement, change, endless going, going with these people, — the spirit of the race in their restless feet! There was always the Desirable beyond at the other end of the line. All the world that could move was in unstable flux, scurrying hither and thither in hot search for the phantom Better — change, variety — to be had for the price of a ticket.

It was a relief to be on the Pullman, seated for a time in a small fixed space, free from the revolving whirlpool of restless humanity, though that fixity itself was being whirled across the land. With a sigh Isabelle leaned back and looked at the passing country outside. The snow had long disappeared, leaving the brown earth naked and forlorn. It was the same landscape, under similar conditions, that Isabelle had gazed at the spring afternoon when she was hurrying back to meet Cairy, his violets on her breast. It seemed to her then that she was happy, with a wonderful happiness. Now she was content. . . . As the train rushed through the Alleghanies, the first faint touches of spring appeared in the swelling stems of the underbrush, in the full streams of yellow water, and the few spears of green grass beside the sheltering fence posts, and the soft misty atmosphere full of brooding changes over the level fields.

Isabelle became eager to get on to her journey's end, to see her husband. Once out there with him, whatever accident befell them, she was equal to it, would see its real meaning, would find in it Peace. She had brought with her the copy of the *People's* and a number of other magazines and books, and as the day waned she tried to interest herself in some of their "pleasant" stories. But her eyes wandered back to the landscape through which they were speeding, to the many small towns past which they darted, — ugly little places with ugly frame or brick buildings, stores and houses and factories, dirty and drab, unlike the homely whiteness of the Grosvenor village street. But they were strangely attracting to her eye, — these little glimpses of other lives, seen as the train sped by, at the back porches, the windows, the streets; the lives of the many fixed and set by circumstance, revolving between home and workshop, the lives of the multitude not yet evolved into ease and aspiration. But they counted, these lives of the multitude, — that was what she felt this day; they counted quite as much as hers or any. She had travelled back and forth over this main artery of the Atlantic and Pacific many times from her childhood up. But hitherto the scene had meant nothing to her; she had never looked at it before. She had whirled through the panorama of states, thinking only of herself, what was to happen to her at the end of the journey. But to-day it was *her* country, *her* people, *her* civilization that she looked out on. The millions that were making their lives in all these ugly little houses, these mills and shops, men and women together, loving, marrying, breeding, and above all living! "All of life is good!" Each one of these millions had its own drama, each to itself, as hers had been to her, with that tragic importance of being lived but once from the germ to the ultimate dust. Each one was its own epic, its own experience, and its own fulfilment. As Renault once said, "Any of the possibilities may lie in a human soul." And in that was the hope and the faith for Democracy, — the infinite variety of these possibilities!

So the literature of "movements" and causes, the effort by organization to right the human fabric, seemed futile, for the most part. If man were right with himself, square with his own soul, each one of the millions, there would be no wrongs to right by machinery, by laws, by discussion, by agitation, by theories or beliefs. Each must start with self, and right that. . . . Yes, the world needed a Religion, not movements nor reforms!

. . . Sometime during the night Isabelle was roused by the stopping of the train, and pulling aside the curtain of the window she looked out. The train was standing in the yards of a large station with many switch lights feebly winking along the tracks. At first she did not recognize the place; it might be any one of the division headquarters where the through trains stopped to change engines. But as she looked at the maze of tracks, at the dingy red brick building beyond the yards, she finally realized that it was Torso, the spot where her married life had begun. It gave her an odd sensation to lie there and look out on the familiar office building where she used to go for John — so long ago! Torso, she had felt at that time, was cramping, full of commonplace, ordinary people that one did not care to know. She had been very anxious to escape to something larger, — to St. Louis and then to New York. She wondered what she would think of it now if she should go back, — of Mrs. Fraser and the Griscoms. Then she remembered the Falkners, and how badly it had gone since with Bessie. It was sad to think back over the years and see how it might have been different, and for the moment she forgot that if it had been different in any large sense, the result would have been different. She would not be here now, the person she was. Regret is the most useless of human states of mind. . . . The railroad operatives were busy with lanterns about the train, tapping wheels, filling the ice-boxes and gas-tanks, and switching cars. She could see the faces of the men as they passed her section in the light of their lanterns. With deliberate, unconscious motions they performed their tasks. Like the face of that lad on the engine at White River, these were the faces of ordinary men, privates of the industrial world, and yet each had something about it distinctive, of its own. What kept these privates at their work, each in his place? Hunger, custom, faith? Surely something beyond themselves that made life seem to each one of them reasonable, desirable. Something not very different from the spirit which lay in her own soul, like a calming potion, which she could almost touch when she needed its strength. "For life is good — all of it!" . . . and "Peace is the rightful heritage of every soul."

The train rolled on towards its destination, and she fell asleep again, reassured.

CHAPTER LXX

At the station in St. Louis a young man came forward from the crowd about the gate and raised his hat, explaining to Isabelle that he had been sent by her husband to meet her. Mr. Lane, he said further, was in court and found it impossible to be there. When she was in the cab and her trunk had been secured the young man asked: —

"Where shall I tell him? The Price house?"

A picture of the familiar empty rooms, of waiting there with her ghosts, aggravated the disappointment she had felt at not seeing John on her arrival. She hesitated.

"Could I go to the court?"

"Sure — of course; only Mr. Lane thought —"

"Get in, won't you, and come with me," Isabelle said, interrupting him, and then as the young man shyly took the vacant seat, she asked: —

"Aren't you Teddy Bliss? . . . I haven't seen you for — years!" She added with a smile, "Since you played baseball in your father's back yard. How is your mother?"

It gave her a sense of age to find the son of her old friend in this smiling young man. Life was getting on apace. . . . The cab made its way slowly into the heart of the city, and they talked of the old times when the Blisses had been neighbors across the alley from the Prices. Isabelle wished to ask the young man about the trial. The New York paper that she had seen on the train had only a short account. But she hesitated to show her ignorance, and Teddy Bliss was too much abashed before the handsome wife of his "boss" to offer any information. Finally Isabelle asked: —

"Is the trial nearly over?"

"Pretty near the end. Cross-examination to-day. When

I left, Mr. Lane was on the stand. Then come the arguments and the judge's charge, and it goes to the jury."

And he added with irresistible impulse: —

"It's a great case, Mrs. Lane! . . . When our lawyers get after that district attorney, he won't know what's happened to him. . . . Why, the road's secured the best legal talent that ever argued a case in this district, so they tell me. That man Brinkerhoff is a corker!"

"Indeed!" Isabelle replied, smiling at the young man's enthusiasm for the scrap. To him it was all a matter of legal prowess with victory to the heavy battalions.

"Federal court-rooms are in here temporarily, — crowded out of the federal building," her companion explained as the cab stopped before a grimy office building.

Isabelle had expected that the trial would be in some sort of public building, which might have at least the semblance of serving as a temple of justice. But justice, it seemed, like most else in this day, had to accommodate itself to the practical life. . . . Upstairs there was a small crowd about the door of the court-room, through which the young man gained admission by a whispered word to the tobacco-chewing veteran that kept the gate.

The court-room was badly lighted by two windows at the farther end, in front of which on a low platform behind a plain oak desk sat the judge, and grouped about him informally the jurors, the lawyers, and stenographers, and mixed with these the defendants and witnesses. The body of the room, which was broken by bare iron pillars, was well filled with reporters and curious persons. Isabelle sank into a vacant chair near the door and looked eagerly for her husband. At last by craning her head she caught a partial view of him where he sat behind a pillar, his face bent downwards leaning on his hand, listening with an expression of weariness to the wrangle of counsel. He was sallow, and his attitude was abstracted, the attitude in which he listened at board meetings or gathered the substance of a wordy report from a subordinate. It was not the attitude of a criminal on trial for his honor! . . .

"That's Brinkerhoff, the big gun," young Bliss whispered to Isabelle, indicating a gentle, gray-headed, smooth-shaven man, who seemed to be taking a nap behind his closed eyes.

The judge himself was lolling back listlessly, while several men in front of him talked back and forth colloquially. The argument between counsel proceeded with polite irony and sarcastic iteration of stock phrases, "If your honor pleases," . . . "My learned brother, the district attorney," . . . "The learned counsel for the defence," etc. The judge's eyes rested on the ceiling, as if he too wished to take a nap. There was a low hum of conversation among the men grouped about the desk meanwhile, and occasionally one of the young men who had been scribbling on a pad would grasp his hat hurriedly and leave the room. Thus the proceedings dragged on.

"They are arguing about admitting some evidence," the young man at her side explained. . . .

Isabelle, who had been living in a suppressed state of emotional excitement ever since that night three days before when she had turned from the newspapers to pack her trunk, felt a sudden limp reaction come over her. Apparently the whole proceeding was without vitality, — a kind of routine through which all parties had to go, knowing all the time that it settled nothing, — did not much count. The judge was a plain, middle-aged man in a wrinkled sack coat, — very much in appearance what Conny would call a "bounder." The defending counsel talked among themselves or wrote letters or took naps, like the celebrated Mr. Brinkerhoff, and the counsel for the government listened or made a remark in the same placid manner. It was all very commonplace, — some respectable gentlemen engaged in a dull technical discussion over the terms of the game, in which seemingly there was no momentous personal interest involved.

"The government's case will collapse if they can't get those books of the coal companies in as evidence," young Bliss informed Isabelle. He seemed to understand the rules of the game, — the point at issue.

Surely the methods of modern justice are unpicturesque, unimpressive! Compare this trial of the cause of the People against the mighty Atlantic and Pacific railroad corporation *et al.* with the trial of the robber baron dragged from his bleak castle perched above the highroad where he had laid in wait to despoil his fellow-men, weaker vessels, into the court of his Bishop, — there to be judged, to free himself if he might by grasping hot iron with his naked hand, by making oath over the bones of some saint, and if found guilty to be condemned to take the cross in the crusade for the Saviour's sepulchre. Fantastic, that; but human — dramatic! And starkly memorable, like the row of his victim's heads nailed along the battlements of his castle. More civilized, the modern tyrant takes the cash and lets the victim die a natural death. Or compare this tedious legal game — which does not count — with that pageant of England's trial of a corrupt administrator at the bar of Parliament! The issues involved are hardly less vital to millions in the case of the People against the Atlantic and Pacific *et al.* than in the case of the races of India against Warren Hastings; but democracy is the essence of horse-sense. 'For these gentlemen before me,' the judge seemed to say, 'are not criminals, no matter how the jury may render its verdict, in any ordinary sense of the term. They may have exceeded the prescribed limits in playing the game that all men play, — the great predatory game of get all you can and keep it! . . . But they are not common criminals.'

At last the judge leaned forward, his elbows on the desk: —

"The court orders that the papers in question be admitted as evidence pertinent to this case."

Teddy Bliss looked chagrined. His side had been ruled against.

"They'll be sure to reverse the decision on appeal," he whispered consolatorily to his employer's wife. "An exception has been taken."

That was apparently the opinion of those concerned who were grouped about the judge's desk. There was no consternation, merely a slight movement as if to free muscles cramped by one position, a word or two among counsel. The great Brinkerhoff still wore that placid look of contemplation, as if he were thinking of the new tulip bulbs he had imported from Holland for his house up the Hudson. He was not aroused even when one of his fellow-counsel asked him a question. He merely removed his glasses, wiped them reflectively, and nodded to his colleague benignantly. He knew, as the others knew, that the case would be appealed from the verdict of the jury to a higher court, and very likely would turn up ultimately in the highest court of all at Washington, where after the lapse of several years the question at issue would be argued wholly on technicalities, and finally decided according to the psychological peculiarities of the various personalities then composing the court. The residuum of justice thus meted out to his clients — if they were not successful before in maintaining their contention — would not affect these honorable gentlemen appreciably. The corporation would pay the legal expenses of the protracted litigation, and hand the bill on to the public ultimately, and the people by their taxes would pay their share of this row. . . . He put on his glasses and resumed his meditation.

"Court is adjourned." At last! Isabelle stood up eagerly, anxious to catch her husband's attention. He was talking with the lawyers. The young clerk went up to him and touched his elbow, and presently Lane came down the room in the stream of reporters and lawyers bent on getting to luncheon. It was neither the place nor the time that Isabelle would have preferred for meeting her husband after their long separation. There was so much in her heart, — this meeting meant so much, must be so much for them both in all the future years. The familiar solid figure, with the reserved, impassive face came nearer; Lane reached out his hand. There were lines about the mouth, and his hair seemed markedly gray.

"John!" was all she could say.

"Glad to see you, Isabelle!" he replied. "Sorry I couldn't meet you at the station. Everything all right?"

It was his usual kindly, rather short-hand manner with her.

"Yes," she said, "everything is all right." She felt as if all the significance of her act had been erased.

"You know your mother hasn't come back from the Springs," he added, "but they are expecting you at the house."

"Can't we go somewhere and have luncheon together? I want so much to see you!" she urged.

"I wish I might, but I have these lawyers on my hands — must take them to the club for luncheon. Sorry I shall be kept here until late in the afternoon. I will put you in a cab." And he led the way to the elevator. As always he was kind and considerate. But in his equable manner was there also some touch of coldness, of aloofness from this wife, who had taken this curious opportunity to come into his affairs?

"Thank you," she faltered, as he looked down the street for a cab. "Couldn't I go somewhere about here for luncheon and come back afterwards to the court-room? I should like to wait for you."

"Why, if you want to," he replied, looking at her with surprise. And as if divining a reason for her agitation, he said: "You mustn't mind what the papers say. It won't amount to anything, either way it goes."

"I think I'll stay," she said hurriedly.

"Very well. I will call Bliss to take you to a hotel."

He beckoned to the waiting young man, and while Mr. Bliss was finding a cab, Lane said to his wife: —

"You are looking very well. The country has done you good?"

"Yes! I am very well, — all well!" She tried to smile buoyantly. "I don't expect ever to be ill again."

He received this as a man accustomed to the vagaries of woman's health, and said, "That's good!"

Then he put her into the cab, gave some instructions to the young man, and raised his hat. His manner was perfect to her, and yet Isabelle went to her luncheon with the bubbling Mr. Bliss sad at heart. She was such an outsider, such a stranger to her husband's inner self! That it was to be expected, her own fault, the result of the misspent years of married life made it none the easier to bear. . . .

Mr. Teddy Bliss exercised his best connoisseurship in selecting the dishes from the printed broadside put before him at the hotel restaurant, consulting Isabelle frequently as to her tastes, where the desire to please was mingled with the pride of appearing self-possessed. Having finally decided on tomato bisque aux crutons, prairie chicken, grilled sweet potatoes, salad and pêche Melba, which was all very much to his liking, he dropped the card and looked at Isabelle with a broad smile. The world and its affairs still had an irrepressible zest and mirthful aspect to young Mr. Bliss.

"You're likely to hear some or-a-tory this afternoon, Mrs. Lane," he scoffed. "The district attorney is a Southerner, and he's going to spread himself when he makes his plea, you can believe. It's *his* chance to get talked about from San Francisco to Washington. . . . Of course it don't cut any ice what he says, but the papers will play it up large, and that's what they are after, the government. You see" — he waxed confidential — "the government's got to save its face somehow after all the talk and the dust they have raised. If they can secure a conviction, — oh, just a nominal fine (you know there is no prison penalty), — why, it'll be good campaign material this fall. So they fixed on the A. and P. as a shining mark for their shot. And you know there's a good deal of feeling, especially in this state, against railroads."

"I see!" In spite of herself Isabelle was amused at the naïve assurance the young man had given her that nothing serious could happen to her husband, — not imprisonment! Mr. Bliss's point of view about the famous case was evidently that of the railroad office, tinged with a blithe sporting interest in a legal scrap. The ill-paid government attorneys trying the case were a lot of "light-weight mits," put up against the best "talent" in the country employed by the powerful corporation to protect itself; in short, a sure thing for the railroad in the final knockout if not in the first round.

"It was bad, their getting in those Pleasant Valley Company books," he remarked less exuberantly. "But it won't make any difference in the end. The papers have made the most of that evidence already."

"Why do you suppose the newspapers are so bitter against the road?"

"They aren't, the best of them; they know too much what's good for them. They just print the record of the trial. As for the sensational ones, you see it's this way, — they don't care, they haven't any convictions. It is just a matter of business for them. Slamming the corporations suits their readers. The people who buy most of the papers like to have the prosperous classes slammed. Most people are envious; they want the other fellow's roll, — isn't that so? They think they are as good as the best, and it makes 'em sick to see the other fellow in his automobile when they are earning fifteen or eighteen per! They don't stop to consider that it's brains that makes the diff."

"So it is merely envy that produces all this agitation?"

"I am not saying that the corporations are philanthropic institutions," Mr. Bliss continued didactically; "of course they aren't. They are out for business, and every man knows what that means. I suppose they do a good many tough things if they get the chance — same as their critics. What of it? Wouldn't the little fellow do the same thing, if he could, — had the chance? . . . What would this country be to-day without the corporations, the railroads? Without the Atlantic and Pacific, right here in St. Louis? And all the work of those men they are prosecuting and fining and trying to put into jail? Why, if the President had his way, he'd lock up every man that had enough sense and snap in him to do things, and he'd make this country like a Methodist camp meeting after the shouting is over! There's no sense to it."

Isabelle laughed at the young man's vigorous defence of "our" side. It seemed useless to attempt to pick flaws in his logic, and it would hardly become her as the wife of his "boss" to betray that she was not wholly convinced of his accuracy.

"Besides, why can't the government let bygones be bygones? Every one knows that the roads did some queer things in the old days. But why rake up old crimes and make a mess? I say let's have a clean slate and begin over. . . . But if they keep on legislating and howling against corporations, like some of these trust-busting state legislatures, we'll have a panic sure thing, and that will do the business for the reformers, won't it now?"

This, as Isabelle realized, was, in the popular language of Mr. Teddy Bliss, her husband's point of view, the philosophy of the ruling class, imbibed by their dependents. As the young man turned from expounding the business situation to his succulent bird, Isabelle had time for reflection.

This young man was sucking his views about honesty, business morality, from the Atlantic and Pacific, from her husband. One of Renault's sentences came to her, "We all live in large part on a borrowed capital of suggested ideas, motives, desires." And the corollary: "Each is responsible not only for the capital that he borrows from others, — that it should really be the right idea for him, — but also for the capital he lends, — the suggestions he gives to others — possibly less stable minds. For thus by borrowing and lending ideas is created that compulsive body of thought throughout the universe on which we all act."

Her husband was on trial for that which he had borrowed and thus made his own, as well as for that which he had passed on into life — to Mr. Teddy Bliss, for example.

CHAPTER LXXI

THE government attorney had already begun his argument when Isabelle, escorted by Teddy Bliss, returned to the court-room. The district attorney was a short, thick-set, sallow-faced man, with bushy gray hair growing in the absurd "Pompadour" fashion, and a homely drooping mustache. Another "bounder," thought Isabelle, one of the hungry outsiders, not in fee to the corporations, who hired only the best lawyers. Perhaps he was aware of his position there in the dingy court-room before the trained gladiators of his profession — and also before his country! The lawyers for the defendants lolling in their chairs settled themselves placidly to see what this humble brother would make of the business. Mr. Brinkerhoff's eyelids drooped over his gentle eyes, as if to shut out all distractions of sense from his brain. The thick-set district attorney frequently scraped his throat and repeated the phrase, "if it please your honor." He had a detestable nasal whine, and he maltreated the accents of several familiar words. The culture of letters and vocal delivery had evidently not been large in the small inland college where he had been educated. These annoying peculiarities at first distracted Isabelle's attention, while the lawyer labored through the opening paragraphs of his argument. In the maze of her thoughts, which had jumped across the continent to the little mountain village, there fell on her ears the words, "In a land of men born free and equal before the law." Was it the tone of unexpected passion vibrating through those ancient words, or the idea itself that startled her like an electric shock? That pathetic effort of our ancestors to enact into constitutional dogma the poetic dream of a race! "Born free and equal"!

— there was nothing more absurd, more contrary to the daily evidence of life, ever uttered. Isabelle fancied she saw a soft smile play over the benign face of Mr. Brinkerhoff, as if he too had been struck by the irony of the words. But to the district attorney they did not seem to be a mere poetic aspiration, nor a catch phrase with which to adorn his speech; they voiced a real idea, still pulsating with passionate truth. From this moment Isabelle forgot the lawyer's nasal intonation, his uncultivated delivery.

He stood there, so it seemed, as the representative of the mute millions which make the nation to defend before the court their cause against the rapacious acts of the strong. This great railroad corporation, with its capital of three hundred and seventy-five millions of dollars in stocks and bonds (a creature, nevertheless, of the common public, called into existence by its necessities and chartered by its will), had taken upon itself to say who should dig coal and sell it from the lands along its lines. They and their servants and allies had, so the charge ran, seized each individual man or association of men not allied to them, and throttled the life in them — specifically refusing them cars in which to transport their coal, denying them switching privileges, etc. . . . The government, following its duty to protect the rights of each man and all men against the oppression of the few, had brought this suit to prohibit these secret practices, to compel restitution, to punish the corporation and its servants for wrong done. . . . "The situation was, if your honor please, as if a company of men should rivet a chain across the doors of certain warehouses of private citizens and should prevent these citizens from taking their goods out of their warehouses or compel them to pay toll for the privilege of transacting their lawful business. . . . And the government has shown, if it please your honor, that this Pleasant Valley Coal Company is but a creature of the defendant corporation, its officers and owners being the servants of the railroad company, and thereby this Pleasant Valley Coal Company has enjoyed and now enjoys special privileges in the matter of transportation, cars, and switching facilities. The government has further shown that the Atlantic and Pacific, by its servant, John Lane, . . ."

At this point the railroad counsel looked interested; even the serene Mr. Brinkerhoff deigned to unclose his eyes. For the district attorney, having disposed of his oratorical flourish of trumpets, had got down to the facts of the record and what they could be made to prove. In the close argument that followed, Isabelle's thoughts went back to that trumpet phrase, — "all men born free and equal." Slowly there dawned in her an altogether new comprehension of what this struggle before her eyes, in which her husband was involved, meant. Nay, what human life itself, with all its noisy discord, meant!

Their forerunners, the fathers of the people, held the theory that here at last, in this broad, rich, new land, men should struggle with one another for the goods of life on an equal basis. Man should neither oppress nor interfere with man. Justice at last to all! The struggle should be ordered by law so that men might be free to struggle and equal in their rights. To all the same freedom to live, to enjoy, to become! So these fathers of the republic had dreamed. So some still dreamed that human life might be ordered, to be a fair, open struggle — for all.

But within a brief century and a quarter the fallacy of this aspiration had become ridiculously apparent. "Born free and equal!" Nothing on this globe was ever so born. The strong who achieved, the weak who succumbed — both knew the nonsense of it. Free and equal, — so far as men could maintain freedom and equality by their own force, — that was all!

(There was that man who begged John to give him cars. Poor thing! he could not maintain his right.)

And every man who complained at the oppression of another either oppressed some one or would so oppress him, if he had the chance and the power. It was, of course, the business of the law to police the fight, — the game had its rules, its limits, which all must obey, when not too "destructive." But essentially this new land of liberty and hope was like all other human societies, — a mortal combat where the strong triumphed and the weak went under in defeat. . . . That was what the array of brilliant counsel employed by the Atlantic and Pacific really represented. "Gentlemen, you can't block us with silly rules. We must play this game of life as it was ordered by God it should be played when the first protoplasm was evolved. . . . And really, if it were not for us, would there be any game for you little fellows to play?"

Egotism, the curse of egotism! This was stark male egotism, — the instinct for domination. And defendants and plaintiffs were alike in spirit, struggling for position in the game. The weaker ones — if they had the hold — would pluck at the windpipe of their oppressors. . . .

So while the attorney for the people spoke on about rate-sheets and schedules A and B, and bills of lading from the Pleasant Valley Company (marked "exhibits nine and ten"), the woman in the court-room began to comprehend dimly the mystery behind this veil of words. Every man felt instinctively this spirit of fight, — the lively young clerk at her side as well as the defendant before the bar, her husband; the paid writers for Mr. Gossom's patriotic magazine as well as the President and his advisers, — all had it in their blood. It was the spirit of our dominating race, fostered through the centuries, — the spirit of achievement, of conquest. Mr. Gossom's clever writers, the President, and the "good element" generally, differed from their opponents only in manner and degree. "Gently, gently, gentlemen," they called. "Play according to the rules of the game. Don't bang all the breath out of your adversary's body when you have him by the throat. Remember, gentlemen, to give every one his turn!"

In the light of this understanding of the nature of the game of life, the efforts of the government to preserve order in a row of this magnitude became almost farcical, — so long as the spirit of man was untouched and SUCCESS was admittedly the one glorious prize of life! . . .

Finally the district attorney ceased to speak, and the judge looked at his watch. There was not time for the defence to make its argument to-day, and so court was adjourned. The lawyers stretched themselves, chatted, and laughed. The raw district attorney had done his worst, and judging from Mr. Brinkerhoff's amiable smile, it was not very bad. The newspaper men scurried out of the room for the elevators,—there was good copy this afternoon!

Lane joined his wife after a few moments, and they left the court-room.

"Are you tired?" he asked solicitously. "It must have been dull for you, all that law talk."

"Oh, no! . . . I think I was never so much interested in anything in my life," she replied with a long sigh.

He looked as if he were puzzled, but he made no further reference to the trial, either then or on their way to her mother's house. And Isabelle in a tumult of impressions and feelings was afraid to speak yet, afraid lest she might touch the wrong nerve, strike the wrong note,—and so set them farther apart in life than they were now.

CHAPTER LXXII

THEY dined in the lofty, sombre room at the rear of the house, overlooking a patch of turf between the house and the stable. Above the massive sideboard hung an oil portrait of the Colonel, a youthful painting but vigorous, where something of the old man's sweetness and gentle wisdom had been caught. This dining room had been done over the year before Isabelle was married; its taste seemed already heavy and bad.

Her mother's old servants served the same rich, substantial meal they had served when she was a child, with some poor sherry, the Colonel's only concession to domestic conviviality. The room and the food subtly typified the spirit of the race, — that spirit which was illuminated in the court-room — before it had finally evolved. . . . The moral physiology of men is yet to be explored!

Lane leaned back in the Colonel's high-backed chair, gray and weary under the brilliant light. At first he tried to be interested in Grosvenor, asked questions of his wife, but soon he relapsed into a preoccupied silence. This mood Isabelle had never seen in her husband, nor his physical lassitude. After a time she ventured to ask: —

"Is it likely to last much longer, the trial?"

"A couple of days, the lawyers think." And after a while he added morosely: "Nobody can tell how long if it is appealed. . . . I have had to muddle away the better part of the winter over this business, first and last! It's nothing but popular clamor, suspicion. The government is playing to the gallery. I don't know what the devil will happen to the country with this lunatic of a President. Capital is already freezing up tight. The road will have to issue short-time notes to finance the improvements it has under way, and abandon all new work. Men who have money to invest aren't going to buy stock and bonds with a set of anarchists at Washington running the country!"

It was quite unlike Lane to explode in this manner. It was not merely the result of nervous fatigue, Isabelle felt: it indicated some concealed sore in her husband's mind.

"How do you think it will be decided?" she asked timidly.

"The trial? Nobody can guess. The judge is apparently against us, and that will influence the jurors, — a lot of farmers and sore-heads! . . . But the verdict will make no difference. We shall carry it up, fight it out till the last court. The government has given us enough errors, — all the opening we need!"

The government had played badly, that is. Isabelle had it on her tongue to demand: "But how do *you* feel about it, — the real matter at issue? What is right — *just?*" Again she refrained, afraid to array herself apparently on the side of his enemies.

"It is all this infernal agitation, which does nobody any good and will result in crippling business," he repeated, as they went to the library for their coffee.

This room, where the Colonel usually sat evenings with his wife and the neighbors who dropped in, was exactly as it had been in the old days, — even the same row of novels and books of travel in a rack on the polished table. Only the magazines had been changed.

Lane lighted a cigar and sipped his coffee. Revived by his dinner and cigar, he began to talk more freely, in the same mood of disgusted irritation, the mood of his class these days, of the men he met at his club, in business, — the lawyers, the capitalists, the leaders of society. Isabelle, listening to his bitter criticism, wished that she might get him to speak more personally, — tell her all the detail that had led up to the suit, explain his connection with it, — show her his inmost heart as he would show it to himself in a time of exact truth! With this feeling she went over to where he was sitting and put her hand on his shoulder, and as he glanced up in surprise at this unexpected demonstration, she said impulsively: —

"John, please, John! . . . Tell me everything — I can understand. . . . Don't you think there might be some little truth in the other side? Was the road fair, was it just in this coal business? I so want to know, John!"

Her voice trembled with suppressed emotion. She wished to draw him to her, in the warmth of her new feeling to melt his stern antagonism, his harsh mood. But as he looked inquiringly at her — weighing as it were the meaning of this sudden interest in his affairs — the wife realized how far apart she was from her husband. The physical separation of all these years, the emotional separation, the intellectual separation had resulted in placing them in two distinct spheres spiritually. The intervening space could not be bridged in a moment of expansive emotion. It would be a slow matter, if it ever could be accomplished, to break the crust that had formed like ice between their souls. Isabelle went back to her seat and drank her coffee.

"I don't know what you mean by fair and just," he replied coldly. "Business has to be done according to its own rules, not as idealists or reformers would have it done. The railroad has done nothing worse than every big business is compelled to do to live, — has made a profit where there was one to make. . . . This would be a poor sort of country, even for the reformers and agitators, if the men who have the power to make money should be bound hand and foot by visionaries and talkers. You can't get the sort of men capable of doing things on a large scale to go into business for clerk's wages. They must see a profit — and a big one, — and the men who aren't worth anything will always envy them. That's the root of the whole matter."

It would be useless, Isabelle saw, to point out that his defence was general, and an evasion of the point she wished to see clearly, — what the real *fact* with him was. His mind was stiffened by the prejudices of his profession, tempered in fierce fires of industrial competition as a result of twenty years of triumphant struggle with men in the life and death grapple of business. He was strong just because he was narrow and blind. If he had been able to doubt, even a little, the basis of his actions, he would never have become the third vice-president of the Atlantic and Pacific, one of the most promising of the younger men in his profession.

Recognizing her defeat, Isabelle asked about the Johnstons.

"I have seen Steve a couple of times," Lane replied. "I meant to write you, but hadn't the time. Steve didn't make good in that lumber business. Those men he went in with, it looks to me, were sharks. They took all his money away, — every cent. You know they mortgaged the house, too. Then the company failed; he was thrown out. Steve was not sharp enough for them, I guess."

"Isn't that too bad!"

"Just what might have been expected," Lane commented, associating Steve Johnston's failure with his previous train of thought; "I told him so when he gave up railroading. He was not an all-round man. He had one talent — a good one — and he knew the business he was trained in. But it wasn't good enough for him. He must get out and try it alone — "

"It wasn't to make more money," Isabelle protested, remembering the day at the Farm when the two men had walked back and forth, delaying luncheon, while they heatedly discussed Steve's determination to change his business.

"He had this reform virus in his system, too! . . . Well, he is bookkeeper, now, for some little down-town concern at eighteen hundred a year. All he can get these days. The railroads are discharging men all the time. He might be earning six thousand in the position I offered him then. Do you think Alice and the boys will be any better off for his scruples? Or the country?"

"Poor Alice! . . . Are they still living in the house at Bryn Mawr?"

"Yes, I believe so. But Steve told me he couldn't carry

the mortgage after the first of the year, — would have to give up the house."

"I must go out there to-morrow," she said quickly; and after a time she added, "Don't you think we could do something for them, John?"

Lane smiled, as if the suggestion had its touch of irony.

"Why, yes! I mean to look into his affairs when I can find the time. . . . I'll see what I can do."

"Oh, that is good!" Isabelle exclaimed warmly. It was like her husband, prompt generosity to a friend in trouble. And this matter brought husband and wife closer in feeling than they had been since her arrival.

"Ready money is a pretty scarce commodity," Lane remarked; "but I will see what can be done about his mortgage."

It was not easy, he wished his wife to know, even for the strong to be generous these days, thanks to the reformers, and the "crazy man in Washington," with whom he suspected she sympathized.

They sat in silence after this until he had finished his cigar. There were many subjects that must be discussed between them, which thrust up their heads like sunken rocks in a channel; but both felt their danger. At last Isabelle, faint from the excitement of the day, with all its mutations of thought and feeling, went to her room. She did not sleep for hours, not until long after she heard her husband's step go by the door, and the click of the switches as he turned out the electric lights.

There was much to be done before their marriage could be recreated on a living principle. But where the man was strong and generous, and the woman was at last awakened to life, there was no reason to despair.

CHAPTER LXXIII

ISABELLE did not go back to the court-room to listen to the remaining arguments, not even to hear Mr. Brinkerhoff's learned and ingenious plea in behalf of the rights of capital, the sacred privileges of property. She felt that John would rather not have her there. But Isabelle read every word of the newspaper report of the trial, which since the district attorney's impassioned and powerful plea had excited even greater public interest than before. Not only locally, but throughout the country, the trial of the People *vs.* the Atlantic and Pacific *et al.* was recognized as the first serious effort of the reform administration to enforce the laws against capital, by convicting not merely the irresponsible agents but also some of the men "higher up." It was John Lane's position in the railroad that gave these "coal cases" their significance.

Isabelle read the report of the trial with thoughtful care, but much of it was too technical for her untrained mind to grasp. All these arguments about admitting certain ledgers in evidence, all these exceptions to the rulings of the court, the dodges, fences, pitfalls, the dust created by the skilled counsel for the defence, confused her. What she gathered in a general way was that the road was fighting its case on technicalities, seeking to throw the suit out of court, without letting the one real matter at issue appear, — had they dealt illegally and unjustly with the public? To her emotional temperament this eminently modern method of tactics was irritating and prejudiced her against her husband's side. "But I don't understand," she reflected sadly, "so John would say. And they don't seem to want people to understand!"

With these thoughts on her mind, she took the cars to

the little suburb north of the city, where the Johnstons lived. Bryn Mawr was one of the newer landscape-gardened of our city suburbs, with curving roads, grass-plots, an *art nouveau* railroad station, shrubs and poplar sticks set out along the cement sidewalks, in an effort to disguise the rawness of the prairie pancake that the contractors had parcelled into lots. Isabelle found some difficulty in tracing her way along the ingeniously twisted avenues to the Johnston house. But finally she reached the two-story-and-attic wooden box, which was set in a little grove of maple trees. Two other houses were going up across the street, and a trench for a new sewer had been opened obstructively. At this period of belated spring Bryn Mawr was not a charming spot. Unfinished edges left by the landscape gardener and the contractor showed pitilessly against the leafless, scrubby trees and the rolling muddy fields beyond. It was all covered with a chill mist. In the days when she lived in St. Louis she had never found time to go so far to see Alice, and she had shared Bessie's horror of the remote and cheerless existence in this suburb, had wondered how an intelligent and well-bred woman like Alice Johnston could endure its dull level of platitudinous existence. But now as she picked her way across the sewer excavation, she felt that the little wooden box ahead of her was home for this family, — they must not lose that! Place and circumstance had lessened in her estimates of life.

Alice opened the door herself, and with a radiant smile of hungry delight enveloped Isabelle in her arms.

"Where did you drop from, Belle?"

"Oh, I thought I'd come on," Isabelle replied vaguely, not liking to mention the trial.

"And you found your way out here, and navigated that ·ewer safely! The boys find it surpassingly attractive, — as a coal mine, or a canal in Mars, or the Panama ditch. I've tried to induce Mr. Jorgesson, the contractor, to hang out a lantern or two at night. But he evidently thinks well of the caution and sobriety of the Johnston family and prefers to take his chances of a suit for damages. So far the family has escaped."

Alice's face showed two girlish dimples, while she talked glibly,—too glibly, Isabelle thought. They went into the dining room where there was a tiny coal fire before which Alice had been sewing. Isabelle's namesake—number two in the list—having been considered by her aunt, was dismissed on an errand. The older boys were at school, the baby out in the kitchen "with the colored lady who assists," as Alice explained.

When they were alone, the cousins looked at each other, each thinking of the changes, the traces of life in the other. Isabelle held out her hands yearningly, and Alice, understanding that she knew what had befallen them, smiled with trembling lips. Yet it was long before she could speak of their misfortune in her usual calm manner.

. . . "The worst is that we have had to take Ned out of the technical institute and send him back to the school here with Jack. It isn't a good school. But we may move into the city in the fall. . . . And Belle had to give up her music. We all have to chip in, you see!"

"She mustn't give up her music. I shall send her," Isabelle said quickly, reflecting whimsically how she had loathed her own music lessons. Alice flushed, and after a moment's pause said deliberately:—

"Do you really mean that, Isabelle?"

"Of course! I only hope she will get more out of it than I did."

"I should be glad to accept your offer for her sake. . . . I want her to have something, some interest. A poor girl without that,—it is worse for her than for the boys!"

Isabelle could see Alice's struggle with her pride, and understood the importance of this little matter to her, which had made her deliberately clutch at the chance for the little girl.

"Belle shall come to me to-morrow and spend the day. I will send for the teacher. . . . Now that's settled, and,

Alice, you and Steve will be better off soon! He is too able a man — "

Alice shook her head steadily, saying: —

"I am afraid not, Belle! Steve is too good a man, that is the trouble. I don't say this to him. I wouldn't take a particle of hope from him. But I know Steve all through: he isn't the kind to impress people, to get on, — and he is no longer young."

"It is such a pity he left the railroad," Isabelle mused. "John says they are turning men off instead of taking them on, or he might have found a position for him."

"Never!" Alice's eyes flamed. "If it had to be done over, even now, we should do the same thing. . . . Steve is slow and quiet, never says much, but he does a lot of thinking. And when he makes up his mind, he sticks. . . . When he saw what it meant to take that position in the traffic department, what he would have to know and do, he couldn't do it. It is useless trying to make a man like Steve live contrary to his nature. You can't bend a big, thick tree any way you want it."

"But, Alice, he might have been wrong!" Isabelle protested, coloring.

"Yes, — he might have been wrong," Alice admitted, her eyes falling. "But Steve couldn't see it any other way. So he had to do as he did. . . . And the lumber business failed. I was afraid it would! Dear Steve! He wasn't fitted to fight with those men, to see that they didn't cheat him."

It was later that Alice uttered the deep cry of her heart. . . . "Don't think, Belle, that I mind the hard times, the work and all; not even the school for Ned, and the poor prospect for the children. After all, they may do as well without the advantages we could have given them. But what breaks my heart is to see Steve, who is bigger and abler and stronger than most men, go down to the bottom of the ladder and have to take his orders from an ignorant little German. It's small of me, I know, and Steve doesn't complain. But it seems to me terribly unjust somehow."

For a moment her feeling overcame her; then she recovered her composure and continued: "But then, it's Steve! And I wouldn't have him a particle different, not for all the success in the world. You see I have my pride, my snobbery. I am a snob about my husband."

The boys came in from school, and the house shook with racketing children.

"They don't know what has happened, really, — they are too young, thank Heaven!" Alice exclaimed. "And I don't mean they ever shall know — ever think they are poor."

The two stood on the porch for a last word, arranging for the little girl's visit to Isabelle on the morrow. The twilight had descended through the mist.

"See!" Alice said, pointing to the white tree trunks across the street, and the vague fields beyond. "Isn't it very much like that Corot the Colonel used to love so much, — the one in the library? We have our Corot, too. . . . Good-by, dear! I have chattered frightfully about ourselves. Some day you must tell me of your stay with Mrs. Pole and of yourself."

"There isn't much to tell!"

Alice Johnston, watching her cousin's agreeable figure disappear into the mist, felt that if with Isabelle there might be not much to tell, at least a great deal had happened these last months.

And Isabelle, picking her way cautiously along the sewer excavation, was thinking of the home behind. The couple of hours she had spent with Alice had been filled with a comprehension, a curiously immediate grasp of the other person's vision of life, — what it all meant to her, — Alice's disappointment, her pride in her defeated husband. For the first time in all the years she had known them, Steve and Alice and the children seemed quite real persons, and their life as vivid, as interesting to her, as her own.

Sad as their little story was, in its pathetic limitations of plans and hopes, it did not seem to her intolerable, or sordid, or depressing, as it once would have seemed. Just as she possessed somewhere in herself a new strength to endure whatever misfortune might come to her, so she had an instinctive feeling of how others endured what on the surface of events seemed merely distressing and disagreeable. And the Johnston house, plain and homely as it was, with all the noisy children, had an air of peace about it, the spirit of those that dwelt there, which Isabelle felt to be the most precious thing on earth. . . . Alice had said, "It's Steve — and I wouldn't have him different for all the success in the world!" The words stung Isabelle. Such was marriage, — perfect marriage, — to be able to say that in the face of worldly defeat. Neither she nor John could ever say that about the other.

CHAPTER LXXIV

THE newsboys were crying the verdict up and down the wet street. Across the front page of the penny sheet which Isabelle bought ran in broad, splotched letters: GUILTY; RAILROAD GRAFTERS FINED; and in slightly smaller type: *Atlantic and Pacific found guilty of illegal discrimination in famous coal cases — Fined eighty-five thousand dollars. Vice-president Lane, General Traffic Manager of Road, fined thirteen thousand six hundred and eighty dollars*, etc. Isabelle crumpled the paper into her muff and hurried home. As she walked numbly, she thought, 'Why six hundred and eighty dollars? why so exact?' As if the precise measure of wrong could be determined! On the doorstep of her mother's house lay the quietly printed, respectable two-cent evening paper that the family had always read. Isabelle took this also with her to her room. Even in this conservative sheet, favorable to the interests of the property classes, there were scare-heads about the verdict. It was of prime importance as news. Without removing her hat or coat, Isabelle read it all through, — the judge's charge to the jury, the verdict, the reporters' gossip of the court-room. The language of the judge was trenchant, and though his charge was worded in stiff and solemn form and laden with legal phrases, Isabelle understood it better even than the hot eloquence of the district attorney. It swept away all that legal dust, those technical quibbles, which Mr. Brinkerhoff and his associate counsel had so industriously sprinkled over the issue. "If the facts have been established of such and such a nature, beyond reasonable doubt; if the connection of the defendant has been clearly set forth," etc. As the penny sheet put it, "Judge Barstow's charge left no room for doubt as to the verdict. The jury was out forty minutes and took one ballot." Twelve men, be they farmers or "sore-heads," had found John Lane guilty of something very like grand larceny. The case was to be appealed — of course.

Even the respectable two-cent paper delivered itself editorially on the verdict in the famous coal cases, with unusual daring. For the *Post* was ordinarily most cautious not to reflect upon matters inimical to "leading interests." To-night it was moved beyond the limits of an habitual prudence.

"Judge Barstow," it said, "in his able analysis left no room for doubt as to the gravity of the charges brought by the government against the Atlantic and Pacific and certain of its officers. The verdict will be no surprise to those who have followed closely the so-called coal cases through the preliminary investigation by the Interstate Commerce Commission and the recent trial. A state of affairs in the management of the Atlantic and Pacific railroad was revealed that may well shock men long accustomed to the methods of corporate control. It was shown that officers and employees of the railroad owned or controlled various coal properties that depended for their existence upon special favors given them by the road, and that these companies were enabled by their secret alliance with the railroad to blackmail independent, rival companies, and drive them out of existence. To put it in plain words, the Atlantic and Pacific favored its secret partners at the expense of their competitors. . . . Apart from the legal aspect so ably dealt with by Judge Barstow, the spectacle of graft in the Atlantic and Pacific must surprise the stockholders of that corporation quite as much as the public at large. Apparently high-salaried officials shared in these *extra profits* together with freight clerks and division superintendents! . . . We cannot believe that the moral sense of the country will long tolerate a condition of affairs such as has been revealed in the case of Vice-president Lane." . . .

This was no academic question of economic policy! No legal technicality. The paper fell from Isabelle's hand, and she sat staring at the floor. Her husband was called in plain prose a "grafter," — one who participated in unearned and improper profits, due to granting favors in his official capacity to himself.

As Isabelle closed the old-fashioned shutters before dressing for dinner, she saw her husband coming up the steps, walking with his slow, powerful stride, his head erect, — the competent, high-minded, generous man, a rock of stable strength, as she had always believed him, even when she loved him least! There must be something wrong with the universe when this man, the best type of hard, intelligent labor, should have become a public robber! . . . Renault's solemn words repeated themselves, "The curse of our age, of our country, is its frantic egotism." The predatory instinct, so highly valued in the Anglo-Saxon male, had thriven mightily in a country of people "born free and equal," when such a man as John Lane "grafted" and believed himself justified.

Lane stood behind her chair waiting for her in the dining room. As she entered the room he glanced at her questioningly. He had noticed that the evening paper was not in its usual place in the hall. But after that glance he settled himself composedly for the meal, and while the servants were in the room husband and wife talked of immediate plans. He said he should have to go to New York the next day, and asked what she wished to do. Would she wait here in St. Louis for her mother? Or join her at the Springs? Or open the Farm? He should have to be back and forth between New York and St. Louis all the spring, probably.

Isabelle could answer only in monosyllables. All these details of where she should be seemed irrelevant to the one burning point, — what will *you* do now, in the face of this verdict of guilt? At last the meal was over, and they were alone. Isabelle, without looking up, said: —

"I saw the verdict in the papers, John."

He made no reply, and she cried: —

"Tell me what you are going to do! We *must* talk about it."

"The case will be appealed, as I told you before."

"Yes! . . . but the fine, the — "

She stopped for lack of the right word. He made a gesture of indifference at the word "fine," but still waited.

"John, is it true what the judge said, what the district attorney said, about — the officials getting money from those coal companies?"

She colored, while Lane eyed her and at last replied irritably: —

"The officers of the road invested their money, like most men, where they saw fit, I suppose."

"But does that mean they take advantage of their position with the road to make money — improperly?"

"That depends on what you call 'improperly.'"

Her mind leaped clear of this evasion; she cried out: —

"But why did you want to make money — so much money? You had a large salary, and I could have had all the money we wanted from my father!"

Her husband looked at her almost contemptuously, as if her remark was too childish for serious consideration. It was axiomatic that all men who had the power desired to make what money they could.

"I certainly never cared to live on your father's money," he retorted.

"But we didn't need so much — "

"I wonder if you realize just how much we have seemed to need in one way or another since we moved East?"

There it was staring her in the face, her share in the responsibility for this situation! She had known only vaguely what they were spending, and always considered that compared with women of her class she was not extravagant, in fact economical.

"But, John, if I had only known — "

"Known what?" he demanded harshly. "Known that

I was making money in stocks and bonds, like other men, like your father's friend, Senator Thomas, like Morton, and Beals himself? Isabelle, you seem to have the comprehension of a child! . . . Do you think that such men live on salaries?"

"But why weren't the others indicted and tried?"

He hesitated a moment, his face flushing, and then there burst out the truth. She had unwittingly touched the sore spot in his mind.

"Because there had to be some sort of scapegoat to satisfy public clamor! The deals went through my office mostly; but the road is behind me, of course. . . . They all shared, from Beals down."

At last they were at the heart of the matter, he challenging her criticism, she frightened at the cloudy places in her husband's soul that she had penetrated, when a servant interrupted them, saying that Lane was wanted at the telephone. While he was out of the room, Isabelle thought swiftly. What would be the next word? Was it not better to accept his excuse? "They have all done as I have done, men who are honored and respected. It is universal, what we do, and it is only an accident that I am put up as a target for public abuse!" If she persisted in knowing all, she would merely divide herself farther from her husband, who would resent her attitude. And what right had she to examine and judge, when for all these years she had gone her way and let him go his?

The blood beat in her ears, and she was still uncertain when Lane returned. His face had lost its color of passion, and his voice was subdued as he said: —

"Steve has met with an accident, — a serious one."

"Steve!" Isabelle cried.

"Yes; I think we had better go out there at once. Alice got some one to telephone for her."

The account of the accident had been in that late edition of the penny paper which Isabelle had seen, but it had been crowded into the second page by the magnitude of the Atlantic and Pacific sensation. Lane bought the papers, and they read them on their way to Bryn Mawr. Johnston had been run down as he was going to the station early that Saturday afternoon. It was a heavy motor, running at reduced yet lively speed through the crowded city street. A woman with a child by the hand had stepped from the sidewalk to hail an approaching street-car, without noticing the automobile that was bearing down behind her. Steve had seen their danger, rushed for the woman and pulled her and the child out of the way, — got them clear of the motor. But he was struck, a glancing blow in the back, as the motor sheered off. He had been taken to a drug-store, and reviving quickly had insisted on going home. The driver of the car, apparently a humane person, had waited with a notable display of decency and taken the injured man with the doctor who had attended him at the drug-store to Bryn Mawr. . . . The reporter for the penny paper had done his best by the accident, describing the thrilling rescue of the woman and child, the unavoidable blow to the rescuer, with all the vividness of his art.

"It was a brave act," Lane remarked, folding up the sheet and putting it in his pocket. . . .

As soon as they entered, Alice came down to them from the sick room. She was pale, but she seemed to Isabelle wonderfully composed and calm, — the steady balance-wheel of the situation. When Steve had first reached home, he had apparently not been badly off, she told them. He had insisted on walking upstairs and said that he would be quite right after he had laid down a little while. So the doctor went back to the city in the motor. But at dinner time, Alice, going into his room, found him breathing heavily, almost unconscious, and his voice had become so thick that she could scarcely make out what he was saying. She had summoned their own doctor, and he had called another from the city. They feared cerebral trouble, due to a lesion of the spinal chord; but nothing could be certainly determined yet.

"Something seems to be on his mind," Alice said in conclusion. "I thought I made out your name, John; so I had you telephoned for. I don't know that it will do any good, but it may quiet him to see you."

While Lane was upstairs, Alice talked on in the composed, capable, self-contained manner that she usually had, — merely speaking a trifle faster, with occasional pauses, as if she were listening for a sound from Steve's room. But the house was painfully still.

. . . "You see," she explained, "Steve doesn't move quickly, — is too heavy and slow. I suppose that was why he didn't succeed in getting out of the way himself. The car wasn't really going fast, not over eight miles an hour, the chauffeur said. . . . But Steve saved the woman and child, — they would have been killed."

He had saved the woman and child, — chance strangers in the street, — possibly at the cost of his life or the use of his limbs. There was an ironical note in the tragedy. This stout man with the character in his slow organism that could accomplish great things — this hero of Alice's — had stepped off the sidewalk to save the life of a careless passer-by, and risked his own life, the happiness of his wife and children, in just that little way.

"It was so like Steve, — to realize but one point, *their* danger," Alice continued with a proud smile. And Isabelle could see the dull, large-framed man, his head slightly bent, plodding forward in the stream of home-goers on the pavement, suddenly lift his head, and without a moment's hesitation step out into the path of danger. . . .

When Isabelle and John left the house late in the evening, he said gravely, "The doctors don't think there is much chance for him."

"He will die!" Isabelle gasped, thinking of Alice, who had smiled at them cheerily when they went out of the door.

"Perhaps worse than that, — complete paralysis, — the lower limbs are paralyzed now."

"How perfectly awful!"

"I think he knew me. He grasped my hand so hard it hurt, and I could make out my name. But I couldn't understand what he was trying to say."

"Do you suppose it could be the mortgage?"

"Very likely. I must attend to that matter at once."

They were silent on the way back to the city, each buried in thought. The verdict, which had stirred them so deeply a few hours before, had already sunk into the background of life, overshadowed by this nearer, more human catastrophe.

"I shall have to go on to New York to-morrow, for a few days at least," Lane said as they entered the house.

"I will stay here, of course," Isabelle replied, "and you can bring Molly and the governess back with you. I will telegraph them." It was all easily decided, what had seemed perplexing earlier in the evening, when she had been occupied merely with herself and John. "I can be of some help to Alice any way, and if he should die — "

"Yes," Lane agreed. "That is best. I will be back in a week." And he added casually, announcing a decision arrived at on the way to the city: —

"I'll have my lawyer look up that mortgage. You can tell Alice to-morrow and try to get Steve to understand, so that he will have it off his mind as soon as possible."

Her heart responded with a glow. Yes, that was the very thing to do! She had money enough to help them, but she did not know just what to do. It was like John, this sure, quick way of seeing the one thing to be done immediately and doing it. It was like him, too, to do generous things. How many poor boys and young men he had helped along rough roads in their struggle up, — given them the coveted chance in one way and another, without ostentation or theory, simply in the human desire to help another with that surplus strength which had given him his position of vantage.

"I will write the note to Mather now, telling him what to do about the mortgage," he continued in his methodical, undemonstrative manner. As he sat down at the desk and drew pen and paper towards him, he paused a moment. "You will see to the nurses, — they should have two. The doctors may decide on an operation. Have the best men, of course."

He struck pen into the paper with his broad, firm stroke. Isabelle stood watching him, her heart beating strangely, and suddenly leaning over him she kissed his forehead, then fled swiftly to the door.

CHAPTER LXXV

ISABELLE waited in the carriage outside the station for her husband and Molly. The New York train was late as usual. She had driven in from Bryn Mawr, where she had spent most of the ten days since Lane's departure. She was steeped now in the atmosphere of that suburban house covered by the April mist, with the swelling bushes and trees all about it. There had been an operation, decided on after consultation with the eminent surgeons that Isabelle had summoned. After the operation hope had flickered up, as the sick man breathed more easily, was able to articulate a few intelligible words, and showed an interest in what was going on about him. But it had waned again to-day, and when Isabelle left, Alice was holding her husband's large hand, talking to him cheerfully, but there was no response. . . . How wonderful she was, — Alice! That picture of her filled Isabelle's thought as she waited in the carriage. Never a tear or a whimper all these anxious days, always the calm, buoyant voice, even a serene smile and little joke at her husband's bedside, such as she had used to enliven him with, — anything to relax his set, heavy features. "How she loves him!" thought Isabelle, almost with pain.

When she left that afternoon, Alice had sent a grateful message to John. "He will come out to-morrow if he can?" she had asked. She knew now that the hours were numbered without being told so by the doctors. And never a tear, a self-pitying cry! Oh, to be like that, — sturdy in heart and soul, — with that courage before life, that serene confidence in face of the worst fate can offer! Alice was of the faith of Renault.

Lane came down the platform, followed by Molly and her

governess. As he raised his hat in greeting, Isabelle noticed the deep lines at the corners of his mouth, and the line above his broad, straight nose. When they were in the carriage, she realized that her husband had been living these ten days in another world from the one she had inhabited, and in spite of his questions about Steve and Alice, he was preoccupied, still held by the anxieties and perplexities of his business in New York, still in the close grip of his own affairs, his personal struggle. So she talked with Molly, who was almost articulately joyful over her escape from the country, at the sight of streets and motor carriages.

As they were going to dinner a servant brought word that a reporter wished to speak to John. Usually Lane refused to see reporters outside his office, and there turned them over to his secretary, who was skilled in the gentle art of saying inoffensive nothings in many words. But to her surprise John after slight hesitation went into the library to see the man, and it was a long half hour before he returned to his dinner. The evening was another one of those torturing periods when Isabelle's heart was full and yet must be carefully repressed lest she make a false step. After a little talk about Molly, her mother, the Johnstons, Lane turned to open his mail that had been sent up for him from the office. Isabelle left him absorbed in this task, but she could not sleep, and when at last she heard him go to his room, she followed him. Laying her hands on his arms, she looked at him pleadingly, longing now not so much to know the facts, to reason and judge, as to understand, perhaps comfort him, — at least to share the trouble with him.

"Can't you tell me all about it, John?"

"About what?" he demanded dryly, his dislike of effusiveness, emotionalism, showing in the glitter of his gray eyes.

"Tell me what is troubling you! I want to share it, — all of it. What has happened?"

He did not answer at once. There was an evident struggle

to overcome his habitual reserve, the masculine sense of independence in the conduct of his affairs. Also, there was between them her prejudice, the woman's insufficient knowledge, and the barrier of the long years of aloofness. But at last, as if he had reflected that she would have to know soon in any case, he said dryly: —

"The Board has voted to relieve me of my duties as general manager of traffic. I am assigned to St. Louis for the present, but the duties are not specified. A polite hint — which I have taken!"

"Did Mr. Beals do that?"

"Beals went to Europe on his vacation when the coal cases first came up. . . . Besides, it would have made no difference. I think I see in it the fine hand of our good friend the Senator, — smug-faced old fox!"

Isabelle felt how much this action by the directors had stung him, how severely he was suffering.

"It was . . . because of the verdict?"

"Oh, the general mess, the attacks in the press, complaints from stockholders! They want to get under cover, show the public they are cleaning house, I suppose. They thought to shelve me until the row fizzles out, then drop me. But I am not the sort of man to sit around as a willing sacrifice, to pose for the papers as a terrible example. They will know, to-morrow!"

Isabelle understood why he had consented to see the reporter. Hitherto, he had refused to speak, to make any public defence of himself or comment on the trial. But after this action on the part of the directors, after the long smouldering hours on the train, he had decided to speak, — at length. It would not be pleasant reading in certain quarters near Wall Street, what he said, but it would make good copy.

Biting fiercely at his cigar, which had gone out, he struck a match sharply and talked on: —

"I am not a back number yet. There is not another road in the country that has shown such results, such gain in traffic, as the A. and P. since I was put in charge of traffic five years ago. There are others who know it, too, in New York. I shan't have to twiddle my thumbs long when my resignation is published. The prejudiced trial out here won't stand in the way."

In the storm of his mood, it was useless to ask questions. Isabelle merely murmured: —

"Too bad, too bad, — I am so sorry, John!"

Instead of that dispassionate groping for the exact truth, justice between her husband and the public, that she had first desired, she was simply compassionate for his hurt pride. Innocent or guilty, what right had she to judge him? Even if the worst of what had been charged was literally true, had she not abandoned him at the start, — left him to meet the problems of the modern battle as he could, — to harden his soul against all large and generous considerations? Now when he was made the scapegoat for the sins of others, for the sin of his race, too, — how could she sit and censure! The time would come for calm consideration between them. There was that something in her heart which buoyed her above the present, above the distress of public condemnation, — even disgrace and worldly failure. Coming close to him again, she said with ringing conviction: —

"It can make no difference to you and me, John!"

He failed to see her meaning.

"The money doesn't matter, — it isn't that, of course. We shan't starve!"

"I didn't mean the money!"

"Sensible people know what it amounts to, — only the mob yaps."

"I didn't mean criticism, either," she said softly.

"Well, that New York crowd hasn't heard the last of me yet!"

His lips shut tight together. The spirit of fight, of revenge, was aroused. It was useless to talk further. She drew his arm about her.

"You will go out to see Steve to-morrow, won't you?"

"Yes, of course, — any time in the afternoon."

She kissed him and went back to her room.

One precept out of Renault's thin book of life was hard to acquire, — Patience. But it must be acquired, — the power to abide the time calmly, until the right moment should come. The morrows contain so many reversals of the to-days!

CHAPTER LXXVI

It was probable that the dying man did not recognize Lane, though it was hard to say what dim perception entered through the glazing eyes and penetrated the clouding brain. The children had been about the room all the morning, Alice said, and from the way the father clung to Jack's hand she thought there still was recognition. But the sense of the outer world was fast fading now. The doctor was there, by way of kindly solicitude, — he could do nothing; and when the Lanes came he went away, whispering to John as he left, "Not long now." Alice had sent away the nurse, as she had the night before, refusing to lose these last minutes of service. She told Isabelle that in the early morning, while she was watching and had thought Steve was asleep from his quieter breathing, she had found his eyes resting on her with a clear look of intelligence, and then kneeling down with her face close to his lips he had whispered thickly. Her eyes were still shining from those last lover's words in the night. . . .

When John went back to the city, Isabelle stayed on, taking luncheon with the nurses and little Belle. Neighbors came to the door to inquire, to leave flowers. These neighbors had been very kind, Alice had said often, taking the boys to their homes and doing the many little errands of the household. "And I hardly knew them to bow to! It's wonderful how people spring up around you with kindness when trouble comes!" . . .

Meanwhile, overhead the life was going out, the strong man yielding slowly to the inevitable. Twilight came on, the doctor returned and went away again, and the house became absolutely still. Once Isabelle crept upstairs to the door of the sick room. Alice was holding Steve's head, with one arm under his pillow, looking, — looking at him with devouring eyes! . . . Gradually the breathing grew fainter, at longer intervals, the eyelids fell over the vacant eyes, and after a little while the nurse, passing Isabelle on the stairs, whispered that it was over, — the ten days' losing fight. Presently Alice came out of the room, her eyes still shining strangely, and smiled at Isabelle.

When they went out the next afternoon, there was in the house that dreary human pause created by the fact of death, — pause without rest. Flowers scented the air, and people moved about on tiptoe, saying nothings in hushed voices, and trying to be themselves.

But in the dim room above, where Alice took them, there was peace and naturalness. The dead man lay very straight beneath the sheet, his fleshy body shrunken after its struggle to its bony stature. Isabelle had always thought Steve a homely man, — phlegmatic and ordinary in feature. She had often said, "How can Alice be so romantic over old Steve!" But as the dead man lay there, wasted, his face seemed to have taken on a grave and austere dignity, an expression of resolute will in the heavy jaw, the high brow, the broad nostril, as though the steadfast soul within, so prosaically muffled in the flesh, had at the last spoken out to those nearest him the meaning of his life, graving it on his dead face. Lane, caught by this high, commanding note of the lifeless features, as of one who, though removed by infinite space, still spoke to the living, gazed steadily at the dead man. And Isabelle felt the awe of his presence; here was one who could speak with authority of elemental truths. . . .

Alice, her arms resting on the foot-rail of the bed, was leaning forward, looking with eyes still shining at her husband, her lover, her mate. And her lips parted in a little smile. Large and strong and beautiful, in the full tide of conscious life, she contemplated her dead comrade.

A feeling that she was in the presence of mystery — the mystery of perfect human union — stole through Isabelle. The woman standing there at the feet of her dead man had had it all, — all the experience that woman can have. Had she not loved this man, received his passion, borne his children, fought by his side the fight of life, — and above all and beyond all else cherished in her the soul of the man, the sacred part of him, that beauty unknown to others hitherto, now written plain for all to see on his face! And her lighted eyes seemed to say, 'What place is there here for grief? Even though I am left in mid life, to struggle on alone with my children, without his help, yet have I not had it all? Enough to warm my heart and soul through the empty years that must come!' . . .

Tears dropped from Isabelle's eyes, and convulsively she grasped the hand that rested beside her, as though she would say, 'To lose all this, what you two have had, how can you bear it!' Alice bent down over her tear-stained face and kissed her,— with a little gesture towards Steve, murmuring "I have had so much!"

They walked slowly back to the city in the warm April night. Neither had spoken since they left the little house, until Isabelle said with a deep solemnity: —

"It was perfect — that!"

"Yes! Steve was a good man, and Alice loved him."

Each knew what lay behind these commonplace words in the heart of the other. These two, Steve and Alice, in spite of hardship, the dull grind of their restricted existence, the many children, the disappointments, had had something — a human satisfaction — that *they* had missed — forever; and as they walked on through the deserted streets silently, side by side, they saw that now it could never be for them. It was something that missed once in its perfection was missed for all time. However near they might come to be, however close in understanding and effort, they could never know the mystery of two who had lived together, body and soul, and together had solved life.

For mere physical fidelity is but a small part of the comradeship of marriage.

CHAPTER LXXVII

Miss Marian Lane was such a thorough cosmopolite that she had no discernible affection for any place. She referred to Central Park, to the Farm, to the Price house in St. Louis, to Grosvenor with equal indifference and impartiality, as she might later to London or Paris or Rome. She did not even ask her mother where they were to spend the summer. That there was a Park in St. Louis, as in all properly created cities, she had confidence, because she asked Miss Joyce to take her there the day after her arrival. Isabelle's own childhood had been strongly colored by places, — the old house in K Street, this ugly Victorian mansion, and especially the Farm. Places had meant so much to her in her youth, her feelings reflecting their physical atmosphere, that they had been more vivid than persons. But Molly was equally content anywhere. She needed merely Miss Joyce, a Park, and pretty clothes.

Clothes, indeed, were the only subject that aroused a semblance of passion in Molly's sedate soul. "Oh, we shall go shopping, mamma!" she exclaimed with the first real animation Isabelle had seen in her, when her grandmother remarked that Molly had outgrown all her dresses this winter. They were sitting in the large front bedroom that the Colonel and his wife had always occupied. Mrs. Price had just returned from the Springs, and was already talking of spending the summer in Europe. Since the Colonel's death she had become a great globe-trotter, indefatigably whisking hither and thither with her reliable maid. It seemed as if after all these years of faithful economy and routine living, the suppressed restlessness of her race, which had developed at an earlier age in Isabelle, was revenging itself upon the old lady. "Mother's travels" had become a household joke. . . .

"Can't we go to-day? Miss Joyce and I saw some lovely things at Roseboro's, mother!" Molly urged, jumping up from the lounge, where she had been telling her grandmother about Grosvenor. "Oh, yes, grandmother," Isabelle had heard her say in a listless voice, "we had a pleasant time in Grosvenor. Miss Joyce took me coasting with James Pole. And we had sleigh rides. Miss Joyce was afraid to drive the horses, so we did not go except when Mrs. Pole took us. . . . Aunt Margaret was very nice. Miss Joyce gave us all dancing lessons." . . .

It was always Miss Joyce this and Miss Joyce that, since Molly's return, until Isabelle had impatiently concluded that the faithful English governess with her narrow character had completely ironed out the personality of her charge. As she listened to Molly's conversation with her grandmother, she resolved to get rid of Miss Joyce, in order to escape hearing her name if for no other reason.

"I suppose you'll wait to get her clothes until you are back in New York," the practical Mrs. Price observed; "they are so much cheaper and more tasteful there. The stores here don't seem to be what they were, — even Roseboro's can't compare with Altman's and Best's for children's things."

"We may not be in New York this spring," Isabelle replied, waking from her meditations on the subject of Miss Joyce and her daughter. "John's plans are uncertain — and I don't care to go without him."

"You can try Roseboro's, then; but I don't believe you will be satisfied."

"Oh, mamma, can't we go in the motor now!"

And Molly ran to Miss Joyce to dress herself for the expedition.

Isabelle had scrutinized her little daughter with fresh interest the few days she had been with her. Molly had always been an unresponsive child since she was a baby.

In spite of her beautiful pink coloring, carefully preserved by country life, she was scarcely more alive than an automaton. Whatever individuality she had was so deeply buried that her mother could not discover it. Why was it? Why was she so colorless? She had been "moved about" a good deal, like many American children, according to the exigencies of the family, — to St. Louis, the Farm, the New York hotel, the New York house, Europe, Grosvenor, — a rapid succession of panoramas for one small mind to absorb. But Molly had never seemed disturbed by it. One place was as good as another, — one set of children, provided they had nice manners and were well dressed, as agreeable as any other. If she were put down in a Pasadena hotel, she found playmates, judiciously selected by Miss Joyce, of course, who supervised their games. In all the changes of scene Isabelle had been most scrupulous in her care for diet, exercises, régime, and as long as the child seemed content and physically well she had seen no harm in taking her about from scene to scene. Now Isabelle had her doubts.

The little girl came downstairs, followed by the capable Miss Joyce, who was brushing out a fold in her white broadcloth coat and arranging a curl, and looked in at her mother's room, with a pretty little smile and a gesture of the fingers she had copied from some child. "All ready, mamma, — shall we wait for you in the motor?" As she passed on, followed by Miss Joyce, — the figure of dainty young plutocracy and her mentor, — Isabelle murmured, "I wonder if it has been good for her to move about so much!"

Mrs. Price, a literal old lady, took up the remark: —

"Why, she looks healthy. Miss Joyce takes excellent care of her. I think you are very fortunate in Miss Joyce, Isabelle."

"I don't mean her health, mother!"

"She is as forward as most children of her age, — she speaks French very prettily," the grandmother protested. "She has nice manners, too."

Isabelle saw the futility of trying to explain what she meant to her mother, and yet the old lady in her next irrelevant remark touched the very heart of the matter.

"Children have so much attention these days, — what they eat and do is watched over every minute. Why, we had a cat and a dog, and a doll or two, the kitchen and the barn to run about in — and that was all. Parents were too busy to fuss about their children. Boys and girls had to fit into the home the best they could."

There was a home to fit into! A cat and a dog, a few dolls, and the kitchen and the barn to run about in, — that was more than Molly Lane with all her opportunities had ever had.

"There weren't any governesses or nurses; but we saw more of our father and mother, naturally," the old lady continued. "Only very rich people had nurses in those times."

The governess was a modern luxury, provided to ease the conscience of lazy or incompetent mothers, who had "too much to do" to be with their children. Isabelle knew all the arguments in their favor. She remembered Bessie Falkner's glib defence of the governess method, when she had wanted to stretch Rob's income another notch for this convenience, — "If a mother is always with her children, she can't give her best self either to them or to her husband!" Isabelle had lived enough since then to realize that this vague "best self" of mothers was rarely given to anything but distraction.

Isabelle had been most conscientious as a mother, spared no thought or pains for her child from her birth. The trained nurse during the first two years, the succession of carefully selected governesses since, the lessons, the food, the dentist, the doctors, the clothes, the amusements, — all had been scrupulously, almost religiously, provided according to the best modern theories. Nothing had been left to chance. Marian should be a paragon, physically and morally. Yet, her mother had to confess, the child bored her, — was a wooden doll! In the scientifically sterilized atmosphere in which she had lived, no vicious germ had been allowed to fasten itself on the young organism, and yet thus far the product was tasteless. Perhaps Molly was merely a commonplace little girl, and she was realizing it for the first time. Isabelle's maternal pride refused to accept such a depressing answer, and moreover she did not believe that any young thing, any kitten or puppy, could be as colorless, as little vital as the exquisite Miss Lane. She must find the real cause, study her child, live with her awhile. The next generation, apparently, was as inscrutable a manuscript to read as hers had been to the Colonel and her mother. Her parents had never understood all the longings and aspirations that had filled her fermenting years, and now she could not comprehend the dumbness of her child. Those fermenting years had gone for nothing so far as teaching her to understand the soul of her child. The new ferment was of a different composition, it seemed. . . .

Isabelle was to find that her daughter had developed certain tastes besides a love for clothes and a delight in riding in motor-cars. . . . Molly was in the library after luncheon, absorbed in an illustrated story of a popular magazine, which Isabelle glanced over while Miss Joyce made ready her charge to accompany her mother to the Johnstons'. The story was "innocent," "clean reading" enough, — thin pages of smart dialogue between prettily dressed young men and athletic girls, the puppy loves of the young rich, — mere stock fiction-padding of the day. But the picture of life — the suggestion to the child's soft brain? Isabelle tossed the magazine into the waste basket, and yawned. Molly had left it with a sigh.

On the way to the Bryn Mawr house Isabelle tried to explain to Molly what had happened to the Johnstons through the loss of the father, telling her what a good man Steve was, the sorrow the family had to bear. Molly listened politely.

"Yes, mother!" And she asked, "Are they very poor?" An innocent remark that irritated Isabelle unreasonably.

The children played together downstairs while Isabelle discussed with Alice some business matters. It had not sounded very lively below, and when the mothers came down they found Molly and Belle sitting on opposite sides of the little parlor, looking stiffly at each other. The boys had slipped off for more stirring adventures outdoors, which Molly had refused to join, as she was making a formal call with her mother. In the motor going home Molly remarked: "The boys haven't good manners. Belle seems a nice girl. She hasn't been anywhere and can't talk. That was a very homely dress she had on; don't you think so? Does she have to wear dresses like that? Can't you give her something prettier, mamma?"

Isabelle, who thought her god-daughter an interesting child, full of independence and vitality in spite of her shyness, wondered, "Is Molly just a stick, or only a little snob?"

Molly was sitting very gracefully in her grandmother's limousine, riding through the parks and avenues with the air of a perfect little lady accustomed to observe the world from the cushioned seat of a brougham or motor-car. Catching sight of a bill board with the announcement of a popular young actress's coming engagement, she remarked: —

"Miss Daisy May is such a perfect dear, don't you think, mamma? Couldn't Miss Joyce take me to see her act next Saturday afternoon? It's a perfectly nice play, you know."

Repressing a desire to shake her daughter, Isabelle replied: "I'll take you myself, Molly. And shan't we invite Delia Conry? You know she is at school here and has very few friends."

"Oh!" Molly said thoughtfully. "Delia is so ordinary. I should like to ask Beatrice Lawton, — Miss Joyce knows her governess. . . . Or if we must be good to some one, we might take Belle."

"We'll take them both."

"I don't think Beatrice would enjoy Belle," her daughter objected after further reflection.

"Well, I shall ask Delia and Belle, then, to go with me alone!"

(She had looked up the Conry child at the school where Vickers had sent her, and had arranged to have her brother's small estate settled on the girl, as she felt he would have wished. Delia, whose mother had never been heard from, was a forlorn little object and Isabelle pitied her.)

When her temporary irritation with Molly had passed, she saw there was nothing unnatural in the child's attitude. Probably she was a little snob. Most children brought up as Molly had been, most of her friends, were little snobs. Their governesses taught them snobbery, unconsciously; their domestic habits taught them snobbery.

Isabelle resolved more firmly that she should dispense with the excellent Miss Joyce. A beginning very far down would have to be made, if she were to reach the individuality of this perfectly nurtured modern child of hers. There was nothing bad about Molly; she was irritatingly blameless. But what she lacked was appalling! At eighteen she would be unendurable.

And the mother had no warm feeling, no impelling affection for her daughter, any more than the child had for her. That lack would make it all the harder to do what must be done. Here, again, as with her husband, she must begin to pay for all the years that she had shirked her job, — for the sake of "her own life," her intellectual emancipation and growth, — shirked, to be sure, in the most conscientious and enlightened modern manner.

For nobody could call Miss Lane a neglected child.

CHAPTER LXXVIII

It would be very simple for Mrs. Price to provide Alice with a comfortable income, — the Colonel would have done so; and when Isabelle suggested it to her mother after the funeral of Steve, the old lady agreed, though she was not of a philanthropic nature and recalled the fact that the marriage had been a foolish one. But Alice flatly refused the arrangement. She had been trained to work; she was not too old to find something to do, and she had already taken steps to secure a place as matron in a hospital. "I am strong," she said to Isabelle. "Steve has left it for me to do, — all of it. And I want to show him that I can do it. I shall be happier!"

John had a better comprehension of her feelings and of the situation than either Isabelle or her mother. "Alice is an able woman," he had said; "she will not break down, — she is not that kind. And she'll be happier working."

So he took care of her little life insurance money. He also obtained a scholarship in a technical school for the oldest boy, and undertook to fit the second one for college, as he showed studious tendencies. Isabelle would look after Belle's education. In all these practical details of readjusting the broken family, John Lane was more effective than his wife, giving generously of his crowded hours to the Johnston affairs, ever ready to do all that might be done without hurting the widow's pride and vigorous will.

And this, as Isabelle knew, came in the days of his greatest personal perplexity. His resignation as third vice-president had been accepted after protest, negotiations, and then had elicited a regretful communication to the press (emanating from the Senator's office) of an eulogistic nature, concluding with the delicately phrased suggestion that "Mr. Lane's untiring devotion to his work necessitates his taking a rest from all business cares for the present. It is understood that he contemplates a long vacation in Europe."

John handed the paper to Isabelle with an ironical smile.

"You see we are to go abroad, — the usual thing! That's the Senator's crafty hand. He wants everything decently smooth."

But the public no longer cared. The coal cases had gone up to a higher court on appeal, and when the final decision was handed down, the "street" would be interested not in the question of John Lane's guilt or innocence, but in the more important question of whether the Supreme Court "would back up the President's campaign against capital."

Meanwhile, there was none of the social stigma attached to the verdict against her husband that Isabelle had resolutely expected. As soon as it was known that the Lanes were established in the city for the spring, their friends sought them out and they were invited to dine more than Isabelle cared for. In their class, as she quickly perceived from jesting references to the trial, such legal difficulties as John's were regarded as merely the disagreeable incidents of doing business in a socialistic age. Lane, far from being "down and out," was considered in the industrial and railroad world a strong man rather badly treated by a weak-kneed board of directors, who had sought to save themselves from trouble by sacrificing an able servant to the public storm. No sooner was his resignation published than he received an offer of the presidency of a large transit company in the middle West. While he was considering this offer, he was approached by representatives of another great railroad, which, though largely owned by the same "interests" that controlled the Atlantic and Pacific, was generally supposed to be a rival. Lane was too valuable a man to be lost to the railroad army. The "interests" recognized in him a powerful instrument, trained from boyhood for their purposes, — one "who knew how to get business." The offer flattered Lane, and soothed that sore spot in his inner consciousness. He saw himself reinstated in his old world, with a prospect of crossing swords with his old superiors in a more than secondary position.

Isabelle knew all about this offer. She and her husband talked together more freely than they had ever done before. The experiences of the past weeks, — Steve's death, the planning for Alice's future, as well as the emotional result of the trial — had brought them nearer an understanding. Lane had begun to realize a latent aptitude in his wife for grasping the essential matters of business, — investments, risks, corporation management. She understood far more than the distinction between stock and bond, which is supposedly the limit of woman's business intelligence. As the warm May days came on they took long rides into the fresh country, talking over the endless detail of affairs, — her money, her mother's money, the Colonel's trust funds, the Johnstons' future, the railroad situation, — all that John Lane had hitherto carried tightly shut in his own mind.

And thus Isabelle began to comprehend the close relation between what is called "business" and the human matters of daily life for every individual in this complex world. There was not simply a broad mark between right and wrong, — dramatic trials; but the very souls of men and women were involved in the vast machine of labor and profit.

She was astonished to discover the extent of her husband's interests, his personal fortune, which had grown amazingly during these last ten fat years of the country's prosperity.

"Why, you don't have to take any position!"

"Yes, we could afford to make that European trip the Board so kindly indicated."

"We *might* go abroad," she said thoughtfully.

A few years before she would have grasped the chance to live in Europe indefinitely. Now she found no inclination in her spirit for this solution.

"It isn't exactly the time to leave home," her husband objected; "there is sure to be a severe panic before long.

All this agitation has unsettled business, and the country must reap the consequences. We could go for a few months, perhaps."

"It wouldn't be good for Molly."

And though she did not say it, it would not be good for him to leave the struggle for any length of time. Once out of the game of life, for which he had been trained like an athlete, he would degenerate and lose his peculiar power. And yet she shrank unaccountably from his reëntering the old life, with the bitter feeling in his heart he now had. It meant their living in New York, for one thing, and a growing repugnance to that huge, squirming, prodigal hive had come over her. Once the pinnacle of her ambitions, now it seemed sordid, hectic, unreal. Yet she was too wise to offer her objections, to argue the matter, any more than to open the personal wound of his trial and conviction. Influence, at least with a man of John Lane's fibre, must be a subtle, slow process, depending on mutual confidence, comprehension. And she must first see clearly what she herself knew to be best. So she listened, waiting for the vision which would surely come.

In these business talks her mind grasped more and more the issues of American life. She learned to recognize the distinction between the officials of corporations and the control behind, — the money power. There emerged into view something of a panorama of industry, organized on modern lines, — the millions of workers in the industrial armies, the infinite gradations of leadership in these armies, and finally far off in the distance, among the cañons of the skyscrapers in the great cities, the Mind of it all, the Control, the massed Capital. There were the Marshals' quarters! Even the chiefs of great corporations were "little people" compared with their real employers, the men who controlled capital. And into that circle of intoxicating power, within its influence, she felt that her husband was slowly moving, — would ultimately arrive, if success came, — at the height of modern fame. Men did not reach the Marshals' quarters with a few hundred thousands of dollars, nor with a few millions, with savings and inheritances and prudent thrift. They must have tens of millions at their command. And these millions came through alliances, manipulations, deals, by all sorts of devices whereby money could be made to spawn miraculously. . . .

Meanwhile the worker earned his wage, and the minor officers their salaries — what had they to complain of? — but the pelf went up to the Marshals' camp, the larger part of it, — in this land where all were born free and equal. No! Isabelle shuddered at the spectacle of the bloody road up to the camp, and prayed that her life might not be lived in an atmosphere of blood and alarms and noisy strife, even for the sake of millions of dollars and limitless Power.

One evening in this period of dubitation Lane remarked casually: —

"Your father's friend, Pete Larrimore, came in to-day to see me. Do you remember him, Isabelle? The old fellow with the mutton-chop whiskers, who used to send us bags of coffee from his plantation in Mexico."

"Awful coffee, — we couldn't give it away!"

"He wanted to talk to me about a scheme he is interested in. It seems that he has a lot of property in the southwest, Oklahoma and the Texas Panhandle, some of it very valuable. Among other things he has become involved in a railroad. It was started by some people who hadn't the capital to carry it through, and now it begins nowhere and ends in the same place. Larrimore and his friends think they can get the capital to carry the road south to the line and up north, and ultimately will sell it perhaps to one of the big systems. . . . They are looking for a man to build it and push it through."

"What did you say?" Isabelle demanded eagerly.

"Oh, I just listened. If they can get the money, it might be successful. That country is growing fast. . . . It would be a chance for some young man to win his spurs, — hard work, though."

He talked on, explaining the strategic position of the new road, its relation to rivals, the prospects of that part of the country, the present condition of the money market in respect to new enterprises; for Isabelle seemed interested. But when she interrupted with sudden energy, "Do it, John! Why don't *you* take it?" he looked puzzled.

"It is a young man's job, — pioneer work."

"But you are young — we are young! And it would be something worth doing, pioneer work, building up a new country like that."

"There's not much money in it," he replied, smiling at her girlish enthusiasm, "and I am afraid not much fame."

Not money, not the fame of the gladiator, the fame of the money power; merely the good report of a labor competently performed, the reward of energy and capacity — and the thing done itself. But to Isabelle this pioneer quality of the work appealed strongly. Her imagination expanded under the idea.

"I can see you living for the next ten years in a small Texas town!" he jested. "However, I suppose you wouldn't live out there."

"But I should!" she protested. "And it is what I should like best of all, I think — the freedom, the open air, the new life!"

So from a merely casual suggestion that Lane had not thought worth serious consideration, there began to grow between them a new conception of their future. And the change that these last weeks had brought was marked by the freedom with which husband and wife talked not only about the future, but about the past. Isabelle tried to tell her husband what had been going on within her at the trial, and since then.

"I know," she said, "that you will say I can't understand, that my feeling is only a woman's squeamishness or ignorance. . . . But, John, I can't bear to think of our going back to it, living on in that way, the hard way of success, as it would be in New York."

Lane looked at her narrowly. He was trying to account for this new attitude in his wife. That she would be pleased, or at least indifferent, at the prospect of returning to the East, to the New York life that she had always longed for and apparently enjoyed, he had taken for granted. Yet in spite of the fixed lines in which his nature ran and the engrossing preoccupations of his interests, he had felt many changes in Isabelle since her return to St. Louis, — changes that he ascribed generally to the improvement in her health,— better nerves, — but that he could not altogether formulate. Perhaps they were the indirect result of her brother's death. At any rate his wife's new interest in business, in his affairs, pleased him. He liked to talk things over with her. . . .

Thus the days went steadily by towards the decision. Lane had promised his wife to consider the Larrimore offer. One morning the cable brought the startling news that the president of the Atlantic and Pacific had committed suicide in his hotel room in Paris the evening before he was to sail for home. "Bad health and nervous collapse," was the explanation in the despatch. But that a man of sixty-three, with a long record of honorable success, a large fortune, no family troubles, should suddenly take his own life, naturally roused the liveliest amazement throughout the country. Nobody believed that the cable told the whole truth; but the real reasons for the desperate act were locked tight among the directors of the railroad corporation and a few intimate heads of control — who know all.

Lane read the news to Isabelle. It shook him perceptibly. He had known Farrington Beals for years, ever since at the Colonel's suggestion he had been picked out of the army of underlings and given his first chance. Isabelle remembered him even longer, and especially at her wedding with the Senator and her father. They were old family friends, the Bealses.

"How terrible for Mrs. Beals and Elsie!" she exclaimed. "How could he have done it! The family was so happy. They all adored him! And he was about to retire, Elsie told me when I saw her last, and they were all going around the world in their yacht. . . . He couldn't have been very ill."

"No, I am afraid that wasn't the only reason," John admitted, walking to and fro nervously.

He was thinking of all that the old man had done for him, his resentment at his chief's final desertion of him forgotten; of how he had learned his job, been trained to pull his load by the dead man, who had always encouraged him, pushed him forward.

"He went over for a little rest, you said. And he always went every year about this time for a vacation and to buy pictures. Don't you remember, John, what funny things he bought, and how the family laughed at him?"

"Yes,—I know." He also knew that the president of the Atlantic and Pacific had gone across the ocean "for his yearly vacation" just at the opening of the coal investigation to escape the scandal of the trial, and had not returned at the usual time, although the financial world was unsettled. And he knew other things; for already clubs and inner offices had been buzzing with rumors.

"I am afraid that it is worse than it seems," he said to his wife on his return from the city that afternoon. "Beals was terribly involved. I hear that a bank he was interested in has been closed. . . . He was tied up fast—in all sorts of ways!"

"John!" Isabelle cried, and paused. Did this old man's death mean another scandal, ruin for another family, and one she had known well,—disgrace, scandal, possibly poverty?

"Beals was always in the market — and this panic hit him hard; he was on the wrong side lately."

It was an old story, not in every case with the same details, but horribly common,—a man of the finest possibilities, of sturdy character, rising up to the heights of ambition, then losing his head, playing the game wantonly for mere pride and habit in it,—his judgment giving way, but playing on, stumbling, grasping at this and that to stop his sliding feet, breaking the elementary laws! And finally, in the face of disaster, alone in a hotel room the lonely old man — no doubt mentally broken by the strain — putting the pistol to his head with his shaking hand. And, afterwards, the débris of his wreck would be swept aside to clear the road for others!

Farrington Beals was not a single case. In this time of money disturbance, suicide and dishonor were rife in the streets, revealing the rotten timber that could not stand the strain of modern life, lived as it had been lived the past ten years. It was not one blast that uprooted weak members of the forest, but the eating decay of the previous years, working at the heart of many lives. "The frantic egotism of the age!" Yes, and the divided souls, never at peace until death put an end to the strife at last, — too much for little bodies of nerve and tissue to stand, — the racking of divided wills, divided souls.

"John!" Isabelle cried that night, after they had again talked over the tragedy; "let us go — go out there — to a new land!" She rose from the lounge and swept across the room with the energy of clear purpose — of Vision. "Let us put ourselves as far as possible out of this sort of thing! . . . It will kill us both. Do it for my sake, even if you can't feel as I do!"

And then there poured forth all the story of these years, of their life apart, as she had come to see it the last months, in the remote and peaceful hills, in the court-room, in the plain pathos of Steve's death and Alice's heroism, and now in this suicide,—all that had given her insight and made her different from what she had been, — all that revealed the cheapness of her old ideals of freedom, intellectual development, self-satisfaction, that cult of the ego, which she had pursued in sympathy with the age. Now she wished to put it away, to remove herself and her husband, their lives together, outwardly as she had withdrawn herself inwardly. And her husband, moved in spite of himself by her tense desire, the energy of her words, listened and comprehended — in part.

"I have never been a real wife to you, John. I don't mean just my love for that other man, when you were nobly generous with me. But before that, in other ways, in almost all ways that make a woman a wife, a real wife. . . . Now I want to be a real wife. I want to be with you in all things. . . . You can't see the importance of this step as I do. Men and women are different, always. But there is something within me, underneath, like an inner light that makes me see clearly now, — not conscience, but a kind of flame that guides. In the light of that I see what a petty fool I have been. It all had to be — I don't regret because it all had to be — the terrible waste, the sacrifice," she whispered, thinking of Vickers. "Only now we must live, you and I together, — together live as we have never lived before!"

She held out her hands to him as she spoke, her head erect, and as he waited, still tied by years of self-repression, she went to him and put her arms about him, drawing him to her, to her breast, to her eyes. Ten years before he had adored her, desired her passionately, and she had shrunk from him. Then life had come imperceptibly in between them; he had gone his way, she hers. Now she was offering herself to him. And she was more desirable than before, more woman, — at last whole. The appeal that had never been wholly stifled in the man still beat in his pulses for the woman. And the appeal never wholly roused in the woman by him reached out now for him; but an appeal not merely of the senses, higher than anything Cairy could rouse in a woman, an appeal, limitless, of comradeship, purpose, wills. He kissed her, holding her close to him, realizing that she too held him in the inner place of her being.

"We will begin again," he said.

"Our new life — together!"

And this is Influence, the work of one will upon another, sometimes apparent, dramatic, tragic; sometimes subtle, unknowable, speaking across dark gulfs. The meaning of that dead man's austere face, the howl of journalists on his uncovered trail, the old man dead in his hotel room disgraced, the deep current of purpose in his new wife, — all these and much more sent messages into the man's unyielding soul to change the atmosphere therein, to alter the values of things seen, to shape — at last — the will. For what makes an act? Filaments of nerve, some shadowy unknown process in brain cells? These are but symbols for mystery! Life pressing multifariously its changing suggestions upon the sentient organism prompts, at last, the act. But there is something deeper than the known in all this wondrous complexity. . . .

John Lane, the man of fact, the ordered efficient will, was dimly conscious of forces other than physical ones, beyond, — not recognizable as motives, — self-created and impelling, nevertheless; forces welling up from the tenebrous spaces in the depths of his being, beneath conscious life. And at last, something higher than Judgment swayed the man.

CHAPTER LXXIX

THE private car Olympus had been switched for the day to a siding at the little town of Orano on the edge of the Texas upland. The party within — the Lanes, Margaret and her children, and several men interested in the new railroad — had been making a leisurely tour of inspection, passing through the fertile prairies and woodlands of Oklahoma, stopping often at the little towns that were springing up along the road, aiming south until they had reached the Panhandle. These September days the harvests were rich and heavy, covered with a golden haze of heat, — the sweat of earth's accomplishment. The new soil was laden with its fruit. The men had been amazed by the fertility, the force of the country. "Traffic, traffic," Lane had murmured enthusiastically, divining with his trained eye the enormous possibilities of the land, the future for the iron highroad he was pushing through it. Traffic, — in other words, growth, business, human effort and human life, — that is the cosmic song that sings itself along the iron road.

Margaret had said mockingly: —

"Wouldn't it do our New York friends a world of good to get out here once a year and realize that life goes on, and very real life, outside the narrow shores of Manhattan!"

That was the illuminating thought which had come to them all in different ways during this slow progress from St. Louis south and west. This broad land of states had a vital existence, a life of its own, everywhere, not merely in the great centres, the glutted metropolitan points. Men lived and worked, happily, constructively, in thousands and thousands of small places, where the seaboard had sunk far beneath the eastern horizon. Life was real, to be lived vitally, as much here in prairie and plain as anywhere on the earth's surface. The feeling which had come to Isabelle on her westward journey in March — the conviction that *each one* counted, had his own terrestrial struggle, his own celestial drama, differing very little in importance from his neighbor's; each one — man, woman, or child — in all the wonderful completeness of life throughout the millions — swept over her again here where the race was sowing new land. And lying awake in the stillness of the autumn morning on the lofty plateau, as she listened to the colored servants chaffing at their work, there came to her the true meaning of that perplexing phrase, which had sounded with the mockery of empty poetry on the lips of the district attorney, — "All men born free and equal." Yes! in the realm of their spirits, in their souls, — the inner, moving part of them, "free and equal"! . . .

"It's the roof of the world!" Margaret said, as she jumped from the car platform and looked over the upland, — whimsically recalling the name of a popular play then running in New York.

An unawakened country, dry and untilled, awaiting the hand of the master, it lifted westward in colored billows of undulating land. Under the clear morning sun it was still and fresh, yet untouched, untamed.

"It *is* the roof of the world," she repeated, "high and dry and extraordinarily vast, — leading your eyes onward and upward to the heavens, with all the rest of the earth below you in the fog. How I should like to live here always! If I were you, Isabelle, I should get your husband to give you a freight-car like those the gangs of track-layers use, with a little stovepipe sticking out of one corner, and just camp down in it here, — on the roof of the world."

She lifted her thin, delicate face to the sun, reaching out her arms to it hungrily.

"We must sleep out to-night under the stars, and talk — oh, much talk, out here under the stars!"

During the past year at Grosvenor her frail body had

strengthened, revived; she was now firm and vigorous. Only the deep eyes and the lines above them and about the mouth, the curve of the nostril and chin, showed as on a finely chased coin the subtle chiselling of life. And here in the uplands, in the great spaces of earth and sky, the elemental desire of her soul seemed at last wholly appeased, the longing for space and height and light, the longing for deeds and beauty and Peace. At last, after the false roads, the fret and rebellion, she had emerged into the upper air. . . .

"How well the little man rides!" Isabelle remarked as the children went by them on some ponies they had found.

Margaret's face glowed with pride.

"Yes, Ned has improved very fast. He will go to school with the others now. . . . The doctor has really saved his life — and mine, too," she murmured.

So the two slept out under the stars, as Margaret wished, with dotted heavens close above and vague space all about; and they talked into the morning of past years, of matters that meant too much to them both for daylight speech. Isabelle spoke of Vickers, of the apparent waste of his life. "I can see now," she said, "that in going away with that woman as he did he expressed the real soul of him, as he did in dying for me. He was born to love and to give, and the world broke him. But he escaped!" And she could not say even to Margaret what she felt, — that he had laid it on her to express his defeated life.

They spoke even of Conny. "You received the cards for her wedding?" Margaret asked. "The man is a stock-broker. She is turning her talents to a new field, — money. I hear the wedding was very smart, and they are to live on Long Island, with a yacht and half a dozen motors."

"I thought she would marry — differently," Isabelle observed vaguely, recalling the last time she had seen Conny.

"No! Conny knows her world perfectly, — that's her strength. And she knows exactly what to take from it to suit her. She is a bronze Cleopatra with modern variations.

I think they ought to put her figure on the gold eagles as the American Woman Triumphant, ruling her world."

"And on the other side the figure of a Vampire, sucking at the souls of men." . . .

And then they talked of the future, the New Life, as it would shape itself for Isabelle and her husband, talked as if the earth were fresh and life but in the opening.

"He may do something else than this," Isabelle said. "He has immense power. But I hope it will always be something outside the main wheels of industry, as Mr. Gossom would say,—something with another kind of reward than the Wall Street crown."

"I wish he might find work here for Rob," Margaret said; "something out here where he belongs that will not pay him in fame or money. For he has that other thing in him, the love of beauty, of the ideal." She spoke with ease and naturally of her lover. "And there has been so little that is ideal in his life, — so little to feed his spirit."

And she added in a low voice, "I saw her in New York — his wife."

"Bessie!"

"Yes, — she was there with the girl, — Mildred. . . . I went to see her — I had to. . . . I went several times. She seemed to like me. Do you know, there is something very lovable in that woman; I can see why Rob married her. She has wrecked herself, — her own life. She would never submit to what the doctor calls the discipline of life. She liked herself just as she was; she wanted to be always a child of nature, to win the world with her charm, to have everything nice and pleasant and gay about her, and be petted into the bargain. Now she is gray and homely and in bad health—and bitter. It is pitiful to wake up at forty after you have been a child all your life, and realize that life was never what you thought it was. . . . I was very sorry for her."

"Will they ever come together again?"

"Perhaps! Who knows? The girl must bring them together; she will not be wholly satisfied with her mother, and Rob needs his daughter. . . . I hope so — for his sake. But it will be hard for them both, — hard for him to live with a spent woman, and hard for her to know that she has missed what she wanted and never quite to understand why. . . . But it may be better than we can see, — there is always so much of the unknown in every one. That is the great uplifting thought! We live in space and above unseen depths. And voices rise sometimes from the depths."

And lying there under the stars Margaret thought what she could not speak, — of the voice that had risen within her and made her refuse the utmost of personal joy. She had kissed her lover and held him in her arms and sent him away from her. Without him she could not have lived; nor could she live keeping him. . . .

At last they came to Renault, the one who had opened their eyes to life and to themselves.

"Still working," Margaret said, "burning up there in the hills like a steady flame! Some day he will go out, — not die, just wholly consume from within, like one of those old lamps that burn until there is nothing, no oil left, not even the dust of the wick."

As the faint morning breeze began to draw across the upland they fell asleep, clasping hands.

CHAPTER LXXX

THE rising sun had barely shot its first beams over the eastern swell when Lane came to the tent to call them for the early breakfast before the day's expedition to a wonderful cañon. Isabelle, making a sign to John not to disturb Margaret, who was still fast asleep, drew the blanket over her shoulders and joined her husband. The level light flooded the rolling upland with a sudden glory of gold, except along the outer rim of the horizon where the twilight color of deep violet still held. Husband and wife strolled away from the tents in the path of the sun.

"Big, isn't it?" he exclaimed.

"Yes!" she murmured. "It is a big, big world!" And linking her arm in his they walked on towards the sun together.

In the morning light the earth was fresh and large and joyous. And life, as Renault had said over the body of the dead child, seemed good, all of it! That which was past, lived vainly and in stress, and that which was to come as well. So Alice had affirmed in the presence of her bereavement. . . . Life is good, all of it, — all its devious paths and issues!

"It is so good to be here with you!" Isabelle whispered to her husband.

"Yes, — it is a good beginning," he replied. And in his face she read that he also understood that a larger life was beginning for them both.

As they turned back to the tents, they saw Margaret huddled in her blanket like a squaw, gazing steadily at the sun.

"And the morrow is added to the morrow to make eternity," she was murmuring to herself. "But always a new world, a new light, a new life!"